THE FIRST TO DIE AT THE END

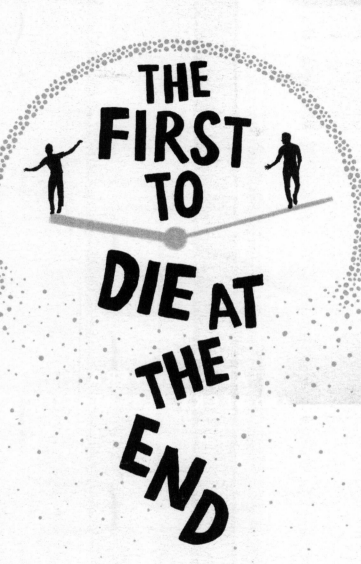

THE FIRST TO DIE AT THE END

ADAM SILVERA

SIMON & SCHUSTER

First published in Great Britain in 2022 by Simon & Schuster UK Ltd

First published in the USA in 2022 by Quill Tree Books,
an imprint of HarperCollins Publishers

1 3 5 7 9 10 8 6 4 2

Simon & Schuster UK Ltd
1st Floor, 222 Gray's Inn Road
London WC1X 8HB

www.simonandschuster.co.uk
www.simonandschuster.com.au
www.simonandschuster.co.in

Simon & Schuster Australia, Sydney
Simon & Schuster India, New Delhi

A CIP catalogue record for this book
is available from the British Library.

HB ISBN 978-1-3985-1997-8
eBook ISBN 978-1-3985-1244-3
eAudio ISBN 978-1-3985-1245-0

Printed and bound by CPI Group (UK) Ltd, Croydon, CR0 4YY

For those who've been with me since the beginning.

Shout-out to Nicola and David Yoon,
my favorite neighbors with the biggest hearts.
They show me time and time again what love should look like.

PART ONE
Death-Cast Eve

Everyone wants to know how we can predict

death. Tell me this. Do you ask pilots to explain

aerodynamics before boarding the plane or do you

simply travel to your destination? I urge you to not

concern yourselves with how we know about the

deaths and instead focus on how you'll live your life.

Your final destination may be closer than you think.

—Joaquin Rosa, creator of Death-Cast

July 30, 2010
ORION PAGAN
10:10 p.m.

Death-Cast might call at midnight, but it won't be the first time someone tells me I'm going to die.

For the past few years I've been fighting for my life because of a severe heart condition, straight scared that I might drop dead if I live it up too hard. Then an organization called Death-Cast appeared out of nowhere and claimed they could predict when—not just if—we're about to die. It sounded like the premise of a short story I'd write. Real life never hooks me up with wins like that. But everything got really real, real fast when the president of the United States held a press briefing where he introduced the creator of Death-Cast and confirmed their abilities to predict our fates.

That night, I signed up for Death-Cast.

Now I'm just hoping I won't be one of the first to get an inaugural End Day call.

If I am, at least I'll know it's game over, I guess.

Until then, I'm going to live it up.

3

And that starts with attending a once-in-a-lifetime event: the Death-Cast premiere.

Death-Cast is hosting so many parties across the country, I think to lift people's spirits and get them hyped about this program that will change life and death as we know it. They're already underway in so many places, like the Santa Monica Pier in California and Millennium Park in Chicago and the National Museum of the United States Air Force in Ohio and Sixth Street in Austin, to name a few. Of course I'm at the best one—Times Square, the heart of New York and home to the first Death-Cast offices. I love my city, but you'd never catch me out in Times Square on New Year's Eve—it's way too cold to do all that. But I'm chill hanging out on this hot summer night for something so historic.

It's wild how much bank Death-Cast must be dropping across the country. Or even in Times Square alone. These jumbotrons are always promoting a million things at once, everything from soda products to TV shows to new web addresses, but not tonight. Every screen has been replaced with a digital black hourglass with a radiant white background. The hourglass is almost full, signaling the End Day calls that will begin at midnight. But it feels bigger than that. It's almost like the product that Death-Cast is pushing is time itself. That marketing is working because people are lining up to the information booths as if a new iPhone is on sale, all to talk to the Death-Cast customer service reps.

"Imagine working at Death-Cast," I say.

My best friend, Dalma, looks up from her phone. "I could never."

"For real. It's like every call is saving someone's life, but also, not really. How do you sleep at night knowing everyone you spoke to that day is dead?"

"I know you always got death on the brain, Orion, but you're killing me."

"I got death on the heart, technically."

"Oh my god, I hate you. I'm going to get a job at Death-Cast just so I can call you."

"Nah, you can't live without me."

I don't add how she's going to have to at some point. No one's banking on me living another eighteen years. Not even Dalma, even if she'll never admit it out loud and always talks about everything we'll get to do together in life. Like her dreams of my first book signing whenever I get serious enough to pursue publication of my super-short stories or the novel I'd love to write if only I believed I'd live long enough to finish it. Or cheering Dalma on as she takes the tech world by storm. And ragging on whatever dates we bring home, which has always felt unbelievable because there's no way we'd ever be bold enough to say what's up to guys we think are cute and/or interesting. If I didn't have this stupid-ass heart, we could have all that and more.

I just got to be present. I might not make it to the future, but I can live in the now.

Though it's kind of hard to get death off the brain—yeah,

brain, not heart this time—when some fortysomething dude walks past us with a sign that reads *Death-Cast Is Ending The World*. Like, okay, he's not a fan of Death-Cast, but claiming that they got the power to end the world? That's a lot. He's not alone, though. Since Death-Cast was announced at the start of the month, these doomsayers have been running their mouths about boiling oceans and sweeping storms and crumbling grounds and burning cities. I get that apocalyptic and dystopian novels are hot right now, but people need to take a breath and chill.

Freaking out about death every minute isn't a good life, and yet, tons of people are freaking out about death every minute.

It's like the end of the world is actually beginning.

In the past few days there's been a record number of supermarket break-ins as looters stock up on canned goods and gallons of water and toilet paper. There've been too many killing sprees because life sentences won't last long if the world ends as quickly as the doomsayers are predicting. But nothing hits harder than hearing stories about those who've taken their own lives because we're speeding toward a future with too many unknowns.

I was pissed after hearing about those deaths.

How could Death-Cast have access to this info and not prevent the murders, or intervene with the suicides? But apparently that's never been in the cards. Death-Cast claims they can't pinpoint someone's cause of death, only their End

Days to prepare them. And unfortunately, once someone's name comes up in their mysterious system, their fate is written in stone—and later on their headstone.

Death-Cast may not be all-knowing, but they'll do wonders for my anxiety. If I don't get the End Day call, I'll be good to live more boldly instead of second-guessing, triple-guessing, quadruple-guessing every damn thing I do out of fear of pissing off my heart and triggering cardiac arrest. I'll also never be caught off guard again by loved ones dying. Like I was at nine years old when my parents went into the city for a meeting and were killed after a plane was flown into the World Trade Center's south tower. My parents obviously didn't have Death-Cast back then, but I'm forever haunted thinking about how there must've been a clear moment when they were certain they were going to die.

I swing at those heartbreaking thoughts, knocking them all back.

Death-Cast will make sure I'm never denied a goodbye ever again.

Well, the chance to say my goodbyes.

I know I don't have all the time in the world, I feel it in my heart.

I got to go live my firsts—maybe even lasts—while I can.

VALENTINO PRINCE
10:22 p.m.

Death-Cast can't call me because I'm not registered for their service. Not that they would anyway since my life is only getting started.

If anything, I feel like I've been reborn today.

Rebirths feel appropriate as someone born and raised in Phoenix, Arizona. Now it's time to restart my life in none other than New York. From the Valley of the Sun to the Big Apple. I've been dreaming about this city for so long that after I printed out my boarding pass at the airport and saw PHX → LGA, I broke down and cried. That one-way ticket meant I would never have to see my parents ever again. That I could build a new home with my twin sister.

I probably shouldn't have booked the window seat on my flight over. I did my best to keep it together as the plane bulleted down the runway and shot into the sky. It turns out my best is awful. As all the buildings and roads and mountains kept shrinking from view, I cried in the clouds. My seat-mate seemed judgy, admittedly. It made me wish even more that my sister was next to me as she should've been before a last-minute work opportunity came up. Thankfully, Scarlett will be on the first red-eye out to join me in our new apartment.

Five hours later, when New York came into focus, everything felt right, even though I'd never stepped foot among those skyscrapers and parks. Then we landed and I rolled my suitcases straight to the taxi line, where everyone else seemed miserable waiting, but I was so excited to finally ride inside these classic yellow taxicabs that I'd seen on TV and as props in magazine ads. The driver could tell I'd never been here before since I never stopped watching the street life. That first step onto the curb felt like a movie moment, as if cameras should've been flashing; there will be time for that later.

As of tonight, as of now, I can call myself a New Yorker.

Or maybe I have to wait until my landlord finally greets me with my apartment key so I can be certain that I wasn't scammed after finding this studio on Craigslist. While I'm waiting, I'm taking in my little corner of the Upper East Side. There's a tiny pizzeria right next door that's trying to lure me inside with the smell of garlic knots. Honking cars pull my attention back to the street, where someone old enough to be my grandfather is screaming into his phone to be heard over the music blasting from the bar on the corner.

This city is loud, and I love it.

I wonder if I'll ever miss the quiet of my old neighborhood.

The door opens behind me, and there's a man wearing nothing but a white tank top and basketball shorts and slippers. He has a thick mustache and thinning black hair, and he's glaring at me.

"You going to come inside?" he asks.

"Hi, I'm Valentino. I'm a new tenant."

The man points at my suitcases. "I can tell."

"I'm waiting for the landlord."

He nods but doesn't leave. As if he's waiting for me to come in.

"Are you Frankie?"

He nods again.

"Nice to meet you," I say.

He reluctantly shakes my hand. "Are you moving in or what?"

I was warned that not every New Yorker will be nice to me, but maybe Frankie is tired since it's pretty late. I grab my suitcases and enter the building. It's a warm night, but once I'm inside, I understand why Frankie is dressed like he's grabbing the morning paper in Arizona. It's so hot in here it's as if I walked straight into the pizza oven from next door. The hallway is narrow, painted this mustard yellow that is not fun on the eyes, but I respect the choice. There are steel mail-boxes built into the wall with packages on the floor waiting to be picked up, and a trash bin overflowing with junk mail including Death-Cast flyers. I take it many people in this building aren't registered for the End Day calls. I'm personally not either, because my parents are total skeptics, but that paranoia is another inheritance of theirs I need to abandon.

Frankie pauses while going up the first flight of stairs. "Where's the other one?"

"The other one?"

"Your twin."

"Oh, she's flying in tomorrow morning."

Frankie continues ascending. "Make sure if any other big boxes arrive you handle them in a timely fashion. Carrying all your deliveries up these stairs was bad on my back."

"I'm so sorry." I had to ship some things early, like an air mattress, blankets, towels, pots, and pans. Though I'm guessing the biggest culprit for his back pain were the five boxes of clothes and shoes and accessories, which are just as essential as making sure I have somewhere to sleep until my proper mattress can arrive on Tuesday. "Is the elevator broken?"

"It's been broken since my father ran this place," Frankie says.

I see. I'm not sure how legal it is to advertise the building having an elevator if it's purely decorative, but I'm going to make the most of it. All those years spent in my family's small

home gym have prepared me for this life. I haul the suitcases, knowing they're about fifty pounds each, since I had
to weigh them at the airport. Frankie makes no offer to assist,
which is okay. By the third flight up I'm remembering that
my new apartment is on the sixth floor. Sweat is building on
my lower back, and I'm positive I can skip leg day during all
future workouts. I'm out of breath at the top, but—actually,
no buts. This is all part of the initiation of the city. Nothing
makes me feel like a real New Yorker than being able to say
that I live in a sixth-floor walk-up on the Upper East Side.

There's no ceremony when I'm led to apartment 6G. No
welcome to the building, no congratulations on my first home
away from home. Frankie simply opens the door, and I follow
him inside, leaving my suitcases in the narrow entry hallway.
The bathroom is to my immediate left, and while I know I'm
going to spend hours in there every week doing my extensive
face routines, I'm interested in exploring the space where I'll
be doing most of my living. The wooden floor creaks under
my boots as I step into the studio. My delivered boxes are up
against the left wall where I'm planning on putting my bed.
There are two windows facing the street and a third above the
kitchen sink that offers the view into another neighbor's apartment. That's not a problem. I'll buy curtains this week.

However, the biggest problem is how small this apartment is. Scarlett and I are using the money our parents
reserved for college to pursue our dreams—modeling and

photography—and we're hoping to stretch it as long as possible, hence the studio.

"The photos online made it seem bigger," I say.

"I took those pictures," Frankie says.

"They were really pretty. Are you sure you uploaded the right photos for this listing? We were expecting more space."

Frankie stares. "You had the option to visit before leasing."

"I didn't live here yet. I only just arrived."

"That's not my problem. You and your sister shared a womb. You'll figure it out."

Here's hoping this studio apartment expands to fit our needs like our mother's uterus.

Luckily for Frankie, I'm not confrontational. I can't say the same for Scarlett, but that's a lesson he'll learn once she arrives. On the bright side, it's only my first night in New York and an iconic feud with my landlord is already beginning. This is a yearlong lease, and I'm sure by the end of it I'll have so many stories to share with all my new friends about this time in my life.

There's a knock on the door, and a young boy walks in. I'm bad at guessing ages. Is he five but really tall for his age or ten but really short? There's something familiar about him, but I honestly can't place why.

He's wearing pajamas and waves. "Are you our new neighbor?" he asks with a smile.

"I am. My name is Valentino."

"I'm Paz."

"Cool name, Paz."

"It's short for Pazito, but only my mom calls me that. I like your name too."

This is the most welcomed I've felt tonight.

Before I can thank him, I notice Frankie glaring at Paz.

"Why are you out of bed?" Frankie asks.

"I'm scared because of Death-Cast."

Frankie rubs his eyes. "Death-Cast is not real. Go to sleep."

Paz starts tearing up. "Okay, Daddy." He drags his feet toward the door, looking over his shoulder as if he's waiting for his father to change his mind. Nothing. He goes down the hallway without another word.

I really want to stop Paz and comfort him about Death-Cast, but I suspect I shouldn't try to undermine Frankie in front of him. I'm sure another opportunity will arise.

"Nice kid," I say.

Frankie doesn't acknowledge Paz again. He only places two sets of keys on the kitchen counter. "Big key is for your apartment, medium for downstairs, small for mail. I'm directly down the hall, but don't knock before nine or after five."

"Understood. Thanks so—"

Frankie leaves, closing the door behind him.

"—much, Frankie," I say to no one.

The studio doesn't seem any bigger without Frankie, but it's not as cold thankfully.

I look at the time—10:31—and want to FaceTime Scarlett. New York is three hours ahead of Arizona, so I call now, hoping to catch her before she leaves to photograph the big Death-Cast party happening in Phoenix. That job is going to pay one month's rent and leave enough change for train fare and modest lunches. I sit on the counter while I wait for Scarlett to answer, spotting Frankie through the kitchen window. Of course it's his apartment that I can view. Frankie grabs a beer out of his fridge, and hopefully he's a sleepy drunk because he's already pretty insufferable.

The call goes through, and Scarlett's face cheers me up.

"Val!" Scarlett props her phone on the bathroom sink as she does her makeup. "Are you in our new home?"

"I am indeed."

"Let me see, let me see!"

I flip the camera around to reveal our space. It doesn't take long.

"Is it just me or—"

"It's not just you. It's smaller than advertised."

"Did our rent shrink too?"

"The landlord literally said that we'll make it work since we shared a womb."

"If I had time to stop putting on my mascara to roll my

15

eyes, I would. I need to jet in a minute. Please tell me you're going to Times Square."

Between Scarlett's gig and this huge modeling campaign I booked, our dreams have gotten in the way of celebrating Death-Cast Eve together. But that hasn't stopped Scarlett from pushing me to attend the Death-Cast party in Times Square.

"I don't know, Scar. The jet lag—"

Scarlett makes a buzzer sound. "Wrong answer. You lost three hours, but you're not tired. Try again."

"I should still rest for tomorrow's shoot."

"You're going to be too wired to actually fall asleep, Val. So instead of tossing and turning on that cheap air mattress, go experience what's either going to be a historic event or the biggest prank that's ever been played on this country."

"I'd love to see Mom and Dad's faces if Death-Cast is proven to be real."

"Me too, but I'm not hanging around to photograph them."

"You're leaving straight from the party?"

"Absolutely. Especially after how they treated you earlier."

I'm still a little in shock. It's like the sting that comes from scraping my elbows and knees when I've fallen during my runs. "I appreciate the solidarity."

"I'd be a horrible twin—and human—to not be on your side. But let's not give them the power of thinking about them tonight or ever again. In the very near future, Mom and Dad won't be able to ignore you as your face pops up all over the country, including their magazines."

"I bet they'll unsubscribe."

"Which means you've won. Now get out to Times Square before you take that over too."

I take a deep breath, knowing she's right. "I wish you were here with me."

"Same, but the money I make tonight will buy us front-row seats to our first Broadway show."

"Don't you mean one month's rent?"

"We need to live a little."

"That sounds like living a lot."

"You say that like it's a bad thing, Val."

"Good point."

I moved because life has been suffocating with my parents ever since I came out. They made me feel like a stranger in my own home. I thought it would be different when I was rolling my suitcases through the living room. But they didn't say anything, not even when Scarlett said it was their last chance before we were leaving for the airport. Mom and Dad stayed quiet, as if they had only one child. I stared at the cross on our front door, praying it fell off as I slammed the door shut and left that life behind.

Freedom should be freeing, but that doesn't mean it can't be heartbreaking.

I'm going to find my own way now.

"Keep me posted on your party," I tell Scarlett.

Scarlett grabs her jacket and turns out her light. "Speaking of, I have to leave five minutes ago. I love you."

"I love you same," I say, our favorite saying born out of our twinness. "Drive safe."

"Always do!"

She does always drive safely. The same can't be said for everyone else.

Back in May, Scarlett was almost killed because of a reckless driver. I was forced to imagine this nightmarish world without her shine, something I haven't experienced since being born two minutes ahead of her. I'm never going to exist without her again. Even tonight feels weird, since she's not in New York, but I'm okay knowing she's alive and well in Phoenix. I'd rather be planets apart as long as she's still breathing on the other side of the galaxy.

Surgery saved my sister's life, though our parents claim it was all God. At the time I thanked the doctors and God, but these days I'm struggling with mysterious forces. That includes Death-Cast, an organization that expects us to trust them with no real proof. Part of me wants to be a believer and the other half has experienced firsthand how faith can backfire. Unlike my parents, I'm open to having my mind changed so that I never have to be scared of losing my sister out of the blue. Maybe we'll all know more in a few days.

God bless those—

I stop myself, still recalibrating everything in my head and heart.

Good luck to those who are basically going to be the Death-Cast test subjects.

As for me, I've been reborn and I have a lot of living to do.

ORION

10:34 p.m.

Even if the world was ending, that wouldn't stop people from
selling things.

The vendor tables in Times Square are usually too tour-
isty for me to give a flying fuck, I have no use for magnets
of the Empire State Building or taxicab key chains with my
name. (Not that anyone ever puts any love into manufactur-
ing things for the Orions of the world.) But even though it's
only been a month since Death-Cast first announced their
program, the street vendors were on top of their shit with
producing thematic souvenirs: a *Smoke 'Em If You Got 'Em*
cigarette lighter; shot glasses with a skull sticker; sunglasses
with red X's painted on; and lots of apparel like shirts and
hats. There's a damn cute beanie I'm tempted to buy, but I'm
already wearing my Yankees snapback that belonged to my
dad, and this thing always lives on top of my curls whenever
I'm out and about. I wouldn't trade this hat for anything in

the world. Okay, that's a big stretch, I'd swap out this hat for a healthy heart in a millisecond, but you feel me.

"This isn't even clever," Dalma says, picking up a shirt that reads *Death-Cast is dying to call you!*

It's so corny I want to set it on fire.

"Yeah, I'm not buying that one."

Then a shirt does catch my eye. It's white with *Have a Happy End Day!* written in a typewriter font across the chest. It's kind of classy even if I don't believe an End Day can be happy. What's so great about dying? But I guess it's more inspirational, and I can't knock that. If nothing else, it'll be a cool-ass souvenir and something to show off when people inevitably ask *Where were you when Death-Cast went live?*, kind of like how people ask *Where were you on 9/11?*

Hopefully nothing traumatic goes down tonight.

I don't need any more grief in my life.

I buy the shirt, throwing it on top of the navy shirt I was already rocking to go with my skinny jeans. This look works too.

"You getting anything?" I ask Dalma.

"A headache," Dalma says, back on her phone. "My mom won't stop checking in."

Our family—but really Dalma's actual family—are visiting her stepfather Floyd's parents in Dayton, Ohio, for the week, and it's the first time they've left us alone to fend for ourselves. Her mom, Dayana, takes her responsibility as my legal guardian very literally, especially to honor my mother, aka her childhood best friend.

"She's just trying to keep us alive," I say. "At least she actually let us hang back."

"A moment of silence for Dahlia," Dalma says, closing her eyes.

We grieve her half sister's vacation plans since she didn't have a choice but to go visit her grandparents, who are getting so old they might be the first people Death-Cast calls. My lita and lito are out in Puerto Rico and we catch up on Skype whenever my cousins are around to set that up for them. I've only met them a couple times, but it means a lot to them whenever we chat, since I'm the spitting image of my dad, apart from my mom's hazel eyes. I don't correct my lito or lita when they call me Ernesto by mistake. That name fills hearts that have long been broken since my parents died.

Dalma deep sighs, killing the silence. "I feel much better now. Gracias."

"De-fucking-nada."

"Let's send Mom a picture so she knows we're alive."

Dalma rotates with her new iPhone 4's selfie cam, struggling to find the right lighting with all these glowing Broadway marquees. She stops when she finds the best angle, the digital hourglasses high in the background.

We squeeze together for the photo, smiling like we're living it up on Death-Cast Eve. Then the fun part is looking it over, aka obsessing over every detail that I hate about myself. Dalma is gorgeous, an easy 10/10 with her brown eyes, silver mascara that matches her lipstick, glowing dark brown skin, and her black hair braided into a topknot. All I got going for me is that I tower over her at six feet, but otherwise I'm a mess. I love that my eyes are hazel, but I don't get why the left one is always uneven, like it's trying to go back to sleep. The brown curls creeping out from under my hat are clumping together and getting frizzy in this heat and it's not cute. My nose and cheeks are still red from last week's sunburn from chilling on our brownstone's rooftop. I begin reaching for my ChapStick when I see how busted my bottom lip is looking. And no matter how many compliments I get on the daily about my sharp cheekbones, I stay swearing I look gaunt and near death, which, I guess, is fitting.

"You hate it," Dalma says. It's not even a question.

"It's whatever. It's just for us anyway," I say.

"We can redo it if you want."

"Nah, I'm good."

We keep it moving, stopping like ten seconds later to watch this raffle where a Death-Cast rep is offering free subscriptions. If the line wasn't so long, I'd hop on too, because their service isn't cheap. A woman wins a free month, which is worth $275. You can pay as little as $20 for one day or $3,000 for the whole year. My medical bills are wild enough, but my guardians still invested in the annual charge anyway

23

because my heart condition won't exactly take a day off. It must be nice to not need to drop that much bank and only opt in when you're planning on doing something super adventurous, like skydiving or rafting. (You'd probably skip jumping out of a plane or traveling down rapid waters if you find out you're about to die.)

Unfortunately, Death-Cast is yet another thing insurance doesn't cover. Which I guess doesn't matter if you've got thousands on thousands on thousands on thousands in your pocket.

"Did you read that article about people wanting platinum memberships?" I ask Dalma.

"I did not. Do I want to know?"

"More like do you want to punch someone in the face?"

"Never, but hit me with it."

"Some rich-ass clowns were campaigning for Death-Cast to have a platinum tier where the operators would call them before anyone else dying."

Dalma stops dead in her tracks. "Rich people are why we can't have nice things."

Meanwhile, we've got Dayana and Floyd investing fifteen grand of their life savings on annual memberships for everyone in the house, not getting greedy for how fast the Death-Cast warning comes as long as it arrives on time before any of us can die.

I stop watching the raffle after seeing someone disappointed that they've received a free subscription for only one day. It seems like they were hoping for more, like maybe they can't afford one of the bigger fees. There's a lot in this world that I wish were free, and I'm adding Death-Cast to the list. People's lives are at stake here.

Dalma and I keep it moving and stop at those newish red glass benches that rise like steps, giving Times Square this urban amphitheater vibe for those who want to chill while the city bustles. There's a full audience and a woman on a small stage. First I think she's some Death-Cast rep with the way she's talking about how she expects this service will change things. I spot an A-frame sign, like the one propped outside the barbershop where I get my shape-ups, but this one isn't marketed to invite you inside for a haircut that'll make you feel good about yourself. It reads *Tell Your Death-Cast Story*. This woman isn't a rep. She's talking about why she signed up. As she finishes sharing her experiences with sickle cell disease, an actual Death-Cast rep behind a table picks a name out of a glass bowl and invites a girl named Mercedes up to the stage to tell her story.

For years, I've dreamt about what it would be like to do a reading at a bookstore, packed with strangers who want to hear my story. Of course I'd want my friends there too, but they're practically forced to show up. There's something magical about my words summoning people to one space. I don't think I'm going to live long enough to actually publish a book of my own—novel, short stories, the world's slimmest autobiography. Anything! But that doesn't mean there isn't a chance tonight to tell my story to this audience.

I go up to the Death-Cast rep, write my name, and drop it into the glass bowl.

This is one of those firsts that can double as a last.

VALENTINO
11:09 p.m.

Google Maps pretty much laughed when I asked for the fastest route to Times Square.

New York is known for its convenient transportation, but it's pure chaos on Death-Cast Eve. Especially in Manhattan. I could've taken the 6 and transferred to some shuttle, but that trip was estimating one hour. I couldn't find any buses going downtown, so I figured my best bet was getting in another taxi. I started walking in the general direction, hailing down cars like I've seen so many NYC characters do in movies, but I must've been doing it wrong because no one stopped. Then halfway there—much like going up the stairs of my newly realized walk-up—I accepted the only way to my destination was to embrace the journey.

That's what I've been doing, and don't get me wrong, I'm excited to experience the subway, but I would've been denied all this sightseeing if I were underground. I walked down Fifth Avenue, passing the entrance to the Central Park Zoo, seeing the famous Plaza Hotel, and Rockefeller Center, where I'll absolutely be visiting in December to see that massive Christmas tree. It's been really exciting to glimpse so many iconic buildings in real life, but also lonely. I'm looking forward to experiencing all of this with Scarlett and all the new friends we'll make along the way. I'm sure I'll see things differently.

Perspective is everything. When I'm modeling, I am who I am, but how I appear depends on who's behind the camera. Some photographers will find my strong and flattering angles. Others won't. Which shots I personally prefer ultimately depends on my perspective. But perspectives shift over time too—years, months, weeks, days, hours, even minutes. Earlier today—though I guess technically tonight, as I jumped time zones—I was sure that nothing could be more beautiful than being on that plane and watching New York come into focus. I was wrong. Nothing is more beautiful than my first glimpse of Times Square.

In the sky, everything below looks like a world for insects. On the streets, I'm the insect.

The buildings are towering, and I find myself leaning my head back like when I'm modeling because I love the pop of my Adam's apple and the stretch of my long neck. But this angle isn't to make me look good right now. It's to appreciate the beauty around me.

I stopped taking pictures blocks ago because these cell phone cameras aren't doing the city justice. Scarlett will arrive in the morning, and we can use her real camera to document our new lives. For now, I'm remaining present.

That first step into Times Square is overwhelming, admittedly, because there's so much life happening from every corner. Someone tries selling me bootleg DVDs of movies that are still in theaters. Shops and restaurants are so closely packed together that I wouldn't even know where to start. I record a quick video of the Death-Cast hourglasses on the mega screen for Scarlett, though we'll probably find better-quality footage on YouTube later. I get distracted by these two men shoving each other, one arguing to settle their debts in cash before the world begins ending tomorrow; he's one of those people. I can't believe I escaped all those conspiracy theorists back home to immediately find one in Times Square, but that's the beauty of this city, right? New York is this nexus for everyone in the world. Including Arizonan models wanting to take their life to the next level, dreaming of their faces on these billboards for all to see.

I walk deeper into the Square—is that what New Yorkers call it? I need to learn fast—and pass someone in an Iron Man costume as he talks to someone mostly dressed up as Elmo, the massive head on the ground as if decapitated as the woman smokes a cigarette. I love this city with my whole heart already. I can't help but sneak a picture of that for

Scarlett too, in case that's a one-time sighting.

I keep going and stumble onto some teen on a stage. At first I'm expecting him to sing a song into his mic, but instead he's speaking with this haunting sadness about the brain aneurysms in the family and the dread of dying from one himself. It's heavier than I expected on a party that's been billed as a celebration of life, but then I find the sign that reads *Tell Your Death-Cast Story*, and everything makes sense. That stage is for people talking about how this service will change their lives.

It can't hurt to listen in on why people are willing to believe Death-Cast.

There aren't any more seats on these red glass bleachers, but I don't mind finding a place to stand. There's a spot next to this beautiful Black girl with incredible style and this cute white boy whose curls are creeping out from under his baseball cap. The boy looks like he's having a hard time keeping it together, wiping the tears from his cheek.

He must have a huge heart.

ORION

11:17 p.m.

These Death-Cast origin stories are breaking my heart.

(Even more.)

But I can't stop listening, not even as I feel like I'm being ripped apart: a woman's fiancé died in a limo accident on the way to their wedding; a child drowned in a bathtub after her big brother got locked out of the home while taking out the trash; a girl's best friend got knifed to death on her birthday, forever staining that day; an older man's wife and child died during a complicated pregnancy, and while Death-Cast can't predict the fate of fetuses, the man still could have braced himself for this tremendous hole in his heart; and then there was a girl who got orphaned like me when she lost her parents in a tornado.

"We have time for one more story," the Death-Cast rep says. She looks to be in her early twenties with a young teacher vibe, like she's about to call on a student for the last presentation of the day. She reaches into the glass bowl, ready to fish out a name.

It's got to be mine.

It has to be, this is the only time I'm ever going to be able to tell my story and—

"Lincoln," the Death-Cast rep calls.

A boy comes down from the red glass benches, really carefully, as if he's scared he might trip and fall and die before he can share his story.

Before it goes unheard like mine.

Lincoln makes it safely to the microphone and tells us about his cancer diagnosis, pointing to his mother and sister in the audience and how Death-Cast will allow them the opportunity to stop resisting the inevitable if that's truly what's in store for him.

I don't have it as bad as him, but I get what it's like to want to tap out of the fight.

Then his story is over. The Death-Cast rep thanks the crowd for their time, and a security guard escorts her away. And everyone goes about their lives—their really difficult, complicated lives.

"I'm sorry," Dalma says.

"For what?"

"That your name didn't get called."

I never outright said how badly I wanted this, but my best friend gets me.

"It's all good," I lie.

I look at the digital hourglasses on the jumbotrons, watching sand, aka tiny black blocks, fill the bottom. Until a tall guy—I bet he's my age; I've got a good eye for this—passes by and breaks my focus. And I mean really breaks my focus because dude is beautiful; I can't help but watch him as he takes a seat at the far corner of the glass bench, looking up at the hourglasses as if they're stars.

I want to know his story as much as I wanted to tell mine.

My heart is going for it; it's wild how being attracted to someone can feel so exciting and dangerous, like he can be everything good and bad for me.

I can't tell the color of his eyes, but man, I want to know.

He's pale, but he could also be pretty white-passing like me.

I think we're the same height if you ignore his dark floppy hair or the classic Timbs giving him a mini boost.

He's undeniably muscular with his broad shoulders, thick neck, the kind of arms that guarantee him the win in any arm-wrestling match, and pecs that must be suffocating inside his fitted black V-neck.

"Earth to Orion," Dalma says, snapping her fingers. "What are you— Oh."

"Yeah. I bet he's a model."

"You swear everyone cute is a model."

"And it's a crime to society every time I'm wrong."

I rip my gaze away from him even though I really, really, really, really, really want to keep staring. Fuck it, I'm weak. I don't last a whole second before I'm sneaking another peek, half hoping he doesn't catch me looking, half hoping he does. But for what—he might not even be into guys, though I'm always down for more friends, especially once Dalma begins clocking mad hours at Hunter College this fall, but I don't know if I can orbit around someone this beautiful and not just fall in love, stay in love, and die in love.

Knowing my luck, he's a straight tourist who I'll never see again.

But maybe not. I'm not psychic; I can't rule anything out.

"I should go say what's up."

"I'm loving this attitude, O-Bro, but are you thinking with your dick by any chance?"

"I think I'm thinking with my heart?"

"Not exactly a reliable source either."

"I'm getting a good vibe from him. He doesn't seem like he's taking in the city one last time before he lives out the rest of his days in an underground bunker, or about to go on a killing spree just because."

"You have such a low bar for boys."

"And you're supposed to be my hype woman."

"So true. If you're really feeling this boy, then go carpe that diem."

I begin turning but snap right back.

There's been so many times over the years where I crush on someone around the city—Dave & Buster's, Central Park, Barnes & Noble, the 5 train—but I never know how to jump from fantasy to reality. Then even when I knew someone personally, like a couple guys in high school, I couldn't act on it because I wasn't out to anyone besides Dalma until after graduation last month.

Even after coming out, I still don't know my way in.

"What the hell am I supposed to say?" I ask.

"Speak from your heart," Dalma says. "Not your dick."

"Speak from my heart, not my dick; speak from my heart, not my dick," I mutter like a mantra.

I don't want to miss my chance to say hi to this guy, the probability of ever seeing him again in New York would be one in . . . I don't know, some big-ass number that would take days to count to.

"I got this," I say with zero confidence.

"Yeah you do," Dalma says with zero believability.

I get a move on, thinking up questions to ask him with every step:

Where are you from?

Are you here with anyone?

You look like Clark Kent. Do you ever dress up as Superman?

Do you play on my team, aka are you into guys?

Oh, you're straight? Do you have an identical twin who is into guys?

Then I'm suddenly standing over him. His eyes—an icy blue that make me suck in a sharp, cold breath—go wide. At first I'm expecting him to freak out, kind of like how I did this one time I stepped out of my local bodega and found some white dude in my face threatening to kick my ass if I didn't hand over my cash and candy. (I went home without cash and candy.) But this guy doesn't look scared of me. His heart-shaped lips actually part into a smile, and I'm lit up like a flaming match to paper.

"Hi," he says.

"Hi," I repeat, like he's teaching me a new language.

"How's it going?"

He's not supposed to be leading the conversation, *I* approached *him*.

"It's going good, I mean, as good as the end of the world can go," I say. Then I realize this could be dead before it begins if I don't make it clear that I don't think the world is going to end at midnight. "Not that I think we're all about to die. Some people have to die obviously, unfortunately, tragically . . . yeah, tragically . . . but I don't think the whole planet is about to blow up in flames or drown or cave in or anything like that." I try taking a deep breath, but I feel like my body is rejecting all air so I can take a whole second to shut the fuck up. For some mysterious reason this dude hasn't run away. "Anyway, I came over here because you were staring at the hourglasses, and I was wondering if you were thinking about all this Death-Cast insanity too."

He looks up at the jumbotron again, another minute down even though I feel like it took me a thousand years to get to the point.

"Definitely thinking about Death-Cast. And life."

"Kind of the same thing now, right?"

"Kind of." He stands, and his eyes find mine again. "I'm Valentino, by the way."

Shit, that name fits. I don't know what I mean by that, but I'm one hundred percent right, and I'll swing at anyone who says otherwise. I mean, I would definitely lose that fight, since I'm zero for one million in fights, but I would fight, fight, fight that fight anyway.

"I'm Orion."

"That's so funny, you're literally the fifth Orion I know."

"Really?"

Valentino smiles. "Not really."

Wow, I'm so damn dumb. "I'm too gullible, you can't play me like that."

"Ha-ha, I'm sorry! You're the first Orion I know," Valentino says. "I promise."

Seriously, my name in his mouth is straight fire to my face, like extra sunburn. And being this close to him has got my insides tight, like all my cardiac veins are choking out my heart because it owes them money. But Valentino seems totally chill, I doubt I'm rattling him at all. One glance at his full, bottom lip reminds me that my own is chapped, so I grab my Chap-Stick to correct that. He watches me glide it across my lip, and he's got to be thinking I'm prepping for a kiss, which I mean, I'm not, but also, I wouldn't be mad at that at all.

Damn, maybe I am thinking with my dick.

I also keep making an ass out of myself.

I can't be left alone with Valentino right now.

"Dalma!" I wave her over, and she comes to the rescue ASAP. "Dalma, this is Valentino."

"Hi," Dalma says, shaking his hand; I didn't even get to shake his hand.

"Nice to meet you," Valentino says. "Your boyfriend here—"

"No, no, no, no, no, no, no," Dalma says. Deep breath, then: "No, no, no, no."

I stare at her, slightly—nah, majorly insulted at how long she was living in those no-no-no's. "Okay, calm down, I'm not trying to date you either."

"He's practically my younger brother," Dalma says.

"Younger by two months," I say.

"As if the world couldn't have ended in the two months it took for you to be born."

"You always say that, like you're trying to have me killed off."

I don't get it, are we throwing down for Valentino? We're eighteen, not eight, but I saw him first, said hi first, made an ass of myself first. I get to see where this is going first.

Thankfully he doesn't seem completely turned off of us.

"You definitely have the practically sibling bickering down," Valentino says, not a beat of judgment in his voice. "I'm the same with my twin."

Holy shit, there are two of him.

I mean, I got to wonder at this point if I've already died and moved on to the afterlife where there are two Valentinos. Maybe Dalma and I don't have to compete at all—we both get to bring a Valentino home and live happy lives.

But wait, I'm getting ahead of myself.

"Twin bro or sis?"

"Sister," Valentino says, which means the fight for his heart is still on.

"Where's she at?"

"Scarlett is back home in Arizona."

Back home. So he doesn't live here.

This is why I need to stop getting ahead of myself.

As a writer, I'm always telling stories before I even know what they're about, getting carried away and turning words into sentences, sentences into paragraphs, paragraphs into chapters, chapters into love stories. Maybe winging it like that works for novels, but for life, your imagination can set you up for a heartbreaking ending.

"That sucks that she's missing out on this party," I say, trying not to get too bummed out. I really got to stop investing so fast.

"She's actually photographing the party in Phoenix. Then she's flying in tomorrow morning for more New York adventures."

"How long are you visiting for?"

"I actually just moved here," Valentino says, looking around again at Times Square.

His words get my heart racing.

So does his smile again.

Valentino has this happy glow while looking around the city as a newly minted New Yorker. Who knows how long he's been waiting to make this happen. It could be a month, a year, a decade, his whole life. Were things bad back in Arizona? Did Valentino and Scarlett need a change? What's good with their parents—or guardians? Are they also moving here? I have so many questions, and it might take a minute to get some answers, but I know I got time now too.

"Welcome to NYC," Dalma says. "So you're alone tonight?"

"I am. I arrived a couple hours ago and came right back out for the party."

"You can chill with us if you want," I offer.

"Some company would be nice. You sure you don't mind?"

"Hell no. It's not like you know anyone else in the city."

"I'm actually very popular. My landlord is pretty much my best friend."

"I can't wait to meet him," I say, which is just so damn bold.

"He's actually the worst, but I'll have to have you over soon anyway," Valentino says with that damn smile.

All right, all right, all right—if this isn't a thing, then I'm giving up on ever making the first move again. I'm going to need a guy to swear on my parents' grave that he loves me, and I won't even tell him that those plots are empty so that he doesn't get funny and lie.

But because Valentino's got me weak, I wouldn't need all that.

His smile alone has got me cashing in.

VALENTINO
11:32 p.m.

It's my first night and I'm making friends already.

Friends with beautiful names. Beautiful faces too.

I stare at Orion, whose cheekbones are worthy of every magazine cover and his hazel eyes, which I suspect have seen too much for someone so young. I realize I'm staring too long when he begins blushing. I'm pretty confident that Orion is gay. I guess he could be bisexual, but at the very least I'm sure he likes other boys too. It's obviously not a bad thing that I can tell. I'm jealous that he seems so open and has been probably given the chance to do so. I should find a way to make it clear that I'm into boys too.

"What's got you hyped about New York so far?" Orion asks.

I could spend the rest of the night answering that question. "I really want to do everything. Just live like a tourist so I don't take any day for granted."

"That's really smart," Dalma says. "I love this city, but I'm over so much of it."

"Like what?"

"Subway showtimes. The first few are amazing, but then you get over it and stay focused on whatever you were doing before the dancers arrived."

"And praying you don't get kicked in the face," Orion adds.

"I hope I don't stop finding it magical" is all I say.

Orion must see some of the excitement vanishing from my eyes. "Don't let us kill your buzz, we're both born and raised here. You're going to be all in, all the time."

"That's the plan."

"What's epic about New York is that you're never going to be able to do it all."

"That's epic?"

"Hell yeah. It means there's always something to do. Some new neighborhood to explore, knowing every street will tell its own story. I'm happy to be your tour guide if you want."

I smile, excited for Orion's own stories as he takes me around the city. "That sounds like a lot of fun. Thanks so much."

"You got it."

A big group of people in lime-green shirts and headbands pass by. They look like they've time-traveled from a St. Paddy's Day celebration, but I know better. They're extraterrestrial believers who are certain UFOs will surface at midnight and beam them up; we have a lot of those back in Arizona. These believers are mostly harmless—bad eggs in every group, of course—but they're all in for reality checks really soon when they're still grounded here tomorrow with nine-to-fives to work and taxes bleeding them dry.

I'm about to take a picture for Scarlett when Dalma asks me a question.

"Are you switching schools for the fall?"

"I'm actually putting college on the back burner. I'm pursuing my dreams instead."

"Which are . . . ?" Orion asks.

I still get a little nervous sharing what I do because people can be judgmental, and if that's true for Orion and Dalma, it's better to know now before I get too invested. I can't be around people who won't let me be me anymore. "I'm a model."

Orion's eyes light up as he turns to Dalma. "I told you!"

"Did you think I wasn't one?" I ask her.

"You're obviously handsome, but Orion says that about every cute guy."

"I don't know whether to feel special or not."

"Feel special," Orion cuts in. Then he's blushing. "I mean, yeah, of course your face should be everywhere."

"Thanks for believing in me and my face."

"Anytime. Anything we would've seen you in?"

Only the really famous models have direct answers for this, and that's certainly not me.

My first job was for these nameplate necklaces last year, and to make me even less recognizable, they had me sporting a *Leo* necklace. Then I was in a brochure for Prescott College, which is the only time anyone will see me on that campus because that tuition is too rich for my blood. Since then I've done a bunch of local ads where I've posed as a big brother, a baseball player, a driving student, and an employee to promote the Phoenix Bat Cave in Paradise Valley.

But soon enough, when someone asks if they've seen me in anything, I can point to this very corner of New York City.

"Not yet, but . . ." I gesture around at Times Square, imagining my face as high as these mega screens and billboards, and as low as the subway ads. "Tomorrow morning I start shooting for my first national campaign. It's for this queer clothing line made by queer designers that puts out special items year-round instead of just for Pride month. It means a lot to me as a gay boy who couldn't have gotten away with wearing any of these pieces growing up." I see the smile creeping onto Orion's face like he's just as happy to have confirmation that I'm gay as I am to get it off my chest. As I always will, no matter who has a problem with it. "Hopefully that campaign pushes my life forward."

45

Orion claps, which is pretty cute. "Congrats, Valentino! That's so dope."

"We can say we knew you when," Dalma says.

"You absolutely can. What about you both? What are your dreams?"

I've stopped asking people where they go to school or what they do for work. I know how bad it was making me feel when people looked down on me for not going to college, or how modeling isn't seen as a credible profession until you're being paid millions to smile for the camera. That will be me one day, but I have to start somewhere.

"I'm a short story writer," Orion says.

"That's amazing! What kind of stuff?"

"Like genre? Mostly weird fantasy stuff. Some sci-fi. One fairy tale."

"Will you let me read some of it one day?"

Dalma laughs. "Good luck!"

Orion is the shyest I've seen him. "Maybe one day. I kind of keep it close."

I suspect there's more to that story, but I don't want to push him. "No worries, Orion. If you ever change your mind I'd love to read something you've written." I turn to Dalma. "So between the three of us we have a model, writer, and . . ."

"I'm a programmer," Dalma says.

I honestly would've thought she was a model too. This is why you don't judge a book by its cover.

"I really want to get into apps, but I haven't cracked that code yet."

"Is code really hard to learn?"

"Oh, no, I was talking about metaphorical code, not literal code. Literal code is easy."

"Dalma doesn't know what kind of app she wants to create," Orion says.

It's funny how even though they're not twins, let alone siblings, Dalma and Orion's relationship reminds me of my own with Scarlett. There's bickering, sure, but there's also speaking on each other's behalf, as if there's some magical telepathic link.

"What about a new game?" I suggest. I used to play *Snake* all the time on my Nokia, but since switching over to an iPhone nothing in the app store has caught my eye.

"Games are fun, but I want to create something game-changing," Dalma says. "Honestly, I've been trying to figure out something from the Death-Cast angle. Something that would be timely and evergreen."

So she's not a Green Shirt Person. Noted.

"Uh-oh," Dalma says.

I look around, nervous. "Uh-oh what?"

"You got silent after she mentioned Death-Cast," Orion says.

"Do you not believe in Death-Cast?" Dalma asks.

"Let's put it like this: I don't think I'm going to be abducted by aliens at midnight."

Orion laughs, and when he does, he covers his mouth with his hand and leans forward. I wonder why he's hiding his smile. My guess would be his chipped tooth. It's not significant, but I've developed an eye for noticing these things through my work. After signing with Future Star Model Management, I had my own bottom chipped tooth restored to make me more sellable. Orion could do the same with good dental insurance.

"But you don't believe in Death-Cast," Dalma says.

"There's nothing to believe in," I say. "The creator hasn't offered any proof."

"A lot of theories but no answers," Dalma says.

"I think it's some kind of magic—it's got to be," Orion says.

"Really, scarily accurate science," Dalma says.

"The devil, according to my parents," I say.

Magic, science, and the devil. But no alien believers in this circle.

"Okay, so I get not having proof," Orion says. "But do you have any reasons why you would sign up? Kind of personal, my bad. You don't have to answer if you're not an aggressive open book. I know we're strangers."

"I'd call us friends-in-the-making," I say.

"I like that," he says.

"Do you dish for friends-in-the-making?" Dalma asks.

I nod. "The short story is that my sister, Scarlett, got into a really bad car accident in May. Getting that call that she was being rushed to the hospital didn't make sense. She's my sister, my twin. She's also a dream driver. I've definitely texted a few times while driving, but never Scarlett. Her phone is off and her eyes are on the road. But this distracted driver crashed right into her."

It's not fair how someone can do everything right and still be hurt because someone else does one thing wrong.

"Holy shit," Orion says.

"I didn't know how I was supposed to live without her. Every thought in that direction seemed so horrific, even the simple things. There's no way I could've eaten birthday cake that's for both of us. Or acted like the right side of the couch wasn't automatically reserved for her."

"I'm so happy she's okay," Orion says.

"She sounds like an incredible spirit," Dalma says.

"Though I bet you're pumped to swap cars for trains," Orion says.

"That's what's so funny about Scarlett," I say. "Once she recovered from surgery, she got right back behind the wheel. She wasn't going to let that near-death experience stop her from living her life."

I'll never forget how tense it was when Scarlett drove again for the first time. I got in the car with her, which couldn't have helped with the pressure of driving again, but

I wasn't not going to be there for her. Scarlett was great—she started the engine, checked her mirror, pulled out of the driveway, and drove one test lap around our gated community before turning off onto the highway, bringing me along for her errands to replace all her camera equipment that got damaged in the crash.

Just like a phoenix, she was reborn.

"Anyway, that's why I'm tempted to sign up for Death-Cast. I don't ever want to mistake another day as ordinary again." I look around, wondering who has and who hasn't opted into the service. "I understand that the person who gets the Death-Cast call isn't the only one dying. If you really hold someone in your heart, you die too."

I take a deep breath, knowing I'm fully alive.

"I feel like I'm missing a whole chapter of your story," Orion says. "You're fresh off this accident. I'd think now more than ever you'd jump at the chance for Death-Cast to give you some peace of mind."

"I'm definitely at a crossroads. I recognize Death-Cast's value, but I'm not sure how ready I am to believe in another force that feels too mysterious. Not after the way my parents used religion to turn their backs on me."

"I'm so sorry," Dalma says. "That's horrible."

"That's total bullshit," Orion says.

I almost tell them it's okay and don't because it's not. There may be a lot I'm still processing about where I stand on faith since coming out, but my parents weaponizing God against me isn't right. "Thanks for siding with me," I say. It really is nice to have more support. I couldn't find enough of it at home and now I'm finding it in a new city.

Orion looks up at the mega screen, watching the hourglass. "I get why you're torn."

"Maybe you can be the tiebreaker for me. Why did you sign up for Death-Cast?"

ORION
11:44 p.m.

Why someone signs up for Death-Cast tells you a lot about them.

Here's Valentino—former stranger, now friend-in-the-making—who wants to buy into the End Day calls because of a near death but not death.

There's a huge difference, obviously.

I'm not dead, but I regularly feel like I'm living that near-death life. I know that motherfucking grim reaper keeps inching closer and closer, almost like he moved into our brownstone, starting off with a cute little lounge across the couch, and then got lonely so he rolled out an air mattress in my room, but then his scythe popped all the air out the mattress and he had no other choice but to cozy up with me in my twin bed. I might have that death breath all up on me, but I'm still here.

When it comes to near death and death, I know both sides of that coin.

I'm not alone in that.

Dalma has been through it too, and we swap looks, like we're trying to see who's going to spill first on why we signed up for Death-Cast.

"You wanted to tell your story," Dalma says. "Now's your chance."

I'm nervous now, feeling the pressure to actually sell the service to Valentino.

"I'll just go first," Dalma says flatly, buying me time. "So my dad died from kidney cancer. I was three, so I don't remember a ton, just little things, like he lost a bunch of weight even though all he did was sleep all the time. My mom told me he was sick, so I would bring him ginger ale and crackers, but it never helped." There's no heartbreak cracking up her voice, it's all in the past. "Then one day he was gone and I didn't understand why, and he kept being gone and eventually I understood."

I've known Dalma my entire life, but I've never heard her describe her grief that way. Like it was riding a bike with a tiny hole in the tire, leaking just enough air that it's slowing you down but takes a while before you understand the full problem. Except no, that analogy has to be trashed because unlike that tire that can be replaced or resealed, no one could pump more air into her father and bring him back to life. And Dalma is quick to shut someone down if they talk about her stepfather as a replacement, no matter how much she loves him.

Man, I'm ready to offer condolences like this is fresh when Valentino beats me to it.

"I'm really sorry for your loss. It's not fair that you lost him so young."

"It happens," Dalma says with a shrug. "Unfortunately, it happened to me."

I bump shoulders with her, knowing that she's always down for a hug, but she's only going to let herself be so vulnerable in front of strangers—and friends-in-the-making. Back home, we're always swapping stories about what it's like not having our fathers or my mother around anymore. Like after our graduation party, when it was just the two of us, we talked about missing her father and my parents in the audience cheering with everyone else, though we'd never say any of that around Dayana or Floyd because we don't want them to feel bad. It's wild how we protect the grown-ups like that. But also, not really.

Life doesn't care how young you are. It forces you to grow up anyway.

"That's my fun little Death-Cast origin story," Dalma says. "Your turn, O-Bro."

Her story wasn't fun, and mine isn't either. There's got to be many someones across the country who are signing up for Death-Cast just because, no strings attached, no trauma lived. Must be nice.

"I've got a heart thing," I say, and it immediately shocks

Valentino, like that first slap of winter air when you step out the door.

"Are you serious?" he asks. "But you look healthy."

"Hey, it's what's on the inside that counts, right?" I throw that line at people a lot, can't lie. But it fails to draw a smile out of Valentino. "I got diagnosed with viral cardiomyopathy a few years ago, which can be super dramatically translated as my heart trying to kill me. If you want boring medical details, then WebMD can give you the CliffsNotes."

"Two different websites," Dalma says.

"Whatever. The point is that it can happen whenever, wherever."

"Now Death-Cast will help you breathe easier," Valentino says. "Orion, I'm so sorry that this is something you even have to worry about. I'm in awe of you."

I probably shouldn't tell him that kind words like that get my heart going. I'm not trying to die, but death by compliment sounds nice.

"If only that was everything," I say.

I kind of want to stop, feeling guilty that we're swinging at Valentino with all this death talk when he came to Times Square tonight to live his life. But with Valentino's concerned, raised eyebrows and soul-gazing blue eyes, I get the vibe that he's waiting for me to drop this other chapter in my story.

"So I lost my parents on 9/11," I say, giving it that pause

that everyone needs to swallow that down. But I've also learned that you can't wait too long because if you're not running your mouth, someone else will start running theirs to tell you their own 9/11 story.

That's what happens when your city lives through a traumatic disaster like that.

Everyone felt something across the city, across the country, across the world. But there's a time and place, and I've lost count of how many times I tell people about losing my parents only for them to jump at the chance to let me know how they couldn't catch a bus home, or weren't allowed to play outside for a week. What am I supposed to say to that? I know what—*I don't care*, and *Your life went on; my parents' didn't*, and *You got your life back, but mine changed*.

This is where outsiders like Valentino are blessings.

He's quiet, either too stunned to find the next words he wants to say or knows no words can change anything. No matter what, I know he's not bursting to tell me what went down with him that day. Lips sealed, eyes glistening.

Tonight, more than ever, I feel nine years old all over again as I relive that day.

It was a Tuesday. Fourth grade, two days into our first full week of school. I was already chosen to be on the safety patrol squad because I was a tremendous ass-kisser, though all that really meant was I got to wear this lime-green reflective belt and make sure everyone was in their classroom in time for morning announcements. I remember really feeling myself too, walking down the halls in my new navy FUBU jumpsuit and bright white sneakers, stuff my parents bought me during back-to-school shopping.

"It seemed like an ordinary day," I say.

And it still took me a minute to catch on that it wasn't.

My shift was over, so I returned my belt to the security desk, where the guard and vice principal were watching the news on one of those big-ass TVs that were always being rolled from classroom to classroom, depending on which teacher called dibs on it first.

"The footage looked like something out of an action movie, but it was so, so real. I saw the towers upright and burning, and then they cut to the collapse." I feel a buzzing in my head and an emptiness in my stomach. "If you want to know how stupid I was, I didn't know this was even going down in New York at that point. My vice principal had called the buildings the World Trade Center, but I grew up only knowing them as the Twin Towers. So I wrote it off as some video game company in another country, and I was so relieved that it wasn't happening here because it looked so scary, and I went back to class without giving it another thought."

I don't know why I'm giving every damn detail like this, maybe I've got more of a novel in me than I give myself credit for, because I'm painting one hell of a picture.

Then I share the thought that haunts me the most.

"I had no idea my parents were dead at that point."

I wipe away some sneaky-ass tears and stare at the ground, I can't even look at Valentino or Dalma.

I start trying to wrap it up, but these memories are rolling fast like a montage, it's got me thinking about how everyone says you see your life flashing before your eyes before you die. Maybe my body somehow knows that I'm hours, or even minutes, away from an End Day call.

If this is the last time I'm going to share this story, I'm going to tell it right.

Classes began as normal, but by lunch, there was a shift. Teachers were abandoning their lesson plans and telling us to do independent reading or chat quietly among ourselves as they stepped out into the halls to have their own conversations. No one was telling us what was happening. Then parents started arriving and picking up their children. Still, no word on why. But we started making a game out of it in class, betting on who would go home next.

"Then I finally overheard someone say the Twin Towers were attacked."

There are so many things I remember about that day, but there are little gaps too, like not knowing who it was who dropped those words on me like a bomb, or how long I sat in that chair trying to process what that meant. But eventually I got up, kind of zombie-walking to my teacher Mrs.

Williams's desk and told her that my parents were in Manhattan that morning for work. She was gentle, using that voice she always had whenever I asked to go to the bathroom or needed her to repeat something for me that I didn't understand. Then I realized I had to make it clearer for her.

"My parents had a meeting at the Twin Towers," I say, and I've said those words a hundred times, a thousand times, a million times because everyone wants to know why they were there. It's not like they were walking down a bad neighborhood's dark alley late at night, they were conducting business in a business building during business hours.

My teacher, a woman who studied Shakespeare and expanded my vocabulary and assigned my reading, had no words for me after I told her where my parents were.

I still held out hope. My mom was always running late, like putting on makeup five minutes after she was supposed to be out the door already. I kept thinking that maybe they were late to their meeting because of her, and that I'd have so many more years of teasing her for that little character flaw, that for that day, we'd be thanking that procrastination bone in her body.

"You hear a lot of stories like that—about people who were supposed to be in the towers that morning but overslept or got stuck in traffic or rode the wrong train or felt sick so they stayed home." I take a deep breath. I can't believe I've been talking so much, and I can't believe no one has stopped me. "But my parents weren't lucky like that, so I was the last kid in the whole school."

And that's when I bust down, crying hard.

I don't need to get into how Dayana was called to rescue me as my emergency contact, or my transition into living with Dalma and her family, or all the nightmares I had and the nightmares I have now and what's changed and what's stayed the same. I probably couldn't even get the words out if I tried, I got myself so deep in those memories that I swear that Death-Cast must have gone live hours ago while I was too busy thinking about the towers falling with my parents inside.

"Can I hug you?"

Valentino's words surprise me, cutting through the air like there are no other sounds—no cars honking, no Death-Cast reps with microphones, no sobs coming out my own mouth.

I nod, still crying, like I'm still that kid who needed to be comforted over and over because I felt so lonely.

My heart is pounding as he wraps his arms around me. The hug is tight, his pecs pressed against my flat chest.

"I hate that you lived through that," Valentino says. "I'm sorry I asked."

I shake my head, my chin dragging along his shoulder. "Nope, we started it."

Dalma clears her throat. "I did some light teasing, but you popped the question first." She winks, swearing she's cute with that little turn of phrase, and it's actually solid but mortifying when I'm hugging this guy who is into other guys but that doesn't automatically mean me.

I break the hug, way too self-conscious now.

"One last thing," I say, wiping away my tears.

"For real?" Dalma asks, then flashes a smile. "I'm kidding, but for real for real, it's almost midnight."

I turn to the jumbotron, and that hourglass is almost full at the bottom.

"I'll be fast," I say.

"You don't have to be," Valentino says.

I rest my hand on his shoulder, the same shoulder my chin was just on. "Look, maybe we'll never talk again beyond tonight, but there's one thing I'd love for you to take away from this encounter."

He leans in, attentive.

"You said that if someone you hold in your heart dies, then you die too. I love my parents so damn much, every time I got to talk about them in past tense like they're nothing but ghosts instead of the living, breathing, solid people they were, it breaks me." We're minutes from midnight. "Here's the truth no one ever wants to admit when death is on the horizon, or when you're deep in that grief—as long as you keep existing, you'll keep breathing, and if you're breathing, one day you'll start living again."

I know it's stupid, but I swear I can see in his eyes that he

61

gets me, that he's burning those words into memory for that tragic day he loses someone, that he's really taking it to heart.

"But no matter how much you're living, Valentino, it's still going to be haunting if you don't get the chance to say good-bye to someone you love. Especially if given the chance."

Valentino looks at the hourglass. "I should sign up before it's too late."

VALENTINO
11:52 p.m.

I'm registering for Death-Cast.

Thankfully I don't have to wait in line since I have a smartphone. I go to death-cast.com and create an account. I skim the contract language and get right to inputting my name, social security number, birth date, phone number, and list Scarlett as my emergency contact. The next slide runs through how the Death-Cast ringtone can't be changed like other government warnings, such as the Amber Alert. Then it's time to pay. I don't want to invest for the full year, and even a month costs too much for all my new expenses in the city, so I opt in at the one-day rate to see how it feels to lean in to Death-Cast. I confirm my plan, and I'm greeted with one final slide:

A Message from the Founder
Welcome to Death-Cast, where you are taking your life—
and your death—into your own hands.

Here at the company, we refer to those who are dying as Deckers. "Why Deckers?" you ask. We want you to remember that you are all the captains on the decks of your own ships, setting sail on your own journeys. Stay in motion, or, more simply put, live your life.

Don't wait until your horizon is fast approaching.

But if it is, Death-Cast is here for you.

—*Joaquin Rosa*

"Done," I say, pocketing my phone.

"How do you feel?" Orion asks.

"Okay? I only paid for a day, in case it doesn't feel right."

"Good call," Dalma says.

"I hope you'll never need it," Orion says.

We shouldn't say never since I don't think anyone wants me modeling at two hundred, but I understand what he's saying. I really hate that Orion had to get so smart about death. But not as much as I like how much he's going to be in my life now.

I'm starting to wonder if destiny is real.

The way Orion was talking about those near misses of people avoiding the towers, I'm wondering if that was all destiny or dumb luck. What about meeting Orion and Dalma tonight? Was that destiny? Would it have happened if I had left the apartment sooner, or later? What if I had tried riding the train instead? Who's to say if our paths would've ever crossed. What I do know is that I've met them and they're both incredibly strong people. I'm impressed that they're still standing.

Especially Orion.

He wears his heart on his sleeve more than Dalma, as if that's some side effect from the viral cardiomyopathy. It's so endearing. Anyone who makes blanket statements about New Yorkers and their harshness hasn't met vulnerable Orion.

Dalma checks her phone. "Couple minutes until life changes as we know it. Let's lift our spirits a bit. What's something you want to do moving forward? I want to figure out my app and start mapping my designs."

I have a long list of things I want to accomplish. Magazine covers, Met Gala appearances, walking down the runway at Fashion Week. Though that won't be accomplished this year alone. I have to put in the time and the work to reach that status. That's what I'll keep doing. I'll book more gigs and keep bulking up so more scouts take me seriously. But after everything I've been feeling tonight while walking through this new city, and meeting new souls, I'm inspired to say, "I want to make great memories. Something to look back on whenever existing seems hard."

Orion grins and nods. "I like that."

But even behind his grin, I can tell he's masking some pain. "What about you?"

"Be fast," Dalma says.

I really wouldn't mind if Orion wanted to tell another story.

"I don't want to die," Orion spits out.

"Didn't I say let's be uplifting?"

"Fine, I want to keep living."

I appreciate his spin, but he doesn't seem as amused by himself as I am.

We all turn our attention to the mega screen. But Orion's eyes are closed like he doesn't want to look at the hourglass. He's shivering even though it's pretty warm except for the occasional breeze. No, he's shaking. His bottom lip is trembling. I think he's nervous about dying, as if Death-Cast is really going to call him in this next minute. I say his name, and Orion peeks, but then shuts his eye closed again. He's fighting back more tears. There's no need to hide a good cry, I've been there—multiple times today, in fact.

I lean into his ear. "You're going to be okay."

It's a promise I can't make, but I'll hope every day that it's true.

ORION
11:59 p.m.

I write short stories because I am one.

I wish I was a novel.

Breaths away from midnight, I know my final chapter is close.

I look up at Valentino, wondering what life could've offered if I had more pages in me.

PART TWO
DEATH-CAST

Death-Cast won't just tell people when they'll

die. We'll make sure their lives don't go unlived.

—Joaquin Rosa, creator of Death-Cast

July 31, 2010

JOAQUIN ROSA

12:00 a.m.

Death-Cast might call Joaquin Rosa to tell him he's going to die, but it would be a shame for the company's creator to not live long enough to see how his creation changes life as we know it.

Truth be told, there are many people who would like Joaquin dead.

People fear change, and this is the biggest change the world has experienced since the internet. It doesn't help that Joaquin won't tell the public how his company can predict when someone will die. He understands the curiosity behind this life-changing service. He's even been amused by the more outrageous theories, such as psychics with futuristic crystal balls, a league of assassins killing people to create balance in an overpopulated world, and—his personal favorite—time-travelers jumping into the future and returning with the next day's obituaries. Nonetheless, Joaquin is remaining tight-lipped because he doesn't believe the world is ready for the truth.

Once that door opens, there will be no closing it.

Shortly after Death-Cast's very discreet inception years ago, Joaquin disclosed everything to Central Intelligence. And by everything, he means everything. Death-Cast has become Joaquin's life's work—a mission even greater than fatherhood—and that work could easily be shut down without governmental support. The process was absolutely draining, so much so that he was tempted to quit before he could begin. But the service Death-Cast will provide is far too important to every living soul who has been robbed by the grim reaper without warning. Sure, some of Joaquin's intentions have ultimately been limited by the government, and he's dreading the day that Death-Cast's power is abused, but for now, he's been cleared to start the work.

The moment is finally here.

Inside Death-Cast's flagship headquarters in New York City, Joaquin Rosa is ready to change the world.

He's going to make history by calling the first Decker, the official name he decided his staff would call those who are about to die. He believes every Decker must be treated as if they're on the decks of their own ships, the captains of their journeys, with their final destinations on the horizon.

There's a quote by the author John A. Shedd that Joaquin thinks of often: "A ship in harbor is safe, but that is not what ships are built for."

He likes to think he's giving people the opportunity for one last sail.

Earlier this evening during his CNN special, Joaquin was asked if opting in to End Day notifications was doing a disservice to how life should be experienced without warning of when it's all over.

"If people want mystery, perhaps they should pick up a detective novel," Joaquin had answered with a crooked smile. "If these lives are truly our only ones, we're better off living them without the mystery of when it will all be over. You know what you can't do once you're pronounced dead? You can't make sure your finances are in order for your family. You can't finally do the thing you've been scared to do your entire life. You can't tell someone you're sorry. You can't tell someone you love them." Joaquin had uncrossed his legs and leaned forward, closer to the interviewer, like he was about to share the universe's biggest secret. "Death-Cast won't just tell people when they'll die. We'll make sure their lives don't go unlived."

Joaquin knows the devastations of losing someone unexpectedly.

It's midnight, but no one is celebrating.

All eyes are on him, sitting at a computer in the heart of Death-Cast's headquarters.

The call center has colorful walls, happy and healthy plants, and stone fountains with water cascading onto white rocks. It's a beautiful backdrop for photo shoots, yes, but this was designed by his wife to be a soothing environment for the operators—known as heralds, since they're the ultimate messengers—during their harrowing shifts. This job can mentally scar someone, Joaquin knows this. That's why instead of psychics and assassins and time-travelers, the world will find therapists and crisis counselors and social workers operating the phones to console the Deckers while being mindful of protecting themselves.

He casts a quick glance at his wife, Naya, and their nine-year-old son, Alano, who are waiting with the same bated breath as everyone else. His family has been put through the wringer since Death-Cast was announced on July 1, but they're finally going to see the fruits of Joaquin's labor.

He'll make it up to them one day.

Joaquin picks up the phone.

The sounds of camera shutters clicking drown out the soothing fountains. This is the only time Joaquin will allow photographers inside the facility. They're all here to capture history. He's already wondering which photograph will be used on all the front pages later and if it will be iconic enough to act as the cover of his inevitable memoir too.

More pictures are taken as Joaquin switches on the computer, the monitor angled away from everyone so only his eyes are on the screen. One of Joaquin's many promises to the public has been that privacy will always be protected, and he will never betray that trust.

He reads the name at the top of the list and dials their phone number.

It's time to call the very first Decker and tell them they are going to die today.

ORION
12:01 a.m.

Death-Cast is calling.

So this is it, that bastard grim reaper is finally getting me. I won't get to see how this first year of Death-Cast plays out or the one after and so on and so on and so on and so on. I might not even make it through the hour before I become past tense. I can't breathe, and I feel like I might drop dead right now. My heart is beating, pounding, hammering, and it's pulsing even faster than the Death-Cast ringtone, which sounds like a church bell being rattled around by some kid. The alert is getting louder, louder, louder as all the demo videos warned it would to make sure the calls don't go missed. And even though the alert is only for me, it's ending all the life around me—everyone is reaching for their own phones before realizing it's my End Day, not theirs, because they have all the time in the world.

I'm huddled up with Dalma and Valentino, but I can't

look at them, I can't see it in their eyes how real this is.

One minute ago, Death-Cast went live, and now I'm going to die, something I've been prepping for the past few years of my life, and I'm still not ready to go—I'm still not ready; I don't want to go; I want to stay, stay, stay.

I grab my phone even though I don't want to answer my End Day call. But then I see the phone is dark, still, and silent. No *DEATH-CAST* caller ID, no vibration, no ringing.

They're not calling me.

My heart doesn't slow down, it's still hammering as I look up and see Valentino holding his phone as it screams the warning of a lifetime.

VALENTINO

12:02 a.m.

Death-Cast is calling to tell me I'm about to die, but my life is only getting started.

This has to be a mistake.

Orion and Dalma and a bunch of strangers look horrified. They shouldn't, though. There's no way I'm dying. Death-Cast is new, and they're bound to get some things wrong. Once I clear this up, we can all go back to partying.

"Don't worry," I say to Orion and Dalma. "I'm sure a bunch of people just got calls they're not supposed to receive."

"Like a pocket dial?" Dalma asks. "I don't think Death-Cast heralds are—"

"I'm sorry to interrupt, but the heralds are humans too." I nod over at the extraterrestrial believers with their eyes to the sky, waiting to be abducted. "So unless the heralds are actually aliens and we got all this wrong, we should leave room for human error."

"Totally," Orion says, but I don't believe he believes me.

"I literally just signed up. It's got to be some mistake."

There are so many eyes on me, and this isn't how I want the world to see me.

It's time to prove everyone wrong so we can move on.

I slide my thumb across my phone's screen to answer this pocket-dial End Day call.

"Hello?" I ask.

"Hello, I'm calling from Death-Cast," a familiar deep voice says, the one we all know well ever since the day he was standing beside the president and announcing this new program. "I'm Joaquin Rosa. Is this Valentino Prince?"

Hearing Joaquin Rosa—Mr. Death-Cast himself—say my name is a shock to the system. It's like being stabbed by cold air all the times I left the house at 5:00 a.m. to go for a run. There's always that temptation to return inside where it's warm and cozy, where I can rest instead. But I'm someone who keeps it moving because that's how you go forward in life. Even now, I feel an urge to hang up this call and pretend it's not happening, but then this cloud will be hanging over my head. I'm sure Joaquin is calling because someone in customer service noticed an error with my registration, and since it's a busy night for everyone, Joaquin is personally seeing to it that there will be no issues when Death-Cast is actually calling about my End Day decades from now. It's awfully kind of him to take the time on this big day.

"Hi, Mr. Rosa. This is Valentino. Everything okay?"

There's a pause on his end. I almost check to see that he

hasn't hung up. "Unfortunately not, Valentino."

"Well, what's going on?" I ask. "Did I mess up my registration form?"

"Valentino, I regret to inform you that sometime in the next twenty-four hours you'll be meeting an untimely death," Joaquin says. "While there isn't anything I can do to suspend that, I want you to know that you still have a chance to live."

I'm shaking my head like he can see me. But Orion and Dalma and a ring of strangers can. I don't mind Orion and Dalma, but everyone else is crowding me like they're waiting for me to break-dance, to put on a show. I wish Times Square would go dark right now, sort of like how all the doomsayers have been prophesizing. Except I don't want the world to end for anyone, myself very much included.

"Are you sure you got the right person?" I ask. "This has to be a mistake, I'm—" I want to say I'm healthy, but I make eye contact with teary Orion, who doesn't need to be reminded that between the two of us he's the one people would vote Most Likely to Receive an End Day Call. Then I remember that being healthy doesn't matter when a car hits you. My sister almost lost her life because of an accident, and now I'm going to be losing mine?

"I just signed up right before midnight. This has to be a mistake," I conclude with no evidence to suggest otherwise.

"I'm afraid it isn't," Joaquin says.

"But how do I know that? How do *you* know that? You can be wrong."

"I'm not wrong, though I wish I were."

"You might be, Mr. Rosa. Maybe you have me confused with another Valentino Prince."

Others exist, I know. I've been typing my name into Google Images as I've done more and more modeling and my pictures have been burying the other Valentino Princes across the country. It felt a bit like winning a popularity contest. There's supposed to be—there *will* be more pictures of me for years to come.

"I understand this is difficult news to receive," Joaquin says. "It breaks my heart to deliver it."

"I didn't even know you'll be making calls."

"I won't, but seeing as this is the first official End Day call, it's mine to make."

The first.

This is the first End Day call.

The first time Death-Cast is calling someone to tell them they're going to die.

This is not how I want to go down in history.

"I don't want to go first," I say. I must sound like I'm a kid all over again, begging my parents to send Scarlett into the bath or dentist chair before me.

"Unfortunately, I don't know at what point today you'll meet your untimely end, but being called first doesn't mean you'll necessarily die first."

I might faint.

I'm actually on the line with Joaquin Rosa, minutes after

his Death-Cast program has gone live across the country, and he's very confident that I—Valentino Prince, the first known Decker—will die today. But he doesn't know how, or what time. That's his claim at least, and something tells me that begging for the truth since the secret could die with me won't go very far.

"Valentino, how may I support you right now? Are you alone?"

No one standing in Times Square is alone, but it feels that way. I'm the only one going through this right now. Then my eyes find Orion again, like magnetism, and he's more than familiar with this fear of dying.

"I'm not alone," I say.

"That's good news," he says.

If I were more confrontational, I'd challenge him. I may not be alone, but the right people aren't here. Scarlett doesn't arrive until the morning, though maybe I should stop her from going and book my own flight back home so I can see everyone. Scarlett, high school friends, kind neighbors. Maybe even my parents will give me the time of day now. But time is so limited. Hours spent at the airport and on the plane could be spent living.

All these thoughts are too surreal.

I came to New York City to change my life, and instead I'm going to die here.

I refocus on the call, ready to move on. "Unless you have

something more concrete to share, I guess this is it."

"Before you go, Valentino, I'd like you to know that on death-cast.com there are various resources on how to talk about your End Day with loved ones, written by some top-tier grief counselors. There will also be different activities updated throughout the day that may be worth participating in," Joaquin says.

Does Death-Cast really think Deckers are going to sit around doing nothing?

I already have plans today. I'm going to sleep in my new apartment before my photo shoot in the morning. Then Scarlett and I are going to explore the city and set up our home and probably celebrate everything by eating dinner on our hardwood floor and using our boxes as tables. And some-time after, or many hours before, I'm apparently going to die.

"I have plans" is all I say.

"Very well. I'll leave you to it," Joaquin says. "On behalf of Death-Cast, we are sorry to lose you. Live this day to the fullest."

No one is going to lose me. I'm not going to be lost.

I'm going to live.

Right as I'm about to hang up the phone, a gunshot echoes across Times Square.

ORION

12:06 a.m.

Just when I thought the Death-Cast ringtone was the scariest thing I'd hear tonight, there's a gunshot.

Gunshots.

Everyone who's been surrounding Valentino starts fleeing in different directions, like roaches when the lights come on. Then a white man with a skull mask appears out of nowhere, firing his gun. Dalma tugs at my wrist so we can get the hell out of here, but I brake when I see Valentino standing still like one of those living statue performers. I wonder if Valentino is shocked at the skull-masked man aiming his gun at him or if he's simply accepted his fate.

But I haven't.

I run at Valentino, knocking him down onto the concrete, right as the gun has been fired. Another gunshot goes off, this time from the police officers as they chase down the skull-masked man who's running away, past Dalma, who's hiding behind an overflowing trash can. She's terrified, I got to get her out of here too, we all got to bounce.

But I can't move.

I feel like high-pressure air is inflating my chest, threatening to explode so fiercely it'll pulverize my bones. There's a burning pain between my shoulder blades, and I don't know if a bullet hit me or not. Maybe I haven't noticed because of adrenaline, or how fast life has been changing and ending since midnight. I want to pat myself down to see if a bullet caught me, but sharp pains are running up my arms, it's like someone is dragging knives along them—up and down, up and down, up and down. I'm going into cardiac arrest, this is the kind of heart attack that I've always thought of as seismic. I try massaging my chest and sitting up to dull the pain, but it's too miserable, and I fall on my back, my face next to shell-shocked Valentino's.

Did I just save him?

If so, by changing his fate, did I change mine too?

Am I going to die instead of him?

Or will we both die by the end of this day?

JOAQUIN ROSA
12:07 a.m.

"This is the way the world ends / Not with a bang but a whimper."

That iconic quote by the poet T. S. Eliot is the first thing Joaquin Rosa thinks about after hanging up with Valentino Prince. He already knows how he'll tweak it for his memoir:

This is the way the first Death-Cast call ends, not with a whimper but a bang.

Joaquin fully expected some whimpering after telling the first Decker he would die today, but instead there was a bang—a gunshot. Many gunshots, to be precise, each one making him want to jump in his seat as if he were being hit by all the bullets. He's safe, mercifully, but he can't say the same for today's remaining Deckers who may be victims of this attack.

Is Valentino Prince a victim, or is he the attacker?

Solving that mystery isn't Joaquin's job.

Removing mystery from the equation of death is.

Joaquin jumps out of his seat, turning to the heralds who have been waiting in the wings for his command. "Begin the End Day calls," he says, doing his best to keep his composure. The call was private, so no one else heard the gunshots, but it won't be long before it's pieced together that an act of violence occurred moments after speaking with the first Decker. He knows that Death-Cast will be blamed for this, scaring off the investors he needs to go global with the program.

The heralds look like ghosts as they float across the room in their white button-down shirts and light gray slacks and ties. Joaquin prepped them to look cool, calm, and collected, the very image the world needs to see to understand the strength and professionalism of the people on the other side of these phones and computers. He releases a deep sigh as the heralds take their seats, switch on their monitors, and get to work.

One look at Naya and Joaquin knows his wife senses a disturbance. He'll clue her in after the media has been dismissed, but he'll have to be fast because once all those reporters and photographers have their phones returned to them, they'll discover the attack and everyone will blame Death-Cast.

He can't ever say it out loud, but he knows that one person's ending is simply a contribution to this company's beginning, and *not* a result of Death-Cast's existence. No matter what anyone says.

As Joaquin looks between the heralds and the photographers, there's one thing at the forefront of his mind: There's an undeniable frontrunner for the cover of his memoir. After all, there's nothing like the bang of a gunshot to get a man's life flashing before his eyes; he just hopes the camera caught Joaquin's reaction.

If not, it would be a waste of a tragic moment.

VALENTINO

Everyone is running for their lives, but not me.

I no longer have one to run for.

I've always done my best to move forward when life is challenging me—morning jogs, jumping up to the next weights during sets, all those casting rejections that made me feel horrible about myself—but what am I supposed to do when life is ending? Just accept it?

When I heard that gunshot, I froze up.

I never expected to see bullets flying around tonight. Is that how I'm going to die?

It's such a terrifying thought that I can't get my body to do anything except lie here on the ground, shivering like an animal that's been abandoned in the cold. The stampede continues around me. There's footsteps running past me, others skipping over my whole body. I even get kicked in the back. One moment, Orion is lying down with his eyes on the sky, and the next, Dalma appears out of nowhere. She's helping him sit up as she yells for help—as she yells *my* name for help.

"He's having a heart attack, Valentino, please help!" Dalma cradles Orion to her chest, slipping some pill into his mouth and telling him to swallow. "Hold on, O-Bro, I'm going to get you help."

It's so strange how we tell someone who's dying to hold on, as if they have a choice.

Do I have a choice? Can I just tell the world, *No, I won't be dying today. Try again later.*

"We need a doctor!" Dalma shouts.

Not a single person stops running. How many of them assume Orion must be dead already? Well, they're stupid. I am too. Orion could've run away, but he didn't. He stayed by my side. More than that, he saved my life even though he knows I'm dying.

I was wrong to think I no longer have a life to run for. I do. It's just not my own.

If there's anything I can do to make sure Death-Cast doesn't call Orion too, now's the time.

I don't think about my personal situation, I put all my focus into my body—tapping into my core to sit up, hands flat on the ground to push off, firm stance on my feet. "Let me get him," I say.

Dalma gives me space, picking up Orion's hat that's fallen off his head and revealing a brown forest of curls. I hoist

Orion into my arms, carrying him like I'm Superman after catching a civilian out of the sky. If I do everything right, I just might be a hero.

"Where do we go?"

"This way," Dalma says, leading us away from the stampede and down Forty-Seventh Street.

"Should we call an ambulance?"

"I can't risk them not treating Orion over someone who's been shot."

How long is it going to take for medics to not even bother treating someone if they know they're a Decker? A week, a month, a year?

"So what do we do?"

"I'm looking up nearest hospitals," Dalma says while scrolling through Google Maps. "NYU has a hospital on Thirty-First, but Orion had a bad doctor there one time so we should go uptown to Lenox Hill on Seventy-Seventh instead."

"I live on Seventy-Seventh," I say.

Dalma looks over her shoulder, as if she's expecting me to elaborate on why that coincidence is important. It isn't. "Keep him upright," she says.

I don't understand why keeping Orion upright is necessary, but I do as I'm told. I shift his head so that his face is resting on my shoulder. His eyes are closed, and he keeps pressing his hand into his heart like he's giving himself CPR.

I suppose that's what he's doing. I don't know how much it's helping, since he's also trying so hard to get a full breath in, but he's stopped short every time. This is what it looks like to fight for your life.

Dalma spots a taxi, and it becomes a race between her and someone else. She wins and guards the door to the passenger seat with her life. I do my best to get there as quickly as possible without falling, and when I reach the car, I prop up Orion in the middle and stretch the seat belt over his waist.

"Is he okay?" the driver asks.

"No," Dalma says. "Please get us to Lenox Hill Hospital."

"You should call an ambulance," he says.

"My brother will die in your car if you don't get a move on now!"

"That's what I'm afraid of."

The driver begins our journey, and he keeps watching Orion from the rearview mirror. It's not even during red lights either, it's while he's actively driving. It's drivers like this why my sister was almost killed.

"Can you please keep your eyes on the road?"

The *please* doesn't mask the attitude in my voice, but it does the trick.

As we're driving, I can't help but wonder if I'm endangering Orion and Dalma by being in the car. If I'm marked to die, does that make me a magnet for death? I don't know, but it's a really lonely thought to have. Isn't the whole point of

Deckers getting these End Day calls to give them a chance to get their affairs in order and hug their family and friends one last time? I suppose that doesn't matter, since my family is on the other side of the country.

I reach for my phone, ready to call Scarlett to break the news. But it's not in my pocket. I triple-check my pockets in my pants as if it'll magically manifest since the third time's always the charm. Nothing, of course. Where could it—

Damn it.

I never put the phone away. I never got the chance to. I was hanging up with Joaquin Rosa when I heard the first gunshot and froze. Then Orion tackled me, and the phone must've fallen out of my hand. This is the worst start to my final day on this planet. Returning to Times Square to look for the phone would be so stupid. Fool me once, shame on New York. Fool me twice, shame on me for risking my life so I can call my sister and for holding out hope that Death-Cast might call back to tell me it's not actually my End Day.

The phone is gone. I have to accept that just like my fate.

Besides, it already served its grand purpose.

No other call will be as life-changing as the one that started this mess.

JOAQUIN ROSA
12:21 a.m.

This isn't how Joaquin imagined Death-Cast's launch.

He believed the calls would be simpler.

Statistically, there are big spikes in death rates on holidays. More drivers on the road equals more accidents. Sharing a cigarette with a family member can lead to one's lungs turning on them, and since they can't be treated in understaffed emergency rooms due to the holidays, the day is stained with loss. Not to mention all the suicides in this unforgiving world. It's all painful, but ultimately, not uncommon. But today isn't a traditional holiday.

Perhaps it's still too early, but Joaquin expected some praise to start flowing in by now. How many people are living differently, more thoughtfully since discovering this isn't an ordinary Saturday, but instead their final Saturday, their one and only End Day?

Instead of treating Joaquin as an angel, they're calling him the devil.

"They're talking about me like I'm the villain," Joaquin says to his wife. He's in the company suite, scrolling through Twitter on his laptop while Naya looks over his shoulder. This is all so heartbreaking. And such a slap to the face. No one knows the sacrifices he made to bring these forecasts to the public. "The world knows I didn't invent death, yes?"

"You're reinventing death," Naya says.

"I'm reinventing how we *live* with death," Joaquin counters.

"I'm familiar with Death-Cast's adages, my love." Naya sits beside Joaquin, prying his hands off the keyboard and holding them in her own. "But the rest of the world is still catching on. I warned you that choosing to be so face-forward also means becoming the face of death until people understand otherwise."

If only Joaquin were actually a psychic overlord from space so he could look into the future to know when this abuse will stop. He's itching to read more comments, to find one loud voice to inspire others to view this situation differently, to remind everyone that Joaquin is a human from this planet with a love for life.

"I'm just trying to help," he says, wondering if this was all a mistake.

Perhaps Death-Cast should have remained buried.

"You are helping," Naya says. "But until they believe in you, don't forget who already does."

Joaquin gazes at his brilliant, beautiful wife, praying that Death-Cast won't call either of them until they're at least one hundred so they can grow old together. During his wedding vows, he told Naya that he wants to love her even when she has more wrinkles than any of the shirts he balls up and tosses into the closet at the end of the day. She found him funny even when others didn't, and just like that first time he heard her laugh in a coffee shop, he knew it was a song he could listen to on repeat for the rest of his life.

Together, Joaquin and Naya turn, their eyes landing on their son. Alano is only nine years old, and it took just as many years to conceive him. The Rosas tried and tried, then gave up, and tried and tried again to no success. Joaquin kept blaming himself, furious at all those sperm cells that were strolling during the race and not even bothering to cross the finish line. He resisted all conversations about adoption because more than anything he wanted a child whose DNA stemmed from his own, from Naya's.

A miracle happened and here he is, Alano Angel Rosa.

He's fast asleep on the couch with his new German shepherd puppy as if tonight isn't the start of a true golden age.

Given how the night is unfolding, perhaps it's great that his son isn't witnessing these horrors.

Joaquin may not be the devil, but let everyone believe that if they must.

They'll remember soon enough who the real monsters are and realize that he was the hero all along.

VALENTINO

12:29 a.m.

En route to the hospital, I can't help but wonder what's going to kill me.

Had Orion gotten the End Day call, he would have every reason to suspect his heart being responsible for doing him in.

But me?

It could be anything.

A car crash seems fitting. It's a cruel fate that's just enough to twin Scarlett's accident except actually be fatal this time. I might fall down one of those steaming manholes and bleed out in the sewer. Or I can escape from a fire only to fall off the fire escape. I'd hate that irony. There are endless possibilities for freaky accidents. But so far the biggest threat has been a gunman with a skull mask. He didn't stick around to finish the job, which has me thinking he wasn't really after me. But what if someone *does* target me? Who could I have pissed off so badly? I was nice to the airport employee who helped me find my suitcases at the carousel. I tipped my taxi driver. My landlord doesn't seem to be a fan, but killing me isn't going to get him his rent money. The only other people I personally know in this city are . . .

The only other people I know in this city are in the back seat of this taxi with me.

That's a ridiculous thought. Orion and Dalma are sweet, welcoming New Yorkers who have been through so much. They wouldn't cast that loss on anyone else. Besides, it's hard to imagine Orion being in a position to kill anyone. He's the most vulnerable person in this car. Then again, it doesn't have to be murder. What if being near Orion, someone so close to death's edge, brings trouble my way? This very trip to bring him to the hospital could be what kills me, a car could smash into my door right now and—

I have to stop.

This isn't helping.

Orion and Dalma are no danger to me. If someone wants to kill me, it's probably some other model who wants my campaign gig.

No.

I'm done entertaining thoughts on who wants to murder me.

Last time I checked, I'm not a fortune-teller who can lay out some cards and discover my fate. I've been told everything there is to know: I'm going to die tonight, or later today if I'm lucky. Even if none of this feels lucky at all.

We arrive at Lenox Hill Hospital, and I carry Orion down the halls as Dalma leads me to the emergency room. Everything is moving so quickly as the nurses come around the counter and examine Orion as Dalma fills them in on his condition. I place Orion on a roll-away bed, telling him he's going to be okay.

The nurse wheels Orion behind a curtain. "Family only," she says as Dalma follows.

"I am family," Dalma says.

The nurse seems doubtful. "By blood?"

"By law."

The nurse nods, pulling the curtain closed around them.

"Did Death-Cast call Orion?" I hear the nurse ask.

"No. Let's not give them any reason to," Dalma says.

That nurse's question is unreal. There's been a lot of debate since Death-Cast was announced about what the roles of medical professionals will be when it comes to attending to Deckers. Are resources worth using on a patient who won't live regardless? Should doctors treat everyone without knowing their End Day status? This idea that if Orion had been called by Death-Cast they might not take care of him is horrifying.

That's going to be my reality.

I'm surely going to be involved in a horrible accident

between now and midnight.

Nineteen-year-olds aren't known for dying of old age, or passing in their sleep.

If I'm brought to the hospital later, will the doctors bother trying to save my life?

Or will they stand there and watch me die?

ORION
12:36 a.m.

There's a warm light on my face, like I'm about to move on to the afterlife or something.

But I know this isn't that.

The nurse is prying open my eyelids, studying my pupils while asking for my name. Before I can answer, Dalma beats her to it.

"It's Orion. Orion Pagan."

"We're checking to see if he knows," the nurse says.

"Right, gotcha. I'm sorry."

I can't see Dalma, but I know she's panicking. "It's okay, Dalma," I manage to breathe out.

"He knows my name," Dalma says. "That means he's okay, right?"

Just because I'm not laid out in Times Square anymore doesn't mean I'm in the clear yet. A lot of people don't know this, but heart attacks can go on for hours. Ignore every TV

101

show where the character is clutching their chest one minute and dying the next. It's not like that, even though sometimes that feels more merciful.

For real, every damn blessing to Dalma and Valentino for getting me here ASAP. Even as I'm going through excruciating pain and would've been good with being treated sooner in an ambulance, I know riding to the hospital in style like that isn't cheap. Everyone's always going on about how my life is priceless and that means paying up so I can live it. Still, Dayana and Floyd go days without checking the mail whenever we're expecting another bill. Sometimes I think about what Dalma's family could do with all that money if I just died already.

It's heartbreaking how much it costs to be alive when you're always dying.

JOAQUIN ROSA
12:40 a.m.

Joaquin is in the call center, watching the heralds navigate the inaugural End Day calls.

There are twenty heralds working tonight's shift. Everything moved fast in July. It had to since the company was essentially announced overnight. In under forty-eight hours, Joaquin built his core team, all people he's known for years and would trust with his life. Then came time to find the first wave of heralds. After extensive background checks, candidates had to go through three sessions before being hired. The first was a phone call with Death-Cast's HR manager, who disregarded any candidate asking about the company's secret, seeing it as a red flag that they were more interested in solving the mystery than how best to perform the job at hand. The second session was a ten-minute meeting with Naya, where she asked them about their lives, later ranking them on how compassionate they seemed in a short window.

Having had her own difficult experiences with doctors over the years, she's aware that someone in an industry that prioritizes one's well-being doesn't necessarily make them a good person. The final session was a series of practice calls, all observed by Joaquin personally, to see if the candidate was empathetic and patient, though not too patient at the risk of other Deckers not receiving their alert because the herald is tied up on another line.

And now, Joaquin is seeing his employees in action, moving around the call center like a teacher in their classroom while the students take an exam. How the heralds do tonight will determine their future in this company.

The stakes are too high to be bad at this job.

His star herald is undoubtedly Roah Wetherholt, who switched from suicide-prevention hotlines to calling people to tell them they're going to die with the same care they previously used to save lives. It seemed as if their crisis counseling was weighing too much on their heart, not always knowing if the person went on to live. At least at Death-Cast, Roah knows the fate on the other end of the call. If Roah keeps up the good work, Joaquin anticipates he'll be promoting them to travel the country as the company expands to train future heralds. His most surprising hire was Andrea Donahue whose rather extended résumé was a slight cause for concern, but her fierce love for her daughter really struck a chord with Naya, and the way Andrea handled her calls with tact impressed Joaquin; she's blowing through her calls tonight with great efficiency. The same can't be said for Rolando Rubio, a former elementary school guidance counselor who showed remarkable empathy during the test sessions, especially during the simulation where he had to speak with a parent about their dying child, but he's moving too slowly tonight, stuck on his very first call as if it's his job to help the Decker map out every hour of their End Day. Perhaps he's better off working as a funeral director, where his sympathies will be better appreciated, and most important, where time isn't of the essence.

Joaquin hovers around Rolando, tapping his watch, urging him to finish this call.

"I can't," Rolando mouths with teary eyes, continuing on with the Decker.

Joaquin admires Rolando's devotion. Every Decker is a human being, and all human beings deserve respect. Too many people over the course of time have not been shown dignity while on their deathbeds. But what Joaquin ultimately needs to get across to his employees is that they must find the middle ground.

Minutes later, when Rolando finally delivers the signature parting message, he scrolls through his computer for the next Decker's information, as if Joaquin isn't shadowing him.

"One moment," Joaquin says.

Rolando looks up at his boss. "Is this because I'm not going fast enough?"

"I want you to know that I appreciate all your work

tonight," Joaquin says, hoping to cool down Rolando, who's clearly upset. "The care you're showing will be meaningful to all Deckers and stay with them during their final hours, I'm sure of it. I simply need you to guide more Deckers before night's end."

"It's a lot harder than it looks," Rolando says.

Was Rolando not paying attention when Joaquin made tonight's first call? Is he not aware that Joaquin is Death-Cast's creator and may know a thing or two about the hardships of these jobs? Does he not suspect that although tonight is the official launch of the program that Joaquin is no stranger to telling people they're going to die? Because he isn't.

This may be a first for the country, but it's not a first for Joaquin.

"I understand these conversations are difficult, even impossible," Joaquin says. "But we have a responsibility to everyone who is paying for our crucial services."

"It's not like this old man was asking why his cable box wasn't working. He had no one in his life. I couldn't just hang up."

Joaquin toyed around with the idea of setting automatic timers to the calls, cutting off the line after five minutes so the heralds wouldn't be put in this position. Perhaps it's something to revisit at the end of the first month, using the average time spent on calls to determine that magic number of minutes.

"While you're taking time as you walk one Decker through their End Day, think of those who are dying without ever knowing their time was up," Joaquin reminds him, knowing he has said this over and over during the training sessions leading up to tonight. But now that the heralds are connecting with real people who are really dying, the urgency behind this statement must carry more weight than ever before.

Rolando seems broken down, rubbing his eyes. "I'll do my best."

"Don't worry about your best tonight," Joaquin gently says. "That will come with more experience. Just see if you can improve your efforts so you can reach more people in need of your care."

Joaquin allows Rolando to return to work, hoping he'll make up for lost time.

If not, maybe working in a funeral home isn't a bad idea.

Those who can't be trusted to call people before they die are better off dealing with them when they're dead.

ROLANDO RUBIO
1:04 a.m.

Death-Cast did not call Rolando Rubio because he isn't dying today, though according to his boss, it seems as if anyone who dies without knowing it's their End Day will be Rolando's fault. All because he spent too much time on the phone with one Decker. Pardon him for caring and for grieving a stranger.

It's becoming clearer and clearer that Rolando isn't cut out for this job as a Death-Cast herald. He'll see how he feels by the end of the night, but if this doesn't work out, he expects he'll return to guidance counseling in public schools to help identify any child's issue that's resulting in their grades dropping or acting out in the classroom. Sometimes it was grief, and Rolando was always confused why a parent would neglect to inform him or the child's teachers so they could all be mindful of any behavioral shifts. Rolando excelled at being there for the students. He created spaces for them to cry. He supervised them in the gym so they could blow off some steam. He gave them time to process their loss. That last one is not a luxury afforded to Deckers. They must simply process their own impending deaths in a single moment so the heralds can keep it moving.

He believed having a heart would be a strength for this position, but maybe ripping his own out of his chest would be better for everyone, himself included. If he doesn't have a heart, then that means it can't be broken.

One hour in and he's coming undone.

How could he not?

Rolando's first and longest call was to an elderly man, who awoke to his alert in confusion and fear, thinking this was all a dream. As the Decker, Clint Suarez, came to understand his reality, it broke Rolando. Clint was so lonely that he just wanted to tell his life story to anyone, even the very someone who was predicting his death. So Rolando listened and listened to Clint's story of a dancing career both lived and unlived, and recommended he put on his favorite song and dance one final time before they hung up. How was a call with an eighty-seven-year-old so hard? Rolando's expecting Clint will die of old age, but what if he has a heart attack while dancing? Is that Rolando's fault? Is it Death-Cast's? Is that how he was always destined to die?

He has no answers, and no time to try and find them.

After being scolded by his boss twenty minutes ago,

Rolando is trying to move faster through his calls. But how do you not stay on the line with a nineteen-year-old girl whose whole life was ahead of her? Or feel compelled to call a man over and over when he's not answering the phone, hoping the Decker didn't die before Rolando could reach him?

Truth be told, the only call Rolando would be happy to make right now is to the woman who got away, Gloria Dario, though he prefers thinking of her by her maiden name, Medina. A funny story about her son, Paz, would remind him that life isn't all about death. Unfortunately, his phone is in his locker so he can focus on the task at hand, and it's too late to disturb her anyhow. Her husband, Frankie, would be upset if Rolando woke everyone up; that man's temper is alarming, and Gloria would have to pay the price.

An even greater truth to be told is that Rolando wouldn't mind seeing Frankie's name appear on this computer, promising his death, but unfortunately Frankie's not registered for the service. If he were, that would give Rolando more than enough reason to keep working at Death-Cast.

It would be the one End Day call that Rolando could make with a smile on his face.

ANDREA DONAHUE
1:07 a.m.

Death-Cast did not call Andrea Donahue because she is not dying today, but the same can't be said for the nineteen Deckers she's called in the past hour.

Well, maybe the same *can* be said for them.

Who's to say if Death-Cast is even real?

Not Andrea. She doesn't need to know the company's big secret (though if someone bribed her with an offer worth risking her solid salary and ironically amazing life insurance, she could be persuaded to do some digging. The private school she's hoping to send her daughter to won't be cheap). She minds her business—mostly. She can't help but notice her fellow herald Rolando is terrible at this job. How did he spend forty minutes on a single call? Andrea believes in kindness, but come on. Befriending someone who is about to die has no value; it's like flushing cash down the toilet. This person will not become a lifelong friend who attends your wedding, or your funeral. They will not celebrate your triumphs, or comfort you during your failures. They won't even move into tomorrow with you.

What's the point?

After Rolando hangs up his call that was certainly shorter than his first but still not as timely as it could've been, Andrea knows she must intervene.

"Rolando," she whispers. "Can I give you some advice?"

He nods with teary eyes and no backbone.

"Do yourself a favor and stop thinking of these Deckers as people," she says, turning to her computer and dialing the next number because time is of the essence—the other important lesson her coworker needs to learn. "Just deliver the warning and move on. Getting someone's life story isn't something you should bring home at the end of the day."

He stares, and she knows her words have flown over his head, much like whenever she gives her daughter priceless advice. She has said her piece and won't bother him again.

Andrea goes back to work as her twentieth Decker of the night answers the phone.

"Hello, I'm calling from Death-Cast. . . ."

While the Deckers may no longer have futures, Andrea is positive she will have a long one here at Death-Cast.

VALENTINO
1:11 a.m.

I hate waiting rooms.

The eight hours Scarlett had spent in surgery, I couldn't stay still—I couldn't *wait*. It's like I didn't have that organ in my body. So I stayed busy. When Mom was hungry, I headed to the cafeteria and brought her food. When Dad was tired but didn't want to close his eyes, I found him a nice, strong black coffee from this little diner across the street from the hospital. When the parking meter needed to be fed, I was there at the top of the hour with my pocket change. During all the other still moments, I would pace the halls or wash my face, hands, and hair in the bathroom or get to know the nurses or flip through magazines for fun gossip to share with Scarlett once her surgery was over. Once she was okay.

Waiting to see if someone you love will live is excruciating.

Waiting to die is miserable too.

I wish I was a parking meter, able to buy more time with the drop of a quarter. Especially since Scarlett isn't answering my calls, either because she's too busy or she doesn't recognize the number. The nurse has let me use the desk phone twice so far, and I don't think she's going to care if I believe in the third time being the charm. But my hands are tied here. Scarlett has to know what's happening, especially before she boards her plane in the next couple hours. If the nurse gives me attitude again I might have to play the Decker card. She'll either become extremely sympathetic and pull up a chair for me so I can spam my sister with calls until she answers, or she'll kick me out of the building for fear of me endangering the patients. I don't know what I'll do if I'm tossed out on the streets like some ticking time bomb; maybe that unknown is why anyone would be concerned to host a Decker in their space.

For now, I'm sitting here in the waiting room. There's no one to tend to, so I'm doing what the room was built for.

Waiting.

I'm waiting for Dalma to come out of the ER.

I'm waiting for Orion's heart to settle.

I'm waiting for a premature death that could come around the corner any moment from now, even this very second. . . .

Nothing.

Everything is eerily still. It's as if I've died already and I'm in purgatory, life's ultimate waiting room.

Though I'm guessing I'm alive because there's no way

purgatory has a vending machine like the one across from me. It's humming, like it wants me to know it's there. To spend the money I can't use to buy more time on some Pringles or Pepsi instead. I quit everything sugary a couple years ago since my smile and body are my work. I get up from this uncomfortable chair and stare into the vending machine at all the soda and chips and chocolate and candy. I zone out, remembering so many times where I said no to a dessert menu, or bite of pie, or Slurpee at a movie theater, or anything that would've brought me joy if I didn't think it was going to threaten my body.

Caring so much about my livelihood meant not caring about how I was living.

I feel so stupid now.

I grab my wallet. I'm ready to spend every dollar I have on making up for lost snacks when I hear my name.

"Valentino," Dalma says, coming out of nowhere. "You're still here."

"Was I supposed to leave?" I ask.

"No, not at all. It's surprising that you would wait here, since . . . you know."

I'm stuck here. Going back to my new place doesn't make a lot of sense. The same goes with buying a ticket back to Arizona. I would lose too many valuable hours on the trip alone. Besides, I couldn't do that until I'm in contact with Scarlett to stop her from getting on the plane and making sure we're not ships—planes—passing in the night. Honestly, I don't know what's best for me. I'm too overwhelmed to think straight.

"I'm here for now. How's Orion?"

Dalma settles into a seat, resting her head against the wall. "They've stabilized him. He's going to be okay."

"Is he staying overnight?"

Dalma shrugs. "Maybe. My family's waiting to hear what the deal is before they drive back from Ohio."

"Your family?" Then I remember what happened to his parents. "Oh, right. So he lives with you?"

"We live together. It's his home too." Dalma sits up. "Sorry, I'm not snapping at you. I'm just really protective of making sure Orion never feels othered."

"No, I get it. I find myself walking some tricky lines as a twin."

"Does she know yet?"

"I haven't been able to reach her. I lost my phone in Times Square and—"

"Oh my god, really?"

"I realized it in the car but didn't want to bother you."

Dalma pops out of her seat with her phone at the ready. "Use mine. Do you know her number by heart?"

I nod. Scarlett's number is the only one I know off the top of my head. Our area codes and first three numbers are identical, but the final four digits are unique. We've always considered our phone numbers to be fraternal twins too.

"Thanks so much."

I put in Scarlett's number, desperate for her to answer even though I have no idea how to begin telling her that I'm living my End Day. That in the next twenty-three hours she's going to become an only child. Unless something horrible is going to befall her too. Then we will have entered and left this world together. But I don't want that for her any more than I want it for me. If given the choice, I would want Scarlett alive and me dead. I know it's true because when she was in the hospital I was bothering every doctor and nurse and letting them know they could harvest me for every last organ Scarlett needed to be saved. And even though I'm not as religious as my proud and strict Catholic parents, I sure found a lot of faith when I went to the chapel and prayed to God to take me instead of my sister. It seems he was listening and answered my call.

Unlike Scarlett.

It's okay. This gives me more time to figure out how to break the news.

Time I hope I have.

1:28 a.m.

The End Day calls are managed by the time zone of a Decker's registered city. That means had I been here as a visitor, Death-Cast wouldn't have reached out to me yet. I wouldn't have been the very first Decker. Maybe if I never moved here, I wouldn't be a Decker at all.

Playing those mind games won't get me anywhere.

Instead, I'm worried about Scarlett. She's still living in the past, still living without Death-Cast. The same for everyone else in Arizona. They'll have no reason to drive with greater caution, and what if Scarlett has found herself in another accident and that's why she's not answering the calls?

I feel like I'm not going to be able to breathe until I know she's okay.

After Scarlett's accident, a friend asked if I had sensed something happened to her. Twins don't have a concrete sixth sense to know everything going on with the other, even twins as close as us. I was out shopping for new concealer that afternoon because the shadows under my eyes were getting darker from too many nights where I couldn't sleep because I was questioning my dreams of becoming a full-time model. I wasn't standing in the middle of the drugstore, where I suddenly dropped my shopping basket as if a feeling of dread hammered my stomach out of nowhere. I only felt all that once I got the call from my parents. Though I wish I could close my eyes and concentrate and hear my sister's heartbeat so I know she's okay.

All I hear is the hum of the vending machine and footsteps approaching me and Dalma. The same nurse from before, the one who asked if Death-Cast called Orion, stops in front of us.

"Orion is drowsy, but you can see him now," the nurse says.

"Thanks, Mary Jo," Dalma says, getting up. "Come on, Valentino."

"Really?" I ask. I'm relieved he's okay, I just know I'm not family.

"You can hang back if you want, but you're welcome to see him too."

I follow her. I'm more than okay with finally escaping this waiting room where it feels like time stands still even though precious minutes are going unspent. I'm holding on to Dalma's phone, and I check the signal bars again. It's still three out of four. Dalma attributes that to the hospital's connection.

We enter the ER and stand outside Orion's curtained space.

"Knock, knock," Dalma says.

"Come in," Orion says.

I pull back the curtain, and Orion looks far worse than I expected. Curls are plastered to his sweaty forehead, and his eyes are red as if he's been infected with some virus. He's shivering even though he's wrapped up in a blanket. One of those black Velcro armbands—I absolutely don't know the medical term—is connecting him to the monitor that looks older than the computer in my mom's office.

He weakly nods. "Hey."

"Stupid question, but how are you feeling?" I ask.

"Just another day in the life," Orion says. Then his eyes go wide, like he's taken another jolt to the heart. "Shit, I'm sorry. I hate all this, but I'm so used to it at this point and—"

"You're fine," I interrupt. He doesn't need to get worked up over that comment. "I'm relieved you're alive. I also can't believe you live like this."

"Unfortunately," Orion says.

"Mom and Floyd are talking about driving back," Dalma says.

"Tell them to stay. I'll be fine."

"You know they won't," she says.

"Are you going to be admitted?" I ask.

"Probably," Orion says. "I doubt I'm in the clear yet."

I check the time. "Aren't the Death-Cast calls ending soon on the East Coast?"

"By two o'clock," Dalma says.

A lot can change in half an hour.

Everything can change in one minute.

"You're going to be fine," I say.

Orion shivers. "I'm hoping you'll be good too. I mean, we literally dodged a bullet after Death-Cast called. Maybe we changed your fate."

The thought gives me hope, like I'm not doomed to walk through my last day like some zombie.

"Maybe."

"I should check if any Deckers have even died," Dalma says, taking her phone back. "The whole system can be screwed up."

This is literally day one of Death-Cast. Assuming their predictions are even real, there still has to be room for error. There's no way they're going to get everything right. I could be a mistake.

Now I'm a zombie coming back to life.

My eyeball gets sucked back into its socket.

My unhinged jaw screws back into place.

My bones mend and my skin regenerates.

I should call Death-Cast's customer service number to confirm that my name is no longer on their to-die list or server or however they're keeping track of the Deckers.

Dalma looks up from her phone, doom in her eyes. "I'm sorry. Joaquin Rosa shared a report a few minutes ago. Death-Cast obviously can't track who has or hasn't died, since it's not like we're microchipped, but there have been three confirmed Decker deaths."

Just like that, my eyeball pops back out, my jaw swings loose, and my bones snap and pierce through my skin.

I'm a dead man walking.

"Thanks for investigating," I say.

"All hope isn't lost yet," Orion says.

I shake my head. "It's probably in my best interest to treat today like it's my last."

Orion and Dalma don't waste their breath trying to protest.

All hope has flatlined.

"Thanks for saving my life, though," I tell Orion. "However much of it I have left."

ORION
1:40 a.m.

Surviving this latest near-death experience has taught me something huge: I'm rich in luck.

Don't get it twisted, on most days I'd prefer cold, hard cash so I can do some damage in a bookstore or buy a new laptop that doesn't die whenever it's separated from its charger for more than a minute. But on nights like tonight, when it would've been so easy for my heart to just give up in Times Square, I got to recognize that my wallet is stacked with good fortune. I just wish I could share the wealth and drop some luck into Valentino's empty cup. Maybe luck could save his life too.

I'm still not ruling out that he's going to be okay.

The curtains part, and a doctor enters. Her curly black hair is pulled back in a ponytail, and she's radiating with her brown skin and bright smile as she looks at all of us. "Hello. I'm Dr. Emeterio." She scans our faces again, like she's trying to make sense of who's who to who. "Is everyone here family?"

"I'm his sister," Dalma says, not bothering to give the legal rundown. Props to this doctor for not questioning us given the different shades of our skin.

"I'm not family," Valentino says. "I can leave."

"Please don't go," I say. I don't trust the outside world and that includes anything beyond this curtain. "We've all had a really, really rough night."

"So I hear," Dr. Emeterio says as she studies me and my ECG, aka my electrocardiogram, aka my recorded heart-beats. "It appears your heart didn't get the memo that you were trying to have some fun tonight. Don't you hate when that happens?" she adds with a wink.

She's walking fresh air compared to some other doctors I've worked with who suck up everything good in a room. It's simple, but Dr. Emeterio not blaming me for the heart attack is a huge plus in my book. My primary doctor, Dr. Luke, is always giving me shit for anything bad that happens while I'm out living my life, like I've got some death wish.

I guess I do have a death wish: don't die with any regrets.

"You're eighteen, so I'm happy to keep chatting with you, but are we waiting on your parents?"

"Guardians are out of town," I say, not trying to get into my backstory. "But I'm good to start."

Dr. Emeterio nods. "Noted. Can you walk me through what happened tonight?"

I don't know where to start, or if it's even my place. I lock eyes with Valentino.

"Death-Cast called me," Valentino says.

I hate hearing those words come out of his mouth as much as I hate believing what it means for him. "Then I got shot at in Times Square and Orion saved me."

"And, uh . . ." I'm reliving the horror all over again—the gunshot, fighting for my breaths, staring at the night sky like it would be my last. "My heart went into overdrive."

"I gave him aspirin to buy us more time," Dalma says.

Dr. Emeterio is speechless, and it's like the light has left her eyes. I'm sure she's seen it all in the hospital until she turns to Valentino, a real Decker who's walking, breathing, living proof of Death-Cast's predictions.

"I'm sorry that Death-Cast called you," she says.

Valentino is still, the harsh lights of the ER beaming down on him like he's in the studio. Except no one should take his photo right now because I'd hate the thousand words that picture would say. His arms are crossed as he stares at the floor, lost in his own world—a really fucked-up world where Death-Cast called him and a fucked-up stranger tried to kill him and a fucked-up fate awaits him.

"Can you give him a physical or something?" I ask Dr. Emeterio. Just because someone looks fine on the outside doesn't mean they're not living with invisible threats. "Maybe an X-ray can show us what's going on."

Valentino considers this, not lifting his eyes. "We know what's happening. I've got a case of death."

I hate seeing Valentino so defeated. Since I can't donate some luck, I want to throw some hope his way. It just can't come from me.

"Dr. Emeterio, there's no way every Death-Cast prediction is going to come true, right?"

For a single second, time stops.

Breaths are held.

Eyes don't blink.

No one's dying.

Then a single word unfreezes everyone.

"No."

Hearts are beating.

Hope is building.

"It seems very unlikely that Death-Cast will have a perfect record, especially on the first night of the program," Dr. Emeterio says.

This is seriously music to my ears, and I think Valentino is listening closely too, like this is about to become his new favorite song.

"There's no known science behind the End Days, or if it's science at all, but seeing as I don't have the imagination of my kids, I'm opting to believe Death-Cast's sources are operating in the same field as mine. I'm not getting stressed out over extraterrestrials or sorcery until someone gives me concrete proof," Dr. Emeterio says with a little grin. "What's important to keep in mind is that as life changes and science advances, mistakes are made."

"This is refreshing," Dalma says. "O's doctor doesn't even believe in Death-Cast."

Dr. Emeterio rolls her eyes, immortalizing herself as my favorite doctor. "That's unfortunate. It's a disservice to our patients to not embrace Death-Cast, especially for someone like you, Orion, who may require a transplant in the near future if your heart isn't stable."

"I'm on the waitlist, but my doctor keeps trying to stick a ventricular heart device in me instead."

"It's a solid consideration if you're okay with the necessary recovery time pushing you further down the waitlist," Dr. Emeterio says.

"Which would suck if my match appeared," I say.

Every physician we've consulted agrees that your boy needs a new heart, but they're also quick to let me know my situation isn't critical enough compared to other patients, aka I'm not dying enough for anyone to save my life now.

I'm constantly playing tug-of-war against myself, and it's this never-ending tie. I want to be strong enough to finally get that win so this game can be over.

"There are no easy choices," Dr. Emeterio says.

"But something has to change. This can't keep being my life."

No one gets the toll all this takes on me.

Like waking up in hospital rooms, relieved that I've beat the odds again but dreading when I won't. Or the smell of bleach and just-fine food. I'm even over the get-well flowers that we've stopped bringing home because they attract flies. I'm embarrassed every time Dayana's temper gets the best of her as she fights with doctors like they're personally withholding healthy hearts in the break room's refrigerator. I feel guilty every single time my health gets in the way of my family's life, especially since I shouldn't even be their problem in the first place, since I'm not actually family.

But nothing's changing.

This is going to be my life until I don't have one.

My anxiety is mounting, blowing up my heart like an erupting volcano.

Between my blood pressure cuff and all the electrodes, my ECG monitor is going off.

"Breathe, O-Bro, breathe," Dalma says, rubbing smooth circles into my palm.

Easier said than done, but I don't go off, she's only trying to help. It's just really frustrating being treated like I'm catching my breath after running a marathon when in reality I'm literally lying in a hospital bed and my heart is racing more than someone who's been sprinting. I've been combating with home remedies, trying to get better. First we worked fish into every meal—fish tacos, anchovy pizza, salmon chowder—so I can get all the omega-3 acids I need to reduce the risk of sudden cardiac death. No lie, I was relieved when it wasn't doing the trick because those meals were so gross, one hundred percent not for me; I went full vegetarian after that. Then we experimented with beta-blockers to slow down my heart rate, but my lungs kept spasming, and suffocating is a no-go when you're trying to live. Lately I've done a couple yoga classes with Dalma to strengthen all my muscles, but all that quiet time leads to anxious thoughts and panic attacks, which, you guessed it, makes my heart run wild.

Like now.

When all else fails, I try little exercises that can be done anywhere, stuff like gagging on my finger or hugging my knees to my chest. Though when the attacks are bad, like tonight at Times Square, even something as simple as that is unmanageable.

For now, I do my favorite technique, which is just holding my nose and mouth shut and trying to blow out air. The basic science behind this is to help me relax and slow down my heartbeat and keep me alive. I used to feel mad silly doing this in front of Team Young, aka my new family, especially because Floyd said I looked like a chipmunk with inflated cheeks, but it's better to get laughed at like some fool than mourned as a corpse in a casket.

"Good job," Dr. Emeterio says.

"Keep it up," Dalma encourages, then, "I mean, keep up the good work, but bring down your heart rate."

I can tell I'm about to cry, but I can't lock it down, the tears start flowing because of how much I hate all of this. My ears pop, and I finally exhale—first the breath, then the loud sob that couldn't stay buried.

Valentino stares, looking haunted as he watches me fight for life again.

I close my eyes, focusing on my breath, telling myself that I'm going to be okay. Death-Cast won't call in the next few minutes, as their window for today's End Day alerts is coming to a close. Everything slows down, and I imagine the good things in life I have to look forward to, like writing more short stories and tanning on our brownstone's roof some more and discovering myself and falling in love with a good-hearted person.

Then I open my eyes, and Valentino isn't here anymore.

"How are you feeling?" Dr. Emeterio asks.

There's always a thousand answers to that question. I keep it simple. "I'm fine."

"Good. Maybe you should get some rest."

I can't rest when I'm so restless.

"Where did Valentino go?" I ask.

"I don't know," Dalma says.

"A word of advice," Dr. Emeterio kindly says. "I have no insider info on Death-Cast, but if they called Valentino, it's in his best interest to operate as if their prediction is correct. It's a terrible loss whenever someone assumes they have more time than they do."

So much for expecting mistakes to be made.

But the doctor's right, and I don't always swear by that.

I keep trying to get Valentino to believe that he's got all the time in the world, but that's not going to do him any favors if he drops dead without having lived his End Day right. If Death-Cast is wrong, then that's going to be a happy surprise.

For everyone.

"I need a sec."

I take off the blood pressure cuff and electrodes. I get out of bed against all protests and leave the ER, hoping to find Valentino before it's too late. I'm relieved—and surprised— Dalma isn't following me, but I bet some nurses are going to try to escort me back to my bed before I can find Valentino. Then I stop bugging because the search is over.

Valentino is in the waiting room.

Shit, I'm so relieved. It's killed all suspense on where he's at, which is good for my heart.

"There you are."

"What are you doing out of bed?" he asks.

"Looking for you. You pulled some low-key magic act and vanished."

"I'm sorry," he says, getting up and helping me to the

seats, which makes me feel so damn ancient, but I guess this is how he cares for someone fresh out of the ER. "I just needed to think some things over."

"It's okay, I get it. I just didn't know if you left to go . . . to go do whatever comes next."

"I definitely thought about it, but I think my place is here."

"Really?" I ask, wondering if it's got anything to do with me, which is so stupid because what am I trying to make happen with someone whose future is about to be cut real short? Scratch that, it's not stupid, he's still alive and his life is worth living until the end, I proved that when I didn't just let him get shot in the streets. But I've got to recognize that I've got storyteller bones in my body and I can build, build, build a narrative out of nothing. I bet Valentino is only still here because a hospital is a pretty solid place to be if you're about to die for some mysterious reason.

"Do you have your phone?" Valentino asks.

I wrestle my phone out of the pocket of my skinny jeans.

"Nothing from Death-Cast?"

I click the side button, the screen lighting up with texts from Team Young but no missed calls. "No, but it's not too late," I say, seeing we're one minute away from the End Day calls stopping at 2:00 a.m.

Suddenly, it feels like the last minute before midnight all over again, except this time we're not surrounded by countless

132

strangers. It's just the two of us, watching the phone's clock and waiting to see if he'll be dying alone or if we'll be going out in a blaze together.

The clock hits two, and no one's calling.

VALENTINO

2:00 a.m.

Death-Cast isn't calling Orion because he's not going to die today, and I think I know why.

This night is unfolding like a photo shoot coming together. For once, I'm not the subject. I'm the photographer, and everything is zooming into focus, like I'm switching out lenses until I land on the best one. The background is still a bit blurry, but if I adjust the aperture just enough, light enters and exposes the true model of this photo shoot. The boy with the constellation name. I've only seen some of his stars at work, but I understand the beauty. Orion is the focal point, so I stare at him and the sharpness of his hazel eyes and the hunched framing of his body, and once everything is aligned, just like stars in a constellation, everything becomes clear.

"You're going to live," I say.

"Until tomorrow, I guess."

"You're going to have much longer than you think."

"So you got some psychic Death-Cast powers or something?"

"No, but I think destiny brought us together so I can change your future."

"I don't get it."

"You don't need the waitlist anymore, Orion. I'll give you my heart."

ORION

2:02 a.m.

Once upon a time, I wrote a fairy tale.

Since fairy tales are on the shorter side, it was an easier commitment than a novel. It's wild what those stories get away with. You got pigs building houses and wolves impersonating grandmothers and a lost glass slipper helping you find your one true insta-love.

Then there's mine. Stop me if you've heard this one.

It's about a young man whose heart is dying.

Everyone always says to write what you know, right?

I named the protagonist Orionis, aka my name in Latin because I'm original as shit. When you're constantly running against the clock, you don't take forever choosing names.

Anyway, Orionis was always out and about doing his thing in this New York–esque kingdom when Death appeared out of the shadows and pressed his skeletal finger to Orionis's heart, turning it from red and healthy to gray and crumbling.

"Am I going to die?" Orionis asked, not at all questioning Death's physical existence or anything like that because when you're in a fairy tale you just roll with shit like that.

"You may live if you dance with me," Death said.

"Hell no," Orionis replied, not about that life.

Until a piece of his heart disintegrated.

Orionis didn't want to die, so he embraced Death, dancing nonstop from dusk to dawn. Orionis was exhausted, stopping to breathe at the cost of his heart chipping away some more. As he resumed the dance, Orionis grilled Death, trying to find out why he was targeted since he was perfectly healthy and didn't engage in any risky behavior, but Death never answered. The two danced all day, all night, all week, all month, all year. Anytime Orionis broke away to do anything that would've made him happy, he lost more of his heart. Eventually, he was left with one last piece the size of a pebble.

If Orionis stopped dancing with Death one more time, he'd be his forever.

One day, right when Orionis was ready to hang up his cloak, aka throw in the towel, he crossed paths with an elder whose heart was so golden it shone through his chest like rays of sunshine. He was so carefree as he lived his life—fishing, performing, cooking, even dancing alone so dizzyingly fast that he fell to the ground, laughing at himself until his face was red. But he lost all color when he saw how miserable Orionis was with Death.

And here's where it gets real, and why I got all this on my mind.

"May I cut in?" the elder asked Death.

Blinded by the golden heart, Death turned away. "No. He's my dance partner."

"I was hoping to dance with you," the elder said.

"No," Death echoed. "You're too bright with life."

Having lived with dreams fulfilled, the elder reached into his chest and ripped out his shine, aka his heart, because the darkest fairy tales get real bloody like that. He handed it to Orionis, the glow so bright it warded off Death, pushing him into the elder's arms. Together, the new dancing partners swayed like a tree shedding its leaves, and once they hit the ground, they vanished in Death's shadow.

Alone, Orionis swapped out his gray, crumbling heart for the radiant golden heart and lived happily ever after.

There's so much about that story that always felt like a fantasy to me, especially the promise of a longer life, but now I'm being offered that reality.

Valentino wants to give me his heart.

This isn't some romantic Valentine's Day card shit either; this is literal.

I stare at Valentino for one minute or one hour, I don't know. I'm speechless at his ridiculously beautiful and generous gesture, though there's no way this is serious. I'm lucky, but there's no way in hell I'm this lucky. Also, Valentino hasn't given this any thought, and that's exactly what I tell him: "You haven't given this any thought."

"There's not a lot to think about," Valentino says. "At the end of the day, you'll need a stronger heart and I'll have one to spare."

"Yeah, but—"

"But nothing, Orion. You saved my life even though you know I'm dying. There's no better way to thank you for helping me live longer than by repaying the favor."

"You get that that's not why I saved you, right?"

"Of course I know that. You're not some vulture."

Seriously, swapping my heart for his hasn't crossed my mind once. Since Valentino got his End Day call, I've been too busy dodging bullets and surviving a massive heart attack and mourning a friend-in-the-making while he's still alive to even selfishly think about what this could mean for me.

"Just say yes," Valentino says.

"Look, this is the nicest thing anyone has ever wanted to do for me, but it's not that simple. First, we need to be matches for blood type and—"

"I'm your match," Valentino says like he has access to my medical records. "I have blood type O."

So that makes him a universal donor, aka he's technically everyone's match.

"No one ever knows their blood type," I say. I didn't even know mine was A+ until I was constantly in and out of the hospital. Seriously, I was so ignorant that the first time I saw that A+ on paper I didn't read it as A-positive, I thought it was A-plus, like my blood got dope grades even though I have a failing heart. "Why do you know yours?"

"I was preparing for the worst after Scarlett's accident. I told the doctors I was willing to donate organs and blood if it would save her life."

I'm upset that the world is about to lose this extraordinary human.

"Okay, but let's say everything else is good to go for the transplant," I say, really trying to get it into his head that this is complicated stuff. "It's not like we're trading Christmas presents. This is heart surgery. I could—" I shut the fuck up because I don't need to tell someone who's about to die that I'm nervous about losing my own life.

"Death-Cast didn't call you," Valentino says, shrugging off my stupidity. "If we—or, well, you and the doctors—do this today, then you should be in the clear, right?"

If a cardiologist confirms that we're legit matches for surgery, then this would be game-changing and lifesaving.

I could finally become a novel instead of a short story.

"This isn't fair," I say.

"How you've been living isn't fair either," Valentino says. "But that's not your problem. You deserve to live—"

"I'm not going to!" he shouts, his cheeks flushed.

I haven't known Valentino for very long, but I didn't have

him down for someone who snaps like that. I can't get at him, though, he's the world's first Decker.

He tugs his shirt, trying to breathe.

"I'm sorry. I was just—"

"You were trying to be helpful," Valentino says, shaking his head like he's embarrassed at his outburst. "You can't save me, Orion, but I can save you. You're a true survivor who's made it this far. Let me help you live the long life I won't . . . I won't get."

I wish this were more like my fairy tale.

Valentino should have many decades under his belt before finding peace with passing his heart like a baton to a young person in need.

But unless there's a miracle, our story won't have a happily ever after.

It'll end in tragedy.

VALENTINO

We waste no time getting started.

One moment, we're all together in the ER, and the next, Dr. Emeterio splits us up into our own examination rooms to conduct tests to determine if Orion and I will be a match. Dr. Emeterio personally oversees my blood work and X-rays and other evaluations that I don't pretend to understand, since it's not as if I have to worry about a pop quiz tomorrow on the difference between electrocardiograms and echo-cardiograms.

There's a small treadmill in the corner, and I really want to go for a run. But what if I fly off like some character in a comedy and my neck snaps? Death by stationary running. What a way to go.

If I had my phone on me, I'd probably give in and google how other Deckers have died tonight. Some of the gunshots in Times Square must've found their targets. But what about the other Deckers? Did someone crash their car into another or directly into a Decker who was crossing the road? What about those who've chosen suicide because the uncertainty of how everything will unfold is too much for them? These thoughts are so upsetting and depressing, and obsessing over them won't help me predict my own fate.

I need to focus on life while I still have one.

This whole production for Orion is already underway, but I still need to go over everything with Scarlett. She needs my bank info so she can keep my savings and buy some extra months in New York. I hope she doesn't move back in with our parents. They've been the worst with me, but they haven't been angels to Scarlett either. I'm assuming Scar still hasn't called me back on Dalma's phone, which remains so nerve-racking. She should be wrapping up the Death-Cast party and heading to the airport soon.

"If all goes well," Dr. Emeterio says as she studies my X-ray. "Your contribution today may change the future of all heart transplants."

"I won't even get to see it."

The silence is short-lived, like I'll be. There's a beeping machine that's carrying on. No fear of being turned off or unplugged forever.

"I promise I don't think of you as some test subject," Dr. Emeterio says, meeting my eyes. "I was only hoping to offer some comfort, but I'm sorry for being out of line."

"No, you're fine. It's just strange how I'll be gone and not know how everything turns out."

"If only Death-Cast could clue us in on all that too," Dr. Emeterio says.

If only.

I'd love another call with Joaquin Rosa where he answers all my burning questions. Will I change the future of heart transplants? Will Orion actually survive the procedure? Will Scarlett live a happy life? Then there's the scariest question of all. No, it's not about the afterlife. I'm not concerned about that. Once I'm dead, I'm dead. I'm not expecting much beyond that, especially as I'm struggling with my faith. What I am concerned about is the Big How—how will I die today? Death-Cast isn't like Catholicism where I'm asked to trust in God and his reasons and his heaven without any evidence. There's clearly concrete proof about Death-Cast's abilities that gained the support of the president and the government and beyond.

I'm supposed to believe Death-Cast knows the When, but not the How?

I don't buy it.

Someone has to know.

"I have your results," Dr. Emeterio says.

Deep in my heart, I already know the answer.

ORION

2:17 a.m.

I'm staring at my X-ray like it's ugly art on a wall.

An eighteen-year-old's heart isn't supposed to look like some misshapen potato, but that's what I think every time I'm shown my insides. Doctors were always quick to show me what a healthy heart looks like, like I didn't know already.

"I bet Valentino's X-rays are as good as his pictures," I say.

Dalma picks up a plastic heart replica. "You've never seen his pictures."

"He booked a huge campaign. They've got to be good. His X-rays have got to be model-worthy too."

Then my head drops because this world is about to lose thousands of Valentino Prince pictures.

Dalma hops up beside me on the bed, the paper sheet crinkling under her, and holds my hand. "Hey, O-Bro. Real talk. I'm getting concerned about you."

"Look, if it's not his heart, I'm not sweating it. We'll find a match."

"This isn't about the transplant. I'm talking about your heart-eyes. How quickly you opened up your heart about your parents. Most important, the heart attack you had after saving this boy. Lots of heart-adjacent things."

"You think I'm in love with Valentino? I'm not. I—I'm just—I don't even know if he likes me that way."

"Whether or not Valentino likes you isn't what's at stake here," Dalma says slowly, like she's explaining computer code, but also lovingly, like she's breaking bad news. "Valentino is going to die today, Orion."

I look around the hospital room, knowing damn well why we're here. "What's your point?"

"You can't get too attached. It's not going to end well for you."

"What's not going to end well is Valentino dying at nineteen," I say, hopping off the bed. I really shouldn't be pacing, I should stay put. But I can't stop my feet from taking me back and forth between the wall with my glowing X-ray and the one with anatomy posters and certificates. "Death-Cast has opened the door to a once-in-a-lifetime opportunity. Most donors are not only strangers but they also remain anonymous forever. Why would I shut out the person who wants to give me his heart?"

Dalma hops off the bed and blocks my path. "I'm trying to protect you. Not fight you."

I know her heart is in the right place—physically and

emotionally. But even with my big-ass imagination, I can't imagine not getting to know Valentino while I can.

And by tomorrow, I can't.

There's a knock at the door, and Valentino and Dr. Emeterio enter.

This is it.

Suspense really isn't good for someone with my condition, and every second of silence is brutal.

"What's up?" I ask, wanting to get this over with, one way or the other.

"It's nice that something good will come out of this," Valentino says, pressing his hand to his chest.

My heart skips a beat, two, ten, a hundred, a thousand, a million, and somehow, I don't die on the spot.

In fact, I'm going to live.

I'm going to live, live, live, live, live, live, live, live, live, live, live, live.

But first, he has to die.

VALENTINO

2:22 a.m.

I could have lived my whole life telling people they will live.

One person will have to be enough.

Orion is frozen like a statue, though given his flowing tears, he's more like a fountain.

"Wow," Dalma says. That's all she's got before she's lost for words. She squeezes Orion's hand, and it's like she has some magical touch that unfreezes him.

Orion flies into my arms. "I—I just. I'm so . . . you know . . ."

"I know," I say.

The first time I hugged Orion was after he shared his story about losing his parents. Now it's because of my heart he'll be gaining. This is really nice. It's so soothing how his curls brush against my jawline. The weight of his head on my shoulder makes me feel really grounded, like I haven't been completely uprooted from this planet even though I'm the only one in this room who's dying today. What's really incredible is how our hearts are beating against each other's chests, like they're communicating in their own language as to what happens next.

I realize I don't fully understand everything myself.

I pat Orion's back and pull away. I hand him a box of tissues, and he dries his eyes.

"I should call Mom," Dalma says, about to step out.

"Wait, Dalma? Has my sister called?"

She shakes her head. "We'll keep trying, though."

"Okay," I say, even though Dalma has stepped out.

The more I tell myself that Scarlett is fine, the more it begins to feel like a lie. Just because Scarlett and I came into this world together doesn't mean we're destined to leave at the same time too. In about a half hour it will be midnight in Arizona. Scarlett still has time to sign up for Death-Cast. I hope she's not a Decker too.

"How are we doing this operation?" I ask Dr. Emeterio.

Dr. Emeterio gestures for us to have a seat as if this is going to be a long conversation. Orion and I sit together, our shoulders brushing as we fidget in these uncomfortable chairs. Dr. Emeterio stares like she can't believe her eyes. "I've been a cardiac surgeon for years, but this is a first for me, gentlemen. Living heart donors who aren't participants because of brain death are rare to come by and, even then, it's usually a family member getting involved."

"Not strangers who met at Times Square," Orion says.

"Or anywhere," I add.

"Indeed. This is very generous," Dr. Emeterio says.

"Have I thanked you yet?" Orion asks me.

"You don't—"

"I don't think I did. I just hugged you."

"It's okay—"

"Oh my god, thank you. Also, if you change your mind, it's all good. You don't owe me this. Seriously, I'm not going to get mad or hold a grudge, I'll respect your choice."

"Grudge wouldn't last too long," I say, intending to make a joke, but I sound hollow.

Orion blushes, not finding it funny either. "Right."

It's quiet again. Heart transplants are supposed to feel more dramatic with more noise. Hospital doors banging open. Fast footsteps. Nurses shouting patients' stats. Crash carts being prepared for surgery. But there's been a lot of silence tonight because we have time. Or at least we think we do. That ceiling light could drop on my head now before I even make it to the operating table. Things would really start getting noisy then to claim my heart while they can.

"Am I going to die first?" I ask.

Dr. Emeterio shakes her head. "It's actually critical that you're alive. We will need you in a vegetative state."

"So I'll be in a coma?"

"Essentially. But one of our biggest obstacles is going to

be getting the right people to sign off on this procedure with such a short window. I'm afraid we don't know any more about Death-Cast than the general public, and as doctors, it's in our ethics to support you first."

"To act like I'm not dying," I say.

"Correct. It's like I said before: it's very possible Death-Cast can be wrong. But we're not going to know until . . ."

"Until after I've died."

"Or survived," Orion says.

"Either-or," Dr. Emeterio says.

"So if I survive, then that means Death-Cast can't be trusted. Though if I die it means they're right but it's too late to do anything about it? Is this a dead end? What are we even trying to figure out here?"

"I can discuss this with the board and explore a window of time in which we may be able to safely perform the transplant with your consent, understanding that we won't be able to save you should you go under and that you're making this decision because of Death-Cast. It's possible that if enough predictions are right between now and the afternoon, then we may be able to proceed. But I'm afraid I can't make any guarantees because this is all too new."

I pinch the bridge of my nose, overwhelmed. I'm tired, but my End Day adrenaline is keeping me up. More than anything I want to be home right now, even on my twin-size air mattress that I'm sure is going to be uncomfortable. But not as uncomfortable as being put to sleep and knowing I'll never wake up.

There's an anatomical heart model on the examination bed. I'm drawn to it, like a model to a camera. It's heavier than I expected, and it's as big as my fist. I'd be surprised if this is actually accurate to scale. But what do I know? I can barely keep up with Dr. Emeterio's conflicts, and I'm not exactly being given the time to become an expert on the subject.

I'm going to cut to the chase.

"What do you suggest I do, then?" I ask.

"If you're serious about being a donor," Dr. Emeterio says. "I would stay here at the hospital. Should something happen to you, we'll be in the best position possible to try to save you. But if we can't and you're experiencing brain death, then we'll be in an even better position to perform the surgery."

"And once I'm brain-dead, my heart will be removed. Then once my heart is removed, I'll be dead." Those words leave my mouth, taking the air out of me too. I haven't cried yet, and I don't want to crack now, but I see Dr. Emeterio nodding through the periphery of my watery eyes. "Okay, and after Orion is put under, you'll replace his heart with mine, and he'll be good."

"Theoretically, yes. That's assuming Orion doesn't reject your heart."

"I won't," Orion says. "Oh, you mean, like, if my body rejects his heart."

Dr. Emeterio answers with a nod as Orion's face goes red.

"But Orion and I are matches, right? So shouldn't it work?"

"Every recipient is different, but on average, there are two to three rejection episodes after a transplant. Some small, some bigger. Some early on, some later."

In a new world where we know when someone is going to die, we still don't know how long someone will live.

I shouldn't stress this so hard. This is going to be Orion's choice ultimately. I can't force him to take my heart. But I can't help but worry. I don't want my last act of kindness to kill someone.

The door opens, and Dalma rushes in so fast it scares me. As if there's some ax murderer chasing her like some horror movie and this is how I'm about to die. I almost even brace myself for death, disappointed that it's arriving sooner than I thought—even sooner, I should say. But this isn't what's happening at all. Dalma's phone is ringing and she passes it to me. The caller ID reads *Scarlett (Valentino's sister)*, and I can feel the biggest cry of my life building from within.

I rush outside into the hallway while answering. "Scarlett!"

"Hey, Val! I'm sorry I missed your million calls and messages, I forgot to take my phone off silent after driving. Where's yours? What happened?"

I try making my way back to the waiting room, but I stop dead in my tracks and slide down the wall by the elevator bank. I don't say anything.

"Val?"

Scarlett is the only person in the universe who can use that nickname. Many others have tried, but it always feels wrong. It's like someone is trying to show how close we are when they haven't put the time in. I obviously don't have more history with anyone than Scarlett, and when we were kids she had a hard time saying *Valentino*, so she started calling me *Valley* and eventually trimmed it to *Val*.

"I'm here," I say weakly, like an ax murderer did manage to get me. "You're not driving, are you?"

"Of course not. What's going on? You sound off."

"I'm going to FaceTime you."

"What's happening? Tell me."

"Just answer, okay?"

I click the video camera icon, and it rings once before Scarlett's face appears. There's pure concern in her eyes, like when she opened her first college admission letter and discovered she was rejected. She really struggled and didn't believe she'd have a future until I suggested we move to New York. But I don't know how to walk her through how to live after I die. I can't even tell her what's happening, I'm stammering over every word. But I don't need words with Scarlett. Just like so many other difficult trials in my life—most recently, when Mom and Dad didn't react well to my coming out—all I have to do is look my sister in the eye and cry and let all the tears speak for me. Except there's no way for my death to dawn on her face since I shouldn't even know it's happening.

"I signed up for Death-Cast, and they called me."

She's quiet and so still that I think the call has frozen out in this hallway.

"No," Scarlett finally says.

I don't know the full sequence of the stages of grief, but I know the first is denial.

"Stop crying, Val, this is so not a thing," Scarlett says. Unfortunately, her poker face is worse than ever. "These Death-Cast operators are total newbies. They don't know what they're doing."

"I—I spoke with Joaquin. Joaquin Rosa."

I manage to get those words out because we can't play pretend. If Joaquin Rosa is screwing up End Day calls, then that whole operation needs to be shut down this moment. But maybe Scarlett will have another argument that I can't counter. Something to give me hope.

"Well, did Mr. Death-Cast tell you how he thinks you're going to die? Because if not, then we shouldn't put too much weight on his little educated guess. It might be an uneducated guess! We have no idea how Death-Cast even works. This is why we didn't sign up."

Scarlett tries staying strong, but she cracks. Something else we have in common is we're both ugly criers. I would be mortified if anyone photographed me while I was this red in the face and wiping snot whereas Scarlett might rip out someone's eyes. Even now when it's just us, she's hiding behind her hand, and I can make out the moon in the background.

"Val, this doesn't make sense. You're fine! Why is this happening?"

I shake my head.

"Did you tell Mom and Dad?"

"No. I'm not ready for another talk about how I'm going to hell."

"They better not be self-righteous about this or we'll never talk to them again." That promise is alive and well in Scarlett's eyes for a whole second before she realizes I can't honor it with her. Or that I can, but not in the way she's intending. The next wave of tears flood down her face. "Val, I need to catch my flight. I'll be there by the morning."

"Maybe you shouldn't come," I say, even though it's the opposite of what I want. I need to say goodbye to my sister in person. I'm protective of her, though. "It might be safer for you if you don't."

"There's no way in hell I'm leaving you alone," Scarlett says, unlocking her car door and settling into the driver's seat.

I'm flashing back to the day she almost died. "Scar, stop. You can't drive in this condition. Just sit and breathe."

Once she calms down, we take deep breaths together,

until her heavy cry quiets into a whimper.

"Don't worry about me. I'm not going to be alone. I made some new friends in Times Square. This is Dalma's phone and—"

Scarlett's eyes widen, and she leans forward, like when we're watching a thriller and she figures out the twist. "But what if they're the reason you—"

"They're not going to kill me. They actually convinced me to sign up for Death-Cast. They're really good people."

"You can't know that. They're strangers."

"And despite that, Orion saved my life."

She's quiet, like she's processing how she got the plot twist wrong. "What do you mean he saved your life?"

This is all scary enough. Telling her that I was shot at isn't going to keep her calm enough to drive safely to the airport so she can catch her flight.

"I had a close call, but I'm okay."

"No you're not." She closes her eyes.

I don't ask if she's praying. That's her business.

"Scar, you're going to miss your flight if you don't leave soon."

Scarlett collects herself. "Okay. I should land around nine your time. Do you want to meet me at the airport? No, matter of fact, stay put. Are you home right now?" She squints. "No you're not. We have ugly beige walls that need a paint job, not white. Where are you?"

I can't go into why I'm at the hospital. If I tell her I'm signing off on being a heart donor and need her by my side when I go brain-dead, then she'll never make it to the airport in one piece. We can talk about this in person. "I'm with Dalma and Orion. But I'm headed home soon."

She wants to push for more information but resigns. "Stay put. I'll see you soon."

"Scarlett, before you go . . . you should register for Death-Cast. Okay?"

"Okay."

"I love you, Scar."

"I love you same, Val."

We don't hang up. It's like we're not sure if we'll ever see each other again. We certainly won't see each other if she misses her flight.

"Drive safely, sis. Pay extra attention to the road this time of night."

Putting pressure on her to focus on her journey instead of my upcoming destination is the only way to make sure she doesn't leave this world with me.

ORION
2:38 a.m.

I press my hands to my chest, feeling my steady heartbeats. It's like my heart is finally behaving because it knows we're going to evict it.

I look at my X-ray again, thinking about how if I ever write about this experience, I can use this as the book cover. Or maybe I'll set the X-ray on fire so I don't have to think about all these years where my insides were ugly and murderous like some hell beast. Nah, I can't do that. Turning my back on my past means not remembering Valentino's lifesaving contribution. Shit, that's assuming any of this works. I don't know what we'll do if my body rejects his heart, or how much time we'll even have to try something before I reach my own dead end.

I'm living so many story lines I didn't plot when I began my day.

Man, I'm so beat. Dalma too. We're squeezing together

on this examination bed while Valentino talks to Scarlett and nurses make some insurance calls on behalf of Dr. Emeterio, who is busy trying to reach the board. Instead of passing out, I'm dreaming while awake. Not just about how my life is going to change but for Team Young too. Dalma won't have to spend another night in a hospital because of me. Her family won't have to cut another vacation short because of me. No one's life will be interrupted again because of me. I can't tell you how much lighter that makes me feel.

"I can't believe this night," I say while staring up at the bright ceiling lights like they're stars.

"Me either," Dalma says.

"Everything's changing because of Valentino."

"What do you give a guy who's dying for you?"

"He's not technically dying for me."

"Obviously."

"Why is that obvious? Maybe he would die for me."

"Are you on your side or my side?"

"Neither and both."

Dalma elbows me, and we laugh.

The door opens, and Valentino lets himself in. His cheeks are flushed, and his eyes are red.

"Hey," he croaks, then clears his throat. "Hey."

I hop off the bed, embarrassed that we're in here laughing while he's going through it. "You good?"

Valentino shakes his head, then nods, and it's like he's glitching. I'm no stranger to conflicting-ass emotions. I've been feeling them pretty hard ever since I found out that I'm going to live because someone else is about to die.

"Is Scarlett good?" I ask, nervous as hell that she's not.

"She's alive," Valentino says.

It's the best answer, I bet. His sister clearly wasn't going to take that news well.

"She's signing up for Death-Cast and then headed to the airport and should arrive around nine."

That's not bad. Just got to keep Valentino alive for the next seven to eight hours. That means lifting his spirits too. "Is there anything you want to do while you wait for Scarlett? Get something to eat? Maybe your favorite meal?"

"Makes me feel like I'm on death row," Valentino says.

I want to swallow my whole fist. "That's not what I meant."

"No, I get it. Besides, I don't know where we'd find linguini at two in the morning."

"Oh, dude. There's a million twenty-four-seven diners in New York."

"We can order something, or pick it up for you," Dalma adds.

Valentino drops down into a chair with zero grace for someone who's a literal model. "I finally move somewhere where I can find food after midnight and . . ." He shrugs. "I probably can't eat before the surgery anyway."

I'm instantly spiraling.

His death shouldn't be about me, but it's feeling like that

with every passing second. So what, Valentino isn't supposed to eat whatever the fuck he wants on his End Day? All because of a surgery he wouldn't even have on the brain if luck hadn't thrown us together?

"That's a devastating good point," Dalma says.

"Nope, it's not," I say. "Valentino, if you want some motherfucking linguini, I'll find you some motherfucking linguini."

"No, really. I'll live," Valentino says. Then he pauses as he hears himself, now haunted by his own words. It's wild how a simple sentiment takes on a new life when you're dying. He brushes it off, something he's going to have to do often if he's going to make it through his End Day—I imagine. "I just want to go home and rest. Prepare the place for Scarlett. Then go to my photo shoot in the morning. My first campaign is a cool way to be immortalized."

"Still got to throw some linguini into that plan," I say. "Maybe some legit New York pizza if you're into that."

Dalma's eyes are closed as she's breathing into her cupped palms. She's not keeping herself warm in this chilly room; she's keeping herself shut. But her words break free. "I don't want to sound heartless—"

"Off to a bad start," I interrupt.

"Oh my god, I'm sorry." Dalma talks with her hands a lot, and right now as she's quiet and processing her next words, her hands are frozen in the air, just up until she's going again. "Believe me, Valentino, I hate myself for saying what I'm about to say because this is such a gift you're giving Orion. He's my family, and I'm so protective of him so I got to say . . . I got to say that I'm really scared that you'll jeopardize this operation if you leave the hospital. If something happens to you, then . . ."

Valentino's head drops, like he's being scolded. "I understand."

"Obviously, we'll hold off as long as we can for you to have time with your sister, but the most logical thing we can do is keep you here for the next few hours."

Someone wanting to save my life has never felt so horrible.

"Dalma, I love you, but hard no on all this. We're not giving Valentino deadlines on his End Day."

Valentino fights back a yawn. "Dalma is right. I'm tired and not thinking clearly. Having dinner in the middle of the night or attending a photo shoot shouldn't outweigh everything you'll get to do with my heart."

I crouch beside Valentino, gazing into his reddened blue eyes. "What you want to do for me is so beyond beautiful that I'm already indebted to you, even if nothing happens. But I'm not going to live the life you want for me if it means you not living yours out while you can."

Dalma is staring daggers. "Orion, can we talk outside?"

"Happily," I say sharply.

I squeeze Valentino's shoulder on the way out, closing the door behind me.

Dalma clasps her hands together, like she's in prayer.

"Please let this boy save your life."

"Please stop encouraging him to drop dead fast."

"You're setting yourself and Valentino up for failure. Be logical. If Valentino can basically die in his sleep, isn't that so much more merciful than whatever horrific tragedy awaits him otherwise?"

The longer Valentino lives, the closer he's pushed to his death. I get that. But I can't make peace with deciding when he clocks out. "This has to be his call, Dalma."

"I'm sure he'll be open to your input. It's *your* heart now."

"Nope, it's still *his* heart."

"It won't be *anyone's* heart if he dies."

"Then it's not meant to be."

This little fairy tale might have an unhappy ending.

If only Death-Cast could tell us how someone was going to die so we could try to dodge it, or even what time it was going to happen so we know how many hours—or minutes—we're working with here. The stakes are too high.

"Death-Cast already opened this one door for me. Maybe it'll open another if Valentino's gets slammed in my face."

Dalma is tearing up. "I'm starting to think you don't want this surgery."

"You know I do."

"Then what is it? Why aren't you going to bat for yourself as hard as I am?"

I'm quiet, then: "When we met Valentino, I already couldn't stop thinking about how much I want to get to know him. Hanging out at his place, inviting him to ours. Being his tour guide through the city. I just want to get to know him while I can, especially before I carry his heart for the rest of my life."

There's nothing like speaking your truths out loud. I swear by that.

It's sinking in with Dalma, who sighs. "So what do we do? I'm all good with keeping him company, but we've got to bubble wrap him or something. And make sure he doesn't do anything too crazy."

I take a second, not wanting to start a fight right as we've chilled down. But in my stupid, busted, murderous heart, I know I'm in the right with this. "I think I got to chill with Valentino alone."

Her eyes narrow. "What?"

"I want him to have a comfortable End Day, and I don't know if you're going to give him that space he needs to breathe, or if he's going to be too on edge around you now."

"I'm not going to slap linguini out of his hands if that's what you're getting at."

"Does he know that?"

"Why are you punishing me for trying to protect you?"

"I'm not. I love how you got my back. I just want to have his and make sure that he doesn't die without living first."

Dalma and I are so used to doing everything together, and whenever we go our own ways, it's usually her call. This is throwing her off big-time.

"If this is what you want, I'm set. I said my piece."

I hug her so fast we almost tumble over. "Thanks, D."

"What can I do for you?"

"Can you find Dr. Emeterio and clue her in? I want to get Valentino out of here before she guilts him into staying."

Dalma nods. "You better keep your phone on you."

"I will. Take a cab home and text me when you're there, okay?" I kiss Dalma's forehead and turn for the exam room's door.

"Be really careful, Orion," Dalma says.

"I'm not going to die today. Bright side of Death-Cast."

"That doesn't mean you won't get hurt . . . or heart-broken."

Suddenly, everything feels so tense it's like I might pop into a thousand pieces. I'm embarking on a really dangerous journey to keep someone alive who is destined to die. For every minute I buy him, that's more time getting to know him. The longer I know him, the harder everything will hurt.

I can't predict the future like Death-Cast, but I already know that my time with Valentino will end in heartbreak.

VALENTINO

2:51 a.m.

Orion returns, alone. One star in this bright examination room.

"Are you ready?" he asks.

I'm not sure what he's talking about. Has Orion changed his stance on how much time I should have before we begin surgery? Or is this Dr. Emeterio making the call? If that's the case, then I'm not ready. Scarlett is finally on her way, and I can't go now.

Orion smiles, and I know I must have it wrong.

"Ready for what?" I ask.

"To live."

"I'm confused."

"You want to go home and get the place ready for Scarlett, right? Then let's go do that."

"You're coming with me?"

"Just to back you up, but if you really want to go at it alone, I'll let you do your thing."

I definitely don't want to be by myself. This is all scary enough. But I don't know how this is going to be helpful for Orion. "You sure this isn't going to be weird? Like you're hanging out with the pig before you kill it for dinner?"

"I don't eat meat anymore, and I'm not a murderer."

"You better not be," I say, finally rising from the chair.

"I don't think anyone would throw down money on me overpowering you in a fight."

"That doesn't mean you don't have friends in bad places. You are trying to harvest my heart after all."

Orion looks stunned. "Oh, you got jokes."

I'm surprised too. I really credit Orion for dragging a little humor out of me. The way he's keeping up the energy reminds me of the times I've been the most relaxed on a photo shoot. I've worked with photographers who are trying to get in and get out, which builds pressure on set and tightens my body. My best shoots have been with photographers who are smiling and laughing like they're the ones in front of the camera. When they're having fun, I am too.

Orion is a good person to be around until Scarlett arrives.

I'm nervous about returning to the outside world, but I'm grateful that I get the chance to do so. That's a big leap from where I was a few minutes ago when I was accepting defeat.

"Thanks for buying me some time," I say.

"All good. You're the one who has to cash in," Orion says, putting on his hat.

DEATH-CAST

When I signed up for Death-Cast, there was that paragraph on the website about how Deckers got their name. Joaquin Rosa apparently wants them—wants *me*—to remember that we're all the captains on the decks of our own ships, setting sail for one last journey.

It's nice to have a co-captain.

JOAQUIN ROSA
2:57 a.m.

Joaquin is watching footage of the Times Square shooting when someone bangs at his door. His heart races. He relives what it was like to hear those gunshots over the phone as he delivered the first End Day call. The disturbance startles Naya and wakes up Alano and the puppy. Bucky skitters off the couch and barks at the closed door, scaring no one with his adorable yapping. As Joaquin rises from his chair, there's more banging.

This better be urgent.

He opens the door to find his customer success engineer.

"I'm so sorry to bother you," Aster Gomez says, her hand frozen in her long dark hair like she's considering whether she should rip it all out. She's great with people but had no interest in telling them they're about to die, so she applied for customer service instead. She was so savvy that Joaquin hired her to lead that department, even though she's only twenty-five. "We're having major issues with the server."

"What's happening?"

"Um . . ." Aster looks down the hall. "It's best if you follow me."

Joaquin follows along with the rest of his family.

"It all started when I received a complaint a few minutes ago," Aster says, speed-walking. "This woman's boyfriend was killed in Times Square tonight."

"That's unfortunate," Joaquin says with all the earnestness in the world. He can't imagine his life without Naya. Especially losing her so violently. "I'm curious. Was it Valentino Prince who died? He was tonight's first call."

"No. His name was William Wilde."

Ah, shame. Joaquin would've liked to include that anecdote in his memoir. But back to the matter at hand. "Does the client understand we've done all we can?"

"Except we didn't."

"Pardon me?"

"We failed to do our one job. The Decker never received his End Day call."

"Well, the Times Square shootings began after midnight—after launch. We've never made any promises that Deckers will immediately be alerted."

"Which I explained, but the woman said her boyfriend's phone never rang. Not even after our calls were completed on the East Coast. I checked our records, and we have no outgoing calls to the Decker's number or the emergency contact."

As they all reenter the call center, Joaquin observes his heralds hard at work. He zeroes in on Rolando, suspecting he's to blame for this Decker not being notified of his death; probably absorbing another old man's life story. That egregious failing will result in his immediate termination.

"Is it Rolando's fault? Did he not reach out to the Decker in time?"

"I checked in with all the heralds, and while Andrea totally assisted Rolando with his contact list after completing her own, every registered user on the East Coast received their End Day call."

"Except that poor man," Naya says, grieving this stranger with her big heart.

"I'm so sorry, Mr. Rosa," Aster says. "But since the Decker never appeared in our system for today, could that mean—"

He holds up a hand, silencing her. He doesn't want to alarm anyone else.

But it's too late.

"What's wrong, Papa?" Alano asks, staring up at his father with tired eyes.

Joaquin won't admit that everything is wrong.

How his empire is falling on the day it was set to rise.

How all will be lost if he doesn't discover the source of this error.

How there are currently Deckers roaming the country, unaware that it's their End Day.

PART THREE
THE FIRSTS

Death-Cast is here for you.

—Joaquin Rosa, creator of Death-Cast

WILLIAM WILDE

(Deceased)

Death-Cast was supposed to call William Wilde to tell him he's going to die today.

This evening, William and his girlfriend of five years, Christi, left their one-bedroom apartment in downtown Brooklyn and rode the train to Manhattan to be among the partyers in Times Square for the launch of Death-Cast. William, a celebrated photographer, wanted to capture this historic event on camera, turning down many offers to do so for magazines. But seeing as he was already set to work the next morning, William wanted to do something for himself, for his own private collection. Especially on a night that was going to be extra memorable by having Christi tagging along.

By that, he meant setting his camera on a timer and capturing the moment he proposed.

Not getting shot.

The gunman was wearing a skull mask and muttering about the end of the world before senselessly firing into the crowd, that first bullet striking William in his throat.

His dreams of receiving an End Day call with Christi as an ancient couple surrounded by children and grandchildren and great-grandchildren were over.

He had to settle for dying in her arms, her tears on his face as he choked on his blood.

Times Square was so, so bright until it dimmed and dimmed . . .

"Stay with me, babe," Christi had said. "It's going to be okay. It's going to be okay!"

No one needed Death-Cast to know this wouldn't be okay.

But Death-Cast should've called nonetheless.

JOAQUIN ROSA
3:03 a.m.

Joaquin fears he will soon be calling everyone at Death-Cast to let them know the company is dead.

It's unclear whether this unnotified Decker's death is an isolated incident, but either way, Joaquin must get down to the bottom of it to protect his legacy, as well as make sure no other registered users die without warning.

Back in his office suite, Joaquin rolls up his sleeves and grabs his laptop.

"Make sure no one speaks to the press," Joaquin says. "We don't want to cause a panic."

"Well, we don't want the public to panic," Naya says.

It's as if she knows good and well that there's a riot of nerves roaring in Joaquin's chest.

Alano looks up from his notebook, where he's been drawing a dress, unable to fall back asleep. "How long will you be gone, Papa?"

"I'm not sure, mi hijo. As long as it takes to get everything back on track."

There's a part of Joaquin that knows, deep down, that if he can't resolve the issue, he may not want to return to face the music. But he always does, and he always will. Even when life feels impossible.

"What are you going to do?" Alano asks.

"You know I can't talk about that," Joaquin says.

Alano whines. "I'll keep it a secret."

"When you're older," Joaquin says.

"It's taking too long to be older."

It's amusing how much Alano believes he's ready to know how Death-Cast works when he still believes in Santa Claus. There are many conversations to have first, such as who actually puts presents under the Christmas tree. Not to mention everything about the birds and the bees, and, to be frank, Joaquin suspects it will be more of a bees-and-bees talk, which he will embrace willingly should he discover he's right. Regardless, Joaquin is protecting both Alano's childhood and security by not giving him the tell-all about Death-Cast. Perhaps when he's thirty, they can discuss it over a beer.

Joaquin kisses the top of his son's head and scratches the puppy behind his big brown ears before walking into his wife's arms.

"I'm going to be out of touch for a while," he says.

"I'll see you when I see you," Naya says.

The two part with a kiss.

Then Joaquin is out the door, on his way to a vault where no one can follow.

VALENTINO
3:04 a.m.

I will live my End Day, however long it lasts.

I brace myself before Orion and I leave the hospital. There are millions of ways I can die in the city. I've been thinking about them all night, but everything feels so much more possible now that I'm out in the open. Shot, strangled, stabbed. Or run over by a car or bus or taxi or motorcycle or even a train if I fall onto the tracks. Maybe something will fall out of the sky and crush me, like scaffolding, since every other block I've passed tonight appears to be under construction. I could have a heart attack of my own, which would be a cruel twist of fate, though better for Orion to know sooner rather than later that I actually won't be the one who will save his life.

Even though my apartment is only an eight-minute walk away, I'm nervous as we're walking down the sidewalk. For all I know, that litter on the ground is concealing manholes that can drop me into the sewers or an actual land mine that will blow me up. The options are endless. I'm tempted to walk on the street instead, but this could become a self-fulfilling prophecy where a car kills me and—

"Look alive," Orion says.

"Look alive?" I ask.

"Look. Alive. You're walking like a zombie."

"Still. That's a pretty heartless thing to say."

"Is that a knock on my heart?"

"Only because you told someone who's dying to look alive."

"You right, you right."

Orion is quiet, though I really like him best when he's talking.

"When did everything start with your heart?" I ask.

Orion lets out a whistle. "Oh man. It's funny because I grew up watching my mom in and out of the hospital. That's not, like, funny in and of itself, obviously, but I was so stupid that I never even considered that I could inherit heart issues too. Like, not once did that cross my mind."

"Maybe that's a good thing. You didn't spend your time dreading that problem."

Sort of like how I'm dreading my death.

"For sure, I guess I just wish I had taken it more seriously. Gotten some advice."

"You were a kid."

"A kid who swore my mom was going to die because of

her heart. Then I got hit with that plot twist of . . . Well, you know the story now." Orion tucks his hands into his pockets, slouching as he walks. It's like the weight of the world is literally on his shoulders. "I had my first bad heart attack a couple days after my sixteenth birthday."

"What caused it?"

"Everything? Sophomore year was not great. I was failing classes left and right, and I was stressed all the time, and I swore I was going to get left back. Then during my earth science final the hypertension was too much and I collapsed."

"That sounds horrible."

"It was, but at least the teacher liked me enough to give me a passing grade."

"You were probably their first student to have a literal heart attack during an exam."

"Oh yeah, heart attacks are so damn rare for teens, I'm like a unicorn—and not just because I'm gay!"

"You beat me to it."

Orion is laughing as a couple people up ahead are shouting. One swings a bat into a car, shattering the window and setting off the alarm. Orion's laugh dies down as the attacker's comes to life. Then I think I'm about to have a heart attack of my own when I see they're both wearing skull masks. I grab Orion's arm, dragging him behind this Jeep that's parked along the sidewalk. We crouch for cover.

"What the fuck—"

I shush Orion.

For all we know one of those masked men is the same one who tried shooting me.

Is this how destiny works in a world of Death-Cast? Is my death actually written in stone but when it happens is the only thing that changes? Have I been marked to be killed by this man who missed me earlier?

I jump when I hear another window shattered, another alarm going off. Surely this means the police will arrive on the scene soon to help, right?

Orion wraps his arm around my shoulders and holds me close like he's a bulletproof vest. I don't even push him away. Maybe he can save my life. If even for a bit longer.

Another shattered window, another alarm, another laugh echoing down the street.

The men in the skull masks are getting closer.

What's their deal? I'm guessing they must be among those people who have no concerns about committing crimes because they believe Death-Cast is the beginning of the world ending. If the cops could arrive and arrest them before they beat us with that bat, that would be wonderful.

Another window, another alarm, another laugh.

They're so close. One car away.

Orion looks really scared for someone whose head isn't on the chopping block, according to Death-Cast. A whimper escapes his lips, and I press my palm to his mouth to silence him. I don't think either of the men heard Orion, but I'm still terrified. Orion's hazel eyes are so apologetic. Then the Jeep's window is smashed in, glass raining down on the other side of the car. Orion's nails are digging into my arm, and I keep my breath sucked in as if it could be heard above this chorus of alarms.

As the next car is attacked, I lead Orion to the front of the Jeep, where we can't be seen.

I finally breathe as police sirens can be heard in the distance, approaching us.

"We got to go," Orion whispers.

I shake my head.

"Yes. What if they think we did it?"

He's right. Best-case scenario, we're taken into custody and I lose valuable hours of my End Day. Worst case . . .

I peek around the Jeep to find the attackers fleeing down the street, back toward the hospital. "Let's go."

Orion and I get up and run, and all I can think about is how my heart is racing hard like one of my more intense workouts and wondering how Orion's is holding up. We turn the corner and my boot slams right into the curb and I'm falling forward and Orion sees me and there's nothing either of us can do to stop gravity.

Right before my head slams down on the sidewalk, I know this is how I'm going to die.

ORION
3:10 a.m.

This can't be it; this can't be how this goes down.

I really want to believe this is a prank, but I know it's not, I saw that fear in his eyes as he was falling. I rush to his side, tripping over myself for a sec, and I flip Valentino over to find a big cut above his eyebrow. His blood stains the ground, looking like a Rorschach test that I don't give a shit about scoring well on because I only need to know if he's alive or not.

"Valentino, dude."

He groans, which is great because only living people groan, which means I can breathe knowing that he can too. His eyes flicker open, and his bare hand is shaking as he raises it to his wound.

"Don't touch it," I say. The last thing he needs is an infection. "Let's go back and get you checked out."

"No, I'm fine. I can clean it up at home."

"You sure?" I ask, helping him to his feet.

"I'm sure. Let's just get off these streets."

I make sure he's not dizzy as we continue on, and he seems as stable as someone can be considering they just busted their face on the sidewalk while running away from masked men. This night is fucking insane. He's right that we need to get him home, where he'll be safe. I'm not used to the Upper East Side, but the city grid makes it mad easy to get to Seventy-Seventh and Second.

"I thought I was going to die," Valentino says.

I'm not going to tell him I was thinking the same thing.

"In that moment, I mean," he adds.

"You're good, though."

"It would've still worked out for you probably. Brain damage and being this close to the hospital is a recipe for success."

I can't give air to that thought without feeling like shit for being the one who encouraged him to leave the hospital and almost got him killed and would have benefited from it.

Valentino is quiet, and I don't know what to say. Should I apologize?

"Zombie," he finally says.

"Uh, what? Oh shit, you have a concussion!"

Valentino shakes his head. "No, you had said I looked like a zombie. Before everything. I think that would've been a better name for Deckers."

As someone who has reread the Death-Cast website a

thousand times, I know why Deckers is the official title. "So Joaquin Rosa thinks of Deckers as the captains of their own ships and—"

"I get that. I'm sorry to interrupt."

"Interrupt away!"

"Calling us Deckers feels too intellectual. We're zombies. The living dead."

"Doesn't that feel too obvious, though?"

"Middle ground: Dead Enders."

"That's too morbid."

Valentino stares dead ahead. "Dying is morbid, Orion."

FRANKIE DARIO
3:15 a.m.

Death-Cast can't call Frankie Dario, but that doesn't stop Frankie from calling them.

Someone who works there, at least.

Frankie is sitting in his dark kitchen, drinking stale coffee out of his unwashed thermos while waiting for his wife's best friend to pick up the goddamn phone. He's learned the hard way not to count on Rolando, not after he disastrously forgot the rings for Frankie's wedding and didn't realize it until the ceremony was already underway. But did Gloria blame her best friend who probably wanted to ruin the wedding because of feelings he still has for her? Of course not. Frankie got chewed out for not checking in with Rolando sooner, as if he didn't have a million other duties assigned by her. But Rolando finally has a purpose in life, and that's working as a Death-Cast herald to tell people they're about to die.

Until it's all revealed to be a scam, that is.

Frankie has too many doubts about Death-Cast to register himself or his family for their services; the government already has too much information about them anyway. Things they shouldn't even know. But Frankie isn't an idiot. He knows there's money to be made here by photographing these so-called Deckers in the event they do die. The best part? Getting personal intel from Rolando.

If he ever answers the phone.

The photo series could be what truly defines Frankie's life. He's not good at a lot of things. Take this coffee for example. Absolute shit. But that's fine, he's not some mindless barista who lives to serve the whims of those wanting frosty cappuccinos with three—not two, not two and a half, not two and three-quarters—pumps of caramel syrup. Frankie can't make a cup of coffee, but he can take beautiful pictures. His newest tenant, Valentino, got suckered into putting down a deposit on the apartment because of Frankie's misleading photos on Craigslist.

That's talent!

It's time for Frankie to achieve his dreams of winning a Pulitzer for Breaking News Photography, and he's positive he'll do so for his work on this historic End Day. He'll either capture the first Death-Cast deaths or the relief on a Decker's face after they survive the day.

Frankie's leg bounces, his knee banging into the bottom of the table.

It's as if his soul is itching with how badly he wants to be out in the world and getting pictures already.

A part of Frankie would hate to expose Joaquin Rosa as a fraud since he sees so much of himself in him. They're both Hispanic men who were born in the same municipality in Puerto Rico, their time in Salinas overlapping for one year. It's a shame they didn't meet back then, as Frankie is sure they could've been lifelong friends. Maybe even the best men at each other's weddings, and someone to whom Frankie could confess that he wished Gloria cared as much about her appearance the way Naya does. And in another striking coincidence, both Frankie and Joaquin are fathers to nine-year-old sons. The friendship between these men could be one that is passed on to generations, like his eyes that are as brown as the milky coffee energizing him. Don't even get Frankie started on some of the nonsense he's seen that little boy Alano wearing; he's trying not to judge Joaquin's parenting, but that's been difficult in the past whenever he's had a couple beers. Frankie will continue to make sure that Paz grows up to be a man.

What truly separates the men, in Frankie's eyes, is success. He's a touch older, a difference hardly even worth noting, and yet his ego is still bruised that he's nowhere near Joaquin's level. They both provide for their families, as any Puerto Rican man should, but the Rosas have three penthouses across the country, whereas the Darios live in a shitty two-bedroom in Manhattan and have to deal with all their tenants' issues.

He's tired of just making ends meet—he's ready for great fortunes to start rolling in.

That begins with Death-Cast.

And with Rolando picking up the fucking phone.

So help him if he's not dead.

VALENTINO
3:17 a.m.

Five hours ago, I stood outside my new home for the first time, thinking I had my whole life ahead of me. Now I'm sporting a bloody cut from my near-death experience. The next time might not be *near*.

"This is it," I say as I reach for my keys.

"Right next to a pizza spot," Orion says, pointing at the closed pizzeria before shoving his hand back in his skinny jeans pocket. "Did you get a slice?"

"No. I was rushing to get to Times Square."

I don't have to say anything else. We know how that turned out. Would I have received the End Day call had I stayed in tonight? If I could time-travel, that's what I would have done differently. I would have hung out at home and unpacked and slept before my photo shoot in the morning. Then I would live long enough to see the fruits of my labor and my dreams come true.

"I should've stayed home," I say.

Orion nods. "With a whole pizza pie."

I check all my pockets again, and my keys aren't in any of them. "This can't be happening."

"What's up?"

"I think I lost my keys."

"You think?"

"I absolutely lost my keys."

"And your phone. I got to say, man, your pants are cute, but your pockets suck."

This is certainly not going to be the worst part of my day, but this doesn't feel good. I'm exhausted, and I just want to go lie down for a little bit. "Should we go back to the hospital?"

"No, just call your landlord—oh." Orion looks at the intercom. "Do you know his apartment? Just buzz him."

"He told me to only bother him during business hours. I don't want to upset him."

"He's not going to be your problem for much longer. Act like you're moving out. You got nothing to lose."

I do have nothing to lose. Frankie already seems annoyed with me, and there's no point trying to improve my relationship with him. Not even for Scarlett, who will have no issues confronting him when he's out of line. I only feel guilty about disturbing his family, but this is an emergency. My whole day is an emergency, and I need to treat it as such.

I go to the intercom, pausing because I'll never see my own name listed here. I press the buzzer for Frankie's apartment.

Then after a minute of nothing, Orion buzzes, holding down the button three times as long.

"He's going to kill you," I say. "More likely me."

"He's not going to do shit."

There's static on the intercom before Frankie's voice comes through: "Who is it?"

"Hi, Frankie. It's Valentino Prince. I'm so sorry. I'm locked out."

"Where the hell are your keys?!" Frankie shouts.

I'm regretting this. "I lost them."

We hear what sounds like the intercom phone slamming.

"Okay, maybe he will kill you," Orion mutters.

Judging by Frankie's face as he comes down the stairs, I'd say we're right. It's not too late to turn around and run. Frankie opens the lobby door and stares at my bloody forehead. I'm stupid for thinking that would buy me any sympathy points. He simply glares at me and Orion.

"I'm so sorry to wake you up," I say.

Frankie blocks the doorway. "You lost your keys on your first night. Who does that?"

I'm not walking him through everything I've been through since discovering I'm a Decker. It's not his business, and I doubt he'd care.

"I'm sorry," I say again.

Frankie tightens his bathrobe. "Did you lose both sets of keys?"

"No, the other set is at home. I didn't carry both. . . ."

"Oh, good, you have some common sense."

"Wow," Orion says. "This is how you treat your tenants?"

Frankie looks Orion up and down, then me. "It's three in the morning. You're lucky I came down at all."

"Can you please let us in?" I ask.

"Only because I already cashed your rent check." Frankie steps aside. "Don't bleed on my floors."

I can only imagine how much more dehumanizing he would be if he knew I was a Decker.

The building is still warm, but the air feels different. This won't be the hall where I go into my mailbox for letters and birthday cards and bills. These stairs I'm climbing won't be my daily leg workout. And as Frankie unlocks my apartment door, I understand this is both the first time I'll ever return here and possibly the last.

Before I can thank Frankie and apologize again, he goes straight into his apartment.

"Nice guy," Orion says, closing the door behind him.

I turn on the lights, regretting it immediately. This place is so bare-bones. "Feel free to sit on any box you want."

"After we clean you up," Orion says, setting his cap down on the counter. He runs the water in the kitchen sink, testing it. "Paper towels?"

I go into my suitcase and toss Orion the roll of toilet paper I packed because I wasn't sure what stores were going to be open with my late arrival. Not to mention all the reports of people hoarding toilet paper across the country in anticipation of the world ending. I'll do some shopping with Scarlett in the morning and make sure she's set up with the basics.

I meet Orion by the kitchen sink.

"The water's warm," Orion says.

He steadies one hand on my shoulder and gently dabs my wound with the other. I wince, but relax into it. Keeping my eyes closed while the water continues running makes me feel like I'm being treated at a spa. I'm dangerously close to falling asleep while standing, so I hold myself up on the kitchen counter.

"You're all set," Orion says.

"Thanks, Doctor . . ."

"Pagan."

"Thanks, Dr. Pagan."

"Be right back, I'm going to go knock on Frankie's door and ask for Band-Aids. I'm sure he'll be so hyped to help out his favorite tenant."

Orion holds back a laugh as he turns to leave, and I pull him into a hug, laughing harder than I thought I could on the day I'm going to die.

FRANKIE DARIO
3:31 a.m.

Frankie could kill the new tenant.

Where does Valentino get off on disturbing him in the middle of the night? Especially on his first day here! The audacity . . .

It doesn't matter that Frankie was already awake. That's no one's business. What *does* matter is that Frankie did his job by giving his tenant two sets of keys, per the lease, and Valentino got locked out of his apartment anyway; he probably lost his keys in whatever alley he met that boy he's brought home. Valentino Prince? More like Valentino Princess.

Frankie will be keeping Paz far away from Valentino. There have been enough red flags as is that there's something off about Paz, and so help him if he ever tries bringing another boy home. Frankie will go into his closet so fast and grab his—

Deep breaths.

197

If Frankie is being honest—and he is, you better believe that—what's really upsetting is that he still hasn't heard from Rolando. Hasn't he ruined enough people's lives already? The next time Rolando needs a favor, Frankie will take his sweet, sweet time getting it done, you better believe that too.

He dumps the rest of his coffee into the sink. He looks out his kitchen window, missing when he could look across the way and find that gorgeous, scrappy young woman in her apartment; she was always up late with different lucky men and women. But she's moved out, and now Valentino is there, hugging that boy by the window. Frankie closes his curtain, no longer interested in anything happening within those walls.

He grabs a beer from the fridge and starts chugging, hoping to drown out his many frustrations.

All he wants is a lead on a Decker he can follow around.

How hard can that be?

ORION

3:33 a.m.

This isn't how I imagined a boy bringing me home.

For starters, I'd thought I'd be able to buddy up with his parents or guardians, maybe some siblings and friends too. I'd be true as shit to myself, but also hype up my better qualities, like my writing and how I keep it moving even though I've got this heart that's trying to stop me. Then we'd all crack jokes over some meal before I'm trusted to chill with my guy in his bedroom, where he does a lot of his living.

Instead, I've been playing doctor to a Decker in an empty studio.

But this Valentino hug is mad nice. I enjoy it while it lasts, and as much as I want to keep staring at his blue eyes and heart-shaped lips, I back off so he doesn't get it twisted. I really did come to help him, not mess around.

It's kind of a dark thought, but I bet people are going to pursue Deckers in the future to get off and move on, no strings attached; I make a mental note to tell Dalma to not create that app.

"So where should we start?" I ask.

"I guess I'll unpack the boxes. It's just clothes."

"You can pick out something for your photo shoot."

"RainBrand is going to dress me up in their stuff."

"Yeah, but you got to roll up looking good anyway."

"Very true. I want to make a good impression so they hire me for future work."

I pause from tidying the counter to make sure I didn't depress the shit out of him. "Seriously, if you need me to kill the optimism and just let you feel your feelings, let me know. I will take my optimism out back and dig a hole."

"I like your optimism. It's way better than pretending it's not happening. Please don't stop," he says with a quick smile before ripping open a duct-taped box with ease.

"Optimism lives to see another day."

I go into his tiny bathroom, putting the toilet paper roll on its holder, and flush the bloody tissues. I check myself out in the mirror and if I thought I looked like shit in that selfie Dalma and I took of us before we met Valentino, I'd like to go back in time and let Past Orion know what a beautiful bastard he is. My lips are extra chapped, and my curls have gone rogue. Just everything about my face screams death.

And yet.

I can't get depressed, not when it's my job to keep Valentino feeling optimistic.

Back on track. I wash my face and deal with my lips and return outside.

Valentino is kneeling in his clothes while he removes his shirt, revealing his strong pecs and chiseled six-pack that I've never seen on anyone in real life. Seriously, this is wild. I feel like I'd break my fist if I punched his chest.

"Thumbs up on all that," I say, gesturing at his physique.

"Ha. Thanks," Valentino says as he puts on a white under-shirt that's less snug on him. "I really wish looking like this didn't feel so mandatory to break into this industry. Who knows how many hours I put into exercising all so I could become a buff corpse."

"A lot of shaving too."

Valentino chuckles. "Yeah. A buff, hairless corpse." He's folding his shirts and stacking them against the wall. "Look-ing back on it, I'm not thrilled how many people were running my life. They didn't even care about me. They just wanted to clone me."

"Well, no one is going to boss you around anymore."

"Speaking of . . . I hope I didn't mess with anything between you and Dalma."

"Nah, you're good. Dalma is just super logical, but I didn't want her nudging you on when you should die on your End Day. This isn't about us. It's all you."

Valentino sighs as he unboxes a couple jackets and sweat-ers. "I appreciate that, but just so you don't feel weird, I don't see her as the enemy. I actually understand where she's coming from. I would've behaved the same way if you had the magical organ that could save Scarlett's life."

If the tables were turned, I like to think I'd do exactly what Valentino is doing for me. Maybe if Scarlett does need some saving one day I can be her hero. If she ever needs a heart and I got Valentino's, then it's all hers, no questions asked.

As I'm opening the box for the air mattress, I'm really taking in what a fresh start this move was for Valentino. He didn't even have a proper bed to sleep on. It's not like when I moved out of my childhood apartment and into Casa Young. I had options between the pullout couch in the brownstone's living room, the sleeping bags from Dayana and Floyd's overnight camping trips, and obviously the guest room bed that became mine. Meanwhile, Valentino has the world's loudest air mattress. I almost unplug it from the wall because I don't want to disturb his neighbors at this hour, but I don't give a shit, because Valentino deserves a bed on his End Day—even if it's just an inflatable one.

In a world that currently has no problem leaving people to sleep on the streets, I'm already nervous how Deckers are going to be treated as time goes on.

It's a good thing Valentino won't have to suffer from that nonsense.

VALENTINO
3:41 a.m.

The last box is full of footwear I won't ever wear around New York City.

My Timberland boots did great work tonight, but I was really looking forward to stepping out with my favorite oxfords and blue Chucks and tan loafers. And also going for many morning runs in my Nikes, exploring Central Park. I pull out two pairs of white sneakers, one scuffed up from casual outings and the other reserved for parties where I'm dressing down but want to look fresh. My parents always thought I was ridiculous for owning identical sneakers with different purposes, but they're not as involved in their appearances as I am. When I think I look good, I feel good. I stand by my fashion choices, even now when it might look silly to have been so protective of shoes that won't see the light of day.

Not on me, at least. They'll find new homes on someone else's feet.

Until then, I line them up by the door.

"All done," I say. It's not much, but I've created the illusion that someone is living here.

"What's next?" Orion asks behind a yawn.

I check the time on my watch. "Scarlett should be boarding by now. Mind if I call her?"

"No need to ask," Orion says, sliding his phone across the floor. "Just go for it."

I used his phone right before we left the hospital so I could text Scarlett how best to reach me since Dalma was no longer along for the ride. She responded quickly, which had me nervous because I don't want her texting and driving, but she had responsibly parked before checking the new notification from another unidentified number. Even distressed, Scarlett is still playing it safe, which is great because we still have about twenty minutes before we're certain that she's not also dying today.

I go to his call history and click Scarlett's newly saved name. She answers my FaceTime in seconds.

Scarlett's face and eyes are red, and she exhales immediately upon seeing me. "I was so nervous it wasn't going to be you."

"I'm home," I say, angling the camera so she can see the apartment with what little I have unpacked and Orion in the corner.

"Good. Make sure there's nothing in there that can kill

you. Like the stove or sharp surfaces. Does the window lock? Lock the window so no one can sneak in."

If this were an ordinary call, I might just tell her that everything is fine. But I want to calm her nerves as much as I'll need her to calm mine, so I go around the apartment and make sure it's death-proofed.

"All done," I say.

"Thank you. Don't hang up yet."

"I won't."

I sit on the air mattress, which is firm enough to help me sleep for a couple hours. I watch Scarlett as she checks in at her gate and takes a deep breath. She's only flown twice before and she's not a fan. Now more than ever I regret leaving early. The cell service gets weaker the deeper she goes down the jet bridge because despite all the reports of in-flight Wi-Fi becoming a thing, I don't know anyone who's been on a plane with one yet.

"Scar," I call as she keeps lagging, her face frozen in ways she would hate.

I hang up and send her a text, hoping it goes through: Service sucks. Let me know when you're about to take off. I love you, Scar.

"She's boarding," I tell Orion. "I should probably go to bed. I want to be rested when she arrives."

"You got to get that beauty sleep too before the photo shoot," he says.

"I have enough concealer to hide my shadows and cut."

"So do you have any bedsheets?" Orion asks.

I shake my head. "I was more concerned with packing a million shoes apparently."

"Oh, I got this." Orion hops up, ready to problem solve as he grabs some of the clothes and jackets I took time folding and brings them to the air mattress. He creates pillows by stuffing sweaters into cotton T-shirts so the wool won't be scratchy on our faces. He lays out one towel across the air mattress as bedding and tops it off with the black trench coat as my blanket.

"If I had my phone, I'd take a picture of this," I say. It's really impressive.

"I kind of love it too," Orion says. He puts one of the sweater-pillows on the floor and makes a sleeping bag out of a sweater and my tan suede jacket.

"What are you doing?"

"Just making my bed. Is that cool? I'll sleep under your jacket so it doesn't touch the floor."

"No, I don't care about that. You don't have to sleep on the floor."

"I really don't mind. I appreciate you letting a total stranger crash anyway."

"You're not a total stranger. If we're going to share a heart, we can share a bed."

Orion's face scrunches. "Eh, technically you're giving

me your heart. We're not sharing. But I'm not going to ignore . . ."

"A dying man's wish?" I ask.

"Hey, you filled in the blank, not me."

Orion throws his sweater-pillow and outerwear-blankets on the bed. We take off our boots. I normally sleep in my underwear, but I don't want to make things uncomfortable, so I switch into my sweatpants. Orion sets an alarm on his phone before using my charger; together we form a perfect team. I switch off the lights and get into bed, where Orion is already getting cozy. The room is dark even without blinds, but not pitch-black thanks to the city lights keeping the block awake. I think about buying curtains tomorrow because it's important I get full-night sleeps, especially on the days I work, before remembering that's not going to be my issue.

How many of those thoughts will I have before I fully accept dying?

Hopefully a ton. That means I'm still alive.

This is the first time I'm sharing a bed with another boy. We're not cheating either by lying on opposite ends with our feet in each other's faces. This is head to head with our eyes up at the ceiling. It's really nice and the kind of life I was planning on creating for myself out here in New York. I had some luck back home with talking to some boys, but it never came anywhere near this level. Everything always felt so tricky because of hiding my feelings from my parents and not always feeling safe doing anything romantic as I walked through my red state. I also never felt that right pull to another boy; someone who would've been worth it all.

It's so quiet that I feel like my heartbeats are so loud, like I'm anticipating something.

Orion ends the silence when he whispers, "I have a question."

"You don't have to whisper."

"I didn't know if you were sleeping."

"You'll know. I'm the loudest snorer ever."

"You can't be the loudest snorer ever and have a room-mate in a studio."

"My snoring is white noise to Scarlett at this point." I turn over so I can see him, but he keeps staring at the ceiling. "Please don't smother me in my sleep."

"Only because you have something I want," Orion says, glancing at me before turning away again. "That's what I wanted to ask about, actually. Does Scarlett know about all the heart stuff?"

"Not yet. The End Day was enough to chew on for start-ers. As a fellow registered organ donor, she's going to be supportive. My heart not being in my corpse isn't the thing that's going to make her feel like her life is incomplete."

I groan as a horrible image comes to mind.

"What's wrong?" Orion asks.

"Thinking about all this organ stuff . . . I just pictured

Scarlett dying in a plane crash and knowing her organs can't be donated like she wanted."

I can't shake it out of my head. The screams, the chaos, the fire, the smoke.

Orion sits up, resting his hand on my shoulder. "Don't worry about that. The plane doesn't take off for another few minutes, so unless Death-Cast is about to call all those passengers, Scarlett is going to be okay."

SCARLETT PRINCE
12:59 a.m. (Mountain Standard Time)

Death-Cast has not called Scarlett Prince to tell her whether she is going to die today, but as she's entering this last possible hour for them to do so, Scarlett is white-knuckling her phone, unsure if she wants to share an End Day with her brother or face life without him.

Scarlett is no stranger to this anxiety, having almost died in May.

While she miraculously hasn't been traumatized by cars, even when driving down the very freeway where that careless man crashed into her, there is an undeniable pain that has remained with her since the accident. It wasn't the blood rushing to her head while upside down in her overturned MINI Cooper, or the tightness of the seat belt against her chest, or even the shards of glass that pierced her skin from the shattered passenger's window, leaving some light scarring across her cheek and neck and arm. What hurt the most was the misery of how she was about to die alone, even though that's not how she started her life.

That heartbreak still chokes her whenever she recalls that pain, a pain that her brother won't ever know because she will be right by his side, even if it means witnessing a horrible death that he doesn't deserve.

"I had a thought before blacking out," Scarlett had told Valentino while recovering the morning after the accident. "That since I was the last one to enter this world, I would be the first one out. It's like life got too crowded so people had to be fired."

"You're making death sound more poetic than it is," Valentino had said.

"That's the artist in me. Happy to be wrong."

Scarlett was no longer happy to be wrong.

Valentino was the first one in and will be the first one out.

Unless they depart together, like a plane off to its destination, one-way.

Scarlett glances up to find everyone else in her row on their own phones, as if they're all waiting to see if today will be their last. Then she has a horrible vision of a collective ringing throughout the entire plane, damning everyone even though they haven't taken off yet. She doesn't want to give that thought power, but it doesn't help when she hears bells.

The Death-Cast ringtone.

They're calling someone aboard this flight.

Scarlett's phone is quiet and dark, and she's immediately consumed by solving the mystery of the unlucky Decker. From her seat in the seventh row, Scarlett can hear the bells chiming from up ahead, possibly someone in first class. But everyone in that section is facing forward, staring up at the front cabin.

The pilot of this plane is going to die today.

What does that mean for everyone else?

CAPTAIN HARRY E. PEARSON
1:00 a.m. (Mountain Standard Time)

Death-Cast is calling Captain Harry E. Pearson to tell him he's going to die today, moments before he was about to prepare his airplane for his centennial flight.

From the first officer to the flight attendants to the passengers, all eyes are on the captain. This is the kind of attention one dreams about during in-flight safety demonstrations, but people are often too lost in their magazines and phones to care. But now they're rapt with great intensity, wondering when Captain Pearson will answer his End Day call. He's about to when he feels a deep dread, such as when he used to watch horror movies but had to stop because his aging heart couldn't handle the suspense and jump-scares anymore, and Captain Pearson becomes very suspicious of all on board.

If Death-Cast is calling while he's not even in the air, then does that mean there's someone on this plane who will kill him? A terrorist with intentions to hijack the plane? It can't be a bomb because everyone would have to be a Decker, yes? Who's to say everyone else isn't about to get a call? This is all new territory.

In a state of distress, Captain Pearson makes a rapid decision, a decision that's against all regulations because those guidelines were written for a world without Death-Cast, where one was to prepare for danger but not where you must accept inevitability. If he's to save all his passengers from a hijacking, he must trust no one, including his first officer, who he shoves toward first class. Captain Pearson doesn't wait to see where he lands. He locks himself in the cockpit, heartbroken he won't make his one hundredth flight but proud of his commitment to safety first.

He sits down in his pilot's chair and answers Death-Cast's call while staring at the sky.

SCARLETT PRINCE
1:02 a.m. (Mountain Standard Time)

Is the pilot going to kill them all?

All Scarlett knows is that once the pilot seals himself inside the cockpit, all hell breaks loose. So many passengers go wild like animals freed from cages, charging to the front of the plane and demanding to be let out. Scarlett wants to do the same, but she's terrified she'll be trampled in the pandemonium, so she cowers with her back to the window. Did the pilot attack his copilot because he wants to fly everyone to their deaths? Or is there someone among them in the main cabin who is the greater threat?

It's hard to hold faith in Death-Cast when they've incited this much hysteria.

What if they're getting things wrong tonight?

Scarlett tries calling that boy Orion's phone to reach Valentino, but she can't get a signal.

Maybe a text will go through: Death cast called the pilot..

215

She types so fast, not giving a shit about proper punctuation.

I didnt get a call but everyone is going crazy.

No messages are going through.

I'm scared, Val, she types anyway.

She might as well get used to these one-sided conversations with her brother now.

ORION

Valentino calls Scarlett again, but it keeps going straight to voice mail.

"What if she's talking to Death-Cast?" he asks, setting down the phone.

The thing is, if Scarlett is getting her End Day call, there's nothing we can do about that. I just got to offer some support so Valentino doesn't completely lose his shit.

"If Death-Cast is hitting her up, I bet you anything you're the first person she's going to call once she's off the phone." I find his eyes in the darkness, seeing him understand. "Scarlett is probably still having service issues."

"You're totally right. It took forever for my text to go through earlier on my flight before we took off. The message had just sent before I had to switch to airplane mode, and that was without interference from all the End Day calls."

"Exactly," I say, even though I don't believe he believes

217

in his words. He's trying to talk himself into that truth, and I respect it.

He rests his head back onto his makeshift pillow. Only to pop up again a second later.

"What if those signal disruptions prevent Death-Cast from reaching Scarlett? Or anyone else on the plane? Or everyone else, even? They could be about to take off, not knowing they're doomed. It's not like Death-Cast could call the airlines either and prevent them from departing, since they're not tracking us like all those conspiracy theorists believe, though in this case, it would actually be really helpful to know if the plane is full of Deckers."

I let Valentino vomit out every last word, and he's got me thinking about my parents and all the other 9/11 victims.

If Death-Cast had been around back then and called the thousands of people who died in the towers and the planes and on the grounds, could they have lived? Everything Joaquin Rosa has talked about suggests they would have been killed in other ways, but would I have gotten to see them one more time that day? Would I have watched them die instead of being oblivious for hours that they were dead? There's a million questions I could ask, just like after watching any movie with major time-travel paradoxes, but unless I can actually rewind time, I'm never going to get an answer.

"It's times like this I wish I still prayed," Valentino says. "I'd pray for Scarlett's safety."

I've never really been religious, but I respect other people's shit as long as they respect mine. Like whenever we're at home and about to eat, Team Young takes a second to pray for their blessings and I peacefully sit it out and we all jump into our meal together. It's all good.

"You stopped praying because of your parents?" I ask.

"I'm aware that my story is as old as the Bible, but my parents made it clear that I was sinning after I came out as gay. It felt like I was banned from praying."

There's something so thrilling every time Valentino says he's gay. I feel like the room should've lit up in rainbows so I could've seen the word fly out of his heart-shaped lips. But honestly, the darkness makes sense, like there's a storm still following Valentino wherever he goes because he has parents who aren't giving him the love he deserves. I wouldn't win the fight, but I'd still want to swing at someone in his defense.

"You know that's all bullshit, right?"

"Mostly."

"Look, I don't fuck with religion, but anyone hating on gay people because of shit the Bible apparently doesn't even say can go fuck off."

"I like how you can swear so freely and not come off furious."

"It's a gift."

"Thanks for your not-quite-impassioned take. It's been

really hard to have leaned on my faith for so many years and to have literally prayed to God that my parents would love me anyway and to have been wrong." He rests his hands on his chest and takes a deep breath. "Getting away from them was one of the main reasons I left. It's part of my job to feel comfortable in my skin. To own my bones. How could I do that if I can't be myself at home?"

And now here he is, in bed with another guy on his first night.

"I haven't told my parents I'm dying," he says.

Everything about this is shocking, but for me, the biggest shocker is how *I* forgot he's going to die today. I got so sucked into his history and cheering on his future that I felt like I slipped into another universe where Valentino is going to have the chance to discover himself the way he's been dreaming about. But he's not, because he is going to die today and his parents who drove him away have no idea.

"Are you going to tell them?" I ask, even though it's not looking good that he hasn't already tried to drop this big news.

"What's the point? Their priest has convinced them that only God is omniscient and that Death-Cast is the work of the devil."

I almost turn on the lights so Valentino can personally watch me roll my eyes.

"Maybe they're watching the news and know better by now," I say.

"I'm still undecided. You'll probably think I'm a monster if I don't."

"No the hell I won't. Why do you think I would?"

He gets really shifty. "I don't know. You've lost family unexpectedly, and I'm sure you have a lot you would've said to your parents had you known it was the last time you were going to see them. . . . Did you ever get the chance to talk to them about your heart?"

"Heart stuff didn't start until I was sixteen, remember?"

"I wasn't clear. I'm sorry. I wasn't talking about your heart condition. I was talking about where your heart pulls you, or more who it pulls you to."

I like that even though I never said anything out loud, Valentino still knows I'm gay. Or at least that I'm not straight. Yeah, I was flirting with him in Times Square and I'm sharing a bed with him now, but I'm really proud of how openly I carry myself. This shit can be really scary, don't get me wrong. Especially in the South Bronx, where I've never seen two men holding hands and *gay* is used as an insult. But I've known for years I wasn't going to have forever to come out, so I flew out of that closet when I got the chance.

I'll just always wish it had been sooner.

"I didn't get to talk about it with my mom and dad," I say.

"Do you think they would have been okay?"

221

"Okay with the gay?"

"Okay with the gay," he repeats. "Don't feel like you can't be honest just because my parents weren't ideal about it."

"You sure-sure?"

"I am sure-sure."

"My mom and dad always wanted me to be happy. I think they always felt guilty that they didn't make more money to buy me whatever I wanted, so they did their best everywhere else. Like getting me a library card when I needed new books to read, or stealing printer paper from work so I could write my stories. So I don't think they would've given a flying fuck who I brought home as long as they made me happy."

Valentino throws up a fist. "Well done, parents of Orion. No wonder you've turned out so great."

I blush in the darkness. "I got to give shout-outs to Dayana and Floyd too. They've been really dope guardians. I can't think of a better place to have moved to than the home of my mother's childhood best friend. We got to grieve her together, and Dayana's always been letting me find my way and make my own mistakes, even when she wanted to step in. Like Times Square."

"She didn't want you to go?"

"Nope. Dalma's parents wanted us to stay in, but I was itching for an adventure."

"Wow. If you hadn't been there . . ."

"Yeah, yeah. I saved your life, I'm a total hero. We get it."

"I was going to say that if you hadn't been there and tack-led me, then maybe I'd still have my cell phone," Valentino says, a smile in his voice. He playfully nudges me, and I feel like we're one millisecond away from wrestling on this air mattress and saying "No homo!" even though we're both gay. "I'm really glad you were there. That clearly wasn't my finest hour, but it could've been a lot worse."

"You could've lost your wallet too."

"And my life," he says, fully serious.

This first day of Death-Cast is so dizzying.

One moment, the Decker whose life I saved has his spirits lifted, and the next, he's haunted.

Maybe this is the biggest advantage to how life was lived before—you don't spend any time grieving yourself when you're not expecting to even die in the first place.

"Seriously, I'm happy you're alive. I'll save you as often as I can."

"Happy," he echoes.

There's something sad about the way he says *happy*.

He could be tired. It's late as fuck—four o'clock in my body, one o'clock in his. But I think it's a life exhaustion weighing him down.

"Valentino?"

"Yeah?"

"I'm not a fan of your parents. Straight-up. If they can't meet you where you're at, that shit is on them. It's their loss because you're fucking awesome. If you think you got something to gain by talking to them one last time, I say go for it. But please, please, please only do it for yourself. You don't owe anything to people who don't want to see you happy."

Valentino reaches over and squeezes my arm. "Well, I'm really happy I've met you. It's nice to know my heart is going to a good person."

"Only good? You called me great before. How can I regain some points?"

"Let me think," he says.

If Valentino asked for a kiss, he'd find my lips on his so fast.

It's hard being this close to him and not being with him.

I feel like we're connecting, I'm not just telling myself some story. I legit believe that if Death-Cast hadn't called Valentino, then I would have put my number into his phone and we would've made plans to hang out—maybe even directly called it a date—and gotten to know each other at a fast-and-steady rate. But we don't get a tomorrow; we're barely getting a today. Soon, his sister will land in New York and they'll spend as much time together as they can, and if all goes well, we'd reunite at the hospital for the surgery, where it will be too late to live like we are right now—two guys sharing a bed in the middle of the night, opening our hearts to each other like when we first met.

I don't want to regret not saying anything—not taking action.

"Valentino?" I whisper.

I wait for him to say my name back, but he only answers with a gentle snore, one that rumor has it will erupt through this empty studio in no time. I stay up as long as I can, listening to Valentino sleep before I finally pass out too.

SCARLETT PRINCE
1:09 a.m. (Mountain Standard Time)

The plane was supposed to take off now, but instead, it remains grounded with the pilot still sealed away in the cockpit—and armed forces outside. Scarlett assumes the pilot himself must've alerted someone. Before anyone could even escape through the emergency exit, security and police officers surrounded the plane, instructing everyone to stay inside as they investigate the threat.

"Remain calm," the pilot had said after quelling all concerns about flying everyone to their deaths.

But how can people remain calm if they were never calm in the first place?

Passengers are banging on windows and threatening the copilot and flight attendants.

Scarlett is scared for her life, but knows she shouldn't be.

If she were going to die, then Death-Cast would've called.

NAYA ROSA
4:30 a.m.

Death-Cast did not call Naya Rosa because she isn't dying today, but how can anyone be sure after a Decker has managed to slip through the cracks of their system?

And then another and another and another.

Four lives gone without warning. These are only the reported cases so far. How many more stories will come out by the morning? How many souls will have moved on without anyone to even announce their untimely passing?

The birth of Death-Cast was supposed to be the death of worry.

But worry is all Naya feels in her heart right now.

Is her son safe? Her husband? Herself?

What about all the dedicated employees who are still working the phone lines, closing out this final hour as they reach out to Deckers on the West Coast? Naya is concerned for their mental wellness too. How many of them are ready to snap under the weight of grief?

Originally, the government had pitched Death-Cast being operated through robocalls for efficiency. Joaquin was very close to leaning into this idea when Naya spoke up. In the same way that doctors personally deliver unfavorable diagnoses, Naya believed that calling to tell someone they were going to die needed that human touch. Discovering your life was over by some prerecorded message was too cold.

In advocating for the Deckers, Naya knew she must take care of the heralds too.

She first designed this open-floor plan to protect the heralds' well-being, not wanting them isolated in personal offices or divided in cubicles. There are four long glossy white tables, each able to sit five people. Everyone is encouraged to personalize their spaces with joyful pictures of loved ones, pets, anything that keeps the threads to their own lives strong so they never become hopeless. And while Naya had toyed around with the idea of stationing little speakers around the call center that played calming music, she decided to have fountains installed to keep everyone connected to actual nature while working their shifts.

Once the End Day calls have concluded tonight, all the employees—both heralds and customer service reps—have mandated group counseling with the option for private sessions too. Naya will also make herself available for personal feedback on how best the company can meet their needs.

Hopefully there will still be a company after tonight.

Naya steps away from the heart of the call center and joins Alano and Bucky in one of the private booths reserved for heralds who need a moment after any interaction that brought them distress. She doesn't know who has more energy right now, her son or the puppy, but watching them play together brings the biggest smile on her face.

"You should go back to sleep," Naya says.

"I like being up late," Alano says.

"Don't get used to it. Regular bedtime tomorrow."

This includes herself, desperate to be asleep in her own bed.

This year has been beyond exhausting. The public only became aware of Death-Cast on the first of July but so much work has gone into the program behind the scenes. Everything had to be done discreetly. For instance, the architects believed they were building a customer service center for a new phone that will be releasing; something that is part of Death-Cast's long game but not happening for another few years.

Once the news was out, things really began taking a toll on the Rosas. Close friends were frustrated that Joaquin and Naya wouldn't share the secret behind the company's predictions and were disturbed that they've had access to it for years and hadn't shared the wealth sooner. Naya's own family has been turning on Joaquin, viewing him as some mustache-twirling, greedy supervillain for not offering these services for free. Neighbors and strangers have turned their noses down on them at every chance they get, believing the family is running some scam that will inspire an Oscar-worthy film in the years to come. Though what breaks Naya's heart the most has been how often Alano was bullied by friends and even harassed by some parents at the park; adopting Bucky last week isn't going to solve all of Alano's struggles, but the puppy has been a wonderful distraction that keeps him from crying every night.

Failing these Deckers won't help earn the public's trust.

Naya won't admit it out loud, but should Joaquin be forced to shutter the company, she will mourn what Death-Cast could have done for the world while celebrating her family's return to normalcy.

That's her purpose in this life.

Even if it sadly isn't her husband's.

JOAQUIN ROSA
5:00 a.m.

Death-Cast's inaugural End Day calls have come to a close in the continental US.

Joaquin is upset he isn't present with his team to commemorate this moment, but he's still investigating the issue. If he can't solve it by the time the heralds are released from group counseling, offering overtime to those who stay, he will simply have to work the call center alone upon his return.

No more Deckers will die unwarned on his watch.

NAYA ROSA
5:11 a.m.

Once a herald finishes their call, there's a stillness in the air.

That was the last End Day call for the night.

Naya is about to encourage everyone to take deep breaths when the very lovely customer success engineer Aster Gomez comes out of nowhere and attempts to start a round of applause for jobs well done. The heralds remain frozen in their seats. All but one. Andrea Donahue is a woman who wastes no time as she goes straight to the wellness room. She will have to wait for the rest of the group, since it is indeed group counseling, but Naya trusts everyone to know their own needs. For Andrea that could have been removing herself from the station where she just spent the past five hours telling people they were about to die. For the other nineteen heralds it appears they need a minute or two or five.

"This job isn't easy, but it's important work," Naya says from the top of a chair where she can be seen. "We thank you for being the voices of this company."

Still, none of them speak.

Not even as they finally file into the wellness room, shaking Naya's hand as she looks each of them in the eye and thanks them by name. Everyone seems so haunted, as if they're being followed by the ghosts of all the Deckers they called tonight. Perhaps it's a good thing they don't know about the Deckers who died and will die without warning today.

Each and every one will be Death-Cast's ghosts.

FRANKIE DARIO
5:16 a.m.

Frankie is back in bed, watching the news.

He's clutching the TV remote in one hand and his phone in the other. He finds holding other objects prevents him from punching walls and people when he's upset. And he's far past upset—he is pissed off. Rolando has ignored all seventeen of his phone calls. If he's dead, Frankie won't mourn him. He never liked the guy, but if Rolando is alive and couldn't even bother to respond to one of his texts, then Frankie is going to punch his teeth in, he swears. A night in jail would be worth it for the fortunes and awards Rolando has cost him.

The news is reporting on a shooting that happened earlier tonight in Times Square, shortly after midnight. It takes a special kind of idiot to be in that crowd, and while the world is apparently down many idiots, Frankie wishes he'd been smart enough to attend the Death-Cast festivities. Of course something explosive was going to happen! If he'd been on the scene he could have scored some brutal, devastating photographs that would have improved his life.

Gloria stirs under the blanket and looks between Frankie and the TV. "Can you lower that?"

"I could if Rolando answered my calls."

"You're calling him now? He started working at Death-Cast," she drowsily says.

How stupid does she think he is? "No shit. But I needed his help."

"With what?"

"Don't worry about it."

He's never in the mood for a lecture, but especially not at five in the morning on no sleep. His wife has always been so unsupportive when it comes to his dreams. That's because she has no real artistic eye, no ability to see into the soul of his photographs. Instead, she expects Frankie to be practical, as if he wants to fix radiators and plunge toilets and deal with tenants who disturb him at three in the morning for the rest of his life.

Meanwhile, Gloria is playing manager and carting off Pazito to every audition every chance she gets. Here's the thing: If Pazito were actually a good enough actor, he would've been booking work more easily after appearing in one of those Scorpius Hawthorne films. Having a small role in arguably the biggest fantasy franchise of their time surely should have led to other opportunities by now, but if that wasn't enough to brighten his star, then that kid isn't shining.

Maybe Gloria should raise their nine-year-old to develop some practical skills sooner rather than later so Pazito doesn't grow up to be "distracted by big dreams" as she once accused Frankie when he forgot the anniversary of their loveless marriage.

He's too upset to even focus on the news anymore. He gets out of bed, leaving the remote, and carries his phone back to the kitchen to see if he can reach Rolando while treating himself to another beer.

Frankie knows this End Day is his ticket out of debt and—if he's lucky—this family.

GLORIA DARIO
5:19 a.m.

Death-Cast did not call Gloria Dario because she is not dying today, not that she should even be reachable, since her husband doesn't want this family registered for this service, but Gloria signed up everyone behind his back anyway.

All her life, Gloria has been a planner.

Every morning she wakes up and knows what she's preparing for breakfast, lunch, and dinner. Every night she checks the weather and lays out her clothes for the next day. She keeps running to-do lists in tiny spiral notebooks that she purchases from the ninety-nine-cent store to stay on track, and practically lives for that thrill of checking off her tasks, no matter how small. She arrives to every appointment at least forty-five minutes early because the subway can be so unpredictable. She preps Pazito's Halloween costume in August with fittings in September and final dress rehearsals in the first week of October. (Thankfully Pazito never changes his mind at the last minute, though she has a bin of fabrics and crafts in the closet just in case.) And even though it's grim business and she doesn't have much to leave behind, Gloria prepared her will during her first year of motherhood and pushed Frankie to do the same to ensure that Pazito will be taken care of after they're gone.

Planning her life has always helped Gloria feel in control. But death has never been something she can plan as accurately until now.

Gloria had cried the entire time she was filling out the Death-Cast registration form, tempted to click out after answering each question in fear of Frankie finding out and hurling insults—maybe even more—for providing private information that has already been shared freely to other places, such as hospitals and even their cable provider. She could tell he was recycling conspiracies from third parties, and she's long given up on trying to get her husband to see reason. All he does is lash out whenever they're in disagreement. Which is why Gloria was crying while registering for Death-Cast. Yes, she's devastated whenever she thinks about how she'll spend her End Day with Pazito, knowing that even a master planner like herself can't possibly squeeze in everything she hopes to do with her son before dying, but more than that, she was heartbroken because she knows that her husband is primed to be the one who kills her.

She discussed this with Rolando—her best friend in this life, and her lover in another—who very understandably hates Frankie and only plays nice to keep her safe.

"Why not just leave him?" Rolando had asked a million times over the years, most recently when she confided in him that she registered herself for Death-Cast. "It feels like you're accepting he's going to kill you."

If Gloria put herself first, she likes to think she would've walked away years ago. Just packed all her things while Frankie was out and left, the only evidence that she was ever there being a signed note about what a monster he is. Who's to say if she would've actually gone through with this. She's known many strong women, her mother included, who have stayed in marriages like this for their own reasons. For Gloria's mother, it was the financial security that was necessary while raising Gloria and her sisters. For Gloria, she stays because her son doesn't see his father as a monster. How could she tear Pazito away from Frankie, especially at a young age?

Over the years, the time to leave has never felt right.

First, Gloria thought things would change when she was pregnant.

She was wrong.

Gloria thought things would change when her son was born.

She was wrong.

Gloria thought things would change when her son slept through the night.

She was wrong.

Gloria thought things would change when her son started speaking.

She was wrong.

Gloria thought things would change when her son began preschool.

She was wrong.

Gloria thought things would change when her son booked a movie.

She was wrong.

Gloria thinks things will change.

She hopes she's not wrong.

But she's planning to be, thanks to Death-Cast.

Moments after Frankie leaves their bedroom, upset at Rolando again for some new mysterious reason, Gloria is struggling to fall back to sleep. She listens in on the news, which is still covering the fatalities from Times Square tonight. She had stayed up with Pazito watching the celebrations when she heard the gunshots. Quick on her feet, Gloria switched off the TV and told him those were fireworks, and when he asked to stay up just a little bit longer to watch them—that boy loves him some fireworks—she apologized and sent him to his bed. She wants to keep her son as young as she possibly can and not force him to grow up too soon.

Who knows what traumatic thing he could've seen if she hadn't turned off the TV?

Now she has her answer. The camera teams present to capture the night managed to get some disturbing footage, including one man being shot in his neck by someone in a skull mask. Then there was a close call as a teen boy bravely tackles another to the ground, saving his life. What a hero. The reporters cut back to an image of the assailant in his mask, sharing that he has not been identified or caught at this time.

Gloria shivers and switches the channel where another news station is reporting on a grounded flight in Arizona where Death-Cast called a pilot minutes before takeoff. Her heart goes to that Decker's family, but she's relieved at how Death-Cast potentially saved the lives of all those passengers. It's unclear if more people would have died had that pilot flown that plane; it's hard to say without knowing how Death-Cast knows who is and who isn't dying, but she's choosing to believe this is a miracle.

Before she rolls back over, hoping to get some more shut-eye before she has to take Pazito to an audition for a commercial later, Gloria checks her phone to make sure that she isn't such a heavy sleeper that she slept through the ringer that is said to be impossible to sleep through unless you're dead. There are no warnings from Death-Cast.

She isn't dying today.

Sadly, this doesn't bring her the comfort it should. Not dying doesn't mean she can't be hurt, and that dread is alive and well. It may not always be that way.

Gloria thinks things will change.

She hopes she's not wrong.

NAYA ROSA
5:55 a.m.

Naya can't speak for everyone else, but she found the group counseling to be very soothing.

Then again, she didn't deliver any End Day calls tonight.

The group therapist guided everyone through meditation with her calming voice. She passed around crayons and paper and asked them to draw a lovely memory, and while Naya could see that some of the heralds, Andrea Donahue especially, were resistant to this exercise, they came around, and even now Andrea seems proud of the art she produced about her daughter's first birthday. Though if drawing was putting some people off, Naya can only imagine if they had gone with the dance party as originally planned; the heralds who are already considering not returning tomorrow would have absolutely been pushed over the edge.

Naya takes the stage for the final event, one Joaquin planned on doing himself.

"Before we send you home, I'd like to read the names of the first Deckers, to both memorialize them and celebrate you all for giving them the opportunity to live before their passing."

It's unclear if this will be done at the end of every shift, but commemorating the firsts seemed important in recognizing that Death-Cast as a company cannot exist without them.

"Valentino Prince, Rose Marie Brosnan, Max Foster, Jacqueline Eagle, Chris Van Drew . . ."

When Naya completes the list, she asks for a moment of silence, in which she thinks about the Deckers who've died without warning from any of these hardworking heralds.

"May they all live while they can, and then rest in peace."

ROLANDO RUBIO
6:06 a.m.

Rolando throws away that drawing the first chance he gets.

That whole group therapy session was born out of good intentions, he knows that. He's just not interested in keeping souvenirs for arguably the worst night of his life. Logically, he trusts that he changed a lot of people's lives today, but he also somehow feels responsible, as if he pulled their names out of a hat and decided they were going to die. But hey, nothing undoes all that grief like drawing that time he went to the beach with Gloria and Paz; it was indeed a happy memory since Frankie didn't go, but nonetheless, it's not serving Rolando's mental wellness—unwellness.

Right as he's about to go into the employee break room and collect his things, he goes down the hall, where he finds Naya and Aster, their conversation turning to whispers.

"Can I speak with you, Mrs. Rosa? Alone?"

Aster steps away, returning to the customer service area.

"Please call me Naya," she says, looking over her shoulder where her son is lying down on a rug with his puppy. "What can I do for you, Rolando? Did you want a private session with a therapist?"

"Oh god, no."

Naya fails at masking her shock but cracks a quick smile. "I know that group counseling wasn't for everyone."

"No, it's not. It feels so culty to tell people they're going to die all night and then try to brush it off with a little meditation and an art project like we're in kindergarten."

"I'm open to feedback on how you think we should manage."

"I have no idea, Mrs. Rosa—Naya. But just not that. That was horrible."

Naya nods, even though Rolando has offered nothing productive. "I understand you were having some difficulties tonight."

He stares point-blank. "Yes . . . I was finding it hard to tell people their lives were over." There's a pause, as if Naya is expecting Rolando to apologize or backtrack because he's so tired or something, but he won't lie. "If the other heralds didn't struggle, I don't know what to say. Maybe they were on the phone pushing printer paper while I was getting in trouble for comforting a lonely old man."

"Your compassion is why we hired you. It's just that we have more Deckers to—"

"Yes, more Deckers to reach. Like the teenage girl who

has plans to go on her first date tomorrow except she'll be dead by then. Or the husband whose wife returns from deployment next month and he'll be too dead to welcome her home. I didn't ask for anyone's story, but I'm getting them anyway."

"That's all so upsetting. Truly," Naya says with tears in her eyes. "Are you sure you don't wish to speak with the therapist?"

"I'm sure."

Deep down, Rolando knows this would be helpful, but he's not in his right state of mind. How could anyone be after working this shift? The amount of people who asked him to help save their lives tonight, as if he hasn't already done everything he can for them. More than anything he wanted to tell Deckers that maybe Death-Cast is wrong, but he has no proof to support that. He would only be feeding empty lies and giving hope to Deckers who will die thinking they would make it to tomorrow, all because Rolando misled them.

"Death-Cast has a beautiful purpose, but this is a terrible job," he says. "I don't want to become numb to people dying. I quit."

And just like that, Rolando can feel himself slowly returning to his body, as if he were a ghost who was slipping away.

This was the right move.

No drawing was going to save his life.

247

DALMA YOUNG
6:16 a.m.

Death-Cast did not call Dalma Young because she is not dying today, but she witnessed the first Decker receive his End Day call. That moment will stay with her for as long as she lives.

When that Death-Cast alarm went off, Dalma was terrified they were calling her childhood best friend Orion Pagan. Lord knows that boy is one bad heart attack away from joining his parents and her father in heaven. But instead the heralds were calling Valentino Prince, the beautiful stranger they'd met less than an hour before, and while she feels for him, she was relieved she wasn't going to lose her best friend. In fact, Valentino has generously offered to donate his heart to keep Orion alive.

Unfortunately, all hope for that transplant has been thrown in the trash, as if that heart was no good.

Dalma will continue living in fear of Orion dying. Fantastic.

She isn't petty; she has plenty to focus on instead of clinging to grudges. But Orion sacrificing his second chance at an
easier life to tend to someone whose time will be cut short?
Irresponsible and inconsiderate. Dalma isn't sure she'll ever
be able to forgive that. She wonders if she's to blame. For the
past few years she's shielded Orion from what she's feeling,
not wanting to add stress to his heart. He doesn't know how
it's rare for an hour to pass where she's not concerned that he's
having an attack and whether he's battling it by himself—if
he'll even win. He doesn't know how her grades drop every
time he's in the hospital because she keeps up this guise that
she can handle it all. He doesn't know that she doesn't know
how she'll live if he dies.

Dalma is family, and Valentino is a stranger.

And yet, Orion chose the stranger over family.

Even over himself.

She was stunned that Orion, who always wants her company, told her to leave him alone. But Dalma can't ever play
that card because if she ever chooses anyone else—even
herself—over Orion, she runs the risk of regretting it if
Orion drops dead while she's away.

Now here she is, back home in her bedroom, tired but too
upset to fall asleep.

Dalma is cuddling with Moon Girl, her childhood doll
with white button eyes and brown skin like her own. She's
always loved space. She sleeps under galaxy lights and dreams
on pillows designed like constellations. Her walls are white

except for the one behind her bed that's wallpapered with dotted white stars. And her most prized object is the Cooper refractor telescope she won in her senior-year science fair; shout-out to the mummified mouse that got her the win. Maybe she should spend more time stargazing than obsessing over Mr. Constellation and his bad decisions.

Or reading the news on her phone about a shooting she experienced firsthand.

She gets out of bed and sets her phone to charge at her desk.

The desk is an old DIY project with a chest of ebony drawers that her stepdad, Floyd, found at a garage sale. He tried helping her out so they could have a fun little bonding moment, but she was determined to do everything herself. The women in her family are builders. Her gran was a seamstress on the Upper East Side, and Dalma isn't saying that people started walking around with more holes in their clothes after she retired, but it's a hell of a coincidence. Her mother, Dayana, runs a small business where she gets paid bank to design websites for bigger businesses. Dalma first fell in love with user interface engineering from sitting side by side with her mother as she wrote code and made the internet a prettier place. Dalma herself will become a worldwide famous programmer once she comes up with her idea. And as for Dahlia, she's got no clear vision just yet, though Dalma trusts her little sister will come into her own over time. Whether she's a builder like the other women or more of a healer like her father or something else entirely, Dalma will back her up.

Because that's how you show up for your family.

But since Orion rejected her help and Dalma is home alone, she's going to choose herself.

Dalma opens her laptop, a present from her mother and stepfather for getting accepted to Hunter College. This really was the gift of gifts because it was impossible to download all the necessary software on her family's desktop computer. Here she has a solid starter package for writing code and designing her future app, the very thing she's focused on right now. She fights back a yawn, but she's no stranger to working through the night. She's going to get shit done.

Since Death-Cast is so hot right now, Dalma wants to create an app that ties into that program, knowing it's the smartest, fastest way to get her work on everyone's radar. Whatever it is, she wants it to be free. She doesn't want to exploit Deckers, even if they might find themselves with savings they no longer need to hold on to.

She bites her nail, thinking.

Her earliest idea was to create a running feed like Twitter, but for Deckers to share their thoughts on how their End Day is going. She thought it would be a lovely way to humanize them in their final hours. Except she remembered how toxic social media apps are, and if people are already this horrible in life, how will they behave when they're sure they won't have any long-term consequences? Dalma is sure someone else will create a similar app and make billions, but she won't create a stage for those voices. Especially not after everything she's already endured as a young Afro-Latina in tech.

She could build something with a charitable component. Like what if a Decker sets a personal goal they've always wanted to achieve, and people cheer them on with donations? Similar to what people do for a track runner in a marathon. All the proceeds could go to that Decker's family or a charity close to their hearts. That could work.

What if there was an app that's basically Craigslist for Deckers who want to have an open house to get rid of their furniture? Though also what's stopping Craigslist from creating that function themselves? Nothing.

Moving on.

Something that could also be very useful to the general public is to know where Deckers are congregating so they can choose to stay away if they don't want to find themselves at risk of a sudden blast that may not kill them but could harm them. Ugh, no. Dalma hates everything about it. It not only tracks Deckers and doesn't give them privacy, but it would ward people away from them like they're lepers. Wow, Dalma hates the idea so badly she backspaces every last letter of that thought. She'd hate to die and have her family find this file and think less of who she was in life.

Maybe Dalma needs to keep the app simple, like a little to-do list for Deckers. But what sets that apart from all the others? Sure, feeling accomplished feels good and that feeling might be magnified for Deckers, but it's not special enough. Anyone could have come up with this idea.

When Dalma starts wondering about creating a quiz app where you can find out what Scorpius Hawthorne character you are based on your End Day, she knows it's time for bed.

She looks out her window, and sunlight is beginning to wake up her Bronx neighborhood.

It's the start of a new day—and the beginning of a stranger's End Day.

VALENTINO
6:30 a.m.

The alarm scares me awake; it's like getting a Death-Cast call all over again.

It would've been nice to wake up and mistake my End Day for an ordinary Saturday, even for a few moments, but that wasn't in the cards for me. At least I got to sleep for a couple hours where I didn't have to worry about dying. No weird dreams or nightmares either. I silence the alarm and turn to find Orion still asleep, his lips slightly parted. I'll let him rest for a bit longer.

I get out of bed with Orion's phone, expecting to find some texts or missed calls from Scarlett when I remember she's still in the air for another couple hours. There are messages from Dalma and Dayana asking Orion if he's okay and I'll leave those for him to answer.

I usually begin my mornings with mixing some electrolyte powder into my water bottle and going for a run. I can feel my body ready to go, but with the timing for my photo shoot, it's simply not on the agenda today. My body also wants food, even something small like a handful of almonds, but according to Dalma I shouldn't eat anything without risking the surgery. It's a good thing my fridge is empty so I can't be tempted, I guess. I use the bathroom and brush my teeth and then hop in a cold shower, which is great for circulation, but I've always loved hot showers, so I should bask in that too while I can. I switch from cold to hot, and I'm surprised the water runs well, considering so much about this building has been a lie so far.

I get out of the shower and wipe the fog off my mirror. I start applying my concealer, like I always do to hide my dark circles and look more alive. Except that's the thing. As I look into the mirror, I don't see a Decker looking back at me. I already look alive and well because I am alive and well. The only real suggestion that something is wrong is the cut on my forehead from banging my head on the curb, and I didn't exactly bleed to death on the streets or in my sleep. I'm okay. Then why am I living a day where my sister is on her way to say goodbye and a boy is in my bed waiting for my heart? How come instead of focusing on all my hard work that has earned me this photo shoot, I'm spending the morning upset that life has other plans for me? I don't know why life wants me dead.

This feels like a bad way to start the day. Though maybe

that only applies to ordinary days, not End Days. On End Days there are no rules, so you can be angry and smash your reflection so you can actually see yourself shattered and look the part of someone who doesn't have their life together. But maybe I'm wrong. Maybe there are rules for End Days and I have no way of knowing because this is the first one ever and I won't get to see if this changes as time goes on.

I wrap a towel around my waist and go back into the studio space, dripping, to get some clothes. I crouch by my folded shirts and pants and try to figure out what's the last outfit I'm choosing for myself before I'm fitted in RainBrand clothes for the photo shoot and a hospital gown for the surgery. I've only worn this sheer black top once, but it might attract some heat. My sportswear could be comfortable, but what if I die and become a ghost in a tracksuit? That's not the way to go. I have tees from brands like Supreme and OriginalFake but they're not setting the mood. I settle on the plain white shirt that really accentuates my shoulders, pecs, and arms, and I'm going to tuck it into my black jeans. I'll pair that with my white sneakers that haven't properly seen the light of the day; it's time to wear them in while I can.

I'm returning to the bathroom to get dressed when I slip on a puddle of water and slam right down on my back.

The fall knocks the breath out of me, but another follows. I'm not dead.

Orion shouts my name, probably thinking I am dead.

"Are you okay?" he asks.

"I'm alive."

"Great start. But are you okay?"

I have a headache, but I'm suddenly self-conscious that I'm only wearing a towel. In all my modeling gigs I've been shirtless once but never had to be in my underwear. Which means this is the most exposed I've been in front of another boy. I sit up, my abs squeezing like I'm beginning a crunch, and my towel is thankfully concealing my business.

"You going to lie down there all day?" Orion asks.

"Maybe. It's my End Day, I'll do what I want," I say.

"Respect." Orion gets down on the floor with me, side by side like we're back in bed. "How are you feeling?"

The wood planks are cold on my back, but it's becoming soothing the longer I'm down here. "I should be fine. My head hurt more last night."

"Good to know. How about with everything else?"

"You mean my End Day?"

"Yeah."

"This morning has been hard. There was something really final about waking up. Nothing killed me last night, but today is definitely the day. Then I almost just died because I don't know how to dry myself after a shower. Can you imagine? The first Decker getting taken out by a puddle?"

"Definitely one for the history books, but not how you want to go down."

I almost find the whole thing funny. "Someone out there is going to start ranking dumb Decker deaths, aren't they?"

Orion turns on his side, hovering over me slightly. "If you die a dumb Decker death I'll tell everyone you died saving the world."

"Or something more realistic, like I rescued kids out of a burning school bus."

"Kids in a school bus on a Saturday isn't realistic."

"Neither is saving the whole wide world!"

Orion laughs. He hops up. "Okay, we can brainstorm more brilliant ways for you to die while we're out living your life."

I take his hand while also holding the towel over my junk. Orion helps me up, and our eyes meet, and his smile gets one out of me. He's pulled me out of my dark headspace already. I break eye contact and stare at his white shirt: *Have a Happy End Day!* in bold black letters. It's the kind of spirit I need to carry me throughout today.

"Since you're getting my heart, can I take your shirt?"

Orion looks down at his shirt like he's forgotten what it is. "Really? You want to be a Decker walking around in an End Day shirt? Isn't that so dark?"

"I think I should keep that message close to my heart."

"Literally?"

"Literally, I guess."

"If you say so." Orion takes off the shirt, and right when

I think I'm about to glimpse what he looks like shirtless, he has another underneath.

That's a shame.

I get dressed in the bathroom and admire my reflection in the End Day shirt.

I step out into the studio space to give Orion a turn in the bathroom while I fight my way into my white sneakers that are so fresh they need some breaking into. I'm sure the downstairs neighbor is rightfully annoyed to hear me stomping at six forty-five in the morning, but they can't possibly hate me more than our landlord. I can't concern myself with either of them. This is my End Day, and I know a model centering himself seems obvious, but in my case it's deserved. I need to take care of myself and my people. Even if that means disturbing my downstairs neighbor as I walk around to make sure this apartment is tidy for Scarlett. I leave the bed alone since we'll go and get new sheets for her together; I also personally like letting this memory of my last sleep live a little longer.

Once Orion is done, he comes out of the bathroom applauding my look. "I hope they're paying you the big bucks because you make a twenty-dollar shirt look expensive."

The money for the job is great, and I have to make sure they can wire it directly into my account so Scarlett can claim it. Maybe I can even ask for a cash payment.

"That's really nice. Thank you," I say.

"My weather app says it's kind of chilly this morning. You might want to throw on another layer."

"You too, then."

"Oh, I'm definitely robbing you, I don't fuck with the cold."

We go through my shirts, and Orion chooses a navy hoodie and I put on my solid gray collared shirt with the buttons undone so my End Day messaging doesn't get lost.

Then one foot out the apartment.

A trip down six flights of steps.

And I pause at the lobby door.

The last time I left this building, I thought everything was beginning. I had all the hope in the world and years of dreams I would be working to make come true. Now as I push the door open, I'm building steel nerves to get me through what I can only hope to be the best End Day a Decker can possibly have.

ROLANDO RUBIO
6:56 a.m.

Rolando is exhausted when he steps out of the building, putting Death-Cast behind him.

He's not sure what he will do for work now. He could try begging for his old job at the school. If they won't rehire him, he can move back to Staten Island and spend some time with his mother. She's been lonely since his father died and could use some company. But Death-Cast can't pay him to return to that call center, that's for sure.

Breathing in that crisp morning air, Rolando is unsure where to go next. He doesn't want to return to his depressing apartment after such a depressing night. He'd love to see Gloria and Paz and celebrate life while he can. Who knows how long it will be until Death-Cast calls him like he did with so many Deckers. Another part of him wants to see if he can find that old man, Clint Suarez. No one should be alone on their End Day.

Rolando checks his phone, and there are more than twenty

missed calls from Frankie. He's nervous and imagines the worst. Then he remembers that Gloria and Paz can't be dead because their names weren't read out loud during the commemoration ceremony this morning. But Death-Cast doesn't call for near-death experiences, and what if Frankie has beat Gloria so badly that she's been hospitalized? It wouldn't be the first time, and he's unsure when it will be the last.

He calls Frankie to put himself out of his misery.

"Finally," Frankie answers. "What took you so long?"

"I've been working. What's wrong? Is everyone okay?"

"I need your help on a project that'll be huge for me and the family."

Rolando rolls his eyes. He's sure this is going to be like that time where Frankie wanted to borrow money so he could buy a car "for the family" and to "keep Gloria and Paz safe from the trains" and "so they can take more trips to the beach," only for Frankie to blow that loan while gambling in Atlantic City. If Rolando had savings, he'd know better than to trust Frankie with any money again.

"What's the project?" Rolando asks, already thinking up excuses to not help Frankie.

"I want to take pictures of Deckers."

Rolando waits for more information, but nothing. "Like as a service?" He wouldn't be surprised if Frankie was trying to make quick cash off Deckers who aren't sure what to do with their money.

"No, I wouldn't charge. I just want to be around and capture their final moment."

What an absolutely horrific intention. Rolando stops in his tracks. "How is that going to help the family?"

"Come on, it's obvious. Getting pictures of a Decker on the first End Day could sell for loads of money. The only Deckers I know from the news are already dead. I need names so I can find them and follow them around."

"So you want to stalk the Deckers."

Frankie is quiet, just like he gets right before he explodes. Except Rolando isn't the one who will be hurt. If Gloria is telling the truth, Frankie has never laid a hand on Paz, but Rolando is scared that day isn't too far away. Then Rolando has an idea. Instead of letting Frankie be the explosive one, he can push Frankie toward an explosion—toward the death of a Decker just like he wants. Maybe Frankie can get hurt along the way and he won't be able to harm Gloria ever again.

"I'll help you," Rolando says, his heart hammering.

He's violating the lives of these Deckers who registered for the program at their discretion. But he's turning his back on ethics if it means protecting a woman and young boy who are at risk simply because of the man in their home. He doesn't want to send Frankie to Clint Suarez, the elderly Decker whom Rolando spoke to for nearly an hour. That man hasn't lived that long for it all to end with Frankie in his presence. He's thinking back to the commemoration ceremony, still fresh in his head. There were a lot of names that stuck out, but none like the very first because he thought it was too charming for a real person.

"Joaquin Rosa called the first Decker. I don't know if he's still alive, but his name is Valentino Prince."

FRANKIE DARIO
7:01 a.m.

Frankie almost drops his phone.

Did he just hear that right? His new tenant is a Decker? The first Decker? Called by Joaquin Rosa personally? This is going to be the best day of his life. Frankie's obviously, not Valentino's. Though Frankie won't be grieving Valentino, he's very ready to exploit his death. The new tenant is going to be his golden ticket out of this building.

There's no way pictures of the first Decker dying won't sell for millions.

Frankie hangs up on Rolando and rushes to his window, drawing the curtain to look into Valentino's apartment. The lights are off. He's probably still sleeping. Or he could have been murdered by that other boy who was trying to be smart with Frankie. Serves Valentino right for picking up strangers in the streets. He runs out into the hallway and bangs on Valentino's door.

265

"It's me, Frankie!"

Still nothing.

Silence is good. Silence means he's not alive to answer.

Frankie returns to his apartment to grab the key to 6G, just used in the middle of the night when Valentino locked himself out.

"What's wrong, Daddy?" Paz asks, eating cereal at the table.

He leaves without answering. He unlocks the door, and if anyone gives him trouble for doing so, he'll rat out Rolando for sharing this Decker's name and Frankie will tell the authorities he was very concerned for the well-being of his tenant. When in reality, Frankie opens the door and steps inside, hoping to find a crime scene.

Nothing, again.

Just an air mattress and clothes and shoes.

He swears under his breath and returns home.

Gloria looks him up and down, finally taking an interest. "What's going on?"

Frankie finds Valentino's number and calls him. But it keeps ringing and ringing. "Why do people have phones if they never answer them?!"

"Why, Daddy?" Paz asks, not understanding that it was rhetorical.

Frankie drags a chair from the dining table—these floors have long been scratched up, and he won't be living here for much longer anyway—and props the chair against his front door to make sure he can see and hear Valentino coming home.

That Decker will change Frankie's life today.

VALENTINO

7:06 a.m.

I love the morning sun on my skin, but I come alive as we go down into the subway, like I'm in a whole new world. Orion isn't nearly as fascinated as I am by the fact that we're suddenly underground. Then we need to buy our MetroCards, and I'm looking between the teller booth and the ticket vending machine as if it might be my only chance to do so.

"I'm torn."

"Human or robot?" Orion asks.

"Most humans have been pretty rude since I got here."

"Robot for the win," Orion says.

"Glad to be checking out of here before a robot apocalypse."

Ripped apart by a cyborg is not one of the creative ways I want to die.

We go to the vending machine and there are options ranging from single ride for $2.25 to an unlimited pass for $89.00.

"I guess a day pass is enough, but I'll just get the monthly pass. I can leave the card for Scarlett and encourage her to go out and use it instead of hanging around the apartment."

I tap all the buttons and pay, and my first MetroCard slides out. It's yellow with blue lettering in what I think is that same Helvetica font I used for so many school Power-Points over the years. I had originally planned on framing this MetroCard along with any other NYC mementos. I hope Scarlett puts it to good use.

I swipe my way in at the turnstile smoothly.

"You're a natural," Orion says.

We wait on the platform with other riders. There are beams with chipped paint. Posters along the wall that have been graffitied by an artist with a penis obsession. An over-flowing trash can. I'm surprised I don't see any rats up here like they're waiting for the train too, when I remember that they're mostly down on the tracks. I want a closer look at the train tracks, but I know better than to be a Decker who ignores the painted yellow lines at the edge of the platform, signaling for everyone to keep their distance at risk of falling in. I press my back to the wall so someone can't accidentally knock me in—or even intentionally. I wouldn't put it past anyone after having a gun fired at me.

"Should I have stayed home?"

Orion doesn't even look puzzled. "We can go back if you want."

"It's not what I want, but it feels like the smarter choice."

"Then let's go."

I'm dragging my feet back toward the turnstiles, thinking about how I can be home in five minutes. I pause at the emergency exit gate. "I'm freaking out."

"I get it."

I almost tell him that he doesn't, except he does. Orion has lived with this panic for years. No, he's never known for a fact that his death was certain. But that doesn't mean he hasn't questioned every little choice he makes. "What's the point of Death-Cast calling if you're too scared to live?"

Orion doesn't have some immediate joke. It's like he has some inner detector that lets him know when I need to be distracted and when I need to be engaged. "This is your End Day, Valentino. Only you can make the call on what to do."

The train rumbles as it begins pulling into the station.

"How do I know what's worth it?" I ask.

He taps the End Day message across my shirt. "Ask yourself if it'll make you happy to do it, and heartbroken if you don't."

When I'm on my deathbed later, looking back on my life—my End Day in particular—I want to feel like I made the most out of it. That I made my dream come true, and got the chance to live it before I die. I should honor my heart before it's pulled out of my chest.

The train doors open, and I turn around, running straight

toward the car while yelling at Orion to follow me. We squeeze in right as the doors close. If I had space to jump and pump my fist, I would. I'm so empowered by Orion's words. Before I can thank him I smell something horrible. I look around to identify the source when I realize why it's so crowded. Everyone is cramming together on this side of the car because at the other end is a massive pile of vomit, probably courtesy of someone who got sick from Death-Cast partying. I'm immediately nauseated, and my appetite has been killed. I hold my gray shirt to my nose, breathing in the Hugo Boss cologne I spritzed on it back in Arizona that smells like plums and citrus.

"Welcome to New York," Orion says with a smile before hiding behind his nose inside the hoodie.

This is not an experience I was particularly interested in having.

Unfortunately, the train is running express and holding us hostage for several stops, so when the doors open at Sixty-Eighth Street, we get out and switch cars. Orion wants distance from the overflow going directly into the next car, so we jog down the platform and hop back on the train before the doors close. This time we're able to sit, our backs to a map of New York with blue, red, green, orange, yellow, purple, brown, and gray lines that each represent a different path.

"We're on the green line," Orion says, tracing where we

started and down to Union Square. "And here's where we're getting out."

I gesture at the map. "Do you think I could travel all of this in one day?"

"I don't know, but honestly, why would you? The trains are mad gross. That hellhole we just escaped from is not rare."

"I originally dreamt about visiting every corner of New York. At least by riding the train I could say I passed through them."

"But the best parts of New York are out on the streets."

"Like when I got shot at?"

"Like when you got shot at!"

"Terrifying."

"Fucking terrifying."

I hope they catch that guy.

Minutes later, the train stops at Forty-Second Street, close to Times Square, where everything changed. The doors remain open too long, and I shudder thinking that man in the skull mask could be any of these passengers filing in. He could think I recognize his eyes and need to finish this job. Choosing to embrace possibilities like this by not retreating home doesn't make things less terrifying, but all I can do is hope for the best today.

As we're approaching Union Square, I look up and down the car. People are holding on to the poles while reading a newspaper or on their phone. Someone else is dozing off, their head snapping back upright as their chin touches their chest. Others are sitting quietly, traveling from A to B or even B back to A. But I really thought there would be some kind of show, like young people turning the train into a jungle gym as they swing around the poles and flip around while blasting music. We reach our stop, and before I step onto the platform, I wait one extra moment to see if a show is about to begin, but nothing.

"First thoughts on your first ride?" Orion asks as we climb the stairs.

"More ordinary than I thought. Where were all the dancers? Is it too early?"

"Nah, I'd see them on the train rides to school a lot of mornings. That really pissed off people. Maybe the usual performers were out doing their thing last night." He squeezes my arm as we leave the station. "I bet you'll catch a show on the way back."

"Hopefully."

I can't imagine I would be heartbroken on my deathbed by not having seen people dancing on the train, but it's one of those daily occurrences in New York I've been imagining for so long that it feels weird to not have been granted that instantly. Especially when time is so limited. It just shows that no matter what's happening in your life, the world doesn't only spin for you.

However, Union Square is a breath of fresh air. There are

chess players sitting on top of crates, basking in the sun. One woman has the biggest smile on her face as she walks eight dogs. Two women are holding hands and coffees as they enter this little park. That could actually be a nice place for a cozy, autumnal photo shoot. I can already picture myself standing on a bench with the flaps of my gray wool coat thrown open, revealing a white tee and . . . I stop planning the outfit I won't be able to wear this fall.

While waiting at the crosswalk, we stand at the curb and I stare at the sky and watch an airplane flying over us. I can't wait until Scarlett gets here.

"Have you ever flown before?" I ask as we cross the street.

"Nope."

"Why not?"

Then I stop in the middle of the street with my hands to my mouth. I'm asking Orion why he's never flown after a hijacked plane killed his parents and uprooted his life. That was so stupid and careless. Orion looks over his shoulder to see I'm not following him at the very same time I remember I'm a Decker who can be run over at any moment. I don't even look both ways, which is probably as foolish as stopping in the middle of the street in the first place. I would be terrible at playing Frogger, though I miraculously make it to the next block in one piece.

Orion grabs my shoulders. "You got to be careful!"

"I'm sorry."

"It's okay. It doesn't matter if cars have stopped, assume there's an idiot behind the wheel."

"I always do," I say, thinking about the idiot who almost killed Scarlett. "But I'm sorry for forgetting about your parents. I won't even blame it on being tired or because it's my End Day. I just wasn't thinking."

Orion shrugs. "You're not the first to slip. It's all good."

I shake my head. "No it's not. But I'll be better from here on out. However long that is."

Orion's hands are on my shoulders again, this time gentler. "If you really want to make it up to me, you won't make it so easy for anyone to kill you."

7:38 a.m.

We arrive at the Future Star Model Management offices.

This is a newer agency that promises to be behind the biggest faces in the modeling world. I'm really grateful they saw my potential after reviewing my online portfolio—their favorite photographs were taken by Scarlett—and after one fun Skype interview I signed with the team. Their company is currently located in some generic commercial building, and I like to think they will make good on their promise and turn people into superstars.

Even though Future Star is new, I still thought the office was going to be glossy with magazines laid out on a glass coffee table. Instead, it feels like this place hasn't gone through any renovations from whatever business was here before; I'm going to go ahead and guess this was a dentist practice since it still has that tooth-dust smell that I remember well from having one of my own ground down before being restored to match its neighbor.

What really gets me is how I was so sure there would be a receptionist with a headset who would instantly recognize me. This man has no idea who I am. There are a dozen head-shots taped to the wall under the company sign, and mine isn't one of them. Was I supposed to bring one with me? No, I'm a client. They also have a massive printer right there in the corner. Even then, I booked a major campaign for this company. You'd think my face would be worth highlighting. It's not, though.

I'm still a Nobody around these parts, and won't become a Somebody until it's too late to get the star treatment.

"Good morning. We're only open today for private meet-ings," the receptionist says.

"I'm Valentino Prince. I'm one of the agency's models. Laverne told me to come straight here for a fitting."

The receptionist nods very slowly. "I see." He punches in a number on his landline the old-fashioned way. No head-sets. I can hear ringing two doors down. "Hi, Laverne. I have a Valentino Prince here to see you." There's a muffled voice. "Uh-huh. Uh-huh. Okay." He hangs up. "Laverne will be out in a moment. You can have a seat if you'd like."

I'm certain the three chairs against the wall are leftovers because they're too lived-in for a new business. Orion and I sit anyway, and he pats my knee.

"This is so exciting," he says.

"It is."

"Wow, you sound so unexcited."

"No, I am. I'm trying to contain myself."

"Why?"

I lower my voice so the receptionist won't overhear, even though he's about eight feet away. "Whenever I pictured this moment, I told myself to play it cool because it's cooler to be cool about something big. I want to be seen as professional and hirable again."

Orion nods. "Okay, I get that, but . . . you know. Get hyped while you can."

"What would I do without you?"

"Probably nothing," Orion says with a smile that belongs on the wall with the other headshots.

A door opens, and out comes my agent, Laverne, an older white woman with gray streaks in her black hair. She's wearing a simple periwinkle-blue sweater with jeans—very casual Saturday attire for a modeling agency.

"Valentino, Valentino. So wonderful to meet you in person," she says as she pulls me into a hug.

"You too!" I say enthusiastically. "Thank you so much for taking a chance on me."

"Oh, please. Your parents laid the foundation of your look and you built it up."

I feel weird about giving my parents any credit given how they disowned me. But she's not wrong. I have my father's eyes and the shape of my mother's face, nose, and lips. They can't deny that I'm their son. Though I'm not going to give them credit on my build. It was all my hard work that got me to where I am today.

"Laverne, this is my friend Orion."

"Beautiful name," Laverne says as she stares at his hair. "And beautiful curls. Why are you hiding them under that hat?"

"It belonged to my dad," Orion says.

"Are you a model too? I can easily find you work in a shampoo commercial."

Orion shakes his head. "Not my thing, but thanks." He squeezes my shoulder. "But this guy is ready to crush his photo shoot."

Laverne looks puzzled. "Didn't you get my voicemail?"

Am I about to find out I got fired? On my End Day?

"I lost my phone last night."

"Ah. I hate to break it to you, but the photo shoot has to be postponed."

"For how long? A few hours?"

"A bit longer. We need to find a new photographer."

"What happened to William?"

Laverne takes a deep breath. "William was murdered last night in Times Square."

I fall back into my seat, and Orion's hand flies to his mouth. I feel transported back to Times Square. The gunshots . . . I never in a million years in a city of millions would've thought I'd know the person who died. Even peripherally.

I wonder if he was registered for Death-Cast.

"That's horrible," Orion says, turning to me, just like when we were at the hospital. "We were actually in Times Square last night."

Laverne's eyes widen. "Wow. Thankfully you're both okay."

Orion doesn't say anything else. Just like at the hospital, he doesn't tell my story for me.

"I'm only sort of okay. Death-Cast called me last night."

The receptionist peeks up from the front counter, stunned.

Laverne laughs. "You're going to be fine," she says, waving off this big bomb I just dropped like it was only cigarette smoke. "You can't possibly believe that those Death-Cast people can actually know when someone is going to die."

"We do," Orion says. "And they've been right already."

"It hasn't been a full day. There are many opportunities for their predictions to be proven wrong."

"Valentino can't risk waiting around for that," Orion says. "So is there something we can do to get this photo shoot going on today?"

Laverne is no longer charmed by Orion. She turns to me.

279

"If you truly believe that Death-Cast is right, then why are you even trying to do this photo shoot?"

"I've been working hard for a moment like this."

"But you won't be around to reap the rewards."

"I like knowing my work is out there. That I was seen."

Laverne nods slowly. "I hear you. Fortunately, I'll have a new photographer by Monday. Tuesday at the latest. We can make your dreams come true then."

Orion is about to fight for me, but I grab his hand. We both stop and exchange a look.

I got this, I say with my eyes.

If you don't, I will, Orion seems to say back.

Then I look at Laverne, and she can't seem to read my mind even though she once said she could see my soul through my gaze. "I will be dead by Monday," I say.

Laverne sits beside me. "You're scared. I understand why. Our president has lied to us about Death-Cast and is creating hysteria. But I lived through this already with Y2K back in 2000. We were told that this millennium bug was going to affect all computer systems and result in banks shutting down and government records being exposed and people getting stuck in elevators and technology turning against us. I was terrified . . . until the clock hit midnight and we were all fine. You will be too because Death-Cast isn't real."

I'm so disappointed. It was one thing seeing people in Times Square not believing in Death-Cast, but it's another to see it coming from someone I trusted with my career—with my life. "Moments after getting my Death-Cast call, I was almost killed in Times Square. Probably by the same person who killed William."

"A nearly tragic coincidence," Laverne says. "I'm relieved you lived—and that you will. We're going to do incredible work at the photo shoot next week."

We're not going to change each other's minds. The only way I can prove her wrong is by dying, and I don't want to do it any sooner than I already will to make a point.

"Is there really nothing we can shoot today? My sister will be arriving in New York really soon. Scarlett's a photographer. You loved her work. So did the RainBrand team."

I don't know which stage of grief bargaining is, but I know that's what's happening here. I'm desperate to make this work, any way I can.

"Scarlett has a wonderful eye, but she's not here," Laverne says.

"I can do it," Orion says. "How hard can it be?"

"Exceptionally," Laverne says. "The RainBrand campaign will need a veteran to helm it nonetheless. I'm looking forward to introducing you to whoever that turns out being in the coming days."

I'm fighting a losing battle, so I'm going to step out of the ring.

"Thanks for seeing me," I say. "I'm sorry this didn't work out today."

"I am too. Is there a new number we should take down

until you replace your phone? Maybe Scarlett's?"

"That won't be necessary. Thanks for your time."

I take one last look at the wall with the headshots, accepting that this agency won't ever turn me into a star.

Not even after everything goes dark for me, like an empty night sky.

SCARLETT PRINCE
5:00 a.m. (Mountain Standard Time)

Scarlett Prince is finally being let off the airplane.

There are still investigations to be held, but the police force wants the plane emptied so they can conduct their searches as they sweep for bombs or weapons, and escort the pilot somewhere safe. Which means Scarlett will be released back into the airport without her luggage but she will have improved phone service. Over a dozen text messages that have been written to Valentino over the past few hours will immediately be sent to Orion's phone. That one-sided conversation with her brother didn't settle her nerves. She couldn't stop reliving the fear she last felt when she was upside down in her car moments after the accident, terrified that she would die alone. She's dreading this to be true for Valentino.

Once Scarlett is off the plane, she fights all urges to break down.

Time is of the essence, and that time must be spent with her brother.

VALENTINO

8:00 a.m.

Dreams don't come true on End Days.

Everything upstairs could have gone differently if I had an agent who believed in Death-Cast in the first place. Calls could have been made to move heaven and earth to help me fulfill my life's dream. All I got was someone who won't even mourn me because she believes we'll see each other in a few days. I'd love for her to be right, but I know she isn't.

I don't look back when we exit the building. I don't even know where I'm going. I just walk down the sidewalk wanting as much distance as possible from this place.

"Slow down," Orion says.

I don't.

I keep going.

"Wait for me!"

His voice sounds further back. Not as strong. I turn, and Orion is leaning against the wall, eyes closed with his hand pressed over his heart. I snap out of my misery and return to his side.

"Are you okay?"

"Yeah, I'm just . . ." Orion takes a deep breath, then another and another. "Blood pressure running high and then speed-walking was a bad combo."

"I'm sorry."

"Not your fault. Mostly not. I'm pissed at what went down upstairs."

"That was definitely disappointing."

"And completely fucking infuriating."

There's an empty bus stop bench a few feet away, but Orion slides down the wall and sits in a crouch. I join him even though my legs are sore from yesterday morning's run and workout and my two fun trips up my six flights of steps. I don't say anything as he catches his breath and fights his inner storm.

I want to thank him for trying to stand up for me at the agency when his phone rings in my pocket. The Death-Cast trauma has burrowed deep instantly, but this is an ordinary ringtone, so I'm able to calm down before my heart reacts as badly as Orion's.

"It's Scarlett," I say. I answer her FaceTime immediately, and she's sobbing hard. I start tearing up instantly. I can see that she's in the airport. "Did you land already?"

Scarlett can't get her words out. Her cries start breaking

up as a series of text notifications begin buzzing, all from her. I keep swiping them away so I can talk to her.

"Scar? What's going on?"

"I'm still in Arizona," she says.

Orion's eyes open at this.

"What do you mean you're still in Arizona?"

"The pilot got his End Day call before we could take off."

As she's telling me everything about how the passengers were going crazy on the plane and how police are investigating the issue, I'm shivering thinking about what could have happened if the pilot had begun the journey and damned everyone else to an early death. I can't know if that's what would have happened, but I'm sure Orion has wondered this countless times too as he reimagined 9/11 in a Death-Cast world.

"Death-Cast didn't call you, did they?" I ask.

Scarlett shakes her head. "No, but my service sucked on the plane, and I couldn't call you sooner and I was so scared you would be . . ."

"I'm not. What's the plan now? Are you going to find another flight?"

"As soon as they determine the passengers weren't a threat to the pilot, yeah. I'll ditch my luggage, I don't care."

"Have you told them it's my End Day?"

"They don't give a shit. It's all about that pilot."

This has got to become a big change in airlines moving forward. No flights can take off unless they're positive the pilots aren't Deckers. The passengers too. That'll resolve any plane crashes, right? Assuming people register for the program in the first place.

"I'm so sorry," Scarlett says. "I'm going to keep trying."

If she could grow wings and flap her way across the country, she would do it one trip. But even in this real world where death can now be predicted, people still can't fly, so she's grounded in that airport until then. I think about other impossibilities like Scarlett driving from Arizona to New York even though that trip is more than thirty-five hours and she's on no sleep. Just because Death-Cast didn't call doesn't mean she can't get into another accident by trying her best to drive here. Another plane is her only option.

I just want something impossible to become possible on my last day alive.

Is that too much to ask?

Apparently so.

"How are you?" Scarlett asks. "Why are you outside?"

I tell her about the bombed photo shoot in as few words as possible.

"What are you going to do now?"

"Go home, I guess. I'll wait for you."

"No!" Scarlett shouts. She turns apologetically to a woman I glimpse next to her. "You didn't move to New York to hang around waiting for me. Go safely explore. I'll be there soon."

"You promise?"

"I promise."

We both know this can't be promised as we hang up, but it's something to hold on to. Scarlett will do everything in her power to reach me. She could bribe someone off the next flight out so we can have more time together, or sneak into the cargo bin and get battered by suitcases for five hours. I don't know, but I do know she will figure it out.

As sure as I am that I'll see my reflection when I look in the mirror, I'm certain that I will see my sister before I die.

That's the most important dream that needs to come true.

ORION

8:12 a.m.

Today is the first time I'm positive I will live no matter what, and I never thought it would feel so fucking shitty.

Don't get me wrong, I'm still not trying to die, but watching Valentino live through his End Day has been rough. It's hard not to feel like the author of his story is some cruel bastard who won't give him any wins. There's so many ways he could've died by now—gunshot or beat down with a bat or smashing his head on the curb or that fall back at the apartment or run over in the middle of the street—and he's surviving for what? To get rejected by his agent, and find out his sister is still stuck back home? I can't celebrate my life knowing his final hours are not working out for him.

"This End Day can't get worse, can it?" Valentino asks, staring off into space and fighting back tears. "That's a stupid question. Of course it can, and of course it will. Death-Cast had no idea what they were talking about when they called

289

Deckers the captains of our own ships. Everything about today shows that I'm not steering my way through this End Day. It's like my wheel is spinning out of control and I'm about to crash into an iceberg and drown." Valentino cracks, crying so damn hard. "I should drop dead now."

That shit breaks my heart.

I try wrapping my arm around his shoulder, and he shrugs me off.

"You should stay away," Valentino says, getting up from the ground. "Just because you can't die today doesn't mean I'm not poison. Everything bad is spreading around me. My heart is probably dangerous too. Orion, I don't know, you should figure out another solution, or find another donor."

"Fine, fuck your heart! I don't care about that. You're not poison or a ship that's about to crash or whatever other analogy you're going to spit out to scare me away. I'm your friend, Valentino, and I'm not leaving you alone on your End Day."

He runs his hands through his hair as he inhales, exhales, inhales, exhales, inhales, exhales. He stares at the brick wall like he wants to punch it but his breaths keep his fists down at his sides. He's unraveling, big-time, but we're going to get through this.

"There are millions of things you can't control," I say as he breathes. "But you can still regain control of the ship and steer yourself—sorry, I'm going to drop this metaphor. I'm starting to really fucking feel like we're out at sea." I step to him, proving I'm not scared of us crashing together in the worst ways imaginable. "You can't bring the photographer back to life or make your sister appear in an instant. That's the kind of shit you can't control. But there are a lot of things we can."

Valentino's ocean eyes look up at me. "Like what?"

"You tell me. What have you been bursting to do in New York?"

"The photo shoot was number one."

"Then let's do it. I'll be your photographer."

"The agency won't accept that. You heard her."

"Screw their photo shoot. We're creating yours now. It can be an album about your life in New York."

"That doesn't sound like a very big album."

"I bet there's a lot of pictures we can take in one day."

"Good point. Hundreds get taken during a one-hour photo shoot, even."

"Hundreds? I was thinking like twenty, but okay. Challenge accepted."

He wipes the last tears from his eyes and smiles. "Maybe we can photograph a lot of my firsts in the city."

"Yes!" I'm hyped to see him getting into it; it's like he's coming back to life so quickly after thinking he should drop dead. "I know your super handsome face was supposed to be all over Times Square; I get that this is different now. But just because the whole damn world won't see these pictures doesn't mean the people in your world won't."

"I really love that. I can show Scarlett the pictures when she gets here."

"I love that too—I mean, it was my idea, but I'm into it."

Valentino is lost in thought, and I'm scared he's going to back out. "I have one condition."

"Anything," I say, and I mean it.

"If you're going to be my photographer, we need to get a really good camera. No phone pictures."

"Done deal. One really good camera, coming up."

We're going to turn this End Day around.

Not like a fucking ship but like two boys who are determined to make every last moment count.

"Thanks for not leaving me alone, Orion."

My eyes travel from his heart-shaped lips that I want to kiss straight to his gaze.

"I'm your friend to the end, Valentino."

VALENTINO

8:38 a.m.

Nothing is open yet on my End Day.

These department stores being closed feels like another slight against me, even though I know it's just bad timing that I'm dying on a Saturday. I don't have the luxury of waiting until ten or eleven to buy a camera. Hopefully some businesses are planning more overnight operations for the Deckers who won't be starting their End Days at the crack of dawn with everyone else.

"I think I found a spot," Orion says, reading something off his phone. "It's a pawnshop that's open twenty-four-seven. I don't know if they'll have a camera, but worth checking out."

"Is it far?" I'm already thinking about getting back on the train to see if my luck changes with the subway performers.

"Three blocks back."

As Orion leads the way, I read all of Scarlett's text messages that chronicle her time on the plane. She was panicking—scared that the pilot was going to fly everyone to their deaths, scared that she would be proof that Death-Cast was wrong, scared that I would be dead before we can see each other again one last time. All her words and every last typo from frantic typing burn into my brain, and I hate that she had to experience this fear. I want to apologize, as if dying is my fault; I guess it sort of will be if dying safely for the heart transplant is an option.

Scarlett won't want me to go through with the operation.

"You're walking straight into your grave," she'll say.

Then I'll tell her, "I'm going to die anyway."

"But what if Death-Cast is wrong?" she'll ask.

That's the big gamble. If I roll those dice and still die, then Orion might too.

I want to live, but I can't risk that, can I?

It's unfortunate that my End Day is Death-Cast's first day. If I had more information on their accuracy record I could know if my call was an error after all. But I don't, and I won't get it. It's just yet another reason why I'm dying with bad timing.

NAYA ROSA
8:40 a.m.

There have now been eleven reports of Deckers dying without Death-Cast calling.

Naya is back in the company suite, resting on the couch while Alano uses her lap as a pillow and Bucky is asleep at her feet. She can't move without waking them, and she doesn't know where she would go if she could. The company's future is on fire, but she can't be the one to put it out. She's sitting there in fear, feeling much like her grandfather who told many stories of what it was like waiting for Naya's grandmother to return home from the war. She wants the door to be flung open with Joaquin emerging, even if he couldn't solve the problem, couldn't win the war. She simply wants her husband to be a survivor.

But what if Joaquin is among the Deckers who died without warning?

VALENTINO

8:51 a.m.

The pawnshop's awning has *ITCHY PALM GEMS* spelled out in colorful light bulbs.

It looks more like one of those Broadway gift stores that sell magnets with your name on it instead of a place where I can find a camera. But considering it's tucked between a CVS and a Domino's, the pawnshop is doing a great job at standing out; it's like a brooch pinned to an otherwise plain outfit. Though unlike its neighbors, it also stands out because Itchy Palm Gems has shards of glass piled where their front door once stood.

"They're definitely open," I say.

"Whether they like it or not," Orion adds. "Fucking looters."

I glimpse a man inside, sweeping. This must be where he works because I can't imagine someone cleaning up after themselves after breaking in.

Orion starts trying to push me back, but I stand strong. "You should get away. Just in case."

"Just in case of what?"

"Who knows, but you shouldn't be the first to find out."

"Then let's just go. The camera isn't worth it."

"Yeah, it is," Orion says, staring into my eyes. I know he means it and that he cares. "Look, we know it's not my End Day, so I should wield that like a superpower."

"Except you're not invincible."

"Nope, but I'm stronger today. Just hang back at the corner for a sec."

I accept defeat, though I draw the line at hiding around the corner. I wait right here.

Glass crunches under Orion's boot as he knocks on the doorframe. "Hey, good morning."

The man stops sweeping and comes to the doorway. "We're closed today."

"Everything okay?" I ask from the sidewalk.

He stares like it should be obvious that everything isn't okay. I struggle with maintaining eye contact because he's really handsome for an older guy. Salt-and-pepper beard on his diamond-cut jaw. Black hair in a quiff style with streaks of silver on the side. Strong and defined arms with the veins showing under his brown skin, which gets celebrated in the gym as if that's the only mark of someone putting in the real work. His pecs are popping through his black T-shirt with the cuffed sleeves, sweat staining his pits. And as someone who can't get a tattoo without scaring off agencies, I'm a huge fan of the white moons tattooed down his bicep, completing the package of this man who belongs on magazine covers.

"Shop got broken into early this morning," the man says. "People wanted to steal other people's shit instead of pizza dough apparently."

I feel safe enough to approach, not expecting this pawnbroker to beat me to death with his broom. "I'm really sorry."

"It's not your fault. Unless you were the looters."

"No, but fuck whoever it was," Orion says.

"I like that fire," he says, giving Orion a fist-bump.

Orion grins. "Is it cool if we pop in real fast? We're looking for a camera."

The man sighs. "A lot was stolen last night. I don't even know what inventory I have at the moment. Feel free to swing by tomorrow when we've reopened. I'll hold any cameras I find on the side for you." He begins turning away.

"Hold up." Orion looks at me.

He always respects my business, even with strangers I'll never see again. I'll have to let him know I'm fine with him supporting me.

"I won't be around tomorrow," I say.

"Out-of-towner?" the man asks.

"Decker," I say.

Then the moment of truth: Will he challenge the reality of Death-Cast, or trust that I'm dying?

The man shakes his head. "That's tragic. I'm sorry to hear that. You're so young. . . ."

I'm relieved that he cares, but of course my truth stings anyway.

"Come on in. You can have a look around," the man says. He shakes our hands. "I'm Férnan."

"Valentino. This is Orion."

"Nice to meet you both. Orion, mind the swearing if my son comes out from the back. He's ten and already cursing like me whenever the Mets are losing."

"That's a lot of fucking cursing, then," Orion jokes, tapping his Yankees hat.

It feels like we're entering a crime scene. The glass counter has been shattered, and all the jewelry boxes have been emptied. Workout weights are still in the corner because I guess the looters weren't lifters. Two bikes on the wall, one yellow and the other steel gray. A microwave is upside down, probably tossed about during all the action. Shelves of sneakers with minimal scuffs, which I'm sure is great for anyone wanting to act like their sneakers are fresh out of the box but life happened while wearing them out, like my white sneakers are already experiencing. Then the floor is littered with so much more, like action figures, baseball caps, tools, video games, DVDs, a couple electric guitars with broken strings, cracked vinyl records, and a bunch of other things that have their own stories. Reasons they were brought here to set someone up for success out there. As if theft wasn't a big enough crime standing on its own two feet, I think about all the stolen treasures that people cannot buy back. That's the biggest crime here.

"How long you been in business?" Orion asks.

"Few years, but thinking about getting out of it soon," Férnan says.

"How come? Because of all this?"

Férnan shakes his head. "This didn't help. I just don't have the heart for this business. I hate putting price tags on people's priceless belongings. I've lost count of how many times people put their wedding rings on layaway for cash."

At least those people got to have weddings. That means they got to fall in love.

That's not in the cards on an End Day.

I continue searching for a camera, remembering that it's something I can control. There are dozens of books fanned out on the floor; I guess the looters aren't readers either. There was no camera hiding underneath the books, though I pile them into a neat stack so it's less work for Férnan later. I look under Frisbees and behind a broken printer but nothing.

The back door swings open, and a young boy comes out. He looks like a young Férnan but without the grays and beard and tattoos. He's wearing a blue sweatsuit. He finishes the last bite of a McDonald's hash brown and wipes the grease off his mouth.

"I thought we were closed, Pops," the boy says.

Férnan is crouched behind the shattered counter. "We are. But these young men were gentlemen, and I decided to let them in. See how manners work?"

"Yeahhh."

"Why don't you see if you can help them find a camera?"

"Can I finally get that bike if I do?" he asks, pointing at the steel-gray bike on the wall.

"It's still not for sale."

"Just say it was stolen, Pops."

"Rufus . . ."

The boy sucks his teeth. "What?!"

Férnan comes around the corner and the boy—Rufus—crosses his arms. "Go to the back and wait for me."

"I didn't do anything."

"You keep talking back like I'm one of your friends."

"We're not friends, Pops?!"

"Stop being a smart-ass."

"If I can't be smart, then stop yelling at me when my report cards suck."

"Rufus, go wait for me in the back. Now."

There's a tense stare-down before Rufus sucks his teeth again. To make matters worse, he kicks a crate and sends it flying into a wall. Everything goes quiet. Orion and I don't move, like we've just discovered we're on a minefield and one wrong step can blow us up. The only explosive in the room is Rufus's temper. Then before any discipline can happen, Rufus seems to diffuse himself as his eyes light up in wonder.

"Found one!" Rufus shouts. He picks up a camera. Férnan extends his hand, but Rufus skips past him and comes straight to me. "Here you go."

It's a digital camera, a Canon PowerShot. I don't know much about this particular model, but it should do the trick.

"Thanks so much, Rufus."

"You're welcome."

Rufus then peacefully retreats to the back.

Férnan sighs as he returns behind the counter. "Don't ever have kids."

"Not a problem," I say, handing him the camera.

Férnan is inspecting the camera against his records when he looks up, eyes wide. "I'm so sorry, Valentino. I forgot."

"Don't worry about it."

"I didn't mean it anyway. I love Rufus, and he's a great kid. His temper sometimes gets the best of him. I was the same way when I was his age. He'll grow out of it." Férnan wipes sweat off his forehead. "Am I making it worse? I'm sorry. This is a first for me, and I don't know how . . . especially with someone so young and . . ."

Orion rests his arm on my shoulder, bringing a casual energy to this moment. "We're all figuring it out, but mad thanks to Rufus for finding us this camera. We're going to make some memories on Valentino's End Day."

Férnan's eyes water as he steals glances at me. He sees someone young. Rufus will be my age in a few years, and maybe Férnan is dreading what it would be like to watch his son live his End Day. I don't wish that on them.

"How long have you two been friends?" he asks.

Orion counts under his breath. "Ten hours–ish."

Férnan has many questions, but he doesn't ask any of them. He simply finishes cross-referencing the model of this camera with his records and says, "This was a sale, not a loan. So it's all yours."

I reach for my wallet, which I haven't miraculously lost today like my phone or keys. "Great. How much?"

Férnan hands me the camera. "No charge."

"Wow—thanks, man—"

"No," I interrupt Orion. "I want to pay. Especially after your break-in."

"That's really noble, but your hundred bucks isn't going to save the shop. I selfishly want to know that you're out in the world making incredible memories."

This Decker discount doesn't make me feel great. I feel like I'm robbing a store that has already seen enough loss. "Fine. I'll accept the camera if you let me buy that bike for your son. I can just leave the money for whenever it becomes available and you can—"

"It's available now," Férnan says. "I've just been telling Rufus it isn't because he keeps acting out. But why does Rufus getting that bike matter to you?"

Orion seems confused too and then catches on.

"My parents weren't great. It'd be nice to know that a father who loves his son is actually showing his son that he loves him."

Férnan looks up at the bike, like he's imagining the memories he'll create with Rufus. "You got yourself a deal."

We work out the price. He tries to undersell me; I try to oversell. It's the most backward haggling I've ever experienced. We land on a middle ground that makes us feel as good as we're going to be and we shake on it. Férnan has a firm grip, and I feel like he's telling me to be strong without using any words.

I look at the bike, imagining Rufus on it with Férnan cheering him on. It's a really nice thought.

"Have a good day," I say on the way out.

"You too," Férnan says, and cringes. His eyes find my shirt. "Actually, yes. Have a happy End Day, Valentino."

"Thanks, Férnan."

We leave the shop.

I power on the camera. It doesn't have a full battery, but it should be enough to get through the End Day. I hand it to Orion. "Would you mind? I think the first picture should be taken outside the store where I got the camera."

"Happily," Orion says.

I get in position and tuck my hands into my pockets. It feels strange smiling in front of a looted pawnshop, but this is how we closed out this chapter in my End Day and that's how it should be remembered.

Orion snaps the picture.

The first of many hopefully.

FÉRNAN EMETERIO
9:09 a.m.

Death-Cast did not call Férnan Emeterio because he is not dying today, though he's struck by the generosity of a young man who will be.

Of all the stores Valentino could have walked into this morning, he chose Férnan's, hours after it had been looted by those fearing the end of the world. Férnan didn't ask why Itchy Palms of all places, but he knows his mother—may she rest in peace—would have said that luck brought them together. She was a very superstitious woman, up until her passing a few years ago. There wasn't a stray eyelash she didn't blow on, or a purse she wouldn't leave on the floor at the risk of her money running away, or a single New Year's midnight minute that wasn't spent eating twelve grapes, a true Cuban tradition. Férnan believes that Valentino was nudged his way, possibly by his mother in the heavens.

The timing couldn't have been better.

Lately, Férnan and Rufus have been at odds. He has his difficulties too with his eldest, Olivia, but she likes her space and will often listen to classical music in her bedroom and not bother anyone. But Rufus, at ten, is trying to become the alpha of the house, just like he is at school or at the park with his friends. He seems to have more respect for his mother, but Férnan believes that's because they don't spend as much time together since Victoria is a cardiac surgeon who works eighty hours a week and mostly evenings; she even got stuck at the hospital for an extra few hours trying to get the board's attention for a special transplant. This summer break is what's sending Rufus over the edge. He's away from his posse and stuck hanging with the parent he doesn't respect and the sister who wants nothing to do with him. Férnan looks to the bike, thinking that might release a lot of Rufus's pent-up energy.

A father-son talk could get them on the same page. Which it sounds like wasn't the case for Valentino and his parents. Férnan would rather fight with his son every day than turn his back on him. Do Valentino's parents even know that he's dying? Or that he's resorted to hanging out with a boy he met ten hours ago? One's final hours should be spent with their family. He can't even imagine Rufus spending his End Day with a stranger. Férnan will make sure he never puts his son in that heartbreaking situation.

Férnan takes the cash for the bike and puts it into the

empty tray of his cash register.

He stares at the bills, thinking about his mother again. Férnan was at a crossroads for work, torn between continuing on as a technician or opening his own business. Then his mother passed, and he thought often of her many superstitions. His palm itching was one of them. It meant his luck was turning around and he would receive money soon. The thought of being a pawnbroker soon followed, knowing he could honor his mother's spirit by being the reason someone's luck turns around during hard times. For all he's done for the community, today someone brought him money.

This is a sign to rebuild his business and his relationships.

Férnan closes the cash register and takes the bike off the wall.

Family first.

ORION
9:39 a.m.

Capturing Valentino's firsts on camera is hella fun:

First time visiting a bodega to get a hot black tea to stay awake and fill his stomach. He even played with the cat after I made sure he wasn't allergic and about to drop dead next to kitty litter.

First time seeing a pay phone, which he said is different from the ones back in Arizona. He posed as if he was on a call, head tilted down but blue eyes up at me. That look did something to my heart and dick, that's all I got to say.

First time buying a bacon, egg, and cheese roll off some dude on the streets. He's still refusing to eat because of the possible operation, which bothers me, especially as he breathes it in. I can tell he wants to rip apart that aluminum foil and devour that sandwich in one bite, even if the hotness sets his insides on fire. But instead he gives it to some woman who's asking for money to eat; we don't document

309

that, obviously.

First time passing the legendary Strand Bookstore, and Valentino wishes he could tuck himself into a corner and read one last book.

And now his first time buying a copy of the *New York Times* from a newsstand. His expression is moody, and I wonder if he's going for some intense, scholary vibe. Then I see the newspaper's headline: THE END DAYS ARE HERE. The photograph on the cover is of Joaquin Rosa in the Death-Cast call center as he's on the phone.

I almost drop the camera when I realize what this means.

"This is when he told me that my life is over," Valentino says.

It's hard to process something so wild like this.

"You okay?"

"It's strange seeing the other side of this call in print."

"It's history, I guess."

Valentino trashes the newspaper. "I'm not history, Orion. I'm here."

Then he's not here because he's walking away from me.

"I'm sorry, I didn't mean it like that. I just—I kind of went through something similar with my parents the day they died. The morning newspaper was already out, but they had released another at some point. I'll never forget, the *New York Times* had some headline about the United States being attacked and how hijacked jets destroyed the Twin Towers.

Right there on the cover were the burning towers. The fire and the smoke . . . I remember squinting hard, like mad hard, thinking I might've been able to find my parents in a window."

Valentino stops and stares at me.

"I was nine and stupid, sue me."

"No, I'm not judging you. It's really sad."

"Yeah, well. Same deal with you and that Joaquin photo. Everyone thinks that moment is only Death-Cast history when it's your history too."

"And 9/11 history is also your history."

"Proof of our lives changing, all on page one."

"You won't find our faces, though."

"I'm not mad at that. I looked like shit that day. You're fucking glowing, though."

Valentino is either blushing or the sun is cooking his face. "Even with my scar?"

"You're going to keep that shit trending, trust me."

"Thanks, Orion." He wraps his arm around my shoulders, and our bodies pushed together is seriously where it's at. "What's next?"

"That's your call."

"I'm calling on you to pick a place for me. A lesser-known gem."

It takes a sec because I'm still caught up on Valentino's arm around me and how freeing it feels to explore a space like this here in lower Manhattan than I would back up in the South Bronx. But then I remember a spot I haven't even hit yet, one we can discover together.

A first for the both of us.

ROLANDO RUBIO
9:47 a.m.

Rolando is in a café, hoping to meet his first Decker.

This wasn't planned. In fact, it's in the guidelines that Death-Cast heralds aren't to arrange meetings with the Deckers. The company set this boundary between heralds and Deckers as if they're therapists and clients who shouldn't be friends, but Rolando doesn't buy that this is simply because of professionalism. He suspects that Joaquin doesn't want any of his operators held hostage by any Deckers or grief-stricken loved ones with nothing to lose and something to gain by getting Death-Cast's secret. As if Rolando knows how the Deckers are identified, but Death-Cast not trading the secret to save an employee's life would certainly be bad publicity.

Fortunately for Death-Cast, Rolando is no longer employed by them.

It's also fortunate for Rolando, who no longer has to live by Death-Cast's rules. Especially when it comes to the first

313

Decker he called last night and spoke with at length—too long if you ask Joaquin or Naya or Andrea or anyone. Being a good human made him a bad employee. Thankfully, he learned a lot about Clint Suarez on that call. He loves dancing. He was an investor. He once won the lottery for eight hundred grand by playing the numbers of his mother's birthday. And that he spends every Saturday morning, at ten on the dot, by coming to Carolina's Café in Union Square, where he likes to sit by the window and enjoy a late breakfast while people-watching.

So Rolando is sitting by the window and enjoying a late breakfast while people-watching. Nothing interesting was happening for a while. One woman walking a bunch of dogs, a florist trying to sell their bouquets to drivers at stoplights. Then there were these teen boys, one photographing the other as he bought a copy of the *New York Times*, which hardly seemed newsworthy to Rolando, pun intended; it didn't get interesting until one boy saw Joaquin Rosa on the cover and shortly thereafter trashed the entire newspaper. Something escalated very fast. As the boys walk off, Rolando keeps people-watching, waiting for someone who could be Clint. This is where the hope comes in. It's very possible that Clint's routine may be broken because he's dead.

Then one minute to ten, the door opens, and in walks an elderly man with dark gray hair. There's a newspaper tucked under his arm, and Rolando wonders if this could be Clint, if it makes sense for someone who is about to die to care about current events.

"Good morning," the man says to the kitchen staff.

Rolando recognizes the man's voice off those two words alone. He didn't even need to hear everyone call back, "Good morning, Clint!"

He really is a regular. He scans the tables by the window, finding none that are empty. There's a slight frown on his wrinkled face, but he doesn't seem fully dispirited.

Rolando stands. "Excuse me, sir. Would you like a seat?"

He wonders if Clint will recognize his voice, but Clint doesn't seem to.

"Oh, that's okay."

"Please, I insist."

Clint resigns and takes a seat, laying out his newspaper on the table. "Thank you very much."

Rolando feels weird, like he's crossing a line, but what he really wants to do is help. "This might be weird . . . My name is Rolando Rubio. I worked at Death-Cast. Last night."

Clint looks up with tears in his eyes. "Rolando. Rolando! Have a seat, have a seat."

Rolando is relieved that his appearance is welcomed. He sits. "I'm sorry to pop up like this. I didn't like the idea of you being alone on your End Day, and I wanted to check in on you. You had mentioned this café and—"

"Good memory," Clint says.

Rolando wonders how bad Clint's memory is that remembering something from less than twelve hours ago is impressive. "Is there anything I can do for you? Do you need help?"

"Is this part of some Death-Cast package?"

"No, I actually . . ." Rolando decides against telling Clint he quit the company. "This is all me."

"That's very sweet of you. There's one thing I'd like."

"What's that?"

"Join me for my last breakfast."

Rolando does so, hoping that if he's fortunate to live as long as Clint, and unfortunate enough to be as alone, that someone shows him this very same kindness on his End Day.

VALENTINO

If I had to spend my End Day somewhere, I'm glad it's in such a walkable city. How much time would have been spent driving back in Phoenix, my eyes on the road and missing all the beauty around me?

I bought a Fitbit in March, having wanted one since Christmas. It's this watch that basically tracks how many steps you take. It was amazing to have on my morning runs and usually inspired me to up my daily goals. Of course I didn't realize I forgot my Fitbit in my bathroom back home until Scarlett dropped me off at the airport, but she assured me that she'd pack it for me. Now there's a chance she won't even arrive with her luggage. It's a small thing, but it would've been cool to see how many steps it took for me to get from my apartment to Times Square last night, or even around Manhattan this morning as my personal tour guide shows me the city.

It gets me thinking.

"I have an idea for an invention. You can make it."

"Do I get to take all the credit?" Orion asks.

"Only if you want me to haunt you."

"That's not the scary threat you think it is. I'd like having you around."

"Okay, but you can't change your mind later when I'm tapping your shoulder every time you slouch."

"Yeah, you're right, I'd be calling an exorcist so damn fast."

There's something comforting about becoming a ghost. Especially because I don't think Orion would have me exorcised. I could watch over Scarlett too. Maybe even make sure my parents don't get a good night's sleep ever again.

"So what's this invention, Casper?" Orion asks.

"Basically, it's a tracker that shows a Decker's journey on their End Day. Friends and family can retrace your footsteps and feel closer to you if they couldn't be with you."

Orion aims the camera and takes my picture.

"What was that for?"

"I wanted to document your first dumb idea."

My jaw drops. "You're a jerk."

"A jerk? Come on, call me an asshole or a dickhead or a bitch. You're not in third grade."

"I don't really swear. Catholic upbringing."

Orion freezes at the corner. "This is perfect. You're not about that life anymore, right? What's going to be your first curse word or swear word, whatever the fuck you want to call it? Howl that shit at the sky and wake up all these mother-fuckers trying to sleep in."

I do some counting. "Three swear words in ten seconds. Well done."

"That's fucking nothing, but thanks. What you got?"

As someone so open today, I grew up so caged. There were so many things I was never allowed to say. I couldn't swear. I couldn't question God. I couldn't talk about my crushes. Then I came out of the closet, and my parents wanted me to go right back in. But Orion isn't asking me to filter my thoughts or feelings. He's asking me to release everything.

Standing on a street corner in New York City, I feel the word bubbling up, and I throw open my arms and shout, "I'M FUCKING FREE!"

Orion takes my picture. "Great fucking choice!"

Before I can thank him, a window slams open above us and a man pokes his head out. "Shut the fuck up!"

I'm so embarrassed that I'm frozen.

Orion snaps another picture before dragging me away, laughing. "Your first time getting told to shut the fuck up in the city. You've been christened as a real New Yorker."

I might find that photograph funnier after my heart has calmed down a bit.

Orion holds on to my wrist as we go down the street and only lets go when we find ourselves somewhere that looks abandoned. There's something suspicious about how peaceful this is. Just empty cars underneath these overhead train tracks. Orion starts going up the stairs slowly, and he picks up the speed a little bit. I try getting him to slow down, but he ignores me. He seems to be enjoying this moment where a simple activity doesn't feel life-threatening. Just because he won't die from a heart attack doesn't mean he won't slip on these stairs and fall back into me. I hold on to the railing for dear life, and Orion is waiting at the top with the biggest smile.

Once I'm up there, I can't believe my eyes.

This train station is a forest. Bright green bushes and flowers are basking in the morning sunlight. Right where the train tracks should be is a pathway that's been paved clean. I'm staring at everything in confusion when Orion snaps a picture of me.

"How does this train station operate?"

"It's no longer a train station. It's a park called the High Line."

It's not ringing a bell. "I've never heard of it."

"It opened last summer. There's more to come, but they have huge plans to grow this park. I thought you should see what they got so far."

This city is so huge that even someone who's been excited to move here didn't know about this place. What other wonders are out there that I'll never see? Not even just in the city or the state or the country. The whole world. I kind of wish I could go into space and do a lap around the planet. Then I could say I saw it all. I can't imagine NASA is going to launch a Decker into space unless it's a suicide mission, so I'm going to enjoy this slice of the world I never even knew existed.

"It's really gorgeous," I say as we walk down the pathway.

"And kind of creepy too, right? Like we're on the set for some postapocalyptic movie."

"What made you think to bring me here of all places?"

"Don't punch me in the face, but I thought it might inspire you on your End Day."

"In what way?"

"Way back when, this area was called Death Avenue. Hundreds and hundreds of people were getting straight wrecked by the trains, it was bad. It got to a point where they—I don't remember who *they* were, but *someone*—hired fucking cowboys to stop people from trying to cross the tracks. Like, legit dudes on horses."

"You're making this up!"

"I shit you not! They—again, I don't know who *they* are—decided to elevate the tracks. Then the rest is kind of a blur."

"Pardon my English, but you're a shitty historian."

Orion laughs. "I'm not trying to compete on *Jeopardy!* or anything."

"Alex Trebek would have you banned for answering every

question with a swear word."

"For fucking real."

I stumble onto the train tracks, the plants growing around them like a garden bed.

This place is really something.

"You still haven't told me how this is supposed to inspire me today."

"I was about to before you started hating on my story-telling."

"I apologize for expecting you to be a know-it-all. I guess everyone needs a flaw."

"My heart is a pretty huge flaw."

"It won't be for much longer."

Then we're just two boys who are silent as we continue crossing this postapocalyptic, retired train line. There's no one else in sight, almost like the world wants us to be present in our future. I listen to the wind and my thoughts, which are both depressing and uplifting. I might not be around to laugh for much longer, but Orion will be if all goes well. It will go well. I'm putting my full faith into that; whatever that means these days.

Orion stops and stares at the plants emerging between the train tracks. "This is my first time here too. I wanted to visit last summer when everything was super fresh, but my heart got in the way. I spent the day at the hospital instead. I took it as a sign that I shouldn't try to go somewhere that was known as Death Avenue. But I was just remembering how the High Line was supposed to be demolished. Just straight wiped from the city until people in the neighborhood fought for it to find new life and it got turned into this dope park." Orion looks at me with his hazel eyes. "I hate that you're dying, Valentino, but I want you to remember that everything isn't over just because you're a Decker. I'm going to keep fighting through whatever your End Day throws your way to turn your life into something beautiful."

There's no doubt in my mind that Orion means every word.

I bumped into the perfect stranger in Times Square.

"It's almost like when I die and you have my heart, I'll live on through you," I say. "A new, beautiful life."

My chest feels tight as Orion and I stare into each other's eyes.

"Totally," he says, breaking contact, and I look away too. "I'll become a walking park."

"What you lack in history, Orion, you make up for in metaphors."

"I'm a writer. I better get that shit right."

We stop and rest our arms on the railing. We have a calming view of the river. I'm guessing it's the Hudson River, but even though I'm a newly christened New Yorker I didn't suddenly download all the knowledge of one. I just watch the water and the boat slowly creeping along its surface.

"I've never been on a boat," I say.

"It sucks, but please don't fight to make that one of your firsts."

"You going to ride up on a horse and stop me like one of those cowboys you made up?"

"Yeehaw," Orion dryly says. "But for real, it's your life. I selfishly don't want to risk watching you drown. I don't give a shit about what Death-Cast thinks, there's no way I'd survive that."

In the same way I'd like to take a trip in a spaceship, it'd be nice to get on a boat and sail across the river and experience something I haven't before. But Orion is right. Drowning sounds like a horrible way to die, and I don't want to test that theory. I wouldn't want anyone witnessing that either. That would be too haunting.

It's hard to live when it feels like death is lurking around every corner.

"I'm going to spend my remaining hours living life from a distance, aren't I?"

"Nope. You're going to live it up close," Orion says.

"How?"

"By making the most of what we can do. If you don't die happily, then I failed you."

"Tough task."

"Game on."

I half expect us to shake on it. Instead, we watch that boat until it slips behind a building; I hope it has a safe journey. Orion steps away to aim the camera at me.

"You should also be in the picture," I say. "This is a first for you too."

"Nope, your End Day is about you. I've made it enough about me already with the whole heart attack and donor situation."

"This End Day would've long been over without you. You're part of my journey."

Orion sighs, defeated. He comes under my open arm and we squeeze together, our heads leaning against each other. Figuring out the right angle is tricky without a phone's mirror.

"How the hell did people take selfies before phones?" Orion asks.

"Luck. I also hate the word 'selfie' so much. Do you think that'll die out soon?"

"I hope so. That word outliving you is upsetting as fuck."

"Agreed."

The longer we take to figure out how to take a selfie on the camera, the longer we're pressed together. I'm not upset at this by any means.

"I'm going to go for it," Orion says. "If I fuck it up, I fuck it up."

He counts us down from three and instead of looking up at the camera, I'm smiling at Orion and thinking about the quality moments we can be sharing from the warmth of my studio. But when anyone looks through this album of pictures, all they're going to be able to see is a Decker whose End Day would've been worse without this new friend who forced him to take his life into his own hands.

CAPTAIN HARRY E. PEARSON
8:05 a.m. (Mountain Standard Time)

There's something very wrong.

Captain Pearson's plane has been emptied of all the passengers, so why does he still feel threatened? There's this knot in his chest that's been squeezing tighter and tighter ever since Death-Cast called. Is this a major case of anxiety? He's been sweating profusely, but who wouldn't? It's stressful knowing that there were almost three hundred people on board who could've been plotting to hijack his plane. Maybe he'll feel better after some fresh air.

But when he unlocks the cockpit door and steps into the main cabin, where police officers are waiting to safely escort him to a private room in the airport, Captain Pearson collapses to the floor.

This is his first heart attack.

And last.

ORION

11:06 a.m.

This End Day isn't about me, but I feel lucky to be along for
the journey.

When I first met Valentino, I knew I wanted to be part of
his life. Yeah, my dick was doing some of the talking because
he's gorgeous, but it was more than that, it was always more
than that. He had stars in his eyes and wanted to grow up in
this city. He'll never be able to do it all, but I'm happy he's
hitting a lot of firsts.

Our next first: riding the bus, since a boat is too dangerous. Or at least it will be our next first if it ever arrives. I
check the time on my phone to see how long we've been
waiting when I realize something historic in the world of me
and Valentino.

"Yo, it's been twelve-ish hours since we met," I say.

I wish I knew the exact minute.

"Really?" Valentino asks. "It feels . . ."

"Feels like what?"

"I was going to say it feels like yesterday."

"Probably because it was."

"Which is why I stopped talking."

"No, don't ever stop talking. You have a nice voice, and I like the stuff you say."

I tried burying that compliment about his voice that I want to listen to all day and that I'll miss, but I did a pretty shitty job covering it up. I'm feeling all these feelings, and I know I shouldn't because this doesn't make sense, but they're fighting their way up anyway. I should write a story about a lovesick zombie crawling out of a grave, wanting a heart to hold, not eat. Oh, wait, zombies are gunning more for brains, not hearts, though I guess they'll eat anything from the body that's fresh. Fuck do I know, I'm no more a zombie dietician than I am a historian.

"You like the stuff I say?" Valentino asks. "What else would you like to hear me say in my nice voice?"

"Don't be a dick."

"Don't be a dick," he parrots with a smile.

"If the bus ever arrives, I'm going to push you in front of it."

Valentino surrenders. "I'm kidding. What do you want to know?"

"I mean, so much. I remember thinking that I liked your name."

"My name? My name is nothing compared to Orion."

"No, I love your name. You've got tons of nickname opportunities. I got O, that's it. Oh, actually, I also had people calling me 'Oreo' in high school. Hated that."

"That's bad, but at least you didn't have to deal with 'Valentino's Day' every Valentine's Day. I had to ask out my friends' crushes for them like I was Cupid."

"I'm so sorry, Cupid."

"It's okay, Oreo."

The bus finally pulls up, and I don't shove Valentino in front of it. Instead, I take his picture as he pays the fare—the driver is confused as shit as to why this is worth documenting—and another as he chooses one of the few available seats in the middle. There's no destination in mind, but we thought it'd be fun for him to get some sightseeing in. Maybe call something out if it interests him. Plus we can take a break from the sun and enjoy some air-conditioning.

"Tell me about Valentino, Valentino. How'd the name come about?"

He's staring out the window. "I never told this to the other kids at school, but my mom was born on Valentine's Day. She grew up loving the holiday because she was always shown love on that day, whether she had a valentine or not. Then my father went and proposed on Valentine's Day like the original thinker he is. My mother wanted us to have names with ties to the day. Mine is obvious, and Scarlett because that's the color of hearts."

"I hate it, I hate it, I hate it. That's a horrible origin story."

"It was going to be worse. Scarlett was almost named Valentina."

"Valentino and Valentina . . . that's some psycho shit. It's almost as bad as them being homophobic. I bet your house was a shitshow on Valentine's Day."

"Absolutely. You know how intense some people are about Christmas? Every threshold had streamers, and there were too many bowls of candy hearts all over the house."

"The ones that taste like chalk?"

"The very same."

I can't believe a beautiful name like his has such a dark, dark, dark history.

"Wait . . . When's your birthday?"

Valentino is shaking his head. "I don't want to say."

"Don't fucking say Valentine's Day."

"No. It's November eleventh."

"What's so bad about . . ." I shudder as I do the math. November is nine months after February. "Oh, they—"

Valentino slaps his hand over my mouth. "Don't."

Not the point, but I'm zero percent mad about my lips being pressed against his palm. It's just like when we were hiding from those masked men with bats, except the stakes aren't super high this time. When he does move his hand, I'm too stunned about the revelation of his parents conceiving him and Scarlett on Valentine's Day to even say anything. I let my face do the talking for me.

"Horrifying," Valentino says. "Thanks for reviving that trauma on my End Day."

A couple passengers on the bus turn to him, staring at Valentino like he's an alien.

"Sorry to hear that," a woman says, holding her child a little closer.

"Thanks," Valentino says, like someone just blessed him after he sneezed.

I'm not sure what the etiquette is for when someone says sorry when they find out you're dying. It might be a minute before society lands on something that feels right.

Valentino shifts back to me. "How did you get your name? Please feel free to be bad at history again if it also involves your conception."

I elbow him in the side for ragging on me again about the history business.

"So my mom's name is Magdalena, and her mother thought it would be cute if I was named Jesus. As if I would've been the first Hispanic Catholic with that name. Like, for real, I'll take Oreo all day, every day, if it means people aren't asking me to turn water to wine or having every dinner known as the Last Supper just because I'm there. Bless my parents, they weren't trying to set me up for failure. Then I was almost Ernesto Jr., but my father didn't think that was fair either."

"Why not? Could your father resurrect himself too?" Valentino asks.

"Oh, totally. He's living his best life back in Puerto Rico. We Skype on weekends. Anyway, my parents wanted something that had no ties to the Bible or anyone in our family. Achilles was the frontrunner for a while."

"Your heart could've been your heel!"

"Shit, that's great! I never even thought of that."

Valentino's proud smile makes me want to give him a million bucks. I mean, I don't have a million bucks. I barely have a thousand bucks, and even that's only because Dayana was really generous on my eighteenth birthday. Point is, I'm not rich, but just like I felt twelve hours ago, I want to fully cash in on this guy. Even if that means the money will go unspent after he dies; at least he'll have known how much he was worth to me.

"When did they land on Orion as a name?" Valentino asks.

"My mother started looking into constellations, and once she saw Orion, there was no changing her mind. Not even when my father brought up how my name means 'mountain dweller.' She didn't give a shit. Everything didn't have to have meaning. Sometimes something that was beautiful was just beautiful."

"I wish your mom could've told my mom that."

"Again, I hate the origin, but love your name."

333

"You don't think Valentino Prince is too charming?"

I bust out laughing. "Oh shit, I forgot about your last name! Yeah, no, that's too much."

"I'd stop being a Prince if I could."

The woman who offered her condolences is still eaves-dropping on our conversation apparently because she seems confused. Same for her daughter, who asks her mother why Valentino doesn't have a crown if he's a prince.

I lower my voice so we can have as much privacy as possible on public transit. "Have you given more thought to calling them?"

"Here and there," he says. This isn't one of those things where he's guaranteed to have the chance to do it later if he's leaning toward it. "There's a part of me that wants to so that I can see them feel bad about how they've treated me. But what if they don't? The fact that I don't know if my own mother and father will grieve me shows how twisted this relationship is. I wish I had parents like yours."

"Me too."

It's not lost on me how lucky I got with my mom and dad. I didn't get the chance to come out to them, but knowing they would've been down with my happiness helps me sleep at night. They would've never chased me out of the city like Valentino's parents did with him.

"Do they have a memorial somewhere?" he asks.

My chest tightens. "Yeah, they technically have headstones

in a cemetery, but I know they're not there. We obviously don't have any of their . . ." I can't bring myself to say that we had nothing to bury. "We don't have any of *them*."

"Do you ever visit the site? Where it all happened?"

"I haven't. I always think it might be healing, but I'm also scared I won't survive it."

"Death-Cast thinks you will," Valentino says, and then he grabs my hand. "I do too."

I try not reading into the hand-holding—tons of people hold hands! Dayana holds Dalma's and Dahlia's hands, and they're family. My mom would hold my hand too, even as I was getting older—my dad not so much, which is cool with me—though I now regret every time I shrugged my mom off because I thought eight years old was too old to be holding my mom's hand. That was stupid. Just like I'd have to be stupid to compare all these people to Valentino, who is staring at me with his blue eyes in a way that sets him apart.

"If you want to go to the site," Valentino says, "I would happily go with you."

"Once again, I can't make your End Day about me."

He lifts my hand, squeezing as he presses it to my chest and then his. "We're in this together, Orion. I want to help heal your heart in every way possible. But only if you're ready."

I think I could be a hundred years old and not be ready to step foot at Ground Zero, where my parents and thousands others died. But waiting until it's your End Day to start living means you won't have time to do it all. Your life will be divided into *firsts* and *lasts* and *nevers*.

I don't want to die never having stood where my parents last did.

I'm going to make this a first.

CLINT SUAREZ
11:12 a.m.

Death-Cast called Clint Suarez last night to tell him he's going to die today, or more specifically, the man sitting across from Clint in his favorite café is the one who told him that his life is over. And just like last night, his operator, Rolando Rubio, is listening to Clint's life story.

It's a long one.

Back when Clint was a little boy—eleven years old, if memory serves him right—he boarded his very first flight with his mother. He couldn't believe how fast planes bulleted down the runway. It was the kind of impossible speed he'd seen before only in the fairly new Superman comic books. Clint was so excited for the adventure to the States back then, not fully understanding that he'd been leaving Argentina so his mother could escape his father. As Clint got older, his sweet mother helped him better understand why they had to leave his monstrous father behind; if Clint ever returned home, he would be sure to dance on his father's grave.

The story seems to strike a chord with Rolando.

"What made her finally leave?" he asks.

"She didn't trust me to be raised by him . . . should something happen to her."

"Do you mean if your *father* happened to your mother?"

All these decades later, and Clint is still furious at everything his wonderful mother had to endure. He grabs the napkin and wipes his tears.

"There's a woman I love," Rolando says.

"Does she love you back?"

"She's married."

"That's not what I asked."

Rolando sips his coffee. "I hope she does. I think she does. But she won't leave her abusive husband because of their son. I wish Gloria had the common sense to leave like your mother. I'm scared her husband is going to kill her one day."

"Have you told her this?"

"It hasn't felt like my place."

"When will you tell her? Her funeral?"

Rolando's eyes water.

Clint thinks about that plane ride again. "I think it's time for you to leave, my friend."

"Did I say something wrong?"

"It's about saying something right to the person who matters the most. While you can."

Rolando tries paying, but Clint gestures him away.

"I've got this," Clint says, waving Rolando's money away. Clint has made a lot of money and invested in many places, including a dance club. "Go help Gloria."

"Are you sure there isn't anything else I can do for you?"

"Be a good role model to Gloria's extraordinary son. Show him what a father should be."

Clint himself never had any children. That's a story for another person.

"Good luck with the rest of your day, Clint. I'm sorry we'll lose you."

"I hope you have a long life, Rolando."

The two hug, and Rolando runs to the street, standing outside the window as he makes a phone call.

In all of Clint's years of people-watching, this is the most connected he's felt to someone outside his window.

It goes to show that even on your way out, there's still time to let people in.

GLORIA DARIO
11:22 a.m.

Gloria wants the best for her son—always has, always will. But sometimes she worries about the career path Pazito is pursuing. For as long as she can remember, there have been horror stories about child actors with bright futures becoming unhappy adults, and the many ways in which they try burying that unhappiness.

When Pazito booked his first role as Larkin Cano in the last Scorpius Hawthorne film, she wasn't worried about her son losing his childhood, since Pazito was only acting in a flashback scene as Howie Maldonado's young self. Even though Howie plays Scorpius Hawthorne's bitter rival, he was beyond lovely on set with both her and Pazito, and considering he's grown up in front of the public eye, it gave Gloria hope that Pazito would be fine as well. Still, there have been a couple opportunities for Pazito to star as a series regular in sitcoms, and though Gloria will never admit it out loud, she was relieved when her son didn't get the parts, even though it broke her heart to share the news.

Is it so wrong for a mother to want her child to be a child for as long as possible?

Gloria doesn't want the answer.

She can't face that question without thinking of the many times she's failed her son by exposing him to the horrors in their home.

No child should grow up watching their parents fight.

Well, is it even a fight if one parent doesn't ever hit back?

No, it's not. That's an attack.

Gloria keeps it together, not wanting to cry in front of the other adults and children in the waiting room. Whenever she's away from Frankie, she tries not to think about him. Distance means he can't harm her. It means she can bury the fear.

The most peace she's known since being in this relationship is when she traveled to Brazil with Pazito for the Scorpius Hawthorne filming. Everyone was so welcoming. The cast showed Pazito all the rooms in the castle, sets he wouldn't have stepped foot in since his only scene was in the library. Howie gave Pazito lots of pointers and encouragement and praise. The crew made sure Pazito's dietary needs were met. And Pazito was surprised when the author of the original series, Poppy Iglesias, a queer trans woman, showed up on his last day of filming with a signed copy of the first book, the very book that Gloria believes has been instrumental in helping Pazito better understand himself, even if he hasn't come out with those words himself. Watching her son be loved was the peace Gloria gulped down like fresh water, nourishing her soul. She was very tempted to stay in Brazil, but when Pazito kept talking about how he couldn't wait to show his father the signed book, and all the pictures with his new friends at the castle, Gloria got on that plane with her son, dreading the entire flight home.

The door opens, and Pazito steps out along with a handler who nods at Gloria before accompanying another child into the audition room.

"How do you feel?" Gloria asks.

She doesn't like asking Pazito how he thought he did during an audition because if he believes he did his best and doesn't get the job it's made him sad in the past. Focusing on how the work made him feel instead has led to less disappointment down the line.

"I had a lot of fun!"

"Good. Did you thank them for their time?"

"Yup! And they thanked me for mine too!"

"Great job. You want to go get some lunch?"

"Okay."

Gloria grabs her purse, but right before she gets up, her phone buzzes. She's immediately uncomfortable, almost like her heart is being pinched, but it's not Frankie calling her home. It's Rolando, and Gloria is able to breathe again.

"Hello?"

"Gloria, hey. How are you?"

"I'm good, I'm good. Pazito and I are about to leave an audition."

"He's a star."

Gloria plays with Pazito's hair. "He sure is. How are you?"

"Having a bit of a day," Rolando admits. It hurts her heart to hear a heaviness in his voice. "Are you and Paz headed home right now?"

"We're actually about to go find some lunch. Take advantage of being in the city."

"Do you mind if I join? I'd love to see you."

Gloria freezes. "You're more than welcome. Pazito would love to see you."

Rolando is quiet long enough that Gloria wonders if she said something wrong. Before she can ask, Rolando says, "Do you know where you'd like to eat?"

"I think we're going to do McDonald's or Burger King."

"How about we grab a bite at Desiderata's?"

The restaurant where Rolando first told Gloria he loved her, back when they were babies in college. Gloria knows she should think this is inappropriate, or even that it's harmless because not only does Rolando know she's married—he was a groomsman at her wedding, after all, since Frankie is short on friends—but Rolando also knows she's a mother who would never break her family apart.

Not even if she wants to follow her heart elsewhere.

But what if she did?

What if instead of waiting to follow her heart, she picks it up and carries it where she wants to go?

Gloria tells Rolando, "Desiderata's sounds wonderful." And before she can hang up, she adds, "I'd love to see you too."

ORION

11:33 a.m.

I'm going to Ground Zero.

I send the text to Dalma, and she calls immediately. I'm not surprised. I always imagined my first visit to the site would be with Team Young, especially Dalma, who also knows the pains of losing a parent. I bet she envisioned it that way too.

"Hey," I say into the phone, signaling to Valentino that I'm taking the call up the block. I keep an eye on him as he leans against the wall, just in case any trouble pops up.

"Whoa," Dalma says. "Is this really happening?"

"I think so. . . . We're like a block away. I could turn back, but I don't think I want to."

Then it's quiet, but we're still on the line. I'm kind of glad this is a straight-up call and not FaceTime because I'd hate to see Dalma's face if she's feeling betrayed. I legit feel guilty, like I'm cheating on her. I just got to own it. "I wish you were here. It's all happening so fast, and I'm trying to go with the flow, just like I'm pushing Valentino."

"It's okay, O-Bro. You know I'm always willing to drop everything for you, right?"

"No doubt about it."

"Then I'm cool. Download me later on why you changed your mind?"

"I'll include every 'uh' and 'um' and 'oh' and my other Orion-isms."

A light laugh, then a sigh. "How are you both doing?"

Valentino is pressed against that wall like he's on a roof's ledge.

"No day is perfect, but we're trying," I say. I don't need to get into the near-death experiences or the canceled photo shoot. I'll save that for story time when . . . when the day is done. "Dalma, he's good-hearted."

"He better be. He's your match."

"You know what I'm saying."

"Are you being careful?"

"Sort of. We're out and about, and I'm not letting him hop on boats and shit like that, but it's his life to live."

"That's good, but I'm not crossing that line anymore. I was asking if you're being careful about how invested you get."

"Yeah, I've got a condom on my heart, don't sweat it."

"I'm serious, Orion."

I keep my eyes on Valentino, wanting to kiss the hell out of him. Holding back my feelings is like sinking into quicksand; the deeper and deeper I'm buried, the more desperate

I am to breathe. "I'm serious too. It's just getting harder and harder acting like I don't like him. Every minute that passes, I care more."

"Do you think it's extra charged because it's his End Day?"

"I was feeling my feelings before I knew he was a Decker. My heart knows what's up."

"Then you better get back to him," Dalma says, meaning it. "Tell him I said hi?"

"I will. I love you, D."

"I love you too, O."

We hang up, and I feel more at ease, like I've got one less hand gripping my heart as I get ready to hit Ground Zero.

I rejoin Valentino. "Dalma says hi."

"Tell her I say hi back next time you speak to her. Is she okay?"

"All good." I look down the street, knowing that when we turn the corner, everything I've been avoiding for years will come into view. "You still want to do this? Legit zero offense if there's somewhere else you want to go."

"I'm still in. Are you?"

"I am," I say.

Half-lie, half-truth.

I take the first step, aka the most important one. The rest follow. I don't turn back at the last second. I keep moving forward into this strangely chilling ghost town. This is supposed to be the city that never sleeps, but it's almost noon, and it's quiet and dark, the sun blocked by the high-rise buildings. I immediately think about writing a story about a boy who follows the sound of footprints left by invisible spirits, and when they step into the sunlight, they're revealed to be his parents, giving him the chance to finally say goodbye. I have a small, stupid envy for that fictitious kid who gets closure.

The deeper I go into the darkness, the eerier it becomes.

"I'm starting to feel like you shouldn't be here," I say.

"I'm not going anywhere," Valentino says.

If he dies here, not only am I never returning to this spot, I'm getting the hell out of this city.

Another minute in, things start feeling less like a graveyard but still alarming. This is the construction site where they've been building the memorial for the past few years, and it's heavily guarded. There are steel barricades and blue wooden barriers and chain fences and cinder blocks and police officers standing outside their cop cars. No one is getting through. Security is going strong, as if someone might launch another attack during the construction of the memorial; it reminds me of making sandcastles at the beach when you have to dig moats if you don't want the waves destroying everything you've built. I can't even see any of the memorial-in-the-making yet, I'd have to climb up one of those cranes to get a bird's-eye view. But I already know what's there—and what's not there. It's a hole in the world where the Twin Towers once stood, and I feel like it's sucking me in, like a whirlpool.

THE FIRSTS

As a family member of the fallen, I've gotten occasional updates about all the ways they want to memorialize the victims. There will be twin waterfall pools where the towers were. This Survivor Tree that was in the area, and, well the name kind of tells you the rest. Some stone monoliths studded with Trade Center steel they recovered during cleanup. And, of course, inscribing the names of everyone who died, from those in the planes and towers and the Pentagon to the first responders and recovery workers. But I'm not going to be able to see any of it until next fall for the tenth anniversary; if I even make it to then.

I toy around with the idea of asking a cop if there's somewhere we can go where we might be able to glimpse what construction is looking like, but things have been too intense in this neighborhood. It's been almost nine years and the fact that cops are still hanging around shows that the city means business. I've heard stories of residents who couldn't even get back into their own buildings because they didn't have IDs updated with their current addresses. I don't want to get kicked out of here, or risk something worse going down, especially with a Decker by my side.

Something feels off.

Nah, not something.

Someone.

That someone is me.

I feel off, like my heart's switch has been flipped.

"I thought I would cry."

"Is it because I'm here? I could give you some privacy."

"No, I want you here."

"Okay. Then what is it?"

"Ground Zero's emptiness reminds me of the funeral." I keep staring at the hidden memorial, waiting to feel something. "I didn't even want to throw a funeral because that meant accepting my parents were dead instead of holding on to hope that they were going to be recovered. No body, no proof. Kind of like how if you don't see a character die on the page or on TV, you wait for that plot twist to blow your mind. I was thinking wild shit, like how my mom and dad were never at the towers that morning and instead assumed new identities and lived happily ever after somewhere else. And of course they had to leave me behind to protect me, like classic dead-but-not-really parents."

Valentino is trying to read my mind. "Thinking your parents abandoned you didn't actually comfort you, did it?"

"Telling myself that story helped me get my first full night's sleep back then." I still remember waking up that morning, so rested that I wasn't even thrown off by waking up in Team Young's guest room. I just thought it was one of our many sleepovers. That was a win for everyone in the house, since I had spent the other nights screaming; poor Dahlia had to go stay over at her abuela's house because she wasn't getting any sleep. "I got to a point where I stopped telling those stories, even though no remains were ever found."

Valentino stares at the construction site. "I'm sorry to say it, but I think your parents died in the towers. Maybe it's because I'm not a storyteller like you, but I can't imagine them living different lives and not coming back for you by now. I've only known you for twelve hours, and I couldn't even abandon you in this dark, cold corner of the city that's heavily patrolled. You're too special, Orion."

Dude is trying to blow up my heart. "You're just saying that because you don't want my parents to haunt you."

"Can ghosts haunt other ghosts?"

All it takes is one second—one impossibly long second—to forget that he's dying.

"I don't know, but if you all hang out, tell them I love them."

"I will. I'll make it really clear that you've grown to be a great man . . . who sucks at history."

"They know that shit already."

"I'll have to find something else to share, then."

Okay, that shit comes off flirty, but whatever idea he's got brimming, that's not something I want him talking about with my mom and dad.

I pull out the camera from my coat's pocket and snap a picture of Valentino.

"What was that for?" he asks.

"You're the first guy I've brought to meet my parents."

Valentino is blushing, definitely not sun-kissed cheeks. "Hopefully I'm not the last, Orion."

Why does moving on feel so heartbreaking?

He's not my boyfriend, and we're not in love.

He's going to die today, and I'm going to live.

All this answers my question.

We're not going to get the chance to become boyfriends who fall in love.

His journey ends here, and I'll keep going until I can't.

Living doesn't feel so heartwarming in this moment.

Valentino takes the camera from my hands. "Let's get a photo of you visiting your parents."

I don't fight him. This is a memory I'll be able to share with Dalma and the Youngs.

I turn to the construction site and stare, thinking about how twelve hours ago I was with Valentino in Times Square telling him about my ties to 9/11 and now I'm here for the first time since my life changed.

In my head, I rebuild the towers, level by level, window by window, and once I finish, I watch the airplanes that crashed into the buildings fly overhead instead, and my parents walk out the front door, along with every other soul that died, and go home.

That's how that day should've ended.

Unfortunately, my memories are stronger than my imagination.

Many didn't go home.

The airplanes didn't stay in the sky.

The towers collapsed.

Then came my life unraveling. Sleepless nights. Screaming. Jumping at every doorbell thinking it would be my parents covered in ash. The stories I told myself. Skipping school. Funerals with empty caskets and the eulogy I never delivered. Pure anger. The guardianship paperwork. Saying goodbye to my first home. Starting over in the brownstone. Pure sadness. Giving DNA samples to test against discovered remains. Dreaming about where my parents would want their ashes scattered. Thinking I might keep their ashes next to me forever, even if one speck was found. Too many condolences when I returned to school. Guilt when I laughed for the first time. Totally lost and trying to find myself in stories. Shame for having a crush. Regret for not coming out. Not going to Ground Zero on the one-year anniversary or the year after or the year after or the year after or the year after or the year after or the year after or the year after.

Now I'm here, alive—not always well, but alive.

I'll keep standing tall for my parents, and living the kind of life they would've loved to have watched me live.

SCARLETT PRINCE

8:59 a.m. (Mountain Standard Time)

The pilot died of a heart attack, and if it weren't for Death-Cast, it's possible he would've taken down the entire plane with him. This is Scarlett's second near-death this summer, and while she feels for the pilot's family, above all, she feels for her own. It's as if her heart is being shredded because if Death-Cast was right about the pilot, then maybe that means they'll be right about her brother. No matter the outcome, it's been urgent that she reaches Valentino. This is what she's told the investigators and officers who relayed the news of the pilot to all the passengers who thankfully released her ahead of everyone else so she could get a head start.

Scarlett arrives at the customer service counter, gasping for breath.

"I need the next flight to New York. Death-Cast has called my brother."

VALENTINO
12:00 p.m.

In one precious moment your life can change.

You can go from being an only child to a twin brother. You can start running and never stop. You can find your passion. You can almost become an only child again. You can come out of the closet. You can land the gig of your dreams. You can move to a new city. You can meet a boy. You can say goodbye to your future when Death-Cast calls.

It's been twelve hours since I became the first Decker.

There's no doubt I've only made it this far because of Orion. It started with him saving my life and has evolved into him changing how I live it.

"What's next?" Orion asks, the World Trade Center's memorial site blocks behind us.

"Why don't we ask Death-Cast?"

They seem to know everything. Joaquin Rosa himself told me to check out their website for events that are happening today. I log on to death-cast.com and select New York in their city tab, and I'm presented with many options for the day. There's an amusement park in Coney Island, which would be a lot of time spent on the subway. A list of restaurants that I would love to visit, but I still can't risk the heart transplant going wrong because I wanted a nice Italian meal.

"Oh shit, a Broadway show?" Orion asks, looking over my shoulder.

"I can't put my finger on it, but I'm not interested in revisiting Times Square for some reason."

"Hmm. Yeah, I wonder if it has anything to do with the dude who pulled a gun on you."

"Probably more because it was really crowded."

"Good point, good point. Anything else jumping out at you?"

"Not really." I close the website and right as I'm passing the phone back to Orion it begins ringing. "Scarlett."

"Get it, get it, get it!"

I put the phone to my ear and answer. "Hey."

"I got a flight!" Scarlett shouts while breathing hard, sounding just like when she'd join me for a run and would yell at me to slow down whenever my thoughts carried me ahead of her.

"You did?!" My smile tells Orion everything he needs to know. "For when?"

"They're about to begin boarding. . . . I don't even have

my suitcases!" She's panting and telling people to excuse her as she charges past. "It sounds like . . . a Decker has been pulled off the plane . . . airline sees it as a risk . . ."

Hopefully the Decker wasn't trying to go home to see family. In the event they are alone, I hope they find someone who can help make their day count. Like I have.

"I feel horrible for them, but I'm grateful I'll see you."

"Twin thoughts. I'm here, I'm going to board. I love you, Val. Be safe so I can see you soon."

"I'll guard my life with my life."

We hang up. I'm so happy that I start shaking. I might even cry.

"Scarlett's coming!" Orion says.

"She sure is! She's boarding her plane now."

"We just got to guard your life with your life," Orion says, smirking.

Five-hour flight with another hour for traffic. I have to survive another five hours. I'm not good at math, so I don't know what the probabilities are of seeing Scarlett with just under twelve hours max before my End Day concludes, but the odds are feeling great. I'm no longer exhausted and starving, I'm rested and satisfied. I would take off into a run right now with my hands thrown up in the air as if I'm breaking through marathon tape, but now's not the time to overexcite Orion's heart or risk falling into a manhole.

"What should we do? How about something iconic?

Maybe the Empire State Building?"

Orion winces. "I'm not going to hold you back, but I don't really do super tall iconic buildings anymore."

"Say no more."

"I'm happy to go with you, I'll just hang out downstairs."

I try to make sense of how that would work in this new world of Death-Cast. If Orion—someone who isn't dying today—doesn't accompany me up to the Empire State Building, does that increase the risk of something catastrophic like the attack on the World Trade Center? Or if he did go up with me, does that thwart death? I'm sure the world will get its answer one day, but I'll die without it. It doesn't feel like a true loss in the grand scheme of things, and the same goes for not visiting the Empire State Building.

"No worries. It would've been cool to feel like a king of the world and swear at the sky again, but I'll save that for another life."

He's quiet, and I feel bad. I don't want him down on himself, because he's not holding me back. He's been pushing me forward.

"I'm sorry. I was only kidding."

"No shit," Orion says with a smirk. "Come on, I'm not that soft."

It's funny how well I feel I know him and how much more there is to learn. The one bright side to Scarlett not being here yet means I get to spend more time with Orion.

Hopefully I'm able to introduce them to each other. Not only because Orion will be carrying my heart but in the hopes he can look after Scarlett in New York when I'm gone.

"What are you thinking about, then?" I ask.

"The next two stops in your End Day adventure. The first is somewhere most New Yorkers haven't visited, and the second is iconic. Do you want to know or be surprised?"

I choose surprise. That's a welcome gift.

Wherever Orion is taking me, it's also downtown and only a few minutes away from the street corner where Scarlett called with the best news. The best news given my situation, that is. It's dawning on me that even if I reach out to my parents this second, it would be pretty impossible for them to see me in person one last time. Should I feel guilty? Do they deserve that chance? What do I owe them as the son they raised? Then before I can voice any of these feelings, I remember Orion's wisdom from last night. I'll speak to my parents if I have something to gain. But I owe myself peace more than I owe them anything.

Today is beginning to feel like I'm doing years of growing up within hours.

"Earth to Valentino," Orion shouts. "I love your little lost-in-thought moment but I kind of have to blindfold you quickly."

"Why?"

"So you can't out my organ harvesters, duh."

"Cool. Just wanted to know."

Orion removes his hoodie—technically, my hoodie—and wraps it around my head. His smile is the last thing I see before the sleeves are tied around my eyes. The hoodie is snug around my face, and the darkness is more peaceful than I'd imagine. A shiver runs up my spine when Orion holds both of my hands. This alone could be the surprise, and I'd love it. He starts leading me to our destination, and I'm walking awkwardly like that time I put on my mother's high heels as a kid, nervous I'm going to fall and snap an ankle.

"Trust me," Orion says.

"I do."

"We're about to enter a train station, but the sign spoils everything."

"Hence the blindfold."

"We have to be really careful going down the stairs. We'll take our time, okay?"

"Okay."

At the top of the staircase, Orion places one of my hands on the railing and keeps holding the other. He guides me, step by step, though the first few are the most nerve-racking. My calves are tingling, and it takes a bit before my feet find the rhythm, like we're dancing. The overall experience feels like a roller coaster where you begin with regret and doubt and then you release all that and enjoy yourself. I let out a deep sigh when we reach the landing, but it turns out that's not the only set of stairs. Orion doesn't let my hand go as he reaches into my pocket for my MetroCard and swipes me in, then doing the same with his own.

"Can I take off the hoodie now?"

"Nope. There's still signage everywhere."

He leads me down the next set of stairs, and I grip his hand, increasingly nervous that this is all going too well and my desire to be surprised is going to get him hurt and me killed.

"Almost there?" I ask.

"Almost there," Orion says.

An overhead announcement begins, and Orion leans into my ear and mumbles nonsense to drown out the message. Feeling his breath on my face gives me goose bumps.

"Sorry about that. We haven't come this far for Train Operator Number One to spoil the ending."

"I appreciate your dedication."

"Do you have an iPod on you? Or I can use the songs downloaded on my phone. Maybe more annoying noises?"

"Can you talk to me instead?"

"And say what?"

"Tell me a secret."

Orion is quiet, but this time I can't read his face. I only know that he hasn't walked away because he's still holding my hand, even though we're not moving.

"What kind of secret?" he asks.

"Something personal. Something you wouldn't even admit out loud."

"Unfortunately, you're the perfect person to tell a secret to."

Any secret dies with me. "Exactly."

"Okay, but you got to wait until we're on the train."

It's like my whole body is vibrating. Is this because of the incoming train roaring through the subway? Am I secretly on the tracks? Or is it pure anticipation on what Orion will share with me, hoping it's what I would say if he asked me?

The train doors open, and I manage to hear "last stop" before Orion hums loudly into my ear and guides me inside, straight into a seat. I no longer even care about where we're going. I want to know what he's going to reveal about himself. He stops humming to tell me to keep my head down, and I fold into my lap, dizzy in the darkness. I would fall forward if it weren't for Orion holding his arm across my chest. Then right as the conductor begins announcing what the next stop will be, Orion's lips graze my ear.

"I'm scared I'm going to die and never have been in love."

It's so silent that I hear the doors close.

The train leaves the station.

Orion unwraps the hoodie, and the light bothers my eyes, but not as much as his confession that he can't possibly believe is true.

"I can tell you want to say something, but we don't have a lot of time."

"A lot of time for what?"

Orion gestures at the rest of the train car. There's no one sitting in the blue and orange seats or holding on to the railings while playing on their phones. It's empty except for us.

"Is this rare in New York?"

"Not at all, but we're going somewhere that we're not supposed to . . ."

Childhood memories of the thought of going to hell resurface. It doesn't help that I'm alone with another gay boy. "Should I be nervous?"

"You should be careful, and not let go of me." Orion ties the hoodie around his waist, and he pushes open those folding doors that connect from one car to the next. "We're about to pass by a secret train station." He steps out onto this metallic bridge and holds on to a black rubber strap with one hand. He extends the other to me.

There's a sign that reads *Riding or moving between cars is prohibited* with a black silhouette between two train cars being shamed for doing so within a red stop symbol. But the bottom reads *unless there is an emergency, or as directed by police or train crew* and I'm going to declare my End Day an emergency.

I take Orion's hand, half stepping onto the bridge and holding on to the rubber strap with the tightest grip. The wheels screeching are ten times louder out here, and the winds are blowing back my hair like we're on the top of a building. It's exhilarating without being as dangerous as skydiving. This is a first, but neither of us are stupid enough to try to document this with a picture. The fact that we're doing this at all is already plenty stupid. But I'm not going to die here like some self-fulfilling prophecy from when I was panicking earlier about all the different ways I can die.

The train slows down slightly as it turns, breaking out of the dark tunnel. The secret station is illuminated by the sun casting through the skylight. I'm blown away by how different this station is from the one I was in this morning. This feels more like Grand Central, which I've only experienced through movies where characters arrive in New York for the first time and do that classic spin that screams, "I've made it!" If I weren't so scared of falling onto the tracks, I'd probably spin right now too. It's magical experiencing this hidden corner of New York and I'm shocked more people aren't risking their lives and breaking the law to stand out on this crossway to see this for themselves. The sign on the bricked wall reads *CITY HALL*, and there are green and white tiles running along the vaulted ceiling. The most surprising piece would have to be the literal chandeliers that are switched off or don't work, but to think they once lit up a train station like it was a ballroom? Showstopping.

As we're returning into the darkness, Orion howls in euphoria, and I do the same, our voices echoing through the tunnel.

I'm aching to stay out here, but he wisely nudges me back inside.

"So?" Orion asks, flipping his thumbs up and down.

I don't even know what to say. This is one of those pas-sages that you can only stumble on if you don't get out of the train when you're supposed to, and I got to live something that most New Yorkers won't in their entire lives.

I answer Orion's question with a hug. "Thank you for being the most thoughtful person ever."

Orion squeezes. "You kidding? You won that award when you offered me your heart."

The train pulls into the station, and I don't want to let go. I don't care if thousands of people pour into the car. That'll only push us closer together. I want to hold on to Orion because he's under this ridiculous impression that someone won't love him in what I have faith will be a long, long life after the transplant. But I have to let go because Orion says, "This is our stop." I get out and follow him up the stairs and outside the station with a new mission before I die.

Make sure Orion knows he deserves the world.

GLORIA DARIO

12:15 p.m.

Gloria tries breathing.

In, out. In, out.

Why does it feel like she's a breath away from an asthma attack?

The restaurant is a little stuffy. She removes her light jacket and tucks it into the corner of the booth where she's sat across from Pazito. Her son is telling her all about one of his assigned books for summer reading, but Gloria is struggling to focus, to keep her eyes away from the door where Rolando is expected to walk in any moment now. She wonders if he'll be carrying a bouquet of sunflowers like he did their first—and last—time here at Desiderata's, the day where Rolando told Gloria he was deeply in love with her.

The day where Gloria regrets not saying it back.

The truth is, Gloria knew she loved Rolando, but she wasn't as certain that she was in love with him. Those lines can be blurry, especially when you're young and haven't known love yet—or known what it's like to be in a relationship where things aren't as they should be.

A marriage, even.

The early days with Frankie were passionate, as if they were floating above everyone else in their orbit, to the point where whenever Gloria was brought back to earth, she missed that high. So much so that she ignored the red flags billowing in the winds.

Who would have thought that falling in love could take you to the skies?

But people don't have wings, and walking through life is how you get to be in it.

It's up close, it's personal, it's real.

Gloria regrets not having kept her feet on the ground, especially after how often she found herself being thrown to the floor by the man who once took her to impossible heights.

Here she is now, seated at the restaurant named after her favorite poem, written by Max Ehrmann as if he was staring into her soul as he put pen to paper. Desiderata is about what you need in life, what you desire, and when the door opens and in walks Rolando, Gloria breathes as if he's the oxygen she's been craving.

It doesn't even matter that he's not carrying sunflowers.

"Uncle Rolando!" Pazito slides out of the booth and

rushes to Rolando, almost crashing into a waiter.

"Hey, Paz-Man!" Rolando hugs Pazito with a love and tenderness that Frankie doesn't.

Gloria thinks—no, she believes with her whole heart that Rolando will be an amazing father one day. She's mostly sad that she didn't realize this, oh, twenty years ago when he confessed his love for her, but it's okay. Gloria's greatest creation is Pazito, and she wouldn't change a single hair on his head or bone in his body, and that means accepting some of those hairs and bones come from Frankie too.

She gets out of the booth with a smile and a hug.

"Great to see you," Rolando says, as if it's been years since the Fourth of July when they last saw each other for a barbecue in Althea Park, the same day he applied for the Death-Cast job.

"You too," Gloria says. Even though she wants to hold on to Rolando for dear life, she lets go and sits opposite of him and Pazito. "So . . . tough day?"

Rolando's tired brown eyes seem to say so. "I should've known what I was getting into with that job."

"Did you cry a lot?" Pazito asks. "I think I would cry a lot."

"That's because you have a big heart," Rolando tells him. "I'm going to be honest, I haven't cried."

"So you don't have a big heart," Pazito says.

Rolando chuckles. "I like to think I do, Paz-Man."

Gloria is a breath away from agreeing before her son fires off his next question.

"Have you found out how your bosses know who's going to die yet?"

"No, I haven't. I actually won't—"

"I think everyone has a prophecy," Pazito interrupts. "And Death-Cast somehow knows everyone's destinies. Prophecies are a big part of the Scorpius Hawthorne books."

"You might be right, but I won't be able to find out the big secret. I quit this morning."

Gloria leans forward. "You did? Why?"

Before he can answer, the waiter approaches, asking if he can get anything started for the table. Gloria still remembers how long it took for her and Rolando to place an order last time, promising their waitress they would take a look at the menu in just a moment, but the two kept joking around and laughing so hard that they were fighting for their next breath. She's mourning a life of love and laughter and light as she orders a hot tea and waffles with maple syrup.

"I'll just have a black coffee," Rolando says.

"Nothing to eat?" Gloria asks before the waiter can.

"I just came from a . . . a meeting, you can say. I ate a bit there."

A meeting? He's not normally so vague.

Gloria wants to ask with who, but for the first time in a long time, the answer scares her.

What if Rolando had a breakfast date? Who's the lucky woman? Will Gloria be strong enough to attend that wedding? Can she hold back the tears when meeting his child?

She will.

Gloria is a planner, and she plans to be happy for her best friend.

Once the waiter steps away, Gloria follows up with Rolando. "You quit?"

"It wasn't a good fit for me. It's probably too heavy to talk about right now," Rolando says, glancing at Pazito. "Are you both going straight home after lunch? Maybe we can go to the park? We can talk some more then."

"Park!" Pazito shouts, scaring the patrons in the booth behind him.

"It looks like we're going to the park," Gloria says.

She won't be able to spend her life with Rolando, but they can have today.

ORION
12:38 p.m.

"Next stop: Brooklyn Bridge," I announce in my best train conductor voice.

The bridge is a couple minutes away from the train station, the perfect one-two punch for Valentino's tour. He doesn't seem super hyped, though, or even slightly hyped. The Brooklyn Bridge is an iconic part of New York where he can take in views of the city; I can even point out where the Twin Towers once stood. But Valentino seems . . . pained?

"You good?" I ask. "I promise the bridge isn't going to collapse under us."

"I'm not concerned about the bridge. That sounds nice."

"Okay, cool. Then what's up?"

"I'm thinking about your secret."

"The secret that stays in the secret station?"

"I implied I'd take it to my grave. I never said we wouldn't talk about it."

We begin crossing the bridge, the first minute of what could be an hour journey as we walk to Brooklyn with the East River beneath us. That's a long time to dig through this deep pain of love feeling out of reach, like it's buried in the center of the world and I don't have a shovel. But if Valentino wants to claw through the ground with me, I can't knock that.

"What do you want to know?" I ask, unwrapping the hoodie from my waist and putting it back on, cozy inside it like I was when wrapped in Valentino's arms on the train.

"Why do you think no one will love you before you die? Because you're expecting you'll die young?"

"It's wild, but I could live until I'm a hundred and I think I'll still never know love. Like, legit love. This world isn't built for guys like us, you know."

"That doesn't mean there isn't someone out there for you."

I want to scream that I think he's that capital-s Someone. "I came out last month too and it's not like a bunch of dudes started lining up outside my house."

"Probably a good thing."

"I had a shit ton of crushes in high school, and I didn't know for sure, but I got some closeted vibes from a couple of them. I swore they were prob into me too, though no one hit me up with any confessions once I was out."

"I'm sure someone wanted to, Orion. It's possible they weren't ready or were still figuring themselves out."

There's a million reasons why someone won't come out. What might seem like no big deal to one person is the whole universe to another.

"True. There's also shitty parents," I say, thinking of Val-entino's.

"Maybe they would've been kicked out of their house. I got lucky."

Parents not kicking you out of your home because you're gay shouldn't be luck. That should be the expectation when you bring a kid into this world. If you can't do that, then fuck off, fuck off, fuck off. I'm done playing this shit where we got to be nice to people who hate on us for how we love. They're the reasons why we got it so hard, why we lock away our feelings even though it means we'll die without knowing the happiness that comes to others so easily.

"Did you ever have any boyfriends?" I ask, feeling sick with envy in my empty stomach.

"No, but I had a big crush back in March."

"What was he like?"

Though I already suspect I know the answer: muscular, beautiful, pearly white smile.

"He's another model."

You don't fucking say.

"We first met during this photo shoot a couple years ago. I was this student driver acting like I didn't know how to drive, and George was posing as my instructor, though he actually doesn't know how to drive. The casting people did not care. George played a really convincing and kind instructor."

"Was he actually a piece of shit?"

It's stupid and immature being so competitive with someone in his past, someone who isn't spending Valentino's End Day with him. But I'm stupid and immature when it comes to these things, back off.

"George was a good guy. We bumped into each other in an audition room and hung out that entire day. Then it started getting dark, and before I could go home he leaned in for a kiss."

I want to fucking catapult myself off this bridge, I'm so jealous.

"I backed away," Valentino says.

Okay, never mind, maybe I'll take up flying instead.

"Why'd you back off?"

Valentino steals a glance my way. "I wanted my first kiss to be memorable."

"I like that a lot," I say. Some things are worth holding off for. "Do you believe in soul mates?"

His blue eyes stare out into the river, then the skylines. "I think so. I believe there are people you're destined to meet, but it's up to you to do the work. The work always seemed really intimidating and even impossible."

"I feel that. I love being gay, but fuck, this shit is hard sometimes."

"No kidding. It's not even legal for us to get married."

My heart stops—not really, but really, you know—and it only starts pumping again when I realize he's speaking about the general *us*, not the Orion-ampersand-Valentino *us*.

"Is marriage something that's been on your brain?" I ask.

"Absolutely. I was looking forward to meeting my man and proposing and planning the wedding and stressing out about vows. Scarlett would be my maid of honor, of course. I originally pictured my parents being there, but when I realized that wasn't going to happen I thought I'd invite so many friends and friends of friends to fill the venue so I wouldn't even notice they weren't there. This is probably one of the saddest things about dying today: I'll never know if this was going to change."

"I wish we could know if your parents would've come around, it's just—"

His hand finds my shoulder. "I'm sorry to interrupt. That wasn't about my parents having a change of heart. It was about the government and the church and society accepting gay marriage. It would've been nice to know this was even a possibility in my lifetime."

If Valentino had been in love and wanted to cement that by marrying his partner before death do them apart today, he couldn't.

This is not a problem most couples have, my parents included. My mom and dad put up with a lot of shit as Puerto

Ricans, but no one stopped them from making it official, no one was disgusted by their love, no one killed their dream of starting a family. We should've had decades on decades on decades with each other, but who knows what that would've looked like. They could've gone all their lives watching me fight a war they never fought in, watching me never have what they have. In all my years of imagining what my parents' terrifying final moments looked like, I like to think they were holding each other. My dad hadn't stepped out of their meeting for one of his million bathroom breaks and my mom wasn't trying to find a hot tea. They were so close that they could hear every *I love you* over the screams, over the explosions.

They were together, as the world has always allowed them to be.

"How about you?" Valentino asks.

"How about me what?"

"Have you thought a lot about marriage?"

"Honestly, no. I never thought I could even think about it. I've been too busy freaking out about trying to survive the day to even dream about the future. Like, I don't know what Old Orion could look like or ever picture any Little Orions running around."

"You'd be amazing with kids. You're so incredibly thoughtful."

"Do you want—" I stop myself, hating how Valentino will die before I get this right. "Did you want kids?"

Valentino nods. "I had names picked out too."

"Please tell me you weren't going to keep up the Valentine's Day theme."

"I absolutely would've! I wanted Rose for a girl and Cupid for a boy."

"You would've been doing your son dirty. How about, um—what's Cupid's Greek mythology name? Eros!"

"I know we're joking, but I don't hate Rose and Eros as names."

"I kind of don't either. What did you actually pick out? They better be better now."

"No pressure." Valentino seems nervous sharing. "I really like Vale because it feels like the fraternal twin to my name. Alike, but not identical because they're pronounced differently. It's also unisex, which I love."

I genuinely love the name too, but I'm too choked up to say anything. He really gave this a lot of thought, and it will never happen. There are some bucket-list boxes you can check off on your End Day and others that are impossible. Like Valentino getting married to the love of his life and having a child named Vale.

"I hate that you're being robbed of all these moments."

"What moments?"

"Everything you want. Falling in love, walking down the aisle at your wedding, holding your baby for the first time, all of that."

"I hate it too. I like knowing that it doesn't die with me. You're the first person I've spoken to about Vale."

"Not even Scarlett?"

"No. I'm like you that I'm not sure how realistic all that was. I certainly believed I'd have more time to make those dreams come true, but there were still so many barriers. I didn't want Scarlett to get so excited only to not watch it all happen. Especially because she wants a big family of her own; she's hoping for triplets. She would've offered to name a kid Vale for me, but that would've meant giving up on my Vale. I might have to take her up on that now."

Story idea: a graveyard for dead dreams, headstones marking each one.

I hope I can find a happy ending for that.

"If something happens, will you tell Scarlett for me?" Valentino asks.

"Of course. This world will have a Vale Prince, even if I got to name my kid that."

He scoffs. "You're just saying that."

I stop and grab his wrist. "Hell no, I'm serious. I'd never lie to you. First name, Vale. Middle name, Prince. Last name, Pagan."

"Vale Prince Pagan," Valentino says, testing it out. He stares out into the city skyline, like he's imagining this child growing up in the city he didn't get to. "They'll have your curls and loud laughs."

"It sucks that they won't have your blue eyes."

"Hazel is really beautiful too," Valentino says.

He turns to me with this intense gaze.

I press my hand to his chest and walk my fingers up to his collarbone.

"I'm happy the kid will have your heart."

"Technically, you'll have my heart."

There's a fire growing inside me, but this isn't a heart attack.

This is life lighting me up.

"You've had my heart since the start, Valentino."

I'm burning, burning, burning.

"And you've given me the best End Day, Orion."

"It's not over. There's still lots of firsts ahead of you."

"There's one I'd love more than others."

"Then carpe fucking diem—"

Valentino's heart-shaped lips shut me the fuck up.

VALENTINO
1:01 p.m.

One second into my first kiss, and I already hope it won't be my last.

It's gentle even though I've been starving for a moment like this for years—and during the best parts of my End Day. It's like Orion and I are savoring each other until we become greedy. The kiss builds from slow to fast, soft to strong, like my heartbeat. It's so passionate that my head knocks the baseball cap off of his. I have half a thought to leave it there on the ground, but that's from his father and deserves more respect. I somehow manage to break the kiss and bend down for the hat. As I'm rising, I lift Orion by his hamstrings and he wraps his legs around my waist. I've always wanted to carry another boy like that.

Orion kisses me from above, and I'm seeing stars.

Add this kiss to the list of things I don't want to end. But whether it's a morning jog or the perfect kiss, all good things must come to a stop when you need to breathe.

Orion unwraps his legs from around me and slides down my body until we're face-to-face. I put his cap back over his curls, and he adjusts it just as he likes it; I'll get it right next time.

"Hi," he says.

"Hi. That was memorable."

"Hey, I might suck at history, but I can make it."

The Brooklyn Bridge offers many views. At the very top, there's an American flag waving in the wind. There are the cars driving beneath us and the river flowing further down. The buildings that I won't have time to visit but can appreciate here. And the gray skies above everything. It's all beautiful, but it doesn't beat the boy who brought me here.

I sigh deeply. "You have made my End Day so hard, Orion."

First, there's a flirty glint in his hazel eyes, then concern when he sees I'm not smiling. "Shit, I'm sorry, did I—"

I slide my palms up his, pressing them together.

"Thank you for giving me a glimpse into the life I moved here for. It's not going to be a long life, but I'm getting to live it because of you."

"I don't know how long I got either, but if you're my first and only, then I could—"

"Don't say you'll die happy."

"Then I could die . . . miserably . . ."

"That's not great either."

"How do I win, then?"

"By not accepting defeat. I'm honored to be your first, but I don't want to be your only."

"Things don't exactly work out for me. You're the best guy I've ever liked and . . . "

I bring his hand to the inside of my overshirt, my heart beating against his palm. "After the operation, you're going to have more time. Please use it wisely so you're not trying to squeeze in everything in one day. Write the longest novel ever. Look for love. Start your family."

Orion is tearing up. "Why are you hitting me with a goodbye speech right now?"

"I can't hold off on anything anymore." I kiss him again. "Especially not after my favorite first with you."

"There's still time to one-up it."

"How so?"

"I'm going to take you on your first date, Valentino."

JOAQUIN ROSA
1:11 p.m.

Joaquin has returned to the Death-Cast headquarters and stares at the empty call center. The heralds have gone home for the day, but will there still be jobs to return for tonight?

He goes straight to the company suite, expecting to find his family around the table or watching TV, but no one's in here. He can hear the TV on in the bedroom and gently knocks on the door before letting himself in, where he finds Naya and Alano asleep on the king-size mattress, a luxury Joaquin invested in knowing his family would occasionally find themselves staying overnight. The puppy leaps off the bed and rushes Joaquin. Joaquin sweeps Bucky into his arm and snuggles him, already feeling his blood pressure drop. He really needed this.

Everything he's been through since he left has been difficult and frustrating and disappointing and heartbreaking.

Joaquin turns off the Scorpius Hawthorne movie on the TV and goes to the restroom to wash up, cleaning his face and drinking water straight out of the faucet too. The time spent in the vault always leaves Joaquin feeling out of touch with himself, but now, Joaquin is starting to feel like, well, Joaquin.

"Hi," Naya says from behind with tired eyes. "Any luck?"

They never openly talk about what's inside the vault or what happens in it. For the rest of their lives, Joaquin and Naya—and perhaps one day Alano—must live as if there are tiny cameras everywhere they go, planted by someone wanting to know the secret behind Death-Cast.

"Some luck, but not enough. Have more deaths been reported?"

Naya nods. "There have been eleven reported deaths. All registered. None notified."

Joaquin feels unanchored again. "I have to release a statement."

"Is everything over?"

He can hear the slight hope in her voice for a dream he can't make come true.

"No. But if my understanding of the issue is correct, this glitch isn't done."

"What do you mean?" Naya asks. She holds up her hand, understanding he can't expand into too many details.

He shares what he can.

"I'm under the impression this issue caps at twelve deaths."

That means there's still one Decker living their life, unaware it's their End Day.

ORION

1:24 p.m.

Valentino and I hold hands like a couple as we continue down the bridge.

We're spitting out different ideas for our first date, trying to find something that won't risk the heart operation later, something he's more dead set than ever on protecting. Sitting down at a nice fancy restaurant is a classic move, but smelling the hot food we can't eat would be torture. And as much as I'd like to watch Valentino ask a bartender to serve him his first ever drink before he dies, we probably shouldn't be drunk before surgery. There are safer options, thankfully. Like strolling through Central Park and riding the carousel, maybe even together on the same horse or unicorn if we want to be extra gay about it. There's also Bryant Park, where some New York Fashion Week stuff goes down, but there's nothing for Valentino to get out of that today.

"A lot of options," I say.

"We'll figure it out," Valentino says.

The bridge is more crowded on this end. I'm more alert, as if someone here will be a threat to Valentino whereas he's relaxed to the point where he asks a stranger to take our picture. I feel everyone's eyes on me, so aware that I can't imagine being comfortable having another guy hold me this close in the Bronx. Then I stop giving a shit about what the world thinks when Valentino pulls me into a kiss, like I've seen so many guys and girls do in the past. I love that this moment documented on camera is both a cliché and a fuck-you to everyone who doesn't want to see two boys kissing. Valentino and I haven't looked over any of the pictures taken today, and this is one I'm pretty hyped to relive when we do.

We slow down past this fence that has so many colorful locks clipped onto it.

"That's a lot of locks."

"Seriously, they need a collective noun." I think for a sec. "An embrace of locks."

"Well done. Dare I ask what they are, my favorite historian?"

"It's barely history, I think this shit started last year. They're love locks. Everyone bragging about their indestructible bonds and blah blah."

"You sound like a big fan."

"I guess I'm still carrying some bitter energy."

Most of the locks have writing on them: LUIS & JORDIN; HOWIE + LENA; NICKI AND DAVE; and CARLOS

AMA PERSIDA, to name a few. Others are dates for anniversaries I'll never know.

No locks with the names of two guys.

I wish I had one, dyed like a rainbow.

"This is really cool," Valentino says, trailing his fingers down the fence before continuing down the bridge, taking me with him like a current.

"I should've brought a lock for you. Why the hell isn't anyone up here selling any? They could make a killing."

Valentino laughs. "You can always come back and leave one in honor of me."

"Nah, I want to make moments while I have you."

It's not the end of the world, since Valentino and I have the pictures, but I want to commemorate the journey we've taken since being on this bridge. From our starts to our stops to our new beginnings to bracing our ending. If I had a marker, I could write our names into the steel. Then I spot a wooden bench, there for any tired travelers. I grab my key and get down on my knees and begin carving—V-A-L-E-N-T-I-N-O—as he takes a picture of me vandalizing the city. When I'm done with his name, he pulls out Scarlett's home key and starts scratching mine into the bench. It doesn't take him as long to finish. It all reads like one word:

I like how his *O* flows into mine, as if he's passing it on along with his heart. I'll take every letter and kiss and breath from him before it's time to live without him.

"I know where I want to go for our first date," Valentino says.

"Where?"

"Times Square."

"But that's where—"

"Where I found out I was going to die."

"And almost did."

"It's also where we met. I'd like to go back."

"You sure it's about us and not because you want to find your phone?"

"See? You know me well."

I sigh. I can't deny a dying guy's wish. "Let's go back to where it all started."

JOAQUIN ROSA
2:00 p.m.

Joaquin stands in front of the camera, a mic pinned to his collar.

He's sitting in one of Death-Cast's privacy booths, intended for heralds who need a moment to themselves once the weight of the job begins crushing them. Joaquin himself is very tempted to scream right now after having read many of the ugly things being said about him and his company online. No, they didn't have a flawless launch, but all their predictions have been accurate. Unfortunately, some slipped through the cracks because of . . . he can't get into it. He must compose himself as his broadcast on the Death-Cast website goes live.

"Hello. This is Joaquin Rosa coming to you from the Death-Cast offices with some news. It has been brought to our attention that there was a flaw in our system, and while I can't disclose what caused this error, I must own that it has happened, and as a result, we not only betrayed the very promises made to our users, but we failed our mission to begin this new age of no longer worrying about unexpected departures. I will be haunted by those losses until the day I die. I offer the deepest apologies and will be reaching out to the affected parties personally in the very near future. If they'll take my call, that is."

Some might say Joaquin shouldn't apologize for something that isn't his fault. He certainly believes that he's not fully responsible for everyone in his company as if he's hovering over everyone's shoulder and proofing their work. But he can't divulge any details as to what happened so just like Death-Cast's successes, he must also be the face of its failures.

"But Death-Cast won't die today. While we have failed to call some Deckers to alert them that today was their End Day, we are tracking a one hundred percent success rate in the predictions we have made. Unfortunately, those we've called have died, or we believe, will be dead by day's end. We can hope to be wrong there, but ask that you continue to operate as if we aren't."

Joaquin takes a deep breath, giving any viewer a chance to let that sink in.

"As for today's error, I believe the issue has been resolved for all our users, beginning tomorrow. For the next ten hours, I ask you all to remain mindful. Live life to the fullest, but don't live it as if you're invincible."

VALENTINO

2:02 p.m.

Life moves fast when you stop waiting around for what you want. When you go for it.

To think Orion and I started our trip on the Brooklyn Bridge talking about why love is hard for boys like us to coming out the other side holding hands is as amazing as our first kiss.

Now the only time I'm able to spend in Brooklyn before I die is walking to the Court Street station so Orion and I can return to Manhattan for our first date in Times Square, where we first met.

Am I concerned I'm destined to die in Times Square? Maybe a little. But I don't want to keep giving power to things that are beyond me. This is a choice I am making. This isn't part of some higher being's grand plan.

I'm going back to Times Square, where my life should've ended, and I'm going to enjoy my first date with the boy who saved my life.

Maybe after, we can go back to my place for some alone time and safely wait for Scarlett to arrive as the hands on my clock keep moving forward.

We board the R train and the car is packed. I'm pressed against the door with Orion's back leaning into me, my hands locked around his waist. He rests his head on my shoulder. I'm glad his eyes are closed because he can't see the passengers stealing glances at us as if we're doing something wrong. This city can be scary, but I'm not going to show fear. I won't get a long life of little moments like this one with Orion, and I want to embrace the feeling of someone's body against mine while I can.

"You think I'll finally get to see one of those showtime dances?" I ask.

He looks at the subway line map. "Someone better dance between now and your place."

"Is it too crowded, though?"

"You'd fucking think. People back up real fast once they hear that music kick in."

The trip is enjoyable enough though it's pretty obvious that I get my hopes up every time the connecting doors open, thinking dancers are about to announce themselves. So far it's just been other passengers moving through the train and one kid selling candy out of a shoebox to pay for his basketball team jersey; I give him my remaining cash.

After a few stops, enough people have filed out that Orion

and I are able to take a corner bench. He wraps an arm around my shoulders and lounges a leg across mine. I kiss him when he smiles at me, thinking about how everything is beginning for us, just like it should for two people who only met less than twenty-four hours ago. I don't think we would've moved as quickly if I had all the time in the world, but that doesn't mean I would've enjoyed the secret subway station and long walks on the bridge any less. I would've just wanted more, as I do now.

"I think I'm going to have to make an ass out of myself for you," Orion says at the next stop.

"What do you mean?"

Orion squeezes my thigh. "I'm waiting for a sign, one sec."

I look around the train, trying to see what he's paying attention to. Then we exit the tunnel and pull into the next station, and I see the very literal sign: *PRINCE STREET.* I gasp and quickly snap a picture of it. I want Scarlett to come visit. I still don't understand how Orion is going to make an ass out of himself. He gets up, and I do the same, thinking we're getting off early, but Orion gently pushes me back into my seat. He removes the hoodie and drops it into my lap.

"You better appreciate this shit," he says.

"Appreciate what?"

The train doors slide closed.

Orion takes a deep breath and shouts the magic word: "SHOWTIME!"

My jaw drops while everyone else on the train glances

up, seeming more annoyed than excited. Most are curious enough that they keep their eyes on Orion. I'm stunned that Orion is even willing to do this. It takes a lot of heart; the soul kind of heart, not the organ.

"Showtime on the R train! This very special showtime is dedicated to our newest New Yorker!" Orion points at me, and I'm blushing. He's clapping, working extra hard to get a scatter of applause from the other passengers. "Thank you, thank you!"

Orion pulls out his phone and starts playing some techno song. It occurs to me that I don't know what kind of music he's into, that these are the small ways that we're still strangers. And yet, here he is, about to perform this big gesture for me. He places his phone on the floor as he slowly starts swinging around the pole in the center of the car, and with his first hop onto the pole, I can already tell this is not some hidden talent he's been waiting for the perfect moment to reveal. This is going to be the most charming catastrophe, and I'm going to love every second of it. Orion slides down and crab-walks against the door and then clumsily rolls forward. I'm laughing so hard at how wonderfully stupid he looks while other passengers stare at Orion like he's drunk. I can't speak to what Orion would look like intoxicated, but this can't be far off. I start taking pictures as Orion jumps up and swings on the ceiling's handrail that's for the tallest of the tall. Everyone remains thoroughly unimpressed, and

I'm surprised and relieved no one is booing him.

"Main event!" Orion shouts. He removes his baseball cap and tosses it up and tries catching it with his foot. He fails the first time, the second time, the third time, the fourth time, and though he comes really close on the fifth time, he misses.

"You got this!" I shout. I start a slow clap, and surprisingly, other passengers join in. "Come on, Orion!"

The next moment isn't perfect, even though Orion has strangers rallying for him, but he sneaks a smile for me anyway. Then he focuses as he flips the cap up and kicks his foot straight into it, and he catches himself on the pole before he can fall.

My palms hurt from how hard I'm clapping.

Orion grabs his phone off the floor, and goes up and down the car with his cap for donations. He returns to me with a one-dollar bill, some loose change, and a kiss.

"Are you completely embarrassed to know me?" Orion asks.

"Not at all. That was the best show of my life."

"Well, that's fucking depressing," he jokes. At least I think he's joking.

"Thank you so much, Orion. That was everything."

"I think it's nothing compared to what's going to happen next."

"What's that?"

"You putting on a show."

"I think it might be too dangerous for me to swing around the train."

"Nah, I'm not asking you to do all that. I want you to walk your first runway."

Orion's grin is so mischievous. He's the king of making memorable moments.

I turn to the clear aisle, able to easily imagine it as a stage. Instead of chairs, there are train benches with an audience to watch me. There's no way I'm passing up this incredible opportunity. "Let's do it," I say.

Orion shakes my shoulders in excitement. "This is going to be epic! Okay, so they are a tough crowd, but I can hype this up as a one-time event. You game with being introduced as a Decker, maybe even as the first Decker? I want you to get all the love you deserve."

Even if no one else pays attention, I think I'd be happy with Orion watching me walk the train. "Whatever you think is best."

He hands me his phone. "Pick your song."

I wanted to know what music Orion is into, and now I'm getting the chance. There's such a range, between Linkin Park and Alicia Keys and Evanescence and Death Cab for Cutie and Carlos Santana and Celine Dion and Eve and the Pussycat Dolls. There's so many songs by women, and it gets me thinking about my personal playlist of songs I'd listen to whenever I had the house to myself. I never really felt comfortable listening to pop music around my parents, especially if the artist was a woman. That's how it was before and after coming out. If they were home and I wanted to listen to my favorite songs that they would disapprove of, I'd have to listen to them discreetly on my iPod; it felt like hiding my porn habits all over again. But now my parents aren't around and I'm not stuck in my bedroom. I'm free to listen to whatever I want by whoever I want whenever I want.

There's a song in Orion's playlist that was also on mine: "Release Me" by Agnes. It feels appropriate.

"Attention, attention!" Orion shouts. He hops up on an empty train bench, his arm outstretched like he's sailing on the deck of his ship—my ship. He's been an incredible co-captain, like I thought he could be.

"Don't worry, I'm not going to dance again," he says after a couple passengers groan as if their entire afternoons will be ruined by another interruption. "But we've got a really special show for you. This is Valentino Prince, and he's not only a Decker, but he's the very first Decker—he got his call from Joaquin Rosa!"

For the first time, everyone's paying attention.

No one is on the phone or reading a book or talking among themselves.

Death makes people pay attention that way.

All eyes are on me.

Orion's too. "Valentino moved to New York to be a model, but since today is his End Day, I'd love it if we could hype up Valentino as he turns this train into his first and only runway. Can we give it up for him?"

There's instant applause, like I'm a household name every-one has been waiting to see.

Orion presses *Play* on the song.

All my nerves get stomped flat with my first step, and I walk my imaginary line, one leg over the other like an acrobat on a tightrope; one misstep and you can die. My arms swing and hips sway naturally as I lean back, my chest puffed out and my head held high. I stare straight ahead as the music follows me thanks to Orion. Passengers are cheer-ing me on and taking pictures on their phones, maybe even recording. I can't let that break my focus. Every model should have an objective, something they're selling to those who are watching. For me, it's making your dreams come true by any means necessary. At the end of the car, I throw open my overshirt and slide one hand in my pocket and return down the aisle, stopping to flourish my free hand at the same train pole Orion swung around. He whistles, and others join in, this song that I've only heard in my imagination, and it's a dream come true to live this moment.

It doesn't matter that I'm not walking for one of the big Fashion Weeks in New York or London or Tokyo or Paris or Milan. I'm getting to be seen by real people, people who will have seen me strut in a way that I wasn't able to do in my own home.

As I'm making another lap down the train, I realize we're one stop away from Times Square. Some passengers offer me condolences before stepping out as others board.

"This is your last stop to see the one and only Valentino Prince!" Orion shouts, taking pictures.

For my last act, everything is coming off.

I start removing clothes like it's an old life to shed.

First, the overshirt gets thrown over my shoulder, until I pass Orion and give it to him.

Next, I show off the *Have a Happy End Day!* shirt before removing it.

Finally, I'm in nothing but jeans and boots.

Everyone is cheering, and Orion is collecting cash in his cap as the song comes to an end and we arrive at Times Square. Most of the passengers give me a standing ovation, and I blow everyone a big kiss before picking up my shirts and grabbing Orion's hand and dragging him out of the train and onto the platform. I throw my clothes down again and pick up Orion, just like I did on the bridge, and his nails dig into my sweaty back.

We're both laughing over how exhilarating that experience was, and then we give New Yorkers a third show with a passionate kiss that proves Orion and I aren't strangers.

None of them know how I almost died in Times Square and how amazing it feels to be here right now.

Not only alive, but living.

"You were amazing," Orion says. "You should, like, be a model."

"I'm in the market for a new agent. But I got to ask: Do

you believe in Death-Cast?"

"Hell no I don't."

"Fantastic. The job is all yours." I wipe the sweat off my chest with my button-down before getting dressed. "You made my dream come true, Orion. Thank you for everything."

"Sorry you had to see some super shitty showtime dancing."

"That was a highlight."

"Then you have bad taste. I really can't believe I did that."

"It was very adorable, but just know if you're that embarrassed, it dies with me."

"And lives on with every other New Yorker who saw it!"

"Well, think twice next time. Better yet, don't think twice. Isn't life more freeing when you just let go?"

Orion doesn't think twice about kissing me. "Like that?"

"Just like that."

I take his hand as we climb the stairs and step out into Times Square like it's my first time. It's different from last night. The sun is high and the mega screens are showing regular ads instead of the Death-Cast hourglass. Tourists are going in and out of shops. A crowd is surrounding two break-dancers, looking like street ballerinas as they spin around on flattened cardboard in white tank tops and sweatpants. Cars are crawling through Times Square so slowly it's like they're driving through sand. A hot dog vendor is haggling with someone, and I'm sure he could hustle me into buying one for fifty bucks, I'm that hungry. Spanish music is blasting from a boom box behind me.

There's so much life happening in Times Square.

Even though a man was killed here last night.

Even though I was told I'm going to die.

But what Death-Cast really wanted was for me to live. I've done plenty of that now.

Hopefully there's more to come.

SCARLETT PRINCE
11:15 a.m. (Mountain Standard Time)

Scarlett needs this plane to take off.

It's bad enough that she's reliving the trauma of the first flight, but she can put all that behind her as long as she's in motion, as long as she's moving forward. Her time with Valentino is already so limited and she's not just talking about how his End Day is halfway done. Scarlett and Valentino were supposed to see each other through long, full lives, and that's being robbed from them. Scarlett doesn't even know what she will do with Valentino when she arrives, what even has to get done besides spending time together, but she simply wants to be in New York figuring that out with him already.

Scarlett cannot believe this day.

Why is the plane still grounded?

What's going on this time?

Haven't the pilots been cleared? Or are they not registered for Death-Cast?

She's about to join the chorus of passengers in bothering the flight attendants for some answers when one of the pilots addresses everyone.

"Attention, passengers. I have some news."

Deep in her heart, as if Death-Cast is calling, Scarlett knows—she just knows.

ORION

2:37 p.m.

Valentino and I are becoming inseparable, as if we're the living, breathing versions of our inscribed name back on the Brooklyn Bridge—ValentinOrion, all one word, the O bigger because it belongs to both of us. If I'm not holding his hand because he's taking pictures of Times Square, I'm touching his shoulder or hooking my finger through his belt loop. It's like I'll float away if we lose contact. More like he will, I guess.

We're holding hands as we walk through Times Square, back toward the area where people were telling their Death-Cast origin stories. Where I first met Valentino. The stage I never got to stand on is gone, but the red glass benches remain as a new fixture, tons of people sitting there.

"Okay, so I was pretty bummed out by not getting to tell my story, but then you walked past me and I was . . . I was into you from the jump."

"That fast?" Valentino asks.

"That fast. Did you think I was a total weirdo for saying what's up?"

"No, I thought you were cute too. And I actually spotted you first."

"Wait. What?"

"I was just walking through the Square—"

"No one calls it that!"

"Well, start that trend in my honor."

"I'll hate it, but okay. Go on. Tell me how you thought I was cute as fuck as you were walking through the Square."

"I was walking through the Square, and that Death-Cast presentation caught my eye—"

"And then I did too!"

"Do you want to tell the story of how I thought you were cute or do you want me to?"

"Are you for real asking a storyteller if he wants to tell—"

"Anyway, I saw you—"

"But you didn't say hi!"

"Probably because I knew I wouldn't get a word in!"

I zip up my lips and hand Valentino the make-believe key. He clenches it in his fist.

"Knowing my luck, I'll probably lose it like my phone." Valentino looks over his shoulder as if there's a chance he's going to find his iPhone on the ground just waiting for him. "I didn't say hi because I didn't know that was a thing that people actually do. But I'm really glad you did what I didn't have the heart to do."

I want to snatch the key out of his hand so I could ask him if the pun was intended, or to rag on how he definitely doesn't want my busted heart, but Valentino unlocks my lips with his own.

"Just so you know, I legit never walk up on cute guys. I was really trying to live it up."

"Thank God you— I'm really thankful you made that first move, Orion."

"Thanks for not scarring me with some huge-ass rejection, Valentino."

He doesn't take his eyes off me, like I'm the most interesting part about this city.

I grab the camera out of the hoodie's pocket and point at the bottom corner of the bench. "Go sit. I want to take a picture of the spot where I first met you."

"I'm not taking that alone. We're in that together."

Valentino and I sit on the bench, and I extend my arm, hoping to get the right picture. I'm about to snap one no matter how shitty it is when someone taps my shoulder. It's an older Latino man sitting beside a young curly-haired kid in glasses; I'm guessing father and son but definitely family.

"Would you like some help?" the man asks.

"Oh, uh, sure. You don't mind?"

"Not at all."

We step aside so the man and the kid can get down easily.

The kid seems a little jumpy, like he's about to hide behind the man. I'm guessing he's like nine or ten.

"It's okay, Mateo," the man says.

I give him the camera, though I feel bad about scaring this Mateo kid, who keeps looking around. I get this heartbreaking feeling that maybe it's Mateo's End Day and he's terrified of dying but he really wanted to people-watch in Times Square before he does. Valentino snaps me out of it when he turns my gaze to him, our eyes locked. The man counts us down from three and instead of smiling for the camera, Valentino leans in and kisses me. It means everything that I'll have this moment immortalized, and when we pull apart, Valentino is smiling with his eyes closed, as if he's burning this moment into his memory, as if he's not going to be able to look over the pictures with me.

"Beautiful," the man says, handing me the camera. "This will make for a great postcard to send to your family."

"Not for my family it won't," Valentino sadly says.

"I'm sorry to hear that," the man says. "I'm happy you're living your life as you should."

"Thank you, sir." Valentino shakes the man's hand, and I do the same.

I turn to Mateo. "Sorry if we scared you before. Truce?"

I hold out my fist for a pound, but Mateo goes for a handshake. Then as I open my fist he forms his. He's blushing and seems upset—not pissed like that Rufus kid back at the pawnshop—but disappointed in himself like he can't do anything right. All that shit is valid, I definitely went through a lot of anger and shame when I was figuring out life without my parents. There were never any magic words that made me feel better when I was deep in it, and I don't know this kid enough to even try casting some spell on him. I just keep it real.

"Hey, you're okay," I tell Mateo.

Mateo doesn't seem to believe it.

"Come on, son. Let's head up to the park," the man says, sensing it's probably best for Mateo to back out of this situation. "Enjoy the rest of your day."

"That's the goal," Valentino says with a smile only I understand. We watch the two walk away, the man hugging Mateo close. "It's nice to see a father care for his son like that."

"It reminds me of my dad," I say. I'm so used to talking about my parents so fondly that I forget to filter for Valentino who didn't get so lucky. "Sorry."

"Don't apologize for your loving childhood. I know it's messed up, but I would honestly say I had one too. I can remember what it really felt like for my parents to love me. Tons of gifts under the Christmas tree, big birthday parties, taking care of me when I was sick. We had movie nights where Scarlett and I got to pick what we watched. If Scarlett and I couldn't agree on one movie, our dad would stay up for double features." He looks around at Times Square. "I think if I grew up in New York my parents would've taken us everywhere. The Statue of Liberty, the Christmas tree at Rockefeller Center, Radio City, Empire State Building. Here, of course."

There's a lot about what Valentino has said that makes me sad, even pisses me off. A parent shouldn't love you only through childhood, but I'm glad his life hasn't been total hell. It could've been so much better if he had parents or guardians like mine. Maybe if he had grown up in New York we could've met sooner. It hurts to think about how much easier and harder his End Day would've felt if I'd known him for years.

I can't start cracking now, I got to stay strong.

"What else do you want to do while we're out here? Find an artist to draw a caricature of us? Nah, that's a waste of your time."

"Sitting next to you isn't a waste of my time," he says.

"If you say so . . ." I grab the cash I pocketed from his subway runway and count it out. "Sixty bucks."

"That bad? I thought I did a better job."

"You're shitting me, right? Sixty bucks is amazing. I'm not surprised, look at you."

"Shall we see how I look after the artist is done with me?"

"Hell yeah."

I kiss him, staying in our spot just a little longer.

Then my phone rings.

I freak out for half a sec before I remember it's not a Death-Cast ringtone and that we're outside their calling window.

I release the deepest sigh, like someone is interrupting us. "Place your bets on who it is," I say as I reach for my phone. "Dalma? Scarlett? New contender?"

"Hopefully it's not Scarlett," Valentino says.

True, because she should be on her plane by now.

"It's Dalma," I say. I answer her call. "Hey, what's up?"

"Thank god you're okay," Dalma says.

I'm immediately thrown back into the headspace of 9/11 and everyone's relief whenever they found out someone was alive. "Why wouldn't I be? What's going on?"

"O-Bro, have you not seen the news?"

"No, I haven't. We've been——" I shut up, my heart going crazy. Valentino can see the panic in my eyes. "Dalma, just tell me what's going on. I'm freaking the fuck out."

"There's been a Death-Cast update. Some Deckers have slipped through the cracks, and the problem won't be sorted until tomorrow. I think that's still a big question mark too."

I almost drop my phone.

I'm shaking.

My eyes water.

"What's happening?" Valentino asks. "Is everyone okay?"

This is the fucking thing: I should have an answer.

I should know if everyone is okay because Death-Cast

was supposed to solve these mysteries so we could live our days peacefully if we weren't about to die. But now I'm back to where I was yesterday and every damn day before that. My heart going wild could actually be the beginnings of an attack that kills me.

Has today been my End Day too?

VALENTINO
2:51 p.m.

Orion looks like he's seen a ghost, or more realistically, like he's been called by Death-Cast.

I guess in both cases you see lives that are over.

That doesn't make sense, though. He's not some seer who communicates with ghosts and Dalma isn't a herald at Death-Cast. I'm scared that someone he loves has died, like Dalma's family, but that doesn't make sense because I was under the impression everyone in their house was registered for Death-Cast. A herald would've called if it was their End Day. Could it be something with Dr. Emeterio? Maybe she's done further testing and Orion and I are no longer a match? Or she can't get anyone to sign off on the transplant in a timely fashion? There are hundreds of questions, and the only person who can give me an answer is lost in his head.

"Orion . . ."

He's frozen, staring at the mega screen like the hourglasses are on display again. A tear slides down Orion's face. "What about the Deckers they called already?"

This is about Death-Cast.

This could be about me.

Orion starts sobbing. Is this good? Is this relief? Are we going to have more time?

Am I going to live?

"I'll call you back—I don't know, Dalma, let me call you back . . ."

He hangs up.

I can tell in his eyes that he's not about to personally deliver death-changing news.

"What's going on?"

"Death-Cast fucked up," Orion says, shaking. "Deckers have died today without knowing it's their End Day and . . . there's a chance that . . . there's still a chance that more will die before midnight. Joaquin Rosa is trying to fix whatever went wrong, but he can't promise anything—even though that was his company's whole fucking job!"

This means that Orion could die today.

Scarlett too. She survived her own brush of death when the pilot got his End Day call before takeoff. What if everyone on that plane is destined to die today too?

If Death-Cast has had errors today, what does that mean for me?

Orion seems to read my mind.

"I'm sorry," he says, like he knows he's murdering my hope.

"Don't be." I have spent so much of today accepting how it will end. Orion however has been trusting in the accuracy of this program and has returned to the unknown. "What can I do for you?"

"I don't know, I . . . I'm so tired."

"Do you want to go back to mine and rest?"

"I'm not tired like that. I mean, I am, but I'm . . . I'm tired of living like this. I thought everything was going to be different and it's just all bad news. Like, how can Death-Cast even be sure that you're going to die when they don't know whether I'm going to live? Couldn't they throw some hope our way?"

"We don't know what's happening in those offices. They might not be sure but don't want to cause further hysteria."

"If the product is broken, they should say that shit!" Orion shouts, scaring people around us. "I'm not trying to have you marching to your death if you're not supposed to die!"

"Let's go talk about this elsewhere."

"No! This is our first date, and we need to live it while we can!"

I get up and pull him away. He doesn't fight me, which is upsetting. Orion losing that fire means his spirit is breaking on a day where he's been finding out who he can be in a life where he's not scared of dying. I'm frustrated and disappointed that Death-Cast has ruined this trust. I won't be around to watch the company go under, but they'll deserve it.

His phone rings again.

"I said I'd call her back . . . ," Orion says, reaching for his phone. "It's Scarlett."

"Do you mind?"

Orion shakes his head. I assumed he wouldn't, but I didn't want to turn my back on him.

I answer the call. "Hey, Scar."

Scarlett is crying even harder than Orion. "The airline grounded all their planes." She goes on to explain everything I already know about the Death-Cast updates with no new insights. "They can't risk it, especially after what happened on my last plane. I've tried explaining my situation, but there's nothing anyone can do."

This is how it ends.

I'm going to die without seeing my sister one last time.

"I don't know what to do, Val!"

"Take a breath, okay?"

"I'm going to try a different airline, or see if I can use our rent money and savings on a private jet. Private jets would still fly, right?"

I don't understand how air traffic works, but I know I have to take care of my sister when she's hyperventilating like this. "Scar, I need you to breathe."

She tries taking deep breaths, but she gets overexcited. "Maybe you're not even going to die, since Death-Cast has proven they don't know what's going on."

So Death-Cast clearly doesn't have the grasp on the End Days that we'd all like. But we've seen many of their predictions come true today. I can't expect to be the exception.

I can play along for my sister, even if it's only for a little bit. "Maybe I'll live."

"Then I can see you tomorrow when it's safe to fly."

"And I can take you to this secret subway station."

"There's a secret subway station?"

"Orion showed me it today. It's amazing."

"What else is there to see?"

"The Brooklyn Bridge has incredible views and these love locks."

"Love locks?"

"They're cool. I'll explain when I see you."

"Can't wait. What else?"

"You got to see Times Square. This is where it all happens."

One phone call changed my life. Another is changing Orion's.

"Of course we're going to Times Square."

"Orion can give us some pointers for the rest of the city."

"I'm excited to meet him."

"You'll love him. He's the best." I hold Orion close. I've known that I will be able to help him live after I'm gone, but now that I know he's not as safe as we previously thought, I'm determined to protect him. That starts with getting him off these streets, where I'm not prepared to save him in the event he has a heart attack. "Scar, I'm going to head back to our apartment. I'll call you from there."

Scarlett's voice cracks. "Pl–please call me as soon as you're home."

"I will. I love you."

"I love you same."

I hang up and pocket the phone.

"She's not coming, is she?" Orion asks.

"No." It's painful to admit it out loud. "It really felt like we were kings of the world, didn't it?"

He nods. It's as if he's so speechless he won't even swear about how unfair this is.

"I think we should get out of here. Want to go back to my place?" I know we'll be safe in my tiny studio.

"Don't hate me, but can we go to mine? It's just . . . if something is going to go down, I want to know I got to say goodbye to Dalma and the fam. . . . If you don't want to go, I get it, but I'd love it if you came, though. We don't have to stay that long either, we—"

I give Orion a quick kiss so he can stop and breathe. "It would be really nice to be around some family right now. Especially since I can't be with Scarlett."

"You sure? I don't want to rub salt in the wound and all that."

"Take me home, Orion."

GLORIA DARIO
2:54 p.m.

Gloria is at Althea Park with her family.

No, she's at Althea Park with her son and her best friend.

This is an important distinction.

No matter how much Rolando loves Pazito, he is not his father.

And no matter how much Rolando once loved Gloria, he is not her husband. Even if she wishes she had married him instead. But she must live with the choice she made twenty years ago when she turned down his heart.

"Go play," Gloria tells her son.

Pazito runs toward the park's jungle gym as if all the kids swinging on the monkey bars are friends of his and not complete strangers. He's fearless, something Gloria has always loved about him and recognizes has aided him well in auditions. Pazito never freezes up; he always moves. Well, that's not completely true. Fear freezes Pazito when Frankie raises his voice and hands at Gloria. But she doesn't want to give air to those thoughts right now. She's been having such a lovely day.

Gloria sits on the blue bench, not far off from when she was here for the barbecue on the Fourth. She looks over at the stretch of grass as if she can see the memory playing out before her, like ghosts stuck in the past: Gloria's two sisters relaxing with sangria on lawn chairs; Pazito playing catch with his older cousins; Frankie working the grill, but only because Rolando was originally on cooking duty and Frankie just had to show him up; and Gloria herself on the picnic blanket, hugging her knees and daydreaming about how freeing this gathering would feel if only there were one fewer person.

She returns to the present, to the reality where Frankie indeed isn't here at the park.

Where Gloria is alone with Rolando.

"I'm sorry to hear about Death-Cast," Gloria says.

"Don't be. I'm really proud of myself for quitting."

"In what way?"

"Instead of waiting for the day when an operator calls to tell me I'm going to die, I already understand how important it is to live while I can."

Gloria loves that insight.

Life shouldn't be about to end before someone begins living.

"That's really admirable," she says, watching her son fear-lessly scale the jungle gym, watching her son live like he's going to forever.

"Don't you think you should do the same?" Rolando asks.

"Do what?" Gloria asks.

"To live while you can."

"I am," Gloria says.

"No offense, Glo, but I don't think you are."

He hasn't used her nickname in ages, and Gloria's heart skips a beat. "What do you mean I'm not living?"

"Tell me what your life looks like—and not what you do for Pazito."

Everything that Gloria can think of that doesn't involve her son feels too small, even if it brings her joy. Things like cooking with her mother's recipe for garlic maduros and watching legal dramas and soaking in the tub with only a lit candle alive in the dark bathroom.

"Raising a child should count," Gloria says. "That makes me happy."

"It does, but . . ." Rolando shifts his knee toward hers. "But what are you going to do when Paz has grown up? How are you going to spend your days?"

Sadly, Gloria hasn't planned for life without her son. She doesn't say anything because she has nothing to say and doesn't want to lie. She's lied enough in this lifetime, always pretending everything is good and well.

"Your son is important," Rolando says, and he gently adds, "But so are you."

This isn't the first time Rolando has asked Gloria to think of herself, but it is the first time he's done so with tears brimming in his brown eyes. It's almost as if he knows something that she doesn't, as if Death-Cast told Rolando that Gloria will be dying soon and was given the chance to deliver the news in person instead of having a stranger call her. She can't be sure, but what Gloria does know is that Frankie has never told Gloria that she's important. Once again, she can't be sure, but Gloria would bet anything that her husband has never valued her life, maybe only for keeping a clean home and doing the heavy lifting with raising their son.

Gloria is important.

Gloria matters.

Gloria deserves a better life.

Feeling this in her heart, Gloria breathes deeply, like after a long day where she's been on her feet all day and crawls under her covers for bed. But she doesn't want to wake up to the same thing anymore. "It's too late to change," she says.

"Of course it isn't, Glo." Rolando's hand twitches on the bench, but his fingers don't find their way into hers. "Think of how many people whose lives have changed today because of Death-Cast. It's only going to be too late if you wait until the last minute to start over."

Those words should feel like a warning, but instead Gloria views it as a blessing.

"Are you starting over by quitting your job?" Gloria asks.

Rolando stares into her eyes. "It's more than that. I'm quitting a life that doesn't make me happy."

Gloria wishes she could do the same. "What's not making you happy?"

"You," Rolando says.

It's like her heart has been ripped out by a single word.

This whole afternoon has really been about pushing her away. Perhaps he's too frustrated with Gloria and can't bear to watch her go on as she has.

Before Gloria can apologize for steering her own ship as she has seen fit, Rolando apologizes.

"I'm sorry—you're not the reason I'm unhappy. At least, not in the way you might be thinking," Rolando says, flustered. "I spent this morning with a Decker. This old man who was my first call of the night."

Gloria's shredded heart is stitching itself back together.

So Rolando wasn't on a breakfast date. He was with a man who's dying today—who may be dead already.

"Why did you meet with him?"

And so Rolando tells Gloria about his long phone call with the man named Clint, and how he came to find himself having breakfast with him on his End Day. "I don't want you waiting around for your life, Gloria. And more important, I don't want you waiting around for your death. It might not be my business, but I don't want to regret not saying anything if . . . if Frankie loses control."

As if the worst parts of her life flash by, Gloria shudders.

"I'm sorry to bring this up," Rolando says. "But not as sorry as I'll be if I lose you."

"I appreciate the concern. It's just more complicated than you think."

"I think it's the opposite. It's simpler than you think. You shouldn't be with someone who might be your cause of death. Not when you have so much to live for."

Gloria turns to Pazito, but she understands she should be pulling out a mirror instead.

She reminds herself that she's important, that she matters, that she deserves a better life.

"I'm scared," Gloria finally admits.

"I understand. Frankie is terrifying."

"No, it's more than that . . . I'm scared of starting over."

Gloria looks at the park, finding her son going down a slide. He's one of many kids who will grow up and expect for life to be smooth sailing. But Gloria's journey has been rocky, and she's sure that peace will be on the horizon if she throws her husband overboard. But it's not that simple. Frankie will weigh her down like an anvil, keeping peace out of reach.

"Starting over is scary," Rolando says. "But that's the only way forward."

"It's the only way forward," Gloria repeats with tears in her eyes.

"For me, starting over means not waiting for my End Day to admit that I'm still in love with you, Gloria. Always have been, always will be."

Gloria sucks in a breath, as if she's had the most amazing kiss in her life. But Rolando has not touched her. Not physically, at least. They remain seated apart and staring at one another, the sounds of children living in the background, and Gloria's heartbeat pounding in her ears. Rolando does love her—always has, always will. Gloria believes those words with a fierceness that she never felt for Frankie's vows. The man she should've married was the one standing behind her husband at the wedding.

"I'm not expecting you to divorce your husband for me," Rolando says. "But I hope you'll divorce him for yourself."

Before Gloria can decide if she wants to restart her life with Rolando, she must choose to end this one with Frankie.

Out with the old, in with the new.

Gloria must divorce Frankie—for herself, and for her son who will always be at the heart of every decision she makes, no matter what anyone says. But unlike before, she's now thinking about what she wants her life to look like after Pazito has grown up and moved out to live his. She doesn't want to share a couch or bed or even a hundred-foot radius with her husband, with the man she should have never married.

The man Gloria should have left long ago.

Long ago when he first terrorized her.

When he first put his hands on her.

And after every other time.

Gloria cannot undo the past, but she can forge a new future.

And all's well that ends well.

RUFUS EMETERIO
3:00 p.m.

Death-Cast did not call Rufus Emeterio because he is not dying today.

In fact, Rufus is having the time of his life as he rides his new steel-gray bike around Althea Park. He learned how to ride a couple years ago, ahead of his older sister, Olivia, who has no interest in picking up the skill, and it's all good because Rufus has enough passion for the both of them and then some. Back during his short-lived training-wheels day, his father asked him to take it slow, but Rufus picked up everything fast and was ready to go, go, go. He built up speed through this drugstore parking lot and almost rode his bike into a busy street where a car would have easily killed him if he hadn't hit the brakes. That was the first time he got a big talking-to from his pops, and it certainly wasn't the last, but look at where those lessons and talks have gotten them today: Rufus is riding a bike that he believes is destined to carry him on many adventures, and his father is trusting him to navigate his own journey.

Honestly, Rufus isn't even mad at how his father sprung this chat on him. (And he definitely wasn't mad when he got surprised with his dream bike at the end of it!) The thing is, Rufus loves his pops, but they've been going head-to-head lately when what they needed was a heart-to-heart. His father talked to him about his past, and while Rufus wasn't in the mood for a history lesson, especially during summer break, it actually turned out to be pretty cool. It taught Rufus that it's okay to feel his emotions, even anger, just like his own father often did with his parents when he was growing up. But Rufus can't let anger be the only thing he feels.

Rufus thought about this a lot on the train ride to Althea Park with his pops and sister.

A while back, Rufus and Olivia made up a game called Traveler, where they tell stories about the other people they see out in the world, though usually when they're on public transit. Today on the train there was an old man who dropped a lot of cash into the purse of a young salsa dancer and Rufus imagined that he's a Decker making sure his money goes into the right places before he dies, whereas Olivia was more focused on this woman whom she believed to be a spy for Death-Cast to make sure people are dying as they predicted to protect their reputations.

But if someone else were playing Traveler and saw Rufus, who would they see? Probably a boy who always talks back and is always trying to win a fight. Even against those who don't want to fight him. In reality, Rufus is a cool kid who loves his family, and he would rather show the world that side of himself instead.

He wasn't at the start of today, but right now, Rufus is happy.

Things are good with his pops.

His sister is also hanging out.

And his mom has just arrived, wanting to see everyone before she returns to work.

Rufus is tempted to try to pop a wheelie, even though he's never been successful in executing one, but he doesn't want to stress out his mom over broken bones when her job at the hospital has her specializing with literal broken hearts.

"Nice wheels," his mom says, giving Rufus a high five. "What'd you do to deserve that?" she asks, though she looks more at his dad too for the explanation.

"He talked back," Olivia says.

"You're technically right," his dad says. "But Rufus talked back with respect, and I did the same."

"Happy to hear it," his mom says.

Rufus likes when she's proud of him, and he's going to try harder to make that happen. "I also helped out at the shop."

"How's it looking?" his mom asks.

"Better," his dad says at the same time Rufus says, "Bad."

For a moment, Rufus braces himself to go on the defense, as if he's going to be scolded for saying the truth when what he said is legit the truth. The pawnshop is not in great shape. Yeah, they got all the glass off the floor and the front door has been boarded up, but when they left, it was still a mess. And his father seems to remember that as he nods with a little smile and agrees, "It's pretty bad."

Rufus breathes, relieved that he didn't have to fight.

"It'll be better soon," his mom says, sitting on the park bench.

Rufus doesn't know what his mom has been going through at the hospital, only that she came home exhausted and wanted to try to help out at the shop, and everyone begged her to get some rest instead.

"You good, Mom?" Rufus asks.

"It's been a long day." She looks around at the park, where other kids are playing and laughing, and it seems like the kind of thing she needed. "I'm on call for a surgery tonight. It's for a Decker who wants to pass his heart on to another boy he's only just met. They're both so young and . . ."

His dad seems stuck on a thought. "Wait. Did one have a Yankees cap?"

"I didn't see a cap at all."

He snaps his fingers at himself. "Valentino?"

Her back straightens. "How do you know that?"

"We met a Decker at the shop this morning. They bought a camera off us."

"He was a Decker?!" Rufus asks. He can't believe he met a real-life Decker and he's only just now finding out about it.

His mom sighs. "Though the news is now reporting that Death-Cast has made some mistakes today. Just because they got some predictions right doesn't mean they still can't be wrong. This could complicate things on our end for the surgery, but only time will tell. I just hope those boys are having the time of their lives."

Rufus is itching to ride his bike some more because all this death talk is making him uncomfortable. But he sees that his dad has fallen into some kind of trance. "What's up, Pops?"

"Things weren't—aren't—great with Valentino and his parents. I wonder what his heart is telling him to do." He looks at his family with a steel, teary gaze. "None of us are perfect, but let's never let things between us get so bad that we could know we're dying and still not want anything to do with each other. Goodbyes are the most possible impossible because you never want to say them, but you'd be stupid not to when given the chance."

Rufus lets his father's words sink in.

He would never want to fight with his family so much that he wouldn't try to see them one last time before he dies. He knows the day will come where he's a grown man and his parents are old that he will have to say goodbye. And it will probably feel impossible, but Rufus's father is right, it will actually be possible. Just really difficult. But that's a problem for a long, long, long time from now.

Until then, Rufus is going to be a kid.

He's going to have fun with his bike.

He's going to be a good son and brother and friend.

He's going to live.

MATEO TORREZ JR.

3:14 p.m.

Death-Cast did not call Mateo Torrez Jr. because he is not dying today.

That doesn't mean he isn't still living in fear.

Ever since midnight, when the Death-Cast calls began, Mateo has been scared, staying close to his father. Mateo even slept in his father's bed last night, resting on the left side that once belonged to his mother, who died giving birth to him. Maybe it's all the fantasy books he's read growing up (particularly the Scorpius Hawthorne series, which is chock-full of prophecies) but Mateo has always imagined that he's been marked for an early death because of the life that ended when creating him. He was so sure that Death-Cast was going to call his father last night, sharing the tragic news that Mateo would be dying, but the phone never rang.

So then why can't Mateo breathe?

He's arrived at Althea Park with his father. There's plenty

432

of fresh air, but he still feels like death must be hiding around every corner. Like a pack of dogs could jump all over Mateo, which might seem like a good time for some people, but his allergies are so bad that he could break out into hives and his lungs could close up from anaphylactic shock and he could die.

He'd hate to leave his father alone, especially after killing the woman he loved the most in this world.

The first time his father—Mateo Sr., known to his friends as Teo—sat Mateo down to talk about Death-Cast, all Mateo could think about is how the day he was born would've been different if only his father could have prepared for his wife's death. As Mateo understands it, his mother wasn't expected to die during childbirth, and the death shocked his father, who didn't get the chance to say goodbye to the woman he imagined his life with as he held their only child together for the first time.

Now look at Mateo.

Given the gift of life, and too scared to open it.

Mateo is trying to be brave, but it's much harder than people think. He doesn't agree with those who believe fear to be a choice. There have been many times he would have liked to fight his way out of fear's entanglements, where he would have chosen to live, but it also felt like fear had this impossibly tight grip on him, like tentacles wrapped around his neck and wrists and ankles, holding him back. One of many reasons he admires his best friend, Lidia, is that she carries herself like she was made for this world. She stands up for herself whenever people make her uncomfortable, and while she can be choosy, she can make friends with anyone.

Sometimes Mateo thinks about why anyone would want to be friends with him.

Why anyone would choose him.

He's thinking the same thing now as he looks at all the other kids in the park. Most of them are running across the jungle gym as if there's no risk of falling and hurting themselves. There's a boy on a bike that seems too big for him, but maybe he'll grow into it. As the boy rides past Mateo, he takes a step back because Mateo knows good and well that he is not invincible.

"You don't want to play?" Teo asks.

Mateo wants to, but he doesn't know how to.

And he knows how to, but he doesn't want to.

Actually, he wants to and he knows how to, but he doesn't know how to get out of his head to do anything. He ends up just being stuck.

For someone who's often praised for his kindness and generosity, Mateo sure can be his own worst enemy.

"I'm okay, Dad," Mateo lies.

He doesn't like making people feel bad, especially his father, who works so hard to give him a good life. But today has been difficult. From what he understands Death-Cast really wants people to live, but Mateo still can't help but be confused about how much of life is now free will and how much of it is destined. Would people die if Death-Cast didn't call? Are people now living recklessly because they've been told that tomorrow is still on the horizon for them? Or are the deaths set in stone? The questions hurt his brain, and not having an answer squeezes his heart.

While his father has given him a great life, Mateo must learn how to make his own. There's no telling how much time either of them has—either Mateo will be right that he's cursed to die young or his father will pass before him, just like it should be. He'll never forget the first time he told Teo about the curse and how sad his father got at the idea of having to bury him.

Why can't people live forever?

"Talk to me," Teo says gently, like he's inviting Mateo in and won't be upset if he declines but wants his son to know that he's here and would like his company.

Mateo watches everyone in the park with awe. All they're doing is being themselves, and it's still the most magical thing in the world. Why can't Mateo cast those same spells?

"I just look at everyone, and I don't know how to be like them."

"I love that you're you," his father says. "You're a special kid, Mateo."

"You have to say that. You're my dad."

"Belief is less about what you say and more about what you feel. Since the day you were born, I felt such powerful love and protection for you. I hope to protect you now by promising that there is no one else like you. I'm lucky to not only know you but to call you my son. You don't have to be anyone but Mateo Torrez Jr."

Mateo stares up at the sky, remembering all the times his father brought him to this park and taught him about the clouds while on the swings; doing that instead sounds really nice right now. But a question is clawing its way up his throat and wrenches his mouth open and flies out: "Should I really be myself if no one likes me?" And before Teo can say the obvious, he adds, "Please don't say that you like me. I know that already."

"As long as you know it," Teo says. "What about Lidia?"

"She won't like me forever. She thinks I'm annoying."

"When did she say that?"

"Well, she never said annoying, but she said I'm an over-thinker. Like I'm too much."

"You're very thoughtful, Mateo. You can be too careful sometimes, but we know that."

Over the years, whenever Mateo has gotten hurt, he's done everything humanly possible to make sure it never happens again. There was the time he was running during a recess race and tripped and scraped his knee and he refused to play for the rest of the school year. Even when he was working up the courage to run again and have fun, no one wanted to pick him because they didn't think he was a good sport. He is. Why is it a bad thing to not want to get hurt?

"It's like . . ." Mateo stares at the ground, not wanting to see the other kids playing together. "It's like by keeping myself safe, no one wants to be in my life. I'm not trying to push people away, Dad."

"I know you're not, buddy. Maybe you can try something different. Go pull someone in."

"How?"

"Go talk to someone. Most important, be yourself while doing it."

Mateo doesn't know about this. But then again, how dangerous could other kids be? It's not like when he got scared of those two older boys in Times Square. Mateo thought they were up to no good at first, like a prank or something worse, but it turns out they were up to good. They just wanted a picture taken together, and when Mateo saw them kissing, he felt something unlock within. It reminded him of the conversation he had with his father last month.

"How do you find love, Dad?" Mateo had asked. "Where is it?"

"Love is a superpower," his father had said. "It's one we all have, but it's not a superpower you'll always be able to control. It'll get harder when you get older too. Don't be scared if you find yourself loving someone you're not expecting to.

If it's right, it's right."

Mateo wonders if those two older boys were scared to love each other.

It didn't seem so.

Mateo stands, ready for his challenge. Then the fear comes back and tries shoving him back onto the bench, but he stays strong on his feet. "I'm going to try, Dad. But if I don't make a friend, can we go home?"

"Absolutely. I'll make you a cup of tea, and we can watch a movie."

He would really like that.

But first.

Mateo walks toward the park and goes to the swings. The closer he gets, the more one boy seems familiar. His dark hair is sitting flat, but if Mateo pictures it swooped up, it reminds him of someone else. Then it hits Mateo like the magical blue lightning bolt from his favorite books. He doesn't know the boy's name, but he was the actor who played Larkin Cano in a flashback scene for the adaptation's final movie. It was a small part, but Mateo still thinks it's so cool. This kid actually got to explore the magical castle and meet the people who've played Mateo's favorite characters. This is easy, so easy, Mateo can ask about Scorpius Hawthorne stuff and make a friend. He stands there, like he's waiting his turn to swing, and he opens his mouth—

"Pazito!" a woman calls from a bench, not far off from

Teo. "Let's go get ice cream!"

The boy—Pazito—hops off the swing and runs away before Mateo can introduce himself.

Bad timing.

Mateo is ready to call it a day when he decides to give it one last shot. There are girls on the monkey bars and playing jump rope. A boy goes down the slide backward and laughs as he slams onto the mat. Some teenagers are playing handball and it seems so intense.

Then Mateo sees the boy with the bike again. He's inspecting the chain, and maybe he cares a lot about safety, just like Mateo. Mateo walks toward the boy right as he gets back on his bike, pedaling away.

"Pops, look!" the boy shouts as he leans over his handlebars and glides under a tree's low-hanging branches.

"Great job, Rufus!" the father responds.

Rufus . . . Mateo really likes that name. It's not one he hears enough, but it's nice.

Not believing the third time will be the charm, Mateo spins around and returns to his father. "I tried."

"That's all I can ever ask of you," Teo says. "Home?"

"Home," Mateo says.

Home is the place where Mateo can be himself, where he can live, live, live.

ORION
3:17 p.m.

The journey is off to a rough start.

First, Valentino and I debate the safest way to get home. I think taking a taxi can get us there sooner, but he's nervous about being in a car after Scarlett's accident, especially on his End Day. I can't knock him. The thing is . . . today might be my End Day too. But I let it go because the certainty of his fate trumps my possibility. Not that that makes me any less nervous about riding the train uptown, since I feel that bastard grim reaper shadowing me again. I got to take some blame, I guess, since I've shown Valentino how dreamy train rides can be with running from car to car like it's a race or traveling through secret subway stations or putting on shows and getting standing ovations.

But when you flip that coin, shit gets real.

As the train exits Manhattan and enters the Bronx, I make sure there's space between us on our bench in the corner. Not so much space that we can be targeted individually, but not so close that we draw attention for being together. I hate talking shit about my home borough, because I love the Bronx, but I can't pretend like we've got our act together, like being gay is going to fly with everyone. In Manhattan, it's way less of a risk to lounge my leg across Valentino's lap and rest my head on his shoulder and kiss him. Here, I've got to keep everything to myself. Our lives could depend on it.

The last few stops are the most intense, they feel like the dwindling hours of an End Day. The closer you're getting to your final destination, the more alert you have to be, not wanting it to all go wrong when you've still got time to get it right.

I feel the tension in my chest, like my heart is being choked out. I'm too scared to even breathe because I might breathe too gay. I know that might sound like overkill to someone, but unless they've done years in the Bronx, I'm not interested in what they have to say. Body language is everything when you're trying to stay alive. Think of all the animals in the wild who will bluff and have you thinking they're tough as fuck when maybe they've never fought for their lives before. Valentino has got muscles, but can he fight? I can fight, but I don't have the muscles to win, so I try to blend in, camouflage like a white-passing rabbit in the snow. That means not drawing attention to myself by holding the hand of the boy I really like. It's heartbreaking to even have these thoughts, but that's where we're at up here.

We hit that last stop and arrive in Mott Haven without any predators lunging at us. I never get cocky in my neighborhood either, because there's always people rolling through who you don't know and they don't know you and everyone is sizing each other up and the wrong person makes moves to come out on top. We pass this one dude who's minding his own business, deep in his beef patty. Then another asks us for the time, and I get nervous because sometimes someone is just trying to get you to whip out your phone so they can steal it. I have Valentino check his watch and tell the dude that it's forty past three.

I know my block isn't much, but I love it. There are flags for Jamaica, Dominican Republic, and Puerto Rico in windows doing double duty as country pride and curtains. There's a *no parking!!!* sign graffitied on a wooden fence, and there are always cars in that driveway; that disrespect has become a running joke with Team Young. I haven't stepped foot inside the Congregational church right by this little park, but I like the castle vibes.

Then there's our brownstone in a row of others, all similar in brick and build but distinct by upkeep, decorations, and door colors. This brownstone has been in Dalma's family for generations, and its outsides could use some love but the inside is bursting with it. I'm so relieved when Valentino and I go up the stairs and make it to the front door that's as red as the Times Square glass benches. I pull out the key that I used to scratch Valentino's name into the bench at the Brooklyn Bridge and unlock the door.

We made it.

We're safe.

And I've brought home a guy for the first time.

He might even be the last.

"I'm here," I shout up the stairs.

There are three levels to the brownstone. Dalma and I have our bedrooms on the ground floor where we also have access to a small backyard plus our own private entrance, though we don't really use it because that hallway is practically a storage unit with bins and boxes and furniture that Dalma plans on refreshing for her room but hasn't gotten around to it. The whole thing is a fire hazard, honestly, and something we should correct ASAP. Dayana, Floyd, and Dahlia have their bedrooms upstairs, and there's also a ladder that leads to the rooftop, where I do my tanning and sunburning.

I lead Valentino through the middle floor and into our living room.

"This place is so nice," Valentino says.

He stops by the wall that has all our family pictures. I love all the casual ones, but I don't really get involved with the professional photo shoots at JCPenney because I always feel like an add-on. Almost like they know they have to invite me so I don't feel weird even though there's no evidence that they're thinking shit like that, I get nothing but love from my guardians. I just know that if I weren't living here, I wouldn't be invited to the studios. So why should I go just because they were forced to take me in? This is something I'm going to be working through for years if I get years to work through things.

Valentino taps my school picture from fifth grade where I wasn't smiling. "Bad day?"

"First school picture without my parents," I say.

"That'll do it."

I had missed picture day in fourth grade because I was out grieving. My mom really loved dressing me up those mornings. Ironing my shirts and making me look grown with ties and spritzing my curls with a personal remedy to give them extra shine. When the samples arrived for my fifth-grade pictures, I sat down with Dayana and let her choose her favorite out of all the different poses—fist under chin, arms crossed, a forced smile, and straight-faced.

"This one feels honest," Dayana had said, choosing the picture up on the wall.

I liked that we weren't bullshitting, especially since that particular picture day was a week after the one-year-anniversary of my parents' death.

There are footsteps coming from upstairs, and I immediately know it's Floyd, who walks around the house as if he's got brick feet. Floyd is in a polo and jeans that are buckled up with the same black belt he uses for all his baggy pants. His brown hair is gelled like usual, even though Dalma woke up everyone in the middle of the night to drive back home before my surgery.

"Hey, garrochón," Floyd says as he shakes my hand. He's got that old-school Puerto Rican vibe where men don't hug that much. My dad was like that a little too. "Glad you're back in one piece."

"You too. Floyd, this is Valentino."

Floyd looks at Valentino a little skeptically. It could come off a little homophobic, not going to lie, but I know it's probably more caution over having a living, breathing Decker in the house. He overcomes it with a handshake. "Nice to meet you, Valentino. I'm sorry for . . . you know."

"Thank you, sir."

"Call me Floyd, please. Come on downstairs."

Before I can ask why everyone's downstairs, Valentino turns to me. "What's a garrochón?"

"Tall and lanky, basically."

"Been calling him that since he was a kid," Floyd says as he goes down the stairs. "By the time he was twelve he was taller than me."

"Not that hard," I say.

Floyd laughs, and he's about to raise his hand like he wants to play-hit me, but we've been beating that habit out of him. Yeah, poor choice of words, my bad. Correction: we've been getting him to cut that shit out because Dayana is extra sensitive to domestic abuse after witnessing her father mistreat her mother. She doesn't want her girls being raised in a home where that shit is a joke, or me picking up on that in my own adulthood.

We get to the ground level, and I tell Valentino not to mind all the furniture, boxes, and bins. That shit has us looking so sloppy, so I rush him into our living area, where Dalma and I have laid out a rainbow rug that's got footprints tracked all over it. I expected to find the fam on the couch watching a movie or something because why else would they be down here, but there's nothing but blankets and throw pillows there.

"Surprise!"

I tense up, and we find the ladies of Team Young out in the tiny backyard with a festive blanket thrown over the fold-out table. Dalma is holding roses, and Dahlia is raising a sign that reads WELCOME VALENTINO! with most of the letters covered in glitter, almost like she ran out of time or glitter, maybe both. Dayana is the first to walk over to Valentino and embrace him in her arms, like a mother.

"It's wonderful to meet you," Dayana says, her palms on his face.

"You too, Ms. Dayana," Valentino says. I'm impressed he got her name right with all these D's in here. "You're already living up to every wonderful thing Orion has said about you."

Dayana pinches my cheek, something she hasn't done in a minute.

"Did you know about this?" Valentino asks.

"Hell no," I say, both blown away and shocked. "Can we maybe chill on surprises when a dude with a heart condition is involved?"

"I texted you," Dalma says.

I check my phone, and she did indeed throw a heads-up my way, but I haven't taken my phone out of my pocket since we've been on the subway or when we were walking over so I wouldn't get robbed. "My bad."

Dalma hands Valentino the roses. "I'm sorry for being so insensitive last night."

"Your heart was in the right place," Valentino says.

"But I went about it wrong. I hope you can forgive me."

Valentino hugs Dalma, and I kind of want to collapse on the couch and cry.

Little Dahlia—I mean, she's thirteen, but she's always going to be Little Dahlia to me even if she's about to be Big Dahlia compared to her father—gives me a hug, and I introduce her to Valentino.

"I'm sorry that you . . . that you're going to . . . you know . . ." Dahlia shakes her head. "Thanks for helping Orion."

"He's the one who's been helping me," Valentino says.

"He better help you, you're giving him a heart!" Dahlia

says with the air of *Duh!* in her voice. She turns to her parents. "Can we give him his presents?"

"Presents?" Valentino asks, following Dahlia to the table.

Dalma stops me. "Hey, I hope this is okay. We thought it would be nice to thank him for everything and show him some family love."

"It's perfect," I say. "Or as perfect as an End Day can be with strangers."

"It seems like you're more than strangers."

Unfortunately-slash-fortunately we are.

However this End Day is destined to close out, it's going to hurt far more than I can possibly imagine.

VALENTINO
3:58 p.m.

The Youngs are treating me like I'm family.

I'm sitting at the head of their dining table with my roses in my lap. In no world would my parents ever give me flowers, not even on Valentine's Day. I can't help but feel like this is my very literal Last Supper without the meal or betrayal. Instead, Dalma comes out of the kitchen with a gift bag. She says it's not much, but I'm already feeling blessed. I toss the tissue paper at Orion and pull out a snow globe of New York City, a taxicab fridge magnet, a pizza key chain, and a small brown bag of dried linguini noodles.

"I will personally cook those for you if you want them," Dalma says.

This feels like the ultimate peace offering. "Tempting, but I'm going to pass."

There's a sad relief in Dalma's eyes. "If you change your mind . . ."

"I'll take you up on that." I shake the snow globe, the white powder showering the miniature Statue of Liberty and silver buildings. "Thank you all so much. This was really sweet of you."

"We wanted to welcome you to the city," Dalma says.

Orion is sitting quietly. I can tell how much this gesture means to him, but it seems to be making him really sad too.

"Where did you move from?" Dahlia asks.

"Phoenix, Arizona," I answer.

"Why'd you move?"

"It wasn't the right fit for me anymore. Like a jacket I outgrew."

"Do you think you wouldn't be dying if you stayed?"

Everyone shouts, "Dahlia!"

"Dahl, that's so rude," Dalma says.

Dahlia shrugs so big it seems exaggerated. "I'm just asking a question!"

I want to ease the tension.

"It's a great question. I've wondered if Death-Cast would've called if I'd never left home. But I'm choosing to believe that staying in Arizona would've ruined my soul and that the one day I've had in the city is the most I've lived in a long time." I tell the family about how I've been spending my End Day. How the rejection at the modeling agency led to us buying a camera at a pawnshop and going on a journey of firsts. All the pictures we've taken for my sister and Orion to remember me by. Walking the High Line. Visiting the World Trade Center's memorial site. Being blindfolded and taken past the secret subway station. The journey across the Brooklyn Bridge. Our performances on the train. Returning to Times Square for a first date that got interrupted. "I can't remember the last time I've done so much in one day." I slide my fingers through Orion's and lock them together, knowing that the family sitting at this table will only look at us with pride and not judgment. "If I stayed in Arizona, I wouldn't have met my first boyfriend."

Orion's eyes widen and he smiles. "Boyfriend?"

"If that's okay with you."

"Hell yeah, boyfriend."

We kiss.

Dahlia whispers, "But they just met!" and Dalma whispers back, "Shut up!" and Orion and I break our kiss, laughing along with everyone else.

Together, Orion and I share more intimate details about my End Day and how we've navigated what was safe to do and what was worth a little risk. Dahlia wants to know how bad Orion's dancing was on the train; we let the tips between our performances speak for themselves. Dalma thanks me for keeping Orion company at the World Trade Center site. Orion tries talking about it, but he doesn't get much out. Dayana comes to the rescue with stories about growing up with Magdalena while Floyd talks about the epic World

Series parties that Ernesto would host whenever the Yankees were playing.

"I'm sorry to hear about Scarlett," Dalma says. "Any chance she'll make it out?"

"I'm not counting on it," I painfully admit. Today is about acceptance. Orion has encouraged me to control what I can and accept what I can't. "I'm having a really lovely time with you, but would you mind if I actually called Scarlett? I'm feeling really inspired to set some things straight with my family after being welcomed by yours."

"Do you mean . . . ?" Orion asks.

"Yes."

I'm going to call my parents and tell them it's my End Day.

4:36 p.m.

Coming out as gay was one thing. Coming out as a Decker is another.

I came out as gay to Scarlett our first moment alone while she was recovering at the hospital. "I love you, Val" was all Scarlett said out loud, and her knowing gaze said everything else. I'd wanted to come out to my parents that afternoon too, but they spent so much time praying at my sister's bedside that I knew I should wait. A couple days after Scarlett was home, I knew I had to make my move so I could get everyone to adjust to our new normal instead of returning to our old normal, where I had to be closeted. I sat my parents down in the living room and came right out with false confidence. It was tricky to tell if they already knew. I had thought about all the times my father would say "He's a queer" as an insult or how my mother suspected any single older man must be gay if they weren't married with children. There weren't any knowing gazes from my parents like there were with my sister. But there were lectures—lots and lots of lectures with the headline being that I'm doomed to damnation if I choose sinning over Christ.

Will my parents still tell me I'm going to hell once they discover it's my End Day?

I'll get my answer soon.

I called Scarlett a few minutes ago, and she supports my choice to let our parents know. I don't know how she would have dealt with this if I hadn't come to this decision myself. As far as I'm concerned, she's their favorite, but would they have held a grudge against her for not telling them it was my End Day? We'll never have to find out, I suppose.

I'm upstairs in the brownstone's living room, next to the internet modem so I'll have a stronger signal for the Skype call with Scarlett and our parents. Orion props his laptop on top of this corner desk, its cord plugged into an outlet because it'll die if it's not charging. The desktop background is cluttered with Microsoft Word documents with file names like *Watch Me Watch You* and *Golden Heart* and *Life Hostage* and *Never Right, Always Left*.

"You've written so many stories," I say.

"They're all just drafts," Orion says, drawing the curtain and allowing light in.

"It's still a lot."

"I just get in and get out. I don't even correct typos."

"Only your eyes have been on them. Do you think . . . Are you still only wanting your eyes on your stories? It's okay if so."

Orion smiles. "I'd love for you to be my first reader."

I squeeze his hand before looking back at the laptop. "Thanks. That'll be a nice reward for getting through this call."

"You sure you don't need anything else? I can hang around if you want, I don't have to appear on camera or anything like that. I can just be close if you want me close."

I get up and pull Orion into a hug; I like that I've lost count of how many times we've hugged. It means we're making up for lost time and time that will be lost. "You've been here with me every step of the way today. I need to walk this path myself."

Orion kisses me. "You got this, Valentino."

He returns downstairs as I sit back at the desk and log on to Skype. It always takes forever to start up, but my call to Scarlett manages to get through.

Scarlett is back in her bedroom, using our mother's Dell laptop with the blurry webcam since her own belongings are still stuck on the first plane. Her mascara has stained her cheeks, but she's not crying at the moment. "Hey, Val."

"Hey, Scar."

We don't say anything for a while. We're too lost in how unbelievable this is.

I look at her scars, so grateful she's still alive, and I hope it stays that way.

"Do they know why you're home?" I ask.

"Only that I couldn't get a flight out because of Death-Cast."

"I'm sure they loved that."

"They called the pilot's heart attack a coincidence. I'm still hoping they're right."

It's telling that I could die on this webcam and my parents still wouldn't believe Death-Cast predicted my fate the same way Scarlett will ultimately come to terms with it. Thankfully, I'm not trying to convince anyone that I'm going to die today. I just need to get some things off my chest. There's also the matter of the morbid segue about how I need to get something out of my chest too.

"Scar, there's something else you should know."

She's immediately alarmed as if I finally have some medical diagnosis that will lead to my death. "What?"

"It's a good thing. If I die, my heart will be donated to Orion."

Scarlett has the saddest smile. "That's really beautiful."

"Hopefully Death-Cast is wrong, and I can personally introduce you two. Just know that I was always willing to give him my heart even when he was a really nice stranger, and now more than ever I'm proud that I'm going to have played a big role in helping my extraordinary boyfriend live on."

Her hands press against her own heart. "I'm excited to hang out with you and your boyfriend."

"I'd love that."

I don't think Scarlett and I will have a traditional goodbye. Not when she's still holding on to hope that she's going to see me tomorrow.

I'll have to find another way to say everything I have to say to my favorite person.

"I'm ready," I say.

Scarlett carries the laptop into the living room, where Mom and Dad are on the couch rewatching *It's a Wonderful Life* with their fans blowing. Scarlett grabs the remote and turns off the TV.

"What are you doing?" Dad asks.

"Put the movie back on," Mom says.

She sets the laptop down on my father's ottoman. "Valentino needs to talk to you."

My parents stare at me. Mom is wearing her bathrobe with her planner in her lap. She's the only person I know who manages to see those planners through to the end. Dad is in a white shirt tucked into gray shorts while snacking on those Royal Dansk Danish cookies straight out of their blue tin. They're both quiet, even though there's plenty they can say. They can ask me about my flight. How I'm settling in. Even thank me for getting out of their house. But they look away as if their movie has resumed playing. I don't necessarily want to see them later if all they're going to do is repeat the same behavior that made me uncomfortable in the very house I grew up in.

I'm about to ask Scarlett to return to her room with the laptop so we can spend this valuable time talking instead, but I'm not going to be driven away again.

I'm going to live a first—the first time I talk openly about my life.

"New York has been a roller coaster, thanks for asking. Have you been following all the Death-Cast news? Did you hear about the shooting that happened in Times Square? I was one of the people who got shot at, which was especially scary because it happened moments after Death-Cast called to tell me I'm going to die."

They both turn to the screen like they can't control themselves, like magnetism.

"You're probably wondering why this is news to you since I've known since midnight. It's because I was willing to die without telling you because I don't believe you care about my life. I am your only son. Your firstborn. The reason you became parents, and you never even tried to love me once I told you I'm gay."

They both wince, like I've said a bad word. Like I'm bad.

"There will come a time when you have to reckon with how you made me so unwelcomed that I moved away. But I want to thank you for being so unloving because it pushed me out of your house and into the arms of a boy with the biggest heart. He's made sure my last day on this planet is filled with the love and kindness I deserve, and I'm going to spend what's left of my life with him even if that means I'm going to hell when it's all done."

ORION
5:05 p.m.

My boyfriend—yeah, boyfriend. And what!—is in my house.

This is still blowing my mind.

I wouldn't have ever put down money on meeting someone who goes from "boy" to "boyfriend" in under a day. I should bet on myself some more. Last night, I swore Valentino was so out of my league, and I'm not knocking him now when I say that he isn't. I'm just showing myself some love because I showed up for a stranger who needed some himself without expecting anything in return; I wasn't even in it for the heart. We're in the same league—except when it comes to train performances obviously—and I'm just as great and dope as he is, and we would've done even more great and dope things if we had the time to be great and dope together but the sun is going down and that means it's almost lights out.

I'm getting stressed, feeling like I should Decker-proof

459

the house for Valentino and everyone else: get all the cords off the floor, maybe even unplug everything that's unnecessary; quadruple-check that the smoke alarms have working batteries; clear the hallway for emergency exits; place cushions at the bottom of each stairway in case anyone falls; and barricade the windows to protect us against intruders. All I would be doing is delaying the inevitable when instead I can be living with Valentino while I can. I took the time to finish cleaning my bedroom and setting it up for something great, something that I think might be the relaxer he needs after what's got to be a tough conversation with his family.

I've thanked my people a thousand times for showing up for Valentino like that and hitting him with the love that his own parents wouldn't give him.

"Okay, all done," I say, rejoining everyone at the table.

"He's going to love it," Dalma says.

"I hope so." I rap my knuckles against the table. "Seriously, thanks for everything."

A thousand and one.

"It's our pleasure," Dayana says. She checks her watch. "What timeline are we looking at here?"

"I don't know. I'm not going to force him out."

Floyd sits up. "Absolutely. No one is asking you to march Valentino to his death."

"Please don't start doing it now. We haven't even heard back from Dr. Emeterio—"

"Orion, hear us out," Dayana says. "We love you and want the best for you."

"Then don't try to get me to cut his End Day short."

"We want to increase all of your days, garrochón," Floyd says. "Death-Cast is providing us with a unique opportunity to get you the care you need, but there's a lot of preparation that needs to go into it too."

"That shit can go wrong now," I say.

"Language," Dayana says, looking at Dahlia as if she's not cursing behind their backs.

"Look, I might not be an official Decker, but I could die tonight too. Are you going to feel good if we rush Valentino's death and I also die?"

Everyone is quiet, and Dalma is fighting back words, but just like the middle of the night at the hospital, she loses against herself. "This isn't about us, Orion. You and Valentino have formed this really beautiful relationship, and it's heartbreaking that you won't have more time together. But how are you going to feel if Valentino dies in vain and then you do too?"

I'm pretty damn close to being a smart-ass and telling her I won't feel anything because I'll be dead, but I stay shut because everyone's heart is in the right place and they're just trying to swap out mine for Valentino's. They don't get how hard it's going to be to live because of Valentino and without him. How every heartbeat is going to be him whispering for the rest of my life. I just don't want to hear him telling me from beyond the grave that I pushed him to die so I can live.

Valentino is coming down the stairs, and I rise to meet him at the door. He's carrying my laptop, and the closer he gets, the louder his cries become. I open my arms for a hug instead of clenching my fists like I want to because I'm so pissed that even with death on the horizon his parents couldn't get their shit together. Valentino doesn't come in for the hug, he tosses the laptop on the couch and grabs my face and kisses me. It's not passionate like the first one on the Brooklyn Bridge, which is great because I don't care that my family can see us but I'm not ready for them to watch me go in like that either. Valentino is kissing me like I've given him a present.

"You okay?" I ask, breathing. "How'd it go?"

"They said nothing, but I did. Everything I needed to."

"I'm happy for you. And your parents can kick rocks and—"

"I don't wish ill on them, Orion. Telling them that I'm willing to go to hell to live my life was all I needed to win."

"You said you'd go to hell? That's some king shit."

He wipes his tears. "I'll probably regret that if hell is real."

"Yeah, that'll bite you in the ass. Hell sounds hot."

"Can't be worse than an Arizona heatwave."

"But for real. How'd you leave things? They really didn't say anything?"

"Not a single word, Orion. I honestly thought they would

apologize or tell me they love me or even something snotty about how this is what I get for going against God. But the silence started hurting even more, so I hung up. I thought it'd be better to cry in private."

I wish I had been upstairs with Valentino the second that first tear dropped. I hate the idea of him crying alone, but he didn't need me in his space and face. Valentino is a survivor who needed some help on his End Day, but always had that resilience in his heart and bones.

I grab his hand and lead him back outside, where there's a loving family waiting for him. He doesn't offer a ton more details than he did me, but they're ready to go to war on his behalf too.

Dayana looks nauseated from this story. "I love God, but God would never come between me and my children. If your parents had a healthier relationship with God, it wouldn't have to."

"It means a lot to hear that," Valentino says.

"I'm sorry you're not hearing it from your own mother and father," Dayana says.

"Do they know about . . . about me?" I ask. Then I realize how I sound. "Not about me like as a person, like as your friend—boyfriend. I meant about the transplant stuff."

"They don't know about that," Valentino says. "But they know about you."

"You sure you stuck around long enough to make sure

they didn't have heart attacks?"

"That's dark," Dalma says.

"I can make that joke, the heart attackers are my community."

Dayana stands. "Okay, everyone up and out. Let's give the boys some privacy." She shoos Dalma, Floyd, and Dahlia upstairs.

But Dalma comes back around. "O-Bro . . ."

That's all she says before leaving us downstairs, closing the door behind her. But I know what she's telling me to do.

Well, what not to do.

Don't let Valentino die in vain.

But first things first: a couple more firsts.

VALENTINO
5:23 p.m.

"Welcome to the O-Zone," Orion says, opening the door to his bedroom.

"Great name," I say, my heart pounding as I step inside this cozy bedroom with air blowing from his rotating fan. The walls are painted a light gray, almost white. Thumb-tacked above his wooden desk are pictures of Orion with his parents. The one window offers a view into the backyard where the table is empty with everyone back upstairs. Behind me is Orion's twin-size bed made up with a white comforter, just like mine was in Arizona. Except on top of his bed is also a black-and-gray plaid blanket with his phone, my camera, two champagne glasses, and a white candle resting on a tray.

"What's all that?"

"We never got to have a proper first date," Orion says, taking my hand and leading me to the bed. "I thought we could have it here."

465

"So you literally get in bed on the first date."

Orion laughs. "Only if I like the guy."

"Good for you."

"Good for us."

He acts as if he's striking a match and fake-lights the candle.

"I hope that candle doesn't fall over and set the bed on fire," I say.

"Hard same, that would suck."

We sit against the wall, holding hands and our empty champagne glasses.

"I take it we're not drinking anything," I say.

"Who said that?" Orion sips nothing and then sighs like he's had water for the first time in ages. "Oh man, I really needed that."

I drink air out of my glass. "That was really good."

"No, no, no, no, no, no. You totally faked your way through that."

"As opposed to?"

"Living your way through it."

This is my End Day, and all I've had today is black tea because of the potential surgery, but as I raise the glass to my lips again, I think about all the things I'd want to drink one last time if I could: iced tea with lots of lemon; a root beer float from a diner; the green shakes and vanilla protein smoothies I loved making in the mornings; apple juice that reminds me of sharing sippy cups with Scarlett as kids; and gallons and gallons of water. I'm still really dehydrated when I'm done with this little exercise, but I'm full on the memories of these little things I took for granted. I release a deep breath that's satisfying to Orion.

"Great start to our first date," I say.

"It gets better—I hope."

"If you're thinking what I'm thinking—"

"Oh, I'm thinking what you're thinking, but I'm also thinking about how nervous I am to read you one of my stories."

"The story is what I was thinking about. What else were you thinking about?"

Orion looks into my eyes before he realizes I'm teasing. "I hate you."

"No, you don't."

"No, I don't."

There's a tension between us before Orion grabs his phone. "I wrote this before I knew you, but it was about a heart transplant."

Orion begins reading me his short story "Golden Heart," the same one I saw on the desktop of his laptop. It's not a comedy, but I can't help but laugh when Orion says the main character's name is Orionis. But it gets darker when Death starts aging Orionis's heart and he can only stay alive if Orionis dances with him. His life became this never-ending dance with Death, one he was ready to be over because living like that wasn't life at all. Then he comes across an elderly man with a golden heart who was living carefree and doing everything Orionis couldn't do. But it was breaking his heart to watch Orionis so miserable, just as mine breaks for Orion. The elder gives Orionis his heart as I will for Orion.

Orion closes his phone. "That's the end."

"It's heavy and happy."

"Yeah. I didn't think it could get sadder except for the fact that you don't get to live as long as the elder."

"That's sad, but that's not the saddest part. The elder didn't even know Orionis. I got to spend the day with the person who will have my heart."

"Big facts. I like knowing that I'm not being powered by a total shithead."

Orion is trying to hide behind humor. I think we're reaching that point. That point where we know we're going to have to say goodbye.

I grab his hand.

"Do you think that you'll write about me?"

"There won't be enough words, but you're giving me the time to try to find them."

I pull Orion into my lap and we stare at each other.

"Thanks for welcoming me into the O-Zone."

"Thanks for walking into my life."

"Thanks for saving mine."

"Thanks for saving mine," Orion repeats.

We kiss like it's a challenge to see how long we can before death breaks us apart.

Then as we get more excited, we give in to a special first for both of us.

I flip Orion to the bed, and he fakes concern over the unlit candle but he's speechless when I lift off my shirt. His fingers trail down from my collarbone and through my pecs and trace my abs before unbuttoning my pants. It's much smoother than me wrestling with his skinny jeans that cling to his legs for dear life. But once we're both fully naked, we stare at each other with the biggest smiles.

"Best day ever," I say.

"Best motherfucking day ever," Orion says.

Then we move as if the world could end in the next minute.

He passes me a condom, and I slide it on and slowly move inside him, and it feels so good that I can't believe I'm only going to be able to experience this once.

The only thing I can do is no different from what I've done all day: live in the moment.

Our hands are pressed to each other's beating hearts as Orion and I continue living this incredible first together.

PART FOUR
THE END

On behalf of everyone here at Death-

Cast, we are sorry to lose you.

—Joaquin Rosa, creator of Death-Cast

ORION
6:06 p.m.

That first time was better than I could've imagined—and I'm a fucking writer!

Seriously, I'm surprised I survived it. I'm not saying the sex was wild or anything like that, it's just been tricky dealing with all these hormones as my heart stuff worsens. I was starting to swear sex was going to be too risky, like skydiving or rock climbing. I'm not interested in jumping out of planes or scaling mountains, but sex has always been pretty high on my to-do list, and Valentino was the perfect first partner. It was slow, like I always thought it would be, and he checked in on me every step of the way, never trying to rush through it even though the clock is ticking louder and louder on his End Day. He wanted to live in that first time as long as I did, and it's as if we turned minutes into hours.

But real talk, we're talking minutes here.

Some of my favorite minutes ever.

Now, I'm showering down the hall from my bedroom, wanting to get back to Valentino. The whole time I'm rinsing my hair and body I'm torn between memories of how good everything felt and how bad everything will feel when he's gone.

Something that's only just beginning will be ending just as soon as it started.

His death can happen at any moment.

It could be happening right now.

It could have happened already.

The thought of Valentino being dead in my bedroom scares me.

I get out of the shower, barely drying off even with the sudden memory of Valentino busting his ass this morning at his apartment because he was dripping from his own shower, and I remember that I'm not in the clear yet either, that today could be my End Day too, but I can't stop myself from needing to see him alive, alive, alive, alive, alive. I open my bedroom door, and Valentino is sitting at my desk and talking into the camera.

Or he was talking into the camera until I busted in like the house is on fire.

"What's going on?" Valentino asks, fear in his blue eyes.

"Nothing, nothing." I almost drop the towel wrapped around my waist, which wouldn't be the end of the world now that we've seen every inch of each other. "I wanted to make sure you were okay. I had a bad feel— I got nervous."

Valentino lets out a deep breath and sits. "I'm okay. I'm just recording a message for Scarlett. Something for her to have after I'm . . ." A small, knowing nod. "Do you mind if I finish? I need a minute."

"Take your time," I say. Then: "And don't die." Then-then: "You know what I mean!"

I leave my bedroom, and I'm half tempted to punch myself in the mouth so I can't say anything stupid again. Instead, I return to my bathroom, where I towel-dry my curls because a hair-dryer feels too risky now that my own fate is up in the air again; I'm not trying to get electrocuted. I change into fresh jeans, a bit baggier than my last pair so I won't have to fight my way out of them. And on top of my undershirt I put on Valentino's gray button-down he's been wearing, breathing in the collar that smells citrusy, kind of like his hoodie. If Valentino has a problem with me wearing it, then he's going to have to wrestle it off me, and then maybe he dies or we die together because of a fight over a shirt that I want to keep like a championship belt, like a trophy that will always remind me of the victories on this End Day.

I step on a towel and drag it from the bathroom to my bedroom, drying the puddles.

Then I knock on my bedroom door, which feels weird. "You good?"

Every millisecond he doesn't answer I get nervous.

"Come in," he says after one whole second, alive and well. I open the door and he smiles when he sees me in his button-down. "It's a good look on you."

"You wear it best, but I want to keep it, and you should know I'm willing to fight you to the death."

Valentino rises from the desk and pulls me into a kiss. "It's all yours," he says after.

He seems content in his *Have a Happy End Day!* shirt, though I invite him to raid my closet again now that I've robbed him. He goes through my hoodies as I do some cleaning up—condom and wrapper in my small trash, socks and underwear and skinny jeans in my hamper.

"All good with your message?" I ask Valentino.

"I think so," Valentino says as he slips on an ordinary gray hoodie. "It's not like I have a lot of time to get it right."

"I'm sure Scarlett will love it, even if you just sat there in silence."

"You're probably right."

I begin making my bed. Somehow, it's going to feel so empty without Valentino, even though I only shared it with him once. Grief is a sneaky son of a bitch, trying to knock me out before Valentino is even down for the count. I'm not having much success with tucking the fitted sheets under the mattress, I always get this shit wrong. Then Valentino comes to the rescue, and it's the millionth reminder that he won't be around to help make my bed, to hold me close, to ask how I'm doing.

"We should get going, Orion."

I try speaking, but I can't. I'm not ready for this to be over.

"I thought we could share one last first," Valentino says.

"Don't say our first last goodbye or anything like that."

Valentino holds up the camera. "First stroll down memory lane?"

"I'd love that," I breathe.

"I thought we could do it at my place. Then I can leave the camera behind for Scarlett and we can go straight to the hospital after. Hopefully Dr. Emeterio has figured out something for me . . ."

That something being a peaceful way to die versus whatever else awaits him.

But I'm not giving life to those nightmares. I'm going to live the dream.

"Take me home, Valentino."

FRANKIE DARIO

6:24 p.m.

This day can't get any worse.

First, that Decker tenant of his went off and died, killing Frankie's dreams.

Then his wife's best friend quit his job at Death-Cast, making himself useless to Frankie in the future.

And then Joaquin Rosa went on air and admitted that his company isn't the godsend he claimed it is, ruining Frankie's chances of capturing the shock of any Deckers who survive.

Frankie feels stuck, as if he's unable to evict himself from this life the way he can tenants in his building. He wishes he could get rid of everyone. That way he could go hide out on the first floor whenever Gloria is getting on his nerves; he'd essentially be living downstairs with that in mind. This building . . . why couldn't his father leave him a better legacy to inherit, like a Fortune 500 company? Instead, Frankie has to deal with unclogging pipes and burning himself on radiators and being made out to be the bad guy because other people can't pay their bills on time. How is that his fault? Pay up or get out. This isn't a homeless shelter.

Frankie is watching the evening news in his living room, where the topic is Death-Cast. Surprise, surprise. His apartment door has remained open since the morning, even when his downstairs tenant decided to blast some bachata this afternoon; he was ready to put an eviction notice on her door just because. But Frankie has been hoping that maybe Valentino Prince somehow survived this deep into his final day, though that seems unlikely given how the newscasters are talking about Death-Cast's successful predictions among the registered users they did call. Still, he keeps his door open, knowing that there's less than six hours before midnight.

A lot can happen in that time.

The lobby door all the way downstairs slams shut, a complaint often made by the first-floor tenants, and Frankie continues claiming he'll get around to it and never does and hopes he never has to. Could it be Valentino? Then he recognizes the fast footsteps running up the stairs and he sighs in response.

Paz runs inside. "Dad! Dad! Dad!"

"Yes?" Frankie asks.

"I booked the commercial! I film next week!"

Frankie turns to his son, not giving him his full attention but just enough. How is it possible—how is it fair?—that a child continues getting closer to his dreams than his own father? First it was a small role in that movie, and now it'll be some commercial, and next it'll be a starring role in some TV show. Why is the world ready to show this child more love than a man who has done his time, who has worked hard, who has hustled?

"Good job" is all Frankie says.

"It was so fun," Paz says, plopping down on the couch next to him. "Then we all went to get ice cream. I got a brain freeze."

All?

Frankie can hear Gloria's keys jingling as she climbs the stairs slowly, like usual, as if she's walking up some steep mountain. He will punch a wall if she ever complains about the elevator not working again. He'll also punch a wall, maybe even Gloria herself, if she doesn't have a good answer as to who was hanging around his son today.

Then he hears the man's voice. It's Rolando.

Why are they together?

If she's having an affair, so help them . . .

Hell, Frankie has cheated on Gloria a few times with the broad on the third floor, but that was different. Gloria has no idea, and Frankie would never flaunt that in her face. But bringing Rolando into his home? As if Frankie hasn't voiced a thousand times to Gloria that he doesn't fully trust Rolando only has friendship on the brain?

For the first time since this morning, Frankie is very tempted to slam the door shut—right in Rolando's face.

VALENTINO

6:27 p.m.

Why walk toward your own death when you can drive?

Floyd is driving us down the FDR, a ten-minute journey between his house and my building. But there's a catch: I'm alone in the backseat of the van as Orion sits shotgun. It's a safety decision and one I chose to respect when I got in the car and accepted this generous offer.

Transportation is really tricky on an End Day.

Orion and I tried leaving for the subway, but his family wouldn't allow us. There were too many risks between here and the station, and then the train ride itself presented its own dangers. I thought we could take a taxi, but his guardians didn't trust any drivers, especially since just last week Floyd had to provide medical attention to a cabbie who was responsible for the accident. What if fate was cruel enough to put that man behind the wheel again with us in the backseat? Floyd volunteered to drive but refused to let Dayana, Dalma, and Dahlia get in the car too. He tried suggesting there wasn't enough space for all of us, but it's a van. Everyone could fit. I just know he doesn't want to risk their lives. I'm sure he wishes Orion were in Dayana's car with the girls, but the best he could do was suggest Orion sit up front with him to help navigate a freeway that has been a pretty straight shot.

I'm not upset. I want Orion close to the airbags. The best protection I have back here are comforters and bedding and pillows that Dayana has given me to leave behind for Scarlett. Now Scarlett won't have to sleep under my clothes like I did with Orion.

I love that memory. The first time I shared a bed with a boy.

I reach over as best as my seat belt allows and hold on to Orion's shoulder like it's the edge of a cliff. He turns and kisses my knuckles before covering them with his hand.

The entire ride has been quiet. There's already a level of care that goes into driving without factoring in a confirmed Decker in the backseat. I'm sure Floyd is nervous that this act of kindness he's showing me can lead to everyone's deaths. Orion is paying attention to his side-view mirror for any rogue cars that might spin out of control.

No matter what happens, I still can't help but feel like I'm in a hearse, being driven to my funeral even though my heart is still beating.

ORION
6:30 p.m.

My phone rings, and for a second I feel like I can't answer it, as if I'm the one driving the car and not someone sitting shotgun. Floyd's got those steel nerves thankfully. I check my phone, and it's not Dalma or Scarlett calling. It's a number I don't know.

"Hello?"

"Hi, I'm calling to speak with Orion Pagan. This is Dr. Emeterio from Lenox Hill."

"Oh my god, hey! It's me."

"How are you?"

"I'm okay, I'm really good, actually."

"Does that mean Valentino is still alive?"

"Yeah, we're together right now." I look over my shoulder and tell Valentino that it's Dr. Emeterio on the phone. "So what's up?"

"Is it possible to speak with Valentino?"

THE END

"Totally." I pass the phone back to Valentino.

I'm trying to figure out if Dr. Emeterio calling is a good thing or bad thing. I watch Valentino from the rearview mirror, hoping to get a spoiler of some sort. He's just saying, "Yeah" and "No" and "Uh-huh" and then finally, "Thank you, Doctor. I'll see you soon." That doesn't tell me shit either, we were already planning on going back to the hospital.

Valentino meets my eyes in the rearview mirror.

And smiles.

And nods.

And tears up.

"The board approved the surgery," Valentino says.

It would be a bad idea for my heart to explode right now, but I'm bursting with happiness.

We can't save his life, but we can hook him up with a gentler death.

Death-Cast for the win.

GLORIA DARIO
6:34 p.m.

Gloria has lived too much of her life in fear.

There was the first time Frankie laid a hand on her, furious after losing money during fantasy football, as if Gloria had been the one who drafted the players on his team. Then Frankie beat Gloria when she was pregnant so bad that she was bleeding and thought her child may have been killed by his father. There was also the time Frankie's temper was igniting, over something Gloria has forgotten about, only remembering how she ran out of the bathroom in nothing but a towel and grabbed three-year-old Pazito and hid in a neighbor's apartment as Frankie tried finding her, a puddle building around her bare feet as she clamped her hand over Pazito's mouth so he wouldn't respond to his father as he called out his name, like the worst game of hide-and-seek. And Gloria certainly can't forget about when she was out late for Rolando's birthday, and how Frankie wanted her home sooner and sought her out when she didn't answer her cell phone, as if she was in bed with Rolando, something her heart has called for many times before but she never acted on it because she wanted to be better than Frankie, who had no problems cheating on her—as if she didn't know about the neighbor downstairs. When Frankie demanded she get in the cab, Gloria refused, seeing how furious he was. But Frankie left the cab like it was a cage and hurled himself on Gloria like a wild animal, attacking her in public, in front of Pazito, who cried from the backseat. Hospitalized while Frankie only spent one night in prison, Gloria was scared she might die.

And now, Gloria must do what she fears most.

Leave.

This is the only escape.

The only way out is through, as Robert Frost says.

Gloria goes through, stepping into her apartment for what could be the last time. The door is still propped open, and Pazito is sitting with Frankie, who pays Rolando no mind as he enters with Gloria.

"Hi," Gloria says. A more astute husband would know something is up already. Gloria and Frankie never greet each other. She sets down her bag on the small kitchen table, ready to slip out of her shoes when she remembers she won't be staying long. She can track all the footprints around the apartment that she wants. It will be Frankie's mess to clean for once. "How was your day?"

Frankie grunts. "I told you Death-Cast wasn't the future," he says to Rolando without looking at him. "You sure you weren't fired?"

"I quit," Rolando says.

Gloria can sense that Rolando wants to say more, to challenge Frankie, but all that will do is sour his mood even more. She nods at Rolando, who takes his cue and walks toward Pazito's bedroom.

"Come show me your new train set," Rolando says.

Pazito hops off the couch with the biggest smile and runs into his room. Rolando exchanges an *I'm here for you* glance with Gloria before closing the door behind him.

The fear continues to rise in Gloria, the way hot air does in this building. But soon enough Gloria will be back outside and able to breathe as a free woman. She doesn't sit even though her feet are tired. She wants to appear tall where she is not, and strong like she's always been.

"Frankie, we need to talk."

"About what?"

"I'm unhappy. You are too."

Frankie doesn't look unhappy. There's a fury in his eyes that Gloria has seen time and time again. She flinches off his stare alone, remembering how quickly he can go from being still to on top of her.

"Don't speak for me," Frankie says.

THE END

"You don't speak for yourself," Gloria says. "And I don't ever speak for myself either."

"Then get to the point. What are you saying?"

"I want a divorce."

These are the words she has imagined herself saying for so long, but she cannot believe they're coming out of her mouth now. She almost wishes she could suck them back in, but the words have taken flight and so must she if she's to be free.

Frankie looks murderous before turning to the bedroom door, behind which the biggest parts of Gloria's heart can be found.

"Is it because of him?"

"It's because of me."

The chair gets kicked out from under Frankie's feet, spinning toward the TV set.

Gloria wishes Death-Cast was functioning as promised so she'd know who will make it out of this apartment alive.

489

VALENTINO
6:37 p.m.

Everything is going according to plan.

We arrive at my building safely, parking outside with Dayana's car behind. Everyone steps out onto the curb, and we release this collective sigh of relief. Floyd keeps a watch on the block as people are partying across the street in the bar, as if someone might drunkenly stumble over here and pick a fight. Dahlia goes to the pizzeria and breathes it in, asking Dayana for a slice with pepperoni. Dalma seems nervous, and I'm tempted to invite her inside so she can see everything will be okay, but I really want some alone time with Orion.

"It's loud," Dalma says.

"I love it," I say.

Orion has the pillows in his arms and I carry the bedding. "Should we go up?"

Dayana checks her phone. "Back down by seven, okay?"

"How long is that?" Orion asks.

"Twenty-one minutes."

"That's not enough time."

She looks at her phone again. "Now it's twenty minutes. Your time keeps going down, so you should hurry up."

I reach for my keys, now sporting the pizza key chain Orion's family gave me.

"We should buzz Frankie just to be dicks," Orion says.

"Maybe on the way out."

I unlock the lobby door, and it slams closed behind us. We begin shuffling up the steps.

"I'm sorry if that ride was weird," Orion says from behind me.

"Not at all. Floyd was only trying to keep you alive."

"Keeping you alive too."

"I'm sorry for endangering everyone by existing."

"Shut up, that's not how I feel. I just wish I could've been sitting back there with you. I felt like we were being pushed away because of PDA or some shit like that."

At the top of the first landing, I stop. "Like this?"

I kiss him, happy to have our lips reunited again like we are.

"Like that," Orion says. "Can you hook me up with a kiss on each floor?"

"What a great incentive to stay alive."

We continue up.

"I missed you while I was sitting up front, FYI," Orion says.

"Same. Holding you calmed me down a bit."

"What a coincidence, I also calmed down when you were holding me."

Second landing, second kiss.

Someone's cooking on this floor has my stomach growling. I don't even know what it is.

"That smells amazing," I say.

"For real."

"What's the first thing you're going to eat after the surgery?" I ask.

"Isn't that kind of torturous to talk about?"

"It'll be over soon anyway," I say with a lightness in my voice.

"You choose for me," Orion says.

It's hard to think because at this point I would eat this dirty banister or a human foot. "You got to have some linguini, of course."

"No doubt, no doubt."

"Mashed potatoes drowned in gravy. Roasted carrots. Steamed spinach. Macaroni and cheese that's baked to the point it's burnt."

"I might have to break that up over a couple meals."

Third landing, third kiss.

Someone is arguing upstairs. That noise problem won't be mine for much longer. I'm relieved that I did all my recording back in Orion's so I won't have that in the background, even if loud neighbors are a classic New York staple.

"I'm excited to see these pictures," I say.

"Which ones are you most hyped to see?" Orion asks.

A different memory rises as I go up each step.

Outside the pawnshop.

My first time buying a copy of the *New York Times* before realizing my connection to the cover shot of Joaquin Rosa on the phone.

Up on the High Line with Orion.

The memorial site.

The Brooklyn Bridge.

Everything on the train where we put on a show for the ages.

Kissing Orion in Times Square.

They're all winners.

"The High Line," I decide at the top of the stairs, right as I hear a clattering from above that I can't make out and don't concern myself with because I'm happy in this memory. "It's our first photo together. I want to see how it came out."

"I bet you look amazing, and I look like shit."

Fourth landing, fourth kiss.

"I'm sure you look great too."

"I said amazing! Once again, in trying to compliment me, you downgrade me."

I laugh. "I'm sorry, my amazing boyfriend! You are amazing and I'm sure you look amazing and everything about you is amazing and I'm not amazing enough for you! Are we amazing again?"

"Yeah, sure, sure, sure, we're amazing again, my great boyfriend."

"I could kick you down these stairs," I say, halfway up the fifth flight.

"I'll just land on my pillow. But for real, I wouldn't mind the break. You chose poorly moving into a sixth-floor walk-up."

"I was told there'd be an elevator."

"If you knew me sooner I could've checked that shit out for you."

"Add that to the list of why I wish I could time-travel."

Fifth floor, fifth kiss.

"This moment isn't so bad," Orion says.

This one isn't.

FRANKIE DARIO
6:40 p.m.

Frankie is going to kill Rolando.

He considers grabbing the gun from his closet, but a bullet is too merciful. He wants to personally beat Rolando to death. There are any number of ways to do that: the leg of the chair that just popped off as it crashed into the TV's entertainment center, the TV itself, the boots by the door, the defrosted ham Gloria was supposed to cook for dinner, a kitchen knife, some good strikes with the ring of keys. His fists will do the trick just fine too.

"Rolando, get out here!"

"What are you doing?" Gloria asks.

Frankie points his finger at his wife—at the woman who no longer wants to be his wife. "You brought this man into my house, so let's see how much of a man he is." The door opens, and Rolando steps out. Paz tries following him, but Rolando nudges him back into his room. Rolando turns to Gloria.

"Don't look at my wife!"

"You need to calm down," Rolando says.

"You don't make the rules in my house!"

"We're all happy to leave your house."

Frankie begins closing the space between himself and Rolando. "You can get the fuck out of my house, but you're not leaving with my family!"

"I am not your property," Gloria says, getting in between the two men.

Frankie shoves Gloria into Rolando's arms. "Then you can both get out of here! But Paz isn't going anywhere!"

He has no interest in being a single father, but he'll be damned if another man raises his son.

"Where I go, Pazito goes!" Gloria shouts, brushing her hair out of her face.

"Over my dead body!" Frankie says.

He takes his first swing.

VALENTINO

6:41 p.m.

Orion holds his chest and takes a deep breath. "How's your heart doing because mine—"

The shouting becomes clearer at the top of the sixth floor. It's Frankie.

"You can get the fuck out of my house, but you're not leaving with my family!"

A woman says something, maybe about property?

"Then you can both get out of here! But Paz isn't going anywhere!"

"Where I go, Pazito goes!"

"Over my dead body!"

Then there's a clap, like flesh on flesh, and a thud.

The woman screams "HELP!" before crying out in pain.

I drop the bedding, shaking in fear.

Everything in my heart tells me this is going to be the moment I've been dreading, but nothing stops me from racing up those steps.

"Valentino, no!"

"Stay back, Orion!"

I get to the sixth landing without a sixth kiss.

Frankie's apartment door is open. He's on top of a man pummeling him with nothing but his fists and a woman—I'm assuming his wife—is on the floor with her palm pressed against her devastated face. Then a door opens and that little kid, Paz, watches in horror at his father as he beats someone bloody. Is that man a Decker? I'm frozen over how unreal this is.

Paz sees me. "Please help!"

I don't waste any more time. I run into the apartment and wrap my arms around Frankie and wrestle him off that man. Frankie elbows me in my stomach so hard that I taste acid in my throat, and he backs me up into the wall.

This is how I'm going to die . . . against a man who is fighting for his life.

He's looking at me like I'm a ghost when I punch him in the face.

I won't go down without a fight either.

Frankie is massaging his jaw when I see that Paz has vanished from the doorway. I hope he's hiding somewhere. Maybe I can get Paz out of here, back downstairs where he can be safe with Orion's guardians, who have kept me alive for as long as they did. Then Frankie is swift with picking up a broken chair leg and swings it into my head over and over . . .

THE END

I'm dizzy and stumbling backward and scared and tearing up and being torn up and—

He kicks me square in the stomach and out his apartment and—

Down the stairs, reaching for the banister and—

I miss and grab ahold of Orion instead—

Why is he on these stairs, I told him to stay back—

Am I going to die holding him or—

The memory of our first hug, back before Death-Cast called—

My forehead bangs into a step, and I'm bleeding—

The memory of us running away before I fell onto the curb—

Squeezing Orion tight to absorb the blow—

The memory of his hand against my heart and mine against his—

We're about to slam down onto the landing I think—

These memories are rapid and jumbled—

I hold on to Orion—

Is this what they mean when they say your life flashes before—

PAZ DARIO
6:44 p.m.

Death-Cast did not call Paz Dario because he isn't supposed to be dying today, and he's very confused because his mother isn't supposed to be dying either, but his father is beating her up.

This isn't the first time either, but this time is the scariest.

Normally Paz doesn't see any of this happening. His mother always tells him to stay in his room and put his chair against the door, just like she would when he was scared of the monsters in his closet. The chair is so tiny that it would break if anyone else sat on it. It's been painted to look like a happy dalmatian with its tongue sticking out on the backrest. But Paz knows the chair doesn't keep anyone out because his mother always eventually comes back into his bedroom without him having to move the chair first. She's always crying and holds him close until they fall asleep in his bed together. Other times his father will come inside his room

THE END

and ask him if he's okay, and Paz will say yes, and he will ask how his mother is doing and his father will say she's okay too, and then the door gets closed again.

Paz has lost count of how many times this has happened.

But his mother screaming for help is a first, he knows that much.

So Paz stepped outside his bedroom, wanting to help his mother as his father hurt Rolando so much that he has a nosebleed. But he didn't know what to do until he saw the new neighbor, Valentino, and asked for his help. Then Paz ran into the closet, not to hide, but with an idea of his own on how to help.

People think Paz is a bad guy because he played one in that movie, but he's a hero.

He's a hero who is going to save his mother's life.

Paz runs back into the living room, which doesn't feel like a room for living after he points the gun at his father and pulls the trigger.

FRANKIE DARIO
6:45 p.m.

Frankie is about to land another punch on Gloria when fire strikes him out of nowhere.

He falls on his side.

Paz stands over him, holding a gun, and fires again.

Not even Death-Cast could have prepared him to die that way.

DALMA YOUNG

6:46 p.m.

Gunshots.

Dalma fears she might have her own heart attack.

This is just like last night at Times Square.

Has someone shot Valentino? Orion? Both of them?

Was this always supposed to end in gunfire?

Had Valentino been killed last night, would this be over? Possibly. But it also means he wouldn't have been able to live first. Something that Orion made sure happened.

At what price?

Her family is panicking. Her mother and Dahlia run out of the pizzeria empty-handed and go straight into the car, yelling at Dalma to get in too. Floyd is banging on the lobby door and buzzing every button on the intercom for someone to let him in. Some tenants on the ground level are running out of their apartments, scared for their lives as they should be, as scared as Dalma should be for hers, but the moment that door opens, she shoves past everyone, even Floyd, and runs up those stairs.

Dalma feels as if she is a first responder, determined to save Orion's life, knowing in her own heart that he would run toward danger to save hers too.

ORION

Everything is mad hazy.

I'm seeing stars, but I'm not in space.

My head is on a pillow, but I'm not in bed.

Valentino's arm is across my chest, but he's not holding me close.

There were gunshots, but I'm not dead.

I fight to get my eyes open and then immediately regret it when I see the blood smeared all over my boyfriend's beautiful face like something out of a horror movie. I want to return to the darkness where I can imagine—no, remember—being in bed with Valentino as he holds me close in a room that's quiet except for our breathing.

I try shaking him awake, but he's still trying to sleep, which fine, I get it, we haven't had a ton of rest on his End Day, but we don't have a lot of time left, and we still have to go down memory lane together. Valentino wanted—wants—to

505

see how our first picture came out together, that fucking selfie, a word that we both fucking hate, that's not supposed to outlive him.

Maybe I can wake him up with some Sleeping Beauty–type kiss because this can't be how it ends, please don't let this be how it ends.

I press my lips to Valentino's, but he doesn't snap awake and kiss me back.

His chest is slowly rising.

There's hope, there's hope, there's hope, hope, hope.

I just don't understand something.

If his heart is beating, why doesn't it feel like he's alive?

DALMA YOUNG
6:47 p.m.

Dalma's heart is pounding, scared she might bump into the killer or see her best friend's corpse.

One feels worse than the other.

She makes it to the fifth floor, Floyd right behind her, and at the bottom of the next flight of stairs is Orion and Valentino, surrounded by the donated pillows and bedding as if they decided to set up camp and rest in the stairway. She's relieved that Orion is crying, because crying means he's alive, but her heart breaks for what this means for Valentino.

"Orion . . ."

He doesn't even seem to register her. He's just begging Valentino to wake up.

If Dalma died, this is how she imagines Orion would react, and they've known each other their entire lives. But her best friend is crying this hard over a boyfriend he's only known for a day—not even!—and she knows this pain is just as true as it would be losing her.

This death will stay with Orion for the rest of his life.

Here's hoping it's a long one.

"He's still alive," Floyd says, examining Valentino.

"He wasn't shot?" Dalma asks.

"No, no, no, he got kicked down the stairs," Orion says.

Dalma looks up to the sixth floor, glimpsing an open door and hearing crying.

Could the killer be upstairs? Is there another place they could have escaped, like a ladder to the roof like she has at home? Or will they be rushing down at any moment? If they're not wearing a creepy skull mask like that killer in Times Square, will they take out Dalma and everyone else to leave no witnesses behind?

She wants to drag Orion and Floyd out there, but as long as Valentino is still breathing, Dalma knows Orion won't leave his side.

"I need some space," Floyd says, opening Valentino's eyelids.

Orion refuses to get off his boyfriend.

"He's trying to save his life," Dalma says.

The truth is, Dalma lied.

She can't speak for Floyd, but her eyes and brain and heart are processing what's really happening here. Valentino is beyond saving. He is going to die, as Death-Cast has predicted, possibly any minute now. But it might not be too late for Orion. It doesn't have to be his End Day too.

Everything has been building to this moment, this convergence of lives.

"We need to get you both to the hospital," Floyd says, scooping Valentino up in his arms, surprising strength for someone who's on the shorter end of life.

Dalma locks her arm with Orion's, who won't take his teary eyes off of Valentino, not even as they go down the five flights of stairs. She's surprised they make it down in one piece, and relieved when they make it out of the building alive.

They escaped the killer, and if all goes well from here, they will live to see another day.

Most of them will, at least.

GLORIA DARIO
6:48 p.m.

Gloria's son has killed his father to protect her.

Tears run down sweet, young Pazito's cheeks.

Sweat glistens off Rolando's bruised and beaten face.

Blood pools around Frankie like a spilled bucket of red paint.

"Don't move, Pazito," Gloria says, eyeing the gun still clutched in her son's hands.

Pazito is shaking.

One wrong move and Gloria will find herself dead next to her husband. She knows that Pazito won't harm her, not intentionally, but accidents happen all the time whenever a gun finds its way into someone's hand, especially a child's. This weapon shouldn't have been in their home in the first place, but she couldn't convince Frankie to get rid of it, and it's hard arguing with a foul-tempered gun owner. Gloria feels as if she failed Pazito by not fighting harder, by not trying to leave sooner, by putting him in the position to protect her when it should be the other way around. Now, Pazito will be scarred for the rest of his life, haunted by the ghost of the father he killed, and there are no words for how much that breaks Gloria's heart.

For now, with loving hands, she takes the gun out of her son's.

She sets it down and picks him up, carrying him to his bedroom.

She covers his eyes as if he won't be able to see his dead father in the darkness.

Together, they cry in bed, their final fight fought.

ORION

6:56 p.m.

Last night, my life changed.

Last night, my life also almost ended.

I had the heart attack in Times Square and I was in the backseat of a taxi, tucked between Dalma and Valentino as they rushed me to the hospital. Now we're headed back to the exact same hospital, only this time it's Valentino we're trying to keep upright, trying to save. He's got a chance, I know he does, especially since it's a quick drive to Lenox Hill, even if those three minutes feel like the longest three minutes in the history of three minutes. We waste no time getting Valentino inside, abandoning the car, which Dayana can deal with when she pulls up in her car with Dahlia. I'm too woozy to help carry Valentino, but Floyd has got that handled as Dalma runs ahead of us to alert Dr. Emeterio of our arrival.

Dr. Emeterio appears with a team, surprised to see

Valentino in this state when we were all hoping for something more peaceful. She directs her nurses to rush Valentino away. They're going to try to save his life, like she said they would, but if they can't, I better get ready for surgery. I've had all day to prepare for this, but now that everything is getting really real, real fast, I'm not ready. Death-Cast was supposed to eliminate these fears, but they messed up and now I have no idea if we're both destined to die at the end. I'm taken into the ER. Floyd is bossy with my nurses to make sure I'm not hemorrhaging; I can tell Floyd is unofficially preparing me for the surgery we've wanted for years.

I'm told my heart is fine even though I feel dead inside.

People swear they're going to live perfect lives when you get the chance to say everything you need to say, but the truth is: death is faster than you.

Even when you're warned.

There are things I never got to tell Valentino, things he never got to tell me.

Whole lives of stories we never got to share with one another.

Whole lives we didn't get to live together.

I breathe out his sister's name, the person who did get to spend her life with Valentino, but she won't be here to see him through his death.

"I have to call Scarlett," I say.

I dig my phone out my pocket, and the screen is shattered.

I know why.

The end began when that fucking bastard kicked Valentino down the stairs. I don't know what happened with those bullets, but you won't catch me grieving that son of a bitch if he's dead. Good fucking riddance, I don't give a shit. No matter how much I get to live because of that fucker's crime, I'll never be grateful for how he did Valentino dirty.

I call Scarlett.

"Finally, Val," she says with all the relief and confidence in the world that it's her brother on the line.

"It's Orion," I say weakly.

"Oh."

My silence does some of the speaking for me.

Scarlett breathes. "Can I talk to my brother?"

"He's currently being treated by doctors. He's alive, but . . . it's not looking good, Scarlett."

There's no silence on her end, only anguished cries. "What happened?"

I didn't see everything, but I tell her everything I know. Dalma stays close as I keep cracking through this story. Dayana and Dahlia find us, and Floyd hugs them tight.

"Valentino was being a hero," I say. I stop myself from saying that he died as one.

I stay on the phone, and we cry together.

When the door opens, I'm hoping for a miracle. But

Valentino doesn't enter with all the blood back in his body or all his cuts and bruises brushed away as if they were photoshopped. It's Dr. Emeterio, and she speaks with Floyd and Dayana while glancing over at me. I go to reach for Dalma's hand to find that she's already holding mine. I squeeze so hard that I might pulverize her bones and my phone.

"Is Valentino okay?" I ask.

Scarlett holds back her cries, listening for an answer too.

Dr. Emeterio's face is one big spoiler. "Valentino is showing signs of brain death."

It's like I'm falling down the stairs again, the air being knocked out of me, everything hurting so much that I'm ready to black out. She's talking about his oxygen levels and putting him on a ventilator and additional prep work and tons of other things that I can't process because Valentino's brain is shutting down, aka he's basically dead.

"Are you ready to receive Valentino's heart, Orion?" Dr. Emeterio asks.

I'm so thrown off, I feel like I'm not worthy enough for this. Or even like I'm guilty because the stars were always aligning in a way where he would die so I could live.

"Orion?" Scarlett calls for me through the phone. "You're not going to let my brother's heart go to waste, are you?"

Her question feels two-sided: I shouldn't reject the transplant, and I should put it to good use once it's successfully inside me.

I won't, and I will.

This is what Valentino wanted and this is what I want too.

"I'm going to live," I vow, even though Death-Cast could be wrong about me.

Then the end begins so quickly.

I'm rushed into another room and as they're prepping me for surgery I'm thinking about how it's time to say goodbye to my heart, the one that my parents gave me. It was always supposed to be there, but now it's like someone telling me that my shadow is going to stop following me around. My life is about to be suddenly reshaped because of a sudden death and that's assuming I don't go down too.

I get a minute with Team Young before Dr. Emeterio wants to put me under, and there isn't enough time to tell everyone everything I could say to them and everything I want for them so all I say is "Thanks for making me feel like one of your own." I could live in this group hug forever.

But I can't.

I have one more stop before we can begin.

"I need to see Valentino first."

There's no fighting me on this.

I'm brought in to the operation room where Valentino is on the bed, his face still beat.

I lean in and whisper the words I should've said when I knew he could've heard me, and then I kiss him for the last time.

THE END

Then I'm off to the operating table.

If all goes well, Valentino will live in me for the rest of my life.

But I don't know how this ends.

PART FIVE
THE BEGINNING

I've always loved the expression "Out with the old, in with the new." It holds meaning to every individual person. It can be about anything. A lover, an organ. Even a way of life—a way of death. What does it mean for you?

—Joaquin Rosa, creator of Death-Cast

August 1, 2010
ORION
1:19 a.m.

Death-Cast probably isn't up and running anymore, but if they are, they're probably going to call any second now because I have a hole in my chest.

A metaphorical hole, but it hurts just the same.

I also can't answer any calls because there's a tube down my throat.

I'm so groggy, drugged up from this surgery. But anesthetics are only good for the physical pain. They don't do shit about heartbreak.

Not even when they put your boyfriend's heart inside you.

DALMA YOUNG
1:23 a.m.

Death-Cast could call Dalma Young to tell her she's going to die today, and she can only hope she will live a day as magical as the one Orion shared with Valentino.

Dr. Emeterio tells the family that Orion's surgery was a success, but the celebration is reined in. This is a win that's come at a devastating loss.

Dalma hugs her mother tight, crying over the thought of how many more years she'll get to spend with Orion. She can safely imagine him throwing back shots together for their twenty-first birthdays like their mothers got to do, cheering her on with the rest of the family at her graduation, delivering speeches at each other's weddings, and everything else that precedes and follows. Of course, life is never guaranteed, no matter how healthy you are. That lesson was learned with Orion's parents and now Valentino. And even with a new heart, Orion isn't promised the same odds as those who haven't had transplants.

But Dalma can hope and dream.

And most important, she can make sure time is never taken for granted.

"Can we see O-Bro—Orion?" Dalma asks, wiping her tears.

"Soon," Dr. Emeterio says.

"Thank you for everything, Doctor," Dayana says. "You have no idea how much . . ."

"I only wish I could've saved them both."

Until now, Valentino's death hadn't been confirmed aloud.

"We'll pray for his soul, and his family," Dayana says.

"Only the sister," Dalma says.

Valentino's parents can pray for themselves.

Together, Dayana leads the family in prayer, passing blessings of peace onto Valentino's soul and strength to Scarlett and love and light to them both.

When they're done, Dalma finds Scarlett's number in her phone, saved from last night when Valentino first called her.

She can't help but feel like a Death-Cast employee as she makes this call.

SCARLETT PRINCE
10:29 p.m. (Mountain Standard Time)

Scarlett's phone rings, and she knows it's not her brother. She's forever open to a miracle, but she's not expecting one. It's probably the airline calling about her suitcases as if she cares about the whereabouts of her clothes and camera equipment after losing her other half. But it's not. She doesn't recognize Dalma's name at first, and then quickly remembers she's Orion's best friend—and one of the last people to see her brother alive.

She doesn't bother composing herself. "Hi."

"Hi, Scarlett. This is Dalma Young, I'm Orion's friend."

"I know." Scarlett almost asks what's wrong, as if that's not clear.

"Right. I think the doctor is going to call you any minute now, but—"

"My brother is dead," Scarlett says. She would welcome the news of Valentino being in a deep coma, as long as that means he's still alive, but she's not holding her breath.

"I'm so sorry, Scarlett."

She hates every urge to run out of her bedroom to go cry into the arms of her parents. If they couldn't treat Valentino right in life, they shouldn't get to grieve him or console her. But Scarlett can't deny that the urge is indeed there because that's how alone she feels right now. Valentino isn't around— isn't alive—to hug her.

The loneliness of becoming an only child has already begun.

Scarlett feels hollow. . . . Can someone feel hollow?

She wants to knock on Valentino's bedroom door and see what he thinks.

"Is there anything I can do for you?" Dalma asks.

Scarlett forgot she's on the phone. "Tell me everything else went well."

"It did," Dalma says, her voice tinged with guilt.

What went wrong for Scarlett's brother went right for Dalma's friend.

"Good," Scarlett says. That's what Valentino wanted. "Do you have his camera?"

"I do. Are you still coming to New York? If not, I can mail it to you along with everything else he has in the apartment."

Scarlett can't imagine being in New York without Valentino. "It'll be too lonely."

"No, it won't," Dalma says. "We don't know each other, but Orion and Valentino showed me that doesn't matter. If you come out here, you will never be alone. My family is your family."

They seem like pretty words, something you say to comfort someone who lost the person closest to them. But Scarlett is choosing to trust this stranger. Valentino did the same, and it worked out in all the ways that matter. Besides, it's not as if she really sees herself staying in this haunted house with her parents who drove Valentino away.

She will brave New York to honor Valentino's spirit, not treating it as the city where he died, and instead remembering it as the new home where he lived.

There's a flicker of flame in her hollow chest, like hope heating within, like the fires of a phoenix that will be reborn.

Her life is changing—has changed—and she will need a fresh start to get through her grief, to completely reimagine a future without her twin brother.

But she'll never forget him.

Scarlett doesn't have to carry her brother's heart for him to forever live in hers.

GLORIA DARIO
3:04 a.m.

Death-Cast did not call Gloria Dario because she isn't dying today, but Gloria certainly feels dead inside.

Never in a million years did Gloria predict the first End Day would unfold with her husband dying—with her husband being killed by her son. What's confusing is how Death-Cast didn't even call Frankie. Yes, Gloria registered Frankie for the service behind his back, but it's still his phone number that was listed. Why didn't Death-Cast call? Will these mistakes be prevented in the future? But maybe if Death-Cast had called, Frankie would've killed Gloria in an outrage too. He almost did tonight anyway. She's only alive thanks to her son, but at the cost of his own life, his own future.

In the police station, Gloria holds Pazito close.

While this was an act of self-defense, Gloria is coming to understand that it won't be that simple. There will be investigations and questionings and the idea of anyone seeing her wonderful son as anything but breaks her heart. What if a court tries taking Pazito away? All because he wanted to save her life? Rolando has been assuring her that won't happen due to Frankie's documented abusive history, and Gloria desperately wants to believe him, but when has the criminal justice system been fair? Even if Pazito serves no jail time, what will this do for his soul?

"Mrs. Dario?"

Gloria looks up at the officer. "It's Ms. Medina."

She's reclaiming her maiden name, never taking another man's, not even one who loves her with his full heart. Gloria must be herself first, and only she can define what that means.

"Ms. Medina, is it possible to speak with Pazito alone? We'd appreciate his cooperation but understand if you'd like to wait for a lawyer."

Gloria knows there's no point in fighting, nor do they have anything to hide. She lifts Pazito's chin with her finger. He's staring at her with terror in his eyes.

"They're going to lock me up," Pazito says.

"They just want to talk," Gloria says. As a parent, it's her job to protect her child. That has always meant shielding him from all his fears, whether it was the monsters under his bed or now the nightmarish reality he could be living. "Be honest, Pazito. Do not lie."

"I won't, Mom."

Instead of beating herself up some more about all the different things Gloria believes she could've done to not be here tonight, she pulls her son in a quick but tight hug. They can only move forward, and if all goes well, they'll be able to figure it out together. And if Gloria can find the space in her head and heart, she'll be able to invite Rolando in. That's not a decision to be made lightly, especially given her last big impulsive decision resulted in the death of her husband, a husband she doesn't expect she'll ever find herself mourning. But who knows. Grief is strange, and it can make you miss someone who was never good for you.

Pazito drags his feet alongside the officer, looking over his shoulder the entire way.

Gloria holds it together until her son vanishes into a room for questioning, and the moment the door shuts, she sobs.

"He's going to be okay," Rolando says.

Instead of blaming him for encouraging her to follow her heart, she believes him.

There are dark times ahead, but she's choosing to focus on the horizon, on when the sun will rise and cast light everywhere that's needed nourishing, and Gloria Medina will continue to grow and grow and grow.

August 3, 2010
ORION
2:04 p.m.

Death-Cast didn't call last night or the night before.

I'm starting to believe the surgery was a success.

That I'm going to live.

The tube has finally been pulled from my throat, and I'm able to breathe on my own. The IV lines will be removed later. These machines monitoring me will be used on someone else. I think tonight is the night when I'll be good enough to transfer from intensive care to another ward for specialized cardiac attention. If all goes well there, I could be home soon. It's hard to wrap my head around how much of my life has been spent admitted to hospitals and how once I'm out this time, it could be the last for a while. Probably not forever, but my odds are mad better than ever before.

I've been in and out of it the past three days, but I'm awake now, catching up with the family while trying to get some food in my stomach. After the first night, Dayana and Floyd have been taking turns on who goes back with Dahlia when visiting hours are over to get some rest, but Dalma refused to leave the hospital, in case I woke up and needed her. And I do, but unless she's mastered necromancy, there's nothing she can do.

I'm caught up on everything I've missed.

First, Frankie was killed by his son. The kid who welcomed Valentino into the building. How he got his hands on a gun is beyond me, but he pulled that trigger twice to stop his father from killing his mother. Now it's a big news story and an investigation is underway. The kid, Paz, told police how his mother looked like she was about to die even though Death-Cast hadn't called her, so he wanted to save her life. It's kind of hard to believe that's going to protect him, especially since Death-Cast messed up big-time.

That's the other huge piece of news.

Joaquin Rosa held a press conference where he shared Death-Cast's opening numbers. They had a perfect score on predictions but failed in outreach to twelve Deckers— including Frankie. He said he will be haunted by those losses for the rest of his life and has done everything in his power to ensure that will never happen again. It looks like people are buying into it, especially since there have been no more fuckups while I've been recovering from surgery. The Death-Cast program is going to grow and grow, maybe even go global. This service might still scare some people, but I bet I could change anyone's mind about the possibilities of knowing your fate by sharing Valentino's story.

The End Days have some horrors, but if you commit to living, they can be beautiful too.

DALMA YOUNG
4:44 p.m.

Death-Cast did not call Dalma Young because she isn't dying today, but her game-changing idea has finally been born.

"I finally know what app I want to create," Dalma says, alone with Orion in his hospital room.

"Oh yeah?" Orion asks quietly.

He sounds disinterested, but Dalma knows he's simply not here mentally. This grief is different from a child losing his parents. Back then Orion was screaming all the time and was confused every time he woke up. Dalma could relate, but she doesn't know what it's like to lose a friend. Or a lover. But she now sees the power of finding people before it's too late.

"You and Valentino changed each other, even though you shared only one day together. You gave him peace before his death, and he'll stay with you for the rest of your life," Dalma says, thinking more of Valentino's imprint on Orion's soul instead of the new heart in his chest, but that too. "I think I can build an app that makes sure no one dies alone."

"How would it work?"

"Everyone would create a profile on the app so you can find your best match, but I don't think it should be random selection. This is personal, and the Decker should choose who they invite into their life, especially with time so limited. I can even create the option for Deckers to pair up. Then whoever gets the honor of being chosen to keep the Decker company, they'll help them however they can. It might just be basic companionship as they get their affairs in order. It could be hyping up the Decker to live a lifetime on their End Day."

There's a flicker of life in Orion's eyes, almost like an entire film reel of his time with Valentino is unfolding in his head. "That's going to change a lot of people's lives, Dalma."

"I hope so."

Dalma isn't sure if Orion will ever use the app. It's hard to imagine at this stage. He's strong, but can his new heart handle more heartbreak?

Time will answer that when it's time.

"You know what you're going to call it?" Orion asks.

The name came to Dalma like lightning. "The Last Friend app."

ORION

4:54 p.m.

I was Valentino's Last Friend.

Dalma's app is going to form some incredible connections, but it's a double-edged sword that can't be wielded by the faint of heart. The Last Friend must understand that not only will the Decker die, they may also witness the death. That's scarring. But not all scars are bad. I look down at the one across my chest.

The scar that says I was more than Valentino's Last Friend.

5:17 p.m.

"When did he die? What time?"

Just as I want to know everything about Valentino's life, the same goes for his death.

Dr. Emeterio stops studying my charts and pulls out her clipboard. "Valentino passed at 9:11 p.m."

Nine.

Eleven.

Just when I thought those numbers couldn't become more haunting.

6:17 p.m.

"You have a guest," Dalma says in the doorway of my new room.

I'm guessing my guest isn't one of the fam. "Who is it?"

"Scarlett."

My heart—Valentino's heart—is screaming with heartbeats.

"Are you in the mood for company?" Dalma asks.

No, but there's no saying no.

Not to the twin of the boy who gave me his heart.

It's a good thing that I wasn't surprised by Scarlett's arrival because she reminds me more of Valentino than I expected. Her energy matches his from when Valentino and I were first at the hospital last night—I mean, the other night, time is weird. Valentino was trying to accept his fate, and Scarlett is now doing the same. That's going to take a long time.

Her hair is pulled back into a ponytail, and her face is clean of makeup, and she's paler than she appeared on FaceTime.

"I'll give you two some privacy," Dalma says, closing the door behind her.

since he spends most of the day sleeping off his graveyard shift or busy on numerous calls. Joaquin simply can't afford to not be at headquarters after the opening-day fiasco where twelve registered Deckers met their ends without notice. Haunted, Joaquin puts aside the mounting paperwork and leaves his office. He needs to see that while he isn't able to go where he wishes, doors are opening for others.

Joaquin stands in the call center where his heralds are fulfilling his life's mission.

There's been so much heartbreak and loss across the world, and within Joaquin's own world, to get to this point. To reach these astonishing new heights with a view no one in their right minds ever imagined could be made a reality.

While Death-Cast can only tell someone when they will die, they can't predict how someone's life will change on their End Day. The Decker must make those discoveries themselves by living with the fullest of hearts, down to the last beat.

August 7, 2010
ORION
11:17 a.m.

Death-Cast hasn't called because Valentino Prince saved my life.

I'm finally back home, bracing myself for the first night in my bed since sharing it with him. It's one of those firsts that doubled as lasts, and I love it and I hate it. Thankfully I won't be alone. Dalma and Scarlett are going to keep me company in sleeping bags.

A new family isn't all Valentino left behind.

Upon arriving home today, Scarlett surprised me with a photo album containing all our memory-lane pictures. I'd already seen them from going through them together at the hospital, telling Scarlett all the stories from Valentino's End Day, but now I have my own collection to hold close since Scarlett is keeping her brother's camera. I love all our pictures together, especially the ones from the High Line and Times Square, our very first and our very last.

So much life happened in between.

I'm staring at the pictures of Valentino strutting during his subway runway. I'm tempted to send them to his agent so she knows what the world has missed out on by not believing in Death-Cast, but she doesn't deserve to see him in all his glory.

Even in death, I'm still protective of Valentino.

There's a knock on my door for the thousandth time in the one hour I've been home.

"Yeah?"

"It's me," Dalma says from the other side.

"Me too," Scarlett says.

I'm not really in the mood for company right now just because. I was warned that mood swings and depression are side effects of heart surgery, as if that's what's got me down, down, down, down, down, down, down, down, down, down. I kind of want to be alone until tonight, just resting in bed with bad TV and my photo album. Later when I can't sleep is when I'm going to need the most company.

"What's up?"

"I have something for you," Scarlett says.

"Something else?"

Maybe it's more of Valentino's clothes that I can breathe in, or the cologne he used.

"Can we come in?" Dalma asks. "We'll be fast."

I give in. "Yeah."

Dalma and Scarlett enter my room. Scarlett's hand is closed into a fist, but I'm going to put down money that what she has for me isn't a punch to the face. I don't know what it is, maybe it's something of Valentino's that she's willing to part with and thinks I would like. Maybe a photocopy of his death certificate, which might seem morbid, but I would keep that in my treasure chest along with the news article of everything that went down in his building and all the 9/11 media I've collected over the years.

"So what is it?" I ask.

I'm not trying to be rude, but I'm in pain and feeling really broken even though Valentino's heart is holding me together.

"There was something else on the camera," Scarlett says.

"The video he recorded for you," I say.

She nods. "It's only four minutes and thirty-two seconds, but it took me a couple days before I had the strength to finish watching it. It just hurt too much. I never knew life without him and . . . Valentino may have been the first one in and out, but his last words were lovely. That's helping."

I don't know what Valentino said to Scarlett. That's not my business and never will be unless she decides she wants to talk about it instead of holding it close.

"But there was another video at the end," Scarlett says. "At first I thought it was for me, but then Valentino said your name."

My old heart would've stopped dead.

My new heart is coming to life.

Maybe too quickly, but I'm staying strong.

"He recorded a video for me?" I ask.

Scarlett nods. "I didn't watch it. Obviously. I only discovered it last night, but I wanted to wait until you were home and settled before sharing."

"But what if I had died before—"

Dalma's puzzled look shuts me up.

If there was a chance I was going to die without getting to watch Valentino's video, Death-Cast would have given us that heads-up.

"My bad."

"It's a new world," Dalma says.

"It's going to take some getting used to," Scarlett says.

In more ways than one.

Scarlett opens her fist and reveals a USB flash drive. I already have my own that I've used for homework assignments in the past and for backing up my short stories in case my laptop dies for real. But inside this little memory keeper is a video of Valentino saying my name. Maybe more, and if not, that would still be enough.

"Thanks," I say.

Scarlett smiles. "Back at you."

I almost ask for what, but it's clear what she's thanking me for.

Everything.

"You want to watch it now?" Dalma asks.

"Hell yeah."

My whole life wasn't spent with Valentino, I didn't even get a full day. I need more now.

Dalma props my laptop on my bed, setting it to charge so it stays alive. "I love you, O-Bro."

"You too, sis."

It's the first time I've called her my sister, and not in a she's-pretty-much-like-my-sister way.

Dalma squeezes my hand before she leaves the room with Scarlett.

I plug the USB flash drive into the laptop I'll be using to write stories about Valentino.

To immortalize him.

For now, I click on the file that's been titled *Valentino to Orion*.

There he is, frozen, in my bedroom, at my desk, as if he's three feet away and not out of reach in every way.

I press *Play* on the video, and Valentino Prince comes back to life.

"Hi, Orion."

His blue eyes, my name flying out of his heart-shaped lips, his bedhead from after we had sex . . .

If it weren't for Death-Cast, I'd bet on this video killing me. But knowing I'll survive gives me the strength to watch this now, to want to watch this forever on a loop.

It won't kill me. But it could heal me.

"I don't have a lot of time," Valentino says—said. "Not only because it's my End Day. That's obvious. But you're in the shower after our incredible first time together, and I'm nervous you might pop back in any second now. I just finished filming my video for Scarlett and everything is so uncertain and I wanted to get some things off my chest in case my death catches me off guard."

Thankfully he had that foresight. But I don't want to think about Valentino's bruised and bloody face after that deadly fall down the stairs, I only want to remember him as he was throughout his End Day. Smiling, beautiful, lively.

"I can't imagine what I would do without you," Valentino said. "That might seem strange because I lived a whole life before you, but even though I didn't know you, I know you were the kind of person I was hoping to find. It's easy to say the timing was bad, but it could have been a lot worse, right? I could have never known you, Orion."

Valentino's eyes teared up, like that thought is too brutal.

I'm with him one billion percent.

"One of the downsides of living, Orion, is that you're going to have the challenge of living without me," Valentino said, then cringed. "I'm sorry. That came off more self-important than I meant. You've told me how grief affects you, and I'm not in the same league of your parents, but I know I wasn't a nobody either. I don't want you to fall into a black hole, or think that you have to. I want you to find the light even on the days that feel as dark and—"

Then the door opened because Valentino got interrupted by me, by Past Orion. The camera is still on Valentino—I can't even see Past Orion, who I personally know is standing in the doorway in nothing but a towel because that was me—and it hurts rewatching that fear in Valentino's eyes as if something horrible was about to happen.

"What's going on?" Valentino had asked, popping out of my chair.

"Nothing, nothing," Past Orion said. "I wanted to make sure you were okay. I had a bad feel— I got nervous."

Then relief washed over Valentino as he sat back down and breathed. "I'm okay. I'm just recording a message for Scarlett. Something for her to have after I'm . . . Do you mind if I finish? I need a minute."

"Take your time. . . . And don't die. . . . You know what I mean!"

Past Orion left, and Valentino smiled into the camera.

"I'm sorry for lying to you," he said with a smirk. "I hope you understand. . . ."

If I ever have to lie to someone, I hope it's charming like this.

"What was I saying?" Valentino looked up, like his words were written on the ceiling, a prepared speech. "Please don't give in to your grief. Don't wait for your End Day to live like we did together. If you're having a bad day, maybe you can do me a favor and go for a run. It's what I would do. It's what I did a lot, honestly." He went quiet, like he was lost in his head. But then he found himself again and smiled. "I want you to make more discoveries in your city, and I want you to be brave enough to make the first move again the next time someone catches your eye. And someone will catch your eye again, Orion. Please don't deny yourself that out of fear of losing someone again, or guilt because you're living on and I can't."

Valentino inched closer to the camera, so close that it's like he's a breath away.

"Before Death-Cast called, you told me the truth about grief. How as long as you keep existing and breathing that you'll eventually live again. You have to live, Orion." Valentino tapped his chest. "This heart isn't my heart or your heart. It's our heart. I love you, Orion. Live enough for the both of us."

The video stops there, but my tears only get started.

Valentino Prince loved me—and I got to hear him say it. I get to hear him say it for the rest of my life, even if it's just the one time echoed forever.

I'm no longer a short story. I'm now a novel.

Better yet, I'm a work in progress.

I have all these new blank pages, and I'm going to live a

life worth writing about.

Valentino called me his co-captain on his End Day, and I'm going to treat him as my cowriter through my life.

I'll discover more firsts and never hold back when creating those moments.

I'll go for runs through the city as if I'm still his personal tour guide.

I'll write an epic story about an immortal character named Vale.

And I'll maybe even fall in love again, and I'll make sure I say it before it's too late.

This is the beginning with many more firsts to follow.

I hold my favorite ValentinOrion pictures to my heart.

His heart.

Our heart.

ACKNOWLEDGMENTS

This book tried to end me, but I'm here, YAY!

First, a gigantic thank you to my editor, Alexandra Cooper! Writing a prequel to my favorite fictional universe was incredibly difficult and Alex was so patient and understanding and helpful, even when I would call and say stuff like "Hi, I need to completely rewrite one of the narrators!" and "Guess whose book that takes place in winter needs to be set in the summer instead!" and "Can I have one more week with these edits?" when it was definitely more than one more week. This book wouldn't be what it is today without Alex trusting my chaotic process and all her guidance in helping me reach the heart of this book—in every version I pitched.

My extraordinary agent and fellow night owl, Jodi Reamer, for championing me and reading this book even though *They Both Die at the End* scarred her so badly that she was scared to go turn on the lights in her home. For real, huge props to Jodi for always hearing me out—if you know me, you know I talk a lot and have a billion ideas at any given moment.

Kaitlin López's assisting was TOO helpful! Kaitlin is the one who realized that this prequel couldn't take place on New Year's Eve/Day because of two random details in *They Both Die at the End* that next to no one would've noticed. And as badly as I wanted to shrug off that continuity because switching seasons—especially a holiday season!—was no easy task, I would've been haunted by not doing the work. Props to Kaitlin's editorial eagle eye for making this book make sense. (Don't even get me started on the time zones.)

My publisher aka HarperCollins! Shoutout to Rosemary Brosnan, Suzanne Murphy, Michael D'Angelo (especially for the brilliant title that improved the course of this story!), Audrey Diestelkamp, Cindy Hamilton, Jennifer Corcoran, Allison Weintraub, Laura Harshberger, Mark Rifkin, Josh Weiss, Allison Brown, Caitlin Garing, Andrea Pappenheimer and the sales team, and Patty Rosati and her team for being the absolute best.

Thank you to Sean Williams for his stunning work on the UK cover.

My agency aka Writers House! Shoutout to Cecilia de la Campa, Alessandra Birch, and Rey Lalaoui for all they do to get my books across the world. I'm blown away by their reach.

My friends! Luis and Jordin Rivera kept me sane, and Luis let me spoil this book over and over while I was drafting to keep me hyped about the story, and he hooked me up with great ideas like the secret subway station. Elliot Knight was the first person to hear me read from this book, which was especially meaningful in ways that are obvious to us and don't have to be laid out on this page. Becky Albertalli put up with me as I cycled through a million different potential narrators for this book. David Arnold for staying my bro/fake husband and Jasmine Warga for being the only person I want to eat (vegan) candy with in a bathtub. Arvin Ahmadi for hyping up my third-person writing like it's the best which means a lot since Arvin is the best so there's a lot of best-ing happening here. Sabaa Tahir for always letting me know when I get something right and helping me figure it out when I got it wrong. Robbie Couch for all the pastries I come home to after he's been housesitting for me (and other sweet friend stuff too but mainly the vegan snacks!). Victoria Aveyard, whom I'm starting to suspect doesn't live in Los Angeles because we never see each other here, but I love that we text a lot. Alex Aster, a new friend who became a great friend as quickly as it takes for her to record a TikTok aka super fast. Angie Thomas for writing a prequel before me so I could bother her on what goes into it. Marie Lu, Tahereh Mafi, and Ransom Riggs— I've always admired these incredible humans, and I've been lucky enough to get closer to them during my time out in Los Angeles. Rebecca Serle, I'm so proud of our journeys, both personally and professionally. And Nicola and David Yoon, I love their big hearts—especially because it means they won't unfriend me even though I curse too fucking much.

This book wouldn't have been completed without my group chat switching over to a Zoom room so we could all hit our deadlines. Dhonielle Clayton, our Zoom host who banished me to naps when I yawned too much. Mark Oshiro, our time-tracker who ended our sessions with the voice of a heavenly masseuse. (Unlike that time where I called everyone back with scary demonic growls I found on YouTube.) Patrice Caldwell for not quitting the group chat when we were all freaking out about our deadlines. (And shoutout to Ashley Woodfolk and Zoraida Cordova for their special appearances!)

My mom, Persi Rosa, who has always deserved better than the way I saw her treated growing up. Even though she carries many regrets, she still manages to show grace to those who aren't worthy. I'm in absolute awe of her remarkable strength and gigantic heart. And I'm pleased to report that despite the many echoes between my mom and Gloria from this novel, my mom has found a love that's both safe and true.

As always, huge thanks to booksellers and librarians and educators! Now more than ever your determination to keep books like mine available for customers, patrons, and students like yours is so appreciated. Thank you for fighting that fight.

A new first—thanks to everyone on BookTok/TikTok that helped *They Both Die at the End* find a second, unbelievable life. Special shoutout to Selene from @_moongirlreads who was the first person who made the book go viral, reopening the doors for me to write in this Death-Cast universe. I'm forever grateful.

My readers, for keeping me going creatively.

My therapist, for keeping me going mentally.

My dog, Tazzito, for keeping me going physically. On walks. Many walks.

And, last but not least, Andrew Eliopulos, who was the first person to love this Death-Cast universe. Even though he's moved on—professionally! Not in the death way! He's alive, YAY!—his brilliance will forever live on in all things Death-Cast. And beyond.

CONTINUE READING FOR A SNEAK PREVIEW FROM...

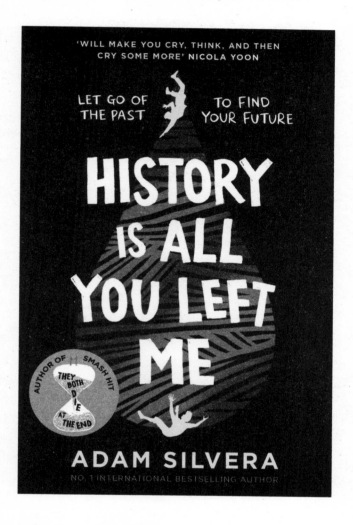

'WILL MAKE YOU CRY, THINK, AND THEN CRY SOME MORE' NICOLA YOON

LET GO OF THE PAST   TO FIND YOUR FUTURE

HISTORY IS ALL YOU LEFT ME

AUTHOR OF SMASH HIT
THEY BOTH DIE AT THE END

ADAM SILVERA
NO. 1 INTERNATIONAL BESTSELLING AUTHOR

'SWEETLY DEVASTATING, PASSIONATELY HONEST, BREATHTAKINGLY HUMAN'
BECKY ALBERTALLI
AUTHOR OF SIMON VS. THE HOMO SAPIENS AGENDA

TODAY

MONDAY, NOVEMBER 20TH, 2016

You're still alive in alternate universes, Theo, but I live in the real world, where this morning you're having an open-casket funeral. I know you're out there, listening. And you should know I'm really pissed because you swore you would never die and yet here we are. It hurts even more because this isn't the first promise you've broken.

I'll break down the details of this promise again. You made it last August. Trust me when I say I'm not talking down to you as I recall this memory, and many others, in great detail. I doubt it'll even surprise you since we always joked about how your brain worked in funny ways. You knew enough meaningless trivia to fill notebooks, but you occasionally slipped on the bigger things, like my birthday this year (May 17th, not the 18th), and you never kept your night classes straight even though I got you a cool planner with zombies on the cover (which you-know-who probably forced you to throw out). I just want you to remember things the way I do. And if bringing up the past annoys you now—as I know it did when you left New York for California—know that I'm sorry, but please don't be mad at me for reliving all of it. History is all you left me.

We made promises to each other on the day I broke up with you so you could do your thing out there in Santa Monica without me holding you back. Some of those promises took bad turns but weren't broken, like how I said I'd never hate you even though you gave me enough reasons to, or how you never stopped being my friend even when your boyfriend asked you to. But on the day we were walking to the post office with Wade to ship your boxes to California, you walked backward into the street and almost got hit by a car. I saw our endgame—to find our way back to each other when the time was right, no matter what—disappear, and I made you promise to always take care of yourself and never die.

"Fine. I'll never die," you said as you hugged me.

If there was a promise you were allowed to break, it wasn't that one, and now I'm forced to approach your casket in one hour to say goodbye to you.

Except it's not going to be goodbye.

I'll always have you here listening. But being face-to-face with you for the first time since July and for the last time ever is going to be impossible, especially given the unwanted company of your boyfriend.

Let's leave his name out of my mouth as long as possible this morning, okay? If I'm going to have any chance of getting through today, tomorrow, and all the days that follow, I think I need to go back to the start, where we were two boys bonding over jigsaw puzzles and falling in love.

It's what comes after you fell out of love with me that it all goes wrong. It's what comes after we broke up that's making me so nervous. Now you can see me, wherever you are. I know you're there, and I know you're watching me, tuned in to my life to piece everything together yourself. It's not just the shameful things I've done that are driving me crazy, Theo. It's because I know I'm not done yet.

HISTORY

SUNDAY, JUNE 8TH, 2014

I'm making history today.

Time is moving faster than this L train, but it's all good since I'm sitting to the left of Theo McIntyre. I've known him since middle school, when he caught my eye at recess. He waved me over and said, "Help me out, Griffin. I'm rebuilding Pompeii." A puzzle of Pompeii made up of one hundred pieces, obviously. I knew nothing of Pompeii at the time; I thought Mount Vesuvius was the hidden lair of some comic book overlord. Theo's hands had entranced me, sorting the puzzle pieces into groups according to shades before beginning, separating the granite roads from the demolished, ash-coated structures. I helped with the sky, getting the clouds all wrong. We didn't get very far with the puzzle that day, but we've been tight ever since.

Today's outing takes us from Manhattan to Brooklyn to see if the lost treasures in some flea market are as overpriced as everyone says they are. No matter where we are, Brooklyn or Manhattan, a schoolyard or Pompeii, I've planned on changing the game up on Theo on this even-numbered day. I just hope he's down to keep playing.

"At least we have the place to ourselves," I say.

It's almost suspicious how empty the subway car is. But I'm not questioning it. I'm too busy dreaming up what it would be like to always share this space and any other space with this know-it-all who loves cartography, puzzles, video animation, and finding out what makes humans tick. On a crowded train, Theo and I usually squeeze together when we sit, our hips and arms pressed against one another's, and it's a lot like hugging him except I don't have to let go as quickly. It sucks that Theo sits directly across from me now, but at least I get the very awesome view. Blue eyes that find wonder in everything (including train ads for teeth whitening), blond hair that darkens when it's wet, the *Game of Thrones* T-shirt I got him for his birthday back in February.

"It's a lot harder to people-watch without people," Theo says. His eyes lock on me. "There's you, I guess."

"I'm sure there will be some interesting people at the flea market. Like hipsters."

"Hipsters are characters, not people," Theo says.

"Don't hipster-shame. Some of them have real feelings underneath their beanie hats and vintage flannels."

Theo stands and does a bullshit pull-up on the rail; his brain gets him top marks, but his muscles can't carry him as high. He gives up and hops back and forth between the train benches like some underground trapeze artist. I wish he would somersault to my side and stay put. He holds on to the railing and stretches his leg to the opposite bench, and his shirt rises a little so I peek at his exposed skin peripherally while keeping my focus on Theo's grin. It might be my last day to do so.

The train rocks to a stop and we get off, finally.

Manhattan is home and all, so Theo never bad-mouths it, but I know he wishes more of its walls were stained with graffiti like they are here in Brooklyn, bright in the summer sun. Theo points out his favorites on the way to the flea market: a little boy in black and white walking across colorful block letters spelling out DREAM; an empty mirror demanding to find the fairest of them all in a crazy neat cursive that rivals Theo's perfect handwriting; an airplane circling Neptune, which is just fantastical enough that it doesn't give me flying anxiety; knights seated around Earth, like it's their round table. Neither of us have any idea what it's supposed to mean, but it's pretty damn cool.

It's a long, hot walk to the flea market, located by the East River. Theo spots a refreshment truck, and we spend five bucks each on cups of frozen lemonade, except there isn't enough of the sugary slush left so we're forced to chew ice to survive the heat.

Theo stops at a table with *Star Wars* goods. His face scrunches up when he turns to me. "Seventy dollars for that toy lightsaber?"

Theo's inside voice sucks. It's a problem.

The forty-something vendor looks up. "It's a recalled saber," she says flatly. "It's rare and I should be charging more." Her shirt reads PRINCESS LEIA IS NOT THE DAMSEL IN DISTRESS YOU'RE LOOKING FOR.

Theo returns her glare with an easy smile. "Did someone pull an Obi-Wan and cut someone's arm off?"

My knowledge on all things *Star Wars* is pretty limited, and the same goes for Theo's knowledge on all things *Harry Potter*. He's the only sixteen-year-old human I know who isn't caught up on everyone's favorite boy wizard. One night we argued for a solid hour over who would win in a duel between Lord Voldemort and Darth Vader. I'm surprised we're still friends.

"The battery hatch snaps off easily and children can't seem to keep them out of their damn mouths," the woman says. She isn't talking to Theo anymore. She's talking to an equally unhappy dude her age who can't figure out an R2-D2 alarm clock.

"Okay, then." Theo salutes her, and we walk away.

We stroll for a few minutes. (Six, to be exact.) "Are we done here?" I ask. It's hot, and I'm melting, and we've definitely seen that some of the treasures are way pricier than they legally should be.

"Hell no, we're not done," Theo says. "We can't leave empty-handed."

"So buy something."

"Why don't you buy *me* something?"

"You don't need that lightsaber."

"No, stupid, buy me something else."

"It's safe to assume you're buying me something too, right?"

"Seems fair," Theo says. He taps his dangerous watch. It is actually for-real dangerous, as in it's not safe to wear. I'm not even sure how or why it got made, because its sharp sundial hands have scratched unsuspecting people's bodies—mine included—enough times that he should throw it in a fireplace and kill it dead and then sue the manufacturer. He wears it anyway because it's different. "Let's meet at the entrance in twenty minutes. Ready?"

"Go."

HAVE YOU READ THEM ALL?

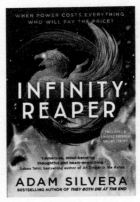

NIGHT WHEREVER WE GO

TRACEY ROSE PEYTON is a graduate of the Michener Center for Writers at University of Texas-Austin where she worked with Elizabeth McCracken and Bret Anthony Johnston. Her short fiction has been published in *Guernica, American Short Fiction, Prairie Schooner* and elsewhere, and her short story, "The Last Days of Rodney", was recently selected by Jesmyn Ward to appear in *Best American Short Stories 2021*.

night wherever we go

TRACEY ROSE PEYTON

b

THE BOROUGH PRESS

The Borough Press
an imprint of HarperCollins*Publishers* Ltd
1 London Bridge Street
London SE1 9GF

www.harpercollins.co.uk

HarperCollins*Publishers*
Macken House,
39/40 Mayor Street Upper,
Dublin 1
D01 C9W8
Ireland

First published in the United States by Ecco, an imprint of HarperCollins*Publishers* 2023

First published in the UK by HarperCollins*Publishers* 2023
1

A catalogue record for this book is available from the British Library

HB ISBN: 978-0-00-853284-0
TPB ISBN: 978-0-00-853285-7

This novel is entirely a work of fiction. The names, characters and incidents portrayed in
it, while at times based on historical figures, are the work of the author's imagination.

Text designed by Alison Bloomer

Printed and bound in the UK using 100% Renewable Electricity by CPI Group (UK) Ltd

This book is produced from independently certified FSC™ paper
to ensure responsible forest management.

For more information visit: www.harpercollins.co.uk/green

NIGHT WHEREVER WE GO

CHAPTER ONE

IN THE COMING YEAR OF our Lord, the 1852 *Farmer's Almanac* predicted four eclipses, three of the moon, one of the sun. It said nothing of torrential rain. No prophecies of muddied fields or stalks of cotton so waterlogged and beaten down the bolls grazed the earth.

By the time the hot Texas sun made its return, glaring its indiscriminate and wanton gaze, it was much too late. The cotton wouldn't mature, instead choosing to rot right there, the bolls refusing to open. It held back the white wooly heads that were so much in demand, and instead relinquished a dank fungal smell that remained trapped in the air for weeks.

The day we were ordered to clear the field, we prayed for a norther, those horrible howling winds that scared us plumb to death our first winter in this strange country. But we knew better. Texas weather was an animal all its own, and we had yet to figure out what gods it answered to.

With no plow, we had no choice but to break it up by hand. We took to the field with pickaxes and dug up the roots, and patch by patch, we set them aflame. It was easy to get too close, to underestimate the direction and sway of the growing fire. We spent the day that way, leaping from one blaze or another, our long skirts gathered in our fists while black plumes of smoke darkened the sky.

The smoke remained long after dusk. It was still there late that night when we shook off sleep and stumbled out of our lumpy bedding to peek outside through the gaps in the cabin's chinking. All the while, we debated whether to go crossing at all. There was a lot of complaining and grumbling about tired limbs and feet, about bad air and threatening fog, about howling dogs, hungry lobos, and angry haints lying in wait. Yet, no one wanted to be left out.

We yanked loose the rags and moss stuffed into the cracks and crevices, but even then, we couldn't see much. Everything appeared to be still and dark. Ahead, a haphazard row of sloping outbuildings stuck out of the ground like crooked teeth. The high brilliant moon made monstrous shadows of them, dark shapes we stared at for long bouts until we were sure there was no movement.

The wind stirred and we could hear the wild swinging branches of half-dead trees just beyond the farm, the knobby limbs that clacked all night. We listened past them, for dogs, for wolves, for any sign of the Lucys.

Opposite the outbuildings was the Lucys' house, a wide double-pen cabin nearly three times the sizes of ours. From our doorway, only a sliver of their house was visible, but it was just enough to gauge their wakefulness by the solid black reflection of their windowpanes, the lack of firelight seeping from the cabin's walls.

The Lucys did not like us moving about at night. Often, they threatened to lock us in after dark. We imagined only the fear of fire kept them from doing so. After all, burned-up property was akin to having no property at all.

A quick word about the Lucys, if we must. To most, they were known as the Harlows, Mistress Lizzie and Master Charles of Liberty County, Georgia. Or really, she was of Liberty County, Georgia, and he was one of the many who came to the Texas countryside claiming to have no past, in hopes of making the land yield some invisible fortune he believed he was owed. But to us, they were just the Lucys, sometimes Miss or Mrs., Mister or Master, but typically just Lucy, spawn of Lucifer, kin of the devil in the most wretched place most of us have ever known.

One by one, we slipped out of the cabin and around the corner and farther still, past the Lucys' property line. There were six of us total, trudging single file into the forest. Junie led the way, followed by Patience, Lulu, Alice, and Serah, while Nan, the eldest, brought up the rear. We slipped deeper into the grove of dead trees, the large oaks and elms skinned of their bark, in various stages of atrophy. This was believed to make clearing the land easier, but it seemed to us wholly unnatural, another sign that the land of the dead maybe didn't reside under the sea as we previously thought, but was somewhere nearby, in some neighboring county in Texas.

⤙

WHEN WE BECAME WE, Texas country was still new, only a few years old in the Union. Navarro County was known as a land of wheat with dreams of cotton. Corn was the surer business, but men like Mr. Lucy came to Texas with cotton on the brain and dragged us along to make sure the land would yield. He had been unlucky before, we knew from Junie, because she had been with the Lucys the longest. She had worked for Mrs. Lucy before she was a Mrs., then was carried off to Wilkes County, Georgia, where she worked field after worn-out field as the couple's debt grew and grew. And she told us how they packed up and left in the dead of night to outwit angry creditors that threatened to seize what little he had left. By then, all Mr. Lucy had between him and sure ruin was thirty worthless acres and three slaves. They took to the road in two wagons stuffed to the gills with furniture, clothes, crockery, and seeds, the Lucys fighting all the while, their two small children screaming in fits. Harlow droned on about a vision from God, about a land of plenty, while his wife called him a fool with foolish ways, her pitch increasing with every mudhole, every windstorm, every feverish river of dirty water. God's favor would surely shine upon them, Harlow assured her. But when their two male slaves were seized and held at the trader's office in New Orleans for outstanding debts, Junie wondered if Lizzie was right all along. She knew she had only been spared a place in the trader's pen because on paper Junie belonged to Lizzie, a dower slave held in trust for Lizzie's children.

Junie never told us much about the two men who had been seized, if they were kith or kin, and if that was the reason she didn't work in the house for Miss Lizzie anymore. Instead, she told us about the tavern in New Orleans where they stayed for a couple of nights. How she sat on the back steps outside the kitchen, eating a bowl of bland rice, while the men's voices, drinking and carousing inside, carried out into the alley. How she was listening for Harlow's voice, to hear how he might go about retrieving the two men and how long that might take. He was sitting at a table a few feet away from the door, downing beer with his uncle Pap, a Louisiana merchant. And she wondered how long Pap would continue bragging before he offered to pay

Harlow's debt, but that offer never came. Instead, Pap told him, start fresh. Take what you have left and invest in women. They are cheaper than men and more versatile—can not only pull a plow and clear land, but can cook and clean, too. And best of all, they can breed, increasing a master's profit year over year every time a child is born. "But be careful, boy, about using your own seed," the man warned. "Out there, you'll want hardier stock and while half-breed gals fetch top dollar down here, outside Orleans, you can hardly get two nickels for 'em."

At the markets in Louisiana, Harlow asked us all the same questions. Had we born children before? How many? And had those children survived? In the back rooms of the auction houses, where they pulled dresses up to the neck, squeezed breasts, thumped hips, examined teeth, more questions were asked about the history of our wombs. Our previous owners or the brokers that negotiated for them were asked about our health. Were we without venereal disease or tumor? Were we verifiably sound and would a doctor certify to that fact? Harlow was teased about his need for certification, while the rest of the planters assured him they could read a slave body like a book, could determine with their bleary eyes and grubby, callused hands all one needed to know.

Alice, Serah, and Lulu were acquired there, along with Patience and her young son, Silas. Nan, having been in Texas prior to the war with Mexico, was picked up in Houston. Too old to be a breeding woman, he was told, but a good cook and doctoring woman, which he figured he would need out in the wilds of the upcountry, where the land was supposed to be better albeit remote.

But like us, the land proved finicky. Nothing grew sure or full under one bout of unrelenting sun after another. Cotton buds fell off the plants, the bulbs never growing full size, or

they rotted with too much rain. The corn planted early survived, while the late corn withered. And so far, not a new babe
born among us.

———

WE HURRIED ON DEEPER into the woods, dodging brittle limbs
and swarms of mosquitoes, while listening for snakes and wolves,
only slowing down once we reached the live part of the forest,
where the grass and moss softened our footfalls and the heavy
green leaves gave us cover. It was darker in this part, harder to
see, but harder to be seen, with a refreshing coolness that nipped
at our necks and feet. After a long day pressed with heat, the
coolness pulled down our songs, had us singing under our breath,
praise-house songs, feeling-good songs, the kind we knew before
ever coming to this place.

For each of us, these songs were different, as all our before-
heres were different, and some days, it's too much work, untan-
gling them. We borrow and steal in good measure, sometimes
throwing all our before-heres in a pot and making them available to the whole of we. She who can't remember her daddy
may borrow the memory of mine. Tell me about your ma, one
of us would say, what she sang to you at night, how she braided
your hair, what kind of dress did she make you for church, what
kind of sweet did she give you when you couldn't be soothed by
nothing else. But, of course, there were things each woman held
back, things she deemed too valuable for the pot or the opposite,
things too likely to spoil it whole.

We finally stopped when we reached The Tree, a large split
oak, growing in two opposite directions, one reaching sky-
ward, the other stretching out, wide and low, as if trying to
reach the sea.

BEFORE THE CROSSING COULD happen, there was a small matter that had to be handled. By this time, Serah knew the drill. She plopped down on the ground while the other women spread out around her, some kneeling and others sitting in the tree. It was important that all of their heads be higher than hers, a clear demonstration of her guilt.

Serah twirled a leaf between her fingers, a practiced blank expression on her face, as she listened to the details of her crime. Yes, she was in "hot water" again, but not because she was a troublemaker. That was solely Alice's purview, let Serah tell it, but more so, because at nearly seventeen, she was the youngest and still unschooled in the ways of life. She didn't yet understand how to manage white folks and their questions, and how often what was being said aloud had little relation to what was being asked or the request being made.

Nan, the elder of the group, dropped a bucket near Serah's leg and tipped it upside down with her walking stick. This was the signal that it was safe to talk, that the bucket would trap the sound and make their dealings under night sky unknown.

"I still don't get," Nan began, "why you opened your mouth."

"I didn't. She asked me," said Serah.

"You could've said you ain't know. Why didn't you?"

Serah stopped her twirling. She could hear the impatience in the old woman's voice, could picture fresh lines of irritation creasing her forehead. She hated being the cause of it. She respected Nan. Didn't want to be the kind of useless woman Nan thought little of, because Nan was one of those women who could do most anything. Nearly every farm had one. Not only could Nan cook and sew, but she could pull a plow, fell a tree, deliver babies, make medicines, and as such, had little compassion for able-bodied young girls, like herself, who could barely haul water. "'Cause Lucy was in a foul mood, waving a poker in my face. You know how she can be."

Stifled tittering broke out among the group.

"Alright, women, what say you?" Nan said, opening up the floor, but the rest of the group just yawned and waved their hands, ready to get the whole subject over with.

"We ain't talk punishment," said Alice, the only woman with a stake in the matter. It was Alice who had actually done the deed in question and had already been punished by the Lucys for it. She had stolen a cut of bacon from the Lucys' smokehouse and, in a panic, hidden it under the cookhouse steps. What Serah was guilty of was the telling. As the youngest of the group, she was still liable to make a wrong move and not necessarily understand why.

"Fine," Nan said. She motioned for Junie to hand over a small sack of corn seed she had been carrying. Nan then emptied the sack onto the ground next to the bucket. "Alright, your punishment is to pick up each and every seed of this corn."

Nan tipped the bucket over and picked it up. "See this," she said, reaching down and feeling for a notch in the wood with her fingers. "It should reach here. If it don't, we'll know you ain't finish and send you back. But the longer the seed is down, the harder it'll be. You ain't got long before the mice and squirrels come calling."

Alice made a whistle-like sound through her teeth.

"What now, Alice?" Nan said.

"She got the easiest one. She should get the hardest. Something smaller, like rice or benne seed."

"You see any rice or benne seed 'round here?"

"No, but in Carolina—"

"This look like Carolina to you?"

"At least make her kneel in it first," said Alice.

The small germ of anger Serah had been tamping down threatened to rise up, her face growing warm, a snappy insult flashing across her mind.

"Oh, shut up, Alice," Junie said, from her place underneath the tree.

"Don't pay her any mind," Nan whispered to Serah, squeezing her shoulder.

Serah nodded, inching closer to the pile of gray seed, its normally pale yellow color darkened from yesterday's tarring. In this country, they didn't push corn into the soil naked. Instead, the seeds were soaked in a mixture of hot water and sticky black tar, then laid out in the sun to dry, in hopes of staving off squirrels and raccoons who'd eat the seed before it took root.

She could smell the tar as she picked faster, her face over the bucket, strangely soothed by the soft tapping sound of the seed hitting bottom. She could feel Alice watching her, the woman's arms folded across her chest, while the rest of the women chatted among themselves, already done with the matter. She knew Alice could be what the women sometimes called a "miserable spirit." Everybody had the propensity to be one, but Alice was of those who embraced the feeling of it, felt more alive in the thrall of it. And if Serah understood anything about the prevailing wisdom of dealing with such folks, it was to handle them with care.

─⚏─

CLEARLY, THE ROAD TO becoming a we was not a honeyed one. The sun of Texas felt different to each of us. It made us crazy for a time and that crazy was called many things—homesickness, grief, drapetomania. What forged us together was more than circumstance. In some ways, we were more different than alike. None of us the same age or born in the same place. Some of us knew the folks that birthed us and some of us didn't. Some of us were born Christians, others came to it roundabout, if at all. Some of us practiced Conjure and practical magic, others steered far clear. Some of us had born children and lost them, while others were little more than virgins. We were bound together by what tends to bind women like us together. Often, that doesn't make folks kin. Makes them trapped. And that can make them hateful toward one another, unless it's redirected and harnessed toward something else altogether.

THE OTHERS BEGAN WITHOUT waiting for Serah, Nan, or Alice. Serah could hear them praying on the other side of the tree. Someone was singing, a throaty drawn-out hymn that sounded like a dirge, more vibration than song.

And it remained that way, low and thrumming, until Nan checked the bucket and emptied the corn seed back into the sack. She tied off the bag and handed it to Alice, and then carried the bucket over to the women singing, where she placed it inside the circle of women and turned it over. Serah and Alice followed her, joining along the outer edge.

Nan moved around the circle, dotting foreheads with oil as the song grew louder. The vibration grew so strong, it felt as if the group was being pulled deep inside it, made weightless, now swaying and rocking, like leaves in a strong wind. Junie moved into the circle and the women locked hands around her.

Serah watched as the woman spun and danced and cried. Moonlight shifted through the trees and lit up Junie's hair, braided and tucked at the base of her head, the long, crooked toes of her bare feet, the faded brown trousers rolled over at the ankle. Junie was the only one among them who wore pants, a set of Harlow's old trousers she wore tied around her waist with a thin rope. And that was often how Serah thought of her—the one who wore pants. It was a holdover from Serah's arrival, this need for categorization, to understand this new world and the people inside it by their habits and tics, their wants and weaknesses. Junie slowed down, turning her tear-streaked face to the light, before stumbling out of the circle and taking her place back along the perimeter.

Patience went next, inching her way into the circle with small steps. She didn't dance or shout. Instead, she just stood there, in stillness, with her eyes closed, her hands clasped together, a strand of rosary beads dangling from her wrist, whispering a prayer. She was the only Catholic among them, but she didn't seem to mind it. If others used their faith to separate themselves from others, she wasn't one of them. She needed the gathering part, she told Serah one day.

When Serah's turn came, she entered the circle, unsure of what to do. She didn't feel much like shouting or dancing. She liked the song enough, liked the sound of the women singing, but she couldn't drop down into it, the way the others seemed to. She wasn't a Christian, but the other women didn't know that, and didn't seem to care, really. This was just a means to open the door. It was your business whose help you sought—whether it be Jesus or the moon or your dead.

She spun around, repeated a prayer she heard others pray, whispering the words over and over while she waited for something to happen. She wanted to feel whatever it was that made the other women so joyful, whatever made them rock on their heels or fan their arms with glee. She wanted to know for herself what created that dazed, wide-eyed expression they often gave her afterward, like they were still somewhere else, and hadn't yet returned to the constraints of this world. She danced and she rocked, but nothing happened past her own self, past her own muscles moving as she directed them to. No Holy Spirit descended upon her. No burgeoning warmth washed over her.

At the edge of the circle, Lulu began shouting, her eyes closed, and fists clenched. The women recognizing the presence of Spirit moved to encircle Lulu, making it safe for her to move deeper into the sacred realm. Just like that, Serah's time in the circle was up, where she thought if anything was to be felt, if any spirit was to make its presence known, it would be there, inside the heat of the women.

Serah rejoined the outer edge of the circle, where she watched Lulu go deeper, jumping higher and pumping her arms, as if on the verge of flight. That seemed fitting. That if anyone would be a vessel, it would be Lulu. Not because Lulu was more righteous or upstanding than any of the others, in fact, most would say the opposite. It was more because there was little veneer between her and the world. Lulu was guileless. She'd say the meanest thing possible directly to your face with no shred of sass or anger in her voice, then get up and make you a cup of tea. She was fully a product of the moment itself, with little regard to the seconds before or after.

And still the sight of Lulu shouting and dancing made Serah feel worse. Locking hands like this was one of the few times Serah felt of the women, when she felt like they were something more than just a gaggle of strangers fastened together. But she found this night, she could take little comfort in it. She knew it took time to figure out a place, to learn its climate and its ways, what flora, fauna, or predators it might kill you with. So, it made sense that it took time for her gods and her dead to find her here, to cross the many miles of land and sea, not to mention, if there were protocols necessary to tangle with the gods here already. Kiowa gods, Cherokee gods, German gods.

However, the presence of Lulu shouting in front of her said different. This woman crying and dancing so freely made it clear to Serah that other people's gods had no problem locating them. So, if it wasn't Texas, with its strange air and stubborn fields, its plagues of pestilence and grifters, then surely, it had to be her. It had to be something wrong about her or in her that kept them from coming, that left her in this strange place with little to no aid in this world.

CHAPTER TWO

Days later, over the din of pickaxes and hoes, we could hear Mrs. Lucy shrieking. One sharp cry, followed by another long high-pitched wail. No one cast an eye in the direction of the sound. We went on pushing oat seed knuckle-deep into the earth, as if the sound of Mrs. Lucy going into labor was the most natural thing in the world.

The shrieking kept on, at turns growing louder, then fading out, only to start up again.

"Think Nan need a hand up there?" Junie said, after a while.

"She'll send Silas if she need us," Patience replied.

We knew Nan would tend to the birth despite Mr. Lucy's incessant railing about finding a suitable doctor to tend to her this go-round. Everyone knew it was all talk. This part of the country was still desolate, with few neighbors to speak of, and even if he had a connection to a bona fide doctor willing to make the journey, it was unlikely he could afford the fee.

The boy Silas ran up, waving his bony arms. He was a thin whisper covered in dust, his shirttail skimming his ashy knees. "Nan want you!" he cried. "Come now."

"Want who, baby?" Patience asked him.

He shrugged, one naked shoulder poking out of the neck of his shirt. She stood up and crooked her index finger at him. *Come here.*

He stared at her for a moment but didn't move.

"I said come here," Patience said.

The boy ambled over.

She sighed. She shifted the shirt so it centered around his neck. "Boy, you are a sight." She licked her thumb and cleared his face of sleep and crust, while he squirmed.

"Who she ask for?" Junie asked him.

He shrugged again.

Patience pinched his shoulder. "Open your mouth when somebody speak to you."

He gave Patience a defiant look and pulled back from her. "Didn't say. She just say come now and bring hot water."

A flash of anger crossed Patience's face. He saw it and ran, back in the direction of the Lucys' house.

"Get back here, Silas!" His legs slowed a moment, so she knew he heard her, but he kept on anyway.

He was skinny and fast, but Patience was faster. Years of worry had made her wiry and taut, and she leaped over to him, in a few quick paces, her skirt gathered in her fist. She grabbed ahold of his shoulder and pinched it hard, turning him toward her. His small face twisted up and he let out a ragged breath. She bent her face close to his. "Don't you run from me. I'm your mother, not them. You listen to *me*, you hear?"

He nodded, his eyes wide.

She wrapped her arms around him, but he was stiff as wood

in her arms. He pulled back from her and leaned his head in the direction of the Lucys' house.

"Alright," she said, dropping her arms. He turned and ran away. She watched him until he reached the edge of the yard, a flicker of disappointment flaring up in her chest. She probably wouldn't see him the rest of the day, and this was how the one moment she had with him went.

She went back to her place on the row and crouched back down, wrapping her fingers tight around the handle of the pickaxe she'd left lying in the dirt. She slammed it into the ground a few times, until she could let the air out of her body slowly and then slower still. She wasn't sure when it happened, the moment when her boy became more theirs than hers. Initially, she didn't protest too much at the idea of him being a houseboy. She figured he'd spend most of his time helping Nan, and that seemed alright, as he was a frail child, often too sickly to follow them around in the fields all day. Most of the time, she worried about harm coming to him in that small evil house, how quickly and often he'd become the target of all the discord that flowed between the Lucys. Every time she got an evening with him, she checked his back, his legs, his arms, for lash marks, for bruises, but she got fewer and fewer evenings with him now. He slept in the Lucys' house, to aid with the Lucys' children, and getting him back to share a meal became harder and harder to come by. "He can't be spared now," she was always told.

And worse, he didn't even bother to sneak away to see her anymore. There was a time when he did, dipping by the loom for a moment to make her laugh or swinging by the cabin, while they were finishing up their sewing. Now, if he came at all, it was because she begged Nan to send him, for a few minutes when he wouldn't be missed. Now, when he came, he'd make it plain how much he didn't want to be there. He no longer liked the ashcake she made in the fireplace, singeing her fingers in the process. He didn't want the small corn-husk dolls she made him. He no longer liked sitting in her lap and listening to tall tales or singing with her. At first, she thought he was just worried about being punished, so worried he couldn't relax, but soon, it became clear to her, that wasn't it. He no longer felt at ease, so far away from the Lucys. He missed them now, it seemed, much like he used to miss her.

Patience ran her fingers over the gaping hole she made. She pushed the dirt around, making a mound and pushing the seed down inside it. It was early, the position of sun in the sky told her, but she felt so tired she thought the sun must be wrong. "Bird, you go," Patience said suddenly, from her place at the end of the row.

"Why me?" asked Serah.

"'Cause you still slow as sorghum syrup . . ."

"Like molasses."

"Slower . . . like cold tar," said Alice.

The women chuckled. "Now, you go on."

Serah groaned and headed off after Silas.

Patience watched her, hoping the girl might tell her something more about what she saw inside the house. All this time, Nan had been telling her not to worry, but it didn't ease her mind any. Instead, she suspected that Nan was holding something back, not in a malicious way, in a protective way. But if her boy was in danger, Patience wanted to know. Even if it didn't seem like there was much she could do about it. What was being somebody's mother, if not that? Sensing danger and putting your body in between it and your child. Maybe she couldn't sing him songs at night anymore, nor wash his face and hands in the morning, but maybe this she could still do.

—✦

SERAH DID NOT RUSH in the hot, humid air. Silas ran on ahead, only slowing down once, to peek over his shoulder at her. She waved him on. "Go 'head. I'm coming."

She peeled off in the direction of the well, where she filled two buckets with water. It took her a few minutes to link each bucket to the opposite ends of a shoulder yoke and balance them proper across the back of her neck. Gingerly, she inched toward the yard, with a close watch on the rim of each bucket, only spilling a cupful before Lizzie let loose another wild, piercing shriek.

When Serah reached the cookhouse, a small building with a large hearth and square table, she transferred both buckets into a large iron kettle and got a fire going.

Nan appeared in the doorway, her face shining with sweat, a long white apron cresting over her ankles. "Why you doing that out here instead of in the house?"

"Oh. I didn't think to—"

"Girl, I declare," Nan said, sighing in exasperation. "Hurry up." She turned and walked away.

Serah ladled hot water into a pitcher, wrapped a cloth around the handle, and carried it into the Lucys' house. She was blinded for a moment by the sudden darkness, an unfamiliar earthy scent washing over her.

"In here," Nan said, calling her from a bedroom at the end of a long wide hallway. Inside the room, Serah placed the pitcher down on the floor next to Nan, without looking at Mrs. Lucy, drenched in sweat on the edge of her chair, a thin slip scrunched around her pale thighs. Serah averted her eyes and headed back out of the room.

"Where you going? Get back here," Nan said, rubbing the pregnant woman's stomach.

"To fetch more hot water," said Serah, though she had no intention of returning to the dank dark room.

"I need a hand. Get behind her."

Serah forced herself to move closer. She didn't even want to be in the same room. The whole process stirred up a wild anxiousness inside her. Whenever women grew big with child, their bodies growing alien and monstrous, she found herself watching them with suspicion, though she couldn't place what it was she found frightening about them. Maybe it was the deep wide bellies, so heavy they could tip a woman over on the row, sending them headfirst into the stalks. Or the sight of them unclothed, a new taut round world affixed to their bodies. Or the muck that descended from them when the babies came spilling out, one after another. Or the incessant need of the thing once it arrived, the swaddled bundles lying underneath a shelter of leaves at the edge of a potato bed, the constant sound of crying and mewling they emitted throughout the morning, only growing louder as the day went on. She couldn't forget how the births turned the women on her old farm in South Carolina adrift, made them wan and stiff-legged as they chopped and weeded, sometimes with the babe hoisted on their backs. They spent the evenings sewing and fighting off sleep, while the child fed or cried, or cried, then fed. But the worst part was the artless rebellion of their bodies after too many births, how their spines tipped forward, or their uteruses descended lower and lower, suddenly trying to meet the air, and how some never healed right after the fifth or eighth birth. How one woman was banished altogether, sent to the woods to live in a cave after her inside parts never mended. The woman lost all control over her bodily functions. Rivers of piss and shit dribbled with such frequency and without warning that all the time, she was afraid to eat or drink, the smallest excretions causing her great pain and great embarrassment.

Ever since then, Serah looked askance at the whole birth enterprise. And while she was surprised Lizzie of all people rekindled this anxiety in her, it just confirmed how little she wanted to do with the entire process. She had no desire to be bedside while the woman shrieked and squirmed. She didn't care to witness the elaborate protocols doctoring women, such as Nan, were insistent about following, in hopes of helping a new soul transition into the world proper. And most of all, she didn't want to be in the thick of it herself, with a trapped soul inside her, sucking her dry and tipping her organs about, or later, nursing at her breasts or cradled in her lap, where eventually it'd be taken away, the moment she allowed herself to love it.

"Rub her back, will you?" said Nan.

Serah ignored the parts of herself that wanted to run elsewhere, that would instead be grateful to be cast back outside in the sticky heat, sowing winter oats with the rest of the women. Instead, she did as she was told and rubbed the woman's back in slow circles, her fingers damp from the sweat-soaked slip. Just how long would she have to do this?

Lizzie let out a loud moan, her body sliding down off the chair. Serah slipped her arms underneath the woman's armpits and felt the woman's weight sink down into her. Lizzie's hair was now plastered to her head, her breathing slow and wide.

Serah looked down at the lolling head, the neck no longer able to support it, and she found herself looking for the seam of the woman, as if there were just a few tired stitches holding Mrs. Lucy together.

"My first lying-in, I had six women in the room with me," Lizzie said. A sudden wave of pain seemed to hit her then and her head snapped back into Serah's chest with a thud.

Nan sat opposite the two, now squatting on a makeshift

stool, waiting to catch the baby. "Mmhmm, who was there?" she said, pressing a warm compress on Lizzie's swollen stomach.

"My ma, both my sisters, Mrs. Kenneally from the farm over, and Mother Amy from the church . . ." Lizzie breathed.

The child seemed to be crowning now and Nan motioned for Serah to hold the woman firmly, lest she sink down when the child slid free. Serah tightened her grip and closed her eyes.

"Send for them, won't you?" Lizzie said, her voice breaking.

Nan began pressing low on the woman's abdomen. "C'mon, Mrs. Lizzie, push a little bit more."

"It was a storm that night and they all had to stay over. There wasn't even enough room for them all, but they wanted to be close to me and the baby—"

A long low moan stopped the anecdote, then a surge of water spurted out from the woman, splashing Nan's arms, so high it soaked her rolled-up sleeves. Serah was startled, but Nan barely blinked. She just reset her footing and urged the woman on.

Within seconds, the baby emerged, the small slippery body coming so fast, Nan almost lost her grip. "I got you, honey," Nan said, gripping the child firmly and placing it in her lap. She cleared its mouth with her finger and wiped it off with a warm, damp cloth. The pale red creature drew breath and screamed.

"Is it a boy?" Lizzie asked.

"Yes, yes, it is."

"Well, that's a relief," Lizzie said, a slow grin spreading over her face. "Let me see him."

Nan wrapped the child up and held him out to Lizzie.

Serah looked down at the wrinkled infant, its mother slumped over and leaning toward him, and couldn't resist the urge to extract herself. She slowly began trying to pull her arms free.

"Where you going? We have to wait for the afterbirth," Nan said.

Serah strengthened her hold and a few minutes later, the dark purple mass slipped down and out, Nan catching it in a waiting chamber pot. Serah could see it, wet and jiggling, the long pink cord extending from its center. Nan set the child down and tied off the cord. She then cut it, firing the end with the flame of a lit candle.

Serah had never seen an afterbirth up close. She just knew there were many folks who attributed a good deal of their misfortune in life to this moment, to the separation of their body from this quivering mass. She didn't know why exactly, only that it needed to be buried at the base of a good tree and it needed to be close by, where one could look after it and visit it, when necessary. She didn't know what the fallout was when one couldn't do that. The afflictions people named were all different—water in the lungs, sickness in the head, a deadening of an arm or leg. Almost anything could be attributed to the mishandling of this sacred thing and one's untimely separation from the tree or hollow where it was buried.

"Here, take him, while I get her cleaned up," Nan said, holding out the mewling, crying child to Serah.

Serah hesitated, before taking the pale pink babe in her arms. She looked down at it, the blue veins crossing its face, the tiny, pursed lips, the heavy eyelids snapping open and closed. He looked harmless, not unlike a sleeping chick. *Oh, what damage will you come to do in this world?* she thought. And because she was holding him and could feel the child settling into her arms, she wondered if they could speak this way. Perhaps she could make her thoughts travel down and out her fingers and into his small soft body. She could plant these notions inside him while he was still wet and forming, like setting seeds in damp soil.

I should dash your head in right now, she threatened, grinning at the child suddenly. *How many lives could I save just by doing that? But you'll be different, won't you? A righteous man in the hell–carnival?*

The child began screaming.

"Bring him here," Lizzie called out from the bed. Serah handed the baby over and watched as Lizzie put the child to her breast, but he couldn't latch on, couldn't draw down the thick yellow milk of the first days.

"Here, take him," Lizzie sighed. Serah took the squirming child back in her arms while Lizzie sat up, squeezing her breast, trying to coax milk out. "I thought this time feeding would be easier," she said. "I didn't have much milk with the first two either, but our old house girls had plenty. We never wanted for milk when they were around. I didn't think much of it at the time, but you know that Roberta had a baby every time Mother did."

Serah felt stuck under the weight of this small pale boy. Nan had disappeared with her tools, motioning for Serah to stay put until she returned.

Lizzie continued pressing on her left breast, until a thick smear of fluid trickled from her nipple. "Ooh, give him here."

Serah gave the child back to Lizzie. He opened his mouth to scream and Lizzie slid the glob into the child's mouth. "Well, Roberta was a married woman. I suppose if I want plenty of milk round here I got to get y'all husbands," Lizzie said, chuckling. "Young Master Will, we got to get these gals married off, now don't we?"

It was all too close. Serah surveyed the room, looking for a task that would get her out of that house. She grabbed a sack and began stuffing all the soiled linens and bedclothes into it.

The baby opened his mouth again and Lizzie jammed her nipple inside, just as a wave of activity bubbled up from the front part of the house. The sound of Lizzie's older children bursting in, now stomping and screaming in the front room. "Go get them," Lizzie said.

Serah stepped out of the bedroom and went down the hall, where four-year-old Louisa was chasing her older brother, five-year-old Ollie, around the table. "Stop it!" Louisa screamed, as Ollie whooped and yelled.

"Both of you stop that running and hush up," Serah said as Ollie ran toward Serah, taking cover behind her legs. "Your ma wants you," she said as she steered the two children into the bedroom.

"C'mon and meet little William," Lizzie said. Louisa and Ollie inched toward the bed as if afraid. "C'mon, he won't bite."

Serah grabbed the sack and beelined for the door as the children crowded around the bed.

"Gal, come back when you're done," Lizzie yelled after her. "You know he won't sleep through the night."

⚞

BEFORE NAN COULD GET dinner started, she needed to get cleaned up. She placed her tools in a pot of water and set them to boil. Any unused herbs needed to be set aside for inspection—that nothing got wet or damp, lest it would mildew and rot.

In a small room off the backside of the cookhouse, she kept her few belongings and the rolled-up pallet where she slept most nights, when she wasn't needed overnight in the Lucys' house. Only on special occasions—such as crossings and holidays—did she wander down to the quarters and sleep some portion of the night alongside the rest of the women.

On a small bench, she poured some warm water from a kettle into a bowl and stripped out of her clothes. With a rag and a small slice of soap, she washed herself, with particular care around her fingers and under her nails. In the corner of the room sat the waiting chamber pot with Lizzie's afterbirth in it. The wriggling purplish mass looked like it might slither away at any moment. She watched it from the corner of her eye as she washed, as if whatever came out of a Lucy could surprise her, if she wasn't careful. She chuckled to herself at the thought.

Now, in a fresh set of clothes, she felt better. The grit and sweat of Lizzie's labor off her, she felt like she could breathe. She pushed the soiled heap of clothing to the side. Scrubbing them would have to wait.

She walked over to the chamber pot and peered down at it. She had already inspected it once, but she did so again, just to be thorough, just to make sure it was whole and hadn't come out piecemeal, otherwise, she'd have to go back and wait for Lizzie to pass the rest of it. A fragmented placenta meant all kinds of danger.

But this one looked healthy and whole. The only concern now was the matter of disposing it. She had to admit she was puzzled. She hadn't delivered many white children, and the few she had were the offspring of indentured immigrants, Irish mostly, half of which were deemed "fallen" due to their relationships with Black men.

For the Black mothers she normally cared for, there were very specific protocols for each stage of delivery. All kinds of things that needed to be done to usher in the new spirit, and to keep bad spirits at bay so they couldn't do harm to the child or mother. Normally, she might bury the afterbirth near the trunk of a tree; other times, she'd salt it and burn it, and protect the ashes for the first few weeks of the baby's life. The burning would take hours, but Silas could watch over it, and set the ash aside, if she explained it to him proper.

Yet none of that seemed necessary. She picked up the bowl and walked out of the cookhouse, and over to the far side of the yard, past the smokehouse and around the barn, to the small pen, where the few hogs the Lucys owned were rustling about. Fat and noisy, they grunted and squealed. A spotted black one moved toward her, sniffing for food. She stood and watched them for a moment, before flinging the bowl's contents over the railing. She watched as the greedy hogs ran toward the bloody material and devoured it.

For all the years she had been midwifing, she felt a tether to the children she had delivered. The ones who survived and ones who didn't. They stayed with her, a genteel chorus that lived in the corners of her life. She didn't mind it, really. The alternative seemed lonelier. But she wanted no binding connection to this one. She'd see him and his mother every day, and that seemed plenty.

All those detailed rituals she usually did were there to help protect the child and mother, but in her estimation, Lizzie and baby William needed no such thing. And if they did, she damned well wouldn't be the one to provide them.

CHAPTER THREE

New cotton was up the first time we saw Zeke. We were eating our midmorning meal of ashcake and coffee, passing a tin cup of the bitter hot liquid around from person to person. This was but another complaint we had against this wily country. Here, *coffee* had come to mean nearly any vile warm drink one could think of. It could be made of anything—pecans, parched corn, even walnuts—and yet, they still called it coffee and served it at every meal.

We only had a few minutes more to eat, so we almost didn't notice the man trailing behind Mr. Lucy like a shadow. On occasion, Harlow rented builders and masons, men we only saw in passing, erecting one leaning structure or another, so the man's arrival didn't trouble us. We didn't wonder after the man, who he might be, or what task he was brought to execute.

Instead, we concentrated on Mr. Lucy, still some distance away, his eyes obscured by the brim of a large hat. We couldn't hear him, though we could see without looking, his head cocked in our direction, his mouth moving, a likely river of instructions and invectives streaming from his lips. All spines straightened, all antennas leaned toward the two men as we shifted our bodies in the opposite direction, palming the last bits of ashcake, draining what was left of the foul now-lukewarm coffee, before heading off in the direction of the potato slips.

Later, when we made lore of this moment, we'd say the opposite. That we saw a monster coming, that the sky darkened, and a lone rooster crowed and flapped its wings, even though the sun was long done rising. Anybody claiming to be a seer would say they felt his presence, that the moment they saw the man, they knew something awful would come to pass.

———

WE DIDN'T SEE THE two men again until dusk. By then, we were sticky with day, our blouses soiled with sweat, our hems ragged and crusted with dirt. We were in the yard again, in the midst of our evening work. Patience was wrestling with the crank, grinding the corn needed to make our dinner, while the rest of us readied a sack of cotton for spinning. We plucked husks, seeds, and lint from the fiber, then carded it—combing the material with long wire teeth until it lay flat and pliable.

We could still smell what Nan had cooked the Lucys, a pungent dish of roasted meat that made our mouths water. We prayed she'd saved some bit of it for us, even if it was just the gravy, flavored with bacon grease. It was her we were listening for, so when Mr. Lucy and the man pushed into our circle, we were sorely disappointed, still wrapped up in our fantasies of corn pone drizzled with gravy.

Mr. Lucy motioned Patience to shut down the crank and sit.

It was then we got our first good look at the man. He was about a head taller than Mr. Lucy, a broad strapping figure, the way we figured Moses might have looked when he parted the Red Sea. He had sleepy brown eyes and a scruffy beard that obscured his mouth. Almost immediately, we began to anticipate the tasks he could take off our hands. He could split rails or help us clear the land on the other side of the farm, where our tiny garden plots were plundered mercilessly by the wandering roots of thirsty trees.

If any of us thought him handsome, she made no indication to the rest. And maybe secretly, for a lone moment, we were gladdened by the idea of him, someone to play the lady for, to adorn ourselves in perfumes and baubles, and carry on harmless, ongoing flirtations. This was true for those among us who enjoyed men. We would have been happy to tease one another about him, to make him believe we were half in love with him and entertain ourselves with silly jealous bouts where we'd force him to choose one of us. And those among us who found men scary or altogether more trouble than they were worth would find our games comical and take bets on which woman might best the other, and it is they who would get in between the two parties, if the game grew sour and someone really got attached to the man in question.

"This here's Zeke," Harlow said. "He gone be with us a while. Help him out, will you, like good Christians should. He'll stay in the barn."

We nodded. The man's face was a blank, his eyes looking past us.

"Nan's cooking up a meal for him," Harlow went on. "Patience, you take it up to him when it's done, hear?"

"Why me? He got two legs."

"Gal, don't mar my peace," Harlow said, glaring at her. "You want some heat on your back?"

Patience didn't answer, and the two men walked away. She went back to the crank, where she muttered under her breath about being chosen for the task. "I ain't his mother. I ain't suckle him." She cranked the mill faster now, the creaky gears drowning out all sound, all voices, making it suddenly too hard to hear one another.

⟶

IT WAS DARK BY the time Patience approached the barn with Zeke's dinner. She stood at the edge of the doorway, peering into its black insides, the dank smell of wet hay rushing toward her. She listened for the man but didn't hear him, only the rustling of a few pigs in the pen adjacent to the barn. Far off, somewhere a dog was howling.

"Hey, mister," she called out. He stepped forward, so sudden and quiet-like he startled her. The moonlight was dim, and she could barely see his face.

"What was you doing in there?" she asked.

"Resting."

"Oh." That struck her as curious, that he seemed to be there without a task or assignment. "They ain't give you a pine knot?"

"Yeah, but don't need it. Dark suits me fine."

"Hmph," she said. Another curious thing. "Here." She shoved the tray of food at him—corn pone with gravy and two slices of ham covered with a clean piece of homespun.

He didn't take the tray, or even seem interested in its contents. He smiled weakly, a small gap between his two front teeth. "It smells good," he said, "but I don't really like to eat until after."

"After? After what?" She tried again, pushing the tray toward his barreled chest until it touched. "Here."

"Come in. You're supposed to stay awhile." He grabbed hold of the tray, putting his hands on top of hers.

Patience jerked backward. The tray tilted, warm gravy spilling onto his hands and shirt. "Dammit. Sorry," she said, uprighting the tray. "Take the food and I'll see if Nan has something else you can change into."

He fanned out the shirt. "It'll dry." Again, that weak, strange smile passed over his lips. He stepped closer to her. "Don't be scared of me. I hate for gals to be afraid of me," he said, looking her in the eye so intensely, she dropped her gaze. "I'll be gentle as I can," he murmured.

It hit her suddenly what he was saying, and she dropped the tray, jumping back when it hit the ground, splashing onto her skirt. He looked at it for a moment, as if only slightly disappointed.

"Never mind all that. C'mon in," Zeke said.

"You a traveling nigger?"

He nodded.

"And you supposed to be a kind one? That it?"

"Yes, miss, I tries to be." And there was that strange smile again, the cautious pleading gaze, like he wanted her to acknowledge this kindness in him, that here he was talking to her plainly and reasonably, instead of dragging her into the barn like another stockman might.

But she was too stunned to care about all that. She stepped backward, watching the man closely as she put more and more space between them. They stared at each other for a long moment, before he turned away, disappearing into the barn.

She spun and ran full speed into the hazy darkness. She was tempted to run as far as she could, but the problem was, that wasn't very far. She had a better idea than the other women what lay at the end of most attempts—more land, little food, and an infinite number of white men with guns. And what she understood more than most about all those white men with guns in this strange and new country was how arbitrary and varied their cruelty could be. Yes, it could be glittering and wild, but more often, it was ordinary and banal and monotonous.

It was this ordinary type of cruelty that disappeared her husband, Jacob. She thought of him as she ran through the yard and back to the cabin full of women. "Damn you." It was Jacob's fault. That she was still here alone, running from a dark barn in the dead of night from a man the Lucys brought for the sole purpose of mating with her.

She thought herself a widow and if anyone asked, she said Jacob had died, though she had no earthly idea whether he was alive or dead. It's not that she wanted to wish death upon him if he was still breathing. It was just the easiest way to finally wrap her mind around the fact that he wasn't coming back. It was the waiting that had almost done her in. That made the days impossible to get through, that made her feel as if she was on the verge of imploding.

She came to this place a wife, newly separated from her husband. And while the couple had lived most of their married days apart, with her fate being tied to the whims of a wealthy widow on a farm in northern Louisiana, and he being a freeman, working the ports, he came up almost monthly, offering the widow free labor in exchange for being allowed to visit his wife and their young son, Silas. When the widow died and Patience and Silas ended up here, Jacob followed. He showed up some months later, not long after they all arrived in Navarro. Harlow was cordial at first. Got Jacob to help him build the first two cabins and even raise the barn. And it seemed like maybe the couple could have a similar arrangement akin to their life in Louisiana, but as time passed, Patience and Jacob realized that was less and less likely.

Jacob still couldn't afford to buy her and Silas's freedom, as that price tag was always a goalpost in motion, but worse than that, freedmen weren't allowed to be in the country long. Texas had a law against them. Without a petition or a white man to vouch for him, he couldn't stay without risk of being jailed or re-enslaved.

Patience begged Harlow to vouch for Jacob, but he refused. Said he didn't believe in free niggers.

"Tell you what, though. I'm not unreasonable," Harlow said to her. "Jacob could sign himself over to me. And that would solve it. The law couldn't touch him, then. And nothing would change. He'd be here working on the farm just he like he been doing."

For days, Patience couldn't even bring herself to mention Harlow's proposed solution to Jacob. Every time she looked at him, the words burrowed themselves deeper into her flesh. It wasn't long before Harlow told Jacob himself. Gave her husband an ultimatum with a ticking clock in the middle of winter. And for days after, she and Jacob fought like they never had before.

"Over my dead body," she told him.

"Ain't up to you. It's up to me."

"I swear you do this, you gone have to marry one of them 'cause we through."

"Woman, you gone quit me when I'm trying to stay with you. You really are touched."

"Maybe. Still don't make what I say any less true."

That was the thing about husbands. You know them better than they know themselves. And she knew Jacob wouldn't survive it. He didn't have the kind of soul that could parse it for long. In short bouts, he managed fine. After that, he had to take off for a long haul on a fishing boat, or a gig managing horses for a stagecoach, or upriver somewhere, where he'd haul freight for any of the companies shipping goods back and forth. Too long here and he'd die.

Besides, didn't he know how fast he'd come to hate her and Silas under this new arrangement? How soon he'd see his family and the coffle as the very same thing. His being there for so long had already changed things between them. She had begun to think the distance they had before suited them better. After all, wasn't love served best in tiny bits, when one could eat it whole, when she could wear her good face and he his, when she could starch her one good dress and do up her hair for the short time they'd spend together—a period so short they never had to watch the other get beaten to the ground or cut real low? Hadn't they been better for it? To never have to look at the other with pity or shame.

By the time she reached the cabin, she was out of breath. She pushed the heavy door wide open, her breathing so ragged she couldn't speak.

"Somebody after you?" asked Alice, sitting up suddenly.

"No, no," Patience said, shutting the door closed.

"What then?" Junie asked, squinting as she broke a piece of thread with her teeth.

Patience didn't answer. She sat down on a stool for a long moment, then immediately stood up. She paced around the front door, pressing it shut over and over again. She wandered over to the lone shelf that held that week's rations and began moving them around. The small sack of corn now on the left, the gill of salt now to the right.

"Pay, what is it?" said Lulu.

Patience shook her head. She squatted next to her own pallet and yanked out all the stuffing—moss, corn husk, hay, old rags—and then, one by one, began stuffing it all back. "He a breeding nigger." She laughed, a high-pitched terrible laugh.

She shook her head again, the stark, outraged laughter growing choked in her throat. "Y'all hear me? Lucy done brought us a breeding nigger."

—≤

THE NEXT DAY, PATIENCE fished her rosary out from its special hiding place and put it around her neck for protection. She wouldn't speak to us, only to it. All day we heard her whispering as she fingered the beads. "Mother Mary, never was it told that any asking your help was turned away. Mother Mary, I run to you for my protection." Those of us who consulted other earthly sources of help were at a loss. None of us wanted to get close enough to the man to collect the required skin and hair or fluids needed to do darker deeds. And maybe foolishly, we hoped it wouldn't come to that. That maybe Patience's prayers would be answered, that the Lucys would grow to see the error of their ways.

And by dusk, we thought maybe it was so, as we hadn't seen Mr. Lucy or Zeke all day. We went about our evening routines, casting lots to determine who would grind that night's corn and who'd have to stand over the hot fire to bake it.

"I don't care what that dice say, I ain't doing it. I did it yesterday."

"So . . ."

"That's your own fault. If you threw better . . ."

And while laughing at us, Patience did a dangerous thing. For one lone second, she forgot about them, the whole ordeal slipping to the back of her mind. Like tales of his namesake, Mr. Lucy could sometimes just appear. All of a sudden, he was there, standing behind her, and without a word or syllable even uttered between them, he snatched Patience toward him with one hand, striking her with the other. In his fist, there was a bundle of reedy branches and ragged green leaves. He struck at her bare skin, her arms, neck, and face. He let go and she sunk to her knees.

"Do it. Or tomorrow will be worse," he said, walking away, disappearing as suddenly as he came.

We helped her up, took her to Nan, who applied thick salves to the nasty, stinging welts that sprung up on her skin. The Lucys were often reluctant to use the long-tail whips so common across the South. Not because they objected to the cruelty of such methods of correction, but mostly because it wasn't economically feasible. Black snake whips and cat-o'-nine-tails flayed the skin, did damage to the muscle, put a person down for days, weeks even, depending on the number of lashes. Not to mention, it could affect resale value. Those were luxuries a yeoman farmer couldn't afford, with only a handful of folks in the fields.

—⤝—

PATIENCE TOOK A NAP and woke up hours later, the heavy numbing effect of the salve wearing off. She blinked at the stars, staring down at her from the holes in the roof, the small gaps where the logs didn't meet all the way, the spaces along the ridge that leaked every time it rained.

She was alone in the cabin and she was grateful for the rare moment of quiet. Muffled chatter began to seep in from outside. She opened the door and the chatter paused to ask her questions she had no use for.

Was she hungry?

Did she need more salve?

Did she want some tea?

She didn't answer, didn't want questions or their eyes or their speculating. Whatever was waiting for her in that barn probably awaited them, too, but not today. She didn't know why that mattered, but it did.

She walked past them and continued up toward the yard. She thought about Jacob, about the dark woods at the edge of the farm, where she could lie out for a few days. Someone else would have to go in her place, and maybe that'd give her enough time to figure out a solution.

She knew just the place, a gully with a thicket of low-slung ash trees, and the memory of it stung her. It was the last place she saw Jacob. After arguing about the ultimatum for a week, Jacob went ahead and signed himself over to Harlow. She was angry about it, but Jacob convinced her he could handle it. Besides, they just needed to wait for the weather to break, he said, then he'd get her and Silas out of there.

Jacob was good at geography, had a bird's sense of direction, so his plan didn't seem far-fetched to her. But that winter was brutal and several months in the cold cramped cabin, with not only a sickly screaming toddler but four other women, changed his tune. He picked fights, with Patience, with the women, with Harlow. "You sure Silas mine?" he'd ask her, whenever he wanted to get a row started. The child was too sickly and frail, he'd claim. She must have been running around with someone else back then. She spent most of the season in a state of silent seething, clutching her rosary beads, and whispering the Pater Noster, which, for some reason she couldn't figure, only made him madder.

He got Harlow to agree to let him build a new addition onto the cabin, but the two came to blows before he could finish. Harlow got a fist in his eye and Jacob took off running into the woods. Late that night, she snuck out to take him a change of clothing, a blanket, and some food. She figured he was in the gully, where they used to go whenever they wanted to be alone, but she hadn't wanted to be there with him in a long time, and almost forgot how to find it. She found him there, shivering and tired. "It'll blow over in a few days," she told him. "Lucy can't afford to lose you."

"We should go now," he said, clutching her arm, wrapping his body around hers.

"We can't. Silas won't make it. Not in this weather." She couldn't see Jacob's face but could feel the coldness in his demeanor return. "You didn't see him on the trip here," she went on. "That cholera going round. He barely survived it."

Jacob didn't say anything for a while. He let go of her, brought his face down to hers, and whispered low into her neck. "Leave him."

The ground underneath her feet shifted; the trees in front of her grew soft and blurry, the branches melding into the dark sky.

"What?" she whispered, shifting her body backward in a futile attempt to see his face. A cold gust of wind sent the branches of the trees clacking. The sound of it felt like it was inside of her. The sharp edge of her heart beating.

"I ain't hear you," she said. *Say it again, you bastard.*

He didn't say anything more, just pulled the blanket around his shoulders, tucking it tight under his arms.

Maybe she didn't hear that. It was just this land playing tricks on her. Jacob would never say such a vile thing.

He rubbed his hands together. "How much food did you bring?"

She handed over the small basket she brought, filled with corn pone and a couple pieces of salt pork wrapped in cloth.

He stuffed a chunk of corn pone into his mouth. "It's not enough," he said, chewing.

"It's enough 'til I get back over here tomorrow," she told him.

"Lucy will cool off in a couple of days and you'll come back. You'll act sorry. He'll make a big show and then it'll be over with. And when it's warmer, we'll figure out a plan," she heard herself say, the words tumbling out fast and jumbled and high-pitched.

He nodded. "You say so."

"I do." She forced herself to kiss him goodbye. Her mind churning all the while, arguing with itself. *He didn't say that. Yes, he did. He didn't say it. You know he did. If he said it, he would've said it again.*

"I'll see you tomorrow," she said, pulling away from him.

He nodded again and she took off through the trees.

The next night, he wasn't there, and she found herself surprised by his absence. He must have moved to another hiding place, she figured. He'd be back around any day now. He wouldn't leave with those words between them. He wouldn't leave without making it right. But he never returned to the farm or the gully. With each day that passed, she was sure the next day would be the day when he'd return. Ask her forgiveness for all his misdeeds. Be the Jacob she knew, the Jacob who showed up after long bouts away. That Jacob was kind and warm, that Jacob was sweet and helpful. But she hadn't seen that Jacob in a mighty long time, and who knew which Jacob would appear if they ever crossed paths again.

She could see the barn up ahead, the ragged shape of it butting against the cloudy night sky. Her face and arms still stung. The top half of her body was swollen and painful. The nettles created rashes that stung and itched, and she shoved her hands in her pockets of her apron to keep herself from scratching the wounds until they bled.

The air was humid, and though she couldn't see Zeke, she could feel him there, waiting and looming, with that crooked unsmiling grin. She felt foolish for trying to stop the inevitable. For what was coming anyway, like a wave rising up over the shore, like rain bursting from a cloud. Some things couldn't be stopped. And wasn't she silly for still trying. She hadn't been able to stop previous times, whether the men were white or Black, slave or free, whether they snatched her from behind and choked her until she suffocated, or just talked and talked and talked while they pulled her dress up over her face. And she hadn't been able to stop the country from eating Jacob, even though she tried.

She stopped at the cookhouse, where a covered tray lay on the table. She picked up the tray and moved stiff-legged to the barn. She made her mind blank as a sheet as she walked into the barn's dark maw, in much the same way her father had walked into the sea. She had never been told what body of water it was, only that he charged forward into the rising water, determined to walk back home. Mother Mary, why did you not bring me a great sea to walk into?

Zeke stirred when he heard her, a pine knot torch catching light. And she could see him in the dim flame, sitting up in a makeshift bed of hay, a soft expression in his eyes.

"You hungry?" she said.

"Starving. But I don't eat until—"

"Right," she said, putting the tray down on a bench.

She went and eased herself down next to the man on the pallet.

"You're very pretty," he said.

"Don't. Just get it over with," she said, lying down. The flame went out and she pulled up her dress.

She thought then about water, how it must feel when boats enter it, the sharp bows that seemed to sever the water in half but didn't. And she thought about Jacob, how he'd kill this man if he knew, but he would likely never know, because he didn't stay.

WHEN PATIENCE SLIPPED BACK into the cabin sometime later, we were still up sewing. We had just finished our allotments and had taken up hers.

"Go to bed. I'll finish," Junie whispered to the rest of us.

We shook our heads.

Patience lumbered past, and we all resisted the urge to touch her, to squeeze her arm or rub her back.

"Nan brought down more salve," Junie said, her voice sounding more like a question.

Patience didn't respond. She walked over to the pitcher on the table and filled a bowl with water.

We finished our sewing without speaking while we listened to Patience behind us, washing the man off of her.

Once she was done, she fished around her bedding, slow at first, then more frantic, tossing out the stuffing, as she had done the day before, but searching this time. Her fingers pulling apart the moss and hay. She shook loose her dress, the pockets. "Where my beads?"

We looked up.

"My rosary beads. Nobody seen them?"

We shook our heads.

"You had them the other day," Serah said.

"I know, but they ain't here now."

We tried to help her look, but the dark shadowy cabin made it hard to see much. We grazed the uneven floorboards with our fingers, checked the hard wooden shoes chucked in the corner.

Finally, Patience stopped. "Alice, you take them?"

Alice paused, scratching her face. "'Course not."

"'Cause if you took them, I won't be cross. I just want them back. Now."

"I said I ain't got them."

Patience walked over to Alice's corner of the room, where her pallet and trunk lay. Patience put her hand on the trunk and drummed her fingers on top of it.

Alice's blank expression grew steely as she rose from her stool. "Don't bother my things."

"Open it, then. Show me they not there. We all know you got a bad habit of taking what don't belong to you."

"So now I'm a thief and a liar?"

"Alice, even the mice in this room know the answer to that there question."

Lulu let loose a low whistle. "Back home, those are fighting words."

"Lulu, shut it."

Alice leaped toward Patience, but Junie grabbed ahold of her arm. "Leave her be," Junie said, with a hard edge in her voice.

"Let her go," Lulu said. "Patience a big girl. She can answer for all them choice words she spitting."

"Lulu, stop," Serah said quietly.

"No one's talking to you, Bird."

"How 'bout everyone shut it?" Junie said. "Let's not add any more dark to this awful day, alright?"

There was a general nodding and muttering, the tension in the room loosening a bit. Junie let go of Alice's arm with an affectionate squeeze.

Patience moved back to her bed. She shoved the stuffing back inside her mattress and lay down, pulling her blanket up over her head. Even in the dim flickering light, we could see her body shaking. Normally, one of us would go over to her and whisper soothing things, but this time, no one did. It was as if we feared the stockman's presence was contagious and whoever touched her would inevitably be next.

CHAPTER FOUR

BEING PAST CHILDBEARING YEARS, NAN was the only one exempt from spending a night or two with Zeke. However, she was responsible for certain hospitable tasks. It was she who showed him where to bathe, washed his clothing, and cooked his meals, serving him breakfast and lunch at the cookhouse daily.

And Nan felt bad for not realizing what he was the moment she saw him. In hindsight, she felt she should have seen it. There was a certain incoherence around the eyes she noticed that first day and, even now, was still trying to make sense of.

Some days, he ate on the cookhouse steps, and when he'd catch her watching him, he'd give her the strangest manic grin, his lower jaw twitching from side to side. The two halves of his face didn't seem connected, deadened eyes and an animated mouth.

Ever since Patience was struck for rejecting the man, Nan had been trying to find something that would help the women's cause. Before sunrise, she crept out into the woods, searching for roots and shrubs that might be useful. She didn't want to kill him, just wanted to make him ill enough that he couldn't perform.

By the time Nan reached the edge of the woods, the sun was just coming up. The dogwood trees were flowering, small red berries glistened from their branches. She could take back some berries that might cover the bitter taste of dogwood bark. Perhaps she could even make him a dessert.

In the understory, tall spindly plants with purple leaves swayed in the faint breeze. Pokeweed. It was poisonous, but the timing was all wrong. The trick with herbs was always timing. Harvesting a plant at the wrong time could be disadvantageous, even fatal. Choosing the wrong day, the wrong moon, could do a person serious harm. And she wanted to show a bit of restraint. After all, he had a family to go back to, he told her as much. Mentioned them with great care for some reason, and she thought it strange then, as she had barely exchanged more than a few words with him.

"You done?" was the only thing she could remember ever saying to him. But no matter what she said or if she said anything at all, he took her presence alone as an invitation to talk. Maybe he was lonely or just wanted this one woman to see him as whole, even if it was just the old lady cooking up vittles in a dark smoky kitchen. The impulse was a reasonable one, she supposed, but she didn't care for it, couldn't oblige him. She just wanted him gone, with as little harm done to the women down farm as possible.

There was some jimsonweed, a white flower surrounded by spiky leaves, but it seemed risky. It could sicken the man, she knew, but it was more likely to create an effect on his brain than his body. More likely to send him into some dreamy, hallucinogenic state where there'd be little telling what he'd actually do in that dark barn.

Some feet ahead, she spotted a chaste tree, its bright purple flowers just beginning to open. She wandered over to it, sensing some vibration calling to her. An unbelievable phenomenon she realized whenever she tried to describe it, but she had known it all her life—this ability to hear plants and trees whispering to her, offering her help. Young women came to her all the time, trying to develop remedies for one ailment or another, as if healing was just a matter of putting together the right recipe. They didn't understand the most important part of her job was listening. That most plants have dueling abilities, easily able to heal or kill you. And their effect on a body could change based on the makeup of that body. It wasn't like baking a pie, she warned whoever would listen to her.

She had learned this the hard way, after years of trying to ignore what her grandmother had taught her when she first began apprenticing. "The gift ain't just here," the old woman used to tell Nan, placing a palm over her eye. "It's here, too," her grandmother had said, motioning toward Nan's ears and heart. "Plants able to do most anything, if you listen to 'em."

Take the chaste tree for instance. In women, the seeds were thought to aid one's fertility, but in men, the seeds acted as a sedative for their lower parts.

She reached past the bright flowers, the fan of green leaves spread out, the thin reeds bearing clusters of black seeds. She took two seeds, crushed them with the edge of her mattock, and inhaled their sweet scent. Yep, these will do nicely. She carefully removed a few clusters of seeds and dropped them in her lap bag.

The sun rose higher, and she rushed back the way she came. She paused for a long second, in front of that dogwood tree she saw earlier, as it was still whispering to her. She put her hand over it and thanked the trunk in advance for its assistance, before peeling off a few pieces of its smooth gray bark. It was another sedative but, in the right amount, could cause nausea and painful stomachaches.

Then, she hurried back to the farm, a remedy already forming in her mind. She'd boil the dogwood bark for a few hours and use the liquid to make Zeke a soup. Then she'd crush the seeds and sprinkle them on top. She'd set it all with a nice piece of corn bread, just ripe for dipping.

Back at the cookhouse, she got the corn bread on the flames and the dogwood tea boiling. And when she saw the women coming in for their midmorning meal some hours later, she left them their coffee and bread without saying much. She didn't want to offer them false hope. The remedy would likely work, but it just as well might not. Bodies and medicines could be unpredictable.

⟶

WHEN LULU'S TURN CAME, she sat down opposite Zeke and emptied her pockets. On the dirt floor, she had laid out an assortment of valuables, one by one. Two silver shillings, a handful of seashells, a small mirror the size of a fist, a speckled barrette, one gold button, and a set of rosary beads.

"And I got a hog, too. I ain't seen him in some time, but can find him, if you want him."

Zeke looked at her puzzled. "All this for me?"

"One hand washes the other, right? They pay for a thing. I pay for the contrary," she said. "Understand?"

His jaw hardened. "I understand you best get those trinkets out my sight."

"I ain't mean you no offense." She held up an iridescent cone-shaped shell. "You ever seen the creatures that live in these? If I had a place this pretty, I'd never leave it." She was rambling now, her words running together as she picked up each object and explained its origin story. "This mirror belonged to my sister. She gave it to me when we parted. And this barrette, too. It's broken now, but I still keep it. Oh, and these beads . . ." She picked up Patience's rosary beads and rolled them in her palms. "These belonged to my mother. My inheritance. I'd hate to part with them, but . . ."

The man's hard jaw softened and his eyes wandered, as boredom overtook his face.

He let her talk awhile longer, before removing the rope from his trousers and lowering his pants.

She talked the entire time. Now contradicting everything she said before. New linkages arising. The shillings handed down from her father when he died. The beads from an uncle, a cousin. The mirror from an old mistress who had taught Lulu her figures. The barrette a gift from her oldest brother.

She had offered Zeke her entire life savings. A treasury of things lifted from all the different places and farms she had been. None of the stories were true, all the people she linked to the objects imaginary. When she first stole them, she had only intended to borrow them, but people noticed them gone before she could return them, and it became much too hard to give them back. The fact that folks missed them, wondered after them, only confirmed what she had gained by taking the items. The closeness born of the object. The gift with all that warm feeling attached. A lineage of kin, blood or otherwise, connected to it. That was the thing she wanted. That was the thing she took for herself.

She wasn't willy-nilly about it. She wouldn't pocket any old thing, and to her credit, she tried to do it less and less. But there were particular times when she couldn't help it. Whenever the world felt particularly dark or more lonesome than usual, the treasure of objects made her feel better. It couldn't be helped that an object's warmth soon wore off and she'd have to obtain something new to keep the good feeling going.

And so it was with Patience's rosary. The wooden beads connected by a frayed piece of twine radiated something unfamiliar to her. The kind of connection an orphan like her had never really known. On her last farm, folks called people like her lost, a no-name—a person sold away from her family so young they were doomed to remain forever unmoored. She had been sold four times and she wasn't an old woman yet. In truth, though, she didn't know how old she was—older than Serah for sure, but younger than Junie and Patience, and likely closest in age to Alice, who believed herself to be twenty-four or so.

To the whole of the group, she lied all the time about the friends and family she'd left behind. Aunt Carrie, who was the funniest, cousin Brendy, who could dance better than any of the neighboring folks. A trail of names from an assortment of farms, names and faces she mixed up now and then, fading as the years passed. Because no one else need know she was a no-name. If they couldn't recognize it, she wouldn't bother telling them. People sensed it, though, even if they didn't know what it was they were sensing. The sliver of desperation was familiar as the smell of rain coming.

She hunted for the telltale signs of it on her and had only recently accepted that there was little to be done about it. She was the kind of woman people disliked immediately, without the need for evidence. An instinct of some kind that remained no matter how much wooing she did. The cache of objects, though, never refused her. They remained perfect and arrested emblems of affection and warmth. What did it matter if that affection and warmth was originally for someone else?

And so, when the man set about his work, she cast him in the same light. She placed his hands where she wanted them. She imagined them a lover's hands. She told him how she much she'd missed him, reminded him how long it had been since they had last seen each other.

"Don't you remember that peach tree?" she whispered in the man's ear, now no longer Zeke but a man she had known two farms ago, or a woman at an outpost near Houston.

"Mmhmm," he answered.

The willful collapsing of memory never adhered to the moment perfectly. The grafting was always lopsided and ill-fitting, but if she squeezed her eyes shut and concentrated, the phantasm held up just long enough.

———

JUNIE HAD ALREADY BEEN working her own plan. She hadn't washed herself or changed her clothes in days. And after many hours chopping cotton under the July sun, the rank smell emitted from her intensified with every passing day. And to make matters worse, she started wearing an asafetida bag around her neck, to ward off a summer flu, she said. The smelly herb mixed with body odor was enough to give anyone a headache. The smell was so strong we slept with the window covering pulled back, the front door cracked, and the fire still going in the hearth, even though it was still unearthly warm at night. Usually, we kept the window covered and the door shut, with a chair in front of it, for fear of lobos or bears or men. But this time, we wrapped our weekly food rations tightly in a quilt and hid them underneath the floorboards. We used up half of that week's salt drawing protective lines along the window's edge and in front of the door.

Whenever we grumbled about the smell, she paid us no

attention, just hitched up her trousers and retightened the rope she used as a belt, her way of letting us know she didn't care nothing about our grumbling, and it wouldn't change her mind. She was stubborn that way.

The night Junie was sent up to the barn, she picked up the tray from the cookhouse and spit in it. She had to remove her cob pipe to do so, and a tiny bit of ash fell into the soup. Ah well. More flavor.

With one hand, she held the tray and with the other, a pine knot torch. It was a moonless night and the humid darkness felt syrupy and thick. She raised her torch high as she stepped into the barn, spotting Zeke sitting in the corner. He waved her over.

He appeared smaller than she remembered, a bit paler, too, his forehead damp with sweat. She put the tray down near him and sat out of arm's length, but close enough for her smell to overtake him.

"Ain't feeling too good," he said.

She continued to smoke her pipe, eyeing him closely, sti-fling a laugh when his eyes filled with water, and he coughed, the smell finally reaching the back of his nostrils, the rise of his throat. He coughed again, and she cackled.

"Say, gal, whose britches you got on?" he asked after a while, peering at her trousers with hazy, bleary eyes.

"They mine. You like them?"

"No," he said, making a puzzled face.

She laughed, his confusion coupled with sickness making her feel more at ease.

"They were a gift," she said. In truth, they started out as a punishment. All the women wore long skirts and dresses, no matter the season, no matter the task. In muddy weather, the hems grew black and soiled. When washing clothing at the creek, the skirts were cinched high around the thighs, but still got soaked by rising water. And Junie was no different until she and Lizzie got in one of their rows.

Out in the reaches of Texas country, Lizzie was horribly lonely, and she liked to summon Junie up to the house to lallygag with her about times back home, as if they were old friends having tea. Junie hated these sessions, but she put up with them, in hopes of securing a bit of news about her children back in Georgia. Whatever affection the woman claimed to have for her, she knew she should treat it like glass, a fragile endangered thing. But sometimes, she failed miserably.

The last time she did, she was too exhausted to hold her tongue and criticized Lizzie's jagged cutting of the cloth set aside for the women's winter garments. The cutting was a task Lizzie always insisted on doing herself, but since she didn't have to sew what she cut, she didn't realize how much extra work she created. Junie listened to the woman chatter on, while slyly trying to steer the scissors straight, but all she could think about was how exasperating it was going to be later trying to make the seams lie flat and the edges not fray. Finally, she interrupted Lizzie midstream and demanded the woman hand the scissors over. "A blind mule could do better," Junie muttered.

After that incident Lizzie took her clothing and left her only Harlow's old trousers and shirt to wear. Most women wouldn't be caught dead in a pair of britches for fear of being seen as mannish or ugly, fears some of them already had by nature of the labor they did. After all, when was the last time anyone had seen a white lady make a road or fell a tree? "Ladies" wore hoopskirts and bonnets. They sat in parlors away from the oppressive glare of the sun, where they sewed or spun. And maybe some of the poorer ones went out and fed the chickens or milked the cows or even churned the butter themselves, but there were certain things they would not do. And because Junie and the others washed the linens of said ladies, they knew that while their clothes and sheets may smell of flesh or musk or urine, they were hardly ever crusted with soil, mud, and the carcasses of dead bugs—all things she and the other women beat from their own clothing and linen regularly.

She didn't take back what she said to Lizzie, initially out of spite, and as time went on, she grew to like the trousers and wanted to keep them. She couldn't ignore how nicely they kept her thighs from chafing in the heat or kept the insects from attacking her ankles in the high grass. The skirt was a tent for things, what got trapped underneath often sank its teeth and claws into her flesh. But no more.

The women ribbed her about wearing the white man's pants. A talisman of his power, his evil. What could it do so close to the skin? It was likely to cause her flesh to rot, they teased.

Zeke moved toward his tin cup of water and drained what was left, putting it down with a loud clatter. His chin wobbled on his neck before pointing in her direction. "Did you bring me a drink?"

"No."

"Fetch me some water? Please."

"No." She returned his puzzled gaze, but her humor was lost on him.

He jolted up out of the barn and vomited, his body heaving and seizing, until finally he set down right there in the entryway, his head leaning against the doorpost, his mouth sucking air in greedily.

Junie stood up and slipped past him, so relieved she could cry. By the time she reached the cabin, she was whistling.

She pushed open the door and grinned. "He down like a rabbit in a trap."

Serah and Alice looked at her, puzzled.

"What you mean?" said Alice.

"He sick."

"How sick?" asked Serah.

Junie shrugged and stretched out on her pallet.

"But won't Lucy think you did something to him?"

"Doubt it, but if he do, maybe it'll put something on his mind. Make him realize this ain't the way."

"He think you did something, ain't he likely to kill you?" asked Patience, without raising her head.

"He can't get the harvest out of the ground without me. He know it and I know it," said Junie, pulling off her trousers. "Besides, that traveling nigger ain't dead. I know dead when I see it, and he not it."

—⤢—

IT WASN'T THE FIRST time Zeke had been poisoned. Since being sent out on this "traveling business" nearly five years ago, he'd been stabbed, burned, blinded, hexed, peed on, and called every name but a son of a God. Husbands, boyfriends, and fathers waited for him in the dead of night, and he didn't like fighting them, but when they came, he was ready. Not because he wanted to hurt them, not any more than he wanted to have sex with their women, but where else was he to put all these things thrashing about inside him?

When they swung at him, he swung back harder, cracked ribs, kicked out teeth, not because he was in the right. He knew if he was in their place, if any man touched his wife or his daughter, he'd do worse. But he had a job to do and the quicker he did it, the quicker he could get home to his own family.

He accepted that it was only a matter of time before someone killed him, before he was castrated or infected, made so sick he withered and died, and every day of every trip he went out on, he woke up wondering if that day had finally come to pass, unable to barely breathe until he returned home and hugged his wife.

That wasn't always so. When he was young and foolish and unmarried, it didn't seem such a bad job then. At least in theory. He was more social then, loved going to frolics and always had a few sweethearts on neighboring farms. And like most young men, he had a ferocious appetite for lying down with them. It seemed like the most natural thing in the world to him, not unlike eating or sleeping. But that changed when he was sent into one smelly back room or another and told to copulate with a crying, fearful woman as if he were no more than a bull or a horse.

And late nights, when he gathered with the men on his home farm to drink rotgut and gamble a bit, they'd press him for lurid details about the women he met, lust gleaming in their eyes. Just once, he wanted to tell them how he hated it, how all the looks of disgust and fear began piling up inside him, how they burrowed under his flesh like a nasty parasite. How he used to love the smell of women, but the musky scent of these scared angry strangers clung to him for days, made him sick. But he knew what the men wanted to hear from him, so he gave it to them. He boasted about all the women he bedded, how sweet the loving was, and the scores of children he gave them. He never told them how he begged his owner to stop sending him out, how he just wanted to be home with his wife, and how Master Simmons just laughed and shook his head. "Knew I should have never let you marry in the first place," the old man said. "You know, Jensen was just by here and he's taking quite a liking to your little boy. Now, I told him he wasn't for sale, but . . ."

This was the cost of keeping his family intact, having his wife and children all under the same roof. And if he only had to "travel" a few times a year, maybe that was worth it.

His face burned with fever, his clothes were drenched in sweat, his stomach roiled like a stormy sea. Someone had finally done it, he thought. And now he could put to rest the idea of stopping it himself. He had seen desperate men take to themselves with an ax, chopping off a finger or a foot to avoid being sent into the jaws of cane country. It never worked. Lying never worked either. It only ratcheted up the evil. He had tried it a few times when he first started out, when the woman was so upset, he couldn't bring himself to do it, and when the door was unbarred, he lied and said they had. He quickly learned it only made things worse, only created maniacal audiences—viewing parties of white men who sat alongside, tittering and ogling, clamoring and shouting like they were at a boxing match.

But maybe that was all over now. He flopped over, a cloud of dust rose up, filling his nose and mouth. He coughed and lay back, opening himself to the full weight of the fever. And when the old cook came in with vittles and medicinal teas, he waved her away. Harlow then dosed him with ipecac and castor oil, which made Zeke's retching worse for a spell before the fever finally broke. Once it subsided and he was finally able to stand again, he had to admit the feeling that washed over him wasn't relief.

~⤙~

SOMETIME LATER, MR. LUCY told Junie to take Zeke his dinner and look after him. It became clear to everyone then that they hadn't succeeded in ridding themselves of the man or his task. Serah took to hiding out after that, disappearing into the woods for hours, sometimes a whole day, hoping she might be skipped in the process. She'd come back, hungry and wan and peppered with purple inflamed pest bites. Nan would feed her and grease the wounds, but at the first opportunity, she'd disappear again. So it wasn't surprising when they put the harness on her, a strange contraption with two irons bars across, one encircling the shoulders, the other, the torso. The two crossbars were connected by a vertical iron spine that towered up over the wearer's head, where a small bell was fixed.

The bell rang all day, and most of the night. Every time she moved and even when she didn't. She slathered wet mud inside it to make it stop, and that would help once the mud dried, but it didn't take long for the mud to dry further and flake off in large chunks, raining bits of dirt into her hair or down her dress.

She wore it nearly a week before they removed it, the sudden absence of the weight making her light-headed and nauseated. And even with it gone, she still heard the ceaseless ringing inside her, between her ears, bouncing around her chest.

One night, Mr. Lucy dispensed with the dinner ritual altogether and walked her to the barn himself. He closed both barn doors and locked her inside with Zeke, the darkening sky still visible through the slats. She banged on the door until she was tired while Zeke whittled on a bench. She slid down to the ground, her back against the door.

"Water?" he said, cocking his head in the direction of a pitcher on the floor.

Her throat was dry, but she couldn't bring herself to say yes to the water. It seemed like saying yes to the whole thing.

He stood up and filled the cup and set it down a few feet from her. His long shadow spread toward her, and she pulled her knees up to her chest to keep the shadow from reaching her feet.

He returned to his bench and continued his woodwork. "I know you hates me and I don't mind it. I don't. But whether you hate me or not, it all comes out in the wash just the same. I can get it over with and you never have to see my ugly mug again."

She heard the wind outside knocking against the cabin walls. An inevitability of a rising storm headed toward her. Neither Patience nor Junie nor Lulu had escaped it. And they were smarter than her, wilier than her. How did she think she could sidestep this thing when they hadn't?

She remembered when she and her brother Jonas were little. They were twins, her being the oldest by a few minutes. Often enough, they took up trouble together, but when their misdeeds were found out and the time came to pay for their sins, oh, how different they were. Jonas would walk right up to their father and take his beating, by sticking his hand out or turning his backside to the waiting hand or tree switch. Jonas would cry when struck, but not long afterward he'd be off, on his next bout of mischief, as if the earlier event had never happened, whereas she prolonged the spanking for as long as possible. She hid out for hours, sometimes a whole night, her father finding her in her favorite hiding spot. He'd pick her up and put her to bed next to her brother, but the next day, the whipping still awaited her. She'd be dragged back to the site of the alleged crime and whipped. And even though her father never hit her as hard or as many times as he hit Jonas, she cried twice as much. Was twice as angry and got spanked for still sulking about it days later.

She missed her brother, but it was hard to remember him without his teasing admonishments. He'd say whatever happened was all her fault, because she made what should have lasted a few minutes go on for days. She heard Jonas in her ear now, below the faint ringing.

And so, she didn't stop the man when he finally pushed her down into the hay. She closed her eyes tight and thought of Jonas on the other side of a whipping, gleefully throwing sticks in the air and watching them fall.

⤚⤙

WHEN ALICE'S TURN CAME, she had already decided. She'd go into the barn one Alice and come out a different one. She had long harbored an obsession with molting animals—snakes, grasshoppers, and frogs that shed skin, leaving their old selves behind. Whatever happened in that dark room need not touch any other parts of her life. She could find whatever was to be found in the barn and leave it there when she left it.

She picked up Zeke's dinner and took it into the barn. She sat down, and when Zeke waved the tray away, she ate his until she'd had her fill. She was always hungry, and it was the first time in months she was able to eat as much as she needed, as much as she wanted. When she was done, she pulled out a small bottle of liquor she had swiped from the Lucys' storehouse. She hadn't shared it with any of the women and she didn't offer Zeke any either. She drank until she had enough, until the dark barn grew darker still.

That was the last thing she remembered. Every blurry thing after became part of this flaky, outer layer of skin she felt molting off her body. Every place he touched. Every patch of skin that met his.

It all would go, sloughing and molting away. Some of it went willingly, but some she had to help later with her fingernails or the sharp point of a twig, or even the dull edge of a whittling knife.

⤚⤙

AFTERWARD, WE ALL FELT at sea. Like Zeke was some strange illness we all caught and couldn't rid ourselves of. Some felt it in the body—congested lungs, rheumy eyes, and stomach pains;

while others felt it in the mind—a thick brain fog or the opposite, a compulsive agitated spinning.

Being so close to one another only made it worse, only made the grime inside pulse and spin and pitch. Whereas by one's lonesome, the muck would settle and harden, without another person kicking it up all the time.

"Stop all that jawing."

We found ourselves splintered then, unable to unstick ourselves nor pull anyone else from the rising, tightening mire. We were incapable of that for a while. All of us except Nan. But we hated her for being spared, then hated each other for not having been.

"Pass me by with all that."

That's how we spoke to each other then, in an exhausting state of seething. Made only worse by the fact that we were stuck together, like appendages of the same hand.

CHAPTER FIVE

A WEEK LATER, AT THE mouth of the creek, under the moon's half-closed eye, we threw in everything but our bodies. We had requests and we had offerings. We had leaves, fronds, and husks marked with sharp rocks and yellow clay and we had stolen apples, wild purple flowers, and fragrant buds of honeysuckle.

We waited for the water to take what we gave it, counted on its ebb and flow to absolve us, to wash our sins and carry them away, toward another town or dam, to be eaten or shredded by beavers or waterfowls, but minutes after throwing everything in, we could see our requests just lying there, floating, a thin soup over a shallow rocky bed.

No matter how many sticks we used to push it down below, a mirror of the muck inside us remained on the surface of the water. We could only watch for so long before clouds of mosquitoes drove us away.

From the creek, we went to The Tree to pray, but couldn't

shake the muck of the river. It felt personal, the muck solidify-ing. It seemed as if it was determined to hang around. Praying felt like a last resort. Some say, it should've been the first. And sure, some of us had been up to it all the while separately, but when gathered together, the power of the thing was supposed to be magnified. But the more desperate we felt, the more impos-sible it seemed.

And whereas usually it was just Serah who felt outside of it, unable to follow the thread deep down into its center, where all the joy and light was supposed to be, this night, it was true of nearly all of us. First, Junie wouldn't sing the song and Nan had forgotten the oil, and Patience led the prayer at whisper level, her voice getting lower and lower as she went on. No one wanted to hold hands or lock arms or get trapped inside the closed circle. No one wanted to close their eyes, even.

The night sky felt full of beings—water spirits and unteth-ered dead, gulls and dragonflies and murky stars—but it also felt empty, like the land was seeping and stretching out beyond its initial borders. The desert to the west, the swamp and gulf to the south. To the east, more dead trees and cleared land, and farms like this one aiming for Eden. And north, miles and miles of what? We couldn't fathom where the end of it might be and where we were in the midst of it all.

No one felt like praying. We wanted to be inside the prayer and song, the deep vibration and sweaty fist of it, but couldn't muster any of the necessary stuff to get up inside it. Some of us understood that these were relationships one remade over and over again. All the time, one was seeking alignment with God, with her Dead, with the trees and animals alike. All these rela-tionships required sun and tending to, but the youngest among us didn't understand the back-and-forth. What did it mean to be saved or spared or favored if only to be thrown out again later? It seemed hard not to be undone by such thirst, how often the spirits needed to be fed, praised, or worshipped. And how at times like these, all that effort felt fruitless.

———

"DON'T LOOK LIKE Y'ALL much for doing this," Patience said, shifting her knees up under her. We were all sitting by then, tired of trying but unwilling to give up just yet.

No one said anything.

"Alright then, I'm going to bed," Patience said, pushing herself up off the ground.

"Wait," said Nan. She poured out the contents of her sack in front of us. A pile of roots, clippings from the cotton plant. "Here. Divvy this up among y'all."

"What we supposed to do with it?" Serah said. We all knew the plant well, the knobby thinness of its stalks.

"If you don't want a baby from that breeding man, take it, chew it but don't swallow it. You'll need to do it for as much as you can, long as you can . . ."

Quiet fell over the group. Serah reached over and started separating the knobby roots into small piles of equal size, one for each woman.

"Don't include me. I don't want them," said Patience.

"How come?"

"'Cause I don't to want to lay eyes on that nigger ever again."

Serah stopped arranging and sat back on her heels. "You think Lucy will bring him back?"

"Why wouldn't he?"

"Lucy too cheap to bring him around again," Junie said. "All week they've been fighting about money. Miss Lizzie didn't even want Zeke here."

Patience made a sucking sound. "I hate it when y'all act simple."

"Watch your mouth," said Junie.

"You ever seen them put a bull to a heifer? They put them together over and over again," said Patience. "And if they don't get a calf, they try a new bull. They don't just stop . . ."

No one moved or spoke. The humid air settling thicker now, as if her words had sucked up all the good breathing air. It was hard to swallow, to think, to hear anything over the blood inside us now rushing up to punctuate her speech.

"The only way to make it stop," Patience went on, "is to let a babe come."

The words felt like a kick in the stomach. Something about the thought laid bare felt not just appalling but dangerous. It didn't feel like a careless thought or even just a likely possibility, it felt like a prophecy. And from the one woman who swore she didn't believe in them, didn't believe any who said they were born under the caul and had the ability to see what others couldn't. And maybe that's why it felt more solid, more akin to fact than fraught speculation.

Junie reached toward the pile of roots and pulled them toward her. "I won't have another . . ."

"Even if?" Patience asked, staring at Junie now, the question hanging in the air.

"Even if. Zeke's lucky he still catching breath. May not hold true next time."

Serah turned her face away. She didn't know who or what to listen to. Everything they said made sense and no sense at all and both possible futures were terrifying. She pressed her fingers into the dirt, the soil underneath cool and moist on her fingertips. She hoped her dead would rise up and speak to her through the soil. She figured all she could do was hold off the horror that seemed the closest. Zeke might come back, but he might not. A child born of him, though, would be here longer. Serah reached over and pulled a pile of roots toward her.

Patience shook her head. "Simple as can be, I declare."

Alice nodded in agreement with Patience.

Nan, who had been quiet this whole time, leaned forward and spoke. "Make up your own mind, but I think y'all have a better chance of the man not returning if y'all all go the same way."

"How you figure?" asked Patience.

"If you grow big and the others don't," Nan began, "then Lucy think something probably wrong with them. Maybe they can't have any more children or caught some women's disease. But if none of y'all bear fruit, then he think maybe something wrong with Zeke."

"But he's had to give women plenty of children before, or else he wouldn't be the traveling nigger."

"Yeah, but maybe he all used up now. He had so many he spent up."

"Maybe." Patience was thinking now, we could tell. Serah slipped one of the roots in her mouth and began chewing. She offered one to Patience, but Patience just stared at her hand for a long while until, finally, she took it and put it in her mouth. And once Patience was in, Alice, Junie, and Lulu followed suit.

———

We chewed the acidic roots for days and days. We kept them around, soggy ground masses tucked in the pockets of our cheeks. The constant chewing made our faces tired, our breath sour, our teeth yellow, but they dulled hunger, dulled the mind just enough to lower the worrying pitch. This we did, until the supply of Nan's clippings dwindled, and by the time the frenzy of harvest was upon us, we had already become so adept at removing one plant or another, in different parts of the row, across the entire stretch of it, that we built up an abundant store of the root, which we buried in the ground underneath the cabin floor.

And when Lucy hired on some workers to help with the picking, the pitch of our worry increased, as we worried the three men might be brought on for some alternative purpose. But we rarely saw them, we worked together in one group, and they another. And we held on to the fact that they were never introduced to us as one thing or another, that we were never even told their names or what farms they came from, as proof that they were just passing through and we should regard them as no more than a cloud drifting over. The men must have found us rude, for the few times they tried to engage, greeting us with smiles or clowning around for our pleasure, we turned away from them. Only Nan showed the smallest sliver of teeth when she fed them a hot meal, but the rest of us remained as still and indifferent as the trees.

CHAPTER SIX

CHARLES HARLOW HAD GOTTEN IT into his head that he had finally found the golden key. He now knew the reason why he had such poor showings of cotton the last two years, even though the oats and sweet potatoes did well as could be expected. And he now knew why last year's visit from the stockman bore no fruit and produced no children, leaving Lizzie without a wet nurse to help pick up the slack when her body refused to produce more milk.

He returned from a trip to the mill in Leesburg with an empty dray, two pieces of mail with past-due postage, and a shiny new book he toted around like the Bible. *Affleck's Southern Rural Almanac for 1854*, it was called, and it included detailed tables tracking the movement of the planets and the moon for an entire year.

At a depot in town, the grizzly store owner showed it to him with infectious reverence. The old man flipped through the pages and showed him the drawing of the Man of Signs, a wavy-haired naked figure surrounded by curlicues and symbols, and bold black lines linking each body part to a zodiac sign. Aries, sign of the Ram, corresponded to the man's head, while Pisces, sign of the Fishes, corresponded to the man's feet. The store owner went on and on about how a farmer should live by this diagram and its surrounding symbols to know when to sow seeds and cuttings and when to geld, wean, or breed stock.

"Cancer is the best time for planting, but if you can't manage that, Scorpio and Pisces is second best. And don't geld in any sign above the knees, otherwise the animal will get sick and die," the store owner told him. It wasn't the first time he'd heard sayings of this kind, but before it seemed the superstitions of old drunken men, who pontificated daily on the weather, with their predictions of rain and high wind, and still never prospered, never owned the land they lived on or the poor half-starved Negroes they rented for one year or another.

When he married Lizzie, he learned his father-in-law swore by the epact, but when the man tried to explain it, in that bored patronizing way that seemed reserved for Harlow alone, he couldn't grasp it. He understood it on its face, a system of determining the moon's age in January so as to predict the moon's cycle the rest of the year, but the math was hazy, with its accounting of solar days and lunar days. And worse, he didn't understand how it was used, how Lizzie's father organized himself and his labors around it, and how the more questions he posed to the man about it, the more foreign and unknowable the whole thing sounded.

It's not like he was out there without a plan of any kind. He had a planting calendar and a weather journal and an assortment of farming methods knocking around in his head. And he had worked enough in various capacities on other farms, from overseer to seasonal hand, to know that no two farmers swore by the same method of sowing seed in the ground or getting a healthy yield. Whether one had some special fertilizer he swore by, pig shit or guano, or another only planted onions during the "blooming days," most seemed subject to the same luck or ill fortune, each bowing to the whims of the most powerful deity none of their kind could ignore—Weather.

The difference now was he had seen men savvy enough to sidestep misfortune when it came. At the depot, he'd hear them talking, those who cut the corn early to avoid a sudden freeze, while most everyone else lost their crops and spent the next couple of weeks replanting. The wise (or lucky) farmers said they owed their good fortune to the almanac, to consistent study and testing of its patterns. Only by doing that were they able to predict what the others couldn't.

"What about breeding?" Harlow said, turning back to the store owner. "Would the best time be in the sign of Scorpio?" He pointed to the sign linking directing to the naked man's loins. "Or would anytime from the hips to the knees be good?"

The store owner didn't know, he said, only that the sign of the Virgin should be avoided. "Is that what happened? You tried to breed them during the time of Virgo?" Harlow didn't know, making a note to check his records against the almanac when he returned home, but another farmer in the store overheard them talking and sorely disagreed, said the timing of the Virgin was one of generation and blooming and he should be free to breed or sow seeds in the sign of "the lady with the flower" as he desired.

The two men began to argue, until a third farmer piped up, saying they were both wrong as a boll weevil. That in times of the Virgo, things were likely to "bloom themselves to death," the flowers taking over the plant and stunting all growth.

He listened as the men nearly came to blows, each pulling

out one story or another as proof, none of which cleared up the matter. He signaled to the store owner to add the new bible to his bill, and he balanced it among the sundries and few luxuries he picked up whenever he came to town—tea, sugar, real coffee, whiskey, laudanum, and castor oil. With that, he hurriedly left the store.

Even though his last attempt had been a bust, it still seemed the best course of action to right the ship. To finally get back in the black. Sure, it wouldn't help him much in the short-term, he thought. He'd still likely have to mortgage Alice or Lulu to pay off the promissory note coming due on the land, but some years from now, if he was patient and diligent, he'd surely see a handsome profit.

With this in mind, Harlow scheduled the stockman's return for the month that followed, arranging for him to come when the moon was in sign of the Scales, which, on the drawing, corresponded to the zodiac man's hips. He'd have the stockman stay until the moon moved lower and lower, until it reached the sign of Capricorn, in the zodiac man's knees. That gave him a good span of auspicious days to work with, seven consecutive days total, to get it right this time.

⟶

WHEN ZEKE RETURNED, WE were so angry with one another we couldn't agree on whether to poison him or conjure him, and whatever tricks we each had in mind for avoiding the deed itself were felled by Mr. Lucy, now lurking nearby, outside the barn or hiding within the dark recesses of it. Half of us spent the week in a dulled blind fury, and the rest, in some semblance of a stupor. Junie had stolen some of Mrs. Lucy's laudanum, and the strange liquid had a distancing effect that placed a welcome haze over that entire week. We looked for ways to extend it, asked Nan what sort of herbs we could forage that would do the same thing.

To add insult, we spent the days trapped inside. Rain fell for three days straight, and we worked in the loom then, the grinding motion of the spinning wheel making a burrowing sound that the walls only made louder.

When the seven days were over and Zeke was carted off to wherever he came from, we still hadn't spoken more than four words to one another. And still hadn't by the next time we were scheduled to meet in the woods at The Tree. Nearly an hour after the fires dwindled in the Lucys' house, we all made our way there. The fact that we all showed up was surprising and it was unclear who was coming to fight and who was coming to pray.

"Told ya," Patience said, and Junie nearly swung at her.

"We knew it was a possibility he'd come back at least once more," Nan said, stepping in between the two.

"With all due respect, old woman, if you ain't lain with that bastard," said Patience, "I don't want to hear nothing from you."

"Damn right," agreed Lulu.

"Shut up," Junie said.

"Fine," Nan said. "Kill each other, then." She stepped aside and looked at the two women glaring at each other. She dropped the bulky sack of cotton roots on the ground between them.

Serah picked up the sack. "We have to do it again now. As proof that it don't work."

"Why in the hell would I do that?" Patience said. "No, if I have one, he'll leave me be for a while."

"No, if you have *one*," said Alice, "he'll bring that water-headed nigger back after every harvest."

We were all quiet then, the thought settling over us like a suffocating blanket. The wind rustled the leaves overhead and a cluster of birds let loose a deafening cry, as if attacked.

Nan began to pray and the rest joined in. It became a teeming hodgepodge of all possibilities, calling forth all helpers and saints: God, the Son, the Holy Ghost; ancestors hemmed between realms, in seawater and ocean, in sky and above it; those already in the next world and those barreling toward this one; the sun, moon, and stars; haints, both walking and stationary, those residing in birds, and those residing in trees; and the gods of our parents, whose true holy names we were never told.

Every tradition now mixed together—binding evil with a blade of grass, burying hair and skin of the stockman in a makeshift grave of clay and dirt and snakeskin, tarrying under moon until we grew dizzy, finally ending in a frenzied ring shout–turned–dirge. By the end, we were all soaked, wet as if we'd been dunked into the creek's heavy gray water, but lighter. We had shaken something loose, moved it out of the way, and could now touch the edge.

Serah reached for the sack and passed out the woody dank roots to each of us. A holy sacrament now. We each took one and chewed it.

—⚡—

BY THE TIME WE were done making candles and soap, and the cold weather of winter began to break, there had only been one slippage, which we caught before it got too far along. Alice miscarried, and we sent the soul back over, saving it for a better time, a better place, though we knew it might not take kindly to what we had done.

Harlow then brought Dr. Lewis in to look us over. A young pale man with barely a hair on his chin and a leather bag of loose jangly tools. Back to the barn we were sent, where he examined us one by one. And for those who had spent any time in the back rooms of auction houses, this was little different. He thumped breasts and hips, made us lie facedown on a short makeshift table, with our shoulders and head hanging off the end. One could look down at the dusty ground, littered with strands of hay, while a cold metal spoon was forced between her thighs.

The dim room grew darker. And one by one, we felt ourselves lowered into the belly of that big whale of Jonah's, but Jonah himself, no-account bastard, was nowhere to be found.

The doctor rummaged around, poking and scraping, until finally he removed the spoon, stepping back and declaring himself done. Outside, he and Harlow spoke, but their words made no sense now, a new language they found between them. The doctor said we seemed "sound," and he was unsure why there seemed to be such trouble with this matter. They talked more out of earshot, but a few words floated down toward us. Feckless, the doctor called us. "Liable to eat their own."

We didn't know who Dr. Lewis declared barren until a few weeks later, when Mr. Lucy took Alice along to help with a mill run and came back without her.

CHAPTER SEVEN

Seasons stack on top of one another and time rolls by as if a single year and not two sandwiched together. We mark the seasons not by temperature so much as by task. Corn goes in before sweet potatoes; sweet potatoes go in before cotton. We rotate planting of the second half of crops with cowpeas or snap beans or oats.

We mourn Alice as if she's passed on. We take a few of her things to the tree—her comb, a pair of woolen stockings, a brass button—and leave them there, so she's with us every time we go crossing. Without her, we feel strange and unmoored. The feeling doesn't pass.

There's too much rain, there's not enough rain. We weed and scrape, scrape and weed. Lay some of the corn by and plant again.

That is, until yellow fever comes and lays us low in the summer of 1856, taking both Silas and Miss Lizzie's youngest, William.

OUT OF FEAR OF contagion, the two children were buried together far in the woods, much to both mothers' chagrin. Patience
didn't want her child buried anywhere near William. Though, in
life, the two were often tethered, Patience hoped for Silas to be
free of the Lucys in death.

Lizzie loudly made it known that she didn't want young
William buried far away in the woods. She told anyone who
would listen she wanted him buried close to the house, where
she could visit him often and his father would have to bypass that
whitewashed cross every day, another reminder of the folly he
had brought upon her and her offspring since he'd brought them
to this godforsaken place.

Still weak with fever, Patience prepared Silas for burial, refusing all help from the rest of the women. She knew this hurt
Nan the most, as she spent more time with him than any of
them, but Patience couldn't help it. "You already got all the time
with him," she told Nan.

The old woman's face crumpled, but Patience pretended she
didn't see it. She turned her back and waited for the woman to
walk away, before she approached the boy's stilled wrinkled body.

Alone, she washed him, rubbed the small calluses on his feet
with oil, cut his hair with a straight razor. The disease had made
him tiny again. She dressed him in white, in a shroud Junie and
Serah had made, with small crosses and cosmograms stitched
around the hem. She made a pocket in the shroud and sewed her
new rosary inside it. This one she had made herself with dried
seeds and twine and so it seemed the most fitting to accompany
him. She washed his face once more and then pulled him into
her arms for the last time. He was so light it stunned her. It felt
like gathering the air.

The burial was quick, the words too few, and even the few things they said made no sense to her. The Father taketh and giveth. Her boy would be welcomed in heaven as he was not welcomed on earth. The words gave her no comfort.

On the way back, she broke reeds and branches, trying to leave markers so she could find her way back there. She promised herself when there was an ounce more of strength in her body, she would gather the women and they would come back here and move her son. They would bury him elsewhere.

THERE WAS MORE RAIN, more fever, and even a frightful battle with locusts in the spring of 1857. Nan kept a tally stick, where she marked the occasions, but the rest of us couldn't read it. And whenever we asked, she'd warn us that the two times the stockman came were different, once before cotton-picking time, and once a ways after, and so if we were looking to the season for clues of an impending third visit, we may not find it there.

Mrs. Lucy gave birth for the fourth time. A baby girl they named Carol. A healthy miracle child arriving on a wave of pestilence. A sure symbol of forthcoming bounty, the Lucys exclaimed.

New neighbors sprouted up to the west and again to the south. Most were small homesteads like ours, but a huge one across the water's edge loomed large like a small city, with rows of small buildings dotting the horizon. We could sometimes hear their cow horn in the morning, or a jangle of different bells summoning folks for one thing or another all throughout the day.

The Lucys were at odds; she ecstatic, him annoyed. Excited by the prospect of friends again, Mrs. Lucy met all the wives, invited the women and their hands over for quiltings, and took

us over to their places for cornhuskings and sheep-shearing parties. Mr. Lucy, however, saw every neighbor as an affront, a wily
bastard who stole swaths of land out from under him, land he'd
been just on the verge of acquiring the second his fortune turned
around.

We no longer asked Nan about the marks on her tally stick.
Someone begged her, she wouldn't say who, to cover over any
nicks marking the stockman's visits. Now, whenever she's asked
to recount the days for us, from the strange freeze that rotted the
bolls or that time a hailstorm punched new holes in the roof, the
awful fact of Zeke is left out.

It was true we loved these new gatherings with these new
neighbors. A cornhusking was alright, but a frolic deep in the
woods was even better. A quilting was pleasant, but a church
meeting under night sky, packed together in a rickety dark praise
house not much bigger than an outhouse, made us all giddy and
light-headed. Some of us loved any excuse to be in the company
of these others. And we loved them most simply because they
weren't us—they offered up news from the world, stories and
songs we hadn't heard, dances we didn't know. A lot of them
were from Virginia or Maryland, others from Alabama or the
Carolinas or Indian Country, and others still were just a foot out
of Africa, smuggled into Texas illegally by way of Cuba. They
spoke various tongues and creoles, unfamiliar and musical, with
different country marks adorning their faces and chests, not to
mention different sects of Christians with newfangled crosses
and rosaries. Others were Muslims, who carried white prayer
shawls wherever they went and dropped to their knees five times
a day. But we were most excited by the spiritual professionals:
two bona fide Conjurers, each making mojos and protective
pouches for any who could pay, and one preaching mystic, who
said the Bible had been written on his heart, so we should hold

him in higher esteem than any of the traveling missionaries who rolled through the area once a season to bring us the Gospel.

This new community was full of quirks and beliefs that felt foreign and strange. We hadn't met them all and probably never would. And while some of us embraced that as means to enjoy these folks with a certain temporary abandon, others put up all efforts to remain at a cool shelflike reserve.

CHAPTER EIGHT

BEFORE SERAH MET NOAH, SHE didn't believe in following her impulses. She thought herself an expert at dulling any ragged urge that felt costly. So much so, by the time Noah became a secret she kept from the other women, she barely recognized herself. How quickly she became a wet ball of desires, wanting, and dreaming all the time. The nakedness of it made her ashamed, but that didn't stop her from willing daylight to speed by, from stepping gingerly over Patience's sleeping body and out of the cabin to go and meet him.

She first met him at one of those Saturday-night frolics deep in the woods, but she had seen him before then, in passing, patching the road with the other men or bringing in kindling when the women were quilting over on his farm. And from the beginning, he struck up a strange compulsion in her, one she found herself warring with. For some reason, her eye was drawn to him whenever he worked or moved about. Even when she forced herself not to look in his direction, she was still aware of him, could still feel his presence somehow a few feet away.

The whole thing struck her as dangerous for a reason she couldn't identify. Her senses kept track of the Lucys in a similar fashion, almost always making note of their line of sight, their physical proximity, a quick cataloging of their gaits and faces for temperature and mood. She felt a similar cataloging happening, but with a different edge entirely. She noticed it at the last quilting. He came in with a stack of wood and greeted all the women. He then set the wood down in the corner and attended to the dying fire in the chimney.

One woman teased him about joining the group, said he boasted to her earlier that he could sew better than her and that he should prove it. All the women laughed, and he smiled with a generous show of pretty teeth, revealing a man-made dimple above his right cheek, triangular like the tip of a sharp blade. He shook his head but soon succumbed to the good-natured joshing of the women.

He took the rag and needle the woman closest to him offered and sat down at the edge of the group. He sewed a few stitches while the women peered over his handiwork, commenting all the while.

"Not bad," said one woman.

"But not better than me," said the original challenger.

They all laughed. And his eyes swept over the group, catching Serah's for a second. She froze, midlaugh, her mouth still open, feeling caught somehow, but just like that, his sweep was over, he handed back over the rag and needle, and stood up. He waved goodbye to them all and quickly left.

And she tried to listen to the gossip that followed, how two women commented on how handsome he was and a third got angry at the two for noticing. She wondered then if the curious feeling he inspired was not hers alone, but something he stirred up wherever he went.

———✍———

IN THE WEEKS BETWEEN sightings, Serah tried to forget the curious feeling. And by the time word arrived that some of the new people were throwing another frolic that Saturday, she had almost convinced herself that it was just a delusion now passed.

She was determined to go, although she heard it was becoming more and more dangerous. There were whispers of rollicking patrols shutting down parties and busting up prayer meetings. Near the property line, she swore she could hear the patrollers some nights. Eerie echoes of high-pitched laughter and drunken singing punctuated by the steady clopping of horses.

So successful were the patrol's outings that there was little chatter or vague invitations to any frolics at all the last couple of weeks. And she had been warned that this one would be harder to get to, more far-flung and deeper in the woods than all the others before.

Only Serah and Patience were willing to risk it, and so the two stepped out alone, late that night. The moon was bright, but the walk was long and the mosquitoes so vicious they almost turned back, only heartening when they heard the soft strains of a fiddle. The two headed on until they reached a small clearing, where the frolic was already in progress. The fiddle player stood at one end, an excited caller goading the crowd, calling out dances to a group of women, dressed in a brilliant array of color, their skirts and dresses dyed berry red, mustard yellow, or deep indigo. Some of them wore hoopskirts, set with twine and starch, so stiff they crackled. Bracelets of copper and wood jangled from their arms. Their hair was plaited and curled or tied up in colorful scarves. The smell of flowers rose up from them, ribbons of honeysuckle and gardenia dangling from their necks.

On the opposite edge, men gambled. A solemn throwing of misshapen dice, made of bone, dotted with gray-black tips. Cheers went up as the dice stopped rolling. Under moonlight, it was easy to mistake one side for another. Three marks for two. Five for three. And the men squinted and shouted and cussed.

"He cheating."

"Don't give *him* the dice no more."

Some men threw up their hands and went to dance with the women.

Two women were racing now, but the most easy-gaited thing you ever did see. They balanced cups of water on their heads and danced toward the edge, arms and legs light and delicate. Whoever spills the water first loses. Whoever gets to the edge without spilling the water wins.

On another side, men and women were telling lies and drinking, filling gourds and tin cups with a strong-smelling brew. Within seconds, Patience dashed off toward the barrel, returning to Serah with a cup full of the strong heady liquid. Serah took a few sips and coughed as the liquid burned her chest. A breeze overhead picked up the leaves and moved through them in a slow languid wave.

Patience drank the rest and dragged Serah out into the crowd by the elbow. Serah saw Noah then, crouched at the edge of the dice game, smoking a cob pipe and making bets. She mimicked Patience's hands and hip motions, but her eyes kept on drifting back to the game. It appeared to be his turn now. He took the dice, shook them in one hand and then the other, blew on them, kissed them up, and tossed them gently. The men shouted as the dice stopped. Some cheering, some cursing. And he rolled again, and then a third time, until the streak was over. He stepped back

from the circle, where a woman-in-yellow threw a long possessive arm around his neck.

Serah turned away, back toward Patience, whose face was
softer than it had been in months. The music sped up, a triangle
now joining the fiddle. And the two women laughed and spun.
Serah threw her head back and caught a glimpse of the night sky,
starry and bright, an almost-full moon hanging above them. A
balmy breeze blew across her face, and she stared at that moon.
Almost full to bursting. That's how she felt, a whole moon somewhere inside her had pieced itself together and now it was nearly
whole again, this weird airy fullness in her chest. A strange joy
tinged with hurt. The two women whirled through the air, spinning and dancing, the two laughing into each other's ears, each
other's chest.

They stumbled out of the circle of dancing, to the edge,
where they collapsed onto the grass. The fiddle slowed down,
and the dancers partnered up, shifting from quick step to slow
drag. Couples danced close; their bodies pressed up against each
other. And she spotted him there in the crowd, dancing with the
woman-in-yellow.

Patience headed to the barrels for another drink, while Serah
sat still, the party whirring around her, the moon lower now. So
large it seemed close, as if it were slowly lowering itself down to
meet her. If she just waited patiently, maybe she could touch it.

"Come on down," Serah hollered toward it. She laughed,
clapping her hands over her mouth.

"Come on down," she heard a voice echo. She turned to see
Noah grinning at her.

"That didn't work. Should we try again?" he asked.

Serah nodded and he dropped down next to her in the grass.
"Come on down," they hollered in unison, before breaking into
laughter.

"Shut up that noise," an older man behind them yelled. "Have the patrollers running through here any minute now with all that foolishness."

They murmured a series of sheepish apologies while trying to stifle their laughter, but the more they tried to contain it, the stronger it became, until they were both tired and out of breath.

They sat there for a moment, just breathing, before he finally turned to her again. "If you got it to come down, what'd you do with it?"

"I don't know . . ."

"You just don't want to say," he said.

"It's silly," she said. "You'll think I'm touched."

"I won't."

She raised her eyebrows at him.

"I swear," he said.

"I think I'd grab hold of it and follow it 'til I get back home. It goes everywhere. Why wouldn't it pass through there?"

He grinned.

"You think it's dumb?" she asked.

"No, the opposite. Wondering why I never thought of it."

They both laughed.

"Especially since they used to say Paw-paw flew home. I wonder if that's how he did it," he said. "But how would you hold on? Wouldn't you just fall off it once it went up again?"

"Maybe, but hopefully I'd be closer than I am now," she said.

"Would you have to go under first?"

"Under? Under where?"

He grabbed a stick and began drawing a shape in the grass. He drew a circle with a cross inside it. He pointed at the median line separating the top and bottom half. "Above—land, sky, us, and below—water, land of the dead."

He pointed to the very top of the circle.

"The sun," she said.

He pointed to the bottom.

She said, "The moon?"

He nodded. "The farthest point in the land of the dead, where the oldest ancestors live . . ."

"I'd have to go there? Through the entire land of the dead and come back round? Oh hell naw."

They both laughed.

"You afraid?" he asked.

"Hell yeah," she said. "And if you're not, you should be. Would you do it?"

"No, not until it's my time, but death don't scare me."

"Really?"

"No."

"You don't have to play tough."

"I'm not. The pain is scary, but if you're just going to the other side for a while"—he pointed to the bottom of the circle again—"where everybody is and then you make your way back over, it's not that scary. You could wind up somewhere better than you were before."

"Do you know if your people made it there? Like your Pawpaw?" she said as she pointed to the bottom half of the circle

He shrugged. "I don't know. He doesn't visit. Seems like he'd visit, if he made it over."

"Back home, I used to try to see my mother. I'd go into the creek and hold my breath for as long as I could. Hoping she'd come back to get me, but she never came . . ."

"Could you see anything?"

"No, not really," she said. "Most of the time, I was too scared. There was all kind of slimy things in the water. That's what made me stop trying. Water snakes."

He laughed.

"And not the tiny ones, but the really big ones." She opened her arms wide.

They were both quiet for a moment, the party still whirring around them. The woman-in-yellow was waving now. Serah pretended she couldn't see the woman from the corner of her eye.

"You think the moon gets lonely up there?" he asked.

"Sure. Everybody gets lonely."

"The sun ain't in hollering distance, but the stars are right there."

"The stars probably awful company," she said. "All that haughty twinkling. Wouldn't that get on your nerves?"

"Okay, what about the clouds?"

"They may be better, but they so some-timey, in and out with the wind, or smothering everything."

They laughed again.

"What's so funny? I want to laugh, too," Patience said, plopping down next to them. "It's not going to last much longer."

They both turned toward her. "The drink. I had to scramble for this little bit," she said, holding her tin cup triumphantly. "You want?" She offered the cup to Serah, before turning to the man. "Who you?"

"Noah from Carolina," he said.

"Hmph. Mr. Noah, if a raft was going by with three women on it," began Patience, "one wearing red, one wearing yellow, and one wearing brown, which would you save?"

"Huh?" said Noah.

"Okay, would you save the tall one, the short one, or the mid-ways one?" Patience asked.

He looked at Serah. "What she talking about?"

Serah shrugged.

"Mr. Noah, get on out of here. You ain't serious."

He stared at the two women, unsure if Patience was joking or not.

"Go on," Patience said, waving him away.

"Fine. A fellow knows when he ain't wanted," he said, standing up in mock disappointment. He winked at Serah as he backed away into the sea of dancers.

"Good, then you a better man than most," Patience hollered after him.

She turned to Serah, now watching Noah talking to the woman-in-yellow.

Patience let out a low chuckle. "Oh, not you, too."

"What?"

"A goner for any fool come grinning in your face."

"We was just talking," Serah said, taking the cup from Patience. "Besides, that girl in yellow's probably his sweetheart."

"No, *he* was just talking. You were doing something else," Patience said, smoothing her skirt and giving Serah an exaggerated flirty grin.

"What you mean? I don't do that."

Patience laughed. "And didn't seem like he asked any of the questions he would've if he was trying to court you proper. Did he even ask if you were unattached?"

"No."

"No questions about spun or woven cloth? Or boats rigged or not?"

"No. Should he have?"

"Bird, did he even ask if he could talk to you before he sat down here?"

"No."

"Well then . . ."

As Patience talked, Serah continued watching Noah and

the woman-in-yellow. They were dancing now. He was trying to make her laugh and the woman was trying hard not to be amused, trying hard to stay upset, but even Serah could see the woman was softening toward him.

Serah wondered what was between the two, if they were, in fact, attached somehow. And while she hadn't considered the conversation between them as anything more than frivolous banter, to have it confirmed as such spawned a growing twinge of disappointment inside her. She stood up and stretched her hand out to Patience. "We should go. Patrollers be through here soon."

Patience took her hand and stood up. The two women drifted away from dancers and the music, slipping back through the woods, where the moon shone bright and full, with nary a cloud in sight.

CHAPTER NINE

HARLOW'S RIGHT HAND ITCHED. NEW calluses forming on top of the old ones, causing the tough white skin to flake and peel. The culprit was likely the handle of his new plow. He had been out there behind it since sunup, lumbering after the two plodding horses, while the women weeded and hilled the cotton for the last time. Any day now, the bolls would start to open and the frenzy of picking would begin.

He rubbed his hands together. In the lore of old wives' tales, itchy palms meant money was coming. Hopefully, there was a grain of truth in that. He had already lost a quarter of the cotton crop to worms, so he needed the rest of it to yield proper. He'd bought the new plow on credit, along with sulfur, vinegar, quinine, saltpeter, rope, and ink, and would need a decent profit to finally get square with all the merchants he owed. Merchants who regularly showed him statements listing out his purchases and the total amounts due. Daunting sums that seemed to tick up and up every time he closed his eyes.

He walked to the house but didn't go in. He was stalling. He should go inside and eat something, and then hurry back out for another round with the plow. He left Junie with it, but he didn't trust her on her own for long. She leaned when she got tired, skimming too close to the crop. But his stomach was jumpy and he couldn't imagine food would make it any better. Once Ollie showed up, he'd be able to eat. Hours ago, he had sent his now-eleven-year-old son over to Levi Sutton's house with a note, suggesting the two men revisit an old conversation they once had about Sutton's interest in purchasing a swath of Harlow's land.

From the second the boy left, Harlow hadn't been able to focus. Ollie should be back by now, he thought, but he had told the boy to wait for an answer, and maybe Sutton wasn't there when he arrived.

Or maybe it was a stalling tactic on Sutton's part, he wondered, and somehow, he had already ceded his hand. Perhaps he should have waited until Sutton sent a response, then he could have been the one delaying. He could've waited a whole day before responding, as if he, too, were so unconcerned by the prospect of buying or selling a measly fifty acres.

He didn't care for his neighbor Levi Sutton much. The man was all airs and bluster, snatching up acreage for miles and miles. It was as if the man was over there building his own town. Beyond the acres and acres of cotton, corn, and millet, there was a big fancy white house, not to mention a maze with an actual orchard of all kinds of fruit trees and decorative rosebushes. Folks didn't even refer to it as Sutton's place, but instead, some haughty moniker, like Greenbriar or Greenwich.

He hated to sell any land to Sutton, hated what it might mean if Sutton had designs on more than just that one strip of land, but he tried not to think that far. Instead, he set his mind on paying down his creditors, on getting his financial affairs out of the red.

He sat on the porch, watching the horizon, waiting for the dust clouds of Ollie's horse to appear. And yes, he knew what was said about watched pots and all, but in his line of work, he watched pots all the time. There was little he didn't put his eyes on and wait for verification that it would do what it was supposed to—grow, yield, seed, sunder.

Where was that boy? Just as likely to have dawdled off the path, if he saw the slightest inkling of something interesting. The boy wasn't worth a gill of hard work. And if the farm didn't turn around soon, he wouldn't be able to set Ollie up with much of anything when the boy came of age in a few years.

The sun shifted from behind the clouds, its angry rays now beaming down on his head and neck. From where he sat, he could hear baby Carol wailing inside. When she was first born, about a year after they buried young William, he and Lizzie thought her a miracle child, but no one used that language to describe Carol anymore. The baby had come into the world with Lizzie's orneriness—a fussy, angry ball of constant caterwauling.

He pushed the front door to the house open. "Will someone shut that child up?" No one replied, but it didn't matter, for at that second, the baby went quiet. He stepped into the dim hot room, smoke lingering in the air, the hearth fire burning.

Dorcas, the new wet nurse, cradled the baby in her lap while Lizzie hovered over them. He could see, now that his eyes had adjusted, that the child had stopped screaming because her mouth was full, impaled by the woman's dark naked breast. The wet nurse had been with them nearly a week, and still, the whole business seemed indecent to him. A stranger, some other man's property, nursing his daughter. A trace of shame flickered inside him.

His gaze met Lizzie's. She narrowed her eyes at him. *Not now.* He walked over to them, where Dorcas lifted her head in his direction, without lifting her eyes. See, the fact that she didn't even have the decency to cover herself in a white man's presence said everything. He reached for the baby.

"Give her here," Harlow said.

"She not done yet," Dorcas said, pulling a cloth up over herself and the suckling child.

"That ain't no business of yours. Give her here. Lizzie will feed her," he said, grabbing hold of Carol's foot.

"The hell I will," said Lizzie, stepping in between them, pushing Harlow backward. "Ignore him, Dorcas. Let her have as much as she wants."

Lizzie steered him away from the wet nurse over to the opposite side of the room. "I've said all I've going to say about this. I got her with my own money."

It was true. Lizzie had done the unthinkable. After the last bout of breastfeeding, she declared herself done with it. No more arduous attempts at latching, at increasing milk supply with herbs and poultices, or nursing despite raw sore nipples and clogged ducts. No matter what she did, she could never produce enough milk for their children. The babes howled day and night, and here she was, having to rely on animal milk and pap, like a serf, since the women in the quarters had yet to bear fruit. This is what she spat at him, whenever he brought up the matter.

This time, though, she had secured a wet nurse herself. She rented a woman with "fresh milk" from an acquaintance in the next county over and paid for her services six months outright, without even consulting him about it. The wet nurse just showed up one day. He came back from the fields and Lizzie was sitting there with her in the front room as if nothing extraordinary was going on.

The couple fought about it for hours that first night, to the point of exhaustion, with him refusing to allow the wet nurse near the baby until finally the child's incessant screaming wore him down.

Even now, so many days later, he was still sore about it. "Is it *my* money that's feeding her? Is she laying up under the roof that I built?"

"Fine. I'll pay for that, too. How much you want for her room and board?" said Lizzie.

"That's not the point."

"Then what is the point?"

He slumped down at the table. He started to say something but stopped. He was tired of explaining himself. Tired of her insinuating that the mountain of debt was all his fault, as if he were a god that could control weather and pestilence. As if he could simply raise his hand and stop rain and drought, or wave away the presence of worms, weevils, or grackles. It was simply a precarious business. Had been since the Panic of 1837 and the great depression that followed it. It made paupers of men smarter than him, and she didn't seem to appreciate how close they had come. That it was he who kept the wind at their backs; he, who had secured the five hundred acres that they lived upon. Even after Alice's buyer sued him for failure to disclose her barrenness. He handled it, hadn't he? Mounted an appeal that got the refund amount cut in half. Sure, he had to mortgage Lulu and Serah to secure a loan to pay the damages and the exorbitant legal fees, but he took care of it. He retained the title to the land, and that was the most important thing. Without that, where would they be?

Maybe her father was the reason she didn't seem to appreciate any of it. The reason she thought she understood more about the workings of his business than he did. The reason why every so often she butted into farm affairs, giving her opinion when he hadn't asked for it, and worse, refusing to allow him to use her property as collateral. He suspected her father was advising her and, worse, sending her money that she wasn't telling him about, but he had no proof, and she wouldn't admit it.

"The point is," he began, "you brought a plumb stranger into this house without my say-so."

"I apologized for that already. It's not like I bought her. I thought you'd be pleased to have peace in the house again. And look, Carol's so happy. I think she's already gained a pound or two."

He sighed.

Nan burst in, heaving a big steaming pot of soup onto the table. Soup in *this heat*. If that wasn't proof Lizzie's judgment couldn't be trusted, then what was?

"I don't want to see no more soup on this table until I can see my breath out there, you hear me?" he said to Lizzie.

But his wife wasn't listening. She had drifted back over to the baby and was now busy cooing at the suckling child.

"Lizzie, you hear me!"

CHAPTER TEN

WHAT SERAH HAD WANTED BUT didn't know she wanted came just before Christmas. The air was cooling and the drop in temperature gave the last few frolics of the year new urgency. She felt it most when the fiddler traded off with Delilah, a statuesque woman with a haunted singing voice. She sang beautifully, but no matter the song chosen or the tempo, it all became a dirge. Call it moon sickness, the way Delilah could stir things up in everyone, a slow unraveling of whatever dark mass was swirling deep down inside. A catharsis of the worst kind emerged, as there were never more fights than when Delilah sang, never more old couplings discarded, and new ones made. And yet, no one could keep her from singing really. Someone always asked her to, always pushed her toward the front and begged for a song, paying her in peaches or shiny apples.

It was during this season of Delilah and her ongoing dirges that their conversations picked up again. Noah would see her at one of these outings and sit down next to her as if they were old friends and he'd ask her about the social life of the moon and stars, as if he were inquiring about the health and well-being of distant kin.

Serah looked forward to these exchanges, no matter how brief they were, no matter how silly they seemed to Patience or anyone else. And over time, a strange web of language emerged underneath, like it was possible to talk about nearly anything under the veil of the moon's mercurial nature or the sun's ruthless glare. If it had been a particularly rotten set of days, she might answer his question by talking about the dead moon and how dark everything seemed without it. "I wouldn't blame it if it didn't come back at all . . ."

These discussions made her even more curious about the women he danced with, the possessive one in yellow whose name she since learned was Clara, and others, too. And until the night he taught her to whistle, she began to think he never would dance with her. Maybe she wasn't a woman he could dance with. Maybe she wasn't the sort to be courted or sweethearted.

That night, she had been telling him about how Nan only pulls a plant out of the ground based on what the moon says.

"If the right face ain't up there, she lets it be."

He responded with a long low whistle. "The sun must be jealous as a clam."

"Do it again. That sound."

He whistled again, now adding another note to it, going one octave lower, in the key of one of Delilah's dirges.

For a moment, it snapped her home somehow, back to standing at the reef beside her twin brother, with him whistling at the fish in hopes of drawing them toward the net.

"I never could do that," she said.

"Sure you can." He showed her how to hold her mouth, how

to relax her face, but she couldn't get any sound to come out. "Watch me," he told her.

The permission to look at him up close felt unsettling, so different from the faraway glances she stole most times. The thick eyebrows and smooth skin, the dimple-like scar on his cheek.

"Give me your hand," he said. She allowed him to put her fingers close to his mouth, so she could feel the shape he was making. "See. Not so forced, easy."

She could feel his breath on her fingers, the warm grip of his hand holding hers, and a strange sensation flooded her body. She stilled herself, trying to follow it, this unfamiliar feeling.

He felt her stiffen and dropped her hand, turned his face away from hers, toward a clattering sound, where Delilah stood, readying her song again.

The strange sensation subsided. A cloud swept in, blocking the moon.

She blew out a spurt of air, then another, without any hint of a whistle at all. "Show me again."

He grinned. He whistled a few notes toward her, the same song as before.

"No," she said. "Show me again." She touched his hand.

And there was that feeling again, a strange tingling wave that spread from her fingers all the way up to her shoulders as he guided her hand to his lips. For the first time, she met his gaze directly.

After that, he didn't leave her side the rest of the evening. Even when Clara came by, he didn't waver, only introduced the two women in an easy manner, and went back to teaching Serah the different notes she could make, depending on the shape she made with her tongue.

—❧—

FROM THEN ON, SERAH saw Noah regularly. If not weekly, then nearly every other. If there wasn't a frolic or a prayer meeting, he came over on passes with a husband going to see his wife on another neighboring farm. Noah never came to Serah's directly, because the Lucys had denied every request from neighboring men wanting to visit. Said they didn't want strange niggers on their property, as who only knew what those men might be capable of. A stance Mr. Lucy would feel vindicated in after the Manigault murder some months later.

The two often met at the creek on those Saturday nights. She'd slip off not long after the evening meal, groaning about how Nan needed her help with some arduous task. She'd then creep to the loom, where she could see the bank of trees just above the creek and wait for Noah's tall lean figure to appear. Over time, she told him things she had never told the women. Things that only multiplied in the gaps between seeing each other when weather or circumstance doubled or tripled the periods between visits. And it wasn't long before their meetings took on a certain ritualized order. Often, the confessions were first. Not necessarily weighty things, just the things each had been holding in to tell the other, only touching after they had talked themselves out.

When she tried to parse out the particular magic of it, it got even harder to pin down. She couldn't explain why he felt safe, why from the moment he sat down next to her, talking as if they were lifelong friends, she never felt the impulse to run away, why with him she remained more curious than afraid. And she never expected to like the sex. She figured it was something that might happen, because it was a thing that happened, regardless of how she felt about it. She assumed at some point its likeliness after realizing what a glutton she was for being touched by him. What was most surprising to her about the act was that it didn't come over her like the weight of the ocean, didn't pass through her like the bow of a steamship. That when it happened, it seemed like the horizon line meeting the earth, the most natural adhering of two things always coming back together. Whereas all sex before felt like a splintering, what she felt with him was the opposite, a deep and sweet mending. Her body became a map of all the places he had touched, and what lingered afterward in the soft soreness of her muscles seemed to her like a delicious telepathy between them in the silence that followed.

———

WE WERE KIND AND held our tongues, and often pretended to be asleep when she crept back in after a visit. We didn't poke holes at her secret and weren't surprised when she couldn't keep it to herself. When she let it slip from her mouth, in that dazed way of beloveds, what he had said last time they had seen each other, how he could make an instrument out of anything, how he had given her a ring, a razor-thin band fashioned from a button.

It reminded us how young she was, how that first rush of love could take you like a strong tide. And who were we to deny her that fleeting joy? We knew some women went their whole lives and never tasted it or had it for what felt like seconds, as searing and haunting as a dream, before it left them and they convinced themselves that they had never known it at all, because that loss stacked among the others seemed the easiest to deny. Because even if you found it, how long before a white man raised his hand and put a body of water in between?

And maybe this was the small hiccup in our generosity.

"It won't last," we said.

"Young people hearts fickle as the moon."

"You know how many sweethearts I had way back when?"

"Mmhmm, could count mine on both hands."

What we were really saying, though, is don't get attached to anybody, if you can help it. If it ain't your kindred, ain't your blood, don't carry anybody's heart into your belly. Men are weak, ever hungry, flighty. Some nights, we'd laugh and tell her stories about men we had taken up with, men who courted us slow and heavy as molasses, only to find out later they had wives and children on a neighboring farm. We'd warn her about the temperature of a man's heart, how quickly it could turn to frost, the same way a northeaster could surprise the plants and freeze them quick-quick.

Serah would just laugh and shake her head. The folly of old bitter women, she must have thought. If she had been willing to listen, she might have heard the steady murmur of something else. The haunting of the disappeared, the husband swallowed up by sea or sky without warning. Sky took him, water took him, earth took him. Easier than saying he was beaten to death after running away, or his master died and he was given to an uncle in another state. Facts weren't friends. They could be fickle as paint. Hard to come by and easily changed.

But we didn't blame her for wanting. We crossed our fingers, made offerings to the saints on her behalf, in hopes they would let her have this one thing she desperately wanted. All week long, she waited to see him, and if he had been sent off on a cattle job, it could mean two or three. And so, when the occasion demanded, we braided her hair special, helped her dye a skirt red or indigo, and made her perfume necklaces of flowers stolen from Miss Lizzie's garden, in hopes she could enjoy this bright thing unsullied for as long as it lasted.

CHAPTER ELEVEN

DORCAS HAD LOST TRACK OF just how many days she had been with the Harlows and how long it would be until she could return home. Her sleep was leaden and thick, and every morning, when she was yanked from it, either by the infant's high-pitched wailing or the angry shadow of its mother shoving the child toward her face, she spent the first few minutes lost and disoriented.

She slept on the floor next to the manger, as she was supposed to anticipate the child's waking, to hear it grunting or squirming before it began wailing, but she never did. The briny blackness of wherever she had gone in her sleep never gave up its hold so easily. She could still feel that heaviness upon her when she took baby Carol into her arms and the child burrowed its face onto her breast. She'd lift her blouse and the infant would latch on, the how, who, where, and why seeping back into her brain.

Carol was solely her charge, from the moment the infant woke up until the second it went to sleep. The child was to be within arm's length of her at all times, and what was worse, the child seemed to know it. The first few days, the hungry infant clung to her with a fierceness that she thought would dissipate in the days that followed, but it never did. It was as if the child decided the key to ending its deprivation was to fix itself to Dorcas permanently. Even once fed, Carol would not allow herself to be put down. If she woke up from sleep and found herself in the manger, she howled until she saw Dorcas was near, until the woman picked her up and held her.

This was disturbing enough, but what Dorcas found even more troubling was the child's ravenous appetite. How it only grew and grew, the babe fattening and lengthening, with swollen cheeks and wide watchful eyes. Not to mention, the growing strength of the child. How it held up its neck to peer around or spread its fingers to grasp at her collarbone, how its small pink mouth began to pull more and more milk from her with graceless ease.

As the milk seeped out of Dorcas, she felt something go with it. Something she couldn't name. She didn't fight the child, not consciously, but some part of her body tensed up, trying to hold something back. But the more she held back, the more the child seemed to want. She felt other things seeping out of her now, her memories and self-made things. A river flowed out of her. She couldn't explain what was floating out on that river, what was leaving her that she could no longer retrieve, or the gray widening blur it left in its wake. Not that there was anyone to explain it to. No one spoke to her, not really. As long as Carol was in her arms, there was no need.

Even Nan, the peevish cook, who came and went and tidied, who set down food and water for her sometimes, always seemed to be looking past her, always seemed to regard her with exasperation. Dorcas had an inkling of why that might be. It was because she refused to take up any task that had nothing to do with the child. If the child was sleeping, she stood by and waited for it to wake up. She would not rinse a cup or a dish or scrub the child's laundry. If that seemed wrong to the cook, she did not care. The house regarded her as a two-legged heifer, and so she would do no more than wait to be milked. That is what they rented her for. They would get nothing more. She said as much the first day and had barely said a word to anyone since.

But the truth was, they took more from her all the time. The child was a thief, and it stole more from her every passing day. She felt weaker, the child heavy and fat in her arms, weighing her down in the chair. Her vision grew soft, and all sound seemed to be coming through a long, winding tunnel. She'd think, *Next time I go down to the privy and relieve myself, I won't return.* But, once she was outside, the weakness always flared up. She couldn't tell one fuzzy tree from another, if she should follow the sun or go in the opposite direction. The one time she wandered way past the privy, the peevish cook spotted her near the loom and assumed she got turned around.

"Lost, huh?" Nan said. "Follow me. I'll take you back." The woman began leading her toward the house.

Don't take me back there, Dorcas wanted to say, but she held her tongue. She didn't know Nan, didn't know what thoughts the woman could be trusted with.

The truth was only her left eye was any good to begin with. The right eye had a cloud in it, ever since she was a child. The left eye compensated and did all the work, so it sometimes grew tired. But never this tired. It never gave up altogether, the way it seemed to now in this house, with this child at her breast. If she didn't give the child any more milk, or rationed it somehow, would some of her sight return on its own accord? Were all her memories and things now buried in the pale jiggly flesh of this squirming baby? What could she break the flesh with? What could she use to pierce the fat thigh or moonlike belly?

Maybe the loss of vision was a blessing and she was being spared from seeing anything more. On particularly hazy days, the soft blur of her vision turned the child into a faint, affable presence. The sucking sound became a lapping body of water, and a pleasant warmth washed over her. She felt faraway then, on the other side of that long tunnel, from where she could see the Harlows milling about, just pale streaks on a distant stage.

Other times, the whole house seemed monstrous to her. A faceless changeling fixed itself to her day and night, her nose was assaulted by a heady mix of curdled milk and soiled diapers, the warping floor planks creaked underneath her feet, and the room was full of ghosts and swirling smoke, while outside, swarms of iridescent blackbirds veered and circled the house, cawing and shrieking all the while.

A sudden cold spell sent the grackles farther south. Gone were their teeming circles in the sky, their shrieking chatter, or their strange presence lined up and at the ready. She felt their absence acutely, the company they provided, the questions they raised inside her.

Without them, the house narrowed, the husband and wife fighting all the time now. About food, about money, about her. "We should just take her back," he'd say. "Get a refund left on the contract before it's too late."

The wife always said no. "Until I see milk oozing out of your teat, I ain't talking about it no more."

And on it went, sometimes growing haggard and nasty between them, with blows flying in all directions. Dorcas did not look. She did not turn her head to see who swung and where such blows landed. She positioned her seat so it faced the window more than the room, and she kept her good eye focused outside.

White people didn't like the help to see them in low moments. They never wanted to be reminded that what stood in the rear of the room, feeding the child, or waving the flyswatter, or refilling the glasses with water, could see and hear their moments of folly and shame.

Soon, Dorcas found she could no longer mount the tunnel of distance she had been able to before. Now, the quarreling couple felt close at her back. The hungry babe lay on her chest, pawing and sucking and taking. She felt weak and light-headed.

And for the first time since her arrival, she produced less milk. There was a growing pain in her left breast, so she let Carol feed from the right and hoped that would be enough to send the child to sleep. It wasn't. Carol squirmed and howled and kicked.

"Try the other one," said Lizzie.

Dorcas shook her head. "I can't. It hurts."

"Sure you can. It's going to hurt sometimes. That's no reason for Carol to go hungry."

"She's had plenty."

"Well, she wants more."

Dorcas leaned over the manger and began to put the kicking child down.

"Don't you put her down when she's screaming like that!"

Dorcas pulled the child back into her lap. She put the child on her left breast and winced when Carol latched on, but as she predicted, nothing came out, and Carol began howling again.

"See?" Dorcas said. *I told you.*

"You're not even trying. Probably just a clog. You have to press out the milk, then. Like this," Lizzie said. She reached toward Dorcas's breast.

Dorcas winced and blocked the woman's hand, her grip loosening on Carol, just as the child wrenched backward. Carol fell to the floor with a loud thud. She lay still in a heap, not making a sound. Dorcas felt something crack inside her, the cloud in her eye seemed to break and seep outward at the sight of the stilled baby.

Lizzie kneeled down and began looking Carol over. The girl opened her mouth and screamed. Lizzie took the baby in her arms. "There, there," she murmured. "Go get Nan," she said, turning to Dorcas.

But Dorcas couldn't move, the seeping cloud made it all gray, hard to determine the boundaries of all the objects surrounding her, the origin of voices speaking. While Carol cried, another baby laughed. Another baby was gurgling, was giggling.

"I'm sorry," Dorcas said to the room, to the gurgling baby.

Lizzie sighed. "You should be. Now hold her. Carefully." Lizzie motioned for Dorcas to sit back in the chair, where she put the howling child back in Dorcas's arms.

Carol grabbed hold of Dorcas's shoulder with her tiny fist, the pitch of her howl lowering then petering out.

"You're lucky she likes you so much," said Lizzie, walking out of the front door, leaving it open behind her. Dust swirled inside the sunlight, now filling the room.

"I'm so sorry," Dorcas said to the child in her arms. In this new amber light, she could see her son's face so clearly. Adam. His small heart beating, a thick gurgling sound coming from his throat. There was his small body, no bigger than a head of cabbage. A bona fide caul baby. With her, then gone, and now back again. Old women always said it was bad luck to go naming a child before their ninth day of life. She couldn't help it, though. She named him early, when he was still just a melon inside her.

The suckling child they pushed into her arms two days after the burial was not Adam. And the pale mewling child searching for her nipple now wasn't either. Somehow, they had swallowed him whole, and she couldn't locate him. The chasm between this world and the one her son lived in felt fixed and vast. No matter what she did, she couldn't cross it. And somewhere stuck between the two worlds lies her grief, a swelling balloon she couldn't reach. It remained a blur, a threatening specter outside her periphery, a piece of hard flint pressing upon the unseeing eye. Until now. Until the sight of the small, stilled body punctured the balloon and its contents broke over her, in one unforgiving wave.

She shut her eyes tight and sucked in big gasps of thick, humid air. She jammed her breast in the child's mouth. She called on the warm solid blankness to come over her, to restore the soft, gray nothing she felt before. *C'mon, child, suck down this grief. Take it all back.*

CHAPTER TWELVE

LIZZIE NEVER TOLD HER HUSBAND about the baby's fall. Carol was fine, more stunned than hurt. There was a small bruise on her leg, but easy enough to keep hidden from him, as he never gave the baby any more than a passing glance. Until the children were old enough to talk, Charles had little interest in them.

She knew if she told him, it would be the final straw in his campaign to get rid of Dorcas. Ever since he and Sutton couldn't agree on a fair price for that swatch of land Charles wanted to sell him, her husband's fussing had taken on a heightened frenzied air. He complained all the time now that they could no longer afford Dorcas. She was just another mouth to feed, and they could barely feed what they had. "Let's take her back," he'd say, nearly every morning before the first cup of coffee. "You know every day that passes, the less money they'll give us on the contract."

"And what am I supposed to feed Carol? Animal milk?"

He'd shake his head. "You fed the other children just fine. Why should Carol be treated special?"

She started to dig in again, explaining the trials and tribulations of nursing, but she stopped herself. Why bother? He didn't listen, nor could he understand why her body wouldn't behave the way he thought it should. So, now, she no longer said anything. She no longer had the energy to explain, to curse, or to argue with him. She was full up with the incessant chatter and shrieking of cranky children, the thunderous screaming of a colicky infant, the noxious smell of sour milk, vomit, and soiled diapers in Texas heat. The rooms were too small, always full up with too many people. Not to mention having to watch another woman nurse her baby. How at first it felt freeing, to not have the infant fixed to her all the time like a new appendage. But as time went on, it felt damning. How dependent she was on this feeble-minded slave who mumbled to herself and stared out the window, as if searching for a sighting of the Lord himself.

Not to mention her foolish, luckless husband. How just the sound of him traipsing through the house could send her into a singular rage. The only thing that checked her anger these days was a small bottle of laudanum she kept hidden in the pocket of her dress. One or two swigs dulled every complaint and worry in her head.

It was only two days after Carol's fall, when she rose to find the bottle empty. It was morning and already Charles was fussing about the wet nurse, about his dwindling line of credit at the shop in town, and how any day now, the shopkeeper would cut him off unless he paid some portion of the debt or handed over some form of collateral.

"He won't cut us off now. He knows the falling cotton prices couldn't be helped," she said as she got dressed.

"Yeah, but everybody else singing that same song, too. Maybe I could give him Patience or Lulu for the season?"

She nodded. "That's a right idea." But she wasn't really listening. She had just slipped her hand into the pocket of the dress she wore last night and found the bottle slick and wet, the cloth soggy. She pulled the dark bottle out, only to find it was empty, nothing but air inside. She must not have corked it tightly.

"But not Dorcas, huh? You would cripple the whole farm to hold on to that teat," he said.

Lizzie's sight went blurry for a second, blood beat at her temples. She licked her wet hand, was tempted to lick the whole bottle, but he was right behind her, glaring at her now.

"Imagine that. No wonder you paid three times what that gal out there is worth. Bet you didn't even ask around. Bet you didn't even nail down proper terms," he sneered.

"'Course I did!" she said, spinning around to face him. "It was my money. And I'll pay as much as I like, since it's been my money keeping this catastrophe afloat ever since I let you drag me to this hellscape!"

He slapped her then, right across the mouth with the back of his hand, the way he often did the female slaves. And even with her face throbbing, the full insult of this action wasn't lost on her.

He stormed off and she sat on the bed, feeling her bottom lip tingle and swell. She opened the bottle and put her lips to it. It was dry as hot sand. She pulled last night's dress down from the hook and found the damp pocket, soaked and pungent with laudanum. She folded the material over so the pocket was exposed and put her lips to the wet cloth. It hurt her mouth to pucker her lips, but she ignored the pain and sucked what she could from the fabric. She drifted off to sleep across the bed, sucking the cloth like Carol sucking her thumb.

—❧—

Lizzie awoke sometime later to the sound of Carol's wailing. She rose from the bed and walked into the front room, where Nan sat, rocking the child.

There was no sign of Dorcas.

"Did she go down to the privy? I told her not to go that far," Lizzie said, storming over to the door and opening it.

Nan shook her head and continued trying to soothe the crying child.

A fly buzzed past Lizzie's face and into the house. There was no sign of Charles in the yard, no sign of the wagon either.

"He take her?" Lizzie asked, but she already knew the answer.

Nan didn't say anything, just held the squirming child out toward Lizzie. "Here. I need to get dinner started."

Lizzie stared at Nan for a long moment, before taking the child in her arms. "Did Louisa and Ollie go, too?"

"No, they down at the creek," Nan said as she walked away.

Baby Carol looked directly into Lizzie's face and screamed. She couldn't remember the last time she had seen a look of such unadulterated disappointment. She didn't want to be left alone with Carol, but she couldn't demand Nan stay if she wanted dinner on the table soon.

"Stop it, Carol. Stop it!" she yelled fruitlessly as the child kicked and flailed. They were stuck together now. An angry baby and its angrier mother. Only Carol wouldn't be assuaged. She let out one high-pitched wail after another.

Alcohol. Maybe just a little whiskey or corn liquor on the child's gums would put her to sleep. Lizzie dashed around the house, looking for a bottle. In the trunk. Under the bed. Where did Charles keep the liquor these days? He was always moving it, from one hiding place to another. Swearing that she or the servants were stealing it from him.

She stepped outside, with Carol on her hip. Maybe he hid

it in one of the outbuildings. The barn or the smokehouse. She swayed in the sun, hoping the movement would calm Carol a bit. Carol grew silent, craning her neck, as if she was looking for Dorcas.

In the yard, Lizzie spotted Serah hanging the family's laundry on the line. The gal had watched William on occasion. She could leave Carol with her for two minutes while she tracked down the liquor.

Lizzie watched as Serah snapped wrinkles out of one of Charles's shirts and hoisted it up over the clothesline. The whole time, the girl seemed to be chewing something, a big unwieldy ball poking out of her left cheek, an activity that she stopped the moment she saw Lizzie draw near.

Charles was right, Lizzie thought with a sigh. *Anything that ain't nailed down.* A good portion of this evening's dinner was probably halfway down this girl's gullet. "Don't you move," Lizzie said, staring at Serah's mouth, her throat.

The girl paused, having clipped the back of the shirt to the line, the sleeves still hanging low. "Ma'am?"

"Don't you dare swallow it. Whatever you're chewing," Lizzie said, lunging toward her. She balanced Carol on one hip and held her palm out in front of Serah's lips. "Spit it out. Now."

Carol began to cry softly, but Lizzie ignored her. The girl spit a dark wet mass into her hand.

It wasn't recognizable but had a pungent earthy smell. "That's it? Open your mouth."

Serah did as she was told and Lizzie peered inside. Still, nothing recognizable. No bits of corn or green leafy bits clinging to her teeth. Instead, what was there was a chalky yellow substance, speckling her teeth and tongue.

"You stealing from me, girl? What'd you take?"

The girl pointed to the ground, to some yellowish rocks at

TRACEY ROSE PEYTON

the far end of the yard. "Just dirt, ma'am. I like the taste. Makes me feel not hungry."

Lizzie dumped the wet lump on the ground and wiped her hand on her apron. "That's disgusting and I don't want to see it again. Now, get these clothes up on the line and go rinse out your mouth."

Carol was crying now. "Hush!" Lizzie snapped at her and swung the child around. She padded over to the smokehouse, but the lock kept sticking. She tried to put Carol down, but Carol began screaming louder. *I bear all things. I bear all things.* She swung Carol to her other hip and marched back toward the house. *Willful children. A foolish husband. Feeble-minded servants. I bear all things through Him that strengthens me.*

She stuck her head in the doorway of the cookhouse and asked Nan to make the child a gruel, but sticky sweet this time. No, she didn't care if it required using the last of the sugar. She wouldn't care if it required every jar of food in the pantry if it won her a couple hours of quiet.

WHEN JUNIE WAS SUMMONED to the Lucys' house after work, she wasn't sure why. Mail wasn't likely. She had seen Harlow leave and he hadn't come back yet. If there was news from home, it wouldn't be until he returned from town or wherever he went.

Junie sighed and scarfed down the last of her scant dinner. She grabbed some needlework and brought it along, as it wasn't good to appear idle in the Lucys' house. But that's not the real reason she brought it. She brought it because it gave her cover, gave her eye somewhere to land, somewhere for her jaw to point its tensions.

She entered the house, where Nan was playing referee between the Lucys' two older children. Nan just nodded and pointed her toward the bedroom. Junie entered to find a strange sight. Carol in the crib, asleep, her body slumped at an odd angle. Lizzie frazzled and wild-eyed, a stack of old letters spread out over the bed. She was reading aloud. "'The ice thawed faster than we expected, almost too fast. Little Phillip will start school this year. It's a shame that he has yet to meet his aunt or his cousins. We have to get them together before they're too old.'"

Lizzie looked up at Junie standing there, as if she'd been speaking to her the entire time. "Little Phillip must be nearly done with school now. Tell me. Did you think we'd be out here this long?"

A rhetorical question. Junie sat down, pulled her needlepoint from her apron, and unraveled it in her lap. She sewed and listened while Lizzie went on reading. Details of a wedding of some distant cousins Junie had never heard of. Junie didn't care to hear about the cake, the feast, or the dress. Or how the fabric came from London, and the house they were going to live in was designed by some lousy Frenchman. Junie only listened out for the gifts, to hear specifically if anyone she knew might be gifted to the new bride and groom.

Her children were owned by Lizzie's brother, Mason, and her mother had fallen to one of Lizzie's aunts, so technically, her kin were "still in the family."

"They'll stay that way," Lizzie often told her, but Junie found no peace of mind in that. For mentions about them in the letters to Lizzie became fewer and fewer. Most of the time, they weren't mentioned at all.

Her children, Hannah and Patrick, would be about ten and thirteen, respectively. And she imagined them tall for their ages, gangly like she was, but Patrick, she decided, would be awkward but fast, like his daddy. The tiny bowlegs she remembered having grown more pronounced as he grew older, just like her husband's. Nelson was a proud man everyone called Ox, who tipped around awkwardly in real time, but in a race could outrun anyone. That combination of speed, agility, and clumsiness made him special in Junie's eyes. And there was a whole alternate universe where her husband and son were known by all in their neighborhood by this shared trait. Big Ox and Little Ox, they'd be called by kith and kin alike.

That sounded pretty in her mind, but what worried her now was that she couldn't picture the children anymore. How time must have changed the small faces she remembered, the ones she'd fed and swaddled and washed with a damp cloth. In the letters from home, they were phantoms, implied in general updates about illnesses and crop yields. "Fever laid low most of the hands the last few weeks, but most are recovering well. All except Gibson, whose cough hasn't improved." And only when she pressed Lizzie to ask about them directly did she get confirmation that they were still on Mason's farm, only a few miles from where they all were born. But even then, the information was scant and thin. "Hannah is a fine hand and suits us well in the house."

After a long passage about the wedding procession, Lizzie stopped reading. "I want to go home."

Junie continued sewing.

"You hear me? I want to go home."

A homesick tantrum was coming on. They surfaced a few times a year. So Junie did what she always did. She got up and stuck her head out of the door, summoned Ollie, and sent him to Nan with a request for tea. She then sat back down, with her needlepoint in hand, and buckled in. These fits usually didn't last longer than an hour. They started slow, and ended high, with Lizzie weepy and needing a nap. And if Lizzie had gotten ahold of some laudanum, that could shorten the whole ordeal to about fifteen minutes.

Her job was to listen and nod fervently. Technically, it was probably the easiest thing she would do that day. She had spent the morning helping patch a fence. The posts were heavy and strained her back, and her hand still hurt from where a splinter broke off and lodged itself under the skin of her palm. All through Lizzie's chatter, she pressed on it, trying to coax it out, but she couldn't see it, could only feel it there. The more Lizzie talked, the more it stung.

Lizzie grew weepy, reminiscing about home the way a lush might. "Do you remember . . ." she'd begin. And she'd rattle off this list: a hiding place under the porch, the grand parades where Lizzie's father and brother would don spiffy uniforms and march with their muskets, the card games with her cousins, and the dances she'd go to with her brother. And the food, the peach pie Junie's mother made Lizzie's family after every harvest or the lemon cake she made special for Lizzie's birthday.

"That was my favorite," Lizzie said, a gleam in her eye. "Nan is a fine cook, but she's not nearly as good as Roberta."

Junie felt a sudden urge to pluck out that eye. How many seconds would it take to retrieve it? To yank it from the woman's silly head. The muscles in her hand jerked and the needle slipped from her fingers, onto the floor.

She hated hearing the woman say her mother's name. Hated hearing the woman flaunt the spoils. The special things Roberta made Lizzie and her family, special things Junie and her siblings weren't allowed and had never tasted.

It was Junie and her siblings who collected those peaches, peeled them and boiled them down, making the sweet jelly-like filling. And if Roberta tried to set anything aside for her children, the smallest portion of jelly after the pies had been set in the hearth, it was Lizzie's mother who'd find it and spit in it, as it was her habit to spit in all the pots after Roberta plated the food for the white family.

Lizzie's mother, Madeline, counted out every cup of sugar, every gill of flour, every cup of butter or cream, with exacting fortitude. She marked every sack, every container, kept copious notes, and wore the key to the pantry around her neck day and night. She didn't take it off to sleep nor to bathe, as Madeline was sure that the only thing that kept the help from eating her family out of house and home and into the red was her grip on that small metal key.

"I always thought we'd be like two peas in a pod our whole lives, just like our mothers were," Lizzie said. "Girls together, then wives and mothers. But I've had more children than you now." Her voice was glum, her weepy affection slipping into something else.

"Peas in a pod" was not how Junie thought of it, but of course, she understood the implication. She was supposed to be a mini-Roberta moving in lockstep with every season of Lizzie's life. She was to have children at the same rate, within months of Lizzie's own, so she could wean her own babies quickly, in order to nurse Lizzie's offspring fully and as long as they needed.

"Trial after trial. Cross after cross," Lizzie went on, waving her arms around. "The soil is cursed. Our wenches barren. All our seeds seem to go unflowered. Got so much debt we can barely see straight. When shall we reap? Huh? When, Junie, when?"

At the sound of her name, the room snapped back into focus. "In His time," Junie said. "Not ours."

Lizzie's glassy eyes focused on hers. "You're right. Absolutely right."

"And that stockman . . . you know God wasn't gon' bless that."

"Charles was desperate."

"Don't sound much like faith to me," Junie said quietly. The splinter in her hand was throbbing. She felt it pushing her to the edge.

Lizzie gave her a pointed look but didn't say anything.

"A fruitful marriage is blessed by God, made of people who choose each other." Junie's word hung there in the air between them, a rare moment of stillness in the house.

Lizzie avoided Junie's gaze, turning back to the letters. She brought them to her nose and inhaled deeply. "Still smells like home. We should go. Just for a visit. It's been ages," Lizzie continued. "I hear the steamboats aren't bad. They used to explode a lot, but they're safer now, I hear. We'd have to get Houston, but from there . . ."

Junie picked up the needle and pushed it through the fabric.

"I know I say this all the time, but I'm serious. A break from all this would be most welcome. And we'd get to see Papa and Mason and Annie. And I bet I could get Mason to bring Patrick and Hannah over. It would be a grand time."

"Patrick and Hannah?" asked Junie. During these tantrums, her children were never mentioned by name. Neither were steamboats or any of the logistics of actual travel. Before, the wish had always seemed desultory, thrown about and abandoned, its appeal dissolving the moment it reached open air.

Junie put the needle down in her lap. She couldn't trust it under her fingers. She needed to get out of that room. It had been years since one of these "letters from home" sessions affected her so. Usually, she felt them like pricks under the skin. She nodded and occasionally chimed in with the spate of required responses. "Oh yes, that sounds real nice." And sure, there were days when Lizzie wanted more than an obligatory nod or parroted response. She wanted Junie to grin and laugh, to participate in the fiction that they were just a pair of close friends, while they sewed or snapped beans. Usually, those days were the hardest, but even then, her family never entered into it.

Junie stood up. "Where is that tea?" she said. "I'll go get it." She stepped out of the bedroom and into the darkness of the hall. It felt thick, a palpable darkness. She pushed herself past the squabbling children. Ollie had grabbed a chunk of Louisa's hair and was pulling for dear life. She did not intervene, only stepped past them and rushed out the front door.

CHAPTER THIRTEEN

WHEN SERAH AND NOAH HAD been together for almost three seasons, she found herself wanting things the neighboring women had. Some had cabins they shared only with their husbands and children. Others had husbands that came to see them twice a week, both on Wednesdays and on Saturdays, when they stayed over until Sunday mornings.

Serah also began to worry about the flirtatious nature of those parties. Although she believed what Noah told her, that his relationship with Clara was just a dalliance, she couldn't help remembering what the women said about the changing nature of men's hearts. She wondered if asking the Lucys for permission to marry him would ease that fear inside her. Though she feared what she'd be inviting in, once the Lucys knew about him.

One muggy night in July, she tried to broach the subject with Noah. He was quieter than usual, sitting on the ground with his hands underneath his thighs. "You ever see a calf being born?" he asked after a while.

"No, don't think so," she said. "What made you think about that?"

He shrugged, not looking at her.

She gently touched his face and turned it toward hers. "Tell me."

"Helped one be born the other day. Haven't been able to stop thinking about it," he said, a look of awe in his eyes. "The mother died. I had it feed it and everything."

There was a fresh bruise on the left side of his face, an angry purple bulge under his eye.

"The calf do that?" she said, grazing the bruise with her finger.

He flinched, inching backward. "Run-in with the patrollers."

He caught the look of worry crossing her face and draped an arm around her shoulders. "Ah, don't you start fretting," he said, with a playful grin. "You know buckra can't catch me." He kissed her forehead.

But they did? She started to say but held her tongue. Perhaps being married might help alleviate this problem, but how could she broach the subject? Maybe she couldn't ask him about the two of them getting married directly, but she could ask if the abroad husbands he knew had ever been denied passes from Sutton. And then slowly tease out what he thought of the practice in general.

"Hmm, don't know if it suits me," Noah began. "Besides, Uncle Ned told me I should look to marry a free woman, so my children be free . . ."

His words gave her a sudden headache, a dull throbbing at the base of her skull. She waited a few minutes, tuning him out, to see if the throbbing would pass. It didn't.

She disentangled herself from his arms and stood up, holding her head. "I feel sick."

She began walking. "I need to go home."

"What's wrong?"

She just shook her head and sped up, climbing up the bank
of the creek, with him scrambling after her. She hurried across
the Harlows' property line, where she knew he wouldn't follow.

She avoided him for a while after that, not going to the
creek or loom on Saturdays. If there was a frolic, she wouldn't
go. She'd stay behind with Nan, quilting or knitting. And when
Lulu and the others returned, she'd pester them with questions
about Noah, if they had seen him and whether or not he had
asked about her.

Lulu was not moved by these pleas. "Talk or don't talk but
leave me be. I ain't your go-between."

The next Saturday, finally ready to talk, she went out there to
the loom and waited, but he never appeared.

———

DAYS LATER, WE GOT word of a murder at the Suttons' place,
the big one to the west, where Noah lived with more than fifty
people. We heard it first from Nan one morning, who fidgeted
nervously while setting down the midmorning meal. She lingered about, scouring the yard for a sign of the Lucys while she
shakily poured out tins of bitter coffee. She whispered what she
had heard on a midwifing job the day before. "A white man dead.
They say Phillis's husband slit the overseer's throat with a bowie
knife."

Lulu let out a low whistle. Junie shot her a look.

"They catch him?" Patience asked.

"Naw, that's how I know. I was in the middle of a birth when the search party came on through. Y'all be careful. If they don't catch him soon, they'll be through here after while."

We nodded, scarfing down the rest of our food, and rushing off to the fields before there was any sighting of the Lucys.

About a day later, Junie confirmed it. She had been summoned to sit with Carol for a few hours one evening. She had gotten the child clean and fed and was finally getting the baby to sleep in a back corner of the house. With Carol was so quiet, they must have forgotten she was there in that dim, smoky room.

Mr. Lucy trudged in, after riding for hours with the search party. He removed his hat and sat it on the table.

"Y'all get him?" Ollie asked, bouncing around excitedly.

"Yeah, got them both."

"Both?"

"The nigger and his wife," Harlow said, sitting down and pulling off his boots. "The two were in cahoots. Teamed up to kill that poor Mr. Manigault. Poisoned him first, then stabbed him. They both gon' burn."

"Can I go next time? Please?" Ollie asked.

"We'll see," Harlow said, petting the boy's head. Harlow began unbuttoning his shirt and walked down the hallway and into the bedroom.

Junie was frozen and remained that way until Ollie followed his father into the next room.

To our faces, though, the Lucys insisted the whole episode was nothing more than a nasty rumor. Sutton's overseer was fine. He was just fired for incompetence and sent away. The Lucys maintained this lie even as they instituted new rules and practices, locking us up into the cabin nightly and then coming by at daybreak to remove the lock from the door.

By the following Sunday, we could tell just how far things had tightened. There was no longer a procession of abroad husbands returning from weekend visits with their families. We didn't hear word of any frolics or even rumors of the kind. There weren't even any invitations to sanctioned quiltings or candy stews.

We saw Harlow less during the day as Nan told us he was off riding with the patrol most nights. And after delivering a baby on the Davidson farm, the drayman who brought Nan back told her how even the Tejanos working cattle on his farm had been run off the land for fear they might collude with our kind.

The Lucys only conceded that the Manigault incident happened when the white folks in the county decided on a public hanging of the couple and brought all the people they owned to witness it.

We won't recount that horrible day in August. Not here or elsewhere. We won't recount what slipped into the eye despite squeezing them shut. Most of us no longer itched to speak for a while. We held each other aloft and while we might have gathered together at a funeral; that, too, was denied us. The white folks kept the remains and did unspeakable things to them. We weren't allowed to wash their bodies nor consecrate them for the hereafter. Without such rites, we worried they'd be forever lost, unable to rest or return home, stuck wandering about the hell of Texas for all eternity.

WHEN ONE PARTNER GOES to glory, its mate soon follows. Patience remembered an old friend telling her that once. How some birds followed their mates even in death. It bothered her now, that she couldn't remember what kind of bird was being spoken of, or how these creatures even made it happen. If the bird's small heart simply stopped beating some hours later, or if the grieving wretch just willed itself to crash into the earth at the first opportunity. Sure, it wasn't akin to what happened to the husband and wife hanged for the murder of John Manigault, but in the weeks since that awful day, those two things became inextricably linked in her mind.

She didn't know the couple, had maybe crossed paths with the wife at a quilting party once or twice. The pair, Phillis and Aaron, were two people who while alive she had never considered, which made it strange that she thought of them all the time now. Of them dying together that way, before a crowd, at the base of a tree, the branches a cross between them. She had kept her eyes shut most of the time, but still it haunted her. More feeling than image. Not one singular sound, but the cacophony, and the weight of the quiet that followed.

It seemed as close to the crucifixion of Christ that she'd ever get to in this life. A strange and holy sacrifice. But for what, she couldn't figure.

"You said you were going to braid my hair, but you just steady sitting there," Lulu said, interrupting her thoughts.

"I'm waiting on you," said Patience. Around her, the women were rushing about, readying themselves for a frolic that, in her mind, no one should risk going to. She didn't try to dissuade them, though. She understood what they were hungry for and some weren't going to be alright until they got it.

Lulu plopped down on the floor in front of her and handed her a comb. Patience carefully took down Lulu's hair, sectioned it off, and began plaiting. No matter the task these days, Patience's mind drifted back to the couple. She knew others were feeling it, too. The rest of the women seemed itching for noise, chatter, or music, to drown out whatever swirled about the moment one grew still. Some may have just felt the need to verify they were alive and couldn't do so without an open-throated laugh bared to the moon, a lazy two-step with someone nice to look at, or a frenzied ring-shout amidst the trees.

"You sure you don't want to come?" Lulu asked.

"Too tired. Maybe next time."

Soon as the lie was out of her mouth, she regretted it but was too tired to tell the truth. The holiness of what she'd witnessed gnawed at her. She came away from it, resolving to give up alcohol, to give up frolics, to be more exacting in the rites of her faith. She'd follow the narrowest road, to feel some bit of comfort around what continued to rub raw in her mind.

"You scared?" Lulu pressed.

She tried to form the words, but she couldn't figure out a way to say it that would make sense to anyone else. That the kind of joy they were seeking that night she saw no point in anymore. She'd wait until they left to begin the calming staid rituals of the liturgy. She found no joy in that either, but there was something comforting about that.

"No, now be still so I can finish," she said. Once she was done with Lulu's hair, she allowed Serah to borrow a skirt, and was glad to see them all go. A new hollow sound filled the small cabin and she met it gladly.

She began her evening prayers with the Act of Contrition. "I hate my sins because they offend thee . . ." Of course, there were moments in that hollow where she grew sleepy, where her mind wandered. How a sudden memory of Jacob could easily up and derail her focus.

How strange of the two of them to survive separately this way, as if they never made a child, never shared a heart. How strange of her to still be alive, with Silas gone. Perhaps Jacob followed him. She couldn't know for sure. But wasn't it stranger still that she hadn't?

Saint Aaron. Saint Phillis. She couldn't help thinking of the couple that way now. The Catholics had so many saints and she never knew what qualified each one as such. Christoph and Francis and countless others. She didn't need a priest or a pope to verify what she had witnessed. The creation of saints.

CHAPTER FOURTEEN

SEVERAL MONTHS HAD PASSED WHEN talk of a secret memorial for the executed couple spread to all the farms. The night of the event kept changing, now that the weather had cooled and the possibility of high howling wind might offer enough cover.

When the night was finally settled upon, it was very short notice, and yet, we all had it in our minds to go. It was a Tuesday, a day when the patrols were typically a bit laxer and more cursory. And we had few worries about getting off the farm, as we knew how to get out of the locked cabin by then. Not to mention, the Lucys had become so nervous about sprees of "murderous Negroes" that come nightfall, they carefully locked their own cabin after bolting down ours.

Late that evening, we pushed the table under the window hatch and hoisted Serah through it. Once on the other side, she grabbed a stool from the loom and placed it down underneath the opening for those of us not so light on our feet.

The walk was long, through a dark, tangled brush, and the strange map someone had drawn on a piece of cloth was blurry and hard to decipher. We bumbled around for a while, until we saw a lookout, a large man posted at the edge of a wide valley who looked us over for a long moment before waving us in. "Watch your step," he said, pointing to a string of grapevine strung low between several tree trunks. We stepped over it and joined the procession of ashen faces, circling two leg-length mounds of dirt. Whitewashed crosses stuck up out of the earth. Several pots were turned upside down to trap the sound of a fading dirge. Every so often, we heard whistling, pairs of lookouts signaling to each other, confirming no danger was near.

The song rose up again. People seemed to come and go, a throng thinning and thickening. And we were unsure if people were leaving, or just trying to lessen the feeling. By then, we were fastened at the elbow, our arms linked, as if the song might unmoor us. A man was preaching, in a low voice, and we all leaned forward to catch the prayer.

We didn't notice Noah behind us until he slipped closer to Serah. We allowed him entry into our line, where he slid in next to Serah, his arm encircling her waist. Her body leaned into his, and he bent down and kissed her forehead.

We let them be, fixating instead on the preacher's voice, the low wheezy tone of it as he spoke about redemption and the riches awaiting us in heaven. He barely spoke about the couple at all and didn't assuage our worries about the ability of the two souls to get back home.

A sharp whistle cut through the dirge. One short piercing blow, followed by two others.

"Patrollers!" someone shouted. The lookout motioned for us all to run west, hopping over the grapevine and leading everyone away from the galloping horses and drunken men hurtling toward us.

One by one, the patrollers hit the strung grapevine at top speed, the horses and riders thrown to the ground. The men yelped and groaned and cursed.

We laughed and laughed as we ran. Pealing bouts of laughter that slowed us down, but we didn't stop running, as we didn't know how long they'd be down for and how many might come after. In the commotion, the large throng split into smaller groups, scattering into different parts of the forest. We slowed down once we got close to Harlow's property line, and it was only then we realized Serah wasn't trailing behind us.

—⚞

SERAH FOLLOWED NOAH TO a large hulking oak tree with a hollow inside, large enough to hide in. They hurried down into it, crouching along the walls of it, on opposite sides of the opening. They could hardly see, and the longer they sat there waiting, their legs cramping underneath them, the harder it got to tell how long they'd have to remain there. The forest grew louder. The buzzing crickets and whippoorwills, the screeching owls and howling wolves.

The longer they sat, Serah felt as if she was stuck in some strange and timeless void. Unable to see or speak, her feet asleep, tingling and heavy, as if they had grown roots and were now a part of the large tree. Inside her were both queasy cold fear and boiling rage. She could hear him breathing and was surprised that even with all that was happening outside, she had the sudden urge to kick him hard. In the leg or the chest even. *Marry a free woman.* The gall.

"I'm sorry," he whispered after a long while.

"Shhh . . ."

"I didn't mean it."

"Yeah, you did," she whispered back.

An owl screeched nearby. She tried to shift her feet, moving the left one first then the right, but they were both so numb she had to push at her ankles to get them to move. "Where you going to find these free women? Maybe they got free brothers."

They both knew the law didn't work that way. The condition always followed the mother, but the words still stung the way she wanted them to. She heard him suck in a breath, heard him moving now, blocking the small opening where she could see a small crack of the outside world. She saw the jagged crack fill then clear, and for a moment, she didn't know if he was inside or out.

"Noah?"

No answer.

He made a noise as he ducked back inside the tree and sat down near the opening. "It's probably safe now but let's wait a bit longer. You hungry?"

He unwrapped a bundle of cloth.

"What is it?"

"Corn cake."

She ate a few pieces and then folded the cloth back over the rest.

"Been thinking a lot about Mexico," he said. "We could go there."

"Yeah? Where's that?"

"Way south. I met a man from there when we was moving the cattle, and he sketched it out. He said to follow the river as far as you can and then you keep going some days more after that. He said it's a long way, and the farther you go, there's hardly any water at all, but it's possible to cross."

"Why would you take me? I ain't your wife," she said. She knew she was being silly, but the wound inside her was still itching and angry and she just couldn't leave it be.

He groaned. "What is it going to take for you to know that I'm serious? If you need me to get permission, to get Sutton to marry us, I'll do it, but why you need their word on things, I'll never know. Their word ain't worth a bucket of spit, far as I'm concerned."

She knew he was right, and she tried to pin down what it was about the whole thing she wanted. It wasn't the sham ceremony with the cast-off dress and the bored white man raising his Bible in the air. Was it the witnesses she wanted—the cluster of friends and neighbors who would hold them to this public declaration? Or was it the step itself and what it signified?

"I got it," he said. "Bind us together."

"What?"

"Don't play dumb. You probably been working roots on me since we met."

"I have not! Whatever you're feeling and doing is all your own self . . ."

"Then bind us together now, husband and wife."

"I can't do it now. I don't have the right things."

"You sure that's it? See," he said, "it's you who's not serious."

She moved closer to the opening and stuck her head out. "Let me look." She crawled out of the tree and stood up, feeling off-kilter and stiff-legged. She foraged together a makeshift kit. Some damp earth, some long reedy blades of bear grass, a splinter off the tree's bark facing the moonlight, and what little she saw of the molted skin of an insect.

"Come out," she told him. "I need the moon. And some of your hair."

He crawled out and sat down opposite her, where she had

laid out all the things she collected. He pulled a skinning knife out of his pocket and unwrapped it from a piece of cowhide. Slowly, he began cutting off a small chunk of curly hair from behind his right ear. She took the hair, rolled it between her fingers, making one long twist. From her own head, she untucked her plaits, fixed neatly at the base of her skull, and from the end of one braid, she pulled loose a few strands of hair until she got a few pieces that were long enough. Then she approximated a ritual where she braided the bear grass and weaved in hair from both their heads.

She had never done a task like it, had always been cautioned against it, in fact, but conjuring elders who warned of the consequences did so because often they were done without the consent of the other party. They were usually employed by jilted lovers, folks desperately seeking people who didn't want to be sought. That wasn't the case here, but she didn't know of any case like hers. And where normally she'd take that as a sign to stop and ask around, she felt as if the void of the tree had opened something, a space that might no longer be available to her in the days to come.

With more hair from both of them, she made three braids in all, whispering a prayer as she worked, placing the corn cake down as an offering.

"You ready?" she said.

"I am. Are you?" She knew he didn't believe much in Conjure, but like most folks had a healthy nervous respect for it, believing in its possibility to hurt him but not to sway his mind to do things he didn't want to do.

She tied one of the braids around his wrist. "I take you, Noah, to be my husband from this day on until death parts us. So help me God, ancestors, and saints."

The words felt strange in her mouth. The silly grin fell from his face.

"You do?" he said.

"Yeah," she said, with a shy smile.

He leaned over and kissed her.

"Your turn now."

He took the second braid and tied it around her wrist. "I take you, Serah, to be my wife from this day on until death parts us."

They kissed again.

She then dug a small hole in the ground and dropped the last braid in. He helped her fill it back up with dirt.

"That all?"

She shrugged. "I don't know. I never married anybody in the woods before."

They both laughed.

"Come here, then, wife," he said, leading her back inside the hollowed tree, where they willed their bodies to merge until light broke in some hours later.

———

As the sun rose higher, Serah's happiness lasted only until she reached the farm's property line. She considered hiding out in the woods another day to try and blunt the wrath she knew was coming, but she wasn't sure if that would make it worse. She went around to the well first, drank until she was full, then crept to the fields. And though she wanted nothing more than to go to the cabin so she could wash herself and change clothes, she thought she might fare better if she went straight to work. Maybe Mr. Lucy had gotten a late start and hadn't noticed she wasn't out there. He was mercurial in his management of the day's work, sometimes stopping by at particular intervals, and other times, just at the day's beginning or end. Only around harvesttime did he remain out there the entire day.

She made her way to the row, without stopping by the main yard to grab a pickaxe or a hoe. Instead, she began weeding with her fingers one row over, as if she had been out there all morning. A few hours passed that way, the sun growing hotter as her stomach growled. She ambled over to Patience to ask if she had brought any food.

Patience put a finger to her lips. *Quiet.* She ducked her head, peering backward over her shoulder. She then fished out a piece of corn bread wrapped in cloth and gave it to Serah. "Lucy knows," she mumbled, before drifting away.

——

WHEN IT WAS TIME for our lunch break, we approached the yard as if it were quicksand. We grabbed some water from the bucket while we waited for Nan to emerge from the cookhouse with a tray of corn bread or ashcake. The door of the small building was closed, which gave us pause. No one could cook in there with the door closed, the hearth produced too much smoke. We shouldn't have been surprised when the door opened and the Lucys came out. He, with a thick bundle of weeds in one hand and a snake whip in the other, and she, with a tray of food.

One by one, they called us up and made us choose between our hunger or the whip, dividing us in two lines. He called every name but Serah's, leaving her to wait and watch. Junie and Nan chose hunger and stood opposite Patience and Lulu, who both said they'd take the whip.

The Lucys exchanged glances. Of glee, or surprise, we couldn't tell.

Harlow then raised the whip, cracking it high in the air. It's an ugly stupid sound.

He struck both Patience and Lulu each ten times, without

stripping them down to the skin. Afterward, Patience was in so much pain, she couldn't eat, while Lulu pushed through and ate so much she made herself sick.

We weren't surprised that Serah's punishment was a combination of the two. No food, surely, and like Patience and Lulu, ten lashes while clothed.

But we weren't dismissed yet. We were still there when they pulled Serah from her knees and made her stand. Lizzie had to hold her up, while Harlow slid the iron harness over her head, the same one he used years ago. It rang and rang as they secured it in place. "Won't be no more sneaking off now," Lizzie said.

"Now get on, the beans aching to be cut," Harlow added, dispersing us back to the fields.

The harness seemed heavier than before, the bell louder somehow than the last time. Serah complained that it cut through every thought, made her teeth ache. We sent her to work on the opposite end, many rows over, where we hoped wind and distance would dull the sound. When we returned from the fields, we hung around the yard longer than usual, hoping Lucy would appear and remove it, but he didn't.

In the cabin, we took up her sewing and made her sit or lie still so we could all have some peace. Serah had brought in some mud to slather up there, but we warned her not to tamper with it, for fear Harlow would burst in if he didn't hear the clanging sound every now and again.

SERAH, WHO COULDN'T FIND a comfortable way to lie down in the harness, tried to sleep sitting up, the upper part of her back propped against a pillow she wedged in between her and the cabin wall. She'd drift off, then shift in a way that sent the bell clanging, jolting her awake. She had stuffed a rag inside it and loosely fixed it with twine, so she could rip it down if Harlow appeared suddenly. The rag helped to blunt the sound, but even then, she still couldn't sleep. Even with the medicine Nan had given her, the pain in her back and legs kept waking her up.

She stared into the pitch-dark of the cabin, where the only light depended on the brightness of the moon and its ability to leak through the holes in the roof. This night, there was no leakage and she imagined herself back in the warm cozy cocoon of the tree she and Noah hid in. She did her best to keep her mind there, like a pin fixing a hem it mustn't let fall. Any worries about whether he, too, had been punished or when they'd see each other again were best left elsewhere, somewhere far from the hollowed tree and the wooded area that surrounded it.

CHAPTER FIFTEEN

TIRED AND SLOW, NAN MOVED through the woods in search of a welcoming tree. A nippy edge in the morning air pushed her to move a bit faster as she pulled her jacket tighter around her midsection.

She swam through it with her walking stick, ducking spindly branches and tangled roots jutting out of the ground. She had been working almost nonstop for the last two days, guiding the arduous labor of Ada, a panicked house girl on the Davidson farm.

This was her fourth job this year, now that the Lucys realized that hiring her out to catch babies could bring in a handsome profit. Farmers paid the Lucys nearly three dollars per successful birth, and she knew she was way cheaper and right more dependable than the young white male doctors entering the trade by the dozens.

After a long delivery, Nan tended to the mother and baby.

She boiled the soiled sheets and bedclothes, got some soup down into the mother, and the child successfully latched on to the woman's breast. She even smoked the clothing and bedding, so the small room would be clear of ill spirits and energies during the child's most vulnerable hours. Technically, the smoking should be done in two days' time, but she knew it was unlikely she'd be able to make it back over so soon.

And now, she was finally onto the last of her tasks, burying the afterbirth in the woods during the long walk home. She just needed a willing tree.

Hardly any seemed pliant. She spoke to two elms and a cedar and nothing. They didn't seem to want any part of it. She wasn't sure of their reasons exactly. The more tired she was, the harder it was to hear them. A wishy-washy oak seemed persuadable. She squatted down at the base of it and put down the two light sacks she was carrying. One contained her midwife tools—a soiled apron, pieces of cord, strips of cloth, scissors, small pouches of pestled sassafras, jimsonweed, and fever grass—and in the other smaller sack, a tangled ball of rags wrapped around the mother's placenta.

Nan started to burn it hours ago, but Ada howled so and plucked it from the hearth with such speed, it surprised Nan. The woman begged her to bury it proper, out in the Texas soil, in hopes that the child would be protected by whatever gods had dominion over this portion of the earth. Nan tried to dissuade her, but the woman wouldn't listen, clearly frightened that something dangerous was already after the child.

Nan prayed with her, but she could tell Ada wasn't soothed by fervent appeals to Jesus. And the more she sat with the woman, she found she couldn't say no. After all, she was the first to hold the woman's son in her hands, the first to watch him draw breath, to stir him to crying and then soothe that cry, the first to wash the boy's tiny head and face and feel the sharp bird-like bones of his back. How could she spend the last two days preparing and making the way for his birth only to deny him this one last thing?

Plus, Nan didn't believe in ignoring the woman's fear. Even though she was a Christian, she hadn't let go of all the old ways either. She knew there were plenty of neighboring Christians who felt like she was straddling, that the Christian path allowed for no other sources of knowledge or help, but that never made sense to her. Why, there were all kinds of things Jesus was perfectly suited for, but there were others, practical immediate things, where He was less so. It seemed foolish to deny oneself all the help that was possible.

She poked at the dead grass with her walking stick. Underneath, it was hard as a rock. Without her small pick, she'd have to use the scissors. She pulled them out and plunged them into the ground, twisting and opening the blades in the dry, packed soil. It hadn't rained for weeks and the dirt was hard and slow to give. She kept digging with the dull scissors until the hole got larger and deeper, but it was still barely deeper than her index finger. Exhausted, she leaned her back against the tree and let her eyes close for a minute.

The minute multiplied and spun. A bird's urgent cry startled her. Her eyes snapped open, and the black lid of sleep slid away. The sky was darker now, the sun having shifted behind the clouds.

Something rustled behind her. She turned to see a possum eating greedily, a couple feet away. Its white pointy mouth stained with a pink wet substance, its furry black body lying among the tangle of rags and bits of bloody raw matter.

"Get," Nan yelled, backing away. The possum didn't move, only opened its mouth and bared a row of spiky teeth at her. "Get," she yelled again, chucking a few rocks at the animal.

The possum raised up on its hind legs and hissed.

She lobbed her scissors at the creature. Hit, the possum screeched and darted off, leaving the tangled mess behind.

A terrible feeling washed over her. What should she tell the new mother now? Ada would think the child doomed. When she had left her, the woman was already stringing together two sets of names for the boy. A shadow name she'd use to derail the evil already stalking her son and the boy's true name, the name that would only be known by a select few. She warned the new mother not to name the babe so soon. It was bad luck to name a child before the ninth day. Before then, the child was merely visiting, the portal between this world and the one he came from still open. He could just as easily turn back toward it. But Ada ignored the warning, pleading instead for Nan to get the afterbirth buried quickly, before the moon showed its face.

Nan assured her she would and left. What else could she do?

Maybe it was best to never mention the possum to the woman, Nan thought. She retrieved what matter was left and stuck it in the hole, but it wasn't much. A heavy feeling settled in her chest. That was the thing about baby catching. The responsibility didn't end once the baby came out, or once the mother was back on her feet. A baby catcher was always tethered to those she had delivered. She understood this earlier than most, when she was just an apprentice, helping out her own mother as a girl.

Back then, she'd hoped to be a seamstress, not a midwife like her mother or a healer like her grandmother. And it seemed strange that she had ended up so much like them, after all this time, when it had been nearly a lifetime since she'd seen either of them.

As a girl, she declared she'd never be woken up at all hours by those sick with fever and boils, that she would never make her own children sit bedside over ailing patients, fanning away fever 'til morning. She'd never have people showing up at her door, day and night, telling her to drop whatever task she was in the midst of and come here, get in this wagon or walk these many miles because so-and-so's fixing to have her baby soon.

Not that sewing and laundering for white folks was trouble free, but it seemed a heap better than cleaning up the deluge of vomit and excrement that flowed so freely from the sick and ailing. But that was ages ago, back in Maryland, when tobacco was still king, and she thought the rest of her life would be spent at the nexus of the Chesapeake.

She'd see the watermen fishing, the Black men who worked the huge nets for the canneries, catching shad and herring. One even taught her how to read the water, how the colors were a code of sorts. How they could tell its depth and what fish may lie underneath by the hue of the water, be it brown, green, or blue.

She was sure she'd marry a waterman one day and have all the fish she and her mother wanted. And she'd learn how to sail, too, how to steer and navigate the tiny boats down the winding rivers with ease.

But cotton intervened. The big churning maw of industry geared up and sucked her and millions of others farther south, toward the Carolinas and Georgia and Alabama, and farther still. And by the time she reached Texas, still then part of Mexico, in an outpost colony riddled with yellow fever and delusion, she convinced herself that her earlier selfishness in regard to the sick was partly to blame.

The sun was shifting again, hotter now. She covered up the hole and retrieved her belongings, trying to think of some way to mitigate what had gone wrong with the afterbirth. It would plague her, she knew.

The path grew denser with brush and moss and she moved slower, watching her steps. In the yellow grass, the scaly green head of a box turtle stretched toward her. That might do just fine, she thought.

She set her walking stick down on top of the turtle's shell and pulled out her scissors. She reached down and grabbed hold of it, the tiny head and legs retracting inside the shell.

"Not gon' hurt you, fella."

With the blade of the scissors, she scraped three symbols into the shell. Two crosses and a cosmogram, a request for protection for the new babe. She turned to the west, holding the turtle so it faced the direction where the sun would set, and she let it go. It remained still, in its shell. She went on farther and when she looked back, the turtle was gone. With the dirt so hard and the river dry, she wondered if the turtle would get very far, but it seemed her best hope for reaching the boy's ancestors. It would be up to them to do what the tree couldn't.

Once she returned to the cookhouse, she fell asleep in the back room without removing her shoes or repacking her sack. But after a few decent hours of sleep, she found the boy's fate still haunted her. She wasn't sure why. She had delivered many babes that grew up to live horrible, stunted lives, no matter how much spirit work she did. And there was little way of knowing if those efforts might be in vain or if they had actually shepherded a soul through a gauntlet of tribulation. It was the reason she got in the habit of keeping a few souls back, returning them to the other-world, so they could choose again—a different time and place, a different mother in better circumstances. It seemed a way to balance the scales a bit.

But she worried now that maybe she hadn't managed to balance anything at all. Evil was always hungry, and maybe more so now. And that perhaps she had only succeeded in starving it, making it so ravenous and torrential in the lives of a few, instead of sporadic and peripheral in the lives of many. Maybe now, it couldn't spread out, all it could do was devour whole the few souls still coming.

Before the week was over, she'd add more animals to the boy's protective army. Another turtle to carry messages to the boy's dead people, and by Christmas two dead chickens. She didn't kill the chickens herself, but instead gave six sweet potatoes to Mariah, a new root worker located on the other side of the creek, to wring their necks and bury them at opposite ends of the new mother's yard, where they would stand sentinel in the spirit world over both the babe and his mother.

CHAPTER SIXTEEN

Even with the harness removed, Serah was fading. Her skin paled to a strange gray. And by the time we were all standing around in the hot sun, watching her marry, she was nearly invisible. Or maybe it was just the heat making everything waver, that made it seem as if she was disappearing.

If the sun was paying us any mind from up there, we must have looked a gay affair, all crowded together and dressed as if for Sunday service. We were all there and the neighbor folk, too, stiff and carefully arranged.

At the fore of the crowd were the Lucys. Mr. Lucy waving a sweaty Bible in the air, and Mrs. Lucy, off to the side, fanning herself, in a light blue dress. Serah and Patience stood closest to them, both stock-still, their faces damp with sweat, pale swishy fabric hanging from their shoulders. Serah's dress was a dingy yellow, Patience's a faded gray, both refashioned from Mrs. Lizzie's old nightgowns.

Mr. Lucy cracked open the Bible and began reading from a turned-down page. "The Good Book tells us 'Two are better than one, for if they fall, the one will lift up his fellow; but woe to him that is alone when he falleth.'"

Serah stared at something low on the ground, a dark seeping oil stain in the dirt. Her arms were folded across her stomach, her fingers fidgeting with what looked like a soiled piece of twine tied around her wrist.

"'If two lie together, then they have heat. But how can *one* be warm *alone*?'" said Mr. Lucy, closing the Bible with a dramatic flourish.

"Amen," said Lizzie enthusiastically.

It was hard to tell if Serah was listening at all, to the white man officiating the ceremony or the man standing next to her, nodding and murmuring along in agreement.

"We are gathered here today," Mr. Lucy went on, "to join Serah and Monroe, Patience and Isaac in holy matrimony."

THE TWO MEN, MONROE and Isaac, came some months ago, shortly after the New Year. They arrived half-starved and ashen, bought cheap off a planter fleeing the malaria of Houston's river bottoms. The first few days, the two men were dizzy and light-headed, barely mumbling a word, while they readily attacked trays of corn cake and drained buckets of water without measure.

Of the two, one was older and broad-shouldered, with a thick beard. The other was lanky, bare-faced, and full-cheeked, like a giant child. We learned later the older one was called Monroe, the other Isaac.

But we didn't care to learn their names. We only wanted to know what purpose they were brought to serve. Were they breeding niggers like Zeke? Or were they just men, who would pull the plow, fell trees, and load the drays, so we no longer had to?

We avoided them best we could, took to eating our meals earlier, and since Mr. Lucy soon employed them in one building project or another, we got our way for a while. They slept in the barn and we retained the cabin and, for once, didn't mind being locked up together inside it.

They built a storehouse and an additional room onto the Lucys' house, and the couple took this as a sure sign that their luck was turning around. A stretch of good weather followed, leading to a good early showing, where we produced the most bales we ever had in a single harvest. Twenty-four bales, almost double what we made most years.

After that, the two men were set against each other in a grand race to build two cabins identical to ours. One on either side of the one where we lived. And it was then that we had to consider them. Look at them, hear them, smell them. They thought us rude and haughty, spoke about us in a dialect we couldn't decipher, and we debated among ourselves whether it was better to be recipients of their love or their hate.

We paid little attention to the race itself, or the chest thumping it brought out between the two. How they enjoyed riling themselves up and putting on a show, and though we were sure this was for our amusement, we didn't give them the satisfaction of laughing. Softening toward them seemed dangerous, and we still hadn't figured out all the contours of this particular danger.

We pretended not to notice their different approaches to the competition. While Monroe concerned himself with speed and the progress of his competitor, pushing himself to get a shoddy shell of the structure up in a day, Isaac moved at his own pace, only seeming to care about the soundness of the logs he chose, the rightness of the pegs, the alignment of his corners. So it was little surprise that Monroe finished first.

The night he finished, Mr. Lucy showed up at our dinner full of praise, the two men following behind him. He broke out a barrel of cider and gave everyone a round, and with a toothy grin, revealed what the reward was.

"I told you I had women, didn't I? Now, Monroe, for your reward, you get first pick for a wife."

Monroe gave a sheepish look at first, then pointed at Serah.

Mr. Lucy clapped him on the back and laughed, the kind of low chest laugh often shared between men. "Good choice. And I expect many portly children, you hear?"

Monroe nodded at him, then at Serah. She turned her face away, shutting her eyes tight.

"Isaac, your turn?" Harlow said.

Isaac shook his head. "Got a wife I like back home, sir. Don't have need for another."

Mr. Lucy laughed and clapped Monroe on the back again. "Tell him he can choose, or I'll choose for him," he said, his voice light and without edge. He turned to Isaac. "Or would some hickory oil make all this go down easier?"

Hickory oil. Another euphemism for a whipping of some kind.

Isaac took a long look at him and at us, while we each prayed to be unseen, invisible, ugly.

And when Isaac didn't answer, Mr. Lucy clapped him on the back, too. He handed him another cup of cider. "Don't ruin a good time, I say." Harlow squinted at us, closing his left eye. We all looked elsewhere, avoiding the roving eye and where it might settle once it landed. "Patience. Yep, she's the one, alright," he said finally. "Now that that's all settled. Monroe, you and your wife will live in the cabin you built. And Isaac, you and Patience will live in the one you built. Isn't that a treat?"

We had all stopped eating by now, the food sour in our mouths. Patience's eyes darkened, a sudden redness around the rim, her fists balled up at her sides. Serah, on the other hand, was surprisingly calm, as if she had heard nothing. The only thing that gave her away was a slight twitching in her face she kept trying to hide with her hand.

—⚞—

THE NEXT DAY, SERAH and Monroe moved into one cabin, Patience and Isaac in the other. That first night, when the sun descended and dark filled the sky and the door of the cabin closed shut, Serah felt as if she had been locked in a small airless tomb. Monroe was there, fiddling with a stubby candle that wouldn't stay lit.

"Why mice love to eat these things, I'll never know." He chuckled. "You not afraid of the dark, is you?"

Serah felt the panic inside her grow louder. All day it had been a low-grade hum, but now it was an incessant clanging, like the bell of the harness.

"Try a pine knot," she said, her voice shaky.

He shook his head. "It's getting late and I rest better in the dark." She could only see the shape of him now, on the opposite side of the room. She was sitting at a small table he had made, carding, even though she couldn't see much. She laid the thick tuft of flax over the metal teeth and pulled and pulled, until the crackly sound of it grew louder.

She heard him lie down on the bed strung up on the left side of the cabin, the cable holding the mattress creaking in response.

For a moment, she felt her own tired body, her aching back and clenched shoulders, and wanted nothing more than to lie down, too. But there was only one bed in the room. A singular bed they were expected to share.

She pushed her work aside and laid her head down on the rickety table and closed her eyes. Within minutes, his loud snoring filled the room. Serah awoke with a jolt and stood up. Carefully, she pulled the front door open and slipped outside. She scoured the area for the Lucys or any trap they might have set. Earlier, Harlow had made a big production out of not having enough supplies to lock down all three cabins, as he had already had the men's leg irons made into other tools. And she worried his whole performance was a ruse to see if she would try and sneak off the farm to see Noah.

She hadn't seen him since the night of the funeral. She had heard from the neighboring folk that he had been laid low with the cat-o'-nine-tails for some weeks, and afterward was sent up to Sutton's ranch to work the cows, but where that was, she didn't know.

She crept outside and pushed open the door into the middle cabin, where only Junie and Lulu lived now. Junie stirred and raised her head. When she saw it was Serah, she shifted over on the edge of her pallet. "Don't let them find you here in the morning."

Serah closed the door and lay down next to Junie. She pulled the covers up to her chin, even though it wasn't particularly cold. She stared at the sky, through the holes in the roof. A distant star winked at her. She gazed back at it but could no longer find joy in it or the lazy stars around it. Instead, the star was a speck of some kind, a strange indifferent witness to Noah and their union, and it seemed cruel somehow to be left with a witness so useless as this one.

IN THE WEEKS THAT followed, Serah never got a full night's sleep. She moved from the fields to the loom to the new cabin in a daze, her hands a moving blur, a glazed fatigue in her eyes. At dusk, she made food for both her and Monroe, grinding enough corn for their dinner, before making ashcakes or corn pone along with a strip of herring.

Whereas the women had always taken a communal approach to dinner, rotating who cooked each night so the rest of the group could get started on that evening's sewing, the presence of the men in the quarters quickly terminated this agreement. When the men first arrived, they stayed in the barn, only steps away from the cookhouse, so Nan was responsible for feeding them. Now that they were in the quarters, that duty fell to the women. And as Lulu and Junie immediately refused to cook for someone else's "rusty husband," the task soon fell to the "wives" alone.

Serah made Monroe a plate and sat down to eat quickly before picking up her sewing for the night. He talked a river while they ate, no matter what happened that day. And she'd nod and make the expected affirmative sounds as required, all the while waiting for him to pass out on the bed and leave her be. Most of the time, his chatter was filled with the same talk. He'd tell her stories about home, about Virginia and tobacco, about working rice in Georgia, about his first wife and firstborn. These stories would run into one another, the links between them porous as rain. She only half listened, unsure if he was talking to her or himself. And only later did she realize that there were things he wanted her to know. He didn't have the women to trade with the way she did, to give things to hold when they got too heavy. But the truth was, she didn't want his things, not his memories or the rough-hewn objects he had begun making her. And she was too young to know that was the worst kind of rejection there was.

Her aim was to keep only the hands visible, as if the constant cooking, washing, darning, and sweeping would keep the man from climbing on top of her one night. She tried, though. She made herself a pallet to sleep on the floor in one corner of the room, where her few belongings lay—some changes of clothes, a lock of hair from her mother, a small cluster of blue beads. Among these belongings, she hid a small treasure of pointed rocks, even carrying one in her apron pocket as she moved about the day. She fed her saints daily and drew lines of protection around the pallet, powdery lines of salt and grave dirt that kept Monroe constantly complaining about the floors and her inability to keep them clean. Sometimes, she'd return from grinding corn and see him sweeping the lines away, fussing all the while. "Where this white stuff coming from? Am I dying? You dying?"

She just shrugged and waited until he fell asleep, before putting down a fresh line, fainter than the one the day before. In the morning, she'd wake up before him, not long before the cow horn blew, and if he stirred during the night, she awoke then, also. This is the bargain she made with the exhausted parts of herself now always threatening mutiny, always threatening unconsciousness at the slightest stillness. The only bit of relief seemed to be in the effect that lack of sleep had on her mind. It razed time somehow, made it so only the smallest square of the present seemed accessible to her. Everything else—be it missing Noah or the other women—felt as if it was lost, somewhere trapped behind a heavy impermeable curtain.

─⤝

AFTER A WHILE, SERAH could no longer live on such little sleep. Her fitful naps transformed into heavy dense slumbers she found hard to wake from.

It was then, one Wednesday night, when Monroe crept

beside her, positioning himself on the edge of her pallet. He pressed himself against her and she wasn't sure how long he had been there, when she woke up in alarm, thrashing and slapping. Her hand hit his back with a loud crack that echoed throughout the room.

"Stop it," he said, grabbing her arms.

But she continued to flail, now thinking of her pointed rocks, trying to grab ahold of one.

"Quit it and I'll let you go."

She paused her thrashing. And he shifted over a bit, releasing one arm while still holding the other lightly. But he was still too close to her, his breath on her neck, his bare thigh touching hers.

"I've been patient, haven't I? Even let you work your little roots until you got comfortable. But my High John the Conqueror ain't never failed me," he said, chuckling softly. It had occurred to her that he might be working roots of his own against her, but when she last swept out the cabin, taking extra care to poke around his few belongings, she hadn't come across anything that appeared to be a charm or a mojo bag.

She kept still as she could, still searching for a pointed rock with her free hand, but there wasn't anything there, just dirt and dust.

"I found your little rocks, if that's what you looking for," he said slowly.

She took in a sharp breath. The room was dark, and she still wasn't used to it, still felt disoriented in the new cabin, the way the chimney was on the opposite wall, the sparse furniture, taller and arranged at odd angles. She wondered how fast she could get to the poker leaning near the firebox. There were sticks there, too. Kindling and such.

"I'm a good man, can be a good husband to you, if you let

me. I can be real sweet to you. Now, we been getting along real good and I say it's about time we start acting like husband and wife." He kept his hand on her arm, his thumb now grazing the frayed bracelet on her wrist.

Serah snatched her arm away and in one deft motion, slid aside, placing her back against the wall and drawing her knees up to her chest. "But we not married. Lucy just put us together like he does the cows," she said. Her mind spun back to the conversation the women had been having the first few days after the two men arrived, if it was better to inspire their hate or their love. In the close walls of the dark room, she instantly knew the latter was her best chance.

"You know a gal needs some things," she continued, "before she can take a man on as her husband. You can't just mount her like a horse and expect her to care for you. You ain't never court me proper or do none of the things I was told a good man does before you can call him your husband. And just 'cause you say you're a good man don't make it true. I need to see for myself. Give me some time to know for myself."

He didn't say anything for a long while. She worried then that he could see the futility of her plea, that there wasn't anything he could ever do that would turn her heart toward him or make her regard his presence with anything more favorable than benign indifference. She would never choose him because she never had a choice in the matter. And the choice was the thing.

"Alright, missy, I'll give you that. Long as you stop with the roots and things. We gots to meet in the middle, don't we?" he said, with another low chuckle.

"We do, yes," she said, though she had no intention of stopping any of her efforts. Already, she was trying to figure out what she could use that might overpower his High John, while she

waited for him to get up and move back to the bed on the opposite side of the room.

But he didn't move. He just lay there, his limbs now spread
out over the pallet, a loud snore erupting from his throat.

—⚘—

NAN HAD LONG SUSPECTED Monroe's tolerance with Serah
would soon wear thin, so she wasn't surprised when Serah came
to the cookhouse, asking about poisonous herbs. At the time,
Nan had her hands full with Carol, so she told Serah she would
think on it but hadn't given the request another thought until
she saw Monroe slinking around the Lucys' house a week or
so later.

She had just stepped outside with a sack of the Lucys' dirty
laundry, when she saw him and Lizzie talking a few feet from
the house.

Monroe stopped talking when he saw her, but Lizzie, her
back to Nan, waved him on, shifting Carol from one hip to the
other.

"Spit it out. What exactly is the problem?"

"She's still . . . cold. Mean. Never kind to me. No matter
what I do for her," he said, lowering his voice.

"Mmhmm," Lizzie said. "And?"

"Ma'am, I'm not a savage. I'm not the sort to thrash a woman
for it. I've been nice. Understanding."

"You want me to whip her?"

"No, that'll just make it worse. She'll probably stop speaking
to me then."

"What do you care whether she's hot or cold at all? Long
as she does as she's told." Carol started to cry and Lizzie turned
back toward the house. Seeing Nan, she pushed the baby toward

her. Nan dropped the sack and came forward, taking the child in her arms.

"Ma'am?" Monroe said, not having moved from his spot.

Lizzie turned and glared at him.

"She say," Monroe began tentatively, "we not real husband and wife, maybe 'cause we never got married proper, you know, like with a Bible and a meeting of some kind."

"Does she now?" Lizzie said.

Nan pinched Carol's leg, causing the child to cry louder.

"Alright, I'll see to it," Lizzie said, waving him away. She turned back to Carol. "What now, little girl?"

Later, Nan worried she caused the conversation to end too early, but she wanted to distract Lizzie before she committed to any real action. Carol kept the woman's mind full, easily diverted from one moment to the next. It seemed likely that if Carol's wailing kept up for the next several hours, the whole conversation might easily slip from Lizzie's mind.

CHAPTER SEVENTEEN

"To honor and obey, until death or distance do you part," Mr. Lucy said loudly, slapping the Bible for emphasis. There was an uproar of clapping and cheering. Mrs. Lucy laughed and twirled. The crowd surrounding the couples stirred to life and rushed forward to greet them.

Only the couples themselves seemed out of time. Isaac whispered something to Patience, and she released her grip on the sides of her dress. Unlike Monroe and Serah, the two were of the same mind about the whole thing. They both had spouses elsewhere and were content to live as siblings under the same roof for now. They'd have to deal with the Lucys and their expectations at some point, but until that time came, they'd manage.

Monroe took a hard look at Serah, searching her face to see if this whole affair had changed anything inside her. Would she hug him? Touch his arm? Or even meet his gaze with a warm smile? He waited a long moment for some signal from her, before reaching out to draw her near. But within seconds, she was already gone, moving through the throng of people to a tall young man standing in the back. The man wore a low hat and an ill-fitting jacket, but he could see the man's eyes were fixated on Serah, and when she reached him, she collapsed against him and buried her face in his chest. The man wrapped his arms around her, whispered something in her ear, and only loosened his grip when he looked up and saw Monroe's eyes narrowing in on him. The two men exchanged looks, a whole conversation of some kind, each accusing the other of being the true interloper.

Monroe started toward them, unsure of what he'd say when he got there. So, this was the reason, was it? All this time, her rejection felt impersonal, more like a skittish deer trying to settle its nerves, but now, seeing the young man, it felt different, more pointed, more offensive. Though in some ways the act of winning her over wasn't personal to him either. He wasn't even sure he liked her. She wasn't kind like his first wife, or a good cook like his second. When she washed his clothes, she left yellow clay streaks that dried and caked in the sun. Not to mention that smelly herb she insisted on wearing, saying it helped with her sinuses, but he had never heard her complain of sinus trouble, never seen her with so much as a runny nose. If he wanted her at all, it was only because she was there. Because he liked the softness of women, how they made the most horrible things feel better. How even when they cussed you, it sounded sweet. And it didn't seem like too much to ask in this godforsaken place to look at one person and have them look back at him with something like kindness in their eyes, even if it was temporary.

That she had already had someone made sense, and seemed like something that shouldn't rub him wrong, but it did. Maybe because she never said as much, or he had never noticed it on her.

Or maybe just seeing them together in that way reminded him of home and what he'd lost. Hating whatever separated him from his family made him feel stupid and impotent at the size of it all, but hating them, this young man in a stupid hat, he was easy to hate. As was she. Easy to make the reason for all that was going wrong now.

Harlow stepped in Monroe's path, put a hand on his shoulder, and grinned a mischievous grin. "This was a mighty expensive affair, but I don't mind 'cause I know you're good for it."

Monroe nodded.

"Let's drink to all the children you'll have," Harlow said, leading Monroe to a spread of food and drink that rivaled any Christmas feast he had ever known. Harlow poured him a shot of whiskey and signaled for the fiddle player to start up. "To a blessed and fruitful union!" he said to Monroe, clinking his cup. "Now, where's Isaac?" Harlow looked around at all the people, milling about, eating and drinking. "Why the Mrs. had to invite all these swill-bellies I'll never know!" Harlow then looked at him and laughed. "Drink up," he said. "I know you'll do me proud, won't you?"

Monroe drained the cup, the liquid burning a line of fire down his throat and into his stomach.

"Whooo. That's good, ain't it, boy? You want more?"

Monroe nodded, his eyes roving the throng for another glimpse of the two lovers. Without seeing them, he imagined them clearly, in the throes of another embrace, rubbing against each other as lovers are wont to do, and laughing at him, at his cast-off faded jacket a size too small, his tattered trousers, his gifts of whittled spoons and furniture, and he had a sudden urge to pummel them both.

PEOPLE ATE, WHILE SERAH and Noah lingered about in opposite directions. She stood at the end of a long table, nibbling a bit
of sweet potato, while he hung around the fiddler. And it wasn't
long before they both vanished from the party, meeting at the
creek the way they had all those times before.

A strange and heady feeling washed over her, being in his
arms now. He was talking fast, a stream of chatter to dislodge
the disorientation of being so close to one another after so many
months apart.

"We tried it your way, but we got to do something else now,"
he said.

"But the patrols are worse than when Manigault got knocked
over."

"It's the only way."

A firefly swam past Serah, moving toward the flat gray water.

"What about Sutton? He's got money to burn."

"No, Mexico is the only way."

Something about the finality of his words made them both
quiet for a long while. Serah stared at the lowering sun.

"I should talk to him. Today," said Noah, speaking about
Monroe. "You know, make it clear."

"Don't do that. You start peacocking and it'll be worse."

"Worse how?"

"Just worse."

"Fine, Bird. What then?"

She tightened her arms around him. "Still got that knife?"
It flashed across her mind. The curved skinning blade he carried
with him that last night in the woods.

Noah's eyes widened. "Not on me. But I can get it. You think
it'll come to that?"

She wasn't sure. If Monroe had a truly ugly side, he hadn't
shown it to her yet. What did Nan tell her he said to Lizzie

that day? That he wasn't a savage sort. But could she trust that? Should she trust that?

She could see now the worry in Noah's face. She shook her head. Maybe she was assuming the worst. "No. I can reason with him."

Noah didn't look convinced, but she didn't bother trying to convince him further.

She kissed his face. "C'mon. We should head back. I'm sure someone's looking for us by now."

Noah groaned. They rose to their feet and headed back to the farm, only letting go of each other once they reached the flat area of the yard, where the party was still in full swing.

"CAN I HAVE SOME?" Lulu asked Monroe, pointing at the cup of liquid in his hands. He gave her a curious look and handed it to her. She sat down next to him and brought the tin to her lips. She took a long sip but didn't relinquish the cup. She felt him looking at her but pretended she wasn't aware, instead looking at the crowd of people eating and drinking. Someone she couldn't see was playing a fiddle and people were dancing to it. A couple of women had moved into the center and were now doing the buzzard lope. She had never learned how.

"You not going to give it back?" he said.

"No," she said, flashing a wide grin at him. "It's mine now."

A look of confusion fell over his face. He opened his mouth to speak and immediately closed it. She wasn't sure what spurred her on—his confusion, the strong heady liquor traveling down her chest, or the sway of the two women dancing. "So, why you pick her, anyway?" Lulu said, turning to him.

"Huh?"

"Serah? I say what made you pick her?" she said, smiling up at him again.

"I don't know . . ." he said, the tension in his arms growing slack. "What do you care?"

"I don't. Was just curious is all . . ."

"You don't have other things to be curious about?"

"Oh, tons," she said, giving him a lingering glance.

He was softening now; she could feel it. "She's young. Figured she'd be easy to deal with. That's all."

Lulu laughed. "Oh, you figured she'd mind you? Do whatever you say?"

He gave her a sheepish grin.

"Well, it's not too late to change," she said, resting a hand on his arm.

"It's not?" he asked.

"What Lucy care for? Where the babies come from don't make him no never mind. Long as they coming."

"I suppose it don't," he said, staring at her curiously. "And you'd like that? Me telling Harlow that I want you instead?"

She stared at him for a long moment, not saying anything. His words came easy, just as she thought they might, but when they washed her over, she felt nothing. Sure, there was a slight rush of triumph, but not the warm feeling she'd hoped for. She closed her eyes for a second, searching around, but no, it wasn't there. All she could feel was his anxious sticky gloom.

"Lulu, that what you want?" he said.

She shook her head, drained the cup, and handed it back to him. "No. I was just saying."

His face changed, his mouth now open in surprise.

"Oh, look, there's the lovely bride now. I should go give her my well-wishes," Lulu said, nodding her head in the direction of the property line, where two figures were standing. From here, it was hard to see them clearly, but that yellow flimsy dress was a dead giveaway. It puffed up with air like a balloon. Serah was wrestling with it, walking toward the party, with Noah trailing behind her.

Lulu turned to see Monroe's face change again, from surprise to anger. She stood up and moved away from him, slipping back among the revelers, and was there in the middle by a table of dessert, in time to offer Serah a slice of gooseberry pie. The girl took the plate and Lulu looked back to see Monroe watching the two of them, a red pall over him.

The sight of him alone and angry confirmed why the warmth wasn't there. It's strange she didn't recognize it before. How alone he was. No one wanted him, not Serah, not any of the women, or neighbors even. Maybe the former wives he sometimes spoke about, but it's likely they were just more pliable than Serah. Women stuck with him who were better at hiding their disdain. Any interest in him, ignited by that initial pang of jealousy she felt when he first chose Serah, was completely gone. She had cured it.

⟶⟵

THE HORRIBLE EVENT OVER, Serah hovered at the edge of the yard. She had already helped the others clear and wash all the dishes. Things Nan said could wait until tomorrow, she took up also. She swept the debris in the yard, in slow, weightless strokes, as she sensed a storm brewing in Monroe's small cabin.

She thought about the land, what was on the other sides of the surrounding farms. How far could she walk, in one direction or another? Could she outrun the dogs? The gangs of white men with guns? Should she trade the certainty of one angry man for the possibility of half a dozen?

She looked for something else to do, something to delay the moment when she'd step into the mouth of the cabin, where she knew he was likely waiting. There hadn't been more than two words between them since the ceremony, but she knew he was angry. She had kept her distance from him most of the day, and yet he seemed always about, a fixed eye glaring at her. It was frustrating. She, who had become very good at going unnoticed, at being softly invisible, could no longer be so. Maybe it was the stupid dress, the flouncy flimsy nature of it, the way it caught light and swam in the wind. Or just that her desire to be invisible was so strong it gave off a smell. The kind that couldn't help catching people's attention, the kind so naked and raw it drew some near or turned others away in disgust.

And since she had little idea what was waiting for her inside those four walls, it seemed the best option was not to return to them. She wished she was more prepared, that she had put together a trick bag by now, with some illness in it to lay him low, some legion of tiny reptiles to take up residence in his leg. That, or some way to pry the High John from his grip, but she still hadn't learned where he kept it.

The moon was hidden by the clouds, which made it even darker. A pocket so black she could barely see her hand, now that they had extinguished the torches and lanterns placed around the yard. One by one, they went out, like a sequence of notes, a low bass falling to the bottom. She thought about Noah, how he felt like a dream evaporating. How long could she lace hope around it? How long could she let the hope of it make her reckless in thought and deed?

She picked up a stick and carried it low, scraping a trail in the dirt. A circle, a pointed arrow, a series of linked curlicues. She was pointing souls now. A whole army of them to nest inside the four walls. And she hoped by the time she got there, a war would be happening between her saints and his. She crossed herself and spun, left then right, as if she was trying to reach some hinge in the air, unlatching some hidden thing where all the otherworldly help could pour out of.

She was so tired. Of the day itself and all that happened and what awaited her next. Tired of the whole mess of it, this strange life that seemed stuck in one place, on one note, like a fiddle with only one string. She was tired of the man's dumb anger, how solid it was, like a large deep rock, and how he kept shoving that rock toward her, as if it was hers to climb.

She pushed open the door of the cabin, one piece of dark opening into another. He wasn't snoring like usual, the only sound the scratching of mice in the corners. She waited for teeth to seize her throat, like a panther or a bear swooping in with lightning speed. And when a wooden post slammed into the back of her head, sending a throbbing blackness over her entire body, she felt a surge of relief, as she waited to see God's face and hear Gabriel's horn.

HE TOOK HER ON the floor, then, with blood in her eye. He took it less because it was the wedding prize he felt owed him, but more because the presence of the other man dared him to do so. He wanted her to know what happened when he wasn't kind or patient. And more so, what happened when one didn't respect the grace they were being offered, when one spat on it plainly, turned their back on it clean. Now that he had literally "put the fear of God in her," he would have no need to be ugly again unless she made him, he told her. It was up to her, he said. She could live in heaven, or she could live in hell. It was her choice.

———

WE BEGGED SERAH THEN to come and stay with us. Lock-ins were few now, but that night had changed her. Noah kept sending her messages, and each time she refused them, telling his little boy messengers not to come back. They kept on coming, one with a handwritten letter she had to get Junie to read to her. "Bird, if you don't love me no more, tell me and I won't bother you again."

From then on, Serah and Monroe's cabin became a battlefield. Each trying to best the other, wound the other, conjure the other. She left mojo bags under the steps, laced his food with sedatives. He'd wake up half-blind and zombified. She set aflame his High John the Conqueror and any other protective work she didn't recognize. Afraid to even touch it, she swept it all into the fire, along with his clothes and shoes. She started working on his senses then. Hearing, taste, and sight. His tongue numb, his foot lame. Each changing with the weather, rotating with the sun.

We dragged her out some nights, but she'd go back, shutting the door on us. And as darkness settled over the yard, a bell went off inside them both. Some nights neither would start up, they'd stay in their protective corners watching each other. Other days, it was bound up in the air and there'd be no stopping it. He'd throw a plate at her, and she'd charge him with a poker, stabbing him in the arm with its sharp end. We didn't know she was that spry, that wily, and it seemed a surprise to herself, that she could wound and hurt this mountain of a man. And then there was no ending it until she drew blood. She was collecting it then— his skin, his blood, his hair, his semen. And she kept pushing to get it. Her pain tolerance growing higher, dulled by sharp blows of her own. This fighting of theirs grew into something we couldn't understand. The way they scratched, slapped, and kicked each other. Sometimes, wrestling on the floor until they both were bruised and sore. How somehow it seemed some dark and twisted catharsis, this bloodletting of rage they unleashed on one other. And how sometimes at the end of it, tired and smarting, she'd mount him, the weight of her hand heavy across his nose or throat, until he was gasping for air. If any sex happened between them, she controlled it, brought order to it, refused to be surprised by it ever again. And slowly he grew thinner and more sickly. So sick, he lay up in their cabin, wheezing like a man twice his age. It was then that he begged her for forgiveness. That if she healed him, he'd do right, he'd do whatever she wanted. And we're not sure we ever saw her happier than she was then, when she had Monroe's whole life in her slim brown hand.

⚊⚊↙

SERAH KEPT NOAH'S LETTER under her clothes at all times, tied around her torso with a piece of thread. Sometimes, it scratched and crackled as she moved about. When she was alone, she'd take it out and trace the funny slanted characters with her index finger. She had memorized it by now, had made Junie read it so many times the paper was soft and stained with grease. And though she worried it might slip out one day, that someone might find it, she couldn't bring herself to get rid of it.

The truth was she couldn't say whether she still loved him. The parts of her that loved him, that lay with him beneath moon and sky, were somewhere else now, inaccessible and unknowable. What she remembered felt like something on the underside of the sea. A glimmering country somewhere far off, much like that Freedom-place neighboring kin whispered about, some place unmapped and ephemeral, its coordinates unknown.

What she had now, in place of her love, was rage. It woke her up in the morning and kept the hoe alive in her hand. Part of her wanted to kill Monroe and the other part wanted him to live a long wretched life, one where she could wreak all kinds of hurt and havoc as long as she wanted.

——⤶

MONROE'S ILLNESS BROUGHT A reprieve. Sickness made him quiet, made him fearful, and thus calm. The Lucys couldn't diagnose what felled him, and fearing contagion, they sent Serah back to the cabin of women. She nodded dutifully, covering a grin with her hand.

Among us, she said little. She was mercurial, at turns joyful and distraught, but still primarily silent. When we asked her what trick she had used to lay down Monroe, what pestilence she had loosened inside his body, she only shook her head and gave a sly close-mouthed smile. Nan dosed the man with calomel and castor oil but didn't press Serah to tell her anything more.

If there was a frolic or a candy stew, she declined going, but wouldn't share with us what she'd rather do instead. And we'd return to find her gone, only to hear her slipping inside the cabin hours later, filthy and wet.

And so we shouldn't have been surprised to discover that she had taken up with Noah again. Though, gone was the girlish giddiness of before—the flowery talk and the silly sweet grin so hard to contain we'd tease her by holding her chin. Maybe she was reassembling herself somehow. Putting herself back in a moment before Monroe and Isaac ever came.

CHAPTER EIGHTEEN

"Tell me about Silas," Isaac asked Patience one night, some weeks later. She found herself stunned by the question. It's not that she and Isaac didn't speak; they did. Quite easily at times about their children, "former" spouses, and such. But most days they were too tired to talk and they both liked silence, didn't feel the need to fill it, the way their neighbors did. Compared to Monroe and Serah, their cohabitation had been largely uneventful. Isaac was a considerate and kind housemate, whose calm temperament often matched hers. Most evenings after they ate, he often helped her with her carding or sewing, and before sleeping, they both spent a good deal of time praying. Separately, of course, as their traditions were different, but he never mocked her the way the others sometimes did. Thinking she was haughty now or putting on airs for not wanting to go out into the woods with them like she used to. He let her be.

And when he was tending to his own spirit ways, he sometimes allowed her to watch. It reminded her of her father. The bowls of water, the symbols and figures he drew in the dirt floor of the cabin.

When she made the mistake of mentioning it to the lone other Louisiana Catholic among the neighboring folk, the woman told her she should report his bedevilment to the Lucys. That if she wasn't going to work to convert him, she should do everything in her power to get out of that house. Patience nodded to get the woman to shut up, but she knew she had no interest in either of those things. She would never report him to the Lucys, and she wasn't sure she wanted to go back to the cabin with Junie and Lulu.

It startled her now, this question of his. So much so, her fingers faltered, and she had to yank out the last two stitches that she had sewn and do them over again. "Why you want to hear about him?"

"'Cause I want you to see something," he said. He sat on the floor, weaving the base of a basket, plaiting thick strands of fever grass.

Patience tried to speak, but she couldn't. The lump in her chest moved up into her throat. She sucked in air and blew it back out. "I can't."

"Close your eyes and try."

Patience put down her sewing and shut her eyes. She sat there a moment, just trying to breathe. In and out, in and out, then a deeper breath, in and out. The dark expanded, the room growing wide around her. She could feel a breeze now, hot rays of sun heating up her skin. A warm concentrated weight in the middle of her back. The boy's breath on her neck, babbling just beneath her ear. She was in that old Louisiana widow's yard, hanging wet clothes on the line. Silas hitched to her spine by a piece of cloth tied around her chest.

In an instant, he was older, now in the Lucys' yard. She was hanging clothes again and she let him put his feet atop hers, and cling to her legs as she moved down the line. He'd laugh and hang on, then fall off, begging to do it again. "C'mon, Ma, again."

"Just one more time and then you got to help. Alright?" she heard herself say.

"Yes, Ma."

He climbed on again, and she could feel him there, his small hands clutching her legs, his head thrown back and laughing. A glorious song.

"You act like he's gone gone. He still here," Isaac said, his voice breaking through the reverie. "Our dead don't leave us."

When she finally opened her eyes a good while later, the room was dark and still. She stood up slowly. "Isaac," she whispered.

"I'm here," he said. He relit the fire in the hearth. "You alright?"

"Believe so."

"Good. Go to sleep. If you have questions, they can wait 'til sunup."

She did have questions, but she was too tired to argue. She felt barely awake, barely alive even, as if she were conducting this conversation from somewhere else entirely. She lay down on her pallet and pulled her covers over her head, her mind already drifting. Her limbs felt heavy, but everything else inside her was so light, it seemed likely to float away.

Isaac tried to explain it to her the next day, but most of it was lost in translation. He knew of no equivalent in English, so he told her in Fula. She didn't understand the words, but some sense of it became clear.

"A door was opened" was all she really understood, but she

wasn't sure how or why. When Sunday rolled around, she set out to make a treat for Silas. She traded a neighboring woman a gill of oats and a thin slice of bacon for two thimblefuls of freshly tapped maple syrup and a small tin of flour.

Back at the cabin, she got a fire going in the hearth, then proceeded to make real biscuits. She combined the flour, salt, and water into a stiff mixture. There was only enough batter for about four biscuits, but that would be fine, she figured, as she set them all in the hearth to bake.

Once done, she set out two bowls and put a hot biscuit in each one. The other two, she wrapped up in a cloth and set them aside for Isaac. A pang of guilt stabbed her in the side as Jacob's face flashed quickly across her mind. No. The act of setting food aside was as sisterly as it was wifely. Nothing more.

She shook off the bad feeling and returned to the two bowls, steam rising from the flaky brown bread. She cut both biscuits open and drizzled each with syrup.

Placing one bowl at the end of the table, she sat down at the opposite end, placing the second bowl in front of her. "If only I got some butter, huh, Silas?" she said. "But I know you won't be able to resist either way." She laughed and closed her eyes until she could feel him there, faint but warm.

"We thank the Good Lord for this food. And this company."

She picked up her biscuit and bit into it. A delightful sweetness flooded her mouth, her chest. She savored each bite, chewing slowly. She sat there, longer still, 'til the warmth of Silas's presence faded.

She rose slowly. She cleaned her dishes and utensils, while leaving Silas's plate undisturbed a little while longer. She'd have to ask Isaac to teach her more about his spirit ways. This small bit he had shared with her had already loosened something inside her.

How full she felt now. So different from when she performed those rites and rituals she'd brought from Louisiana. How pressed down they had always made her feel. Emptied. Hollowed out. That was fine before, but she wanted something else now. Something fuller and sweeter.

CHAPTER NINETEEN

WHEN SERAH SNUCK OUT TO see Noah late one night, she didn't know it would be the last time. She walked the path slowly through the cool air. She couldn't remember ever traveling the path at such a snail's pace. She was always excited before, always in a hurry, but the last few weeks, she could barely muster anything more than mild interest.

Initially, she just thought it was dread, a perpetual worry that whatever she unleashed on Monroe would soon come spiraling back toward her. Even with him gone, that feeling hadn't subsided. He had been away for weeks now, as Harlow had rented out both Isaac and Monroe for the harvest as soon as the ailing man could stand. It should have alleviated her anxiety to know he was miles away, but that only amplified it.

At the bank of the creek, Noah was there already, sitting in the grass, facing the dry riverbed. She tiptoed up behind him, until she was about an arm's length away. She slipped her dress over her head, along with the slip underneath it, and stepped out of her knickers. That first chill of the season crept over her.

She softly called his name. He turned, a grin spreading across his face once he saw her. She remained still while he looked at her in the moonlight, ignoring the crisp edge in the air, and the mosquito landing on her lower back, its sharp beak piercing her skin. She didn't move until Noah gathered her in his arms.

"You sure?" he whispered in her ear.

"Mmhmm."

Ever since the wedding night with Monroe, she wouldn't allow Noah to touch her. Something as simple as his fingers grazing her leg would set her on edge. This was a new body, with new scars, new bruises. A different territory than the one he knew before, and she didn't want him trying to remap it.

He laid her down on the grass and she took him between her thighs. Even with the moon behind him, his face in shadow, she could feel his gaze, watching her, as if he, too, was trying to determine had she only given him her body, because he no longer had her heart.

She didn't know. She wanted to believe she could go back, be the person she was before, doing the things she had done before, but it was becoming apparent now with every moment that passed that she couldn't.

The light of it was gone now. That didn't mean that being with him was without pleasure, without sweetness, but it was different now, as she was different now. She held on to him, wondering if she could be content with that difference. Wasn't that marriage—to weather any shift in altitude, longitude, latitude?

Afterward, he laid his head on her stomach and began droning on about Mexico. His fever for the place was full-blown and he spoke of little else.

"That old vaquero told me so. If we can't get to the Trinity River, we can try Old Bahia Road. That'll take us south, too. We just need to go soon."

She stroked his back. "It's too late now. Cold weather be here soon."

"Then when?"

"After winter."

"That's too late." He didn't say anything for a long while. "You can just say you don't want to go."

"I do want to go." She did surely. She just didn't trust that they could. She knew trouble would find them on the road and she'd be at the mercy of whatever they found, just like she was here. Weren't the two devils she knew better than the dozens of devils they'd cross out there?

"Do you?" He raised his head and looked at her. "'Cause I won't be mad if you don't. But I will be mad if you make me miss my chance . . ."

She nodded. But that wasn't what she was doing. She was saving him from peril, not just keeping him close, but also keeping him alive. Out there was nothing but death and torture—cropped ears, sliced heel strings, and burned flesh. Even if she didn't love him like she used to, she loved him enough to save him from that.

CHAPTER TWENTY

NOAH WAS GONE. SERAH KNEW this before anyone said so. Two weeks went by with no sign of him. On Sunday afternoon, she lingered near the property line, by the split-rail fence, watching the procession of neighboring men heading home after visiting their wives on other farms. Of the two she knew from Sutton's farm, none had recalled seeing Noah, but they reassured her halfheartedly that, though they had not seen him, he was likely fine and there was little to be concerned about.

She thanked them both and didn't hold either up any longer than was necessary. Just a few awkward moments longer than normal, long enough for the men's bodies to betray their words, for their eyebrows to shift suddenly when they averted her gaze, or their fingers to fidget and widen the holes in their tattered pants. She understood the lie and was grateful for it, their attempt to dissuade and temper her worry until the inevitable moment when it couldn't be avoided any longer.

But the lie was still a lie and it left her looking for confirmation elsewhere. She was left trying to read the sky, the filmy surface of creek water, the unwieldy ripple of high grass along its banks. She dissected the cries of birds, the differences in tenor and pitch between owls, grackles, and sparrows, while watching the horizon for the sure descent of crows.

Anything could be a sign. There was no comfort in that, though, just a steady crazy-making. The more she scratched, the less she found. She grew obsessive about rites. About dipping twine in turpentine and stringing it around her navel. About leaving salt and fresh water out for her saints daily. She went tarrying alone and came back with nothing but a rash of fresh insect bites, dotting her arms and legs. There seemed to be no presence she could find that would signal anything to her or lessen the disorientation that missing him created.

———

WE WEREN'T SURPRISED WHEN Levi Sutton showed up looking for Noah one evening in November. Men on Noah's farm told of his relationship with Serah, and Mr. Lucy promptly led him to our door. The rest of us were asked to leave while the two questioned her. We stood outside, watching through the doorway as the two men pelted her with questions about when she last saw him and if he had been talking crazy, with wild ideas about stealing himself and running off somewhere.

She dulled her face. "No, sir, no, sir." She knew nothing of the kind, hadn't seen him in a long, long time, as she was a married woman and her husband didn't approve of her jawing with other men, she told them.

The two men exchanged looks as she rambled.

"Go on outside and wait with the others."

"You believe her?" Sutton said as she came down the steps.

"Hardly. Lying is her second tongue," Harlow said.

From the doorway, we all watched as they searched our room. They rifled through drinking tins, chipped bowls, jars of dried leaves and old coffee grounds. They emptied our pallets of ticking and moss, feeling around for God knows what. They dug their clammy hands into every hidey-hole and crevice, pocketing any silver money we had, dumping caches of our keepsakes onto the floor—colored beads and buttons, rusted coins with crosses etched into them, locks of hair and bits of cloth from lost kin—all into one mounting pile. They grumbled about cleanliness and godliness, about our seeming idolatry of petty objects, our obsession with trifles and trash, while they fingered our dresses and underthings and shuddered at rags stained with menstrual blood.

"You allow 'em to live like this? Just nesting in their own filth?" Sutton asked, shaking his head at Mr. Lucy. "My wife is down at the quarters every week, with a bucket of lime, making sure every cabin is square from top to bottom. And our folks are hardly ever sick. Healthier than the horses, I tell you."

We watched them come down the steps and move into the next cabin, where a newly returned Monroe was inside, whittling.

The two men barged in and we inched up the lane behind them to see what they would do next. First, they ejected Monroe, who rushed down the steps and came over to us.

"What they looking for?" he said.

We shrugged and shifted a bit closer, where we watched them through the open door, a new pile already forming on the ground. Since there was nothing under the bed, they groped the few pieces of clothing hanging along the wall. They shook shoes, emptied more ticking and moss from the mattress, ripped the lining out of quilts and stuck their hands deep inside. They pushed the table around, looking for holes in the dirt floor. A rusty lid glinted. Harlow tried to kick it aside, but it did not move. He bent over and lifted the lid. It covered a hole about three inches in diameter.

"What's in there?" asked Sutton.

"I don't know. I'm not sticking my hand in there."

"You big baby, do I have to everything myself?" Sutton grabbed a poker and stuck it down the hole. He then leaned in close and yanked its contents out. On the ground, he placed what looked like a few small pouches, a rolled piece of cloth that crackled like a leaf, and a bundle of knotty cotton root stems.

—✦—

SERAH WAS FLUSHED WITH shame, seeing the two men paw her things and rip them open, adding them to a growing heap in the center. On the heap were a string of blue beads, the first mojo bag she had ever made, and a piece of cloth from Noah's shirt, with a snippet of the letter he had written her sewn inside it. She was grateful now, she hadn't kept the entire letter, but only one piece of it, the words on it faint, having been touched too many times. Even so, it still worried her. It felt wild and reckless, this keepsake, and she wondered about the smell of it. If his scent on the cloth lingered, she almost wondered aloud about Sutton coming by without his hounds. Only then did she notice the women glaring at her, how Patience was muttering something under her breath, how Junie was cutting her eyes in her direction, and Lulu was still as a stone.

Patience then leaned forward, her chin jutting over Serah's shoulder as she spoke directly into Serah's ear. "You left them inside there? With him?"

The two men exited the cabin and came down the steps. In Harlow's hand was the bundle of cotton root stems. He motioned to Monroe. "You stealing from me? Going to make a go of it with a crop of your own?"

"They ain't mine, sir. You know I wasn't even here during picking time."

"Don't lie. You know I can't stand a liar—"

"They got to be hers," Monroe said, pointing at Serah.

Harlow looked over at Serah, his face hardening. He motioned her toward him, but she didn't move.

Serah watched Sutton instead, a smirk forming as he watched Harlow closely. She looked to see if his interest in the matter grew or flickered out. That would likely determine the length and brunt of this drama.

A pair of hands shoved Serah toward him. She could feel the women at her back, their persistent hot glare on her neck. She had to smooth this over.

Something pulled at her insides. She was afraid of the two white men standing in front of her, but the women spawned a feeling in her not dissimilar. A different shade of fear that was hard to describe.

"It's mine," she said. "But I'm not stealing from you or trying to make my own crop. I use it to make teas when I'm ailing. When my head hurts or my blood comes down. That's all." She tried to look contrite and small and not worth the fight. "I won't do it again," she mumbled.

Harlow's mouth grew thin. He reared back and slapped her, a loud stinging smack, that hurt her pride more than her body. But she fell to her knees under the surprise of it, a loud gasp escaping her lips, her hand rising up to her face.

"What you go and do that for?" Sutton said, offering his hand to help her up. "Don't you know cruelty only hardens them?"

"Says the man whose favorite cowman has gone fugitive."

"That can't always be helped when you own as many as I do. Some are going to run no matter what you do, but most just want to be guided with a decent and firm hand. Isn't that right?" He looked toward Serah for agreement.

She looked at Harlow and then back at Sutton. There was no right answer.

"Answer the man. He talking to you, ain't he?" said Harlow.

Serah nodded, her face still stinging. Harlow's jaw tightened even more.

"Sorry to say every man isn't built for it," Sutton said, wiping his hands on his pants. "The clock is ticking. What about that last one?" He pointed to Isaac and Patience's cabin.

The door was open, and it was plain to see no one was inside. The two men waltzed in, did a cursory kicking of clothing and objects, before turning around and coming back out.

"I must go. You alert me if you see any sign of him," Sutton said to Harlow as they came down the steps and walked away.

For a long moment, everyone was quiet, if not watching, then listening as the two men headed to the north part of the farm. Serah strained to hear and inched a bit closer in the direction of the men, listening for more information about Noah and their pursuit of him. Behind her, unnoticed, a group had formed. Three pairs of eyes had collected at her back. Within seconds, she was gently seized, ushered toward Junie and Lulu's cabin, and led up the steps, the door summarily shut behind them. Reeling, she was, but she knew better than to speak.

Inside, the hands turned her loose. She stood on one side of the room, the others all gathered opposite her, awaiting an explanation. If there was to be some formal council on the matter, deep in the woods under night sky, where Nan would step in and guide all their feverish and disparate temperaments into one cohesive and patient voice, it wouldn't be now. Instead, a low whisper formed in the room growing to a soft cacophony, everyone speaking at once. There were too many faces, too many voices, too much anger and feeling in the room to sift through.

"What the hell, Bird?"

"You left them *there* of all places?"

"How you even have that many left?"

"Told y'all to hide them under the house, not *in* the house."

"They were under the house!" Serah shot back, but she was drowned out.

"I keep mine in the garden now."

"Yep, I bury mine in between the plots."

"How simple!"

"How stupid can you be!"

"I'mma beat some sense into her."

"Me? Didn't know nothing 'bout it, sir. I'm just a simple Catholic who don't consort with them root-wearing daughters of Satan," Patience said, with an exaggerated flourish, eliciting laughs from Lulu and Junie. There was a break in the tension then, as if the whole cabin had taken a breath.

Serah stared at the women and they glared back, but her resolve was collapsing, a tough shell slowly cracking like an egg. Her eyes slid up to the ceiling, where she looked at the holes in the roof. She blinked at the clouds as Junie moved close to her. But when she saw Junie's face blocking her vision, she stepped back, so her body was against the wall, her eyes again drifting to the roof, because Junie's face was too much to take in.

"Didn't mean to leave it there so long. I thought Monroe might have hexed it to get back at me, so I couldn't move it."

"Does he know what it was for?"

"No," Serah said, shaking her head. "I'll fix it. Just tell me what to do."

Junie squeezed her shoulder. "Wipe your face."

"I don't care 'bout them tears. I'm still whipping her ass," Lulu shouted.

"Then you gon' have to beat mine, too," Patience said. "Leave her be."

"Fine. How you want it?"

Patience met Lulu's eyes with a hard glare.

"Lulu, go somewhere," said Junie, with an exasperated sigh.

"Y'all better deal with her," Lulu said as she turned and left, slamming the door behind her.

"What do we do now?" Serah said.

"Wait and see—" Junie said.

"Have a baby," Patience said.

Serah made a face. Patience laughed. "I knew you weren't serious."

"You're joking?"

"Not really."

"Don't scare the girl," Junie said.

"I'm not scaring her. I'm just telling her the truth. It's only a matter of time before they come sniffing around again. They threw a big wedding with a bunch of vittles. They expect a litter in return."

"We didn't ask for—"

"Don't matter. That's what they want."

"Then why don't you have one?"

"Because I didn't mess up. They didn't find the remedy in my place, did they?"

"Pay, stop it. Let's not start that again. If one comes through, they be pairing the rest of us up with Monroe in no time. Or worse, buying new niggers to put us with."

Patience let out a slow breath.

"We just have to wait and see," Junie went on. "And keep our eyes open."

"You say so," said Patience.

They both turned and looked at Serah, who seemed frozen, a glassy look in her eyes.

"It's water under the bridge now," Junie said. "We got to look toward what's coming."

CHAPTER TWENTY-ONE

ONLY WHEN THE STEAMBOAT TICKETS came, did Junie start to believe the trip to Georgia might be real. She had been summoned to the house that evening to help out while Nan was off midwifing, but once she arrived, Lizzie ushered her past the two squabbling children in the front room and into the bedroom, quickly shutting the door.

The sound of Lizzie forcing the door shut stirred Carol from sleep and she began crying. Lizzie picked her up and stuck a strong-smelling cloth into the child's mouth. She then sat down on the bed and leaned against the headboard. "My eyes hurt. Read to me," she said, pointing to a stack of letters on the dresser.

Not since they were girls, back when Lizzie taught her the alphabet, had Junie been asked to read aloud to Lizzie, instead of the other way around. And for a moment, she wondered if it was a trick of some sort. "Please," Lizzie said.

Junie could see Lizzie's face was flushed and teary, and

maybe a bit swollen on the left side. She started to offer to grab a compress but thought better of it. Every minute in this room was a potential tinderbox. It was best to just do as she was told.

She sat down on a chair and began reading. "'I say Valencia is a fool to marry a man with nothing to offer her but himself. She'll find out the hard way, I suppose. Like you did. But I fear she won't listen to me. Write her and tell her yourself,'" wrote Beatrice, Lizzie's cousin. "'Yes, it was rash for Charles to take your wet nurse, but you should have spoken to him first. He has to lead you as Christ leads the Church.'" And between gossip about this person or that, there were details of the bad blood growing between the Lucys, typically over money and mismanagement of the farm. Junie tried to keep the surprise out of her face and read the words in a flat monotone. She knew the Lucys had been fighting a lot recently, but she was amazed to see it laid out so plainly.

"'It's important that you all remain united,'" cousin Beatrice went on. "'Especially in these times.'" Lizzie began blowing her nose loudly. Junie paused and skimmed the next paragraph.

"'We too have had a panic recently. Some plots of insurrection among the slaves in different counties have come to light. I dare say all of the South must watch out for Northerners in sheep's clothing . . .'"

As Lizzie wiped her nose, Junie carefully switched to the letter underneath, and resumed reading aloud the moment the sniffling stopped. "'Dearest sister, I agree,'" wrote Lizzie's brother, Mason. "'A visit from you is long overdue. Please find enclosed five tickets from the Blackwell Ferry company, from Houston to Savannah. The man promised me these are exchangeable . . .'"

She heard the words as they came out of her mouth, heard them swirling in the stale air of the bedroom, but until Lizzie pulled out the tickets from between the pages of a beat-up Bible, it didn't dawn on her fully.

For a moment, she found herself stunned by the array of tickets Lizzie laid on the bed, the bold stark type on the small slips of white paper. She touched one, tracing the lettering with her fingers. March 10th, 1860. It wasn't a trick. It said just what Mason said it did, just what Lizzie said it would.

"When is that?" Junie asked. Her sense of time was fuzzy. Had always been. If the Lucys had calendars, they were never in plain sight. She could track events and seasons, but not the names of the months or years connected to them.

Lizzie sighed. "Not soon enough."

Before today, the Visit was a thing over there, but now it was real. She felt it, a transference of some kind. Even after Lizzie pulled the tickets away from her and slipped them back inside the Bible, she still felt the figures under her fingers.

From then on, the trip became a thing inside her. That night, she dreamed of those tickets and who she hoped awaited her on the other side of that long journey. The next day, she pinched herself whenever the thought arose, but the hope kept rising in her chest. There seemed to be no way to stop it. It was sneaky and clever, seeping into moments both busy and quiet, alike. The thrumming of the loom didn't drown it. Even the work songs she hated didn't crowd it out.

Little upset her then, because she was already gone. A phantom self was moving around doing what needed to be done on the farm, while the rest of her was in Georgia, sitting with her children in front of the fire, telling them stories. They would be too big to sit in her lap now, but she imagined them that way anyhow, nestled in her arms, her cheek against their hair.

She just needed to get the rest of her body there. Over that big swath of land and that big body of water.

—❦—

IT WAS A DAY for churching, but there wouldn't be any church-ing, covert or otherwise. Noah's disappearance had white folks on edge, had them watching everyone as if through a looking glass.

Already, rumors were circulating, and it was easy to guess which ones were started up by Sutton or the Lucys or the Da-vidson family. The fugitive has been captured, they'd say, each spouting a different horrid demise. He'd been eaten by panthers, sundered by ghosts. He'd been flayed and hanged by voracious thieves and ne'er-do-wells en route to California. Or the soul dealers got him and cut his heel strings, before taking him to work sugarcane in the bowels of Louisiana.

Serah was unsure of what to believe. Each possibility awful and haunting. For a time, she believed each new rumor, held it under her tongue, barely breathing until the next one came. And only then did she give up the former. It wasn't long before she didn't believe any-thing, because of how often they shifted, how widely they differed. She even heard that he had been transferred to Sutton's ranching property permanently. The most benign rumor of them all, but she didn't believe it, because Sutton still seemed to be looking for him.

She felt buoyed by the possibility that Noah remained out of their reach. The only thing that punctured that buoyancy was the fraying bracelet around her wrist. Would her binding be his undoing, somehow snapping him back into the vicinity the mo-ment he stepped too far out of range?

She figured the best person to consult might be the root worker, Mariah. And that Sunday, when she saw Harlow's wagon pull away from the farm, with Monroe and Isaac in tow, she figured it might be the most opportune time to go and visit.

Mariah didn't live very far away, only about a mile or two north of the creek, tucked away behind a thicket of black willow trees. Serah knew the way, having tagged along with Lulu once, but she'd never had the nerve to try and consult the woman herself.

Even second time around, the sight of Mariah's place still stunned her. It was a clapboard whitewashed house, with true glass windows covered with bright busy curtains. It had a real sitting porch and a large front yard that was swept and raked daily, its clean furrows still visible.

The front door was closed, and a few people were sitting in the yard, awaiting their turn to speak to Mariah. Serah typically didn't mind waiting, especially if she could overhear a bit of their conversation, but she knew she couldn't wait long. She had only a couple of hours before someone would realize she was gone.

Another person came and left, and now there was just one woman in line in front of her. A handsome young man was now pacing the yard, holding a glass bottle out in front of him. Inside the glass, a large spider inched along to the right a few paces. The young man followed the direction of the spider, flattening the distinct lines in the dirt.

"Hey, Elias." The woman in front of Serah waved and grinned at the man.

He paused and waved back.

"A damn shame," the woman said to herself, chuckling.

"What is?" Serah asked.

"All that man wasted." The woman shook her head. She then turned to face Serah. "You know I'm joshing, right?"

"Of course."

"'Cause I would never go after anything or anybody belonging to Mariah."

"Of course." Serah nodded.

Serah had never seen Elias in the flesh until now, but he was the subject of much talk among the neighboring folk. He was Mariah's husband, and besides him being a handsome, strapping figure, he was also a good ten or fifteen years Mariah's junior. And while Mariah was known all over the region for her ability to win over stubborn hearts for the unrequited or dissolve once ironclad marital unions, a good deal of women put their stock in her solely because of her hold on young Elias. He was never rumored to have a sweetheart or two on a distant farm the way other men were, nor had anyone ever seen him at a frolic hugged up with anyone other than his wife.

The door flung open wide, and a man staggered out, a dazed expression on his face.

"What you want now, Amy?" a voice said from inside. The woman in front of Serah scurried up the steps and into the house. "Harry try to quit you again?" the voice continued, the door shutting firmly.

If the neighboring women were swayed to believe in Mariah's powers by her hold on the young husband, the men among the neighboring folk believed in her for different reasons. For them, it was the house, the swath of land it sat upon, and the seemingly hands-off arrangement she had with the man who retained the deeds to both her and the land.

On paper, she and the land were said to be owned by Martin Robison, a senile planter who split his time between Navarro and San Antonio. And it was rumored to be a strictly contractual agreement, for to be a free woman in Texas created new quandaries, as little could be done without a white man's signature. And so it was a shell game. Robison left her alone and she paid him a small fee annually to cover the taxes of owning her. The land and her mobility were said to be a gift or a payment, depending on who was telling the story, for removing a generational curse from his lineage.

The door flung open again, this time Amy coming out and waving Serah inside.

Mariah stood in the front room and motioned for Serah to sit down at a small table, ornately carved with figures of swimming turtles and slithering snakes. "What brings you, dear?"

To some, Mariah's appearance was the most beguiling thing about her. She didn't look like anybody anyone would assume to be powerful. She had soft worn brown skin and sleepy eyes, and she wore her graying hair into two neat plaits on either side of her head. She looked like any regular old granny. A fact that was remarkable, seeing as most two-headed persons and Conjurers were known by their difference. The presence of the gift was usually visible. A shriveled hand or lame foot, shocking blue gums or catlike eyes. Others were fluid beings—shape-shifting and gender variant, like *omasenge kimbandas* in the old tradition.

Not to mention, she always dressed as if she were on her way to the grandest frolic no one had bothered telling you about. Her blouse was dyed a deep red and her skirt, an intricate weaving of stripes and checkered cloth. A brilliant multicolored blue-and-orange sash was tied around her torso. And if anyone asked her about the mix of color and pattern, if there was a secret to the wondrous ways she put together what would be cacophonous on another body, she'd laugh and say, "Evil follows a straight line. I don't give it a place to land."

Serah traced the figures on the surface of the table. One frog in particular captured her eye.

"I said what brings you," Mariah said, a hint of impatience in her voice.

"How hard is it to break a binding?"

"Depends. On who's bound and what they been bound with."

Serah showed her the bracelet and told her its origin story.

"You only used hair, right? No blood?"

"That's all."

"It's not very strong, then. Don't take much to bust a few strands of hair."

"Oh . . . that's good," said Serah glumly. A weak binding shouldn't impede him getting farther away, but hearing that only upset her. She couldn't help seeing an endless ocean materialize before her.

Mariah's eyes widened. "Honey, you want to make it stronger? If you got something of his, it's not hard to do."

"You can?"

"Yeah, it wouldn't take much. I could web it. That's the cheapest option. For a little more, I could build a dam . . ." Mariah ran down her list of possibilities, each ritual more elaborate than the one before it. "And then it wouldn't take much to call him back to you."

It was tempting, Serah had to admit. "And he'd be unharmed?"

"Can't promise you that."

"What can you promise?"

"Can't promise nothing. The work ain't certain. It's just a strong hand guiding things in a favorable direction."

"Hmph." She was torn. The carved frog on the table seemed to be waiting. Judging. Just how selfish could she be?

"Do you want it or not?" Mariah peered past Serah toward the window. "'Cause it's getting late."

Serah could see the sun setting, a fiery orange spilling into the windows.

"No. He can't come back here. Not now anyway."

Mariah shrugged and tapped the frog on the table. "He'll take your offering." She stood up and opened the door.

Serah placed a blue bead on the frog's mouth and was surprised when the grooves in the table kept it from rolling away.

"If you change your mind, you know where I am," Mariah said, waving goodbye. Serah left the house and hurried back through the woods, the way she had come.

CHAPTER TWENTY-TWO

1

Dear Bird,

The light keeps changing. Not just the brightness or the length of it, but the when and how of it pouring through the trees. I make these letters knowing they'll never reach you. Without ink or paper, the wind and clouds will have to carry these words. And while it's likely they won't do my bidding, I'll keep talking anyway 'cause I know on the other side of this, there will be a reckoning. If and when we gather again, you will have questions. I'll do my best to answer them as I go.

You were right about the strangeness of weather this time of year. The heat has burned off and there's a regular threat of rain. But at least the day is shorter, leaving more hours to travel.

Milly, the old mule, is with me. She's slow, but she's all I could get. And at least there's plenty of corn left on the stalks to eat. We need to get as far south as we can before that changes.

Noah

2

BIRD,

We go as far as we can that first night and spend the morning hiding in the woods. We must be on the edge of a farm though, 'cause I can hear a horn blaring every few hours.

It spooks me. I get on Milly and we ride until she's too tired to go on, but where she stops, there's nothing but prairies. Fields and fields of yellow grass as far as I can see. I kick her a few times to get her moving again. Even the last drop of water doesn't make her budge.

You know how I feel about the plains. I suppose they shouldn't bother me much after so long on Sutton's ranch, but they still give me an eerie feeling now and then. The flat emptiness. How the sounds carry. How the common screech of a barn owl now strikes me as a child screaming.

Last time I ran away, it was the plains that did me in. The smoke from my small fire was visible from miles away and I woke up to a shotgun pressed to my forehead. I like to think I'm wiser now. Can let my stomach go empty longer. A pouch of pecans and a few ears of corn will have to keep me until the land changes again. That is one thing I do know about this place. It will change again. Forest, swamp, desert, or plain. It's all here.

N.

3

Bird,

I was a fool to give Milly the last of my water in a place as stingy as this. We reach the Trinity and it's nothing but rocks, a dried-up suggestion. The banks are empty though, so we lay out and rest for a moment, camouflaged by a hill of large stones.

I kneel down and poke a finger in the dry, light-colored soil hoping to find dampness. All I find is angry-looking beetles with clenched fists. One pierces my hand, drawing blood. I yell out. The blackbirds upriver squawk in response. They circle and swoop, as if trying to determine if we are of any use to them. I wave them away, worried they'll draw attention to us.

I pack up and try to lead Milly away. She's too weak to ride and I pull her behind me. But again, she's stubborn, stamping her feet, and pulling back on the reins. A small sack of dried corn strung over her back falls to the ground and spills. I salvage what I can, losing most of it to the blackbirds.

N.

4

Where the river and the road meet should be a holy place. Especially, when the river is dried up, and the two cross each other like siblings in a shared bed. Won't surprise you it's the opposite. It's rife with soul dealers and smugglers.

Just this morning, I saw a caravan. I was lying in the bushes some feet away from the road, trying to gauge its safety. I had laid there some hours, until I had gotten cold and stiff. Little had passed by. Only an old oxcart hauling some timber. But something told me not to move just yet. And that's when I heard them, the whisper of a hymn floating in the air, the slow clopping of horses.

Three wagons inched by. Behind them a ragged band of men, women, and children hobbling along. I shut my eyes to it. My stomach grew queasy. Their limp hymn poured down into my ears. "Nearer my God to thee," they sang. "Nearer to thee."

You never really forget the coffle, do you? No matter what comes after. The nauseating weight of it. The clinging smell of rust and blood. How confused your limbs get when affixed to someone else's. A man beside you lurches forward and you're yanked along with him. A man behind you passes out and you have to drag his weight along for a mile or more, before he's unhooked.

If I managed to get away with more than a dull Bowie knife, maybe I could be useful to them. José said to make the road proper I'd need firepower, a gun worth a damn and a horse worth more. I have neither, but I couldn't wait any longer.

Whatever they say about me back on Sutton's place ain't true. Not in substance or in deed. Survival looks different after a man has tried to eat you alive with his fingers. When he's tried to lick the bone while you're still inside the bag of skin. No matter how you stare down the wolf, he comes back, with new fangs, new claws.

I hope you understand.

N.

5

BIRD,

Beware of what they call a road here. It's more of an idea than anything else. It peters out and returns, rises up again more solid than before.

Last night, the road took Milly. It was dark, another black night with a dim moon. We were moving slow, as the trail was hard to follow and we didn't want to be led away from it over the plain.

Suddenly, the ground began thrumming, as if it were alive. I couldn't see where it was coming from. It seemed to be all around us. Louder and harder, it grew. Milly was spooked now and I held her bridle tight in my fist. I rubbed her head with the other hand, trying to calm her down, but she only grew more frantic, kicking and rearing back.

Too late, did I see the wave coming, thick plumes of dust billowing up in the air. The first beast sprang through the cloud, a wild-eyed mustang. Behind him, a sea of buffalo, cattle, and horses, all speeding directly toward us. I couldn't see where it ended. Only heard men whistling and shouting somewhere in the distance, in a language I couldn't parse.

Milly reared back again and the reins slipped from my hand. Off she ran. I ran after her, but at the nearest tree, I stopped and flung myself up, grabbing hold of the highest sturdy branch I could reach, and climbed as far I could.

The roar became deafening and Milly got swept up in the stampede. She was carried along for a moment, before she disappeared into a pileup, where I imagine she was soon trampled. I waited for the stampede to clear, the dust to settle, so I could climb down and see, but there were men all about now. Cherokees, I think, from the look of them. Some rode by slowly, sitting high on their horses, their bodies streaked with sweat. Two younger men followed on foot, guiding a team of horses. I feared one of them saw me. He swept the area with his eyes, scanning the trees.

I tried to sense if they would be a help to me, but there was no way of knowing. They could just as easily sell me back or help me make my passage. It wasn't worth the risk.

I remained still. Closed my eyes. Waited for them to move on. I must have dozed off, 'cause the next thing I remember is falling through the air, landing on my arm. The pain was blinding, but I could see it was first light. I lay there for a moment, getting my bearings, before I pushed myself up to see about Milly.

I walked up the road but strangely there was no sign of her. There were a few carcasses. Two buffalo and one horse. A vulture circled and landed. I kept walking, expecting to come across her, but I never did.

Bird, this only confirms to me that this place is more dangerous than we know, and we must leave it. It eats whole so many things, and with such greed and sureness, there's nothing left to mark them by.

N.

6

DEAR BIRD,

Another narrow escape in territory familiar. You know this geography. Crooked plow lines and snaking rows of crops. Some corn, peas, oats, cotton. And the hunch proves right.

I find the lane where the quarters are. A jangle of clotheslines, among them a five-star quilt drying. I see a similar pattern tacked across a window hatch. "A flock of geese" pattern. Could it be a sign?

I knock on the door and an old woman answers. I show her my arm. Ask if there's a healer among them.

She sizes me up for a moment. And I must have looked a sight. Ragged and dirty, weeds and grass in my hair, holding my arm to my chest like a broken wing.

"You running, boy?"

"Yes, ma'am."

She nods and lets me in. She gives me water and lets me drink 'til I am full. Then she rubs a salve on my arm, wraps it tight with a piece of muslin.

And when she makes me a plate, I could cry. Corn bread and salt pork.

"When you done eating, you got to go. Children

be through here soon and you know they tongues too loose."

"Yes, ma'am. I thank you. You done plenty."

She pats my back. "Hurry up now."

I scarf down the rest of the pork and save the corn bread for later. I thank the woman again and leave. At the edge of the lane, there are some men returning from the fields. They give me a curious look but I don't stop. I just keep walking, as if I didn't see them. One calls out to me, but I keep on, moving a little faster now.

But the man is insistent. He catches up to me, gets in my face.

"You hear me talking to you."

"I didn't. Hard time hearing, you know."

"What you doing over here?"

"Visiting."

"Visiting who?"

"My aunt."

The man sniffed. "You don't look like no visitor to me. Look like a fugitive. One who's going to do what I tell him, if he don't want me turning him in to my white folks."

I stopped. "What you want?"

"You got any money? You fugitives always got a little something on you. A shilling or a five-pence?"

"No, all I got is this corn bread and some pecans."

"You won't mind if I see for myself," the man said, reaching for the sack strung across my good shoulder.

"Don't put your hands on me," I tell him, reaching for my knife. I brandish it with my good arm, though I doubt I could make a good wound with it in my left hand. He backs away and I take off running.

I hear him behind me, calling somebody for help. Lucky for me, they're slow in heeding.

N.

7

BIRD,

Whatever mojo I got is fading. Animals no longer skitter past, but stop and stare at me, full-sighted. Even the prairie chicken teases me, as if I'm no threat, which I'm not with one lame arm and no gun, but still. Its yellow jaws swell up full and round, like an omen.

The plains are no place for a man by his lonesome. It's full of secrets. Ditches, graves, and pimple mounds. All the plants have teeth. The tall grasses hide snakes. Berries tempt me, red and sweet, only to sour in the belly, and put me on my knees for hours.

Maybe it's best I don't make these letters anymore. Maybe each day is best left to itself and what's inside of it shut up and left there. The band you tied around my wrist is fraying. Maybe it's the reason I've been circling the same ground.

N.

8

What I thought of as darkness before seems a world apart from this. Sometimes I think I've gone up yonder, all the way round, now on the underside of that cosmogram. The world underneath the world. That would explain the sounds and what I've seen. Or maybe it's the way the mind works on its own after a while.

In the pines near Bastrop, I find others heading south. Among them, a man called Aaron who had already made a life down in Mexico. He married a Seminole woman, had children even, but a white man kidnapped him and dragged him back across the border. He was sold upcountry nearly a year ago and is just now making his way back.

This man, Aaron, warns me about the desert, the strip of land between here and Mexico proper. He gives us options, but none are good. We can go straight down, he says, through brush country, until we reach the river. Or we can go west, also through dry country, toward Eagle Pass, where a band of Seminoles and fugitives have a town there on the borderline. I ask him which is shorter, he can't say. "Which is easier?"

He can't answer that either, but I'm glad for the company and the assistance. Maybe Aaron will prove a better navigator than me.

N.

9

We should've never left the pines, but we grew so hungry after several days. Too hungry to catch anything really. Not even a possum or a squirrel. All our traps failed, and Aaron didn't want to use his last ball of ammunition. There were maybe five of us total, a band of bruised freezing runaways. Three men and two women. All too tired to agree or make much sense anymore.

"We should go toward town," one woman said. "One of the missions will feed us."

"No, we should rest, set new traps. Wait 'til nightfall and then pass on by," Aaron said.

They didn't lie about the missions. There were several in old Goliad. Ghostly white buildings ruined by the war between Texas and Mexico. But they looked unchurched to me, so I didn't trust them. I hung back while the others knocked on the door. A white priest welcomed them inside. I stayed out there in the lane for a while, just watching, thinking maybe I was wrong. That I had cheated myself out of a warm drink and some hearty vittles. And just when my stomach got the best of me and I approached the door, a young Mexican shooed me away from it. He shook his head. *"Mentirosa . . . malvado . . .* a cheat . . ."

I was still unsure what he meant, but I followed the man down the street, where he led me to a small house, where he and his sister fed me and let me trade them a piece of silver for a Mackinaw blanket.

I was still eating at their table, when I heard a commotion outside. They told me not to go out and I watched through the bottom portion of their covered window as Aaron and the rest got hauled away. I could hear the white men doing the hauling arguing about what to do with them.

"The bastard shot a priest. Who's going to buy him when the devil's got a hold on him so?"

N.

10

Bird,

Just wanted to let you know I reached brush country. New terrain. Mesquite, shrubs, prickly pear. But it rains a lot. I make a tent by hanging the blanket between a few shrubs until it passes. When darkness falls and the wind howls, specters loosen from their hiding places and roam free. It's best not to look at them directly. They dance, they sing, they loom large like cornstalks. I don't protest, though they scare me.

When the rain stops, they follow me. More haints come out, some with monstrous blue heads, some with wings and scaly backs. A grand parade following me all the way to the Rio Grande.

N.

11

Oh, what joy to reach the river, but what a surprise it was. It was shallow with white rocks all around it and a few pecan trees along the banks. I walk upstream and barely find enough to cover my knees. I step in anyway, wash myself in the clear blue water, and am thankful to find my net, still tucked away, deep in my sack. I catch as many fish as I can, though I got my tinder wet and had no way to start a fire.

I leave there, thankful and relieved, with a full net of small redfish and bass, convinced the hardest part of my journey is over.

Some hours later, I follow a drift of smoke to a small campsite of vaqueros. One says he'd let me fry up my fish, if I was willing to share. We cook it up and eat well.

And I'm lying there in the dirt, too full to move, when the vaquero breaks the horrible news to me. "Oh, *mi amigo*, that wasn't the Rio Grande. That little gulp of water was the Nueces. You've still got miles and miles to go."

For the second time in days, I could've cried.

N.

12

The strip of land between the Nueces River and the Rio Grande is a hellish one. The men at the campsite told me so. They were heading north, outrunning something else—debt higher than the Sierra Madre.

"Keep every eye open," they warned me. As the strip was full of desperate men—grifters, deserters, and bounty hunters. I did as they said and still, a white man caught me foraging for food and roped me with barely two words between us. "Oh, lucky day. You gone be my ticket, boy." I told him I wasn't running, that I was allowed to hire myself out when I could, but he didn't believe me. Instead, he wrapped himself up in my blanket and dragged me to a blacksmith, where he tried to bargain for a set of irons.

While there, he goaded two or three white men sitting around, each waiting for their turn. "Oh, I'm going to get top dollar for this fugitive. They'll give me at least two hundred. Maybe three!" He directed his comments to a scruffy man swinging a pair of horseshoes. "Barnes, you should come in on this. Let me use your horse and I'll give you a percentage."

Barnes snorted and spat on the ground. "I wouldn't give you a tin of my piss."

The blacksmith refused to front the man a set of leg irons and we had barely gotten more than a few paces away, when Barnes appeared, trying to rob the man of his hot ticket. The two quarreled. Each firing upon the other. I took off, not waiting to see who won. I saw a horse tied to a post and ran toward it. I yanked the tie loose and hopped on. I took off, dipping around the blacksmith's yard and out past the edge of town, going as far as I could.

N.

13

When I reach the Rio Grande, I can see why it's called a great river. It's so beautiful I wish I could gather it up and bring it to you. A mighty winding, careless thing, it is, in the way water can be.

Aaron warned me it's not easy to cross. It's deceiving that way. The current is stronger than it looks. It makes one think he can just walk or swim across it, but the bottom is unsure and the banks aren't safe. Soldiers and Texas Rangers roam up and down the perimeter seeking runaways.

But never mind those no-account bastards, the river says, for it is the true divider of persons. If you manage to look on the surface and baptize yourself in its waters, it likely means a gauntlet lay at your back. Miles of thirst and hunger, wolves and soul dealers of all stripes are somewhere behind you. And now, just one lowly unassuming river.

Like all devils, it seduces. It shimmers in the sunlight and it feels like all I need to do is hoist myself upon it, paddle lightly, and soon I'll reach the opposite side. When it takes me under, I'm surprised for only a moment, but one moment is all it needs.

N.

14

BIRD,

Remember the traveling preacher's talk about heaven. Pearly gates, tables full of food, grinning faces of kith and kin. I still don't believe him. But the Negro colony down here is probably the closest I'll see in this life. I nearly drowned, but the Mexicans who fished me out of the river knew exactly where I was going. And I arrived in Nacimiento de los Negros half-dead on the back of a dray, but I made it all the same.

The town is small and growing every day. Some folks have been down here a full generation or more. But most are like us, running from Texas or Louisiana, or Oklahoma. A few Seminoles from Florida are thrown in, but I suspect they were exiled from the Seminoles' town not too far away.

The folks here got small farms, work their crops, and sell them at the market. It's not perfect. Capture is a steady threat, with the Rangers and other soul dealers charging across the border to kidnap folks, but we're far enough south that it happens less now, or so they tell me.

I wish you could see it because I can't describe it proper. The land is rocky so the crops don't yield much. Most men do some cattle work also, and the songs they sing are both familiar and new, now full of Spanish words.

Listen, this might be my last letter for a while but don't be cross with me. Let me get well. Get a plot of my own to farm and some chickens, too. Let me build you a small clapboard house with a real floor and a real bed.

N.

CHAPTER TWENTY-THREE

BY THE TIME OF THE first frost of the season, Serah had already
begun to suspect what she was feeling in her body was something more than a flu. Her stomach was jumpy, always upset,
always threatening to empty itself. It was tiring, made her sore,
in throat and abdomen. Made others upset at her for wasting
food. Got so others reclaimed her breakfast, her lunch. And she
was too weak from vomiting to fight anyone to keep it.

Every winter, Nan complained about the drop in temperature, however mild. How cold could settle under her joints and in
her fingers. Serah thought maybe that was happening to her, too.
Winter had finally come for her body but instead of her joints, it
attacked the flesh. Made her back ache, her breasts tender, her
stomach a queasy, roiling sea.

She went to Nan, to ask if she had something that might
help with the nausea or the soreness. Maybe she could diagnose
this particular strain of winter illness.

"You ain't catch cold, you caught," Nan said flatly.

"What you mean?"

It was hog-killing time and Nan's hands were lodged deep in the guts of a pig, the shiny loose liver, the translucent slick spleen. The sight usually didn't bother Serah. But this time, the bloody gore of it, the foul smell of it—both sent her reeling. She backed into the wall, clamping a hand over her mouth.

"I mean caught. With child. Now, get out of here before you mess all over my floor," Nan told her.

Serah stumbled outside to retch in the yard. Her head hurt; her stomach ached.

—⚓—

OVER THE NEXT FEW days, Serah spun between two distant poles, wanting it and not wanting it. She spent days thinking of nothing but trying to kill it. She'd chewed cotton root for hours, until her teeth were yellow and chalky, and her jaw tired. And she cursed herself for how sporadic she had been before, only chewing it when she felt like it and stopping anytime she grew tired or bored or hungry.

She had taken to speaking to the spirit directly, willing it to loosen itself from her. She asked her saints to help it along, send it back to the otherworld so it could choose again. Often, she thought of what Junie said that day the cotton roots were found. If she had one, it'd be the stockman all over again, with Monroe put to them all, one after the other, and back again. She had already betrayed the women once. They'd never forgive her this.

But there were days when she couldn't help imagining a family in a white clapboard house, just like Mariah's. Noah would be sitting on its porch, a sweet brown babe asleep in his lap. He'd look up and grin at her, easy as the breeze. And it was then, she got to thinking about generations and lineages, and what if they did kill him, he was gone from this earth as if he was never here. This soul lodged inside her may be the only thing of him that remained. And on those days, she did nothing at all—no cotton root, no camphor, no rue. She followed the women to the fields and back, spun yarn until her sight blurred, and then took her hunger and nausea to bed, as the sun had long set, and nothing but cold dark was to be had anyway.

She was capricious that season. Avoiding the women and then wanting nothing more than the sound of them, the joy of their raucous laughter, the sharpness of their wit. She hated the cold that flooded her body but wanted the feeling of frozenness, of long-standing numbness.

Sharp cold beget a howling colder wind, heavy nausea followed by a black fatigue. There was little she could manage after a day of breaking up the ground or spinning thread all day.

And that didn't change until Harlow showed up one evening and walked her over to Monroe's cabin. Monroe hadn't been back long from his last job, barely a week had gone by. And in that time, the two hadn't said much to each other.

Monroe was sitting by the hearth, warming himself, when Harlow appeared in the doorway.

"Since you're here, thought it was time you got your gal back," Harlow said, pushing Serah inside the room.

Monroe stifled a groan. "Thank you, sir."

"Did you not want her back? You want another?" Harlow asked him.

Serah watched as Monroe's face grew puzzled. Monroe looked at her. Was that all it would have taken for them to be separated? Or was it a trick?

Harlow hadn't closed the door and she looked outside at the blackening sky. She inched toward the door. Maybe she could hide out in the woods a few days, but she'd be on her own. None of the women would bring her any food. They might even blame her for whoever Monroe chose next, if he dared ask.

"Don't know, sir," Monroe began, trying to suss out the temperature in the white man's face. His eyes stopped at the man's waist, where a shiny new revolver sat on his hip. Serah followed Monroe's gaze and saw it, too.

"You can speak freely."

"Well, we alright, but a better match might be made with one of the others," Monroe said carefully.

"How come?"

Both were quiet for a long moment, unsure of how to answer, or what was being asked.

"What a disappointment," Harlow said, sniffing the air. "It's been over a year since I threw y'all that fancy wedding affair and you both promised me portly children." He narrowed his gaze at Monroe. "What good would it be matching you with another, if you can't make butter with the one I give you? You make good on your promise and maybe we can talk about another match."

Harlow turned toward Serah. "Go on, now. Get in." He shoved her toward the bed.

She sat down on it, next to Monroe.

"For God's sake, act like you're husband and wife. Do I have to get in there with you?"

She got underneath the blanket and Monroe did the same.

Harlow moved toward the door. "This time, I'll give you some privacy, but if I come back tomorrow, and y'all still acting like clergy folk, I won't be so kind."

WHAT EMERGED THE NEXT few days between Serah and Monroe was a steely tension. The two sizing each other up, waiting for the first blow. They were both extra cautious about where they sat, where they stood, what they drank, what they ate. They wouldn't share water or food, each preparing their own meals, each securing their own water from the well, and keeping it covered and in sight at all times. They each donned their own protective work, in front of the other. Part ritual, part performance. Serah could tell he was still angry at her for making him sick the way she did that summer, and in truth, he had grown sicker than she expected. And she couldn't say for sure if it was because of the work she had done on him or something else. They all fell prey at one time or another to the mysterious ailments of this country—fevers of all kinds, boils, influenza, dropsy, pneumonia, pleurisy, malaria. Though she knew many who didn't believe in that possibility. If anything befell them, it was because of the malicious root work of their enemies.

His belief that it was her doing wasn't necessarily a bad thing, she figured. It made him cautious, tentative. Made him less of a bully, lording over her with his size and strength. And so, she didn't say much more to dissuade him of the notion. Instead, she narrowed her eyes at him and drew shapes in the air and on the ground. She put down salt around herself, prayed to her saints, whispering loudly enough for him to hear. Neither slept well the next few nights, dozing off and jolting awake, intermittently throughout the night.

One evening, during their nightly chores, she figured she'd at least try broaching the subject of a truce with him. She was sitting at the table, sewing, while he was trying to repair the chinking in one of the cabin's walls. She watched as he pulled moss and rags from the crevices and replaced them with mud.

"You think that'll hold?"

He shrugged. "We'll see."

When he was done, she handed him a cloth so he could wipe his hands.

"How 'bout we call it even?"

He gave her a funny look. "It ain't even. Won't ever be."

"A truce, then. At least until it's warm out. And if you still mad then, we can—"

"Don't care about then, I care about now."

"Fine. What then? You want to poison me. Maybe you already did. You see I can't keep my dinner down half the time. Ain't that enough?"

"Nope," he said firmly.

"When we even then? When I'm dead?"

"Sounds good to me," he said, grinning at her.

───✦───

THE UNSEASONABLY COLD WINTER turned the cabin into a burial pit. A heavy snow collected on the roof one night, and hearing the wood creak under the weight signaled to Serah they were being buried alive together. The temperature inside the cabin grew so cold it became hard to continue the way they had been, seething and wary all the time. They worked together to finish sealing the cabin walls and fortified the blankets with more moss and hay. She knitted woolen socks for them both, while he helped card sheared wool so she could make more things with it.

And while her belly had grown a bit rounder and more taut, it wasn't much more than the usual bit of monthly bloat, which was easy to hide. Besides, she wore most of her clothes all the time now, two dresses layered on top of each other, a slip and a pair of woolen stockings underneath, and a woolen jacket. The hours of daylight were so short, she washed and dressed in the dark each morning and did the same at night.

They made up new rules. Attacks during sleep were off-limits, as was food, because there was so little of it, once Harlow had cut their rations. Whereas formerly they were each allotted one peck of corn per person weekly, now they were given one peck to share, along with the smallest sliver of bacon. More would be given, they were told, once they delivered portly children.

Soon, the performances stopped altogether. They saved the salt for other things. Whatever Monroe hunted from then on, he brought into the house—rabbit, squirrel, quail. From her garden plot, she added turnips, radishes, and onions. They managed a decent meal between the two of them, but she let him attribute her constant chewing of cotton root day and night to pica, a fruitless attempt to assuage her hunger.

The effort of getting sufficient food to eat was enough to make them almost friendly sometimes. But if any chummy feelings managed to develop, the Lucys quickly dashed them.

Harlow's nightly rounds were one thing. These had always happened intermittently, but these days, they were constant. At some point, nearly every evening, he made his way over to the quarters and pushed inside every house, making sure every person was present and there weren't any neighboring folks among them. In Junie and Lulu's cabin, he was usually only there a few minutes, but now, with the couples he lingered. With Monroe and Serah. With Patience and Isaac. He'd pose dirty questions, wanting updates on procreation.

And when he was tied up with duties for the new vigilance committee—all the men in the county had weekly shifts now—Lizzie filled in. On Saturday mornings, she'd barge into each cabin with a bucket of lime in a supposed fit of cleaning. When Lizzie entered Monroe and Serah's, Lizzie would take particular care to sniff the sheets and rifle through Serah's dirty laundry, looking for menstrual rags.

"Don't know why y'all insist on hiding them from me," she'd say, as she did a quick sweep over the floors, using the broom to parse through Serah's belongings, hidden behind a trunk or stacked in a corner.

Afterward, she'd hand Serah a rag and motion toward the bucket of lime. She'd watch as Serah scrubbed, pelting her with questions. "You taking care of all your wifely duties, aren't you?"

This curious behavior left no doubt about what agenda had risen to the top of the Lucys' list. They felt this most acutely on the coldest nights of the year. Long after midnight, Harlow'd show up drunk after riding with the patrol. He'd shove his way inside, and stumble toward them in bed, waving a lit pine knot with one hand, a gun in the other.

"Y'all do it, yet?" he'd say, shaking Monroe.

Say no, and he was just in time for the show.

Say yes, and he'd say, practice makes perfect. Go again.

———

FOR ONCE, MONROE AND Serah were of the same mind. They whispered all the time about killing Harlow. They worried the walls might hear them, that even the rotting logs couldn't be trusted, but they couldn't help themselves. Some nights, it was just a salve, other nights it formed a steely net in their minds— how might they do it, would they need more help than just the two of them? The drunken whooping of the vigilance committee outside would pause this talk, but any sighting of an intoxicated Harlow would unravel it. They buried roots under the steps and scoured the clearings for dark, twisted twigs whose protective power they might harness. It was widely known the effects of Conjure on white people were so-so and fairly unpredictable. No one was sure why—maybe it was the lack of pigment in their skin, the straightness of their hair, or the European gods they brought to the country. But Monroe and Serah kept laying down new tricks anyway, even when the cold weather broke, and it was time for new corn to go into the ground.

—↙—

NOTHING WORKED. NOT ON Harlow and not on the stubborn soul burrowed inside her.

In a fervor, she doubled her efforts. Too much camphor, which made her jittery, rue broke her out in tiny rashes, and juniper had no effect at all. And the days when it seemed to work were the darkest of all.

But then a sign would appear. A strong smell set her gagging; a strange flutter sent a wave of motion over her stomach. And for a full hour or more, she found herself happy. How stubborn this child was, so unwilling to abandon her.

In truth, she had never understood the maternal thing and had seen all kinds on her last farm. Women so besotted with their offspring, loss made them suicidal, and other mothers who couldn't bear to look at what came out of them, let alone hold it or feed it. She wondered now which category her own mother fell into, but she had so few memories of the woman that she had no way of knowing for sure. Her mother had been sold off when she was barely knee-high, so what she had in place of a face or a voice was what little her father had told her and a lock of the woman's hair. Nothing she had, the stories nor the lone memento, could answer the questions that overwhelmed her now.

She feared she would be like those detached mothers, and only in those brief moments of happiness did she consider that she might be the opposite. Both possibilities terrified her. And she worried that the window of time she had to persuade the stubborn spirit was surely closing.

CHAPTER TWENTY-FOUR

RIDING WITH THE PATROL a few nights a week didn't ease Harlow's mind any. If anything, it reaffirmed just how close the edge was, if his labor force ceased to grow. He was stuck with the poorest questionable sort of men—landless louts, slaveless ones, too. Each unable to afford the dues the vigilance committee required to avoid spending half the night on patrol a good portion of the goddamn week.

One cold night, he was fed up. He pulled up to the quarters and slid off his horse. His legs and backside were sore, and there was a fresh gash on one side of his face from a run-in with a low-hanging branch. He wiped a trail of blood from his cheek, while he stood there staring at the three sad leaning cabins. Nearly everything he was worth in the world was asleep in those three dilapidated buildings.

He pulled out his flask and downed a swig of whiskey, but it did nothing to tamp down the watery fury lapping inside him.

There should be double, triple the number of buildings here by now. All with bodies inside them.

He fired up his pine knot torch and charged toward Isaac and Patience's door. He burst inside, gun in hand. "Up, up, everybody up."

The two jolted awake, sitting up on their pallets.

"Y'all know the routine. When was the last time y'all made connection?"

Harlow could see it in their faces, a ripe bound anger so strong it gave off a smell. Neither spoke. Patience looked at the gun, the floor, while Isaac's face was a mask, his entire body stilled. Harlow watched him carefully. The man appeared as if frozen. Harlow couldn't find the hitch in it—his chest didn't seem to rise, his eyes didn't seem to blink. It was strange.

"Cat got your tongues? No matter. Let's get on with it."

The two didn't move.

He cocked the gun in an exaggerated fashion. In the other cabin, that was all it took for the process to get underway, but these two didn't budge.

Finally, Patience said something to the man Harlow didn't catch, in a language he didn't understand. She pulled Isaac's arm and Isaac followed her lead.

She got down on all fours and raised her nightgown. Isaac mounted her and as he began, his eyes locked on Harlow's. He grunted and pushed against her, but kept looking at Harlow, with a look so intense, Harlow felt glued down by it.

Harlow's mouth went dry, the nerves under his skin all began firing at once. His heart sped up in his chest and his groin came alive. Don't look at me, boy, he started to say, but the words wouldn't come out, just a dry stirring in his throat.

He tried to step back, raise his gun with his right hand,

but his body disobeyed. It would do nothing. Only his member raised up and paid any attention.

Isaac kept on staring, kept looking at him, through him. Harlow pulled backward and fell against the door. He then turned and rushed down the steps.

Outside, in the crisp night air, his wits returned. He grabbed his gun and started to charge back inside, but the doorway stopped him. The rectangle shape seemed to be growing somehow, now stretching and towering over him like a huge mountain.

He turned and sprinted away. When he looked back over his shoulder, all he saw was the same tiny cabin amidst the two others. He smacked himself upside the head, in the face. "Get your wits about you," he mumbled to himself as he went on. He wasn't a superstitious man, didn't believe in tales about magical niggers.

Fatigue was making his mind soft. How was anyone supposed to work all day, ride half the night, and still be of sane mind and sound body?

At the house, he locked the front door and checked the windows. He threw another log on the fire and lay down. *Sleep it away.* He almost laughed to himself, but when morning came, the night lingered on his tongue like bile. Before he opened his eyes, the first image he saw was of Isaac, the man's dark eyes boring into his. A smirk appearing on the man's lips.

CHAPTER TWENTY-FIVE

SPRING WEATHER WOULD BE SERAH'S downfall. One day, a sudden swing in temperature left her in sweaty wet clothes for hours. By the time she and the rest of the women got the first quarter of cotton into the ground, the heat had burned off, and she grew chilled to the bone. She made a beeline to her and Monroe's cabin, while Lulu and Junie argued about whose turn it was to grind that evening's corn.

She figured she had the room to herself for a good while, since Monroe often disappeared with Isaac to smoke and blow off a little steam before coming inside. She shut the cabin door and put down a piece of wood to bar it from opening. She got a fire going and then peeled off her damp clothing—the long dress and chemise. She had just stepped out of her knickers, when the door flew open and the wooden bar snapped in two.

She yanked the skirt up and held it in front of her, when Monroe stumbled into the room, a large scaly fish dangling from his hand. "Look what I got—" The words died out in his mouth.

He looked away at first, a reflex, then looked back at her, a slow recognition dawning on him.

"Get out!" she yelled, wrapping the skirt around her midsection.

He closed the door behind him and turned to face her. "That what I think it is?"

"No, now get out."

"The hell it ain't. Prove it."

"Leave," she said, stepping back away from the fire, hoping the dimness made it harder to see her.

"Naw."

The two stared at each other for a long moment. She softened her voice.

"Monroe, out . . ."

"I'll go. Show me your belly first."

Even so close to the fire, she was getting cold. Her feet, her legs. She couldn't stand there forever with the skirt wrapped around her and at the same time, she could think of no way to put it on without exposing herself.

The inevitable had arrived. She dropped the skirt and his eyes widened.

"Now get the hell out."

He shook his head and left.

She laid out her damp clothes in front of the fire. She put on a pair of dry knickers and pulled a shift over her head, and a flannel shirt. She would get dinner started and when he came back, she would talk to him plainly. But what if he was already up at Harlow's, telling the Lucys all about this recent discovery? He wasn't above it, especially if he believed they'd reward his telling with a gift of some kind.

She couldn't hold the spoon without shaking, couldn't stir the bland watery sauce she'd thrown together for the fish without spilling bits of it on the floor. She cut the turnips up, got them boiling, when Monroe came back through the door.

She was mad at herself. She should have been better prepared, she thought, but it didn't occur to her that all of her efforts against the stubborn spirit would be unsuccessful. That her body would betray her and give away the secret while there was still a secret to tell.

He moved to the table, with the fish cleaned and gutted, the stench entering the room before him. Without speaking to her, he fried it up and slammed it on the table, smoke rising up off the singed flesh. Scales glittered on his arms, his pants, his beard.

He sat down at the table and rested his arm between the pan and her. He wasn't sharing.

They sat there in silence. She ate her turnips, he his fish.

"How long you known?"

She shrugged.

"He's been a demon for months now and that would've ended it. You could've ended it," he said. "You must like it, being treated that way."

Serah shook her head. "I don't. But it ain't his business. Ain't yours neither."

"How you figure?"

"'Cause it ain't yours."

He laughed. A slow dark laugh. "And I'm supposed to believe a whore like you. You've been lying since I met you."

"Believe what you want. It ain't yours and it won't be sticking around here."

He ran a hand over his shaved scalp. "You really are touched in the head?"

"I'm sounder than I ever been."

"You harm that babe and I'll put you in the ground myself."

"So you say."

"I promise you that."

"A man of your word, huh?"

"I am."

Serah laughed. Under the tables, her knees were shaking, but she looked him in the eye. "Me and mine ain't got nothing to do with you. This spirit going home."

Monroe laughed. "And where's that, huh? Ain't no home for us niggers. No heaven or hell neither. You ain't figured that out yet?" A wild look came over his face. "Death may be better, but that still don't give you the right."

She laughed. "Why don't it? Didn't you just say you'd kill me yourself?"

"That's different. Ain't got no problem killing you to protect my kin."

"It ain't yours. I swear on my life," she said.

"But it could be."

"It ain't. I know it."

He examined her face for a long moment. "It's that no-account nigger from before? The one at the wedding?"

Serah didn't answer.

"And that man just allow you to run roughshod, huh? Allow you to kill his generations 'cause you say so?"

"He ain't here."

"So what? I ain't letting you do that."

"You don't care nothing about this baby. You just want more rations. You just want Harlow to leave us be."

"Shit, don't you?" He pushed back from the table and stood up. "Do what you want but I'm telling. Thanks to that nigger of yours, my part is done." He moved toward the door.

"Wait," she said, following behind him. She grabbed hold of his arm, but he pushed her aside easily and left.

Not long after, she set off, too, but only got as far as the loom before she heard the dogs howling. She went inside and prayed for a sign. Maybe she'd make it through the woods, protected, made invisible by the powers of her saints, but her faith was waning. She searched her mind for stories of the faithful, those who passed through a forest of demons, who swam through an ocean of sharks, but they seemed abstract, hard to hold on to. There was no tangible thing to pull from, no practice she could apply to what awaited her on either side of the Harlows' property line.

CHAPTER TWENTY-SIX

THE VISIT WAS NOW SET for the end of July. Originally, it had been March but now that there was an established school for Ollie to attend, Lizzie didn't want to rip him out of it before the term ended, she told Junie.

That was fine. Junie kept her hope contained. A manageable size, not too large that it suffocated her, but loose enough to puff up and make the days bearable. But she knew something was wrong when she was summoned early one Tuesday. When she was told to go to the house, they were sowing a second planting of corn and were only a third of the way through.

She walked past young Louisa playing on the porch and into the stuffy house. In the back bedroom, Carol was crying, and Lizzie was retching over a chamber pot, her face red and damp.

Lizzie wiped her mouth on her sleeve and looked at Junie. "It's happening again."

"What?"

Lizzie groaned. "I can't take another. Lord forgive me. Not right now. Not so soon." Lizzie shot a weary glance at Carol.

Junie wet a towel with water from a nearby pitcher and mopped Lizzie's face. She put the chamber pot near the door and ushered Lizzie into bed. "You sure that's the problem?"

"Sure as my hand. My monthly's late. It's almost always near the fourth, but May is nearly over and not a goddamn streak," Lizzie said.

Junie pulled the blanket up over Lizzie's shoulders and then pulled Carol into her lap.

"Finish feeding her," Lizzie said, motioning to a bowl of gruel near the manger.

Junie fed Carol a mouthful. "Mmm, that's good, ain't it?"

Carol bounced from side to side, as if she was trying to nod.

"You talk to her like she can understand you," Lizzie grumbled.

"I always talked to my babies when I fed them. We had some of the best talks then . . ." Junie trailed off, suddenly embarrassed for sharing that thought aloud.

But Lizzie wasn't listening. She was grumbling still, mainly to herself. "Stuck like a pig all over again. And I was so careful. I wrote all the way to New York and paid nearly ten dollars for those fancy pills they sell up there. Dr. Vinter's or something. Guaranteed to make sure your monthly arrives like clockwork! Pure hogwash."

"Aww, it won't be so bad," Junie said, a sinking feeling spreading out over her abdomen. "Fresh air will help. Besides, motion sick, baby sick, it's all the same. You just have to keep moving. The trip will be just the change you need."

"Optimism never was your strong suit," Lizzie said dryly. "She done?"

Carol seemed to be playing now, with the spoon, a bit of

gruel dribbling down her chest. Junie dabbed at the spill with a rag.

"I'll write Mason tomorrow," Lizzie said. "Hopefully, he'll be able to get a refund. And maybe we can go next year. Definitely next year."

The sinking feeling in Junie's abdomen tightened. Next year. There would be no next year or the year after that, she knew. Another infant would make sure of it.

Lizzie might as well have said next decade or century even. The years would stack, and Death would come close, tapping one forehead after another, and soon her children would fall to another member of Lizzie's rotten lineage or be sold at estate.

If Junie was in her right mind at that moment, she would have left, would have gone out into the morning and let her confusion and rage meet the sun, but she was glued to the chair, the gassy child gurgling on her knee.

Lizzie continued her grumbling. "I should sue those Dr. Vinter's quacks. Make them reimburse Mason."

"Can't the pig be unstuck?"

"Huh?"

"I said can't the pig be unstuck?" Junie said louder. "Dr. Vint's can't be the only way to fix your problem."

"What you saying, gal?"

"I'm just asking. Every year, when we kill the hogs, there are certain ways we go about the slaughter. The hog's got to be boiled so the hair can be removed. The hind legs got to be pinned, and the body hung high off the ground, so that first cut down the belly can be done clean. Now, we do it that way, but I'm sure every farmer round here got his own way of doing it, a way he swears is better than the man next to him."

"So?"

"So, are you a sow or a person? 'Cause when a sow is stuck

in the mud, she stuck, but a person has a mind, and all kinds of ability to unstick themselves in whatever mud trying to hold them back. Now maybe I'm speaking out of turn, but it seems like you acting more like a sow than a person these days and have been for a long while."

Lizzie's face turned red. "I should flay your hide, talking to me that way."

"Maybe so, but I'm just saying what cousin Beatrice would say if she were here."

Lizzie didn't answer. She turned her face to the pillow.

Carol began squirming. Junie pulled the baby into her arms and softly began singing a lullaby. A song she knew Lizzie would remember from back home, one they both heard Junie's mother sing many times. "Go to sleep, little baby. Mama went away and she told me to stay and take good care of this baby." She sang another verse and then stopped. The room grew silent and heavy. Junie could feel this one simple dream of hers moving past her, out toward the horizon, climbing farther and farther away in the sky.

"Sing it again," Lizzie said.

Junie sang the song again, the child now asleep. When she finished, Lizzie raised her head, her eyes watery. "I want to go home."

"I know you do."

"I don't want to be stuck," Lizzie whispered.

Junie grew still, barely moving, holding her breath.

"How do I unstick myself?" Lizzie continued.

Junie's mind raced, trying to remember who might have a stash of cotton root hidden somewhere. After the last raid, she burned most of hers. But she couldn't offer up the cotton root, could she?

Junie shrugged. "I'm not privy to those things but I can ask around."

"Would Nan know something I could use?" Lizzie asked.

"She may. I can ask her for you," Junie said.

"But you wouldn't say it was me asking, would you?"

"'Course not." Junie slowly stood up and eased Carol down in the manger. "Y'all rest." Her stomach was roiling. Her performance of indifference was two seconds from buckling. She tucked the blanket around the baby and slid out of the room.

She walked out the front door, a warm breeze hitting her in the face. It wasn't refreshing, but it felt steadying a bit. She realized then she was drenched with sweat. She walked on down farm, out of the sight of the small leaning house.

CHAPTER TWENTY-SEVEN

SERAH HAD TO DIG THE hole herself. A small hole, about a foot deep and a foot wide, just large enough for her belly to fit into. Afterward, she was forced to lie down on top of the hole and then lashed fifteen times with a black snake whip. This was considered light, as it wasn't the customary forty lashes. Here, she put the babe in the earth. Pressed it into the ground, the soil making one shield, her back another. It seemed like an omen.

According to the Lucys, she had finally pushed them to the breaking point. Weeks ago, after Monroe blabbed about the pregnancy and what she had said to him, the Lucys brought her into the house to be under their watch at all times. For them, this seemed a perfect solution to fill in the gap of cooking and housework needed when Nan was away catching babies. However, Serah couldn't abide it. The closeness of the walls, the constant yapping demands of the Lucys, the lack of any sliver of privacy. The proximity was suffocating, not to mention painful.

She knew the Lucys had horrible tempers, but being within arm's reach of them now meant a different level of vigilance. They were hitters—slappers, pinchers, projectile throwers. It didn't help that she was doing everything in her power to be sent back out to the quarters. She burned up meals, singed nearly every piece of ironing, let the wash dry streaky and marked with yellow clay soap. And to add insult to it all, she'd sometimes disappear for hours—going to the well for water and proceeding on past it, just to hide out in the loom for a few moments of peace. The last straw was a half-raw chicken, pink and still laden with feathers, that she served on a plate to a table full of guests.

Facedown in the earth, Serah wondered if what Monroe said was correct. Maybe she was touched. Half-crazy. Moon-sick. Heat-stroked. She had wanted the child in the earth and here it was.

———

AFTERWARD, NAN GREASED HER back with hog lard to ease off the strips of clothing stuck to the open wounds, then coated it with a cool salve. Serah felt dizzy from the pain and the sedative tea Nan gave her. It brought on a strange slippery blackness that came and went. She heard Nan talking, but she couldn't quite hold the thread of her speech.

"They used to tell us when we were little, these marks came from wolves. The long stripes were from the claws and that if we didn't mind, or stay close to home, the wolves would come get us and carry us off into the mountains."

"Did y'all believe them?"

"Sure, for a while. We'd hear the dogs howling at night. And Mama say, 'See, look, they hunting now.' It was a long time before I realized she didn't mean the ones on four legs." Nan chuckled. "Your people never told you that?"

"Nah, but I'd believed it, if they had. You tell your children that?" Serah asked.

"Sure, every living one."

Serah had never heard Nan speak of her children. She tried to raise her head to get a better look at Nan's face, but she couldn't.

"How many children you have, Nan?" Serah mumbled.

"Oh, I don't know. Dozens of children. A hundred grand-children maybe." Nan raised up her walking stick and squinted at it, one side lined with tally marks.

"I don't mean how many babies did you catch? I mean your *own* children . . ."

"They all my children."

All? Before Serah could get her next question out, the heavy black sleep rose up and snatched her again.

CHAPTER TWENTY-EIGHT

One Sunday morning, Junie invited herself on one of Nan's medicine walks. She lied and told Nan she wasn't looking for anything in particular, just wanted the company. "Also, I figured you could use the help . . ." she said, letting her voice trail off, motioning to Nan's walking stick.

Junie had never lied to Nan before, but she would do so now because she knew the old woman would talk her out of what needed to be done. And she didn't need much from Nan, just a bit of guidance in the right direction. She knew there were things other than cotton root she could use. Had heard Serah speak about other remedies with middling results, but she didn't have time for middling. She needed something sure.

She watched Nan approach a cluster of tall spindly plants surrounding a cropping of bushes. Nan moved near them, touched them slowly, surveying the leaves and the underbrush, before pulling out her mattock. She gently dug up the plant, root and all, and wrapped it up in a rag.

"Pokeweed? I thought you stopped using that."

"Nah, I'm just more careful now. It's the best thing I can find for rheumatism."

"What else can you use it for?"

"I only use it for that," said Nan. "'Less I'm cooking up the leaves."

"What other folks use it for?"

"Don't know. You have to ask them."

Hmph, Junie thought. She'd have to try another tactic.

They moved deeper into the trees. Nan paused at a sassafras tree, the leaves sickly and drooping from the heat. Nan circled the tree and peered at it, before peeling a few pieces of bark from it. "Thank you," she whispered, tapping the trunk with her fingers.

Junie stood on the other side of the tree, pulling down a leaf, its shape like the cloven hoof of an animal. "Bird told me," she began flatly, "the cotton root didn't work for her no more. Wonder what else she could have tried."

"Heard she tried most everything." Nan shrugged. "Sometimes a spirit can't be turned back."

"What else she try?"

"A heap of things. As you can tell, none of them worked."

"Would any of them have worked? I mean if the spirit was willing."

"Maybe. But then, you don't need much, if the spirit is willing."

"What you need then?"

"Anything that'll bring down the blood probably fix it."

"Like snakeroot?"

Nan shook her head. "Tansy's better, but hard to find out this way." Nan pointed to a tall hairy stem with tiny leaves. "Like this pudge grass could work. But it can be poisonous, likely to kill somebody if it ain't picked at the right time."

Junie stared at the plant and moved closer to it. What were the odds? she wondered. There had to be other things.

"You hurting? You need something?" Nan asked.

Junie shook her head. "Just wondering."

"Never seen you wonder 'bout such things before? Don't tell me you're caught."

Junie laughed. "Me? Hell naw."

"'Cause the remedy you got is still the best thing. Don't let Bird screwing it up make you think different."

"I ain't caught."

"Alright."

"But what if ain't me?"

"Then tell whoever what I told you."

"What if it was a Lucy?"

"Then I'd let Gabriel and Lucifer sort it out among themselves."

"Even if it means another Lucy in this world," said Junie. "Another Lucy whose first breath will have them looking at us again." Junie picked up a leaf and began rolling it between her palms. "They may even bring that breeding nigger back. Bring him 'round and make us all lie with him again. Well, not all of us . . ."

Junie's words hung in the air. An accusation. A reminder to Nan that she had been spared. Junie hadn't planned on dredging all that up, but if it got her the aid she needed, then she would. She studied Nan's face, the old woman's mouth now drawn into a tight line. "He was awful, remember?"

"You laying that at my feet?" Nan said.

"Not the first time, maybe."

Nan sucked in a breath, as if she had been struck. She turned away from Junie and began walking.

Junie could have told her the truth. Children were one of the few things Nan rarely spoke about. And as such, she knew the old woman would understand the hunger inside her, but she couldn't say it. She couldn't even mention the trip aloud, not outside of Lizzie's bedroom. Outside of those four walls, it sounded like space travel, like some phantasmic dream she had made up. Nan would only unravel it.

Guilt was more reliable. Nan was one of those souls who took on too much responsibility for those around her. Every babe she delivered, every head she dotted with oil and washed, every lone body she healed with herbs and roots, she carried with her somehow. It was a thing Junie had always warned her about. All that webbing and tethering, tangling her up so.

Nan stopped and bent down in front of another tall weed, hairy like the last one. "When it sprouts, maybe. Just the leaves and flowers should do little harm. The oil is the real killer." She stood up slowly, massaging her hip, then raised her eyes to Junie, with a cold and squinted glare.

Junie felt like she had been pierced, but she didn't flinch. Instead, she met Nan's hard gaze with a stony one of her own.

"I'll bring it when it's ready," Nan said. "But after that, we square. Don't ask me again. For that, or nothing else. And if you poison her, don't look to me for help."

Nan began walking again and didn't say another word to Junie the whole way back. Junie followed behind her, her eyes stinging, the yellow sky a shifting blur. She would beg the old woman's forgiveness later, she vowed. After the trip.

After the trip, she'd take it all back.

NAN WAS TRUE TO her word. A few days later, she brought a bundle of clippings of the plant to Junie. Her manner was cold, but she told Junie how to prepare them and how often to administer them.

Junie soaked the leaves and purple flowers in water for hours, then boiled them down a few hours more, and then gave Lizzie the decoction. She made Lizzie this tea twice a day for almost a week, after which Lizzie began spotting. Not a full flow, but enough to signal that maybe the remedy was working. Maybe any day now, a full flow would course down the white woman's thighs, and their plans for the trip would be back on.

The spotting disappeared, but a full flow never followed. Junie went back to Nan to ask for more of the plant, but Nan didn't answer, didn't even acknowledge she heard Junie speaking to her. Instead, she went on chopping onions with renewed vigor.

Junie wandered out there herself, into the woods one morning, but she couldn't tell one leaf from another. So many things looked alike. She remembered the area but couldn't remember the exact plant. Not to mention, she didn't see the little purple flowers anywhere. Instead, she looked for a bare spot where Nan would have uprooted the plant and found a bare patch covered over with grass, but it was hard to tell if it was anything more than some animal's hiding place.

She kept walking until she found a spindly plant with leaves with tiny blue buds that looked similar. She tried whispering to it, asking it as she had seen Nan do, but before she could even get the question fully formed in her mind, she stopped. If it said no, would it change her mind? It wouldn't. Better not ask, then. And what about the possibility of it turning poisonous already? Nan didn't tell her anything more about the timing or how to handle the toxic parts of the plant.

It made her furious, not knowing. She was so close to the

goal. And it had been going better than she expected. Lizzie hadn't complained or fought about drinking the bitter decoction. She'd drink it all down. She'd hand back the cup to Junie and say, "It must be working now. I feel awful."

Junie dug up the plant and prayed for the best.

She was optimistic until she pestled the blue buds some hours later. It didn't smell the same, but she went on, soaked the leaves and flowers, and then set them to boiling. The smell was undeniably different but hard to describe. Less pungent and more woodsy. She tasted a spoonful, then another. It was bitter but not like she remembered.

She couldn't risk using it. She'd have to go back to Nan, and maybe she'd tell her the truth this time. She fretted about it all through the morning's hoeing. And when the women came in for their midmorning meal, Junie went looking for her, but Nan wasn't there.

Later, after work, when Junie came to the yard to grind her corn, Nan still wasn't there. She pushed her way into the cook-house, where she found Serah scrubbing the pots.

"Where's Nan?"

Serah didn't say anything at first, balancing the pot on her large belly while she scrubbed at a stubborn spot with a wet rag. The room was dim and smoky as always, and she couldn't see the girl's face really, only her set, stubborn jaw. She wondered what Nan might have told her.

"What that old heifer say?"

Serah looked at her blankly. "She went to catch a baby on the Ryans' farm. Said she be there a few days, I think."

"Oh. That all?"

"Yeah. You alright? You look funny?"

Junie nodded. "The Ryans? Whereabouts?"

Serah shrugged. "New people, I hear. Friends of the Lucys

some ways from here. They came and got her. But I tell her you looking for her."

"Don't bother," Junie said, stumbling outside. Dusk was falling and the balmy weather was hot and sticky, like the inside of a closed mouth.

It had been a full day and a half since she had given Lizzie her last dose and she needed another. Now.

—⊷

SERAH BEGAN TO WORRY the babe would never come out. Her big widening belly would just continue to expand, until it was able to touch the opposite wall of any room she found herself in. The child would continue to grow and grow inside her, choosing to remain there.

Things ached and swelled. Her back, her feet, her fingers. Her vision blurred; her breasts leaked. A full-scale mutiny from scalp to toenail. And sometimes, it seemed just as likely that it would be she who was expelled, instead of the other way around, the soul having taken over her body altogether. As frightening as that was, the other possibility seemed just as frightening. Any day now, the child would come out, and how easily it might be removed from her sight.

That was the new fear. While her plan to be discharged from the Lucys' house had not worked in the short-term, it seemed a likely possibility once she had the child. But what then? She had no inkling of their plans or inclinations, so she had to do something.

When she stepped outside of the Lucys' house to dump last night's chamber pots and slop jars, she kept on going. She went down farm first and started to knock on Patience's door, but she stopped herself. Isaac must have heard her on the steps for he flung open the door and allowed her inside. He said something to Patience in a tongue Serah didn't recognize. Patience laughed and answered him.

Serah felt the air in the room shift as she entered. She had breached something, she knew, but she went on with her proposal. "Going to see Mariah. Come with me?"

Patience squinted at her for a long moment and shook her head. "The woman's a fake."

Isaac spoke up again, the lilting consonants puzzling Serah. "What he say?" Serah asked.

Patience laughed again. "He say he thinks she's a fake, too."

"Why didn't he just say that, then?"

"He done with English. Says it like poison. Soils the mind."

"And you understand him?"

"More and more."

Serah looked at the two with bewilderment, before focusing her gaze on Patience. "Just come along for the trip. You don't have to see her."

Isaac answered again, in the same musical tongue.

"Nobody was asking you," Serah shot back at him. She turned to Patience, a pleading expression on her face.

Patience shook her head. "You be careful out there."

Isaac opened the door, and just like that, she was back outside on the steps, the door shut firmly in her face. She could still hear Patience laughing. What a unit they seemed to be now. She felt a pang of something, in the back of her throat, but ignored it and hurried on down the steps toward the creek.

At Mariah's, lucky for her, no one was waiting. Elias ushered her inside and she sat down across from the woman. Before Mariah could greet her or even say anything about her big belly, she smacked a handful of blue beads on the table. "Shore up the binding to Noah. And can you bind us to the child, too?"

The beads rolled off the table and onto the floor, but neither Serah nor Mariah moved. Elias picked up the beads, put them on the table, and left the room.

"Sorry. Can't really bind the child to you while it's in there. But if I shore up the binding between you two, maybe it'll help."

Mariah cut Serah's finger, adding blood to the frayed bracelet. The rest of the ritual was a blur. Serah grew light-headed, the busy patterns from the curtain spreading out into a hazy overlay of squiggly lines and circles.

Elias put her on his mule and carried her home. She was housebound again after that, for much of June, but when the cut on her finger ached, she wondered if Mariah was out there, somewhere, calling Noah back. And she'd join in, wherever she was, whispering words she didn't even remember Mariah saying. "Shake-a-canna, Rake-a-canna, bring Noah Dobson back to me."

CHAPTER TWENTY-NINE

JULY WAS A SCORCHER IN ways we couldn't have imagined. The air was hot and suffocating, a wavy wall of thick heat that made it hard to breathe. It felt like putting one's face over an open flame. Crops withered and died; hapless birds rushed into dark houses and barns, breaking their necks. Even in the shade, it was a piping 110 degrees.

We spent those super-hot days in the loom, trying not to faint while spinning thread. The wavy hot air brought bad news that lay suspended in the haze.

Buildings were combusting. A series of fires lit up the state. Half of downtown Dallas went up in flames, and forty miles away in Denton, too. Not to mention Pilot Point, Ladonia, Milford, Sulfur Springs, Fort Worth, Honey Grove, and Waxahachie. All over the course of one long weekend.

We heard the Lucys talking about it, this alphabet of fires spreading like a song. In a matter of days, culprits were named.

The first: newfangled prairie matches. One man said he saw a whole box burst into flames before his very eyes.

Another theory soon emerged in the tense shadow of scorched buildings. A coerced confession from a slave near Crill Miller's farm outside Dallas became a siren call. A new vigilance committee was formed, and every Negro near Miller's farm was interrogated until the right answers were given, and the full view of a conspiratorial plot began to unfurl under a dense white sky.

Men we knew who ran the drays long distances, hauling cotton and timber and wheat, told us what they heard at the mills and the ports. Some were even interrogated and beaten, accused of collusion in a great plot with Northern abolitionists who aimed to destroy the state by fire and make way for insurrection.

We asked them more questions, but they were unwilling to tell us more, warning us how quickly word was spreading from county to county. How they could barely do their hauls without constant checks of their passes, how often they were relieved of their tools.

"Don't repeat what I say here," a drayman would say to one of us. "Of course not," we'd lie. It wasn't a big lie, because we'd only tell one another, under the tree where we still gathered sometimes. And in the dark, looking up at the web of branches under the moon, we'd piece together these bits until a strange thread emerged. A new panic spreading like the flu.

JUNIE HAD NO CHOICE: this time, she'd have to use the cotton root to make Lizzie's tea. It seemed likely that Lizzie might complain about the difference in taste, but she could make something up, about how this new ingredient was important at this stage. She set it boiling in the cookhouse and asked Serah to keep an eye on it, as she knew the girl wouldn't press her and would simply do what she was told.

During the morning meal break, she removed it from the heat and let it cool. Once the temperature had lessened, she strained the liquid and poured it into a small pitcher, before carrying it into the Lucys' house. She knocked on the bedroom door, where Lizzie was rushing around, packing some of Carol's things—diapers, booties, rag bibs. Junie set the small pitcher on the table, as she had done nearly every day for the last two weeks. "This batch may taste a bit different. Boiled it longer this time."

A quizzical look spread across Lizzie's face. Junie felt her legs stiffen, her mouth now dry. She wasn't sure she had answers ready for whatever questions were coming.

Lizzie went over to the pitcher and peered down inside it. She leaned over and sniffed, scrunching up her nose. She rose and gave Junie a pointed look.

Junie froze. Any day now, she was sure the white woman would turn on her. Lizzie would gag on the vile liquid and accuse her of trying to poison her. If not that, then later, when the tea worked, the woman would grow regretful and have her strung up for murder. And if the remedy didn't take, she'd be a liar, a godless root worker who tried to contaminate the woman's mind against Christ, and whatever burden the child became would somehow fall upon Junie's shoulders.

Every day, she pushed these scenarios from her mind, forced herself to only picture the large boat, rocking precariously down a narrow river. Only the hazy vision of her children kept her feet moving, her mouth lying. A stack of lies so tall she worried they'd soon topple over.

"I told you I'm supposed to go to the Suttons' for Emmaline's lying-in," Lizzie said. "But maybe I'll just send word that I don't feel up to it. It can't be safe traveling right now."

Lizzie sat down for a moment. She drank a few sips of the liquid. "Argh, it doesn't get better, does it?"

There was a loud crash in the front room of the house, followed by Harlow bellowing loudly, and the front door slamming. Junie couldn't decipher what he had been yelling, but it jolted Lizzie to her feet, muttering under her breath.

"Probably won't be back from the Suttons' until tomorrow, so I'll need more than that," Lizzie said, her eyes on the bedroom door.

"That's all I got now."

Lizzie rifled through the drawers. "No matter, I guess. I couldn't travel with all that liquid no way. Just bring me the clippings and I'll boil them myself while I'm over there."

Junie felt stunned. Like time had sped up and she was trying to catch up to it.

"Don't just stand there. Go get 'em. The Suttons' wagon will be here soon."

Her mind spun for an excuse, but Lizzie just waved her away. Junie left the room and went out of the house. Her options were few. She could ignore the ask and just return to the fields, or risk giving Lizzie what she requested, a risk that seemed less perilous the more she thought about it. The bigger question was another missed dose. While Junie may not have fully understood the workings of plants and how they affected the body, the one thing she knew for certain was that consistency was key. Like prayer, like tending crops, like raising animals, little worked without regular repetition.

She went to the cookhouse, where a sack of the roots lay hidden underneath the table. She had planned to soak another batch for Lizzie's next dose, but now she wondered what was the danger in handing some clippings over? It's not like Lizzie knew what they were by sight. Of all the tasks Lizzie supervised or tackled with her own hands, the planting of cotton wasn't one of them. Lizzie might know something about cooking or sewing, weaving or canning. And sure, a few times a year, she wandered down to a weigh-in and watched the seed cotton be sacked and measured, before being taken over to a neighbor's gin. Maybe she had even observed Harlow bringing in new seeds, opening pouches of the latest breeds to try, but from the house where she spent most of her days, they were only visible in full bloom. Without the wispy white heads or the spiky hard receptacles that attached them to reedy stalks, they looked like most anything else, like any twig littering the forest floor.

And so, Junie wrapped a portion of the roots in a rag after checking them first for any telltale signs, any remnants of the boll or the head, making sure it looked like nothing more than kindling. She made a tight fist-size bundle and took them into the house, where she placed them next to Carol's diapers. Lizzie nodded and went back to trying to iron the wrinkles out of her best dress.

———

THE SUTTONS' DIM COOL house should have felt like a respite to Lizzie. More than a handful of women were there already, some gossiping over iced tea and lemonade, while others tended to Emmaline, sweating and uncomfortable in a thin nightgown. The women moved easily from bedroom to parlor and back again, while two house girls brought in iced water and coffee, hot water, and towels. Emmaline had in the galley a midwife *and* a doctor at her service. The doctor was some Harvard-educated thin wisp of a man who barely looked old enough to shave, while the midwife was a stocky older German woman with a thick accent and a collapsible chair she carried from room to room, as if it would disappear the moment it left her sight.

While Lizzie should have felt relieved to sit in the parlor, sipping ice water under the vigorous fanning of an adolescent house girl, all she felt was a familiar jealousy even she was tired of. She swirled the cool glass, marveling at the fantastic clinking sound the ice made and the cold shards that lay alive on her tongue. Emmaline still had ice, in this heat. Of course, the Suttons had their own icehouse, but after a month of this weather, she couldn't fathom how they managed to keep anything frozen. If the house girl had leaned over and said a magical fairy delivered it, Lizzie would have believed her.

Carol squirmed in her lap, sucking from a cold wet towel, but the child didn't scream. Even if she did, the Suttons were prepared for that eventuality. A wet nurse was on standby, Emmaline's sister assured Lizzie when she first arrived. "Ready whenever you need," the sister sang, as Carol bucked and shrieked in Lizzie's arms. Lizzie stretched her lips wide in the appearance of a smile, but once she was led into the breezy parlor, and offered a seat next to a mountain of pastries on a silver tray, she decided then that she would spend most of the lying-in opposite that fanning house girl, instead of near Emmaline's swampy bedside.

Lizzie told herself it was because of the smugness on the sister's face, but in truth, she walked in with the intention to do as little as possible. She had no interest in propping up Emmaline in one uncomfortable position after another, while the woman panted and heaved in her face. She didn't want to mop down Emmaline's sweaty limbs with a fresh washcloth or offer middling advice about "bearing pains," or any of the other hundred tasks women came to do at these affairs.

She could hear them now down the hallway, a rising nervous chatter that permeated the house like the drone of a beehive. It wasn't a selective group of women. Any woman nearby was invited and probably a handful more than usual, as it was expected that some would be too fearful to make the trip.

She let herself doze off, only waking when the other women began filing into the parlor and taking seats alongside her. The doctor had chased them out of the bedroom, complaining about how he couldn't do his job with a bunch of meddling biddies in the way. "You shouldn't have come," he told them.

If they were upset in the moment, they were no longer. Now, in front of Lizzie, they mocked him. His flustered, blushing face. How he was downy like a baby, a veritable coating of blond fuzz on his face and neck. How he asked them to help Emmaline back into her clothes, instead of the sheer nightgown she was in when he arrived.

"Modesty is of the utmost importance," he told them, before stepping outside and fastening a long white cloth around his neck.

"What he need that bib for?" A brown-haired woman asked the group.

"Decency. He's supposed to touch without looking, you know."

A few of the women tittered.

"Well, he *is* a child. I declare I got girdles older than him."

"He probably never even seen one up close. Just them scary drawings in dusty textbooks."

"Fancy college or not, I do think it's improper. Some strange man that ain't her husband down there rooting around."

Another woman nodded vigorously. "And wasn't it a school way up north? Don't seem like Sutton to let some strange Northerner in his house, let alone mess with his wife."

"You sound like those nuts in Dallas."

"You must not read the papers."

"I read plenty. Since when every Yankee John Brown? Ran

that last cobbler out of town over an accident of birth. I paid him good money to fix my best pair of boots and now I'll never get them back or the cash I gave him."

"Ladies, I do think we have a bona fide abolitionist in our midst," a blond woman said, letting out a low whistle.

"You take that back, Amelia."

A loud cough from above interrupted the growing hubbub. The doctor stood in the doorway. "Would one of you ladies mind coming in for a spell? It's not proper for me to be alone with Mrs. Sutton."

No one moved, as everyone was eager to see how the two women would resolve what was now fraught and heavy between them.

"Go on, Lizzie," another woman piped up. "You've been hiding out here all afternoon."

All eyes turned to Lizzie, and she directed her gaze to Carol, asleep on the floor, a blanket spread out underneath her.

"She's fine. We'll call you if she wakes up."

The intensity of their pointed gaze pushed Lizzie to her feet, and she nodded, suddenly wanting nothing more than to get away from them all. She followed the doctor to the bedroom.

———

LIZZIE MADE A HORRIBLE witness. She sat in the corner, with her face turned away most of the time. She didn't talk to Emmaline much, didn't hold her hand or mop the sweat away from her face. She didn't even watch the doctor really, stiff and kneeling, one hand wandering around under a puddle of fabric with Emmaline turned on her side, so the two didn't have to look at each other.

In between questions, he rambled on, about the weather and

heat, about a new mill being erected in the county. A stream of inane conversation, about building materials—pine, white oak, cottonwood, and the rumor of a coming railroad, while the woman grunted and panted, sometimes crying out in pain.

Lizzie couldn't keep her thoughts together, and she made an excuse to escape, to send another woman in to take her place. He nodded and she sprung up and bounded toward the door. For a moment, she was ashamed that she couldn't even hold up her end of the bargain. She should at least be able to play the role, to dither and help and gossip and sew. Or even better, to get closer, to assist the man, to unleash a stream of chatter that might assuage the redness in his face and loosen up some free medical advice. Was she bypassing an opportunity to solve her most urgent problem?

The ice water and cooling fans were just a bonus. What she really needed was some medical know-how. Whatever Junie had given her wasn't working. There were moments where she felt grateful, as she knew this time everything would be easier. Serah would wean hers early and she'd finally have a wet nurse of her own for as long as she needed. But she couldn't shake the feeling that it was too soon. She was still apprehensive, though she felt like she shouldn't be. After all, there were women she knew who had a baby every eighteen months, like clockwork. But she didn't feel like she had the constitution for it. After four deliveries, her body already seemed so different. There were all kinds of changes she didn't know how to explain or who even to explain them to. The women in the parlor still felt too far away for that. It was at these times she missed her mother and sisters most. Were these strange fatigues and fevers common? Was it normal to have a bladder that leaked like a sieve or seemed to hold no more than the smallest cup of water? Or for her uterus to slide so low she swore she could feel it peeking out when she peed?

Not to mention her breasts. She feared another babe barreling through would split her in half. Somedays, the fear was muscular. So much so that when Charles moved against her at night, her whole body snapped shut.

She sucked in some air and settled herself back on the chair.

"Dr. Coleson?"

He shushed her, fumbling with his pocket watch, Emmaline crying out in great pain again.

"Ah, that's it. About seven minutes apart, it seems."

"Oh, I can keep time for you." Lizzie gave him a weak smile and offered her hand. He gave her the watch, and she moved her chair a bit closer to the bed.

With a bit of delicacy, she moved the conversation ever closer to points of relevance. Never mind about the pine and white oak of the new mill, or the precise probable location of the railroad post. Instead, how long had he been man midwifing? And if a woman did find herself caught, but she worried her constitution was too weak from the last birth, was there something she could do, to stave it off awhile? Weren't there such methods? Midwives said there were, but he must know better than them old grannies and such. A learned man of science such as himself, more astute, with more knowledge in his left foot than all of them put together.

He blushed, but this time, a different kind of blushing. He puffed his chest out, wiped his damp hands on a rag, and looked her in the eye. "Midwives can't do what we do. They're alright in a pinch, I suppose, but if there's a breech or a more complicated matter, they aren't much use."

"I had this case once"—he leaned toward her now—"where the uterus closed around the fetus like a vise. Everything stopped. The patient was in labor, I could hear her, whenever I stepped outside to talk to her husband, but soon as I came back in, the

uterus tightened like a tobacco plug. What's an old midwife going to do with that? But you see, I got a whole bag of tools at
my disposal." He leaned over and pulled out a metal tool with a
twisted head. He dropped his voice to a whisper, "I had to pry
her open like a walnut. But after that, smooth sailing. Baby came
right on out."

Lizzie couldn't remove her eyes from that metal tool, how
much it resembled cutlery, something used to carve a slice of ham.
She felt her body grow heavy and she sat back firmly onto the
chair, as if it was threatening to slide out from underneath her.

"It's all a matter of balance. Midwives don't understand that,"
he went on. "The four humors: phlegm, black bile, yellow bile,
and blood are the keys to good health. And in females, restor-
ing the menses will solve most problems. Its disappearance is a
telltale sign of imbalance. The human body is more complicated
than we realize, I always say. More delicate, too."

He turned back to Emmaline, who was breathing heavily,
her eyes shut tight.

"What time is it?" he asked Lizzie.

Lizzie shook her head, counting. "Eight minutes?"

"That can't be right."

She handed back the watch and stood up.

He was still fiddling with it when she moved toward the
door.

"Need a break? Send in another, won't you?" he hollered as
she pulled the door shut behind her.

The hive energy of the women was farther down the hall.
Lizzie turned and went the opposite way, back out the front
door. It was dark now, but the moon was bright. It was still unearthly hot, a gust of heat smacking her in the face.

The German midwife, who was sitting in a rocker, jumped
up as Lizzie stepped onto the porch. She was short, with unruly

gray hair she wore tucked in a loose bun. The collapsible chair leaned against the front of the house.

"It's just me," Lizzie said, waving the woman to sit back down.

The midwife settled back into the rocker, smoothing down her long skirt. "How is she?"

"Alright, I guess. She'd probably feel better if you were in there."

The midwife shook her head. "With him?" Her bottom lip turned up into a nasty sneer. "*Nein danke.*"

Lizzie sat down in a rocker next to the midwife.

"She wants me, but husband wants flashy doctor. He win."

Lizzie laughed. "That sounds familiar."

For a long moment, they were quiet in the dark of the porch, watching the wind shift the dry shriveled stalks of what was left of the Suttons' garden. It was even more haunting in the dark, the loose pale sprigs waving like bony figures from the beyond.

Dogs howled, followed by shouting and whistling.

Both women sat up on the edge of their chairs. The patrol was out, circling the area.

"She pushing yet?" the midwife asked.

"No, seemed like the bearing pains were getting further apart."

"Hmph."

"I may have got the timing mixed up, though."

"No, you're right. I've been listening the whole time." The midwife knocked on the wall behind the two rockers. "When your countrymen are quiet, I can hear her just fine." She pulled a folded cloth out of her pocket and unraveled it in her lap, revealing a tangle of dry reedy twigs.

"What's that?"

"Cotton root. It speeds up the bearing pains."

"Oh, like from a cottonwood tree?"

The midwife shook her head. "No, from the crop. If you find yourself troubled and you need to bring on the red king, it works for that, too." She separated a fistful of twigs out and wrapped up the rest, sticking the remainder back in her pocket.

Lizzie cocked her head to the side and stared.

The midwife laughed at the look on Lizzie's face. "I hear the *schwarzes* swear by it. All the time, they chew and chew. It's a wonder y'all have any left." She stood up and moved closer to the house. "She's too quiet."

But Lizzie wasn't listening. She was still following the bundle of twigs in the midwife's fist, her mind spinning a million incoherent thoughts. In a rush, she had tucked the clippings Junie had given her in a sack with Carol's clothes. Maybe here was a better solution.

The midwife pulled open the door.

"Wait," Lizzie said. "Can I have a little? Of the cotton root?"

The midwife nodded. "Once I get Mrs. Sutton on her way, you can have whatever's left."

———

A PICTURE WAS FORMING in Lizzie's mind, but it didn't crystallize until hours later. Until after the midwife had muscled the baffled doctor out and reinstated the party of women. After Emmaline squatted on the collapsible chair, a half-moon cut out of its base, her sister holding one arm, the blond woman holding the other. A slimy head emerged from the fleshy opening and into the midwife's ready hands. An audible cheer went up in the room. Lizzie watched it all, disinterested in the corner, waiting for the moment when the tangle of roots would be handed over to her.

Once Emmaline was cleaned up and the bedding changed, the baby cleaned and dressed, the bundle of twigs was finally hers. She thanked the midwife and slipped off to the empty parlor, where she opened the bundle and compared them against the clippings Junie had given her.

They were identical in color, in slimness, plus similar indentations and discolorations where the limbs had been broken off. She stuck one of the bony twigs from the midwife into her mouth and chewed it, as if it were a delicious dessert she had been waiting for all day. She chewed it over and over until the tough stem broke down into a soft grainy pulp, then spit the mass into her hand. The smell that wafted from it was musky and slightly nauseating. She did this again with a twig from the tangle Junie had given her. They tasted the same, smelled the same.

And more than that, she couldn't shake how familiar the scent was. Serah smelled like that, as did Patience and Lulu. Junie sometimes, but not all the time. She assumed it was a shared bodily odor among them, some mixture of sweat and soil. With her tongue, she could feel a chalky film covering her teeth. She scraped a front tooth with her fingernail, and buried underneath was a yellow substance.

She moved closer to the table, where she pulled the pitcher and plates off the tin tray, and then held up the tray to look at her reflection. She opened her mouth wide and saw her teeth speckled with yellow grit. The tray slipped from her hands.

That speckle of yellow grit. That, too, was familiar. A strange interaction in the yard one summer. She had seen Serah outside, hanging the family's laundry, and she had caught the girl chewing yellow clay. She remembered the girl had said it was to stave off hunger and she never forgot it, because the answer always unnerved her. Sure, she could write off pica as just another childish trait of the people she and her husband owned. Another way they were fit for their place in their world and she hers. But, in a sea of red balance sheets, the pica said something more about she and Harlow and the enterprise they were running. That not only were they a small farm with fewer than ten slaves to their names, but those few people were so poorly fed that they chewed on dirt and clay to satiate their hunger. She would've happily given the girl twenty lashes for stealing food from the cookhouse, without looking into it any further, but this wasn't neat in the same way. And she hated that. It stung. Another piece of evidence of their mounting failure.

That old feeling washed over her. And it wasn't fair, to say it was old. It was always there, a shadow in the corner, a fly drowning in the cream. She had barely moved, a portion of her face visible in the silver tray, crooked on the table. She picked it up and walked outside with it. With both hands, she hoisted it low between her knees and flung it out toward the dead garden among the waving dead tendrils. It fell to the ground with a sharp, clanging thud. A glorious sound.

She had the mind to walk home, but there was Carol. And the moon had moved. It was darker now, too dangerous to walk. She'd have to wait 'til morning. She turned back to the house just as Emmaline's sister appeared in the doorway, wide-eyed, a shotgun in her arms.

Emmaline's sister lowered the weapon when she saw Lizzie. "You alright? What was that?"

Lizzie turned to look at the woman standing on the porch, the Sutton's large Greek Revival–style house towering against the dark sky, its paint so white it looked illuminated.

"Nothing," Lizzie said slowly. "I just came out for some air and knocked something over."

"C'mon back in. It's not safe."

Lizzie nodded and followed Emmaline's sister inside. She

went back into the room, where Emmaline and most of the women were asleep. Two women sat in the corner, whispering, and sewing.

"Where's the midwife?" Lizzie asked.

"Back in the kitchen, I think. C'mon, we saved you a space next to Carol. She was an angel. Does she normally sleep that long?"

Lizzie didn't answer. She scrunched down next to Carol, balling a blanket underneath her head.

If she had thought she would be getting any sleep, she would have complained. She would have extracted Carol from the mess of doting sleeping women and moved to the parlor. Instead, she just lay down. She needed the hive energy of the women to counteract what was congealing in her mind. The years in Texas. The nonexistent birth rate. The book of names that went nearly unchanged from year to year, without additions or increase. The needed wet nurse. How the only surviving children came from her womb. They all knew that myth of a plantation overrun with pickaninnies, fruitful mothers with litters of children. She had the plumb opposite, and for years, it plagued her. And now she knew why.

For so long, she wondered if they had been cursed. The fruitless soil, the perpetual bad weather—from strange freezes to hellish droughts, not to mention the death of young William. But all along there had been another reason for their mounting failure. Why, the answer had laid itself out before her so plainly, and she'd do with it what any Old Testament God worth his salt would do. Rain down hellfire until the angels saw fit to intervene.

CHAPTER THIRTY

THE NEXT MORNING, A HAZY fog greeted us. We welcomed it, thinking it might finally be the end of this perilous heat wave. Rain was finally on its way, we figured. The whole of Texas had been waiting on such rain for two months at least. All morning, we worked slow, trying to salvage what corn we could, sniffing the air for sign of a storm. The salvaging was a fool's errand, as most of the corn was withered and desiccated, but we tried anyway. For the first time in a long time, we were out there all together, with Nan and big-bellied Serah among us, trying to squeeze a full day of farmwork into the few tolerable hours of daylight, while Monroe and Isaac were off with Harlow on an errand.

We weren't out there long before the fog burned off and the sun's gaze grew in intensity.

"C'mon, Patience, make it rain now," Serah teased.

"That ain't what I said."

"You didn't deny it," Nan added.

We laughed, all except Junie, who just nodded, with a small closed-mouth smile.

The air grew warmer, a hot wind barreling through, clogging our noses, and making it harder to breathe. The sun bore down harder, a seething inescapable eye. We traded straw hats, draped our aprons around our heads and necks, but the sun and wind pushed in anyway, stinging our eyes, erupting in heat rashes up and down our arms and backs.

When we were done, with barely a bushel to show for the effort, we trudged over to the loom, where we'd normally spend the hottest portion of the day spinning, but it was padlocked. The riverbed near it was waterless, just a winding bed of pale stones.

Stiff-legged and parched, we headed back to the quarters, but the well over there was barricaded now, covered over with a flat piece of wood and a large block of stone we couldn't move. Something was surely awry, but we couldn't think past our thirst or the tingling heat engulfing our limbs. We plodded to the cookhouse, but the mile-long walk felt thrice as long. And by the time we reached the doorway to the small dark building, heat sickness felled us all. We stumbled in, dizzy, so beset with headaches and stomach cramps we could barely move. Patience, Lulu, and Junie were sweating profusely, wiping their faces and necks with the damp sleeves of their blouses, while Serah and Nan complained of feeling dried out, so flush with heat their insides felt aflame.

On the floor, we laid out, grateful to escape the sun. We passed around a small tin of water until there was none left. It clattered to the ground with a most accusatory sound.

"Go get more."

"Why me? Send her."

"You drank the last of it. You go."

Patience dragged herself up and stumbled back outside. She made her way to the new cistern fixed to the side of the Lucys' house. With small hobbling steps, she passed by the side of the house and peered into the window. No one was there. That was strange. She couldn't remember there being a time when no one was ever inside it.

She reached the back of the house, where the cistern towered over the roof. She stuck the pitcher underneath the spout and grabbed ahold of the handle, but before she could turn it, the hot metal scalded her.

She jumped back, cursing to herself, shaking her burned hand, the pitcher rolling away in the dirt. Grabbing hold of the pitcher, she positioned herself back underneath the spout, using the tail of her skirt to protect her fingers.

The spout seemed stuck. She grunted and heaved until it loosened, but nothing came out. It was completely dry.

◃

THE HEAT SICKNESS AND the thirst were deliberate, part of the plan, we realized later. We awoke to Lizzie playing nurse, providing water, and dabbing faces with a damp, cool cloth. She even sent Ollie out to empty the buckets of vomit, and one by one, she had Monroe carry Lulu, Patience, and Serah back to the quarters. Where Isaac was, no one knew.

For Junie, consciousness came and went, until finally she woke up on the cookhouse floor, dizzy and unsure of where she was or how she got there. All morning, she had been a ball of worry, wondering when Lizzie would summon her to the house, to ask for more of the tea, or complain about having missed last night's dose entirely. Those were the scenarios she hoped for.

What really worried her was the idea of the tangle of roots lying about somewhere in the Lucys' house. She bolted upright but felt immediately pulled down by the fatigue of her body. She coughed, her throat dry. A blurry figure handed her a tin of water, only a quarter full. She gulped it down and held out the cup for more.

The morning's dread surged back to her. She had to retrieve whatever Lizzie hadn't used. What if Nan or Serah saw it? Or even worse, Harlow. He'd know exactly what it was.

A trickle of water dribbled into the tin cup and stopped. She reached for the pitcher, but the hands holding it, pulled it out of reach. Junie stared, trying to get her eyes to focus in the dim room.

"No. Not until we talk."

The figure's features slowly grew sharper. It was Lizzie, her limp hair uncombed, a ribbon askew, a strange glassy look in her eyes, sitting at the small table in the corner.

Junie sat up taller, trying to get her bearings. Dusk was falling, but there wasn't enough light to read whatever was flickering across Lizzie's face. Instead, she noted the weird angle of the woman's shoulders, the continuous bouncing of her right leg, almost independent of the foot connected to it.

"You make the tea?" Junie asked slowly.

"No, but I will . . ."

"Your blood come down yet?"

"No, but it will . . ."

"You don't seem worried."

"Well, it worked so well for you and the others. I need not fear, shall I?" Lizzie said, her voice shaking.

Panic rose in Junie's stomach. "What you mean?"

Lizzie sighed. "Don't insult me."

"Miss Lizzie, I don't know what you talking about," Junie said, slowly, trying to keep her voice calm.

Lizzie tittered. "Now, I know you're lying. I can count on one hand how many times you have ever referred to me as such. I must really have your attention now."

The two women looked at each other, unseeing. Clouds passed over, blocking what little light was left in the sky. Dark fell over the cabin, but neither woman moved for a long time, the air growing thick between them.

"How'd Miss Emmaline do?" Junie ventured. A test question.

"Oh, she did just fine. Had a bitty baby boy. What in Hades we need with another one of those, huh?" Lizzie said, laughing at her own joke. A strange cackle that bounced around the walls. "How's your head?" she said after a while.

"It hurts something awful," said Junie. Time seemed to be off-kilter, warped by some strange dullness she felt clouding her mind, soddening her limbs.

Lizzie struck a match. "The men in town think this bitty old match can start a fire by its lonesome. Isn't that something?" she said as she lit a candle. She sighed and offered Junie a scant bit of water. "Here."

Junie gulped it down and held out the cup. "Is there more?" The image of the well came back to her. Covered over and barricaded. "We couldn't get any from the well."

"Oh, just some foolishness with the patrol. Never mind all that. I want to talk about these twigs you gave me." Lizzie pulled out a bundle of cotton root from her dress pocket and dropped it on the table, causing the flame of the candle to flicker.

Junie stiffened, the throbbing in her forehead spread out, a small vise tightening around her skull. "Need me to boil it for you?"

Lizzie pulled free a short brown stalk and put it her mouth. She began chewing, her eyes never moving from Junie's face. "No, I wanna know how long y'all been unsticking the pig," she said, her mouth half-full. "Is that what y'all call it? That is how you put it, remember? 'Can't the pig be unstuck?' I haven't been able to get it out of my head since."

"Ma'am?" Junie breathed. *She knows.*

Lizzie chewed a minute longer, then blew the thick mass of cotton root out of her mouth. Bits of the chewed root flew into the air, onto the floor, onto her dress. "My whole damn life, you've been by my side. Like family, I'd tell anyone who asked, but maybe I was just blind to what you are, what you've always been."

"I don't know what you mean," Junie said quietly. She kept her body still while scanning the room. How many steps lay between her and the door? How far was the rack of pots and pans? Which one was closest? Heaviest? Where were the hearth's poker and shovel? They were usually right there on the left side.

Above the hearth, Junie could see an image forming. The same visual that had been playing in her mind ever since she first saw the steamboat tickets. A large boat barreling through dark gray water, before stopping at a rickety port where her two children stood.

"I hate it when you pull that dumb slave act with me. It's insulting. Now, I'm giving you the chance to explain yourself. Most people in my position wouldn't be as generous. You know that. But then, you always have taken my kindness for weakness. You and Charles, two birds of a feather that way."

"What you asking me?" Junie said, unable to keep the harsh edge from creeping into her voice.

"I want to know how long y'all been using the cotton root? Emmaline's midwife told me all about it. How y'all use it and for what purpose."

Junie felt her stomach seize up. She searched for an explanation just plausible enough to buy her more time to think, but her mind felt plodding and slow. "Who—"

"And before you play dumb, I should tell you I wrote to Mason this morning and told him we should talk seriously about the fate of your offspring. We could use them here . . . but maybe it's best he sell them. The markets in Louisiana are always hungry this time of year."

The large visual on the wall began to darken in spots, as if it was suddenly splattered with a dark, viscous oil. Junie watched as the oil spread and congealed, until it seemed to soil everything. When she could no longer see the boat, no longer see Patrick's and Hannah's small faces, she turned to Lizzie. "You want me to beg you? Is that what you want?"

Lizzie shook her head.

"What then? What we trading for?"

"I want to know everything," Lizzie said, that glassy desperate look appearing in her eyes again.

"And you'll do what? Write Mason?"

"Yes, I give you my word he won't sell them, but you have to tell me everything."

"Pssh . . . I'd be a fool to believe anything that come across your tongue."

"Well, that would make two fools then, 'cause I've never lied to you and you've been lying to me for God knows how long. I expect nothing less from the rest of them down there, but you?" Lizzie stood up and began pacing. "Just how long y'all been using it? Three years? Five? The entire damn decade?" she said, slamming a hanging pot down to the floor, with a loud crash.

Was this the day of Judgment old folks back home used to sing about? Junie tried to remember the hymns, what guidance they offered, what peace . . . but there wasn't any. Just the sick feeling of oil on her stomach, on her tongue, the inky trail of that boat and her children sliding farther away into whatever plane they were fixed to. *May they be protected. May they be safe.*

A cold steeliness came over Junie. "Off and on, we used it. Whenever we needed to."

"Needed?"

"Yeah, needed. Whenever the pig didn't want to be stuck. Like when somebody put a buck to you like you wasn't nothing but an old sow."

"I already told you that was Charles. You can't still be upset with me for that."

A long pause filled the room, the sound of night pushing in. Whirring mosquitoes and cricket songs. A dog howling in the distance.

"And you know what trouble I had breastfeeding," Lizzie went on. "I needed help. If Charles went about it improperly, it's 'cause we were desperate. I was desperate."

"So were we."

Lizzie stared at Junie and Junie stared back. Met the woman's eyes without shielding any emotion or thought inside her, for the first time she could remember.

Lizzie blinked, averting her eyes as if struck. "I'll advise Mason not to sell your children, but I can't save you from the lash. Not this time."

Junie dragged herself to her feet and stepped into the doorway. That black oil seemed to be above her now, covering the sky. She looked for the moon, for the stars, but couldn't find them. She turned back to see Lizzie still watching her, the woman's mouth drawn into a thin frozen line. "Little sister," Junie sang, "when have you ever saved me from anything?"

Junie stumbled down the steps, deeper into that dark, viscous night. She heard Lizzie behind her, tumbling down the cookhouse steps. "You ungrateful wretch," Lizzie yelled. "By and by, you'll soon know what it feels like to go out into the world without my help."

CHAPTER THIRTY-ONE

THEY HAILED FROM HENDERSON, ANDERSON, Freestone, and Ellis counties. They were boys, big and small, the youngest a scrappy ten-year-old and the oldest just turned seventeen, a ragtag gang making its way to Navarro.

They had been riding all summer. These boys, their number growing with the heat. At first, it had just been three or four farm boys from Henderson, ditching work to go to a hanging in Dallas. But one could say it started way before that. Back in their own counties, they each caught the bug.

In the slow winter months leading up to that long hot summer, they had begun ditching school to go to any dustup nearby, and each county had a few. Even before John Brown's execution in December, folks had been prickly. The old preacher's half-baked raid on Harpers Ferry was considered a joke, but the reaction to his death is what got stuck in white folks' craw. In two short months, Brown went from being a certifiable loon and laughingstock to a saint and martyr now that he was on the verge of execution. Had people all over the North singing his praises, over his mettle, his holy conviction, his willingness to die for abolition. The day he was hanged by the state of Virginia, northward church bells were rung in his honor, guns set off in precarious salute, and preachers ministered to solemn congregations. The feeling in the North seemed to be that Brown had been crucified. The line from then on was clearly set. Anyone who didn't boldly declare slavery a blessing was an enemy, anybody from the North was suspect, likely to be a John Brown copycat or an emissary of abolitionist causes.

When the Chapel Hill committee gathered outside the yard of old man Willis, seen talking behind closed doors with Negroes, the boys were there. They were among the crowd when the man was served his "walking papers" and run out of town.

They were there, in Marshall, when a minister accused of being an abolitionist was charged with treason and barely escaped with his life. That one was a sight to see. When the mob pursued the minister and his family and finally caught up with them twelve miles from town, the boys were among the procession that walked the man to the jailhouse. Some of the bigger boys pushed into the middle of the fray and got to lay hands on the preacher, got to pinch his arm and punch him in the back before he was stripped, whipped, and robbed, before being locked away in the calaboose.

For weeks afterward, the boys bragged about it in class, or on the farm, to all the boys who hadn't been there, whose mothers had managed to keep them home. They rubbed it in. All the fun they'd had and how they couldn't wait for the next one.

They were not disappointed. Come spring, there were more events to go to, and the boys blew off school, blew off chores, to travel in rollicking packs to the site of one great affair or another.

In May, they rode all the way to Fannin to see the hangings of Emma, Ruben, and Jess—three slaves hanged for killing their master. The boys outshouted men twice their size in the tussle for souvenirs—a scrap of a shirt or dress, an ear, or a finger. These mementos would go in the small metal box they carried with them the entirety of that summer.

And once the fires began in July, they didn't even bother going home. They traveled as far as Fort Worth to see another accused abolitionist tarred and hanged. And then back to Dallas, where they camped out the night before an execution to secure a good place in the clearing. That morning, the boys feasted on biscuits and ham, drank bitter coffee, and passed around a bit of whiskey, and were woozy with heat and drink by the time Patrick, Sam, and Cato were hanged—the three slaves the Dallas County mob identified as ringleaders of the fires that scorched and decimated the downtown area.

Newspapers warned Texans of a large, detailed plot of insurrection, scheduled to happen on election day in August. All-out war was on the horizon, one editor wrote, detailing a vast conspiracy of Northern abolitionists who had planted emissaries all over the South, who were working in concert with Black people.

Local papers reported of nearby towns being burned to a crisp, mobs discovering stockpiles of guns and strychnine in slave cabins, interrogations ferreting out hit lists of prominent citizens, and more lurid details of the unseemly plot. That day, while the men were out voting, Black men would poison their wells and take their wives. And a murderous few would lie in wait to slaughter the husbands once they returned home.

As hysteria increased, the boys' attentions grew scattered. It was hard to know which events would turn into the large festive parades of the early part of the summer. They could always ride with the local patrol and see what turned up, as it wasn't unlikely for a raid to turn into a small quiet hanging now and then. But those events happened suddenly and rarely made the papers. And often, by the time word spread of a such a hanging in progress, the boys didn't reach the site until it was all over. Sometimes, they could still grab hold of something for the souvenir box, but it just wasn't the same if they didn't see it with their own eyes.

And that created another issue, with the boys being spread so thin. They fought over the box more and more. Who got to keep it and for how long? It got so the boys didn't even want to share what they obtained with the rest of the group.

By the time they heard about an event in Navarro, it was tacitly understood that any boy who wanted a souvenir would have to secure it himself. That morning, they got on the road at first light, in hopes they'd get a good spot before the festivities happened around noon.

WHEN THE LOOM WENT up in flames, we didn't wait to be questioned. Some of us tried to disappear, but there was nowhere to disappear to. The woods were scorched and barren, most of the trees undressed, as if in the midst of a harsh northern winter. The creek was a memory, dry as bone.

The patrols were everywhere. One of their number seemed to be posted every hundred yards. We wondered if these white men even pretended to work anymore, if they had livestock to tend to, crops to water.

We knew about Dallas and Pilot Point and Denton. We knew they'd look to us and ask about the origin of the loom fire, but only one answer would be accepted. Monroe made his claim early. He zipped around, helping Mr. Lucy put the fire out, kept it from spreading, in hopes that his presence would alleviate any question of guilt. A foolish strategy, we thought, but it seemed to work.

They only looked at us. They only sought us. And when they'd caught and penned us all, we saw Mrs. Lucy up ahead, her face a hot red streak, her mouth a twisted spoon. "I know it was them. Those wenches have been plotting against me since creation."

Any other time, we might have been tickled by her turn of phrase, to hear her channel us this way, but the horrible men surrounding us, their wide faces, and grubby roaming hands, made it hard to hear clearly. Without them, maybe we would have realized what she was saying, what she believed was the true crime, the fire itself merely a ruse of her own making.

We were harried and confused while Junie stood still as the trees, locking her eyes on Lizzie.

Lizzie stared back, her face flushed. She pointed a crooked finger at Junie. "No, just her! She's the ringleader!"

The men seized Junie first, before tightening their grip on the rest of us.

"She the ringleader?" they asked us.

Some of us shook our heads no, others remained frozen.

"Just what I thought." One of the men sniffed. He pushed his face close to Patience's. "You look like the ringleader to me."

"Nah, I think it's the old woman," another man answered.

"I said I'm dealing with the rest of them. Just take *her*!" Lizzie screeched.

"Now, ma'am, the Navarro Vigilance Committee has the authority to handle these threats as we see fit," a redheaded man said. "We're taking these wenches to jail. If Charles wants to file a motion, he can do so down there."

The vise around us tightened. We fought, but there were many.

A loud gunshot startled us all. One round, then two. We all turned and saw Harlow firing into the sky. He lowered his revolver and moved slowly toward us. "Paul, you son of a bitch, release my property," he yelled. "Now, goddamit, or this next ball will be in your throat! You, too, Wendell."

Several of the committee men raised their rifles in Harlow's direction. "You step back," a bearded man barked. "You don't like it, you take it up with the council."

"Yep, you agreed just like everybody else, Harlow. Arsonists will be dealt with no matter who they belong to," the redheaded man added.

The bearded man moved close to Harlow until his rifle was inches from Harlow's chest. "You hang back and collect yourself," the man said quietly. "And once we're gone, you go see Reynolds."

"Charles, you bastard," screamed Lizzie. "Are you just going to let them take everything?"

"Shut it, Lizzie," he yelled back.

The bearded man kept his rifle aimed at Harlow's chest, while the rest of the men hauled us away.

They took us to jail, with gleeful words on their lips. We heard ourselves condemned. Damned. However one considers going over, this felt different. Who among us hadn't considered self-destruction? Who hadn't washed clothes at the edge of a river and one day found herself walking deeper and deeper into the throat of it? Who hadn't considered the bottom of a well or any of the other numerous possibilities that might present themselves in a single day?

On the way to the jail, Serah was separated from us. Her pregnant belly deemed her capable of being reformed, and if not reformed, then just valuable enough to be spared.

Inside the calaboose, some women tried bargaining with the

guard, how they could pick more cotton or drive a plow better than any full hand in the county. They were super women, they promised. If their lives were spared, they could do it all. Split rails, have babies, pick a hundred bushels by their lonesome, and cook up a fantastic plentiful meal with nothing but corn, lard, and whatever scraps one could muster.

Junie may have been the only one who didn't bother with any of the above strategies. All her energy was set upon one thing, speaking to her children on this plane. And if it went the way it appeared to be going, maybe at the critical moment, she could fling herself beyond. Her soul could leap toward Georgia and bypass the otherworld altogether.

The march from the jail to the site couldn't have been more than half a mile, but it felt much longer. The sun was high, its furious glare singeing our skin. We walked single file, bounded together by the wrists, past a graveyard of desiccated trees, out to where a large oak towered above.

A cheer went up in the crowd. A sweaty mass of pink swollen faces. They taunted and heckled us.

Together, we sang. "I know moon-rise, I know star-rise. I'll lie in the grave and stretch out my arms. Lay this body down."

Two limbs of the tree were already roped, made to do the crowd's bidding. Those of us who could talk to trees tried to reason with it, accuse it of complicity.

"I'll lie in the grave and stretch out my arms. Lay this body down."

Past those horrible faces, there was a high fluttering in the trees north of us. The dry branches clacked, the dead leaves rustled, our song now stuck in their boughs. "I go to the Judgment in the evening of the day, when I lay this body down."

"Shut up that racket!"

"They singing in code!"

The song rose higher. "And my soul and your soul will meet in the day, when I lay this body down."

Junie. Lulu. Patience. Nan. Each one adding to the song. The melody then breaks, breaking open, rising higher, before adhering itself to the slow movement of clouds passing over.

⟶⟵

TWO OF THE BOYS secured souvenirs, which included: a scrap of Junie's gingham trousers, a lock of Patience's braid, and one toe, but from which woman they cannot remember.

Come September, after the hysteria has died out, a couple of newspapers will run retractions, noting fires reported that never actually happened, wells declared poisoned that were in fact untainted, and substances thought to be strychnine that turned out to be harmless. Some people will begin to wonder if there was ever a plot of insurrection at all. The box of souvenirs will then lose its luster and later be forgotten about, when Texas joins South Carolina and the rest of the South in the call for secession.

⟶⟵

SERAH COULD HEAR THE women's song from the yard of the auction house, where she remained alone. The small building was only a few paces from the jail, as people were often moved between the two structures.

From where she paced, she tried her best to ignore the lower half of her body, cramping in pain, and focused on the sound of the song starting up, then stopping, taken up by the next pair of women, until there was no song at all.

She squatted in the dirt and was surprised that the baby

slipped out easy, as if it had been waiting on her to just stop pacing long enough for it to descend.

The child was alive, a wrinkled baby girl, not much bigger
than her hand. She cleared its mouth, as she had seen Nan do,
and the baby began to cry. She ripped off a portion of her skirt
and wrapped the baby inside it.

Something else was coming. With the child in one arm, she
squatted and watched the slimy afterbirth fall into the dirt. She
searched around for something to wrap it in. She didn't want her
child to be anchored here, not in the yard of a trader's house, or
in Navarro County itself. She wanted no link between her family
line and this terrible place. She let it dry out in the sun; the husk
of the thing would have to go with them. She had nothing to cut
the cord and it seemed most reasonable to her to never cut it, to
never be more than an arm's length from each other.

A decade or so later, when Serah will give birth for the third
and final time, in the white clapboard house she shares with her
family, her oldest daughter, born in the trader's yard, will be the
one person she wants bedside. Though the midwife will frown
at the child's presence and send the little girl off to fetch one
thing or another, Serah will remain steadfast in this one request.
Outside, Noah will pull the plow slow within earshot, tracking the rise and fall of sounds coming out of the small pulsing
house. If it's a girl, he'll burn a piece of tobacco and indigo, and
if a boy, tobacco and corn. When the pain thickens, Serah will
summon the little girl by her bedside once more and tighten her
swollen fingers around the child's tiny hand. And it'll be hard to
say which one is the anchor affixing them to this new world, lest
they be suddenly wrenched back into the old one.

Back in the trader's yard, the newborn hollers, taking up the
women's dirge. Serah can hear the women singing again, a chorus embedded inside the baby's sharp cries.

ACKNOWLEDGMENTS

A first novel is often a marathon and as such, I need to thank those at both ends of the journey. An extremely special thanks to Henry Dunow and Arielle Datz; Sara Birmingham, TJ Calhoun, Shelly Perron, Caitlin Mulrooney-Lyski, Jin Soo Chun, and the rest of the amazing Ecco team; along with Ore Agbaje-Williams of Borough Press. I'm deeply grateful to you all for making this dream come true. An additional hearty thanks to Kiese Laymon and Margaret Wilkerson Sexton.

A big thank you to the Michener Center for all their support. Thank you, Billy Fatzinger, Holly Doyel, and Bret Anthony Johnston for everything and then some! Heart-filled thanks to Elizabeth McCracken, Roger Reeves, Daina Ramey Berry, and my Michener/NWP community of kickass writers, with particular thanks to dear friends/early readers Rachel Heng, Shaina Frazier, Rickey Fayne, Nathan Harris, Desiree Evans, and Shangyang Fang.

I also want give thanks to all the writing institutions and communities that supported me and earlier iterations of this project: VONA, Callaloo (shout out to Ravi Howard); Hedgebrook, Saltonstall, Sackett Street (with immense thanks to Heather Aimee O'Neill, who read early drafts of this novel); CUNY Writers' Institute (special thanks to Andre Aciman, John Freeman, Patrick Ryan, and especially Matt Weiland, who believed in this book when it was just a first chapter); Paragraph Workspace; and Tinhouse (enormous thanks to Alexander Chee, whose insightful feedback set this book on a different trajectory).

This book owes a great debt to the work of black women scholars and historians of African American history, at large. Paula Gidding's *When and Where I Enter: The Impact of Black Women on Race and Sex in America*, Stephanie M. H. Camp's *Closer to Freedom: Enslaved Women and Everyday Resistance in the Plantation South*, and Herbert G. Gutman's *The Black Family in Slavery and Freedom, 1750–1925* are cornerstones of this text. Other important sources include: Anthony Kaye's *Joining Places Slave Neighborhoods in the Old South*, Yvonne Chireau's *Black Magic: Religion and the African American Conjuring Tradition*, Sharla Fett's *Working Cures: Healing, Health, and Power on Southern Slave Plantations*, Deborah Gray White's *Ar'n't I a Woman?*, Stephanie Jones Rogers' *They Were Her Property: White Women as Slave Owners in the American South*, Marie Jenkins Schwartz's *Birthing a Slave: Motherhood and Medicine in the Antebellum South*, Michelle Lee's *Working Cures*, Zora Neale Hurston's *Mules and Men*, Ann Patton Malone's *Women on the Texas Frontier*, Thavolia Glymph's *Out of the House of Bondage: The Transformation of the Plantation Household*, Tera Hunter's *Bound in Wedlock: Slave and Free Black Marriage in the Nineteenth Century*, Michael A. Gomez's *Exchanging Our Country Marks*, James McPherson's *Battle Cry of Freedom*, Nikky Finney's *Rice*, Everett Gillis's "Zodiac

N

Wisdom," and Donald E. Reynolds' *The Texas Terror: The Slave Insurrection Panic of 1860 and the Secession of the Lower South*. The dissertations of James David Nichols and Mekala Audain on the travels of enslaved African Americans to Mexico were vital. And, of course, the testimonies of enslaved African Americans themselves, including Harriet Jacobs, Charles Ball, Katie Darling, and Rose Williams. The lullaby in the book is from Sea Island singer Bessie Jones' album, *Get in Union*. The author of the spiritual at the end, "I Know Moon-rise," is unknown, but documented in an 1867 edition of the Atlantic Monthly.

Last, but not least, tremendous thanks to my family—Mom, Dad, Damon, and the entirety of the Rose and Atwater clans, both those still here and those in the hereafter. I'm eternally grateful for your presence in my life. Deep gratitude to my crew—Carla, Kihika, Beverly, Kimmie, Akiba, 'Drea, Jackie, Maleda, and my All of We sistren, whose unwavering belief in me over the years makes this possible. And special thanks to my Howard film community, whose communal study over the years informs this work—Haile, AJ, Brad, Daniel, Frank, etc.